BRANDENBURG

Volkmann and Erica looked back at the white house, neither of them speaking. They heard Sanchez' footsteps moments later and turned. The detective held something in his hand.

'The pilot,' Sanchez said to Volkmann. 'He found this lying in the bushes. The helicopter blades must have blown it from the fire.'

Sanchez handed him a piece of glossy paper. Volkmann saw that it was the remains of a very old black-and-white photograph. Half of it had burned, the right side of the picture cracked and worn, but the image still discernible. The photograph was of a woman, a blonde young, pretty woman, smiling out at a camera, sky and snow-capped mountains behind her.

The young woman's right hand was linked through the arm of a companion, a man wearing some sort of uniform. Only the man's shoulder, his left arm and part of his torso were still visible. The rest of the photograph had been burned, its black edges ragged, flaking with cinder. But what caught Volkmann's eye was the conspicuous dark band around the man's arm: a black Nazi swastika set in a white circle.

About the Author

Glenn Meade lives in Dublin. A former journalist, he is now a specialist in the field of pilot training, and is currently researching his second novel.

Brandenburg

Glenn Meade

CORONET BOOKS
Hodder and Stoughton

Copyright © 1994 by Glenn Meade

First published in Great Britain in 1994
by Hodder and Stoughton
A division of Hodder Headline PLC

Coronet edition 1994

The right of Glenn Meade to be identified as the author
of this work has been asserted by him in accordance with the
Copyright, Designs and Patents Act 1988.

10 9 8 7 6

British Library Cataloguing in Publication Data

Meade, Glenn
Brandenburg
I. Title

Typeset by Hewer Text Composition Services, Edinburgh
Printed and bound in Great Britain by
Cox & Wyman Ltd, Reading, Berkshire

Hodder and Stoughton
A Division of Hodder Headline PLC
338 Euston Road
London NW1 3BH

**To my parents
Tom and Carmel**

ACKNOWLEDGEMENTS

To all those in Europe and South America who gave their assistance in the researching of this book, my sincere thanks. In particular, I would like to acknowledge the following:

In Berlin: the staff of the Berlin Document Centre, US Mission, especially Director David Marwell and Dr Richard Campbell who allowed me access to their original files; Axel Wiglinsky, Acting Director, Reichstag Security; Dr Bose and Hans-Christopa Bonfert of the Berlin *Senatsverwaltung für Inneres* (Administrative Council for the Interior); the Berlin *Landsamt für Verfassungsschutz* (Office for the Protection of the Constitution); the staff of the *Wermacht Auskunft Stelle* (WASt.).

In Vienna: the administration staff of the Vienna Central Cemetery.

In Strasbourg: Jean-Paul Chauvet.

In Paraguay: Carlos Da Rosa.

Also, I would like to thank Janet Donohue, and Professor Jim Jackson, of Trinity College, Dublin.

There are others, in Europe and South America, who gave their assistance but who wish to remain anonymous; to them, my gratitude.

At Hodder and Stoughton, my thanks go to my editor, George Lucas, for his professionalism, boundless enthusiasm, and commitment to this book. And to Bill Massey for his very insightful and invaluable advice.

'*So we beat on, boats against the current, borne back ceaselessly into the past.*'

F. Scott Fitzgerald,
The Great Gatsby

PROLOGUE

It was summer and the sun was shining on the blue water but the beach was deserted. The young doctor held the boy's hand as they waited at the cottage gate and the boy was trembling with fear but he wasn't crying.

When they saw the little grey Austin come down the narrow sand track the boy's heart started to pound in his chest. His Mama wore a bright blue cotton dress and looked very beautiful but as she stepped from the car and removed the dark glasses he could see the brown eyes had been crying.

As she came towards them the boy let go of the doctor's hand and ran to his mother's arms. He could smell her perfume and feel the love that seemed to smother him and almost at once he began to feel better. He clung to her cotton dress as she bent to kiss him.

'It's OK, Joseph. Mama's here. It's OK.'

As the young doctor came forward he offered his hand. 'Mrs Volkmann, I'm Doctor Rhys. May I talk with you?'

The boy saw his mother look back up towards the small white cottage near the beach. A window was open, its bright green curtains lifting and falling in the cool sea breeze, but in the bedroom where his father was sleeping the window was closed. The tiny garden was pretty with flowers and beyond the billowing curtains the boy could see the polished Steinway, and the silver-framed photographs on the mantelpiece.

His mother looked back at the doctor. 'My husband . . . how is he?'

'I've given him some pills to make him sleep. They ought to help him rest for at least eight hours.'

The woman held the boy's hand tightly as if to reassure him and the three of them walked down towards the beach. Waves

1

crashed and spumed on the wet rocks and the sun sparkled on the pebbled shore.

The doctor spoke as they walked. 'He's pretty bad, I'm afraid. That's why I rang you.' The doctor smiled down at the boy. 'This little chap's been very good. He ran all the way to the village to Doctor Mansfield's to fetch me.' The doctor patted the boy's head then looked back up.

'Tell me about your husband, Mrs Volkmann. Has he always had this problem?'

'Doctor Mansfield didn't tell you?'

The doctor shook his head. 'No, he didn't. He's on holiday. I'm only filling in, I'm afraid. But should it happen again, I'd like to be prepared.'

They had reached the beach and the crash of the big waves on the rocks and the pebbled sand roared in their ears. The doctor went to sit on a dune.

The boy's mother sat beside him. She fumbled in her handbag and found a packet of cigarettes and lit one with difficulty and the boy saw her face looked tired and pale.

'He's had it a long time. It comes and goes.'

'What triggers it?'

'A newspaper article. Something on the radio or TV. Sometimes just the weather, or the season. And then it gets too much and he sinks like a stone.'

The doctor looked puzzled. 'I don't understand. What's the reason for it, Mrs Volkmann?'

There was a crash of waves then and the boy couldn't hear his mother's words because her voice was lost in the harsh pounding of water on rock and the surf rushing on shingle. When his mother had finished speaking the boy saw the look of horror on the doctor's face.

'Good God . . . I had no idea. How truly terrible.' For a long time he seemed lost for words and then he said, 'I assume he's been seen by the necessary people?'

'Doctor, you can rationalise memories, but you can't erase them. Take that from someone who knows.'

'But you've coped. Your experience was equally traumatic, I'm sure.'

The boy saw his mother shake her head. 'I've coped, yes. But what they did to my husband was unspeakable.'

'I'm sorry, forgive me. I simply wish there was something I could do.'

'There isn't, believe me. But thank you for your concern.' Her brown eyes sparkled down at the boy. 'Joseph has helped.' His mother looked back at the doctor. 'To have a child, it was something that helped us both.'

The doctor looked suddenly out of his depth and very young. The waves crashed against the rocky shore again and then there was a long silence. He looked at the boy's mother awkwardly, as if stuck for something to say.

'When I rang the concert hall, the manager said you'd probably have to cancel your performance tonight. It must be awfully difficult. With your husband, I mean.'

'Not really. But when it happens, Joseph and I cope.'

'I heard you play in London once. I enjoyed the performance very much, Mrs Volkmann.'

'You're very kind. Thank you. And thank you for attending to my husband.'

The doctor stood up slowly and brushed sand from his trousers. 'I suppose I'd better be getting back. If he gets bad again give him two of these.' He took a bottle of pills from his pocket and handed them across. 'They ought to lift him for at least eight hours. But do call me again if you need me. Good day, Mrs Volkmann.'

The doctor shook her hand and the boy watched as he walked to his car. He climbed in and drove back down the rutted sand track.

When the boy looked back he saw his mother throw her cigarette in the waves. She was looking out to sea and her face looked sad.

'Mama . . .'

'What is it, my love?'

'What did the men do to Papa?'

His mother looked at him, and then the brown eyes suddenly filled with tears and she pulled him close to her.

'Something very bad, Joseph. Something very bad happened

3

to your Papa. That's why we must always help him. That's why he needs our love so much.'

She was holding him tightly and close to her breasts and the boy said, 'The men, did they hurt you too, Mama?'

His mother looked down at his face and then she turned her head away and held him tighter and the boy knew she was still crying and heard the pain in her voice.

'Yes, Joseph. They hurt me too.'

The boy pulled away and looked at his mother and his hand went out to touch her face.

'The men who hurt you and Papa. They won't hurt you again. I'll take care of you, Mama.'

He saw his mother wipe away the tears and smile, and then her voice sounded like when his Papa was sad. As if by her smile and gaiety she could banish the bad things that had happened to her and his Papa. She laughed down at him.

'Of course you will, my love.'

She brushed the hair from his forehead and kissed him and wiped her eyes again as she stood up.

'Now come, Joseph. Let's go and take care of Papa.'

The small boy held out his hand to his mother and she grasped it tightly and let him lead her back up to the cottage.

PART ONE

Chapter One

Asunción,
Paraguay.
South America

When the doctors at the San Ignatio Private Hospital told Nicolas Tsarkin he was going to die, the old man nodded sullenly, waited until the men had left, then dressed without speaking another word and drove his Mercedes to the corner of the Calle Palma three blocks away.

He parked the car and walked back the last block to the small commercial bank on the corner, pushed through the revolving doors and told the manager he wanted to see his safe-deposit box.

The manager promptly ordered a senior clerk to go down to the vault with the old man: Senor Tsarkin, after all, was a valued customer.

'Then tell him to go. I want to be left alone,' Tsarkin said in his usual abrupt manner.

'Certainly, Senor Tsarkin. Thank you, Senor Tsarkin'; a final, polite bow from the manager and then, '*Buenos dias,* Senor Tsarkin.'

The blue-suited manager irritated Tsarkin, as usual, but especially so this morning, with his bowing and scraping and ingratiating, gold-toothed smile.

Buenos dias. Good morning. *What was good about it?*

He had just been told he had less than forty-eight hours to live, and right now the pain in his stomach was eating into him like a fire, almost unendurable. He felt weak, terribly weak, despite the drugs to quell the pain. What had he got to smile about? What was good about this morning?

7

The last morning of his life, because he knew now what he had to do.

And yet the truth was, Tsarkin felt a strange kind of relief: the lie would soon be over.

He caught a reflection of himself in the cold, stainless-steel walls as the clerk led him down into the cool of the vault. Tsarkin was eighty-two, and until six months ago had looked ten years younger. He had been fit then, ate the proper foods, never smoked and rarely drank. Everyone said he would make the century.

They were wrong.

His reflection in the stainless-steel wall showed him as he was: thin, emaciated, looking like a corpse already, the bleeding in his stomach so bad that he could almost feel the life draining from him. But he had important things to do, no matter what the pain, no matter what the doctors had told him. And once those things were done he could sleep peacefully, forever.

Unless there really was a God and a Hereafter, in which case he would pay for his sins. But Tsarkin doubted it. No just God would have let him live so long and so full and so rich a life after all that he had done. No, you just died, it was that simple, the flesh became dust and you were gone forever, no pain, no Heaven, no Hell. Just nothingness.

He hoped.

The clerk unlocked the metal gates and led him through into the basement chamber. It was a small room, six metres by six, silent, a cold marble floor. The clerk examined the key number he held in his hand, ran a finger along the shining steel boxes along one of the walls, found Tsarkin's deposit box, removed and unlocked the box and placed it on the polished wooden table in the centre of the room. He handed Tsarkin the key, and withdrew.

Tsarkin knew the procedure: he would press the button on the desk when he was ready to return upstairs. He saw the clerk lock the metal gates again and retreat up the marble steps and then Tsarkin was alone.

The vault had the coldness and the silence of a morgue

and Tsarkin shivered involuntarily. *Soon I'll be there*, he told himself. *Soon there will be no pain*. As he went to sit at the table he dragged the small metal box towards him, inserted the key and opened the lid, before removing the contents and spreading the papers out onto the polished table.

All there. The deeds to his lands, the keys to his past. He reconsidered a moment, putting off what had to be done, thought about enjoying one last orgy of indulgence, but truly there was nothing more he wanted to do. The pain made everything unbearable and, besides, he had enjoyed everything life had to offer.

He gathered up the contents of the deposit box in his hands, sorted them neatly into an orderly pile and placed them in one of the old, large envelopes that contained some of the papers. It made a neat, hefty bundle. Then he pressed the buzzer for the clerk to return.

Soon, thought Tsarkin, as he heard the clerk's footsteps echoing on the marble stairs moments later. *Soon it will all be over*.

He heard the metal gates being unlocked as he closed the lid of the empty deposit box. He left the key on the table, picked up the envelope, and walked towards the gates.

The house stood on the Calle Iguazu, on the outskirts of the city. White and large and surrounded by high walls, barely visible from the road. The classiest part of Asunción, and Tsarkin had been able to afford it. He opened the wrought-iron gates with the remote control, drove up the curved sweep of the asphalt road and parked the Mercedes on the gravel driveway in front of the house.

He grunted when the *mestizo* butler opened the front door to greet him. He went straight through to his wood-panelled study and locked the door. It was warm in the study. Very warm. Tsarkin loosened the two top buttons of his shirt as he looked out onto the lush, manicured gardens, the pepper and palm trees beyond the window. He owned a lot of property in Asunción, and three farms in the Chaco hinterland, but this place had always been his favourite.

He sat down at the polished applewood desk and emptied the contents of the envelope onto the gleaming surface and began to sift through the pile.

He looked at the passport first. Nicolas Tsarkin. Fine. Except he wasn't Nicolas Tsarkin. His real name – God, he'd almost forgotten it – and then when it came to his lips, so unreal, he had to smile to himself, weakly. So long to live a lie. He put the passport aside.

He had once been wanted in half a dozen countries. He had once done terrible things in that old, forgotten name. Inflicted terrible deaths and terrible pain. And yet the truth was, when you boiled it down, he couldn't stand pain himself. He chided himself: it was no time for thought. *Do it*.

He sorted through the papers. Old, tired papers, tattered records of his past. He read through them once again. As in his nightmares, it all came back to him: the cold terror on the faces of his victims, the blood, the butchery. Yet he felt no remorse.

He would have done it all again. No question.

He put the papers aside, removed several blank sheets of paper and an envelope from the desk drawer and began writing.

When he had finished fifteen minutes later he sealed the envelope and tucked it into his pocket, before crossing to the fireplace, clutching the papers from the safe-deposit box in his hands, and making a neat pile of them in the grate.

He took a match from the box he kept on the mantelpiece, struck it and set the flame to the papers. Then he crossed to the wall safe hidden behind the framed oil painting, swung back the painting on its hinges and thumbed through the combination.

He selected the papers he wanted, making sure there was nothing left that might incriminate anyone, and crossed back to the fireplace, watching as the flames licked the papers, adding more to the blaze, until there was nothing, only black ashes. He checked through the ashes with the poker.

The flames had done their work. Nothing remained.

When he had done all he had had to do, he left the house.

He drove to the post office four blocks away, bought the stamp he needed and posted the letter, express. He drove straight back to the house, parked the car in the garage this time, and went into his study again.

Do it quickly, the voice in his head told him.

No time for thought. No time for thinking about the pain to come. From the top drawer of the polished applewood desk he took out the long-barrelled Colt forty-five pistol, checked that all the chambers were loaded, then placed the barrel of the weapon in the roof of his mouth, letting his lips form a perfect O around the cold metal.

He squeezed the trigger.

It was all over in less than a second and Tsarkin never heard the explosion that flung him up and backwards, shattering half his brain, as the bullet ripped out through the back of his skull, sending shards of bone and bloodied brain matter flying into the air behind him, spattering the white walls grey and red as the blunted lead of the bullet embedded itself in the wood below the ceiling.

Less than a second of primary pain.

In all, Nicolas Tsarkin could not have wished for a more quick and painless death.

Chapter Two

*Asunción,
Paraguay.
Wednesday,
November 23rd*

Rudi Hernandez waited while the girl checked in at the desk, watching her figure appreciatively as he smoked a cigarette. The airport was busy, crowded with midday passengers, but his eyes were fixed firmly on the girl.

He told himself: *Hey, remember who she is*.

But he couldn't help it, enjoying the rear view of the girl's long, silky, suntanned legs and the perfectly rounded bottom that filled out the tightly stretched, short red summer skirt.

The view was exquisite and he smiled to himself. It was the Dago in him. He liked women. And he especially liked Erica.

Now he saw her turn and smile at him, her business complete as she gathered up her passport and tickets and picked up her hand-luggage from the desk. She crossed to where he stood as he ground out his cigarette on the marble floor.

He smiled back. 'Everything OK?'

Erica nodded. 'Fifteen minutes before I board. Do we have time for a quick coffee?'

'Sure.'

He took her hand-luggage and led her across the hall towards the coffee-dock. He found a vacant table, and ordered two coffees and two brandies. After the waiter brought their drinks he watched as Erica sipped her coffee, wondering whether to say it, whether to tell her how he felt.

Erica said, 'There's something on your mind, Rudi, isn't there? Is it the story?'

Rudi Hernandez went to shake his head, wanting to tell her, no, not the story, but *you*, how I feel about *you*. The girl was five years younger than he – twenty-five – and each time he saw her after an absence she looked even more beautiful. Her long blonde hair had been cut short, and it complemented her pretty face, her high cheekbones. Her figure, too, had filled out since the last time he had seen her. The hips and breasts fuller, more womanly. And she had started to wear make-up: pink lipstick, blue mascara. It suited her.

Rudi Hernandez nodded instead. 'Yes, the story.'

A lie, but how could he tell her the truth? The story he was working on, the story he had told her about, was on his mind, but in the back somewhere, Erica up front, not wanting her to go.

'I want you to promise me you will be careful,' the girl said more seriously. 'Promise me that?'

He smiled easily, looked into the girl's eyes. 'I'm always careful, Erica. You know that. Too careful sometimes.'

With her blonde hair, she looked so different from the South-American women, the dark-skinned women in the *barrios*, and the contrast had turned heads. The Indian woman selling flowers on Calle Estrella had asked to touch her blonde hair, saying it would bring her luck. '*She is beautiful*,' the old woman had smiled as she stroked Erica's hair and looked at Rudi. '*She will bring us both luck. Believe me.*'

And he had seen the Latin men stare at her, knowing what they were thinking, not blaming them. He had thought the same himself. He thought again of the day they had spent in the mountains, up in the rain-forest near the border with Brazil, the day they had taken the guided tour. How close he had been to her then. He saw the look of concern on her face now.

'Did you think of asking Mendoza to help you with the story?'

Rudi shrugged. 'What story? Maybe it's a connection into

something big. But I have no proof, Erica. No *real* proof. Just the word of Rodriguez. And the photographs.'

He did not repeat what he had already told her, not wanting her to be afraid for him. Instead, he remembered the sight of Rodriguez' brown body, lying on the cold metal table in the mortuary of the city hospital, the feeling of sickness in his stomach when the attendant pulled back the white sheet and he had seen the man's pulped, bloodied flesh. He suppressed the shudder of fear he felt inside himself and leaned closer, the sweet scent of her perfume arousing him.

'I have to take it slowly, Erica. Carefully. And hope that something turns up.' He reached across and gently patted her hand, wanting instead to hold her, to caress her. 'But I promise you, I will be careful.'

She smiled at him. He felt himself reacting to her smile. Had he been in a bedroom with her at that moment he probably would have had enough courage to kiss her, pull her towards him, make love to her. He wondered how she would react, this cool, blonde *gringo* girl, wondered would she have gone with it, or looked at him with a crazy, mixed-up look on her face and said, '*Rudi* . . . stop joking!'

Now he watched as Erica sipped her brandy, held the glass in both hands. 'What about the men you say killed Rodriguez.'

'What about them?'

'Won't they come looking for you? Won't they be afraid you might tell the police?'

Hernandez smiled, seeing her fear, trying to sound unafraid, trying to reassure her. 'No chance. For one, the people who killed Rodriguez don't know me, have never seen me. They don't know I exist. I'm certain.'

'But what happens once the story breaks . . .?'

Hernandez took a sip of the coffee; it was bitter. He grimaced, pushed the cup aside. '*If* the story breaks. I could tell the paper not to print my name. That's not a problem. And I have one or two friends – *policia* – who would protect me if I needed protection.'

The girl saw him reach into his pocket, take out a bunch of keys, play with them idly.

Rudi Hernandez was a handsome man. He smiled easily, as if life were a constant joke. His brown hair, cut in a boyish fringe, made him look younger. Even the noticeable scar that ran jaggedly across his right cheek was not unbecoming, gave him an almost dashing appearance. Erica watched as he toyed with the keys, slipping them between his fingers.

He saw her stare at the keys and smiled across at her. 'Like I told you last night, anything I have on these people is in a safe place where no one would think to look. So stop worrying, Erica. I'll be careful.'

He saw the concern in her eyes. She smiled back. Her hand moved to touch his.

He slipped the keys in his free hand back in his pocket. He felt so close to her, so very close.

'Erica . . .'

'Yes . . .?'

He went to speak again, to tell her how he really felt, just as the metallic female voice came over the public address system, announcing the boarding call for her flight. She let go of his hand gently and began gathering up her things.

'What is it, Rudi?'

He shook his head as her eyes met his and he went to stand. 'Nothing. Come, you better board.'

He walked with her to the departure gate, carrying her hand-luggage, and as they stopped at the security desk he handed across her bag. 'Give my love to everyone.'

The blue eyes lifted to his face. 'I will.'

She moved towards him to kiss his cheek. He turned his face and kissed her gently on the lips instead; soft, warm, smelling again the scent of her perfume, her body, wanting to hold her, just as she drew back from him.

'*Auf Wiedersehen*, Rudi.'

'*Auf Wiedersehen*, Erica. Have a pleasant flight.'

He watched as she went past the security desk. At the gate she turned and waved. He waved back before she disappeared from view, lost in the throng of boarding passengers.

Hernandez shook his head and sighed. He should have said

what he had really wanted to say. That he loved her, this woman.

He heard the public address crackle to life again, the girl's shrill metallic voice filling the terminal.

'*Senor Rudi Hernandez, please come to the information desk. Senor Rudi Hernandez to the information desk, please.*'

The girl at the desk had handed him the message. Mendoza, the day editor's number, written on a slip of paper. He found a telephone booth and dialled. Mendoza himself answered.

'*Si?*'

'It's Rudi, I'm at the airport.'

'*Buenas tardes, amigo*. It is well for some. Others have to sweat in a hot office to earn a crust.'

Rudi grinned. 'They paged me. What is it?' He fumbled in his pockets until he found his cigarettes, tapped one out of the pack and lit it.

'You finished your business with that sexy, good-looking *gringo* woman?' Mendoza asked.

'Hey, have a little respect and remember who you're talking about,' Rudi said, smiling to himself. 'OK, what have you got? Anything juicy?'

'Robbery with violence on Calle Enrico and an old guy who committed suicide. Which you want? Victor Estrel is going to cover one, so it's all the same to me, but seeing we're friends I'll let you have your pick.'

'Thanks,' said Rudi. 'Only how come you never let *me* pick when it's a choice between covering a beauty contest and a political rally?'

He could picture Mendoza smiling at the other end.

'Privilege of rank, *amigo*. Besides, pretty girls only distract you from your work, you know that. OK, which you want?'

'What about the robbery with violence?'

'Some kid knifed a *gringo* tourist and stole his wallet. The cops have the kid and the *gringo* is in the city hospital, wound to his hand.'

'And the suicide?'

There was a pause. 'I got a call from our friend at the police

17

station, Casado, twenty minutes ago. Some old guy blew his brains out up near the Trinidad district.'

Rudi Hernandez took the cigarette out of his mouth and reached for his notebook and pen, trying to decide which story to take. After ten years on the paper it didn't matter much which one. He knew all the stories, had seen all the crimes. Crazy Indians and *mestizos* in the *barrios* knifing one another after drinking too much *cana*, corrupt politicians on the make, the street-wise kids who stole the tourists' wallets on the Calle Palma. It was all news copy to him. That's why the story he was working on was so important.

'You still there?' Mendoza's voice sounded irritated. 'Rudi, I haven't got all day.'

'The old guy, you got anything else on him?'

'Just a name and an address . . . hang on, I've got it here, some place . . .'

Hernandez drew on the cigarette. Which one? Robbery with violence or the suicide? What the hell did it matter . . . pick the closest to the airport.

'The old guy's name is . . . Jesus Maria, some name . . . Tsarkin . . . Nicolas Tsarkin. The house is on Calle Iguazu. Number twenty-three.'

Hernandez paused. He felt a small shock go through his body. 'Nicolas Tsarkin . . . you're sure?'

'Of course I'm sure. That's what it says here. How many Nicolas Tsarkin's can there be in Asunción?'

The adrenalin was pumping now through Hernandez' body, remembering the name, the face. Maybe Mendoza had made a mistake?

'The address again?'

'Twenty-three, Calle Iguazu. What's the matter? You heard of the guy?'

'No,' Hernandez lied. 'What about the police?' He could feel the sweat beginning now on his neck, his palms. It was eighty degrees outside the terminal, maybe a cool fifty inside, yet still he was beginning to sweat.

'What about them?' Mendoza asked.

'Are they at the house?'

'I guess so. But I don't know for sure.' Another pause. 'So
. . . which do you want?'

Hernandez paused. It was the same address. He had been
there, parked across the street, watching, watching because
Rodriguez had told him to watch. The day he took the
photographs. The big house with the white walls where the
old man lived, the old man Rodriguez had said was the one
to watch.

And now the old man was dead. The old man *and*
Rodriguez.

Mendoza's voice on the line now, irritated. 'Jesus, Rudi
. . . what the fuck's up with you? Which you want? I haven't
got all day.'

'I'll take Tsarkin,' said Hernandez. 'Talk to you soon.'

Chapter Three

Strasbourg,
France.
November 23rd

It was Sally Thornton's last night in Strasbourg and she knew she wanted to sleep with him.

It was raining hard as they came out of the restaurant near the Opera and when Joe Volkmann hailed them a taxi to take them back to his apartment she knew she was going to stay the night. Men didn't ask a girl back for a drink and then send you home on a rain-soaked night in a taxi. At least not the ones she'd known.

She wore an emerald green blouse that hugged her slim figure and matched her eyes. Her legs were sheathed in black sheer stockings and she knew she had a figure most women would kill for. Good, generous firm breasts and slim hips. But she wasn't an easy lay and she didn't give her sexual favours easily. Nor was she looking for a relationship, but it had to be a question of attraction on her part.

A lot of the guys at DSE Headquarters stopped by her office to chat her up and she knew by the look in their eyes and the bulge in their trousers that their intention wasn't in the least focused on work, or honourable. But not Joe Volkmann. And maybe that was why she wanted him.

She had been in the intelligence services for five years since Oxford and her year's temporary posting to DSE had been fun but now it was time to go home, a week's leave in London before her posting to New York. When Volkmann had offered to help her pack she knew the offer was genuine and not a come-on.

He'd spent the afternoon at her apartment in Petite France,

helping her fill the wooden packing crates with the Sony stereo equipment and the small items of antique furniture she'd bought. When she suggested a meal to repay him he offered tickets for the Opera and dinner afterwards instead.

As she watched him throughout the performance he seemed to listen attentively to the music and though he smiled at her a lot and the evening had a romantic flavour, he didn't try to make a pass or put his hand up her skirt or rub her up. That kind of activity was a speciality of the Italians if you ventured near their offices on the fourth floor.

And he wasn't cold or distant but she got the feeling he didn't push things: so the man was a challenge. Another reason she wanted him.

The apartment on the Quai Ernest was on the first floor, and the balcony entrance overlooked a tiny paved courtyard. The apartment was a small two-bedroom affair and he kept it pretty neat for a guy. There was a Pioneer hi-fi in a corner and some hardcover books and paperbacks and lots of cassettes and discs. Mostly classical, but some contemporary. Some modern albums and a Dvorak collection and a couple by Russian composers she'd never heard of, along with the usual collection of classics. Some photographs in frames and books on a shelf above them.

'What would you like to drink, Sally?'

She went to sit on the couch and crossed her long legs. She saw him look at them briefly and she smiled to herself and said, 'Have you scotch?'

'Sure.'

'Then I'll have a large one. With ice and Coke.'

He nodded and she watched him go into the kitchen. He wasn't handsome in a conventional way, but he was attractive. And he was tall and dark-haired and well built, and he looked more French than British. He was thirty-seven, but he looked younger. And he had something, only Sally Thornton couldn't figure out what. Something in the sensitive brown eyes; the same eyes she had seen in the woman in one of the photographs on the shelf.

He looked like the kind of guy who could protect a woman

but then all the men she worked with looked like that, trained soldiers and intelligence officers and hard-nosed narcotics specialists masquerading as policemen. And besides, she could look after herself, thank you very much.

She figured maybe what it was: he was the kind of man a girl could trust. He didn't come on strong and he didn't use his physical side like a weapon. And it was the smile that gave him away; like maybe he was vulnerable under the detatched, professional exterior.

He came back into the room carrying her glass and handed it across. He had loosened his tie and his shirt was open at the top button. He drank his beer from the bottle and she thought he looked more relaxed than she'd seen him before.

As he drank he looked over at her. When she crossed her long legs they looked even better in the black high-heels, her tight skirt riding up just a little high so the flanks of her thighs could be seen, and she was conscious of his stare. There was a radio in the hi-fi in a corner and when she flicked it on the voice was Edith Piaf's singing *Je ne regrette rien*. The rain beat hard on the window and she looked at Volkmann.

'You're going to miss me, Joe?'

'Sure.'

'Then why are you smiling?'

'Because they're going to love you in New York.'

'Who? The people at the Embassy?'

'Those, too. But I meant the Americans. The men will be beating down your door, Sally.'

'Why, thank you for the compliment. You'll come to visit me sometimes?'

'If you like.'

She smiled and swirled her glass and looked over at him. 'Tell me about yourself, Joe.'

'What do you want to know?'

She shrugged. 'Anything. I've worked with you for almost a year and I know almost nothing about your background. How long have you been with DSE?'

'Eighteen months.'

'You like working in Europe?'

'Sure.'

'And before that?'

'SIS.'

She uncrossed her legs but stretched them so that he could see them better. 'Were you ever married, Joe?'

He nodded and sipped his beer. 'Once. Divorced, but no kids, Sally.'

'What about your folks, are they still alive?'

She looked up at the photographs on the shelf in wooden frames. There were two of a couple and a young boy: one taken outside a cottage and another on a beach. The boy looked like Volkmann and the couple were obviously his parents. There was another of just the woman. She was quite striking in a pretty way and she sat at a piano, a bunch of flowers on the polished wood, and she was smiling. She guessed that was where Volkmann got the smile as well as the eyes.

'My old man died six months ago. My old lady's still kicking.'

'Is that her in in the photograph? Where was it taken?'

'A long time ago, at the Albert Hall. She used to play professionally. She was pretty good in her day.'

'You didn't want to follow her?'

He sipped his beer. 'Nope. I hadn't got the talent.' He looked at her and changed the topic of conversation. 'You're glad to be leaving us, Sally?'

'I'm looking forward to New York. God knows, Joe, we've really nothing to hide from the Americans or them from us. It's just liaison, but it's a good posting and the expenses are great. But it's a bit of a waste having me there. The Ambassador learns more in a week over lunch than our people do in a year.'

'I got a call from Dick Wolsley the other day. He says the Germans and the French are trying to pull out of the operation already.'

'You mean DSE?'

He nodded and swigged his beer. 'Did you hear any rumours?'

Sally Thornton shrugged and played with the top button of her blouse. 'I've heard they've both made a few noises, but that's about all. If it's true, the whole operation will come tumbling down and bang goes joint security co-operation.' She paused. 'Anyway, it's all a waste of taxpayers' money, don't you think, Joe? And the way things are happening, I'd be inclined to believe Wolsley.'

'Why?'

'Because everyone's in trouble financially. The Germans, the French, us. And since the stock market got the jitters they've got the frights. And when nations get the frights, watch out, it's each for themselves.'

'Did you hear Ferguson say if he'd heard any rumours?'

Sally Thornton smiled. 'I hardly talk to the man. He's so bloody stuffy.'

Volkmann laughed. 'What about Peters?'

'All Peters tells me is I've got good legs and he'd like to take me to bed.' She paused, saw Volkmann glance at her legs again. 'And that you're a good intelligence officer.' She looked at him. 'Do we have to talk about work? What time's your flight?'

'Noon. And you?'

'Afternoon. Do you miss London, Joe?'

'Sometimes, but not much.'

Sally Thornton sat far back in her chair. 'I don't. Not one little bit. It's gone down the tubes if you ask me.' She saw him notice her legs again and she said, 'Can I ask you a very personal question, Joe?'

'How personal?'

'Would you like to take me to bed?'

When Volkmann smiled, she smiled back and put down her glass. 'I've got to be up by eight.'

They sat on the bench together and the autumn leaves lay in deep piles about the small park.

It was November and he had come down from the weapons course in Scotland for the weekend. The sun was shining and the sky pale and blue: one of those perfect days in autumn when the air is crisp and clear and it feels good to breathe. His father was wrapped in the tattered old tweed overcoat that always looked a size too big for him. They sat on the bench and the old man looked at him with watery brown eyes.

'Mama tells me they're sending you to Berlin.'

He saw the look on his father's face as he nodded and then he said, 'It's a good posting, Papa. And I'll get home once a month with luck, so it won't be so bad.'

'Is it dangerous?'

He smiled. 'No, Papa. Not dangerous. It's intelligence-gathering mostly. Nothing for you to worry about. They're not going to send me over the Wall with a gun. And the stories you read about Berlin are usually just that. Stories. The kind of thing you read in fiction. It's not like that in real life.'

'Mama said you went there last month.'

'They sent me over for three days just to see the operation. I think they were trying to find out if I really wanted the posting.'

'And did you?'

He shrugged. 'It's a change from Century House.'

'And Anna?'

'She'll join me in a couple of months.'

'What is it like now?'

'Berlin? A little bit like a miniature New York. Good restaurants and lots of night life if that's where your interests lie. The Americans and British and French have given it a weird atmosphere. Not like the old days.'

He saw the old man look away absentmindedly towards the trees, as if lost in some private thought, but Joseph Volkmann recognised the look on his father's face. The old man stood, glanced at his watch, cut off the pain before it started to take hold.

'Your Mama will have lunch ready. We better not keep her waiting.'

'Papa.'

His father looked down at him and Joseph Volkmann saw the pink circle of rutted flesh on his temple, the wound as blatant as the ones inside that would never go away.

He said quietly, 'It's all in the past now, Papa. A long time ago. But sometimes I want you to talk about it. Maybe it would help.'

His father shook his head. 'Believe me, Joseph, talking about it does not help. I tried for twenty years and learned that it is much better to forget.' The brown eyes looked down at him. 'You'll learn that as you get older, Joseph. Bury ghosts if you can, not resurrect them. Now come, let's not keep Mama waiting.'

He watched as the old man moved away, the bony hunched body lost in the big, heavy tweed overcoat.

He stood and followed his father.

Chapter Four

Asunción,
Paraguay.
November 23rd

A high wall surrounded the perimeter of the property, but Hernandez could see the expansive, sun-washed lawns as he drove up towards the hill, the house itself barely visible beyond the pepper and palm trees that lined the long driveway beyond the walls.

House was not the word: the property was more a mansion. It stood on a hill overlooking the city, large, two storeys high, the bland, grey-painted exterior imposing but not inviting attention.

The day was humid, the sky cloudless. He had sweated on the journey, as much from the heat as from the knot of nervous excitement he felt in the pit of his stomach.

Now he saw the wrought-iron front gates were open, was about to drive the rusting old red Buick through when he saw the young *policia* step forward from behind the cover of the wall, hands dug into the leather belt which held his holstered pistol.

He was very young, in his early twenties, fresh-faced, and his uniform fitted him badly. He stepped forward and raised his hand for Hernandez to stop. Hernandez hit the brakes abruptly and leaned out of the window, flashed his press identity card as he smiled, tried to look friendly.

As the young *policia* checked the identity card, stone-faced, Hernandez said, 'Nicolas Tsarkin. Old guy. Suicide. Right? I'm here to cover the story for the *La Tarde* newspaper.'

He saw the young cop study him. 'No one is to go in.'

'Who said so?'

'The captain. Captain Sanchez.'

'Vellares Sanchez?'

The *policia* nodded, uncertain now. Hernandez looked at the cop. The young man had his right hand nervously on the gun he carried in the leather holster. But the use of Sanchez' first name had thrown him and Hernandez saw the opportunity and seized it.

Hernandez looked up at the house in the distance. 'Is Vellares up there now?'

'*Si.*'

'You got a radio?' Hernandez had seen the hand-held radio clipped onto the back of the young man's gun belt.

The *policia* nodded. '*Si.*'

Hernandez gunned the engine quickly. 'OK, you call up Vellares. Tell him Rudi Hernandez is on his way up.'

'But the captain said . . .'

Hernandez quickly shifted the car into drive, ignoring the young man's protest.

'Don't forget the name . . . Rudi Hernandez.'

The red Buick shot forward through the open gates. Hernandez caught a glimpse of the rookie *policia* in the rear-view mirror, frantically fumbling for his radio.

Hernandez smiled to himself. *First hurdle over with. One more to go.*

The old guy, Tsarkin, had had money. Lots of it, for sure.

The manicured lawns stretched up from the house for over a hundred metres. Hernandez could make out the house beneath the red, pan-tiled roof. He glanced left and right as he drove up the asphalt driveway: beyond the pepper trees there were yellow and pink hibiscus in bloom.

The gardens were something else. Mango trees, peach trees, a couple of coconut palms, their fronds heavy and limp in the breezeless, hot afternoon air. The gardeners must have toiled to keep this place in such good shape. They were the best kept gardens he had seen in Asunción.

He kept the old Buick at a slow pace all the way up, taking in the place, remembering how he had wondered what it would look like beyond the white walls that led up from the road below, something telling him there was more to be learned here in this house than what Rodriguez had told him.

Halfway up the hill the Buick's engine started to chug, racking the old rusted chassis.

Shit!

The big old American Buick was ready for the scrap heap. Twelve years old, one-fifty thousand kilometres on the second engine. It had been a trusty old friend for a long time, but he needed a new car badly. It was the auto-choke, he knew of old; cracked, covered with plastic tape, a thing he should have replaced long ago if only he had had the time. He took a little pressure off the accelerator. The car stopped chugging, then started again after another twenty metres. He was coming round the bend now, seeing the house clearly and unobstructed for the first time: big and expensive-looking.

Thirty metres from where the asphalt driveway became gravel the big old red Buick gave out, the engine not responding to his foot, as he pumped the accelerator hard, the car barely coasting along now, the road still a little uphill. He swung the wheel left and pulled in onto the grass verge, slammed the steering wheel with his fist.

Shit!

Hernandez switched off the ignition and looked up at the entrance. There was a stern-looking uniformed cop standing beside a blue and white parked on the gravel driveway. Then he saw the big front door of the house open and the familiar fat bulk of Vellares Sanchez stepping out under the porch, but not moving out into the sunlight, a grim look on his fleshy face.

Hernandez climbed out of the car and waved. Sanchez did not wave back. Hernandez slammed the car door and began to walk up to the house.

Vellares Sanchez was older than Hernandez, forty, over-weight, always looking like he needed a good night's sleep with his dark, hooded eyelids. The flesh seemed to hang tiredly from his fat face and his thinning black hair was plastered across his balding head in thin wisps. The white linen suit he wore was crumpled and ill-fitting. Everything about him looked in disarray; but Hernandez knew it was a deceptive ploy, that behind those hooded, sleepy eyes there was a brain as sharp as a razor.

He was a man of few words, Hernandez knew of old, though not unfriendly. But now his manner seemed cool and distant as Hernandez came towards him. He shook the hand that Hernandez offered limply, a sure sign he was annoyed, and nodded towards Hernandez' car.

'What's wrong with that heap of junk?' Sanchez said, dabbing his glistening forehead with a cotton handkerchief.

Hernandez smiled, trying to soften the fat man's annoyance. 'The auto-choke's been acting up. Floods the engine. It'll be OK once the sun dries it out.'

'I told the man at the gate not to let anyone past,' Sanchez said sternly.

'You know me, Vellares . . . anywhere there's a story.'

The fat man's voice became even sterner. 'I gave orders.'

'Vellares, come on . . . I mean, it's my living. I don't write, I don't eat.' Hernandez shrugged. 'Look, I'm sorry. Mendoza wants me to get the story. I apologise.'

Sanchez looked at the young man standing before him. He was tall, brown-haired, pale-skinned. The hair cut in a neat fringe and a little on the long side, but otherwise clean-shaven and handsome. He wore his clothes loosely, like one of the lecturers from the *Universidad* which he would have passed for, were it not for the jagged scar that ran across his right cheek. The scar gave Hernandez a roguish appearance, the look of a man who fought in bars, but Sanchez knew better.

They had known each other ten years. He was a good journalist, Hernandez, good with words, and his eyes showed kindness, even though Sanchez knew they had seen as much bad as his own.

'So . . . what gives, Vellares?'

Hernandez was looking at him now with brown, twinkling eyes, the transgression shrugged off as if it had never happened, as if everything was a joke, a laugh. A smile on Hernandez' face, but something else, too, Sanchez sensing it. Excitement? Fear? Sanchez took a pack of cigarettes from his pocket and offered one to Hernandez, who accepted the peace-offering gratefully. He lit them both and looked at the young man.

'Tell me what you know,' Sanchez said.

Hernandez blew out smoke into the hot, cloying air. 'Old guy, name of Tsarkin, killed himself.' Hernandez looked around at the lush, tropical gardens behind him, then back at the house. 'And they say money can't buy you happiness . . .'

'It can buy you anything except good health, *amigo*,' said Sanchez, drawing on his cigarette, coughing.

'That why the old guy killed himself? Because he was ill?'

'Maybe. Maybe not.'

Hernandez reached in the back pocket of his corduroy pants and pulled out a wirebound notepad, searched in his pockets for something to write with. 'You mind if I take some notes?'

Sanchez shook his head. 'No. Only my men from the forensic department haven't finished yet. That's why I didn't want anyone coming past the gates.'

Hernandez nodded. 'How long will they be?'

'They're almost finished.'

'You got a pen I could borrow?'

'You still borrowing pens? Reporters are supposed to carry pens.'

'I keep losing them. Holes in my pockets,' said Hernandez, shrugging a smile.

Sanchez took a pen from his pocket and handed it to Hernandez. 'It was the same ten years ago, in the courts. How many pens you owe me now? Holes in your head, *amigo*.'

Sanchez went to turn. 'Come inside. When the men finish you can take a look around.' There was a slight, uncharacteristic enthusiasm in Sanchez' voice now, as he ground out his cigarette with the heel of his shoe. 'You ought to see the place. This old guy, he had money to burn.'

'Tell me . . .' said Hernandez, and followed Sanchez inside.

Hernandez looked around the house in wonder and amazement, but pretending more surprise than he felt, because this was how he imagined a rich man like Tsarkin might live.

The crystal chandelier in the hallway, the sweeping staircase, the dining-room with the silver candlesticks and the hand-carved chairs of solid oak, the kitchen that was bigger than his whole apartment. There was a jacuzzi with gold-plated taps, and a tennis court on the back lawn.

The servants' quarters were near the outdoor swimming pool. There were four servants, Sanchez told him, and three gardeners. They had all left for the afternoon, after Sanchez' men had questioned them, shocked by their employer's death, the old Indian cook traumatised beyond speech.

Sanchez kept the study on the ground floor until last. The forensic men were finishing as they came into the hallway from the kitchen. Sanchez caught one of the men by the arm and took him aside to talk in private. When they had finished Sanchez crossed back to where Hernandez stood, examining an oil painting of a sleek jaguar in a jungle setting. The painting was unsigned, but not bad. A good amateur, Sanchez thought.

'Well?' Hernandez asked.

'Suicide,' said Sanchez. 'No question. Another problem less for me to worry about. We have a little time before they remove the body. You want to see Tsarkin?'

Hernandez nodded and Sanchez led the way.

The door into the study was open, the room large, like all the others. The first thing Hernandez noticed was the painting in a gilded frame swung back on hinges to reveal a safe in the wall, its grey metal door ajar. There were books on shelves along three walls, a window looking out onto the gravel driveway, a big polished desk and a brown, expensive executive leather chair. Hernandez looked around the room but couldn't see the body. His eyes went back to the safe just as Sanchez pointed towards the window.

'He's over there, behind the desk.'

Hernandez crossed to the big polished desk and looked

over, saw the trousered legs of the man first, then the pools of glutinous blood on the grey carpet, the grey-yellow brain matter streaking the walls and curtains and spattered on the floor. The man's head was covered with a bloodied white handkerchief. Hernandez suppressed the nausea he felt in the pit of his stomach and knelt down for a closer look.

'Hey!'

He turned; Sanchez stood nearby, lighting another cigarette.

'Mind if I look?' asked Hernandez.

'It's not pleasant. He shot himself through the mouth.'

Hernandez nodded and turned back to the corpse. The handkerchief was soaked through in sticky, congealing blood. As he pulled back the material he felt the congealing blood come unstuck from the dead man's face. Hernandez almost vomited. The top of the old man's head was blown away to reveal a cavernous hole the size of a fist; the brain matter everywhere, thick ribbons of drying blood runing down the man's jaws and neck.

The face itself was almost unrecognisable above the mouth, the shattered jaw set in a final, contorted grimace, as if the dead man had feared the last moment before the gun had exploded and the bullet penetrated the roof of the mouth, shattering the cranium. The old man's wrinkled claw of a hand was raised and crooked, as if he were waving a grotesque goodbye.

Hernandez let the bloodied handkerchief fall back into place and stood up, seeing the gun then, big and frightening and shining on the grey carpet, a metre away.

Sanchez looked across at him. 'You OK?'

Hernandez swallowed. 'Sure.'

'It must have been quick. No pain. Not the worst way to go, *amigo*.'

Hernandez nodded. 'What about his family?'

'Not married, according to one of his servants.'

'What did he do, this man?' asked Hernandez.

Sanchez went to sit in a comfortable leather chair beside the coffee table. 'He was a retired businessman. Once, apparently, he owned a number of businesses in Paraguay. Import-Export agencies, mainly.'

'An immigrant?'

'With a name like Tsarkin he wasn't a Maca Indian, that's for sure.'

Hernandez jotted down the details in his notebook. 'Old?'

'Late seventies. I'm not sure exactly.' Sanchez drew on his cigarette, coughed out smoke. 'He had a long life. Hope I'm as lucky.'

Hernandez said, 'You mentioned he might have been ill?'

Sanchez flicked ash from his cigarette into a crystal ashtray. 'One of the servants said he was in and out of hospital for the past six months. Also, he had an appointment at a private hospital this morning. He was pretty sick. Cancer, the servant said. He'd lost weight. He didn't look too good.' Sanchez glanced over at the corpse. 'He looks a lot worse now.'

'How did the servant know he had cancer?'

'He saw a medical report the old man left lying around some place. I'm having one of my men contact the hospital he attended. The San Ignatio.'

Hernandez glanced at the body again, felt the sickness return. He turned, moved a couple of paces towards the open wall safe.

'Anything in there?'

Sanchez shook his head. 'Nothing.' He gestured to the fireplace with his cigarette. 'Lots of ashes in the grate. Looks like he burned a lot of papers.'

Hernandez stepped towards the fireplace. It had been his one hope, finding something, *anything*, but the old man must have been prepared, been sure before death to burn everything.

'Not a sliver of paper left. Nothing but ashes.' Sanchez stared absentmindedly at the grate. 'I wonder what the old man had to burn so bad?'

'I wonder?' echoed Hernandez.

Sanchez looked up, stared at him a moment, before looking away again. 'Anyway, it's all over now. And it's a wrap.'

'You ever hear of Tsarkin before now?' Hernandez looked

back at the body, scribbled a few meaningless notes, trying not to sound too interested.

'No. Why do you ask?'

Hernandez shrugged. 'A wealthy man . . . I just thought you might have heard of him.'

'Never. You?'

Hernandez turned, saw Sanchez regard him curiously. 'No, I never did.'

Hernandez wondered if Sanchez believed him. Probably not, but he made it sound truthful. He smiled. 'But then, *amigo*, Asunción is a secretive place, full of anonymous rich people.'

Sanchez stared over at him for a couple of seconds, the hooded eyes watchful, lingering. Wondering, Hernandez knew, if he had been told the truth. Sanchez missed nothing.

'I guess so,' the fat man said finally. He looked away, pushed himself slowly up from the chair with effort. He took the handkerchief from his pocket and dabbed his brow. 'This heat, it kills me. You want a beer? The refrigerator is full. Imported beers, too. German, Dutch, you name it.'

'Sure. A beer sounds good.'

Sanchez moved away. 'I'll be back in five minutes. Don't touch anything.'

Hernandez nodded. The fat detective turned and went out of the door.

Hernandez stood there, in the middle of the study, trying to think. His eyes went from the bloodied body to the wall safe, then to the fire grate. Why? Why had the old man killed himself? Was it ill-health? Or because of the people Rodriguez had told him about? Or maybe they had killed the old man too, made it look like suicide.

He crossed to the big, blackened fireplace and stood in front of it, stared down at the grate. He took a fire-iron quietly from the stand of utensils beside the fireplace and raked the ashes. It was just as Sanchez had said. Not a sliver of paper. Only soot and ashes. What had they been, these papers?

He replaced the fire-iron and moved quickly now towards

the open safe in the wall, careful to tread softly, listening at the same time for Sanchez' return. He peered into the safe; it was empty as Sanchez had said. He crossed quietly to behind the desk, tried not to look down at the body near his feet.

Blood covered the desk's blotting pad and polished surface. Thick, congealed blood mixed with blobs of grey-yellow brain mucus. Hernandez felt queasy again. He swallowed hard, mopped his sweating brow with the back of his shirt-sleeve.

There were three drawers on the left side of the desk. He tried the top drawer first. It was unlocked and slid out quietly. Inside were a pair of scissors, a paper knife made of *quebraco* wood, the kind the Maca Indians made and sold in the streets, and some plain white sheets of bond paper.

He flicked through the sheets of paper. All blank. He slid the drawer shut and tried the next one. It was empty, unused, the smell of the applewood rising up to meet his nostrils. He slid back the second drawer and tried the last. More blank bonded paper, some elastic bands, a box of metal staples. He closed the drawer and looked down at the drying blood that seemed everywhere, at the rigid corpse, at the one hand raised in the air as if waving goodbye. *So long, Senor Tsarkin*.

He saw a drop of his own sweat fall onto the desk. He wiped his brow again, listened for Sanchez' footsteps, but no sound, nothing, only the sound of his own hard breathing.

The old man had been careful. Very careful. Perhaps elsewhere he kept some information. Something that would point a way, open a door for Hernandez, so that he might know what was happening. Gaining access to the house or study again would be difficult, perhaps impossible. This was his one opportunity. He stepped back towards the rows of shelves lining the walls.

There were books on Paraguayan history, the Chaco Wars, a biography of Lopez, gardening books, books on company and business law, heavy tomes on import-export regulations; a beautiful hide-bound set of volumes by Vasquales on Paraguayan history and culture. The rest were expensively bound novels.

Hernandez plucked one from the shelf. It was in Spanish, its pages virgin, unread. He replaced the book and riffled through some more. The same. No thumb marks, the smell of paper strong. The old guy, he hadn't been a reader. They were for show, these books, except perhaps the business books, part of an image that went with the property.

As he replaced the last book the telephone buzzed.

Hernandez froze, his heart skipping a beat, the shrill noise disturbing the quiet of the study. It buzzed a couple of times, Hernandez listening, listening to hear if Sanchez was returning, but nothing, no sound apart from the telephone. He crossed to the desk quickly and lifted the receiver.

'*Si?*'

'Senor Tsarkin, please.' The man's voice on the line sounded prissy. Hernandez thought he heard music playing faintly in the background, Ravel's *Bolero*. He glanced down at the body of the old man on the floor, thinking a moment. If it was a relative, it wasn't his business to break the news.

'What is it?' Hernandez asked, more loudly.

'Senor Tsarkin! I did not recognize your voice.'

Hernandez was about to interrupt but the man spoke first.

'This is the reservations manager at the Excelsior Hotel. I am telephoning to confirm that everything is in order. The executive suite you requested for Friday evening is suite one-twenty. I am at your service and hope everything will prove satisfactory for your guests.'

Hernandez said it, automatically, feeling his pulse quicken, 'Yes, I'm sure it will.' He turned his head sharply towards the study door, thought he heard footsteps off in the distance. Sanchez returning?

'There is a slight problem, however, *senor*,' the man went on, his voice now more stilted, formal. 'We have some regular guests flying into Asunción late tomorrow night. They require several suites, and we are heavily booked. You said you would only require the suite from 7 until 9 p.m. If it is possible, I would like to confirm this, so that our intending guests may be accommodated.' There was a pause. 'Could you confirm this, *senor*?'

'Yes. Until nine.' Hernandez swallowed, hearing his own heartbeat quicken, hearing the footsteps outside become louder.

'Excellent!' said the man. 'Thank you, *senor. Buenas tardes.*'

'*Buenas tardes.*'

Hernandez replaced the receiver and looked down at the body of Nicolas Tsarkin. Maybe not so *buenas*. When he looked up again Sanchez was standing in the doorway, two cans of beer in his hands.

'Who was that?' Sanchez asked as he came into the room.

'My office,' Hernandez lied.

Sanchez looked at him a moment, then offered a can of beer, watching as Hernandez pulled the ring of the chilled can.

Hernandez took a sip of the ice-cold beer, German beer, the brand unknown to him, but the liquid sharp and refreshing. He looked over at Sanchez. 'Good beer.'

Sanchez nodded and said, 'The office, what did they want?'

'They wanted to know if I'm through here.'

Sanchez raised the can to his lips and swallowed. The heat was terrible, not a whisper of wind blowing in through the open study window. There were tiny beads of sweat running down his face. He wiped his forehead with the back of his hand.

'And are you? Finished?'

'I guess so.'

'Drink your beer. Then we'll see what we can do with that car of yours. If I were a proper cop I'd have you in prison for driving a car like that.'

Hernandez smiled. He finished the ice-cold liquid in one long swallow, then tucked his notebook into his trouser pocket, and slipped the pen in after it.

Sanchez said, 'The pen's mine, *amigo*.'

Hernandez smiled and handed it back. '*Gracias*.'

Sanchez put down the empty beer can and nodded towards the door. 'Come, let's get out of here. Dead bodies, they give me the creeps.'

Hernandez took one last look down at the old man's corpse. Then he turned and followed Sanchez outside.

Hernandez drove back to the city through the dusty, hot streets and parked his car in the office lot of the *La Tarde*, the old engine running smoothly now; he promised himself he would get it fixed just as soon as he got time.

He climbed the stairs to the newsroom, greeted his colleagues, before going to sit at his desk and switching on his computer terminal. It took him only fifteen minutes to write up a filler on the old man's suicide, the bare facts, the name, the address, and the background information he had learned from Sanchez, remembering it all, no need for the notebook on the desk in front of him.

It was almost four in the afternoon when he filed his copy with the news editor, time for him to finish work. He looked around for Mendoza, but couldn't see him. Just as well: the little man would want to go for a beer and Hernandez had other things on his mind. He took out his notebook and flicked it open, saw again what he had written there once he had left Tsarkin's house: *Friday, 7 to 9 p.m., suite one-twenty. Excelsior Hotel.*

Two days away. The question was, what was happening? Why had Tsarkin booked a suite for only two hours? A meeting? It had to be a meeting.

If that was it, then what he needed was a plan, a plan to get in there, into the suite, listen to what was being said. He tidied his desk then went down to the lot and drove to the Excelsior Hotel on the Calle Chile.

The hotel lobby was busy. It was a plush palace of oriental carpets and dark wood, the best hotel in the city. He had spent a night there once before; a pretty visiting female journalist with an American newspaper had taken a liking to him when he had been assigned to help her with a feature article. After her research had been completed she had asked Hernandez back to her room. The two of them had spent a pleasant night and day together, indulging themselves in love-making and champagne, having room-service deliver their meals.

Fortunately the girl's newspaper had been generous with their expense account.

Hernandez took the lift to the first floor and found the suite no problem, noting the nearby room numbers, the layout of the rooms on the first floor, before going back down to the lobby again and out to the car park and the old red Buick parked twenty metres from the hotel's fire-exit doors. Hernandez took note of the doors.

The day was still hot, and he kept the windows down on the way to his apartment, smoking as he drove, trying to work something out in his head, trying to come up with a plan. The key to it all had been Tsarkin. Only now Tsarkin was dead. And Tsarkin had been the only real lead he had had.

When he stepped into his apartment twenty minutes later, he heard the gentle whirr of the air-conditioning unit by the window. He had forgotten to turn it off that morning. The room was cool, pleasant, and his body was very hot.

The apartment overlooked the city and had a sweeping view of the river south of Asunción. Rudi loved it. A bachelor's place, compact, one bedroom, a couch in the living-room where he had slept during Erica's stay. He went into the kitchen and poured himself a large scotch, added some cracked ice, then went to sit by the open window, staring out absentmindedly at the river boats plying up and down the Rio Paraguay.

Sometimes he hated Asunción; sometimes he loved it.

He glanced up at the photograph of his mother and father on the bookshelf in the corner of the living-room. Why had his mother chosen to come to such a God-forsaken city as Asunción? And yet it was home for him; he fitted in more easily here than he ever had in his mother's homeland. There were many things he hated about this city, many things he loved. He hated the poverty, the corruption; he loved the girls, the sun, the easy-going *mestizos*.

He finished his scotch quickly, placed the glass on the table. He could still smell the scent of Erica's perfume lingering in the room.

He looked at the photograph on the bookshelf again, his

father dark and handsome and smiling; his mother blonde, pretty, but her Nordic face set in a harsh, strained smile. She should have smiled more, his old lady. But then she had never had much to smile about. That was the one thing the *mestizo* had done to his blood. Made him smile more.

He smiled now, thinking of the suite in the Excelsior Hotel, the plan coming into his head with such ease, so complete, that he picked up the telephone at once and began to call the number, his hands trembling with excitement and fear.

Perhaps the old Indian woman on the Calle Estrella had been right. Perhaps Erica would bring him luck.

He hoped so.

Because if not, then maybe he was dead.

Chapter Five

Richmond, Surrey,
England.
November 24th

There were no pedestrians in the quiet street of red-bricked Victorian houses, the small park it faced empty on this winter's day.

The black taxi drew up outside number twenty-one and Volkmann paid the driver and stepped out. It was cloudy and cold, the sky threatening snow as he went up the narrow front path. The garden was overgrown; dockweed and nettles climbing between the bare winter rose bushes.

As Volkmann unlocked the door and stepped inside, he heard the faint sound of music coming from the room at the back of the house and smiled. Cole Porter's *Night and Day*.

He left his overnight bag by the door and passed the small parlour, its door open to reveal the silver-framed photographs on the mantelpiece and the walnut sideboard, the bric-a-brac the old woman had collected over forty years.

In the kitchen the big Aga range was fired, its metal throwing out a blanket of heat into the small room, the door at the end open, the music louder now, as he stepped towards it.

She sat by the window of the music room, her grey head bent close to the Steinway piano. The silver-topped walking cane lay on top of the black polished wood. She looked up as he peered round the door, smiled before removing her spectacles.

'I was beginning to think you wouldn't come.'

He smiled back warmly and crossed to where she waited and kissed her cheek.

'It's only two days, I'm afraid. I've got to be back by Saturday.'

She touched his face with her palm. 'No matter, it's good to see you, Joseph. How was your flight?'

'Delayed, two hours. Why don't we go into the kitchen? It's warmer there.'

He handed her the silver-topped cane and helped her towards the door, holding her arm as she limped.

'I managed to get some tickets for the Albert tonight. Think you could manage it?'

'Tonight? But that's splendid, Joseph.'

'It's Per Carinni. He's doing the Four Seasons.' He smiled down at the old woman. 'And how's the patient?'

'Much better, now that you are here. Let's have some tea, then you can tell me about Strasbourg.'

It never changed, the house, remained always as he remembered it, each time he returned: the same familiar smells, the same peaceful quiet that enveloped him like a warm cocoon, and always music, somewhere in the background. The radio was on, a Bach medley playing softly.

They sat in the kitchen drinking tea. She had placed a plateful of biscuits beside his cup but he left them untouched, the old guilt creeping in on him again, the thought of her alone in the big old house, shuffling around on the silver-topped cane.

She was sixty-five next birthday and Volkmann remembered her younger every time he returned. He glanced up at the photographs on the wall over the kitchen fireplace: his father and her, taken thirty years before, her dark hair falling about her face as she smiled out at the camera, himself as a young boy sitting on her knee outside the cottage in Cornwall.

'Tell me about Strasbourg.'

Volkmann put down the white china cup. 'There's not much to tell. There's still a lot of work to be done. It's taken the best part of eighteen months to get things off the ground. And there's a lot of distrust about. The French don't trust the English, the English don't trust the French.' He smiled at her. 'And the Italians, of course, don't trust anybody. So much for mutual security co-operation.'

'What about Anna? Do you hear from her?'

'She telephones now and then. She met someone, a staff officer at the military college.'

'Someone you knew?'

'No. He was four years behind me.'

He stood up and placed a hand on her shoulder, smiled down at the old woman's wrinkled face.

'Come. I'd like to hear you play for me. We have some time before the concert. Then I'll call a taxi and have them pick us up at seven.'

The snow started to fall as they travelled in the taxi towards the city. Light at first, it soon became a thick swirling mist of flakes. By the time they reached the Albert Hall there was a blanket of snow covering the London streets, the traffic turning the virgin white to grey slush.

A few people in the foyer recognised her and came over to say hello, and after the concert they joined some friends of hers for supper in an Italian restaurant nearby, people she knew from the old days, the grand concert tours in Europe, one of them an Italian diplomat whom Volkmann had never met before. His mother told him she had met the man and his wife during one of her concerts in Ravenna.

He was in his late fifties, grey-haired, distinguished-looking, tall for an Italian, with a theatrical manner that suggested to Volkmann the man would have been better suited to a career on stage than one in the Diplomatic Service. He hadn't seen the old woman in over eight years but he remembered her with fondness.

'You could do better than the artiste who played for us tonight, *bella madam*. You must come to Rome. I will arrange it.'

It was exaggerated, of course, but it cheered her up.

When the dessert came, the talk at the table turned to politics.

'Everyone is worried, of course. So much instability.' The Italian diplomat shrugged. 'We can only live in hope. My own government, they have ratified a new commercial loan agreement for certain vital industries in difficulty. But the banks, the banks say there is no money. Where will it all end?'

The diplomat gave a heavy, theatrical shrug and returned to his dessert. He would still eat in the best restaurants, Volkmann reflected, still drink the finest wines. And what was happening at home wouldn't affect him in the least. But what the man said made Volkmann think of Sally Thornton's comment.

It was after one o'clock when the taxi turned into the street. The snow had stopped and when they reached the park the old woman told the driver to stop, they would walk the rest of the way, saying the exercise would do her good. Volkmann helped her out and gripped her arm, the snow soft underfoot, the old woman ignoring his protests, saying she felt better; the evening had done her good.

The trees of the park were ghostly white as they passed the entrance, snow outlining their branches, the open spaces a grey expanse in the gloaming.

She wasn't limping now, as they strolled towards the house. For someone of an artistic nature who had fallen ill, his father had once remarked, the doctor ought to prescribe a round of applause, not pills. Volkmann smiled in the darkness, remembering the remark.

She looked up at him. 'Wasn't Carinni divine?'

They had reached the park entrance, and Volkmann looked down at her face.

'I've heard you play better.'

She smiled. 'You're a toady, Joseph. But you know the way to an old woman's heart.'

She stopped to regain her breath, and he watched as she looked around the snowy park landscape, then moved towards the entrance, stepping through the open gates. He stayed close behind her.

'This reminds me . . .' she said.

'Tell me.'

'Of when I was a little girl. Of Christmas. There was always snow in winter in Budapest.' She looked up at him and he could see her face, dimly. 'But that was all such a long time ago. Long before I met your father.'

'Tell me again.'

He had heard it all before, many times, her words like some comforting litany. The season of plenty in Budapest, and the anticipation of Christmas. When the blue flag was up on the frozen lake in Octagon Square, and the ice was thick enough for skaters, and the red candles flickering in the windows of warm houses, warm as an oven, the smell of oil lamps burning and the great, grey plumes of coal smoke rising in the cold air. Budapest long ago, the city of her childhood.

But the old woman was silent. Volkmann looked down, saw her wipe tears from her eyes. He touched her arm gently.

'Come, you'll catch cold.'

She turned her head then, looked out over the cold white park. Volkmann moved to grip her frail arm before the melancholy took hold. As he looked at her face he remembered the young woman she had been on the beach in Cornwall all those years ago.

She looked up at him and he saw the grief in the wet brown eyes. 'I miss him, Joseph. I miss him so.'

Volkmann bent and took her wrinkled face fondly in both his hands, kissed her forehead.

'We both do.'

Chapter Six

Asunción.
Friday,
November 25th

The giant Iberia 747 banked onto final approach and began its descent into Campo Grande airport.

Of all the passengers on board the packed flight to Paraguay's capital that late afternoon, none was probably so tired as the middle-aged man in the crumpled blue suit who sat quietly in row twenty-three.

The flight he had endured earlier from Munich to Madrid had been tolerable, but the long haul from Madrid to Asunción had taken its toll and now his dehydrated body ached.

It was almost three months since he had last visited Paraguay. He hadn't enjoyed it then and it was unlikely he would enjoy it now. Mosquitoes. Heat. Temperamental natives. But this time his visit would be even briefer, twenty-four hours, and for that he was grateful.

The man in the dark blue suit picked up the leather briefcase from the floor in front of him and clicked it open. He flicked carefully through the documents inside, checked that everything was in order.

A pretty air hostess moved down the aisle, a last-minute check on seat belts. The man glanced up, saw the slim hips and tanned legs sway rhythmically towards him. The girl paused, said something rapidly in Spanish as she pointed to the briefcase on his lap before moving on. The man in the blue suit clicked shut the case, tucked it neatly under the seat in front, and sat back.

Beyond the port window he glimpsed the sprawling, ragged suburbs of Asunción: the flat-roofed white and yellow plaster *adobes* and the tin-roofed shacks of the *barrios*. As the bowels of the big plane shuddered, he heard the whirr of the flaps extending and the dull thud of the undercarriage lowering into place.

Five minutes later he saw the yellow lights of the runway rush up beneath him, and then the rumble of wheels on concrete as the giant aircraft touched down to a perfect landing.

He had retrieved his suitcase from the carousel and passed unquestioned through customs twenty minutes later.

In the arrivals area a tall, blond young man who stood out from the waiting crowd held a placard stiffly in front of him: *Pieter De Beers*. Meyer stepped forward and the young man took his suitcase and beckoned for him to follow.

A Mercedes stood parked nearby, its black bodywork muddied, and he saw the three men waiting inside. Schmidt sat impassively like a rock in front and the two men reclined in the back.

Both wore immaculate business suits and both smiled when they saw Meyer.

One was young, in his middle thirties, and wore a light grey suit. He was stockily built and his dark hair gelled and glistened. Not handsome but ruggedly attractive, and his broad face was deeply tanned from years in the sun.

The second man was in his early sixties, but looked younger. He was tall and lean and very handsome. His silver-grey hair was more silver than grey and was swept back off his tanned face. He had the look of a self-assured diplomat. He wore a charcoal-grey business suit, a white shirt and a red silk tie and his gentle blue eyes radiated confidence and charisma. He raised a hand and smiled again as Meyer approached.

The blond young man put Meyer's suitcase in the boot and Schmidt got out to open the rear door for him.

When Meyer slid into the back seat the two passengers shook his hand in turn.

'You had a good flight, Johannes?' the silver-haired man asked.

'*Ja, danke.*'

Meyer took a handkerchief from his top pocket and dabbed his brow. Even in the air-conditioned Mercedes the heat was almost unbearable. He felt physically drained after the long flight, hoped the meeting wouldn't last long, felt certain it would not.

As he turned to the younger, dark-haired man, he said, 'Any problems?'

Kruger glanced at him and shook his head. 'No, but some bad news.'

'Oh . . . ?' said Meyer, feeling uneasy now, wondering if it had anything to do with the project. It couldn't be, he told himself, everything was in order, he was absolutely certain.

'We'll talk about it on the way, Johannes,' said Kruger, as he leaned forward and tapped the driver on the shoulder.

'The hotel, Karl.'

As the car started and pulled out from the kerb Meyer sat back, dabbing his forehead and silently cursing the heat, wondering what the bad news could be.

Rudi Hernandez was tired. He had been up until three that morning, going over the plan in his mind, checking through the equipment Ricardo Torres had loaned him the previous evening.

'Make sure it comes back in one piece,' Torres had said. 'Otherwise my boss kicks me out on my ass and I'm selling nuts outside the city zoo, *comprende?*'

Comprende.

The equipment was expensive. Torres had gone over the operation of the components with him asking, when he had finished, as he had when Hernandez had first telephoned him, 'What you going to do with all this, *amigo?*'

Hernandez had smiled enigmatically and said, 'Undercover work.'

Torres had looked at him, one eyebrow raised archly. 'OK. But any damage, you pay, *si*? Just remember that, Rudi.'

Hernandez had said he would remember. There was no

problem. He just needed to borrow the stuff for one night. He would return it intact.

He had gone to work early at *La Tarde* next morning, finished at three and driven straight to the apartment. He already had everything organised, but went over it one more time, so there would be no mistakes, no hitches.

Afterwards he had thought about pouring himself a drink but decided against it. He wanted to stay clear-headed and sober, didn't want to endanger his plan. Too much was at stake. He thought of telephoning Erica, just to say hello, just to hear her voice, because he was hyped up now, nervous, apprehensive, hoping everything would go all right. If the plan worked the way he intended it to work then he might get lucky.

If the plan worked.

If it didn't then he figured he was in big trouble, unless he could get out of the hotel fast. He remembered the fire exit on the first floor that led down to the rear of the hotel. A bolthole. He might need it.

He stood and went into the kitchen, poured himself a tepid Coke, dropped in a handful of ice cubes and came back out to the living-room. He sipped the Coke as he sat, then lit a cigarette, thinking about the plan, trying to see flaws. No real flaws, only risks, he decided.

He stubbed out the cigarette in the ashtray and stood up again, aware of his restless anxiety. From the bedroom he took the suitcase, already packed with the rest of the things he needed, then came back into the living-room once again.

He lay the suitcase on the couch and flicked open the catches, checked that he hadn't overlooked anything, then turned his attention to the equipment Torres had loaned him, lying on the coffee table.

He took it piece by piece and placed it carefully in the suitcase among the clothes he had already placed there, making sure the equipment didn't rattle around, remembering that Torres had said how sensitive it was. When he had finished he checked through everything again, carefully shut the suitcase and thumbed the combination lock to another set of numbers.

He felt a shiver of fear go through him. He looked down at the palms of his hands. They sweated and trembled. It seemed to him they had been trembling for the past forty-eight hours. He felt hot all over, despite the air-conditioning. He sucked in a deep breath, let it out slowly.

Relax, amigo. Stay calm. Otherwise you're dead even before you start.

He glanced at his watch. Five-thirty.

He just had time to change and then it would be time to go.

The big black Mercedes moved slowly through the evening traffic towards the city. The glass partition between the driver and his passengers was closed, allowing the passengers their privacy.

Meyer looked out beyond the tinted windows at the lights coming on as dusk fell, at the smaller cars moving past either side in the three-lane traffic, drawing him closer to the city, drawing him closer to his final meeting in this dreadful country.

A rusting, battered old yellow pick-up went slowly past the window, a cowboy-hatted Indian and his fat wife sitting in front, a crying child on her lap, windows rolled down, a radio blaring out Paraguayan harp music. In the back of the pick-up, half a dozen restless, brown-faced scruffy children danced about like monkeys. One of them cheekily made a face and bared his bottom as the pick-up went past.

Dirty, idiotic Dagos. Meyer turned his head away in disgust. How had his people endured it here? He glanced at Kruger. Meyer could bare the tension no longer.

'The news you spoke of . . . ?'

'It's Tsarkin. He shot himself two days ago.'

Meyer's eyebrows rose in surprise. 'He's dead?'

Kruger nodded. 'It was only a question of hours, anyway. Cancer. So he decided to take the quick way. He sent a letter to Franz before he did it. Said the pain was too much to bear. He wished us well, said he was sorry he couldn't make it.'

Meyer nodded, understanding, vaguely remembering something Franz had told him concerning Tsarkin's health.

'A great loss,' commented Meyer. And then a thought
striking him, a terrible thought. 'His papers . . . ?'

His face showed concern as he looked at the silver-haired
man seated opposite.

The silver-haired man smiled. 'There is no need for alarm,
Johannes. Tsarkin burned all his papers. Everything. Nothing
can lead back to us. Nothing.'

'Our people checked it out?'

This time it was Kruger who spoke. 'Franz called to the
house after the *policia* had left. There's absolutely nothing
to worry about. Franz checked it out with the servants. The
policia saw it as a straightforward case of suicide.'

'He checked Tsarkin's study and belongings?'

'There were only some old photograph albums. He removed
them.'

'And Tsarkin's safe-deposit box?'

'He emptied it himself. Burned everything before he pulled
the trigger.' He looked across at Meyer. 'I'm certain Franz
has been thorough.'

Meyer nodded and said, 'And the arrangements for the
meeting . . . ?'

'Tsarkin said the hotel was organised as usual but Franz
checked just to be certain. Everything was in order.' Kruger
paused. Then he smiled and said, 'He was a cautious man,
old Nicolas. As cautious in death as in life.'

Kruger turned his face back towards the window. The
silver-haired man reclined further in his seat.

Meyer did the same, relieved.

Hernandez reached the Excelsior at five-fifty and parked the
Buick twenty metres from the fire escape doors that backed
onto the parking lot.

He looked to make sure there was no one in the lot before
he strolled over to the exit doors, placed his palms against the
metal and pushed. The doors were locked by sprung bars that
could only be opened from the inside. He had checked already

to make sure they worked. They did. He probably wouldn't have to use them but he wasn't taking any chances. Nothing must obstruct the doors from opening onto the parking lot.

A row of metal garbage bins stood nearby, twenty metres from the hotel kitchen rear entrance, but did not obstruct the exit. Satisfied, he crossed back to his car, removed his overnight suitcase and left the driver's door unlocked. He walked round to the hotel entrance.

He wore dark-tinted glasses, and a grey business suit he hadn't worn in years. The suit was out of fashion and a size too small, but it looked respectable with the fresh white shirt and the blue silk tie. He had hardly recognised himself in the mirror when he had dressed after his shower, his fringe gelled back on his forehead, his hair looking darker and thicker with the hairdressing he had applied.

As he walked over to the brightly lit lobby and headed straight for the reception, he saw a fat, dark-suited man standing behind the desk, busy sorting through some papers.

The man looked up as Hernandez approached. '*Senor?*'

'I have a reservation for tonight. My name is Ferres.'

'One moment, *senor.*' The fat man turned to the computer terminal beside him and tapped the keyboard with pudgy fingers. Without looking up, he said, 'Senor Ferres. Room one hundred and four. The first floor.' The man looked up, smiled a plastic smile. 'Our last free room. You were lucky.'

I hope so, Hernandez thought. He had telephoned the hotel the evening before last to make his reservation, explaining to the reservations clerk that he had stayed on the first floor before and had enjoyed the view, had a preference for it. He had waited expectantly while the man checked, breathed a sigh of relief when the man had said yes, but only a double. Hernandez had said he would pay for the double.

'Will *senor* be settling his account in cash or by credit card?'

'Cash,' said Hernandez. 'And I would like to pay now. I intend leaving early tomorrow morning.'

'Certainly.'

'Also, I am having some friends call by shortly. I want a

bottle of champagne and some canapés sent up to my room immediately.'

'But of course, *senor*. At once. I will see to it.' The fat receptionist lifted the telephone receiver and called room service, gave Hernandez' room number and order and replaced the receiver, smiled another plastic smile.

'One moment, *senor*, and I will organise your bill. Then I will have someone help you with your luggage.'

Three minutes later Hernandez had settled his bill and stepped out of the lift on the first floor.

The bell-hop carrying his suitcase led him to his room at the end of the corridor, five doors away from Tsarkin's suite and on the opposite side of the corridor. Having the room on the first floor was imperative. And it had been the last one free, a good omen surely? The evening after telephoning the Excelsior he had gone to the hotel once again to examine the corridor layout. The room he had been given was perfect, not too close, not too far away.

As Hernandez followed the bell-hop into the room, the boy switched on the lights, placed the suitcase on the rack provided, waited for his tip. Hernandez obliged; the boy smiled, bade him good evening and withdrew.

Hernandez crossed to the window and stared out: lights coming on everywhere, darkness descending rapidly over the city, making him just a little more worried, a little more fearful about his plan.

And there was real fear in him now. He swallowed hard and checked his watch. Six o'clock. Whoever was going to use the room down the hall would be arriving soon. There was a sharp knock on the door. Hernandez' heart skipped a beat before he realised who it would be.

He admitted the white-coated, smiling waiter, the food trolley he pushed laden down with the champagne and canapés, watching him, the way he worked, listening to the chatter.

The man made a fuss of arranging the trolley in the centre of the room. Hernandez requested him to leave the trolley in the room and the champagne unopened.

'Of course, *senor*.' The waiter bowed and went to leave, but not leaving, a practised art.

Hernandez peeled off some notes from the wad in his pocket. 'That was excellent service. What is your name?'

'Mario, *senor*. Mario Ricardes.'

'Thank you, Mario.' Hernandez handed the man the money and the waiter bowed and left.

Hernandez looked at the champagne and food. The story was costing him a small fortune already. He hoped it was worth it. The champagne was French and expensive, the six sparkling glasses neatly arranged beside the bucket of crushed ice. The canapés looked exquisite: neat, crisped triangles of fresh bread with smoked salmon, anchovies, various cheeses, meat pastes, arranged splendidly on a silver tray. But Hernandez wasn't hungry, the fear in his stomach now like a living thing as he felt the sweat beginning, but trying not to think of what lay ahead.

He went to sit on the bed and opened the suitcase and removed everything he needed, laid the things neatly on the bed.

He went to work quickly, setting everything out in its place. When he was finished ten minutes later he sat on the bed, lit a cigarette, then punched in the number to call suite one-twenty. There was no reply.

Whoever intended using the suite had thankfully not arrived early. Had someone answered he would have pretended a wrong number and put down the phone.

Hernandez checked his watch again. Six-ten. He stubbed out his cigarette in the crystal ashtray and stood up nervously.

It was time to go to the lobby.

It was a different hotel this trip, Meyer noted as the Mercedes drew up outside the Excelsior. But they had used the hotel before, many times, he and Winter. But never together. The meetings to deliver the reports had alternated between both men.

The hotels had been Tsarkin's idea, the location and room

would be different each time so there would be less chance of electronic bugging or eavesdropping. Better than the houses of Franz or Tsarkin where the prying eyes and ears of servants and neighbours were a threat to security.

The house in the Chaco, of course, would have been ideal, but it was too remote and when the rains came the roads were often impassable. Hotels were better, less conspicuous. Businessmen and tourists came and went without regard.

Schmidt and the driver stepped out of the Mercedes and opened the doors, Kruger and Schmidt leading the way into the lobby, Meyer walking beside the silver-haired man.

They waited while Kruger went to the reception desk, carrying his briefcase. Meyer glanced around at the luxurious surroundings. The lobby was quiet. A couple of nice-looking girls in short, thigh-hugging skirts sat in leather easy chairs nearby. A young man wearing a tight-fitting blue suit close by, reading a newspaper. Their pimp? The girls looked tasty, very tasty. Perhaps he and Franz would have time to indulge themselves later. Knowing Franz he would have something organised.

He saw Kruger return from the desk. 'Which room?' Meyer asked, in German.

'One-twenty,' Kruger replied.

They all followed Kruger to the lift.

Six-fifteen.

Hernandez had bought a newspaper and found a vacant chair in the foyer facing the reception desk.

Background music played softly in the lobby, but Hernandez had a perfect vantage point and if he concentrated hard he could understand what was being said at the desk.

A couple of seats away sat two glamorous-looking girls dressed to kill: slit skirts, high heels, perfect make-up. They were professionals, Hernandez knew, doing their rounds of the city hotels. One of the girls smiled over at him. He ignored the smile – difficult – and opened his newspaper, pretended to read, but keeping his eyes on the entrance to the lobby from the street outside.

It was ten minutes later when Hernandez saw the men. His eyes flicked to the entrance instinctively as he heard them come into the foyer. Four men, all wearing business suits, all European-looking. Hernandez was suspicious immediately: the four men carried no luggage, and only two carried briefcases. They could have been simply returning from a business meeting in the city, but a gut feeling told him otherwise.

One of the men was obviously a bodyguard, a giant of a man, looking uncomfortable in his pale linen suit. He walked ahead of the group, big-chested, tightly cropped blond hair. He had a swaggering, slow, awkward gait, and looked like he was made of solid granite. Not the kind of man you tackled, Hernandez thought, unless you had an army behind you.

The second man was rugged, mid-thirties, his dark hair gelled and shining. He carried a briefcase and looked like a company executive. The third was middle-aged, short, overweight, and wore a blue, crumpled business suit. He held his briefcase under his arm and he looked tired, very tired; his fleshy face haggard, as if he had been drinking or endured a long journey.

But the fourth man was the one who stood out from the group. Tall, leanly built, his silver hair swept back off his handsome face.

The dark-haired man approached the reception desk while the others waited nearby. Hernandez listened, trying to separate the faint piped hotel music from the voices, but the man spoke quietly, very quietly.

'*Si, senor . . .*' came the reply from the desk clerk, and then a muttering of words in Spanish. The background music suddenly rose in pitch, almost drowning out the voices. *Shit. Speak louder, amigo. Louder*.

'All ready for you, *senor . . .*' More babble. *Damn!* He hadn't heard the room number. Hernandez went to stand, move closer, but saw one of the men, the tired-looking one in the crumpled blue suit, glance over at the girls nearby, then at Hernandez. He shifted in his seat, looked down, pretending to look at his watch. He did not want the man to get a good look at his face. He was unfolding his newspaper when he heard the voice speak faintly, in German, in his mother's tongue, the language of his childhood, the man in the steel-blue suit, asking it softly of the dark-haired man, as he passed Hernandez by, moving towards the lift.

'*Welche nummer?*'

'*Ein hundert zwanzig.*'

Which number? A hundred and twenty. Hernandez felt a shiver of excitement, and then a terrible pang of fear.

These are the men.

He watched as they crossed to the lift. The eldest of the men, the one with the silver hair, stood in the centre of the group. He made a remark and the others smiled and laughed, but Hernandez couldn't hear what was said, the men too far away.

The lift opened and the men stepped in. Hernandez stood and watched the numbers over the lift halt at floor one.

He waited a minute before moving towards the second lift, reached it seconds later as the doors opened. He felt a knot of fear in his stomach as he stepped inside and punched the button for the first floor.

When they stepped out on the first floor, Schmidt led them to the suite, inserted the card key and went in first, his big blond head touching the top of the door frame. He switched on the lights, checked the room, closed the curtains, his big, muscular bulk awkward but moving fast.

Kruger entered next, followed by the others. As Meyer closed the door behind him, Kruger was already unlocking the briefcase he carried. He took out the rectangular, hand-held electronic detector, held it chest high, turned around in a circle, watching the small red indicator light at the tip of the device, listening for the alarm signal but none came. None had ever come, but it was a precaution.

Kruger placed the device back in his briefcase and said, 'All clear.'

Schmidt took up a position in a chair by the locked door, sat and folded his arms, two bulges evident either side of his broad chest where Meyer knew the holstered pistol and the big, jagged-edged knife were strapped. The man was expert with either weapon, and intimidating all the more because of his perpetual silence. But his presence at these meetings always made Meyer feel secure. No one would tangle with Schmidt and live. One look at the man's frightening bulk told you so.

As the three men sat around the table at the end of the room, the gentle hum of the air-conditioner wafted in tepid air, but still warm in the room, still humid.

Meyer dabbed his brow and flicked open his briefcase and removed his papers, placed them neatly in front of him, before looking up at the two men waiting silently for him to begin.

Meyer said, 'The report on Brandenburg first, I presume?'

The handsome, silver-haired man made a steeple of his slim, manicured fingers and his gentle eyes sparkled as he nodded.

'If you would be so kind, Johannes. I know you must be tired, so let us proceed as quickly as possible.'

Meyer nodded and dabbed the sweat from his brow again. Then he looked down at his papers and began to speak.

Chapter Seven

Asunción

Hernandez sweated as he stood in front of the bathroom mirror. Gone was the grey business suit and the tinted glasses. The white shirt remained, but this time with a black tie. Instead of the suit he wore the waiter's white service jacket, the black trousers and black shoes he had bought the previous day in a small catering suppliers on the Calle Palma. Without the glasses, his hair gelled down even more; he looked different, certainly different. He touched the scar on his right cheek. Nothing could be done about that.

He knew the plan was not perfect. Few plans were, and this one was hurriedly thought up, flawed perhaps, but it was all that he had, all that he could think of.

If they were professionals, these men, and Hernandez guessed that they were, then they would be careful to check the suite for listening devices. That was why he wanted to give them a little time. If his plan worked, he wouldn't be able to record all their conversation, but the men were going to be a while in the suite, so he should be able to hear most of it.

If the plan worked.

He stepped out into the bedroom and took the single sheet of hotel headed notepaper from the bedroom's writing desk, checking the scribbled note he had written. *Champagne and canapés. Suite one-twenty.*

He knelt down beside the food trolley and raised the white linen cloth that hung over the edge. Underneath he saw the tiny microphone he had placed there earlier with the adhesive tape, checked again that it was secure.

Satisfied, he let the tablecloth fall back into place and then turned his attention to the second part of the equipment lying on the bed. It was a Japanese-made receiver-recorder, no bigger than the size of a hardcover book. He had checked the microphone-transmitter and it had worked properly, just as Torres had said it would.

The receiver was battery-operated, and Hernandez had inserted one of the two miniature tapes he had brought. Everything was ready to go. A spare two-hour tape lay on the bed just in case it was needed. He stood up and checked his watch. Six-forty. The men had had fifteen minutes. Hernandez hoped it was enough time.

He felt the sweat dripping down underneath his arms, down his chest, his neck, his forehead perspiring too. He picked up the white waiter's towel – *a nice touch* – and dabbed his brow, placed the towel over his left arm.

He was ready.

For a couple of seconds he hesitated, thinking of Rodriguez, the hideous, pulped flesh of the man's corpse, and a spasm of cold fear shot through him.

He forced the memory from his mind as he walked briskly to the door, opened it and peered out into the corridor.

Empty.

He pulled the trolley out behind him, checked his room key card was safely in his trouser pocket, then closed the door after him.

He listened again in the corridor for any approaching sound.

Nothing.

Hernandez drew in a deep breath and let it out quickly, then started to push the trolley towards suite one-twenty.

It took Meyer twelve minutes to read the report. He kept to the key points, careful to highlight his achievements, his personal contribution, his hard work, the attention to detail on which he prided himself. Now would come the questions.

When he had finished he noticed drops of sweat on the table in front of him: he had been perspiring heavily. He removed his handkerchief from his breast pocket and dabbed his forehead and then the table. His attention had been so solely focused on the facts, on the delivery, on how crucial this stage of the plan was, that Meyer realised he had been in somewhat of a trance. Now he had finished he looked up.

There was a smile on the handsome face of the silver-haired man seated opposite: he nodded his head agreeably.

They all heard the soft knock on the door and their heads turned sharply. Meyer saw that Schmidt already had his pistol out and by his side. Another knock, louder this time and Kruger stood up quickly from the table and crossed to the door, Schmidt calling out in Spanish, 'Who is it?'

Kruger moved the big man aside and put his ear to the door. Everyone in the room heard the voice behind it reply.

'Room service, *senor*.'

Kruger nodded to Schmidt and the big man stood back from the door, pistol at the ready.

Kruger opened the door a crack, but kept his shoulder firmly against it. He saw the room-service waiter standing there, a dumb smile on his face.

'We didn't order anything,' Kruger said curtly. 'You must have the wrong room.'

'Really, *senor*? Oh . . . I'm sorry . . .'

The waiter looked at the slip of paper in his hand, then at the room number and said, 'No, *senor* . . . suite one-twenty. Champagne and appetisers. Compliments of the hotel.'

Kruger opened the door. He saw the champagne wedged in a silver bucket of crushed ice, the neatly-arranged appetisers, then looked back up at the waiter, gave the man a questioning stare.

The waiter showed him the order on headed hotel notepaper. 'See, *senor* . . . it's written here. Suite one-twenty. Champagne and canapés.'

Kruger took the slip of paper, examined it carefully, then handed it back.

The waiter shrugged. 'If you don't want it, *senor*, I can take it back. It's no problem.' He smiled, affably. 'It's a new complimentary service for our suite guests.'

Kruger glanced again at the food trolley. He was thirsty and tired and the suite humid. The chilled champagne and the appetisers looked refreshingly tempting.

'Very well, you may come in.'

Kruger stepped back and the waiter wheeled the trolley slowly into the centre of the room, close to the table where the others sat, several metres away.

As he began to undo the wire around the neck of the champagne, the man with the dark, greased hair said, 'Leave it. We can attend to that ourselves.'

The waiter nodded, a grateful look on his face. 'As you wish, *senor*. If there is anything else, *senor* . . .?'

'No, nothing.'

The waiter patted the linen tablecloth, rearranged two of the glasses, coughed quietly.

Kruger took the hint, impatiently removed his wallet and handed the waiter a single note.

'*Muchas gracias.*'

Kruger stared at him, noticed the scar on the young man's cheek. 'Your name?'

'Ricardes, *senor*. Mario Ricardes.'

'See that we are not disturbed again, Mario.'

'Yes, *senor*. Of course, *senor*. If there is anything else you wish, please, do not hesitate to call room service.'

Kruger nodded impatiently.

Hernandez turned towards the door, away from the silver-haired man, towards the big blond with one hand behind his back, Hernandez almost gasping for breath, feeling a constriction of fear in his throat, as he passed the rock-like blond man who stood by the open door.

Fighting back his fear, Hernandez turned, took one last look around the suite, tried hard not to make it obvious as he smiled.

'*Buenas tardes, senores.*'

He had his hand on the door knob now as he bowed slightly, glimpsed the men at the table; the tired-looking man in the blue crumpled suit, then just a second's glance at the silver-haired man before he closed the door after him, took three, four steps, then let out a long sigh. He could feel the sweat on his back, his neck, his brow.

Jesus . . .

He walked quickly back towards his room.

The three men were seated at the table again.

Meyer felt relieved. The interruption by the waiter had proved a welcome hiatus. His throat was already dry from speaking in the humid room and he was beginning to feel the effects of dehydration after the long flight. The iced champagne looked tempting but it would have to wait. Meyer licked his parched lips. It was time to answer any questions.

The silver-haired man leaned forward, looked directly at him, his tone more businesslike. 'The shipment . . .?'

Meyer nodded. 'The cargo will be picked up from Genoa as arranged.'

'And the Italian?'

'He will be eliminated, but I want to be certain we don't arouse suspicion concerning the cargo. It would be prudent to wait until Brandenburg becomes operational. Then he will be dealt with along with the others.'

The silver-haired man nodded his agreement, then looked at Meyer intently.

'Those who have pledged their loyalty . . . we must be certain of them.'

Meyer said firmly, 'I have had their assurances confirmed. And their pedigree is without question.'

Kruger shifted restlessly in his chair as he looked at Meyer. 'And the Turk?'

'I foresee no problems.'

Kruger said, 'The girl . . . you're absolutely certain we can rely on her?'

'She will not fail us, I assure you.' Meyer glanced over at the elderly man. 'There are no changes to the names on the list . . .?'

The man shook his head firmly. 'They will all be killed.'

'Your travel arrangements,' Meyer inquired. 'Everything has been organised?'

'We leave Paraguay on the sixth.'

Meyer looked at the two men. 'The schedule . . . perhaps I should go through it once more?'

Both men nodded.

Meyer ran a finger round the rim of his shirt collar. Even with the air-conditioning on the heat was unbearably oppressive. Ninety per cent humidity at least. He found it stifling, wished the meeting would end. A matter of no more than ten minutes now, he was certain. Kruger would want to go over the key points again. He licked his dry lips, glanced over in the direction of the food trolley the waiter had brought, the neck of the champagne bottle visible, nestling in the ice-bucket. He could have done with a glass of the fizzy, chilled liquid to quench his thirst. He turned back to face Kruger.

'It's quite warm in here. Perhaps I might have a glass of water?'

Kruger nodded.

Meyer stood up and crossed to the side table where a carafe of water and several glasses sat on a silver-plated tray. He poured himself a glass of the tepid liquid, glancing at the iced champagne on the trolley as he drank. God, he could do with some of that. And the appetisers looked so tempting. He had hardly eaten on the flight. The damned trolley was beginning to distract him. Meyer finished his glass of water and filled another. He would have to move the trolley out of the way, out of sight, it was beginning to bother him, the sight of that delicious, tempting food and the chilled champagne nestling in the ice-bucket.

He leaned across and gently pushed the trolley away from him, was surprised that it moved so smoothly on its wheels, saw it slide away from him rapidly, glide across the carpet and bump into the writing desk in the far corner, rocking the table lamp, almost knocking it over.

Meyer turned and saw Kruger glance up at him from his papers. Meyer returned to his seat, wishing the meeting would soon be at an end.

*   *   *

Everything was going fine until Hernandez heard the click in the earphones.

He sat on the bed nervously smoking a cigarette. The Japanese recorder-receiver lay in front of him, the cores of the tape still turning smoothly. The men had been speaking in German, his mother's tongue, Hernandez hearing the voices clearly as the machine recorded the conversation in suite one-twenty.

In childhood, his mother had spoken to him in both Spanish and German, sometimes Guarani, that curious, expressive mixture of Indian-Spanish that the ordinary Paraguayan preferred to speak. But German was second nature to him, the language his Paraguayan father had hated but his mother persisted in using.

He was getting the conversation, but every now and then he had to stop and think, connect words, dig up phrases from his memory. At least he had the tape, he could replay it, translate the words more carefully. At least he had the tape.

And then he heard the *click* in the earphones.

The voices became muted, more distant, and then nothing, only a faint buzzing sound.

Hernandez swore out loud. He turned up the volume knob quickly, pressed the earphones against his ears. Nothing. Dead, except for a faint buzzing sound. Torres had said the equipment was good, sensitive but good, could pick up the buzz of a mosquito at ten metres. Well, either it was picking up the buzz of a mosquito right now or the receiver-microphone had worked itself loose or been damaged . . .

Or the men had found it.

Jesus Maria. Hernandez sweated, wondering whether to leave, just go, get out now. No, better to stay, because the men wouldn't know which room he was in, wouldn't know where the receiver was situated. And from the room he could always call the *policia*.

Hernandez began to sweat again, grimaced as he pressed the earphones tightly to his ears: he could hear the muted babble of the men, very faintly. He felt the sweat run down his spine, dampen his shirt even more, the material sticking to his back uncomfortably.

Please, God, don't let them find the microphone.

Hernandez sat on the bed another fifteen minutes, smoked two more cigarettes, listening to the faint buzzing in his ears, the sound giving him a headache. Then he heard it. A loud bang like a gunshot. Hernandez' heart skipped a beat. His blood seemed to freeze in his veins with icy fear. Then seconds later came the sudden sound of laughter in the earphones, the thin clink of glasses, the faint sound of voices.

'Prost.'

'Prost.'

'Prost.'

A chorus of *prosts*.

Hernandez let out a loud sigh, began to relax, began to understand. The champagne . . . the men were drinking the champagne. *Thank God*. They hadn't found the microphone.

The three men raised their glasses once more, in silence this time, the meeting concluded. Meyer looked at the silver-haired man, saw him sip the champagne. The man was pleased, very pleased, Meyer could tell. The meeting had gone well.

Finally Kruger put down his glass and said to Meyer, 'We must take our leave of you. It's a long drive back north. The driver will take you to the safe house.'

Meyer nodded. The silver-haired man placed his glass on the trolley and gripped Meyer's hand firmly in both his, a warm handshake, Meyer feeling the pride, the pleasure well up inside himself.

Kruger nodded to big Schmidt, who opened the door, stepped out into the corridor, eyes left, then right. He turned, nodded the all clear.

Meyer and Kruger picked up their briefcases. The silver-haired man followed after Schmidt, then Meyer next, Kruger last, taking one last look around the room to make sure nothing had been left behind, before closing the door after him.

Schmidt led the way to the lift.

Hernandez heard faintly the last words of the conversation in suite one-twenty and then silence. *Damn Torres and his damned equipment.*

But at least he had something on tape. If only he knew what the men had been talking about.

He shivered inside, hearing the sentence in German again in his mind. *Sie werden alle umgebracht.* They will all be killed. Who were they going to kill?

A chill coursed through Hernandez' body like an electric shock. Who were the men? Most likely dealers, big dealers from Europe. The ones who came over once or twice a year to renew narcotics contracts, to discuss prices. But there was something odd about the whole thing, something strange, a gut feeling Hernandez had that wouldn't go away. Two of the men spoke the accented German of immigrants, their vowels softened by the lisping Spanish. Only one spoke pure guttural German, the rough sing-song German of Bavaria.

Hernandez shook his head, confused by it all.

'The driver will take you to the safe house,' the voice had said. Where was the safe house? Right now it didn't matter; right now he wanted to leave the hotel as quickly as possible. But first he had to retrieve Torres' equipment from the suite. If he had time maybe he could follow the men to the house they spoke of. But he doubted it. Unless he worked very quickly. He picked up the telephone and punched in the number.

'Room service,' said the answering voice.

'Ah, room service! My colleagues in suite one-twenty appear to have some difficulty in trying to contact you. They wish a food trolley removed from their suite. At once.'

'Of course, *senor. Pronto.* Suite one-twenty.'

Hernandez replaced the receiver, threw off the waiter's jacket, dark trousers and tie, then dressed again hurriedly in the business suit and the blue silk tie. There was no need for the dark glasses, he decided. He had everything inside the case within two minutes, ready to go, key card to the room in his pocket.

He saw the spare tape lying on the bed and stuffed it inside the pocket of his jacket. He was ready. He opened the door to his room a crack, listened and waited for the room-service waiter to appear.

As they came out of the lift into the lobby Kruger went ahead of the others and crossed to the reception desk. The fat man behind it looked up, flashed a white-toothed smile.

'*Senor?*'

'Suite one-twenty,' said Kruger. 'We are leaving now. The bill has been paid, I believe?'

The man consulted the computer. 'That is correct, *senor*. In cash, when the suite was booked. Everything was to your satisfaction?'

'Yes, thank you. My compliments to the hotel. The champagne and canapés were excellent. *Buenas tardes.*' Kruger went to turn but saw the fat receptionist stare strangely at him before quickly glancing down at his computer again. Kruger hesitated.

He saw the man look up again, a quizzical expression on his face. 'Champagne? Canapés? We have no record of such an order, *senor*.'

Kruger swallowed. 'I beg your pardon . . .?'

The fat receptionist said mildly, 'There is no record of such an order on our computer.' He smiled. 'Obviously a mistake.'

Kruger said nervously, 'The bottle of champagne and canapés delivered to our suite . . . you're saying they were *not* compliments of the hotel?'

The fat man smiled broadly, amicably, as if Kruger were joking. 'No, *senor*. Of course not. But I can check to be absolutely certain. Perhaps an order was sent to your suite by mistake. However, I doubt it.'

Kruger turned visibly pale. The receptionist was already reaching for the telephone beside him, dialling a number. A moment later he spoke into the receiver, rapidly, but Kruger wasn't listening to the man's conversation. Instead he began to sweat, something niggling at him, worrying him. He was a cautious man, a man who never overlooked minor details, a man who checked and double-checked facts before coming to a conclusion. But this was odd . . .

The fat man replaced the receiver and looked at Kruger. 'Room service have no record of such an order sent to suite one-twenty, *senor*. It's most strange.'

Kruger could feel the palms of his hands pumping sweat. He glanced across at the others, waiting for him.

Kruger said rapidly. 'The waiter . . . his name, I think, was Ricardes . . .'

The fat man smiled again. 'It was he I just spoke to.'

'The young man was tall. A scar on his right cheek.'

The receptionist scratched his head. 'No. Ricardes is not tall. And a scar? No, certainly not. I don't understand, *senor*.'

But Kruger did. Kruger understood. Suddenly a terrible possibility dawning, his mind racing, already his hand reaching into his jacket pocket, taking out his wallet, generously peeling off several notes, trying to control the anxiety and the cold fury within himself, smiling a strangled smile with great difficulty as he handed the money to the fat man behind the desk.

'A misunderstanding, obviously. This will more than cover the bill. Excuse me, but I think I've left something in the suite.'

The fat man smiled. 'Of course, *senor. Gracias.*'

Kruger turned and crossed quickly to where Schmidt, the silver-haired man and Meyer waited, the three men staring at him now, sensing his disquiet, seeing the perplexed look on his face. Kruger could feel his pulse race, hammering through his veins, something wrong, something dangerously wrong. He looked palely at the three men.

'I think,' Kruger said, in a voice as cold and icy as death, 'I think we may have a problem.'

Hernandez heard the room-service waiter pass by his door, saw the flash of the man's white coat and glimpsed his face. It was a different waiter this time. He waited until the man had knocked several times, and, receiving no reply, saw him take a plastic key card from his pocket and insert it in the door. As he stepped inside, Hernandez moved forward, closed his door, and crossed the hallway quickly.

He followed the waiter into the suite; the bemused man turned to look at him.

'*Senor?*'

Hernandez pretended to search through his pockets as he smiled. 'I was just about to leave, but I think I have left my spectacles in the bathroom. Would you be so kind as to fetch them for me? There's a good fellow.'

The waiter smiled. 'Of course.' He crossed to the bathroom, switched on the light and stepped inside.

Hernandez knelt down beside the trolley and fumbled for the tiny microphone-transmitter taped underneath.

In the lobby Kruger wasted no time. He acted quickly. In such matters he had sole responsibility and now he exercised it. He gripped Meyer's arm and spoke rapidly, firmly, hardly pausing for breath.

'Take the Chief and go outside to the car. Tell Karl he is to drive you both to Franz's place and wait there until you hear from me. Tell Johannes to stay with the second Mercedes and remain at the entrance to the foyer. Werner is to go to the rear of the hotel. If there's a fire exit, tell him to wait by it. Give Rotman and Werner a description of the waiter who came to our room. Tall, dark-haired, young, perhaps thirty. Scar on his right cheek. As soon as they see him I want him. Dead or alive. Tell them, Meyer. Dead or alive.'

Kruger saw the silver-haired man look grimly at him, an uncharacteristic fury in his voice.

'I want him found, Hans.' The man's voice almost shook. 'I want him found, no matter what it takes.'

Kruger gave a sharp nod of his head. The silver-haired man went past, Meyer beside him, and strode quickly towards the exit.

Kruger beckoned to Schmidt. Both men walked rapidly towards the lift.

'I'm sorry, *senor*, I can't find your glasses. You're sure you left them in the bathroom?'

As the waiter came out of the bathroom, Hernandez smiled and stood up from the trolley. He held up the spectacles in his hand, the microphone-receiver already in his pocket.

'How stupid of me. I must have dropped them . . . here they are. But thank you for your help.'

The man smiled. 'No problem, *senor.*'

Hernandez allowed the waiter past with the trolley. 'I'll just check that I left nothing else behind.'

'Of course, *senor.*' The man left, closing the door after him.

Hernandez looked quickly around the room. The men who had been here were professionals. They would have been careful not to leave anything behind. He checked, nonetheless. Finding nothing, he stepped from the room, closed the door after him.

He crossed the corridor and went into his room. A minute later he had stepped outside again, dragging his suitcase after him. He closed the door, saw the lift open.

As the two men stepped out, Hernandez froze. There was a split second of mutual recognition, a split second in which Hernandez felt his heart stop and saw the two men hesitate and stare at him – the dark-haired man and the big, rugged blond bodyguard from the suite. Then Hernandez saw the blond reach inside his jacket, the butt of a pistol appearing.

Jesus Maria.

Hernandez turned and ran back down the corridor towards the fire-exit doors.

'*Halt!*' There was a rush of feet behind him as the shout in German rang out.

Hernandez reached the exit doors and pushed through. He raced down the emergency stairwell, the heavy suitcase banging against the walls, slowing him, Hernandez cursing its weight, hearing the racing footsteps behind him on the stairs.

'*Alto! Alto!*' The voice shouting in Spanish now, but Hernandez not stopping, ignoring the call, intent on reaching the safety of the car, taking two, three steps at a time, descending the stairwell rapidly, cursing the weight of the suitcase. He reached the ground-floor exit ten seconds later, his lungs on fire, his chest heaving. As he pushed open the emergency doors and burst out into the darkness, he hesitated.

Jesus Maria.

He heard the men racing down the stairwell behind him. If he didn't slow them quickly he'd never reach the car. He scanned the area frantically, saw the row of metal garbage bins nearby. He thrust out his free arm wildly and grasped one of the metal lids, turned in the same movement, placed the lid on the ground and kicked, wedging the lid between the base of the metal doors and concrete. He raced towards the car, not hesitating to look back.

Hernandez reached the Buick just as he heard the fists pounding madly on the doors behind him, the voice raised in frantic anger.

'*Sind Sie da, Werner? WERNER!*'

Fists beat on the metal like a roll of mad drums but the wedge held. Hernandez flung the suitcase into the car and climbed in, the voice from behind the door louder now, desperate.

'*WERNER! SCHNELL!*'

Hernandez fumbled to insert the key in the ignition. The key found its mark and he switched on.

The engine spluttered and died.

Hernandez felt every drop of blood drain from his body. *No! Please! Not now! Start, please start!*

He turned the key again, pumped the accelerator, his body on fire, the sweat pumping from him, turning at the same time as he heard the deafening crash behind him, the grating sound of metal scraping on concrete, as the garbage lid gave way and the sound echoed throughout the parking lot like a crack of thunder and the two men burst out through the emergency doors.

Jesus Maria!

The Buick's engine suddenly exploded into life. Hernandez

hit the accelerator hard and the car shot forward. As he swung out into the exit lane he saw a figure come racing towards him out of the darkness.

A man. Thirty metres away. Hernandez saw him reach into his jacket, fumble for something.

Werner . . . the man must be Werner . . .

Hernandez pumped the accelerator right to the floor. As the Buick rocketed forward he flicked on the headlights and switched to high beam, saw the man shield his face from the sudden, terrible glare as he raised a pistol in his right hand. It was only a split second but it was enough. The man twisted left to avoid being hit, his body crashing into the bonnet of a nearby car, the glare of the headlights catching the look of terror on his face.

Hernandez swung the Buick between two parked cars and drove at high speed towards the Calle Chile.

It took Kruger and the men two frantic minutes to race to the front of the hotel where the second Mercedes waited.

The driver was already gunning the engine, saying, 'What's going on?'

Kruger was like a man possessed. He flung open the door and pulled the driver bodily from the car, climbed in and found the mobile phone in the glove compartment. He punched in the number frantically.

As the number dialled out on the crackling line, Kruger cursed and sweated. He heard the click and the line was lifted at the other end.

'*Si?*'

'Have we a clean line . . . ?' Kruger spoke rapidly, heard his heart beat wildly in his chest, his voice almost breathless.

'One moment.' There was a long pause. 'Go ahead.'

'It's Kruger. I'm at the hotel. We have a problem. I think someone overheard us discussing Brandenburg.'

There was another long pause at the other end.

Then the voice said, '*Jesus* . . .'

Chapter Eight

Asunción

It was dark and the man and the two girls sat around the poolside table of the big house in the wealthy suburb of Asunción, sipping drinks the manservant had brought. There were lights on under the swimming pool and they gave the smooth water a turquoise colour.

Franz Lieber looked across at the two beautiful young girls sitting opposite.

They were both half-caste *mestizos* and very young and very ravishing, no more than fourteen, and they looked like twins. They were voluptuous, as only pubescent young girls can be, their bronzed, silky flesh protruding in all the right places. Cheap jewellery dangled from their wrists and necks and their short, tight summer skirts displayed generous portions of their tanned legs. Both had plump, firm-looking breasts and magnificent thighs.

Lieber smiled and said, 'My friend will be here soon. In the meantime relax, enjoy yourselves.'

Lieber saw the girls smile. One of them leaned forward to sip her vodka, showing her plump breasts to Lieber deliberately. Only fourteen, thought Lieber, but already she knows how to use her body like a weapon. He was definitely going to enjoy these two.

The wiser of the two said, 'Madame Rosa says you are very generous to girls, *si*?'

Lieber grinned. 'I'm always generous to girls who please me.'

The girl laughed and said, 'Then I will please you very much.'

She looked at her friend and they both giggled like school-girls.

Lieber smiled back wolfishly. He was fifty, with thick grey hair swept back off his forehead. His harsh, rubbery face was covered in ugly red boils, the legacy of an adolescent skin disease. He was a big man, and big-boned. He also had big appetites; in food and drink, as his generous belly testified, and especially in women.

Tonight he and Hans were going to enjoy themselves, play some bedroom games with the girls. It was a favour Lieber extended to certain guests, a refreshing, stimulating end to an evening. Lieber glanced at his watch. Hans would be here soon. They would have some cold drinks with the girls first and then go up to the bedroom. In the meantime, he would have some fun . . .

He smiled at the girl who had not spoken. She was fresh, not long in the business Lieber guessed.

'What's your name?'

'Maria.'

'Come here, Maria.'

The girl glanced at her friend. Her friend nodded and the girl stood up slowly, came round to stand in front of Lieber. She looked good enough to eat, this one . . .

Lieber rested his big hand on the girl's leg just above the knee and kneaded the soft flesh. He gave another wolfish grin. 'Lift your dress, Maria.'

The girl obeyed. She pulled up the tight black dress to reveal a pair of skimpy white panties and pouting thighs. Lieber could see the wisps of dark hair protrude from under the tight flimsy cotton and the plump outline of her crotch. He let his hand ride slowly up the back of the girl's bronzed thigh, had just slipped his hand under the panties onto the girl's round, smooth left buttock when the mobile telephone on the poolside table rang.

Scheisse!

Lieber held onto the girl's ass and lifted the phone with his free hand.

'*Si?*'

He heard the voice, recognised the urgency in it. He let his hand slide off the rounded flesh, covered the telephone mouthpiece and turned sharply to look at the girl, then the other.

'I need to talk in private,' he said curtly. 'Go inside and wait.' He gestured to the open french windows behind him, light spilling from a sumptuously furnished room beyond.

The two girls hesitated.

'*Now!*' Lieber roared.

The girls jumped at the sound of his voice, speaking in whispers as they crossed quickly to the open french windows. Lieber waited until they were safely inside and out of listening range, then pressed the button on the scrambling device clipped to the mobile phone.

'Go ahead,' said Lieber.

Lieber listened to Kruger's frantic voice.

When he had finished, all Lieber could say was, '*Jesus . . .*'

Hernandez' clothes were drenched in sweat.

His eyes flicked to the rear-view mirror as he drove towards the centre of the city, not knowing where to go, what to do, only that he needed to hide, find some place safe.

He swung the Buick left onto the Calle Chile, past the illuminated pink dome of the Pantheon on the Plaza de Heros. The traffic was thin, and Hernandez wove swiftly in and out of the lanes. His heart pounded with fear as he watched to see whether the twin beams of a car's headlights would appear rapidly behind him. But none did. No one following him. Not yet.

The red Buick was a problem. Its colour made it easily identifiable, and the men had seen the car, no question. He thought frantically as he drove, realised he needed somewhere safe to hide the car, somewhere nearby. He swung right again, then left, towards the brightly lit Plaza Constitution, keeping watch in the rear mirror, but knew he had had a head start, feeling a little better now as he drove past the Plaza, the car dipping down towards the river where the streets became narrower and darker, Hernandez knowing now instinctively where to go.

The warren-like riverside *barrio* of La Chacarita loomed

ahead, a drowsy dark place of tin and cardboard shacks built on muddy river flats. He could smell the river now, the rotten smell of sulphur and silt and mud, the river low, and a familiar fishy odour swept into the car through the open window. When he reached the river's edge he turned right, drove for three hundred metres and halted outside a shabby house of peeling white plaster.

Hernandez climbed out and pulled the suitcase after him. La Chacarita was for the poorest of the poor, a tough area that even the *policia* avoided. He locked the driver's door and checked the others, before stepping up to the house and knocking softly on the front door.

His body still on fire, his breathing heavy, he glanced up and down the street. A couple of doors away, a group of old men sat chatting on the stone steps outside an old shanty dwelling, drinking *yerba mate* through metal *bombilla* straws as they played cards. They glanced up but otherwise paid him no attention. Hernandez looked behind him, towards the river: there was a full moon, the river silvery, dotted with *camelotes*, floating clumps of matted water-weeds that looked like malignant bumps on the surface of the silver water.

Hernandez heard a scraping noise behind the door and turned back.

A girl's voice called out softly. 'Who is there?'

'It's Rudi.'

He heard the rattle of a metal bolt being slid and a moment later the door opened. A young girl stood there in the dimly lit hallway. She wore a plain white cotton dress that seemed to give her the appearance of an angel and her brown eyes sparkled at her visitor. There was a look of innocence on her beautiful brown face, a look that always brought out the tenderest feelings in Hernandez.

'How is my little girl?' Hernandez smiled.

The girl smiled back shyly and her long brown hair fell about her shoulders as she looked down at the suitcase. There was a sudden expression of fear on her face.

'You are going away, Rudi?'

Hernandez shook his head, spoke urgently. 'No, Graciella. But I need a place to stay until the morning.'

She did not ask why, simply nodded and led him inside and closed the door. She took Hernandez by the hand into a small room to the left, a single ancient wooden bed set against a peeling wall, above the bed a tiny red light flickering below a picture of the Virgin, the room frugal, but spotlessly clean.

'You sleep in my room, Rudi?' The girl's face looked up into his eyes. Her body was full, would have been undeniably tempting to any man, but Hernandez shook his head.

'I'll sleep on the kitchen floor, Graciella.' He smiled fondly down at her and cupped her face in his hand. 'Now, be a good girl and make me some *yerba mate*. Will you do that for Rudi?'

The girl nodded and smiled back at him. As his hand came away from her face she took hold of it silently and led Hernandez towards the kitchen.

It took Franz Lieber five minutes to make the necessary phone calls. When he had finished he sighed and looked reflectively at the turquoise water of the swimming pool, its pale icy blue calm smooth as a sheet of glass. In contrast, there was a rage inside Lieber. Anger fuelled by fear.

Jesus . . .

Just when everything was going smoothly, just when everything was coming together, some snooping bastard goes and fucks it up. The man was dead once they found him, whoever he was, of that much Lieber was certain. There was no place in the city the man could hide.

How could anyone possibly have known about the meeting? Lieber ignored his drink and concentrated hard, searching for weak links, for flaws. But there were none, especially in South America, especially in Paraguay, not here, not on his territory. The only ones who had known about the meeting were top people, and they could all be trusted, of that Lieber was certain. So how?

He sighed heavily. The consequences of failure were too awesome to even contemplate. Years of planning destroyed, millions wasted. *Millions*. Lieber grimaced. He had invested heavily in this, in time and money, and now everything was in jeopardy.

The man would simply have to be found, no matter what resources it took. He had contacted the necessary people: the men would be out looking already. At least forty men scouring the city, watching the airport, the railway and bus stations, the main roads leaving the city. Lieber just hoped the man hadn't got too much of a head start. The description Kruger had given him over the telephone had been vague – tall, young, maybe thirty, dark-haired, a noticeable scar on his right cheek – but the man's car, a big, ancient red American car, that was something, a clue. He had seen few of those in Asunción.

Lieber pushed himself up from the chair angrily, saw that his shirt was drenched in sweat. The Mercedes would be here soon. He would have to get rid of the girls.

'Noberto!'

The *mestizo* manservant appeared moments later, scurrying out from the house towards Lieber.

'*Si, senor?*'

Lieber gestured towards the house. 'Take a car from the garage and drop the girls off at Rosa's.' Lieber produced his wallet and handed the servant a wad of notes. 'Here, give them this. Tell them I don't need them tonight.'

'*Si, senor.*' The servant's face brightened, glad to be entrusted with this small task.

'Do it *now. Pronto!*'

The servant scurried towards the french windows and went in. Lieber saw him usher the girls out through a side door, heard the car drive away minutes later. He stepped into the house, taking the portable phone with him and went through to his study. The room looked out onto the driveway that led up to his property. He poured himself a generous measure of straight scotch and drank half of it in one swallow. As he went to stand by the window the phone buzzed in his hand. It was Kruger.

Lieber switched on the scrambling device and said, 'I've got forty men out looking. Stinnes is doing the co-ordinating.'

'The airport, the railway station . . .?'

'All being covered. Including the main roads out of the city. The men have a description of the car and the man.'

'The others should be with you any minute. We want this *Schwein*, no matter what it takes.' There was a pause, then Kruger's voice said urgently, 'You know the consequences for all of us if he isn't found . . .'

Lieber swallowed. 'Don't worry, he'll be found. Contact Stinnes, he's waiting for your call.'

The line clicked dead. As Lieber put the phone down by the window he saw the headlights of a car sweep into the driveway and bear rapidly up the path. The Mercedes had arrived.

Lieber looked down at his hands. They were shaking.

Chapter Nine

Asunción.
Saturday,
November 26th,
3.02 a.m.

The girl lay sleeping on a tattered mattress by the old blackened stove.

She was seventeen, and Hernandez loved her the way he loved all his women, only this one in a special way, a protective way. Graciella Campos had the body of a woman, but a child's mind, a mind that would have fitted more comfortably into the body of a ten-year-old. In the *barrio* she could have been trodden on, used, abused, this little flower.

Already the men were queuing up to use her body for a handful of *guaranis* a time when he had met her. He had been writing an article on the orphans in the *barrio* when a woman had told him of Graciella's plight. Could Hernandez help?

When he had first met the girl six months before he had been struck by her incredible beauty and innocence. Her grandfather guardian had died and she was penniless and he had taken pity on her. He had offered to pay for a place for her outside the shanty town, this little delicate flower living in the dungpile of La Chacarita. But the little girl in the woman's body had refused, was scared outside her natural habitat. The *barrio* was home to her; a place of refuge despite the grinding poverty.

So Hernandez had become her guardian, gave her what he could afford each week, got her a job with a kindly priest looking after the altar in the cathedral near the Plaza. He arranged for the old woman to call on the girl every day, attend to anything she couldn't manage. But the girl somehow always managed.

The men no longer bothered her. A friend of his, a tough, honest man who worked on the small river boats, acted as her guardian angel. Already the man had cut and bloodied the faces of several men who had not respected his protection.

The house Graciella lived in had three tiny rooms. They were in the largest, the room that served as a kitchen, a room the girl had proudly decorated in a simple, clean way: there were brown clay pots of plants and flowers, flowers everywhere, because the girl loved flowers, and whenever Hernandez came by he had always made sure he brought her something: a plant, some candy, a cheap trinket, to please her, to see the smiling brown eyes look up at him with innocent gratitude. But not tonight.

It was after 3 a.m. now and Hernandez sat restlessly at the rickety old kitchen table. The girl had refused to leave his side and sleep in her tiny bedroom, wanting to be near her protector. But Hernandez was not tired. Too much was going through his mind. The girl had proudly made them a supper of *chipa* bread and *yerba mate* before she had fallen asleep on the old mattress on the floor.

The tape machine lay on the table and he had the earphones on. He had listened to the tape so many times in the last seven hours that he knew the words the way an actor knows his script, every word engraved in his memory, every inflection noted. The girl had been mildly intrigued. When she had seen Hernandez with the tape machine she had smiled and said, 'Music, Rudi?'

Hernandez had smiled back and shook his head. 'No, something more important than music, Graciella.' The girl hadn't comprehended and had turned back to her cooking. It would have been pointless trying to explain; she would never have understood.

Now he looked again at the tape as he smoked a cigarette. What was on there wasn't much, certainly not as much as he had hoped for, but it was something, something to go on. But what?

He rewound the tape, pressed the 'play' button.

'*The shipment . . .?*'

'*The cargo will be picked up from Genoa as arranged.*'

'*And the Italian?*'

'*He will be eliminated, but I want to be certain we don't arouse suspicion concerning the cargo. It would be prudent to wait until Brandenburg becomes operational. Then he will be dealt with along with the others.*'

Pause.

'*Those who have pledged their loyalty . . . we must be certain of them.*'

'*I have had their assurances confirmed. And their pedigree is without question.*'

'*And the Turk?*'

'*I foresee no problems.*'

'*The girl . . . you're absolutely certain we can rely on her?*'

'*She will not fail us, I assure you.*' Pause. '*There are no changes to the names on the list . . .?*'

'*They will all be killed.*'

'*Your travel arrangements . . . Everything has been organised?*'

'*We leave Paraguay on the sixth.*'

'*The schedule . . . perhaps I should go through it once more?*'

He pressed the pause button, sighed.

What was the shipment the men talked of? The white powder? And the men, who were they? Buyers from Frankfurt? The men who came to South America to negotiate contracts. Or were they? Hernandez sensed something did not fit into place, something strange about all of this, something niggling at him, his mind going back to the lobby of the Excelsior, and then the suite where the men had held their meeting, something strange about the older man, the one with the silver hair, but Hernandez didn't know what.

A shiver rippled down his spine. He replayed the last part of the conversation again.

'*We must take our leave of you. It's a long drive back north. The driver will take you to the safe house.*'

He waited a moment, then pressed the stop button.

He made up his mind then that he would phone Sanchez, tell him everything he knew, ask his advice. But already the men would be changing their plans, surely? Hernandez shook his head. In a way, he had risked so much for so little: voices on a tape, discussing something he could not comprehend.

He glanced at his watch. Three-ten. Sanchez wouldn't be on duty until eight, maybe nine the following day. Hernandez cursed silently. He wanted Sanchez to hear the tape. Perhaps he could help decipher it.

He looked down at the angelic face of the sleeping young girl and felt a twinge of guilt. The men wouldn't find him in La Chacarita, he felt certain of that. But no matter how remote that possibility he was putting the girl in unnecessary danger.

And if the men were out looking for him he owed it to her not to allow her to become involved. He would leave after sleeping for a couple of hours; move into the throng of early-morning traffic on the Plaza. It would be safer than to drive across the city towards his apartment.

Hernandez sighed and looked down at the tape machine. He pressed the eject button and the tape popped out. He held it between his fingers. Perhaps it would be better to put it in his safe place until he could speak with Sanchez. Because that way he would have nothing incriminating if the men found him. But he doubted it. Rodriguez had told them nothing, he was certain.

The spare, unused tape lay on the table where he had left it.

Hernandez stood. The girl stirred, turned over, continued her sound sleep. He would leave the car, it would be safer here. It wasn't far to walk to the station where he kept the luggage box. He could take the backstreets and be back in twenty minutes once the tape had been safely hidden. He stepped quietly into the hallway, slipped back the bolt of the front door, and took the spare key from the nail behind the door where the girl always left it.

* * *

The man was tired.

He had scoured the streets of Asunción all night and now it was after 3 a.m. There was a year's pay for the man who found the car or the driver and the thought of all that money was the only thing keeping him awake. The description of the man he was looking for had been vague; really he needed a photograph. But the car, that was a help. It was easier to find a car than a face; and an old red American model shouldn't be difficult. But so far he hadn't had any luck. None of the other men either; he had passed them in their cars as he scoured the city. *Jesus . . . everyone was involved in this . . . everyone he knew . . . what's going on?*

He had met Model and Kaindel at a coffee stand near the Plaza Constitution. They didn't know either. Only that the man or the car had to be found, on Franz Lieber's orders. The money was proof enough that this was important.

The man rubbed his aching eyes and turned his car onto the Plaza. The dark streets of La Chacarita loomed beyond. Not the kind of place you ventured into unless you wanted to risk your life or catch something from a cheap whore. Even the thieves here were legendary for their quickness. They joked about it in Asunción: make sure if you're driving in La Chacarita and you have to give hand signals that you're not wearing a wristwatch.

The man grinned to himself. *Fuck it*. He had the mobile phone beside him to call for help, a forty-five automatic pistol in the glove compartment and a knife under his seat. Any Dago hassled him and he'd blow a hole in the bastard the size of a fist.

He drove across the brightly lit Plaza and the car rolled gently downhill into the dark *barrio* of La Chacarita . . .

It took Hernandez ten minutes to walk to the old railway station through the maze of narrow back streets. He wasn't afraid; many people knew him in the *barrio*. The streets were deserted and he walked slowly.

Fifty metres from the old porticoed station entrance he froze. Parked across the street facing the entrance, visible under a flickering street lamp, were two cars, a dark Mercedes and a white Ford. Two men stood beside the Mercedes, smoking, talking. Hernandez swallowed. Such a sight would not have troubled him normally, but there was something odd about the scene. No trains due for another four hours at least. Men like these, why would they wait outside the station at this hour? Both men wore suits, looked European. Like the men at the hotel. Like businessmen. Hernandez stepped into the shadows, his heart beating wildly.

He looked towards the entrance, caught a glimpse of two more men standing idly under the porticoed entrance. One was young and blond and wore a leather jacket and open-necked shirt; the second middle-aged and burly and casually dressed. These did not look like businessmen, but they were waiting for him, Hernandez felt certain. Covering the station should he try to leave the city.

Damn!

Hernandez began to panic. He felt sweat drip down the inside of his shirt. He took a deep breath. What he had done at the hotel must have set off alarm bells.

Relax. Take it easy.

But what if there were more men inside the station? How then could he get safely to the luggage box?

He sweated in the shadows for several more minutes until a thought struck him. He smiled. Perhaps there was a way. He turned quickly and walked back the way he had come.

Hernandez reached the rear of the station minutes later. A double wooden gate served as a rear entrance, a small judas visible. This was the entrance the railway workers used.

He entered through the judas gate and stepped into a small yard. As he went through he saw a station worker in uniform sitting in a tiny, glass-fronted office reading a magazine. The man stared up at him a few moments then continued reading. People living in the *barrio* took this short-cut all the time.

A minute later he was on the nearest platform. An ancient diesel engine stood silently up against the buffers, the smell of grease and oil thick in the humid air. Where Hernandez stood was deserted, but he could see the platforms nearest the station entrance clearly, perhaps sixty metres away.

There were Indians and peasants sleeping nearby. An old man selling water and pistachios slept at his stand, his head down, nestled in his arms. Women in their coloured shawls, some clutching babies to their breasts, waited with their sleeping children and husbands for the early-morning trains to take them back to the hinterland. But no men in business suits, no burly-looking men like those at the hotel. The locker area wasn't far, tucked away behind the shuttered concession stands, thirty metres from where he stood.

His eyes searched the distant crowd again, but he could see nothing unusual, no men like the ones he had seen outside. Still, it would be prudent to be careful. Hernandez hesitated, saw a railway official sleeping soundly on a nearby wooden bench, hands folded across his chest, snoring loudly. His uniform jacket lay on the back of the bench. Hernandez crossed to where the man lay, saw that no one was watching, took the uniform jacket and tugged it on and continued walking.

When he reached the locker he inserted the key.

'*Senor* . . .'

Hernandez heard the voice behind him and froze. He turned his head slowly, felt the instant fear. He saw the elderly man standing there.

'*Por favor, senor* . . .'

The man's face was dark mahogany, his skin deeply wrinkled from sun and hard work. He carried an old battered suitcase. An unlit cigarette hung from his lips. He smiled at Hernandez and pointed to the cigarette.

It took Hernandez more than a moment to understand. He fumbled with shaking hands in his pockets, gave the old man the cheap plastic lighter and said, 'Keep it. I have another.'

'*Muchas gracias, senor.*'

The man turned and shambled away. Hernandez exhaled. He was edgy, the fear in him making his body tremble, felt drops of sweat course down his temples. Quickly, he opened the metal locker door, placed the tape on top of the envelope containing the photographs and locked the door again. He replaced the keys in his pocket, crossed back to where the sleeping official lay and returned the uniform jacket. Then he walked back towards the rear exit.

The man had decided to drive down to the river and work his way back up, zig-zagging through the warren of dark narrow streets. At the water's edge he stopped, wrinkling his nose at the smell of sulphur and rotting fish that wafted into the warm interior. He wondered whether to turn left or right. He decided right. He had the doors locked and the automatic pistol was out now and on the seat beside him.

He had gone almost three hundred metres, driving slowly, eyes scouring the waterfront and the tiny alleyways that ran between the shanty homes, when he glimpsed the flash of red. He slowed instinctively. An old red Buick, its rear badge unmistakable, its chassis rusting, stood parked in front of a house with white peeling walls. The man's heart skipped a beat. His hand automatically reached for the gun as he pulled into the kerb. He smiled and grabbed for the mobile phone on the seat instead and punched in the number quickly.

The line clicked. A voice said, '*Si?*'

The man said, 'It's Dortmund . . . I think I've found the car.'

Hernandez walked slowly back along the river, taking his time.

La Chacarita was a deserted place of shadows at this early hour. The tape was in a safe place; he would tell Sanchez about it tomorrow, tell the man everything he knew, hope that he could help him. Leaving the tape in the locker had been a wise decision, he reflected. Even if the men caught him he could bide his time, perhaps do a deal if he was forced to. If he had the tape on him and that happened, then surely he was dead. The voices on the tape, what they said must be important. The presence of the men at the station testified to that. He would need time to decipher the conversation. Perhaps Sanchez would be a help.

He was too nervous and excited to sleep. He stopped by the river and lit a cigarette, thinking, knowing that something was happening, something really big, something that was worth killing for, remembering the faces of the men on the first floor as they came out of the lift, knowing with certainty that they would have killed him. He would tell Sanchez all this; it was too dangerous for him to pursue this alone now. The men at the hotel were powerful men; how else had they sent men to look for him? If the railway station was covered, then so was the airport, perhaps even the main roads. Hernandez shivered. His only hope now was Sanchez.

The fat detective would want to know why he had not come to him immediately, why he had withheld information from him that day at Tsarkin's house. But Hernandez would worry about all that later.

He looked at his watch in the light of the moon. He had been away almost half an hour. It was time to get back to Graciella's place and try somehow to get some sleep. He flicked away the lighted cigarette, watched as it cartwheeled into the silvery water, then he turned and started to walk back towards the house.

Five metres from the front door he saw that it was open.

He froze.

He had closed the door after him, he was certain. Or had he? His mind was in such turmoil. Perhaps he had not? *Jesus, anyone could have come in and* . . .

Hernandez heard the *click* and wheeled round instantly, felt the blood draining from him, saw the two men armed with pistols lunge towards him, their faces a blur, because already there was a rough hand over his mouth, stifling his cry, another gripping his hair, jerking his head back, as other rough hands pushed him into the house. As the door burst in he was propelled forward with an almighty force, into the kitchen now, lights blazing in the tiny room, crowded with men . . .

Jesus Maria . . .

Hernandez felt a sharp punch in his side, the hand still on

his mouth, stifling his scream. The faces around him were a blur as more blows rained down, pulped his face, bruised his body, until he could hardly stand, blood on his lips, its salty taste in his mouth. Rough hands pushing him back against the wall, two quick sharp blows to his kidneys making him want to throw up.

Two big men held Graciella, her tiny body like a rag doll's between them. A white towel gagged her mouth and there was blood on her pretty face, terror in her innocent eyes. The recording equipment lay on the kitchen table still. Two men stood over it, two of the men he had seen at the hotel: the dark-haired one who had opened the door to him, and the older, silver-haired man, handsome, maybe sixty. Both men stared at Hernandez with contempt.

The dark-haired man stepped quickly forward, glared into Hernandez' eyes. The hand that covered Hernandez' mouth came away an instant and the man's fist smashed into Hernandez' face. There was the sharp crack of bone breaking and he reeled back in pain, the bridge of his nose shattered, his scream muffled by the hand again over his mouth, then another blow struck him, across the back of the head, blows raining down on him again. Someone gripped his hair and jerked his head up so that he was staring into the face of the young, dark-haired man.

The eyes were steel-grey and cold. He spoke quietly, threateningly, but with urgency in his voice.

'You will answer my questions. If you lie, the girl dies. If you tell the truth, she lives. You understand?'

The man jerked his hand towards Graciella. The two men holding her yanked her head back savagely by the hair, until the whites of her eyes showed. Hernandez heard her muffled cries of pain. One of the men ripped her dress, her small brown breasts exposed. The second took a big silver knife from behind his back, pressed the tip of the blade against the girl's left nipple.

The dark-haired man said again, 'You understand?'

Hernandez wanted to vomit. He nodded quickly.

The man stared into his face. 'How did you know we were at the hotel? Answer quickly now.'

The hand on Hernandez' mouth came away.

Hernandez said weakly, his breath coming in gasps, 'I was at Tsarkin's house the day he killed himself . . . covering the story for *La Tarde* . . . a call came . . . from the Excelsior Hotel . . . I answered the telephone . . .'

The eyes of the dark-haired man lit up, understanding. He suddenly wrenched at Hernandez' pockets, ripped out the wallet and examined the contents. He plucked out the press identity card, scrutinised the photograph, then handed it to the silver-haired man who stood nearby, watching, the one in charge, before he nodded silently for Hernandez to go on.

Hernandez' voice came in short, staccato gasps, thick with fear, as he told him about Rodriguez. What he had been told about the men. About the equipment. About his plan. The dark-haired man turned pale. He turned to look at the older man, whose face was even paler, eyes glaring over at Hernandez.

The dark-haired man turned back, nodded towards the table and said sharply, 'The tape. We checked it, it's blank . . .' His tone demanded an explanation.

Hernandez sucked in air. His body on fire with pain; the blows had almost crippled him.

'Answer!' the man screamed.

'The microphone . . . there was a problem with it . . .' Hernandez began quickly, but the man suddenly cut him short with a sharp wave of his hand, as if he knew, a sadistic smile on his face now, his hand coming up to seize Hernandez' jaws in a painful pincer grip. Hernandez wanted to scream: *No, the real tape is in a safe place, I can take you to it. We can deal.* But the man spoke quickly.

'Rodriguez . . . what he told you . . . who else did he tell?'

Hernandez tried to shake his head. The man's grip still held him. 'He told no one else . . . Only me . . .'

'You are certain? I want the truth.'

'Yes . . .'

'And you . . . did you tell anyone else? Even a word . . . a whisper?' There was an urgency in the man's voice now. His grip tightened.

'No. No one.'

Pause. 'Tell me . . . why did you leave this house?'

'To get some air . . . I . . . I couldn't sleep . . .'

'Where did you go?'

'I . . . walked along the river.'

The man's eyes searched Hernandez' face, searched for the truth. 'The cargo Rodriguez told you about . . . what do you think it was? Answer truthfully now. The girl's life depends on it.'

Hernandez looked at him through bruised and bloodied eyes. 'White powder. You're shipping cocaine,' saying it and not caring, knowing now that he was dead, no matter what he said, knowing Graciella was dead, only hoping for the child it would be quick, without pain . . .

The man released his grip. Hernandez begged, 'Please . . . the girl . . . she knows nothing . . . she's only a child . . .'

The dark-haired man was smiling now, laughing, as if something had amused him. He turned towards the older man with the silver hair. The man nodded his head.

The dark-haired man turned back. He stared madly into Hernandez' eyes.

'You dumb, stupid Dago fuck!'

Then he turned and clicked his fingers. It happened quickly. The man holding the knife in front of Graciella raised his hand. The blade flashed. Hernandez went to scream, but a hand came over his mouth again. He watched in horror as the knife came down, sliced through the girl's soft brown flesh, slit her from the valley between her breasts to the navel of her stomach. Hernandez saw with horror as the blood spurted out in a fountain, the whites of the child's dying eyes looking to heaven, her body suddenly limp, engulfed in blood. Hernandez felt the vomit rise in his stomach.

And then the big, blond bodyguard he had seen in the hotel stepped forward out of nowhere.

Hernandez saw the flash of another blade as the man drew

a jagged knife from under his coat. Hernandez tried vainly to scream, but a hand trapped the cry in his throat, other hands pinning him hard against the wall.

Then it was as if everything was happening in slow motion. Hernandez watched in mute horror as the jagged metal arced and dug savagely into his chest. He felt a searing pain as the blade plunged into flesh like a hammer blow, felt the flow of hot blood as the sharpness sliced down through his gut. Through the fogging mist of pain engulfing him he was faintly aware of the dark-haired man stepping back, the hands that held him releasing their grip, and he slid back against the wall, slid down into the dark, growing pools of his own blood.

And then there was only the darkness washing in like a cold black wave, washing away the terrible pain, and the faint, ever faint sound of footsteps moving away, receding, all sounds receding, even the last dying breath escaping from Hernandez' own lips.

Until there was nothing, nothing – only darkness remaining.

PART TWO

Chapter Ten

Strasbourg,
France.
Thursday,
December 1st

A log fire blazed in one corner of the restaurant, and the walls
had been freshly painted in warm brown colours, giving the
place a cosy atmosphere.

From where they sat by the window Volkmann could see
the spire of the old cathedral rise into the grey afternoon
sky, the patchwork of red and brown slated rooftops of the
medieval centre of old Strasbourg stretching in serried, jagged
rows as far as the eye could see. A cold wind blew across
the Place Gutenberg, and needles of fine rain clawed at the
window.

You could usually set your watch by Ferguson's appoint-
ments, but almost half an hour had gone by and they had
ordered and there was still no sign of him.

The Head of British DSE hated German food, which
was why when they were having their weekly informal
meeting Ferguson always chose a French restaurant. The
one he had chosen for their meeting today was run by
a personable Frenchman from Lille. The food was always
excellent, if the service usually a little slow. Today, it
seemed better than usual, waiters hovering attentively near
every table.

Volkmann turned to stare beyond the window again,
towards the bronzed statue of Johann Gutenberg. The cold
Place was almost bereft of pedestrians despite the nearness
of Christmas. In the window of a nearby shop a fat, red-faced
little salesman was standing on a chair, struggling to hang coils

of silvered decorations among the shop's seasonal window display.

Tom Peters sat opposite, sipping from a glass of Bordeaux. Ferguson's right-hand man and the section's number two, Peters was a stocky, middle-aged Welshman of medium height, his greying sandy hair swept back off his ruddy face.

He looked across at Volkmann and said, 'There was an article in *Le Monde* only last week. Some hack reckoned that within another few months it'll be like the bad old days of the Great Depression.' Peters nodded towards the struggling salesman across the street. 'For that poor sod's sake I hope all the work is worth it.'

Volkmann smiled and drank the red fruity wine Peters had poured for him. 'Did Ferguson say what it was he wanted to talk about?'

They were in a secluded corner of the restaurant on a slightly raised dais, away from the other diners. Peters sipped his wine appreciatively, then grimaced and looked out balefully at the view.

'Something to do with the bloody Germans, old son.'

Volkmann could tell something was up. Krull wasn't at his desk in the German Section, and hadn't been seen for days. Even the people in the French and Italian Sections seemed to be spending more time than usual lingering over coffee. The only lively presence was in his own department, the British, and that of the Dutch. Both sections were busily working at their desks, as if nothing were amiss, incorrigible bureaucrats that they were.

Ferguson arrived moments later. A tall, gaunt man, pasty-faced, pushing sixty, he dressed like an English squire in Donegal tweeds and check shirt and woollen tie, knotted thickly. He took a seat at the table, apologising.

'I see you've started without me.' Ferguson glanced at the open wine bottle, smiled briefly and sat down, accepting a glass from Peters.

'Have you ordered? Then I suppose I had better do the same.'

Ferguson ordered the fillet of sole with lemon sauce,

buttered fresh broccoli and boiled potatoes. He sipped his wine and sat back, glancing out of the window a few moments, at the pigeons swirling around the Gutenberg statue like limp, grey rags. When he turned back he spoke quietly.

'I had a meeting with Hollrich, that's what delayed me. He's been in Bonn for the past week.'

'Anything that concerns us?' Peters asked.

'It's the people in Berlin and Bonn,' Ferguson replied. 'They're talking about money problems, fiscal cutbacks. Considering the circumstances prevailing just now it's as good an excuse as any. They may want to scale down their involvement in security co-operation. Concentrate on the problems closer to home.'

'They would, wouldn't they? Peters remarked.

Ferguson swirled the rich, fruity wine before swallowing. He grimaced slightly as he looked back at Peters and Volkmann. 'Hollrich says it's mainly money. That the mandarins in Bonn are whining about the need to cut back on spending.'

'The whole operation is run on a shoestring, for God's sake. You made that point to Hollrich, sir?' Peters said.

There was a silence at the table for several moments as the waiter brought their orders. Ferguson waited until the man had left before replying.

'It's not as simple as that, Tom,' Ferguson said. He cut his fish with measured care, chewed it thoughtfully before swallowing. 'According to Hollrich the Chancellor is in trouble with a minority government. There's also been a big rise in internal problems. They've had protest marches on Bonn and Berlin every other day. It's the same scenario everywhere, of course. I could quote you figures but doubtless you both read the newspapers.' Ferguson speared a piece of fish before he looked back up at Volkmann and Peters. 'I know it increases the work load for everyone else, but there you have it. I wanted to inform you both of what's happening. I want you to be aware of what's in the air but to carry on as if it's business as usual. I'm seeing Hollrich again on Monday. Naturally, I pressed the importance of staying within DSE. I told him to pass on that message to his superiors.'

Volkmann said, 'What about the French?'

'I'm seeing their Head of Security on Wednesday. He's heard rumours about the Germans from his own people so he wants to have a chat. I think I can deal with that.'

Volkmann said, 'Anything else?'

Ferguson hesitated and glanced out towards the square a moment before turning back.

'There is something, actually. Something I want you to look into. A favour for Pauli Graf of German Section.' Ferguson paused. 'It's a difficult time and I don't want to rock any boats. However, something has come up. Something I think we should look into.'

Volkmann said, 'Which area?'

'I'm not certain. Narcotics, perhaps. According to Graf, Hollrich wasn't remotely interested. He said they hadn't got the time or the manpower.'

Volkmann said, 'So what's the problem?'

'A girl in Frankfurt, an old acquaintance of Graf's, was in South America recently. She claims to have some information that might interest us.'

'Us?' said Peters.

'DSE, obviously,' replied Ferguson.

'Why can't Pauli Graf handle it himself?' Volkmann asked.

'As I say, the Germans don't seem particularly interested just now. Graf got short shrift from Hollrich, and Graf himself is being posted back to Berlin as of tomorrow. Apart from the manpower constraints he seemed to think his department weren't really interested because it's all too vague and the proper channels weren't used. He says this girl thinks her information might be important but she didn't want to talk with the *Bundespolizei*.'

'Any particular reason why not?'

Ferguson shrugged. 'None that I know of. The girl simply said that she wanted to talk with one of our senior people and that it was important. That she had information concerning a smuggling operation into Europe, but she wouldn't elaborate. She said she wants to talk to someone from DSE in person.'

'Who do you want to handle it?' Peters asked.

'I had thought Joseph,' Ferguson said. He looked back at Volkmann. 'You've got the language and the experience in the field. You know your way around. It may be nothing, of course, but then again, no harm in checking.'

'Nothing more than that?'

Ferguson looked mildly irritated. 'No. I've told you everything I know.'

Volkmann glanced over at the fat salesman across the street. The man had finished his display and peered hopelessly out of the window.

Ferguson said, 'No further questions?'

Volkmann turned back. 'What about the girl?'

'Her name is Erica Kranz. Aged twenty-five. Freelance journalist by profession.' Ferguson took a slip of paper from his inside pocket, handed it across to Volkmann. 'I've written out her address and telephone number. I think you ought to pay her a visit, see what it's about.'

'When do you want me to start?'

'You could drive up to Frankfurt tomorrow. But give the girl a call first.'

'Who do I report to?'

'Me. And if I'm not around you can contact Peters and he'll pass it on. I've already requested information on the girl from Koller of the German Section. I should have the file delivered to you tonight. At least you'll be prepared.'

Volkmann said, 'What about the Germans?'

Ferguson smiled briefly. 'I'm sure they'll see it as just routine. Anyway, they weren't particularly interested. If it's something that doesn't concern the British Desk even indirectly, we can send the ball back to their court. That's presuming Hollrich and his people are still with us. The important thing for now is that we keep the wheels turning, whether the Germans stay within the operation or not.'

Volkmann glanced out of the window. The fat salesman across the square was standing at the entrance to the shop, hands clasped behind his back, examining his work. The square was still empty of shoppers.

When Volkmann turned back, he saw Ferguson and Peters observing him. Ferguson's eyes flicked to the fat salesman. The Head of British DSE frowned, then spread thick, hard butter evenly on a crisp white roll and poured himself another glass of wine.

'I think I read somewhere recently that during the Great Depression it was just the same. Everyone still in business chasing after what few pennies were in circulation. A dreadful mess. But thank heavens we can leave such problems in the incapable hands of economists and politicians.'

Ferguson smiled.

Peters glanced over at Volkmann and raised his eyebrows. Volkmann smiled and sipped his wine but said nothing.

The Orangerie Park, with its exotic birds and miniature lake and cascading waterfalls, its landscaped gardens and its pavilion built by Napoleon for the Empress Josephine, lies within a short walking distance of the offices of the DSE.

Unlike the imposing headquarters of Interpol in Lyon, the bland modern offices of the DSE Headquarters in Strasbourg are little known. Situated near the Parliament Building on the Avenue de l'Europe, the six-storey building houses an amalgam of all the twelve European intelligence agencies and specialised police forces, whose representatives pool and act on matters of mutual security within the European Community. Its full and correct title is *Direction de Sécurité Européenne*, but it is more often called simply DSE.

Whereas the main target of Interpol is the international criminal, its actual powers remain limited. Its officers, drawn from the police forces, are confined to providing primarily an information service, processing and disseminating information within three main clearly defined criminal categories: criminals who operate in more than one country; criminals who do not travel at all but whose criminal activities affect other countries; and criminals who commit a crime in one country and flee to another. But since the nations of the world have varying degrees of difference in their respective criminal and legal procedures, Interpol's officers do not have power of arrest, despite popular portrayal to the contrary in books and films depicting agents moving freely from country to country making arrests where they please. The organisation therefore is limited to providing a clearing-house for information on criminal activity, however effective.

The DSE has a brief not dissimilar but concerns itself with four main categories of criminal and terrorist activity and only as they apply to European security and criminal matters. And unlike Interpol its officers are drawn not only from the specialised police forces within Europe but also from the intelligence services of those countries. Its officers also have powers of arrest, albeit these powers are strictly limited by protocol and to within the member states.

Category One covers terrorist activity, both indigenous terrorism and terrorists from countries outside Europe who may use Europe as a base or as a target. Category Two is concerned with smuggling in all its forms, but prime areas of interest are narcotics, arms, precious metals and gems. Category Three covers espionage, as it relates to both national or Community security, and industrial; Category Four, fraud and counterfeiting.

Within DSE, each individual member state has its own section in the Strasbourg Headquarters, representing that country's state intelligence agency and police force. Each section maintains a staff of no more than twelve senior officers and administrative personnel and liaises with other national sections in areas of mutual concern and interest where these areas overlap. Thus the principal *raison d'être* of DSE is to provide a cohesive, united agency to combat all four categories of criminal and terrorist activity and to maintain a comprehensive and shared computerised data base on these activities.

Joseph Volkmann's office in the British Section was on the third floor, which also houses the Dutch Section. Below the window, dotted with bare cherry trees, is a small square, called simply the Platz, empty on this cold December afternoon.

He had arrived back from lunch at two and gone straight to work, sifting through the reports and filing his paperwork. There were the usual subjects: narcotics, smuggling, terrorism; intelligence reports ready to be acted on or filed away.

When he finished over two hours later, darkness had already fallen outside, lights coming on in the office buildings all around.

He took the slip of paper Ferguson had given him and dialled the girl's number in Frankfurt. When Erica Kranz answered he told her he was a liaison officer with DSE, explained that Pauli Graf had asked someone to have a talk with her.

'Can you tell me what this is about, Frau Kranz?'

The girl's voice sounded uneasy and Volkmann thought he detected a trace of fear. 'I'd rather not discuss the matter over the telephone, Herr Volkmann. But it is important. Could we meet?'

'I could drive up to Frankfurt tomorrow morning. Pauli Graf gave us your address. Unless you want to meet somewhere else?'

There was a pause on the line, and then the girl's voice came back. 'I would appreciate your coming here, Herr Volkmann. My apartment is on the top floor. Is midday OK?'

'Midday is fine. Good afternoon, Frau Kranz.'

At five Volkmann cleared away his desk and went down to the car park and drove to his apartment. It was a modest place by Strasbourg's standards, a compact two-bedroomed apartment in one of the old houses along the Quai Ernest, overlooking a small paved courtyard. The window in Volkmann's bedroom looked towards the Rhine and Germany, five kilometres away.

It was after ten when Koller from the German Section appeared with the file, looking irritated. Volkmann offered the man a drink but Koller refused and seemed put out having to call at the apartment.

'Do you mind telling me why you want the girl's file?'

'Nothing special. Just routine.'

Koller inquired no further. 'The file; please see that the copy I've given you is returned.'

When Koller had left, Volkmann ran a hot bath and poured himself a large scotch. After bathing he lay on the bed and read Erica Kranz's file.

It made interesting reading. Different. Certainly different. And one paragraph in particular made him shiver involuntarily. He couldn't help but wonder what it was all about as he went to stand at the bedroom window.

It had stopped raining and the clouds had long disappeared and darkness fallen. He could see the lights of Germany now, burning into the winter's night beyond the Rhine. He never took the trip across the border unless he had to. Ferguson knew he disliked dealing with the Germans. With few exceptions he had avoided social contact with them even when he had worked in Berlin, that least German of cities.

He set the travel clock for seven, undressed slowly and turned off the light and lay in the bed. The lines in the girl's file had disturbed him and he tossed restlessly for some time before he finally fell asleep.

Chapter Eleven

Frankfurt,
Germany.
Friday,
December 2nd

Volkmann found the apartment block with no difficulty, tucked away behind a cluster of red-bricked, pre-war buildings near the Eiserner Steg on the southern side of the river. It was modern, four storeys high with a grey mansard roof. The girl was waiting for him in the open doorway when he came out of the lift.

She was tall and full-figured, with dusky skin and pale blue eyes. Her long legs were clad in tight blue jeans tucked into brown high leather boots and she wore a black loose sweater. Her blonde hair was tied up, emphasising her high cheekbones. She wore hardly any make-up and her face looked tense. Volkmann introduced himself and showed her his identification before they went inside.

In the background he heard a Mendelssohn violin concerto playing softly. The girl crossed to a mini hi-fi on a shelf by the window and lowered the volume.

'I was just going to make some coffee. Would you like some, Herr Volkmann?'

'A coffee would be fine.'

'Please, make yourself comfortable.'

Volkmann watched her as she went into the kitchen. Her file said she was twenty-five but he thought she looked older. But pretty, very pretty. The girl would have passed for a model or a female executive with one of the Frankfurt commercial banks.

The penthouse apartment was spotlessly clean and furnished in a modern style, large and airy, filled with potted plants and bookshelves and pale leather furniture. Framed colour prints of magazine covers hung on the white walls, and on the hi-fi shelf were several dozen discs and pre-recorded tapes. The standard classics mostly, but there was a selection of Puccini's complete operas and some jazz. The bookshelves were full and Volkmann noticed an open book lying on the couch. He picked it up and glanced idly at the cover. It was a book of poetry by Edna St Vincent Millay and as he replaced the book he glanced towards the window.

The view looked down onto the Main river, sturdy barges passing to and fro on the choppy grey waters. A pine desk stood near the window, a computer console on top.

When the girl returned with two cups of coffee and milk and sugar on a tray, she sat opposite Volkmann on a white leather couch, her long legs crossed. She picked up the book and glanced at the open pages before looking up at Volkmann. Her face appeared pale and drawn and now that Volkmann looked closely he saw the blue eyes were red-ringed from crying.

As she placed the book beside her she said softly, 'Are you familiar with the work of Edna St Vincent Millay, Herr Volkmann?'

He half smiled and shook his head. 'No, I'm afraid not.' Then he looked at her and said, 'Perhaps you had better tell me what this is about, Frau Kranz.'

'You are German, Herr Volkmann?'

'British. Your people in the German Section of DSE weren't particularly interested in your case. Pauli Graf has been posted back to Berlin and passed you on to us unofficially.' He looked at the girl's face. 'If it matters, I can ask your people again.'

She shook her head. 'No. I was just making an observation. Your accent, it's a little different, that's all.' She held the coffee cup on her lap. 'Perhaps I should start at the beginning?'

'Please.'

The girl brushed a strand of blonde hair from her face and looked away towards the window, then slowly back again.

'Until last week I was in Asunción in Paraguay on a week's holiday. I stayed with my cousin, Rudi Hernandez.' The girl bit her lip, hesitated before going on. 'During my stay with him I sensed he was troubled by something. When I asked him what it was he told me he was working on a story. Something the newspaper he worked for as a journalist knew nothing about.'

When the girl hesitated again, Volkmann said, 'What sort of story?'

'Rudi had learned from a pilot he knew in Asunción, a man named Rodriguez, that certain people were smuggling cargoes out of South America into Europe. A week before I arrived in Paraguay, this pilot, Rodriguez, telephoned Rudi and asked him to meet him. He told Rudi he had a favour to ask. He wanted Rudi to write a story, a newspaper article, but not to publish it, to hold it, somewhere safe, with a lawyer perhaps. If Rodriguez was killed, Rudi was to publish the story.'

The girl hesitated again before going on. 'Rodriguez had worked for these people who did the smuggling. They had hired him and his aircraft to transport a number of cargoes. His business was smuggling and he was used to dealing with such people. But now he was certain these men who had hired him had been watching him and wanted to kill him.'

'Do you know what these cargoes were?'

The girl shook her head. 'Rodriguez told Rudi he thought they were narcotics, but he wasn't sure. All he could say was that there had been several consignments, all delivered to Montevideo in Uruguay over a period of almost a year. The consignments were packed in sealed wooden boxes. Rodriguez said he had been very well paid by these men. He also gave Rudi a name. The name of the man who had hired him to do the work. But Rudi wouldn't tell me the name.'

'Why?'

'I think he was afraid for my safety. I think he thought the less I knew about these people, the better. That they were dangerous. Very dangerous.'

Volkmann nodded. 'Go on, Frau Kranz.'

The girl sighed and bit her lip before she went on. 'Two days after Rodriguez had delivered the last consignment for

117

these people, he noticed that he was being watched. That's when he became afraid and contacted Rudi. He told him he thought he had become involved in something over his head, something very big, and that these men meant to kill him. So Rudi agreed to go along with Rodriguez' request and write the story. I think he thought he might be on to something big, a good story, and that Rodriguez would allow him to publish it regardless. But three days later Rodriguez' body was found in a street in Asunción. He had been killed by a car. There were no witnesses and the car didn't stop. Rudi was certain the people Rodriguez had worked for had murdered him. That is what had been troubling him.'

'What made him so certain these men had committed murder?'

'The way Rodriguez had died. And Rodriguez had told Rudi the men he had worked for were very secretive. Their secrecy was almost obsessive. Rudi said they killed Rodriguez because they wanted no one to know what they were doing.'

Volkmann hesitated, put down his cup. 'Did Hernandez inform the police in Asunción about all of this?'

'No. Rudi wanted solid evidence first. He wanted the names of the people involved, and he wanted to be sure of the cargoes, what they contained. And that what these people were doing was definitely illegal.'

Volkmann looked at the girl a moment, then turned away towards the window. The sky was grey beyond. He hesitated, then turned back.

'Frau Kranz, I really don't see how this matter concerns DSE? You have no solid proof.'

The girl was silent a few moments. 'No, but Pauli Graf told me once that the department he belonged to concerned itself with many areas . . .'

'Yes, but South America isn't exactly our territory.'

'There is something that might concern you in all of this.'

'Tell me.'

'Before I left Asunción, Rudi had asked me to check up on something for him. He needed certain information. Four days ago I telephoned Rudi's apartment to tell him my progress. There was no reply. So I telephoned his office. A reporter at the newspaper, he told me . . .' The girl's voice trailed off, her head bowed. Volkmann could hear the Mendelssohn concerto, muted, barely audible, the music filling the silence.

'Told you what?'

'He told me Rudi was dead. The police had found his body in a house in Asunción. The house of a young girl. They had both been murdered.'

The girl took a handkerchief from the sleeve of her sweater, wiped her eyes.

Volkmann said, 'How do these murders concern DSE?'

She looked at Volkmann steadily. 'Before Rodriguez was killed, he took Rudi to a big house on the outskirts of Asunción. The house of the man who had hired him. They watched this house from a short distance away. Rudi wanted some photographs for the story. He had a telephoto lens fitted to the camera. Two men came out into the grounds of the property, walking together. Rodriguez pointed out the man who had hired him. But what interested Rudi was not the man Rodriguez had pointed out, but the second man present, walking with him. You see, Rudi recognised him, had seen him before. In Europe, not South America.'

'I don't understand.'

'Rudi had met this man five years before at a party at Heidelberg University, where I was a student. His name was Dieter Winter.'

'Go on.'

'Rudi was staying with my family at the time, and I had brought him along to the party. Winter had a heated argument with Rudi that almost came to blows. Rudi remembered him vividly. He said it was the first time he had ever wanted to hit someone. Rudi showed me one of the photographs he had taken of the men in the grounds of the house in Asunción. An old man and a young man strolling together. The young man could have been Dieter Winter, but I wasn't sure. He had been a student on the campus but I hardly remembered him. So Rudi asked me to check up on him as soon as I returned home and to send him a photograph of Winter if I could get one, just to be certain.

'When I returned to Frankfurt I checked up on him. I discovered his name had been in the newspapers here in Germany. The police found his body in an alleyway in Berlin a week ago. He had been shot to death.'

The girl reached across for a large buff envelope which lay on the coffee table. She removed a newspaper cutting, handed it to Volkmann. It was no more than a couple of paragraphs and described the discovery of a man's body in an alleyway near the Zoo U-Bahn in Berlin. He had been shot five times at close range. There were no witnesses and the man's identity was given as Dieter Winter. There was a request by the *Bundespolizei* for anyone to come forward with information.

Volkmann handed back the cuttings. 'This man Winter, what was so strange about him being in Paraguay?'

The girl shrugged. 'It just seemed strange to Rudi that Winter should be there, so far from Germany. And the fact that he might have been involved with these people who killed this pilot, Rodriguez.'

'Have you mentioned this matter to anyone else?'

'Only Pauli Graf. But I knew Pauli was just a small cog in a big machine. I wanted to speak to someone in authority.'

'Why didn't you go to the police?'

'I got the feeling Pauli seemed to think it a matter for your people. And besides, the *Bundespolizei* are really only interested in what happens on German territory. But your people, Pauli told me, don't only work in Europe.'

Volkmann put down his coffee. 'What exactly do you want me to do, Frau Kranz?'

The girl looked at Volkmann intently. 'I would like to know why Rudi died, and who killed him. I intend travelling to Paraguay again early next week. Rudi would have wanted someone to follow up his story. I'm a freelance journalist, that is my profession. But my interest is also a personal one.'

'You haven't answered my question.'

The girl hesitated a moment, as if struck by Volkmann's

bluntness, then said, 'You have contacts in the police and security services of other countries. Perhaps you could give me a letter of introduction, suggest someone I could talk with in Paraguay. Or even advise me.'

'I advise you to leave it to the Paraguayan police. Use the proper channels and leave Pauli Graf out of it.' Volkmann looked directly at the girl. 'Tell the *Bundespolizei* what you told me. They'll pass it on to their own people in DSE if they think it's important enough.'

There was a hint of impatience in the girl's reply. 'That's what Pauli Graf told me. But that takes time and I'm leaving for Asunción the day after tomorrow.' She looked at Volkmann steadily. 'I would appreciate any help you could give me, Herr Volkmann, despite your advice. It would make things easier, I'm sure. Besides, as I said, the *Bundespolizei* don't normally concern themselves with a crime that happens on the other side of the world. But your people . . . Pauli Graf told me their brief is wider. But then, perhaps I have been mistaken.'

'Pauli Graf seems to have told you a lot.'

'Not really. He is a friend. I knew him when I was a reporter on the *Frankfurter Zeitung*. He told me just enough to realise that yours was perhaps the only avenue open to me. But then, as I say, perhaps I have been mistaken.'

The Mendelssohn concerto rose and fell faintly in the background as the girl continued to look at him expectantly. Suddenly she looked like a young girl and Volkmann saw the pain in her eyes.

'To be honest, I'm not sure this is DSE's territory.'

'I understand, Herr Volkmann. But thank you for listening.'

Volkmann stood up. 'Your flight to Asunción, when does it leave?'

'Sunday next. From Frankfurt-Main.'

'I'll check with my people. I can't promise anything, but if there's anything I can do to help I'll telephone before you leave.'

'Thank you, Herr Volkmann.'

'Good morning, Frau Kranz.'

The girl watched as Volkmann crossed the corridor to the lift. She closed the door after her and went to stand by the window. The Rhine barges were having a bad day of it; the sturdy vessels tossing about in the grey swell. She saw Volkmann cross the street below towards a parked car, his raincoat flapping about his legs.

There was something distant about the man, she considered. So different from Rudi who had always smiled, and yet the same soft brown eyes. And there was something else, too. She had sensed an almost palpable dislike in his manner towards her. A formality she found disturbing. And she had seen the tension in his eyes and around his mouth.

She watched as he walked away, then dismissed the niggling thought from her mind as she went to wash the coffee cups.

It was after four when Volkmann arrived back in Strasbourg. Ferguson and Peters were both out and Volkmann wrote his report and delivered a copy to Ferguson's secretary along with a copy of the girl's file.

She told him Ferguson was in Paris and wasn't expected back until later that evening. Volkmann sent a security fax to the *Bundespolizei Hauptquartier* in Berlin requesting information on Dieter Winter, giving what details he could about the man, and requesting a photograph, if available.

He read the copy of the girl's file again. Born in Buenos Aires, Argentina, of German-born parents. She had one older sister, married to a Frenchman and living in Rennes. Her father had died in South America when she was three, and Erica Kranz had returned to Germany with her mother and sister the same year.

A graduate of Heidelberg University, majoring in journalism, she had once dabbled with several minor political parties at university but had no known political affiliations at present. Single. No known vices, no convictions. She worked as a freelance journalist from home and had contracts with many of the major popular German glossy women's magazines.

The paragraph relating to the girl's father, even though

it was history now, long past, had influenced Volkmann's attitude during their conversation, no matter that he had tried to push it from his mind. Manfred Kranz had been a Major in the Leibstandarte SS Division during the last war. He had once been wanted in connection with war crimes committed in two of the occupied countries. Twenty male inhabitants of a small village in Southern France called Ronchamp had been publicly executed during the German retreat. Manfred Kranz was the unit commander responsible. And in Russia, he had been implicated in the execution of two hundred prisoners of war during the German assault on Kiev. He had never been brought to trial, the Argentinian authorities refusing to co-operate in his extradition.

Volkmann left the office two hours later, arriving at his apartment a little after six. At ten o'clock Ferguson telephoned.

'I read your report. A little nebulous but interesting.'

'Any reply to the request I sent to the BP?'

'It arrived this evening. Along with a copy photograph.'

'What did they say about Winter?'

'Graduated from Heidelberg five years ago, majoring in history. Involved in several right-wing groups during his student days, but no arrests. He had been unemployed since graduating. The BP have no idea why he was killed. The area where it happened is a stamping ground for petty drug dealers. They tried that tack, however, and came up with nothing.'

'Had Winter any narcotic convictions?'

'None. But considering the area where the shooting happened, that's the angle the BP hinted at.'

'Nothing else?'

'The weapon used in the Berlin shooting is the bit that interests us. A Walther pistol, calibre nine-millimetre, but South American-manufactured ammunition. The BP think it was the same weapon used in the killing of a German industrialist named Pieber in a Hanover restaurant a year ago. A British business colleague of Pieber's named Hargrove was wounded in the same attack and died a couple of days later.'

'What do you think, sir?'

'God only knows. It could be anything. Personally, I think you ought to take the trip along with the girl. This journalist in Asunción, he could have been on to something that might concern us. And it may shed some light on the Hanover and Berlin shootings.'

'You really think it's necessary?'

'Bearing in mind what the girl said about the cargoes, yes, I think so. We can always bill the expenses to the Germans if it ends up in their court. And besides, Hargrove was a British subject, after all.'

'So what do I tell the girl?'

'Just that we're probing. That Winter's death interests us. See Peters about tickets first thing tomorrow morning. I take it the girl won't have any objection?'

'I shouldn't think so.'

'Good. I'll make contact with the people in Asunción and send them a report copy of the girl's statement, translated, of course. Goodnight, Joseph.'

Volkmann heard the line click and put down the receiver. He sat on the bed, half undressed, before turning off the bedside light. He stared out into the darkness beyond the window as he smoked a cigarette, his mind going over the meeting with the girl; the sighting of Winter in Paraguay and the shooting in Berlin; the murders the girl had spoken about in Asunción. How did they connect? Or did they connect? There were no answers, not yet, there couldn't be, only more questions; a pebble thrown into a pond, eddying in endless circles.

There were boats moving along the Rhine. He could see their lights, pinpricks of silvery white in the dark distance. Beyond the blackness lay the rolling shadows of the Black Forest. He thought about the telephone conversation with Ferguson.

He had left the copy of the girl's file with his report. The paragraph on the last page would have stood out, yet Ferguson had not mentioned it. It was a long time before the girl was born. It would have been of no concern to

Ferguson, but it was to him, and he shivered now in the darkness recalling the single paragraph in the girl's file.

North-Eastern Chaco,
Paraguay.
Sunday,
December 4th

Darkness had long descended as the tall, silver-haired man sat in the cane chair on the veranda. He wore a fresh white shirt, open at the neck beneath his pale linen jacket, and his light cotton pants were neatly pressed.

Beyond the wooden veranda the rain fell in heavy sheets. A bright full moon peeped between heavy black rain clouds, but the light was on overhead, moths buzzing about the shade. The man's silver hair shone under the light and his tanned handsome features looked sallow.

The boy served him iced lemon tea from a silver tray. He watched as the boy added two spoonfuls of sugar to the cup, then he turned his face towards where the jungle began. He saw the dark mass of the lush green forest beyond the downpour, the thick stems of bamboo and the fragrant mango trees.

He stared out at the torrential downpour, at the tangle of jade-green jungle plants, obscure in the gardens beyond the sheet of water.

In a while the rain would stop; the dark, pregnant rain clouds over the nearby rain-forest would deplete. And in the morning the sun would shine again, and the gardens and the trees would steam as the heat evaporated the rain water.

'Nature's cycle,' a tutor had told him once, when as a child he had noticed the phenomenon. Remembering the words, he smiled to himself.

But for now it was dark and grey beyond the incessant rain. He heard the footsteps echo on wooden floorboards in the hallway and saw Kruger appear moments later, smoking a cigarette. He wore a grey sweater, the sleeves pulled up to reveal the dark thick black hair of his muscular arms, and his dark hair was swept off his face. He sat in the cane chair opposite.

The silver-haired man turned to the servant boy and said, smiling, 'Leave us, please, Emilio.'

The man's voice was gentle and polite and the nut-brown face of the young boy smiled back at him. '*Si, senor.*'

When the boy had gone, the man lifted the sweet lemon tea to his lips, sipped the refreshing liquid. Then he looked at Kruger, his stocky frame creaking the cane chair. An insect crawled across the table; Kruger flicked it away.

'You contacted Franz on the radio?'

Kruger nodded. 'Nothing to worry about.'

'You're absolutely certain, Hans?'

'The journalist was working alone. There's no question.'

'And the tape?'

Kruger drew on his cigarette, blew out smoke. 'Definitely blank. I had Franz have the tape and the equipment thoroughly checked. The microphone was faulty. Apparently, the only sound that could be picked up was at extremely close range and even then only very faintly. But he recorded nothing.'

'There's no doubt?'

'None. Franz's technician is thoroughly reliable. According to him the equipment was highly sensitive. Handled without care it could be easily damaged. Franz had the equipment disposed of.'

The silver-haired man sighed, a sigh of relief. He lifted the cup and held it in both his slim, manicured hands, sipped the lemon tea. Then he looked out at the jungle, beyond the rain falling in heavy sheets.

'And the travel arrangements, they are all in order?'

'The helicopter arrives at nine. When we reach Mexico City, Konrad will take us to Halder's place.'

The silver-haired man thought a moment and said, 'The journalist, I still want his background thoroughly checked, Hans. But discreetly. Tell Franz. And I want no more hitches. The pilot and the journalist, they will be the last of our problems. What happened at the hotel must not happen again.'

Although the man's voice was soft, the admonition was clear.

Kruger nodded silently, wanting to say that there would be no more problems, that he was certain, that Franz's men had made sure of that, had checked every avenue thoroughly. But the elderly man was speaking again and Kruger listened respectfully.

'Before we leave, I want everything destroyed. Everything in this house we are not taking with us burned. There must be nothing left behind. Nothing. As if we had never been here. As if we had never existed. You will see to it, Hans.'

Kruger inflected his head in reply.

'That will be all, Hans. Thank you.'

Kruger stood and left quietly, his footsteps echoing on the wooden floorboards.

The silver-haired man remained seated, watched as Kruger crossed the veranda, stepped inside the house.

Alone now, he stared up at the rain-forest beyond the sheeting wall of water.

He hesitated, then slowly removed his wallet from the inside pocket of his linen jacket, took out the copy of the photograph. The grainy photograph of the blonde young woman and the dark-haired man.

A moment later the servant boys appeared, Emilio carrying the silver tray, Lopez behind. They came to stand beside him. The silver-haired man smiled over at them fondly, their faces full of adulation.

Then the boys stared at the photograph in the man's hands, before smiling up at him.

The man patted their heads in turn as the boys came to stand beside him.

As he pointed down at the photograph, the man said in Spanish, 'You'd like to hear the story again?'

The boys nodded eagerly, their faces smiling up at the gentle blue eyes.

The silver-haired man carefully replaced the photograph in his wallet and began to speak.

Chapter Twelve

The detective who welcomed Joseph Volkmann and Erica Kranz in the Arrivals area that Monday morning wore a crumpled white suit that looked a size too large for his stocky, overweight body. His fat face appeared pale and rubbery, and his dark eyes looked tired. He spoke good English, several gold teeth flashing as his fat lips moved. He introduced himself as Captain Vellares Sanchez and led them to an unmarked police car and drove towards the centre of the city.

A shimmering wave of intense heat had hit them as they stepped from the aircraft, the air dry and breezeless, hot enough to hurt their lungs. It was summer in Asunción, trees and flowers in bloom, eucalyptus and palm trees lining their route, palm fronds hanging limply in the scorching afternoon air.

Volkmann sat beside the girl in the rear, the windows rolled down but still the heat oppressive. The fat detective mopped his face with a handkerchief as he drove. He barely spoke, except to inquire of his passengers if they had had a pleasant flight.

The city they drove through was a riot of colour and noise; a mixture of old and new; nineteenth-century facades and yellow-bricked *adobes* and tin and wood shanty-dwellings existing side by side with modern buildings and apartment blocks. Ancient yellow trolley cars screeched noisily along the main avenues and on bustling city street corners Indian women sat in the sun beside barrows of fruit and flowers and trinkets.

The detective's office was on the third floor of the *Comisaria Centrico*, the Central Police Station, on Calle Chile. It was a drab, hot place with peeling grey walls and ancient furniture. An old rusting filing cabinet stood in one corner; an electric fan whirred overhead. On a wall by the door hung a laminated cardboard map of South America, its glaze stained sepia by a film of nicotine.

A young recruit brought them strong, aromatic Paraguayan tea. '*Yerba mate*,' explained Sanchez. 'You have been to Paraguay before, Senor Volkmann?'

'Never.'

'The tea is an acquired taste. But as good as beer on a hot day.'

Sanchez removed his jacket and loosened his tie, waited until the young recruit had left before he unlocked a drawer in his desk and produced two files. His own file and the one containing the report the *seguridad* had received from the people Volkmann worked for, translated into Spanish. He had read the report yesterday morning over coffee, had two men from his department check out the information.

Now he smiled briefly at the girl, remembering Hernandez talking about her, appreciating her beauty. Striking. Long legs. Sexy. Like one of the girls you saw on the cover of the glossy, gossipy American magazines. A figure that would bring an instant reaction from men.

He put the thought from his mind as he opened the files and looked up at the *gringo*, Volkmann. The man could have been a cop, but Sanchez knew he wasn't. Something more than a cop. The *seguridad* had telephoned him late the previous day, sent him a copy of the report they had been sent from Europe, asked him to co-operate, told him to let the *gringo* see the necessary files, asked if he needed a translator.

Sanchez told them he didn't: he spoke English, this was an opportunity to get some practice. He wondered, not for the first time, why the two had travelled together, wondered what more there was to the deaths of Rodriguez and Hernandez and the young girl, now that he had read the translated report.

He looked up. He didn't need to read the reports in the

files again; he remembered all the details, had gone over them relentlessly, searching for clues. There was a photocopied map of Asunción City on his desk, a mark in red indelible pen to indicate the area where the bodies had been found. He turned the map round so that they could see it, indicated the street where the house of the young girl stood, as he cleared his throat, spoke slowly.

'We found the bodies here, on the morning of the twenty-sixth, in a house in the district of La Chacarita near the Paraguay river, a short distance from the main railway station. Rudi's car we found parked outside the house. The keys of the car we found in the grass outside, as if someone had thrown them there.'

When the detective paused, Volkmann said, 'The house, who does it belong to?'

'The young girl whose body was found with Rudi Hernandez. Her name was Graciella Campos, aged seventeen. But her mind, it was the mind of a child, you understand? The girl had no family alive. She rented the house.'

Sanchez saw the girl lean forward, saw the look of pain in her blue eyes. 'This girl . . . did she know Rudi?'

'*Si*. I have learned that he gave her money. To pay for food and rent and clothes. It was a kindness, you understand? Not a payment for anything else. They were simply friends.'

Sanchez paused, wondered if his English sounded OK, wondered if his visitors understood him clearly. Erica Kranz's face was pale, not from the heat, but hurting inside. She nodded, Volkmann too.

Sanchez lowered his voice out of respect. 'The girl and Rudi had both been killed with knives. A drunk old man who sometimes sleeps in an alley near the girl's house found the bodies. The girl usually gave him some hot tea in the mornings. When she didn't answer his knock he tried the door. It was open. When he discovered the bodies he told a local priest, who called the *policia*.'

Volkmann said, 'How long had they been dead?'

'Not long. Maybe four, five hours.'

Sanchez took several police photographs from the file,

careful not to let the girl see them, handed them across to Volkmann. Sanchez looked at Erica Kranz. 'Forgive me. But I would prefer you did not look at these, *senorita*. They are not pleasant.'

There was a sudden look of anguish on the girl's face as she turned away. Sanchez had asked Volkmann quietly, as they stepped from the car outside the station, if it was OK to talk in front of the girl. He had said yes. But the photographs were different. Not for the girl's eyes.

There were five photographs, taken by forensic, all in vivid, horrific colour. Volkmann examined them carefully. Two were of the body of Hernandez, two of the girl, one photograph of both of the bodies lying close together, faces up. The brown face of the young girl looked pitiful in death, eyes closed as if she were asleep. The savagery of her wounds shocked Volkmann. The knife had slit her stomach open from chest cavity to navel, exposing the internal organs, the viscera. The simple white frock she wore was ripped apart above the waist and drenched in blood.

He looked next at the photograph of the body of Rudi Hernandez, tried not to allow his expression to change, for the girl's sake. The man had suffered much the same fate: the torso had been slit from chest to groin, the man's innards spilling out onto the bloodied floor.

Volkmann grimaced and handed the photographs back to Sanchez who quickly replaced them in the file. He looked at the girl; she held back her tears bravely, but her face was contorted in an expression of pure pain.

Volkmann said, 'Senor Sanchez, did the forensic people find anything?'

Sanchez looked at him blankly. The girl looked up suddenly, translating quickly into Spanish, *forense*, Sanchez remembering the word now, smiling at the girl, a brief sad smile, telling her he understood her grief.

'You speak Spanish very well, *senorita*,' Sanchez told her.

'I was born in Buenos Aires,' the girl answered quietly.

Sanchez nodded. Hernandez had not told him that. He looked at Volkmann again.

'The forensic people believe different knives were used to kill both victims. Both blades were hunting knives. The one used to kill Rudi had a very big blade. Perhaps a Bowie knife, they think. But other than that nothing much. No fingerprints. Some faint footprints, but nothing they think would really help. There were bruises on the arms and faces of both bodies that suggest several people helped in the murders. But whoever they were, they were careful not to leave anything behind. No prints, no real clues the forensic people could use. And a knife is not like a bullet. Sometimes it is more difficult to trace such a weapon. My men searched the area around the house and the *barrio* itself. Nothing was found. No discarded knives or bloodied clothes. Nothing.'

Sanchez saw the girl wince as he spoke, wondering if he should be so explicit. He picked up the cup of steaming tea and sipped the green, aromatic liquid, put the cup down again. His visitors had so far left theirs untouched; he should have ordered Cokes, he told himself, the *yerba mate* was sharp to the taste and steaming hot.

He paused to take a packet of cigarettes from his pocket, offered them to Volkmann and to the girl. When both refused he lit one for himself and loosened his tie some more as he saw the girl lean forward slightly. She spoke quietly, her voice strained.

'The place where the bodies were found. Did no one see or hear anything? Were there no witnesses? Surely someone must have heard something?'

Sanchez blew out smoke and shook his head. 'The old man I spoke of saw and heard nothing. He had drunk a lot of *cana* the night before. I have spoken also to many people in the *barrio*, in La Chacarita. It is the same story. No one saw or heard anything. And believe me, they would have talked. The girl's death shocked them all. Some old men saw Rudi arrive at the house about seven-thirty in the evening before he died. They did not see him come out. And a man who sleeps down by the river says he woke and thought he heard a car drive along the waterfront very early in the morning while it was still dark. What time, he was not sure. But he said he heard nothing unusual.' He paused a moment before going on. 'There is one small thing, however. It may be important.'

Sanchez hesitated again, saw his visitors look at him, then said, 'The day after Rudi and the young girl were murdered, *La Tarde* published a story about the deaths. There was a photograph of Rudi and the young girl on the front page. A night watchman at the central railway station on the Plaza Uruguaya came to see us. He said he saw a man who looked like Rudi come in the back of the station very early on the morning of the murders, maybe three o'clock. But he could not be certain. He was tired, had been on duty since three the previous afternoon.' Sanchez shrugged. 'Perhaps Rudi was at the station, perhaps not. Perhaps he meant to leave Asunción, take the girl and go some place if he thought he was in some kind of danger. But the ticket office was closed then. Or maybe, if it *was* Rudi, he simply had something on his mind and went for a walk, to get some air.'

Sanchez looked directly at Volkmann. 'Of course, the report your people sent, it changes matters, I believe, when we consider what Rudi said he was doing, writing this story. Also, there are two other things that are important.'

The fat detective tapped his cigarette ash into a cracked glass ashtray on the desk in front of him. 'Number one, Rudi's press identity card was missing. And also his wallet. Yet he still had money in his back pocket. Not much. But enough. And a gold ring and a watch he wore were not taken.'

Volkmann sipped the bitter tea and looked at the detective. 'You're saying whoever murdered Hernandez and the girl didn't intend to rob them.'

'*Si*. I think we can forget about a simple robbery that went wrong. And the girl was not sexually assaulted. We must eliminate all the irrelevant motives. For this reason I think your report to us suggests that Rudi and the girl may have been killed for other reasons. A robber would have taken all the money and the gold ring and the watch unless he was disturbed at his work. I don't believe that happened. No one reported hearing any disturbance and the bodies were not discovered until seven that morning. Also, the way the killing was done. It was not an ordinary murder. To kill like that, brutally, with knives, you must be someone crazy. You understand? So I don't think the motive was to rob. I think it was to kill.

'There is a clue to this. Rudi borrowed some equipment from a friend he knew, a man named Torres. He is a technician with an electronics company. Torres went to the newspaper office when Rudi had not returned this equipment to him. When they told him Rudi had been murdered he came to us.'

The girl leaned forward and Volkmann said, 'What sort of equipment are we talking about?'

Sanchez drew on his cigarette, exhaled slowly. 'Special electronic equipment that would allow a person to hear and record something spoken a distance away. Japanese, and expensive. A very small microphone-transmitter and a receiver which work on a very high radio frequency. I am sure you have heard of such equipment, *senor*. The equipment was borrowed by Rudi two days before he was killed. We questioned Torres. He said he asked Rudi what he wanted the equipment for. Rudi said that it was for *trabajo clandestino* . . . undercover work.'

Sanchez glanced at the girl, to make sure his words were correct, saw that she understood. He looked back at Volkmann as the *gringo* spoke.

'That was all Rudi told Torres?'

'*Si*. No more. Not where he was going or why exactly he needed the equipment. Only that he would return it safely the next day. We have not found the equipment. It was not in the girl's house, or in Rudi's car or apartment. Perhaps it is still lying around somewhere, wherever Rudi used it, if he did use it. Or perhaps the people who murdered him and the young girl have it, or have destroyed it.'

Sanchez paused, looked at Volkmann, speaking softly. 'I believe Rudi used the equipment the day or night before he was killed.' Sanchez tapped a file in front of him. 'The report your people sent us . . . concerning the people Rodriguez was smuggling for, perhaps Rudi thought he could record something, get more information before he published his story. But these people they found him and killed him. The young girl, too. Perhaps she helped Rudi in some way, or was simply a witness to what happened to Rudi. It is only my . . . my *teoria* . . . my theory. But it makes a little sense, you understand?'

Volkmann nodded and said, 'What can you tell us about Rodriguez?'

Sanchez sat back. 'Noberto Rodriguez was a smuggler. His body was found two weeks ago in the city. Our forensic people said he had been killed by a car. The car, it drove away, did not stop. There were no witnesses. We thought it was an accident that someone did not report, a drunken driver, perhaps. Or even a fellow criminal. But my men, they would have heard whispers in the underworld. In Rodriguez' case, they heard nothing. But now I know from your report that something else is possible . . . that these people he had worked for, perhaps they killed him.'

'What kind of work did Rodriguez do?'

'He was a middle-man who smuggled goods from the supplier to the purchaser. He chartered an old DC4 he owned. He flew cargoes mostly to the ports of Montevideo in Uruguay or Porto Alegre in Brazil, for shipping on to Europe and America.'

'Are we talking about narcotics?'

Sanchez nodded. '*Si*, narcotics, of course. But also whatever made a good profit. Gold. Jewels. Leopard skins. Rodriguez was one of the best, I am told. Very, very good.' Sanchez allowed himself a brief smile. 'So good we never catch him.'

Volkmann loosened his tie, the heat in the small room cloying, even with the fan whirring away. He sipped the aromatic tea; it tasted sharp. He put the cup down.

'Rodriguez' friends, people who knew him, people who might have worked with him, have you talked with them?'

'Rodriguez had no real friends. He nearly always worked alone. And concerning the people he did work for, he told no one. To tell would mean death.' Sanchez paused. 'However, there is a man he sometimes worked with, a man named Santander. A smuggler also. We are trying to find him, but so far we have no luck.' Sanchez shrugged. 'And even if we find Santander, he may know nothing. Rodriguez was not the type to talk about the people he did business with.'

'Have you talked with Rudi's colleagues at the newspaper, his friends?' Erica asked. 'Perhaps he confided in one of them about his story?'

Sanchez nodded briefly. 'They knew nothing about any special story Rudi was working on. We also checked Rudi's desk and locker at *La Tarde*. Also his apartment. There was nothing in any of them that would suggest such a story. And no photographs like the ones you spoke of. Nothing that would help us.'

'Rudi said that anything he had he kept in a safe place . . .'

Sanchez flicked a glance at Volkmann, then looked at Erica and nodded. '*Si, senorita*, I read that in the report I received. I must tell you that I had every bank in Asunción contacted yesterday. Rudi Hernandez had an account in one of them. But no deposit box. Not in any of them. I am also having the banks outside Asunción checked just in case. But that will take time.' He looked intently at the girl. 'I have read the report Senor Volkmann's people sent but I would like to ask you myself. Did Rudi say anything else concerning what information or evidence he had?'

'No.'

'Did he suggest where this safe place might be?'

Erica Kranz shook her head. 'All he said was that what he had was not much. But that it was in a safe place. That was all he said. A safe place.'

'The older man in the photograph he showed to you. Could you describe him?'

The girl bit her lip, thought hard. 'The photograph was taken from a distance and wasn't very clear. Old, perhaps seventy. Very thin. That is all I recall.'

The detective nodded. 'I will have a photograph of Rudi shown to the bank people my men spoke to, in case another name was used. Do you remember if Rudi said anything else?

Anything, no matter how small, no matter how unimportant it seems to you?'

'No. I'm certain.'

Sanchez tapped the file, the file containing a translation of Volkmann's report. It was all there: Hernandez and Rodriguez observing the men at the house, what Rodriguez had told Hernandez, in the girl's words. It had helped. Opened a door, even just a little. He looked at the girl again.

'And this house,' Sanchez probed. 'Rudi did not tell you where the area was in Asunción?'

'No. I'm sorry.'

'What about the place where the photographs were taken. Do you remember anything?'

'It was a garden, or a park maybe. I can't be sure.'

'There was nothing in the background?'

Erica shook her head. 'Not that I can remember. Just maybe trees, and open space. But I can't be certain.'

Sanchez nodded again, glanced at his watch and stubbed out his cigarette. There was a long silence. All the questions had been asked. There was nothing more to be said. Nothing until his men turned something up, if they were lucky. The heat in the small drab room had become unbearable. He went to close the file, the meeting at an end, but hesitated and looked at the girl.

'Rudi's parents, they are dead, *si*?'

Erica Kranz nodded.

'His belongings . . .' Sanchez said solemnly. 'Rudi's things . . .'

He paused, saw the girl nod once more. She understood. He removed a set of keys from an envelope in the file and handed them across to her.

'These are the keys to Rudi's apartment,' Sanchez explained. 'In case there is anything from it you wish. Something personal, photographs, perhaps. I have kept copies of the keys myself.'

Erica Kranz accepted the keys. 'Thank you.'

Sanchez pushed his fat bulk from the chair and stood up, picked up his jacket.

'And now, *senor, senorita*, I will take you to your hotel.' He looked at the girl and said gently, 'Perhaps I might speak with Senor Volkmann in private first? I have some police business to discuss.'

Erica Kranz nodded and stepped out into the hallway. Sanchez watched her leave, then turned to Volkmann.

'The security police in my country, the *seguridad*, they keep a file on certain citizens. Rudi Hernandez was a journalist. Journalists are, shall we say, a special case. Because of their work, you understand.'

He saw Volkmann nod his head and Sanchez crossed to behind his desk, removed a file from a drawer and came back and handed it to Volkmann.

'This is a copy of the file. It's not much. Hernandez was not a troublemaker. There is nothing of much interest. But perhaps it may help you understand the man.'

Volkmann took the file.

Sanchez said, 'The man named Winter you asked us to check on. My men are checking with the immigration people. I will let you know as soon as I have something.' Sanchez pulled on his coat. 'The report your people sent. You have nothing more to add?'

Volkmann shook his head. 'You received a photograph of Winter?'

'*Si*, I have it here.'

He removed a wired photograph from a file on his desk. A head-and-shoulders shot, enlarged. The man in the picture was young, blond, sharp-featured, thin-lipped. Sanchez stared at the photograph then looked up.

'It is a difficult case, I think, Senor Volkmann. Strange. Most strange. And Rudi, he was a good man. I want to tell you I will do everything I can.'

'You were friends?'

'*Si*. For many years.'

'The bodies are still at the morgue?'

'No. The funerals were three days ago. Had I known the girl was coming I would have delayed the burials. But the forensic people had finished their work. And the police morgue is full.

Tomorrow, I will take the girl to the cemetery. She may wish to say a prayer. I have also arranged for a police artist to meet with her. Together they may be able to come up with a picture of the old man Rudi told her about.'

'I'll tell her. Thank you.'

'I will also take you to see the girl's house where the bodies were found. And we can talk with Mendoza, Rudi's editor, and the man Torres, who loaned Rudi the equipment.'

The detective buttoned his coat. 'And now I will take you to your hotel. Your people, they have made arrangements?'

'The Excelsior,' said Volkmann.

Sanchez said, 'It's a nice hotel.'

Chapter Thirteen

Asunción

Volkmann and the girl checked into the Excelsior and after dinner he ordered a taxi to take them to Rudi Hernandez' apartment.

It was seven and dark when they arrived. Volkmann turned on the lights in the living-room and found the air-conditioning switch and flicked it on, the heat in the small apartment stifling.

It was a bachelor place; a bedroom and kitchen and living-room and a tiny bathroom. An old portable typewriter stood on a writing desk near the window, below a cluttered bookshelf and a portrait of an ancient railcar pulled by a wood-burning steam-engine. There was a large framed print of a section of the old Berlin Wall being torn down near the Brandenburg Tor, crowds waving the federal flag as they demonstrated their jubilation, another of the ruined Kaiser Dom taken at night and a couple of Indian woodcarvings. An electric fan hung from a hook above the writing desk.

On one of the bookshelves were half a dozen photographs in small silver frames. Hernandez' family, Volkmann guessed. One of a blonde woman and a Latin man, the man smiling broadly, the woman's face serious, unsmiling. There was a silver-framed photograph of Erica Kranz taken in a Bavarian inn, looking much younger, her hair long, laughing out at the camera and holding a stein of beer, her arm around a young, handsome, smiling man.

Volkmann looked at the girl now. She appeared tired and drawn. The long flight and the seven-hour time difference between Frankfurt and Asunción was taking its toll, and she was thinking, he guessed, of the last time she had been in the apartment. He saw her pick up the photograph from the shelf and stare down at the image silently.

'Rudi?' Volkmann asked.

She looked up and he saw the faint smudges under the blue eyes. 'Yes.'

The girl replaced the photograph and sat quietly on the couch, subdued, while Volkmann went to look around the apartment. The police had been untidy in their work: there were drawers open in the bedroom and clothes left in disarray. In the kitchen, cupboard doors had been left ajar. There was an empty scotch bottle in one, an unopened quart of vodka and some soft drinks beside it.

When he came back into the living-room he found the girl staring silently out of the window. The lights of the city twinkled beyond the glass, a clear view down to the Rio Paraguay, boats moving back and forth in the encroaching darkness.

As he moved closer the girl turned and he saw there were tears running down her cheeks. And then she was burying her face in his chest, her body racked by a fit of crying. He held her until the tears ebbed away and then she pulled away from him slowly.

'Forgive me. I . . . I kept remembering. The last night I was here with Rudi. And what the detective said today . . . about the way Rudi died.'

'It's been a difficult day. How about I pour us both a drink?'

The girl nodded. Volkmann turned and went back into the kitchen.

The vodka and soft drinks bottles were on the coffee table, a bowl of ice between them. There were small beads of perspiration on Erica Kranz's forehead and she had taken off her shoes, Volkmann unable to ignore the long, smooth legs, the perfect body. He was attracted to the girl physically, and as she sat opposite he found himself watching the full smooth breasts, the curving hips; the same tanned, dusky skin you saw on some of the South American girls he had seen in the streets. He tried to push the thought away.

'Tell me about Rudi.'

'What would you like to know?'

'Anything you can tell me.'

There was a look of pain on the girl's face. 'He was a good and kind man, and a good journalist. He loved life. Rudi was always quick to laugh no matter how black things were.' The girl shrugged. 'I really don't know what more to tell you.'

There had not been much to read in the police file Sanchez had given Volkmann: two pages of flimsy in English, translated especially, personal details, political affiliations, age, family background. But he wanted to hear the girl's story, wanted to know if there was more; hidden things, private things, things that all men keep to themselves or share with a woman. Some small clue, something that would open a door for him.

He took a packet of cigarettes from his pocket, offered one to the girl, lit them both.

'Tell me about Rudi's background.'

'You mean his family?'

'Yes, his family.'

She stared down at her drink a moment, then looked up. 'Rudi's mother and mine were half-sisters. After the war ended they were brought as children to Argentina by my grandparents. Years later, Rudi's mother met a Paraguayan, a biologist, who was studying at the university in Buenos Aires. When he graduated they married and went to live in Asunción where Rudi was born. He was their only child.'

The girl toyed with her drink, looked up at the photographs on the shelf. 'Rudi was very much like his father. He always laughed at life. Rudi's mother was sterner. She was not a happy woman, I think.'

Volkmann glanced up at the picture of the blonde, pretty woman. Pretty, but not smiling. 'Why?'

Erica Kranz brushed a strand of hair from her face, looked at him. 'My mother told me a story once. She and her sister lived in Hamburg during the war, when they were children. One night the city was being destroyed with firebombs. It was the worst of the air-raids. In the bomb shelters people were praying and everyone was frightened. When a bomb fell

143

nearby, the ground shook and the lights went out. People were crushed in the chaos. Rudi's mother was only a child and she was frightened. She ran out of the shelter, distraught. But what she was to see outside on the streets was even worse and always remained in her memory afterwards. Burning buildings, corpses, the inferno of that terrible night. Childhood friends she had known, relatives, many were dead. She became withdrawn after that. She was a sensitive child and the experience affected her terribly. Rudi used to say she relived that night every day of her life. She was always a sad person.'

'Rudi's parents. How did they die?'

'My uncle often took his family with him when he worked on biological surveys. A light aircraft they were passengers in crashed in the southern Amazon. Rudi was a passenger, too, but he survived. They found him four days later, badly shocked and bleeding. His face was permanently scarred. For a long time afterwards he was devastated. He began to visit us more often in Germany, because we were the only relatives he had left. But he couldn't live there, he said, even though he spoke the language. I think Rudi found the Germans too stern, too serious. The Paraguayans were his people.'

The girl looked down at her empty glass. 'May I have another drink?'

Volkmann poured another for both of them, spooned in the ice cubes. 'Why did your family return to Germany?'

Volkmann looked at her intently. She sipped her drink, held the glass in both her hands. 'My mother had met my father and married him in Buenos Aires. He was a businessman, a German immigrant, and much older than her. But he died when I was three, so I don't remember him. My grandparents had died also, so I guess my mother felt a little lost.

'She sold my father's business and decided to return to Germany. She still had relatives there and thought that it was better for me to study there. After I graduated she married again and moved to Hamburg. We drifted apart after that. The whole family did. But Rudi and I always wrote. He was like an older brother.'

Volkmann saw the girl look away, her eyes wet. He sipped his drink, and looked across at her. Something about her made him want to reach over and touch her, comfort her, but he didn't know how she might react.

'Dieter Winter, the young man Rudi thought he saw at the house. Did he say what they talked about when they met in Heidelberg?'

Erica Kranz frowned. 'I asked Rudi that same question. It was just small-talk, he said. Winter was very drunk when they met, but seemed intrigued by Rudi's background, the fact that he was half-German and from South America. That's another thing Rudi thought strange when he told me he had seen Winter in Asunción. At the party, Winter asked Rudi if he socialised among the German colony in Paraguay. Rudi said no, that they bored him. He preferred the easy-going Latins. He said Winter seemed to take the remark as a personal insult and became quite aggressive.'

'Is that what made Rudi dislike him?'

The girl shrugged. 'He said he found him pompous and a loud-mouth. And Winter had said if Rudi thought so little of Germans he should go back where he belonged. Just like the immigrant workers in Germany, Winter said. Germany didn't need another *mischling*.'

She put down her glass. 'That word. I'm sure you know it's not a nice word. It's used to describe someone who is only half-German, a half-caste.'

Volkmann nodded.

The heat that came and lingered in the small apartment was stifling, despite the air-conditioning. Volkmann stood up, placed the empty glass on the table, looked down at the girl.

'Sanchez said he'd call tomorrow morning to take you to the cemetery to visit Rudi's grave.'

'Will you come too?'

'If you want.'

The girl nodded. 'Yes, I would prefer it. Thank you, Herr Volkmann.'

'Call me Joe.'

He gestured to the telephone nearby. 'You think you could call a taxi to take us back to the hotel?'

Erica Kranz nodded.

Volkmann picked up the things from the coffee table and went back into the kitchen.

It was after eight when they arrived back at the Excelsior. There was a pre-Christmas party in progress in one of the hotel's function rooms. In the lobby, tuxedoed men and beautiful, olive-skinned women in sleek dresses stood around an illuminated Christmas tree sipping drinks.

The girl looked tired in contrast, her mascara smudged. As the taxi passed the offices of *La Tarde* the girl had suddenly started crying. In the dim cab Volkmann had reached across and held her hand, felt her lean into his shoulder, smelled the scent of her perfume, her blonde hair brushing his cheek. She had stared out of the window, wiping her eyes but holding onto his hand until they had stepped from the taxi.

They took the lift to the fifth floor and their adjoining rooms. Volkmann opened her door for her.

'If you can't sleep or you want to talk, I'm in the next room.'

'Thank you, Joe. You've been very kind. Please forgive me for crying, but it's been a hard day.'

Volkmann waited until the girl had closed her door, then went into his own room. The air-conditioning was on, but the room was still warm and humid. He undressed slowly and lay naked on the bed in the cloying darkness.

He could still smell the scent of her perfume as he closed his eyes and fell asleep.

The telephone rang in Volkmann's bedroom an hour later. He switched on the bedside lamp, and picked up the receiver sleepily, hearing the stilted English, recognising the voice.

'Sanchez here, Senor Volkmann. Did I wake you? My apologies . . . the time difference . . . I remembered just as I rang.'

'What's the problem?'

'No problem. Something has turned up. The man you are interested in . . . the German.'

'Winter.'

'*Si*, about him. And something else. The man, Santander, I told you about . . . the one who sometimes worked with Rodriguez. He was picked up by the local *policia* in San Ignacio late this afternoon. A place not far from the border with Argentina. He is being taken back to Asunción tonight. It would be best if you came to my office.'

Volkmann said, 'I'll phone for a taxi.'

'No. Rest for now. My men have to check some things out first. I need a little time. I'll send a car to the hotel for you at midnight. Bring the girl if you wish.'

'Midnight,' repeated Volkmann.

'*Si*. Rest my friend,' said Sanchez, and then the line clicked dead.

Chapter Fourteen

North-Eastern Chaco,
Paraguay

Kruger stood on the veranda smoking a cigarette, watching the men as they worked. Dusk, clouds obscuring the moon, the stars of the Southern Hemisphere barely visible, faint pinpricks of light beyond the brooding blackness of the rain-forest.

The electric generators were on and a flood of light circled the property, spilling out onto the dark edge of the jungle, out beyond where the heavy truck and the small pick-up stood parked, the light making the jade-green leaves of the jungle plants beyond the gravel driveway shine as if they had been polished brightly.

The rain had long stopped, but the air was humid again. Kruger's blue cotton shirt was open at the neck, damp patches of sweat under his arms and on his chest.

Schmidt was supervising the three other men loading the truck, and carrying the heavy boxes himself, two at a time from the garage to the truck.

Kruger watched him. You wound Schmidt up and pointed him in the right direction. Tell him to kill and he killed. Tell him to leave your company and he left unquestioningly. All brawn, no brain. But useful, very useful.

Kruger ran a hand through his black hair and glanced at his watch, then across at the garage, light flooding out through the open doors, the garage filled with wooden and cardboard boxes. There was still much to be done. All the papers travelling separately to Mexico City in steel fireproof boxes. Everything was on schedule and the house would be emptied by morning. His only worry was that the truck would not be large enough to accommodate everything, but Franz had assured him that it would.

He looked at Schmidt again, muscled flesh bulging and straining beneath his blue overalls. The big man looked as if he had been hewn out of rock.

Kruger caught a sudden movement out of the corner of his eye and turned sharply. The curtain of the room nearest him moved. Then he saw the brown face of Lopez. A moment later the face of the second boy, Emilio, appeared.

Both were no more than fifteen, glad of a bed and food, diligent young workers once you watched over them. No one had told them what was happening and they watched the loading of the boxes with curiosity, their soft faces like those of young girls: awed, innocent, interested, watching the men move back and forth to the garage in a steady rhythm. The boys themselves would never have asked what was happening, knew their place, too grateful for having a full belly ever to question anything. One of them, Emilio, turned towards Kruger, and smiled. Kruger smiled back. The faces disappeared and the curtain fell back into place.

A moment later Kruger heard the footsteps approach the veranda from the hallway. He exhaled the smoke and dropped the cigarette onto the veranda, ground it out with his shoe.

The silver-haired man stood beside him now. He wore a light cotton dressing gown over his white pyjamas, ready to retire.

Kruger said, 'The men will have the truck loaded by midnight. Anything we're not taking with us Schmidt will burn.'

The man nodded silently, then placed a hand on Kruger's shoulder as he stared out at the edge of the jungle.

'Are you glad we're leaving, Hans?'

Kruger smiled. 'It's been a long time. Too long.'

'But you won't miss this place?'

Kruger shook his head. 'It's been a prison.' He shrugged. 'When I was younger, perhaps it didn't seem so hellish and claustrophobic. But now, I'm just glad to be leaving.' He turned his head to glance at the silver-haired man as his hand came away from his shoulder. 'And you?'

The man smiled weakly. 'It holds memories, of course, Hans. Fond memories.' He fell silent as he looked out towards where the men worked, dressed in blue overalls, moving smartly as they carried the metal and wooden boxes from garage to truck. Almost everything of importance he possessed was packed in the boxes: his personal belongings, his paperwork and files, years of hard work.

He said quietly to Kruger, 'The boys?'

'Schmidt and I will take them up to the rain-forest.'

This time the silver-haired man turned to face Kruger, and his hand touched Kruger's arm lightly. There was a tone of compassion in his voice.

'Make it quick, Hans. I don't want them to suffer. No pain, you understand?'

Kruger nodded, saw a look like grief cross the man's handsome face.

The man turned away, walked back across the veranda towards the hallway and entered the house.

Kruger waited until his footsteps had died away, then he turned back to watch Schmidt.

North-Eastern Chaco.
Monday,
December 5th,
11.57 p.m.

There was no traffic as the pick-up truck bumped along the rutted jungle road. Not at this hour, not in this part of the Chaco, so remote, empty, vast. The rich sweet smells of jungle and earth wafted in through the open window, a slight breeze cooling Kruger's face. The pick-up travelled at no more than a bumpy thirty kilometres an hour, its headlights washing the rich green undergrowth ahead in silvery light.

Kruger sat in the passenger seat. Now and then he glimpsed the eyes of jungle creatures staring out at them, pinpricks of reflected light amidst the silvery green, before they disappeared, scurrying off into the bushes.

As the truck came round a sharp bend one of the boys laughed and pointed beyond the windscreen. Kruger looked ahead, towards the headlights sweeping the road: a mongoose scurried across their path before disappearing into a clump of mango trees. The boys giggled.

Kruger smiled down at them in the darkness of the cab. The four of them were squashed into the pick-up's cabin: Kruger, the boys, and big Schmidt, his granite face staring blankly ahead as he drove slowly along the narrow dirt road.

Kruger saw the gap in the jungle just ahead and tapped Schmidt on the shoulder. The big man swung the pick-up left, onto a narrow overgrown path, the ground rising up suddenly, the engine straining a little, whining, as the truck moved up towards the mountain.

They were an hour from the house. Another five minutes to go before they reached their destination. Kruger kept his arm in from the window while the truck cut slowly through the dense foliage either side of the track, bits of plants and leaves flying into the cab as the vehicle brushed too close to the sides.

The place was remote, the path hardly ever used, furrows in the soil where a truck or car had driven in the rainy season months before. Kruger had climbed it once, this mountain. He knew the terrain, it was the last place on earth anyone would look.

The truck bumped hard, dipped in and out of the rutted track and Kruger heard the reciprocal thump of the wooden crates in the back as they lurched then settled back down. The boys laughed again. Kruger smiled down at them. He could see their brown faces dimly, eyes bright, smiles of innocence. The trip was an outing and they were enjoying themselves, no hint of fear.

'Are we there, *senor*?' a thin voice asked.

Lopez was looking up at Kruger, who smiled. 'Soon. Almost there.'

The engine strained even more now, the last steep portion of the drive before they reached the small clearing at the top. Schmidt changed gear. The vehicle bumped again. The boys laughed once more as the wooden boxes in the back bumped and slid and settled down again.

The boxes had been Kruger's idea. They made the ride in the pick-up seem all the more plausible. A chore for the boys to perform once they reached their destination. He had told them he needed their help in disposing of the wooden crates. The boys looked like the young, sweet boys you saw in church choirs, their frail bodies more suited to housekeeping and cleaning and waiting at table than manual labour. But they had jumped at the opportunity to travel in the truck.

They had been brought to the house three years before, after the old housekeeper had died. Kruger understood the reasons: the boys were illiterate, barely understood their own Indian language. But they asked no questions and were happy in their own company.

Now the engine's whine receded and Kruger looked up sharply. The vehicle began to level off its climb. Schmidt changed gear as Kruger stared ahead. The foliage had become thinner in the higher atmosphere and now the headlights suddenly illuminated an open space beyond. They had reached the edge of the chasm. The stars in the blue-black sky sparkled, unobscured now, the night sky stretching out vastly before them.

Schmidt swung the steering-wheel round and the pick-up truck turned in an arc and came slowly to a halt. The engine sputtered and died. There was nothing but silence for several seconds, then came the sound of the hot engine clanking as it cooled, and the night shrieks and clicks of the humid jungle. The boys shifted restlessly in their seats.

'Here, *senor*?'

'*Si*, here,' replied Kruger.

'We carry boxes now?'

'*Si*.'

Schmidt and Kruger opened their doors and stepped out; it was a little cooler up here in the mountains. The chasm lay ten metres away. A deep rock cavity that seemed bottomless. No one went down there, only scurrying, foraging animals.

Kruger took the heavy-duty torch from behind the passenger seat and switched it on, aimed the beam at the ground. He glanced at his watch. Midnight.

The light was good, even without the torch, the headlights of the pick-up on dim, the sky above their heads awash with moonlight. He was tired, very tired. He could gladly have slept there and then, but this had to be done first, this last thing.

He looked at Schmidt and both men turned to see the two boys moving away, towards the back of the pick-up, ready to unlock the pull-down at the rear.

Kruger nodded. Schmidt reached inside his overalls, took out the long, silenced pistol and placed it behind his back. Kruger saw the hilt of the big Bowie knife protruding from the man's overalls at the knee pocket.

He turned to look at the boys as they were about to unlock the pull-down, talking quietly among themselves in their Indian dialect. The faint babble of excited conversation could almost have been a final prayer.

At that moment Schmidt stepped up behind them. Kruger saw the silenced pistol appear, saw the weapon being raised and aimed smartly at the back of the taller boy's head.

Phutt!

A split second, then the second boy's head, just as he turned, his mouth open in horror.

Phutt!

The two bodies pitched forward violently as the sounds of the pistol ruptured the silence. There had been the faintest cry from the second boy as the bullet had smacked into the nape of his skull, then no sound, only the ceaseless noises of the jungle.

Kruger pointed the torch to where the bodies had fallen. Blood flowed from the tiny wounds at the base of the boys' skulls. One of the bodies twitched in the light, a sharp spasm and then the brief sound of air expelled. Schmidt saw the movement, aimed instantly and fired again. The tiny body bucked, fell still. Kruger nodded to Schmidt and the big man fired again, this time into the second body. Kruger played the torchlight over the bodies once more. No sound, no movement this time.

He turned to Schmidt. 'Strip them.'

Schmidt placed the pistol on the bonnet of the pick-up. Kruger turned away, took out a packet of cigarettes and lit one. He heard Schmidt at work, grunting as he knelt over the bodies, removing the clothes.

By the time it was done, Kruger had finished his cigarette. He stubbed it out in the pick-up's ashtray. He was careful to leave nothing behind. So careful that he and Schmidt wore soft, flat plimsoles. So careful that he had told Franz to remove and burn the tyres of the pick-up once he had returned with the vehicle to Asunción.

Now the bloodied clothes were in a heap a metre from where Schmidt stood. Kruger crossed to where the thin bodies lay and examined them.

He nodded to the big man. 'You know what to do. Take your time. Do it properly.'

Kruger watched as Schmidt set to work. He had to watch, had to make sure the job was done correctly. He had seen men killed, had killed men himself. But he had never seen a body stripped of its flesh before. The faces and the fingertips. Not that the boys' fingerprints had ever been taken, not that it was likely the bodies would ever be found, but Kruger was not prepared to take that chance, had to be certain no one could trace them back to the house.

He watched as Schmidt took the big jagged-edged Bowie knife from the knee pocket of his overalls and set to work. He picked the body closest to him, turned it over. Emilio. The face looked up at the sky, eyes wide open. Kruger watched, fascinated and revolted at once.

Fifteen minutes later Schmidt had finished his work.

Kruger played the torch over the bodies. Mutilated beyond recognition. Bloodied hollow gore where the innocent brown faces had been, the whites of the skulls eerily visible, the hollow eye-sockets gaping black.

Kruger helped Schmidt carry the corpses one at a time to the edge of the chasm and fling them into the void, heard the sounds of each body seconds later as it flailed against rock on its downward journey into the black pit of the crevice. Then Kruger shone the torch down into the chasm. Nothing visible, only a tangle of green and rock, the bodies swallowed up.

There was blood spattered on Kruger's hands and overalls. He wiped his hands on the grass and saw Schmidt do the same. The blood would wash away with the first fall of rain. Schmidt packed the clothes into a black disposable bag, wiped the bloodied knife on his overalls, before removing them. The overalls went into the black disposable bag with Kruger's.

Schmidt stowed the bag in the back of the pick-up and climbed into the driver's seat. As Kruger went to climb in beside him, he paused to shine the torch about the clearing. Nothing had been left behind. The jungle animals and vermin that inhabited the chasm would finish their work. Pick the bodies clean of flesh.

He glanced at his watch: 1 a.m. Eight more hours. Eight more hours and he would be gone from this hellish country. He might still manage a couple of hours' sleep before the helicopter arrived. He ached all over now, limbs tired.

As he climbed wearily into the cab beside Schmidt, the engine throbbed to life. Then the pick-up turned in an arc and drove back down the narrow track.

Chapter Fifteen

Asunción.
December 6th,
1.02 a.m.

Sanchez was seated behind his desk.

There were dark rings beneath his eyes, and his face looked swollen from lack of sleep. A coffee pot stood on a tray beside him, three cups poured, a half-smoked cigarette lying in the glass ashtray on the desk. Volkmann and Erica sat opposite him.

Despite his tiredness, the detective was alert and interested, Volkmann wondering if it was because he had known Hernandez personally, or because Ferguson had pulled the right strings. It didn't matter; the man was with them, helping.

The small drab office was cooler now, the fan still whirring away on top of the rusting filing cabinet. Sanchez opened a fresh file and stared down at its contents, several sheets of hand-written paper in Spanish.

'This man, Winter. He visited Paraguay eight times in the last three years. Each time at intervals of approximately four months, each time for a stay of only two or three days. The reasons on his immigration card said "company business".'

Sanchez glanced up, then back at the file. He had already explained to Volkmann that the details, Winter's date and place of birth registered on the immigration card, matched with the information that Volkmann's people had sent in their report to the *seguridad*.

'On each immigration card a hotel address was given for the period of his stay. On each occasion he flew into Paraguay he landed in Asunción. Four times from Miami, America, three

157

times from Rio de Janeiro. All connecting flights these, from Europe. The other time was direct from Frankfurt. The last time Winter visited Paraguay was three months ago. Then he stayed at the Excelsior Hotel. Before that the Hotel Guarani. Before that the Excelsior. Before that two small hotels. But mostly the Excelsior or the Guarani. I have a list, you may see it if you wish.'

Sanchez handed Volkmann a page and he examined the list.

When Volkmann looked up, he said, 'You've checked with all of the hotels?'

Sanchez shook his head. 'So far, only the Excelsior and the Guarani. The list I received from our immigration people only late in the evening. My men have still to check the others. It may take some time.'

'The immigration cards Winter filled in before landing. Was there a company name given on any of them?'

'No. None.'

'So who paid Winter's hotel bills?'

'In the two hotels we've checked so far, Winter paid himself. In cash. Always in cash. And in each case he used a suite, not a room, although he was the only guest registered.'

'What about telephone calls Winter might have made from his suite? Do the hotels you've checked keep a record?'

'*Si.* They keep a record of all local and long-distance calls made by their guests, that is the law. But the hotels my men checked so far, the Excelsior and the Guarani, they have no record of any calls made by Winter. The only things on the bills were meals and drinks.'

Sanchez picked up his coffee, sipped the black liquid, replaced the cup. Seeing the still-lit cigarette he puffed on it once more before crushing it in the ashtray.

'No company name,' said Volkmann. 'No telephone calls. What about the car-hire firms? Have you checked with them?'

'I have a list of all the car-hire firms in the city. They will be checked as soon as my men have time.' Sanchez consulted the file again. 'The photograph your people sent of Winter. I had my men ask at the hotel if any of the staff remembered him. But of course no one did.' Sanchez shrugged again. 'Big hotels, lots of new faces every day. My men are still checking the last few hotels on the list, small places, but probably the same answers, I would guess.'

Sanchez looked across at Volkmann. 'On night shift, I have fewer men. There are other things to be attended to. Things happening now. Murders, crimes, you understand. When my men get some time free, they will check at the other hotels.' Sanchez turned to Erica Kranz. 'But at least we know now Rudi was not mistaken about this man Winter, about seeing him in Paraguay.'

Volkmann said, 'But there's no record of Winter being in Paraguay the time Rudi Hernandez claimed he saw him?'

Sanchez shook his head. 'No. But a man can cross a border in a remote place or use a false passport. Or perhaps a record was not kept. This sometimes happens. I have also sent a request to all border posts, just in case the immigration card was not returned to Asunción.' He shrugged. 'Officials in such remote places can be forgetful of their duties.'

'You said in both hotels you checked, Winter always hired a suite.'

'*Si*. Always.' Sanchez consulted the file again. 'On eight occasions.'

'That suggests he meant to entertain, or impress. Or both.'

'Perhaps. But we need more information.' Sanchez shrugged. 'And that may take a little time.'

Erica Kranz leaned forward in her chair. 'What about this other man? The man who sometimes worked with Rodriguez . . .?'

'*Si*, Miguel Santander.'

'Have you questioned him?'

'*Si*. Before you arrived. He has heard about Rodriguez' death. I told him we are now treating the case as murder. Santander thinks we consider him a suspect. I allowed him to think this. He says Rodriguez' death had nothing to do with him. He claims he has been near the southern border for the last two weeks. Up to no good, of course. But he cannot come up with a good alibi.' Sanchez smiled briefly. 'That suits us. That way he is scared. And he has talked a little.' He stood up wearily. 'Maybe you ought to hear for yourself. He is downstairs in one of the interview rooms. Come, I will take you.'

The interview room had the same grey, peeling walls as Sanchez' office. Apart from three chairs and an ancient wooden table the room was bare of furniture.

When Sanchez led them in, Volkmann saw a thin-faced man who looked about thirty seated at the table between two young standing *policia*. The man was deeply tanned, unshaven, his stubble making his dark face appear even darker, his features more Indian than Spanish. His grubby hands fidgeted nervously.

He wore a stained Adidas T-shirt, torn at the neck, and blue faded jeans and scuffed leather cowboy boots. His dark eyes blinked at them nervously. Sanchez gestured to the two *policia* to leave them.

When the men withdrew, Sanchez offered the two chairs to Volkmann and Erica Kranz. The girl accepted; Volkmann remained standing.

'This is Miguel Santander,' Sanchez said. 'He speaks a little English. Or if you prefer, I can translate.'

The man named Santander smiled weakly. 'Please, I speak English. I like to practise.' His smile broadened, showing a row of stained, uneven teeth as he looked at Volkmann and the girl.

Sanchez did the introductions, explaining nothing, only that his two friends were interested in Rodriguez' death. He offered round cigarettes to everyone, including Santander, took one himself, lit them.

He said to Santander, 'I want you to tell my friends here what you told me. Slowly. So they can understand you. *Comprende?*'

'*Si.*' Santander looked at the man, then the girl. He glanced back at Sanchez. 'From where do I begin?'

'From when Rodriguez asked you to help him.'

Santander nodded and drew on his cigarette nervously. There were beads of perspiration on the man's brown forehead as he glanced continuously from Volkmann to Erica, and his hands were restless.

'One month ago Rodriguez come to me.' He began to speak, his voice strained, staccato. 'He say he need help. He need to hire plane from friend of mine for some work he is doing. His own plane, it is old, and he need part for an engine generator. So until he get part he need to hire other plane.'

Santander glanced at Sanchez, then back at Erica and Volkmann, as if waiting to be told he was understood. When no response came, he carried on. 'This work, the work of Rodriguez, sometimes it can be dangerous. For my friend who owns the plane, I need to know it's going to be OK, that there are no problems. No risk. Or perhaps only small risk. Because if Rodriguez have trouble, my friend, his plane, maybe it is taken by the *policia*. So I say to Rodriguez to tell me about this work he is doing, so I know if it is OK to hire him my friend's plane.'

Santander looked at the faces around him and shrugged. 'Rodriguez, he don't want to tell me anything at first. But he need plane, so he must tell me. Some people, they use him to fly cargo across the border. To Montevideo. Already he has done many trips. These people, always they want Rodriguez to work alone. No one else. And always he must fly at night.'

Santander drew on his cigarette and glanced uncertainly at Sanchez; Sanchez nodded for him to go on.

Santander wiped his mouth with the back of his hand, then looked up at them again. 'Each trip is always the same. No change. Rodriguez, he fly plane to quiet place up north in the Chaco. There is no runway in this place. Just field. A field in the jungle with lights. He land there and men are waiting. They put boxes on plane. Boxes made of wood. He fly these boxes to Uruguay, to near Montevideo. He fly low, at night, so the radar don't see him. In a field near Montevideo it is the same. No runway, just field with lights. When he land, men are waiting to take boxes off plane. Then Rodriguez, he do the same again, once maybe in two months. This happens over maybe one year.' Santander shook his head. 'And no problems. Never any problems.'

Santander paused, scratched his stubble nervously. 'I trust Rodriguez. To me, he never tell lies. He say to me there is nothing to worry about. The plane of your friend will be safe. He said he only had to do one last trip. And this last trip, it is a special cargo. Just one small box. Then he is finished working for these people.' Santander paused again, looked up at Volkmann. 'Rodriguez, I know he is good pilot. The best. So I say, OK, you got the plane. But before I get him the plane he phone me and tell me he don't need it. He get the part for his engine generator.'

Santander sat back, looked at Sanchez. 'That is all I know. Rodriguez, he was a friend. Me, I would have no reason to kill him. I never kill person in my life.' He glanced at Erica Kranz, then Volkmann, a plaintive look on his face. 'This, you must believe.'

Sanchez said to Volkmann, 'Do you have any questions for Senor Santander?'

Volkmann nodded and looked down as the man's dark Indian eyes flicked nervously up at him.

'When was the last time you saw Rodriguez?'

'One month ago. When he ask me about the hire of plane of my friend.'

'Not afterwards?'

'No, I swear. He phone me in a bar two days after I meet him to tell me he don't need to hire plane. I don't see or speak to him again.'

'The name Rudi Hernandez. Did you ever hear Rodriguez mention that name?'

Santander thought a moment, shook his head. 'No, *senor*.'

'Hernandez. Rudi Hernandez. You're certain?'

'Certain. I never hear him say that name.'

'Did Rodriguez mention the names of the people who hired him, the people he flew his plane to Montevideo for?'

Santander shook his head. 'No names. Rodriguez never

tell names. In such business sometimes people you work for, they don't give you names. It is better that way, you understand?'

'The places Rodriguez picked up and dropped off the cargoes of boxes. You know where they are?'

'Rodriguez did not say exactly. Only that they were empty places, quiet places. Places with no towns, no villages. The place in the Chaco where he picked up the boxes he did not say. When I ask Rodriguez, all he would say is that it is one of the old German *colonias*. There are many up north, *senor*.'

'The men who loaded and unloaded the boxes. Did Rodriguez say what they looked like? Did he ever describe any of them?'

Santander thought a moment. 'No. He say only that these men, they are good at their work. They work quick. Rodriguez only have to wait for ten, maybe fifteen minutes and boxes are loaded. The same in Montevideo.' Santander thought a moment. 'But I think Rodriguez say that in the *colonia*, there was an old guy in charge.'

'A German?'

Santander shrugged. 'I guess.'

'Did Rodriguez describe him?'

'No, *senor*. He only say that he was old.'

'How many men did the work of loading and unloading the plane?'

'I don't know, *senor*. Rodriguez did not say.'

'Did Rodriguez know what cargo was in the boxes he carried?'

Santander scratched his stubble again. 'He did not tell me. I don't think he know. But these boxes, they are heavy, I think. Except the last one.'

'Why do you think they are heavy?'

'Rodriguez, he say he need a lot of runway. A long field. To lift off. And also a lot of fuel in the tanks.'

'He said nothing else?'

'No, *senor*. I am certain. Nothing. I tell you every-thing.' Santander looked up at Sanchez. 'I tell the truth. Believe me.'

Volkmann sighed, feeling the tiredness taking hold of him. There was no air-conditioning in the room, the humidity high. He paused before going on.

'How many boxes did Rodriguez carry each flight, before the last one?'

'I don't know, *senor*.'

'Big boxes, small boxes?'

Santander shook his head, shrugged his shoulders. 'Sorry, *senor* . . .'

'These people Rodriguez worked for, how did they pay him?'

Santander shook his head again. 'Rodriguez, he tell me nothing about that. But I think cash. After each trip. In such business, that is how it is done.'

'How did Rodriguez meet them?'

'Rodriguez did not tell me.'

'Is there anyone, anyone close to Rodriguez, someone maybe he might tell things to, about his work. A woman, a friend maybe?'

'No, *senor*. Rodriguez, he always keep things to himself. Even when he was drunk he did not talk about his work. To nobody. I am certain. That way, there is no one to tell the *policia*.'

Santander looked from the detective to the girl. She had great legs, really great legs. A good one to have in bed beside you. He had wondered what way they were involved in this, the *gringos*, the girl and the man, but knew it was not his right to ask. He looked back up at the *gringo*.

The man said, 'There is nothing else you remember? I want you to think hard. Anything. No matter how small.'

'Nothing. I swear it.' Santander made a sign of the cross.

Sanchez said, 'If I discover you are lying to me, *amigo* . . .'

'As God is my judge. Rodriguez was a friend . . .'

Sanchez grimaced and stubbed out his cigarette, turned away, towards Volkmann. 'You have any more questions, *senor*?'

Volkmann shook his head.

* * *

The three of them were seated in Sanchez' office again. The detective had more coffee, fresh and hot, brought to them. It was after two, the room silent now, except for the gentle whirr of the fan overhead.

Volkmann glanced at Erica Kranz. She looked tired, tired but preoccupied, something on her mind as she sipped her coffee thoughtfully. He turned to Sanchez.

'You think Santander is telling the truth?'

'*Si*, I believe him. And he is not the type of man who kills. Just a petty smuggler. I think he told us everything he knew.' Sanchez picked up the coffee cup. 'What he said about the old man in the German colony, it helps a little. But there are many German colonies in Paraguay. People who came here before and after the last war. Immigrants.'

Sanchez sipped the hot coffee, placed the cup on the desk. 'What Santander said, it was not much, but it makes the picture just a little clearer. These people Rodriguez worked for, they wanted to keep what they are doing secret. When the work is finished, they decide they want Rodriguez killed. No witness. No one to talk. But Rodriguez, he senses these people plan to kill him. So he thinks up a plan himself. He gives Rudi Hernandez a call and tells him his story. The story is Rodriguez' insurance. I am certain he would have meant to tell the people he had worked for that the police would come looking for him if anything happened to him.' Sanchez shrugged. 'But maybe he never got the chance. Or maybe he told them and they decided to kill him, and Rudi also.'

Sanchez thought a moment, looked away towards the window, then back again. 'There is another possibility. Somehow Rudi learned of a meeting of these people. So he tries to record a conversation, find out a little more, get some evidence. Only his plans go wrong and he and the young girl are killed. What I don't understand is how the young girl was involved.' Sanchez shrugged. 'Maybe she was just in the wrong place at the wrong time. Or helped Rudi in some way and paid for it with her life.'

Volkmann thought a moment, then said, 'The electronic

equipment Hernandez borrowed. What distance could it work over?'

Sanchez shrugged. 'Not far, maybe a kilometre.'

'Hernandez could have been anywhere the night he was killed.'

'I agree. The only clue I have as to where he was the morning of his death is the word of the night watchman. The man who works at the station who claims he saw him.' Sanchez shrugged. 'Who knows what Rudi was doing there, *if* he was there. Maybe he used the recording equipment there, but I don't know, I don't think so. The man at the station says the man he saw carried nothing and was in the station for perhaps only five minutes, maybe a little longer. But the equipment, Torres' equipment, you would have needed something to carry it in. A bag, a small suitcase perhaps.'

Volkmann looked at the fat detective. 'Let's say Hernandez was at the station. Why does a man go to a railway station in the early hours of the morning? And why enter through a rear entrance?' He was thinking aloud, but he asked the question, saw Sanchez frown.

'Perhaps it was the quickest way?' Sanchez replied. 'Rudi, he meant to buy a ticket on a train to some place, leave Asunción. But the ticket office was closed at the time, until later in the morning.'

'Wouldn't he have known that?'

Sanchez nodded. 'I understand. It leaves a question. If Rudi *did* go to the station and stayed for only a short time, it suggests perhaps that he had a purpose. But what purpose? I do not know the answer. Why do people go to a train station in the early hours of the morning? To catch a train, or to meet one, if there is one. But neither is possible in this case.'

Sanchez glanced at the girl. She looked up then, met his eyes a moment before looking away again. She was listening to the conversation but not listening, preoccupied with something, her hands restless, a frown on her face, Sanchez thinking: she is still grieving, that one.

He looked at Volkmann. The *gringo* was thinking, too, weighing things up in his mind, going over words said.

Volkmann said finally, 'What about the other hotels on the list?'

'My men have not called in yet. I will have the communications desk call them up.'

Sanchez stood up, shuffled the pages of the file on his desk before closing the folder. He turned towards the filing cabinet and took the heavy set of keys from his pocket, unlocked the cabinet and pulled out one of the drawers, placed the file inside and carefully locked the metal cabinet again.

When he turned back he saw the girl look up at him, a strange expression on her face, her lips pursed, her brow furrowed in concentration. For the first time Sanchez looked directly at her hands, not her face or her exquisite legs.

In her right hand she fingered a bunch of keys, the keys to Rudi Hernandez' apartment and car. He remembered the girl had been toying with them while he spoke with Volkmann. Sanchez looked down now at her face; her eyes were fixed on his own hand, the hand he held the keys in. He looked down at the keys he was holding, then back at the girl.

Now she spoke softly, in Spanish. 'You asked why Rudi might have been at the railway station. At the station . . . are there boxes . . . for luggage, for people to leave things?'

Sanchez raised an eyebrow. He looked down again at the bunch of keys in the girl's hand; she was holding one of them between thumb and forefinger. He answered her in Spanish.

'I believe so.'

The girl hesitated. 'Rudi, maybe he had one of those boxes?'

Sanchez looked at her blankly.

Volkmann looked at them both, wondering what they were saying.

The railway station faced onto the Plaza Uruguaya.

Inside the old porticoed hall a half-dozen drunks slept it off in quiet corners. Indians and *mestizos* with young families, their babies wrapped in colourful blankets, sat or slept under the concession shops. Poor people from the north and south waiting for the early trains; soft, pitiful brown eyes and looks of bewildered innocence on their lost faces, too penniless to afford even one of the cheap hotels nearby.

Some of them watched sleepily as the three people walked briskly through the station. The smell of diesel oil hung in the humid air. Sanchez looked at the curious, waiting people and pitied them.

The station had not changed much. He remembered travelling on the ancient, wood-burning steam-engines to his grandparents' house in Villarrica. The left-luggage boxes, he vaguely remembered, were off to the right, near one of the concession stands.

They turned a corner and saw the serried rows of several dozen metal boxes set against a concrete wall, black numbers stencilled on their doors. Sanchez stopped, facing the middle row.

'The keys, *senorita*.'

Erica Kranz handed the detective the keys.

Sanchez examined them again. There were two keys that had nothing to do with Hernandez' apartment or car or office desk or locker, Sanchez knew. He had wondered about those keys. The way the girl had wondered. He had asked her at the police station what had made her think Rudi might have kept a luggage box at the station. The girl had shrugged. A feeling. An intuition.

The Indians in his country had a word for it: *mon-ia-taah-ka*. A voice from the world beyond. Perhaps the girl was right. Perhaps Rudi had kept a box here. The safe place he had told the girl about.

Now Sanchez fingered the key that looked closest to the size of the keyhole in the nearest locker facing him. Number twenty-seven was stencilled in big letters on its metal door. He inserted the key. It went all the way in. He tried to turn it. The key moved a little, but no more, Sanchez feeling the resistance of the lock levers.

He turned to the girl and Volkmann as he removed the key, saw the looks on their faces. Hope, urgency.

He pointed to the left, where the row of boxes began, and smiled very faintly. 'Perhaps we should start at the beginning. It is always a good place to start. *Si?*'

Chapter Sixteen

Asunción.
December 6th,
3.45 a.m.

The air in Sanchez' office was grey with cigarette smoke.

Volkmann looked across at the fat detective as he sipped the hot, freshly made coffee the duty sergeant had brought. Sanchez' face looked swollen from lack of sleep. The man's dark hooded eyelids appeared darker still, his skin grey in the thick, smoke-stained air.

Erica, in contrast, appeared very much awake. Awake and silent.

Volkmann, his mind restless, his body racked by tiredness, said nothing, the coffee and the cigarettes staving off the ache for sleep. The conversation on the tape, the conversation in German, had confused and perturbed him.

They had found the tape and the six photographs in the locker marked number thirty-nine. Each photograph was of the same two men. One old, one young, taken obviously with a telephoto lens at brief intervals, the men walking in the grounds of a white house, the property visible in the distance.

One of the men was Dieter Winter, the man's blond hair and thin, sharp features unmistakable when compared to the head-and-shoulders shot Sanchez had received. The second man in the photographs, Sanchez thought he had faintly recognised. On the journey in the car from the railway station to his office he had racked his memory until it finally came to him, remembering the white house in the photograph first, then connecting the house with a photograph of the old man named Tsarkin, the old man who had committed suicide two

171

days before Rudi was killed. He had remembered seeing the photograph in one of the bedrooms in Tsarkin's house, picking it up, looking at the face of the man whose face no longer existed in the study downstairs. The house in which he had last seen Hernandez alive, Sanchez explained to Volkmann and the girl. At least now there were connections, thin wisps of a web, something beginning to come together.

Except the tape.

They had listened to the tape eight times. Erica had translated the conversation for Sanchez, then transcribed it in Spanish, the fat detective reading the girl's writing slowly, questioning the inflection of words in the handwritten script, like Volkmann curious, perplexed, reading the cryptic words over and over, asking Erica to translate again from the German, making sure the transcript was right, no nuance ignored, no word overlooked.

In the smoke-filled office now, Sanchez looked across at Volkmann and said, 'You want to hear the tape again?'

Volkmann nodded, said yes, he wanted to hear the tape again. Sanchez pressed the play button on the cassette player lying on his desk, before lighting another cigarette and sitting back.

Volkmann listened, hearing the deep, guttural voices on the tape fill the silence of the room once more, almost knowing the words from memory now, but wanting to hear them again.

'The shipment . . .?'

'The cargo will be picked up from Genoa as arranged.'

'And the Italian?'

'He will be eliminated, but I want to be certain we don't arouse suspicion concerning the cargo. It would be prudent to wait until Brandenburg becomes operational. Then he will be dealt with along with the others.'

Pause.

'Those who have pledged their loyalty . . . we must be certain of them.'

'I have had their assurances confirmed. And their pedigree is without question.'

'And the Turk?'

172

'*I foresee no problems.*'

'*The girl . . . you're absolutely certain we can rely on her?*'

'*She will not fail us, I assure you.*' Pause. '*There are no changes to the names on the list . . .?*'

'*They will all be killed.*'

'*Your travel arrangements . . . Everything has been organised?*'

'*We leave Paraguay on the sixth.*'

'*The schedule . . . perhaps I should go through it once more?*'

There was a long pause on the tape until Volkmann heard a voice speak again.

'*I'm sorry, it's very warm in here. Perhaps I might have a glass of water . . .?*'

They heard the clink of glass a few moments later, the sound of water poured, the long silence, then the *click* on the tape, followed by a faint buzzing noise.

Sanchez leaned across and pressed the forward button. There had been another long period of silence on the tape, only a muted buzzing noise, until the sound of voices came again, but this time very faintly, the words fuzzed, crackling, barely audible.

'*Prost.*'

'*Prost.*'

'*Prost.*'

Another pause, then very faintly, '*We must take our leave of you. It's a long drive back north. The driver will take you to the safe house.*'

Silence.

Sanchez waited a while to make sure the conversation had finished, hearing what he thought on the tape was the faint sound of a door being closed, then he leaned across and switched off the machine.

Volkmann looked down at the scribbled notes he had already written on the fresh page of his notebook, his own shorthand of the taped conversation. Sanchez had asked what the word Brandenburg meant. Erica had explained that it was the name of a city west of Berlin, and was also the name of a German province that had once contained part of the state of Berlin. The famous Brandenburg Gate that stood near the Reichstag, the old German parliament building, had once been the original entrance to the territory.

Hearing the answer, Sanchez had nodded, but scratched his head, a confused look on his face; the explanation had not helped. He was more perplexed than ever.

They had discussed the tape for the last hour, played it over and over, but there was nothing that would open a door for them, nothing concrete, nothing that would point a way immediately.

Volkmann tried to concentrate on the tape. Three different speakers, Volkmann had decided, listening to the tones, the words, the timbre in the men's voices.

'*Your travel arrangements . . . Everything has been organised?*'

'*We leave Paraguay on the sixth.*'

The sixth. Today.

Volkmann had asked Sanchez to rewind the tape on those lines. He had listened again to the faint voice that had spoken the reply, the same voice, Volkmann felt certain, that had later said, '*We must take our leave of you. It's a long drive back north . . .*' North, where was north? They had discussed that line also, he and Sanchez. North in Paraguay meant a vast area of jungle and swamp and scrubland called the Chaco. Sanchez had pointed to it on the nicotine-stained map on the wall.

North could even mean over the border . . . Brazil . . . Bolivia. Or simply a suburb far north of the city. Anywhere.

Volkmann looked across at Sanchez and said, 'This old man, Tsarkin, the suicide case. Tell me again what you know about him.'

Sanchez had the file open on his desk, the file on the old man's case, the coroner's report, the letter from the oncologist at the San Ignatio Private Hospital. He had explained it all briefly to Volkmann and the girl, now he glanced at the file again.

'All I know at this time is what I have in the report from last week, the report I filed after investigating the suicide.

The man was aged eighty-two, a retired businessman, a naturalised citizen of this country for many years, and a former director of many companies. On November twenty-third, in San Ignatio Hospital, he was given less than forty-eight hours to live by the doctors who attended him. He had stomach cancer. The bleeding had become very bad. The doctors who treated him at the hospital were not surprised when they learned the old man had shot himself. He was in pain, and very weak, despite drugs to help him.'

'You're certain it was suicide?'

Sanchez nodded. He yawned, put a pudgy hand to his mouth, blinked several times. 'There was no question. He was alone in the room at the time. And considering the evidence of his poor health there was no need to probe much into his affairs. But now it is a different matter. I have asked one of my men to find out more about this Senor Nicolas Tsarkin. I will have the relevant files in the office of immigration checked as soon as the office opens this morning. My man is also checking Tsarkin's house, to see if there are any papers he might have kept. Anything that might help us.'

Volkmann looked at the tired detective. 'You said there was a safe open in the study where you found the body. And embers in the fire grate.'

'*Si*. But this sometimes happens when people kill themselves. Private letters, personal things, they destroy them beforehand.' Sanchez shrugged. 'Especially if they have something to hide. In Tsarkin's case, we know now that is most likely true.'

Sanchez thought a moment before going on. 'When Rudi arrived at Tsarkin's house he seemed a little anxious. He seemed curious about the old man, but tried not to show it, I think. Something else. I left the study for several minutes where the old man's body lay while we waited for it to be taken to the morgue. When I returned Rudi was putting down the telephone. He said it was a call from his office. But I'm not so sure. My detective is also checking this. And the calls made from Tsarkin's house recently.'

It was dark still beyond the office window. Sanchez could hardly keep his eyes open, the action of smoking helping to keep him awake. He should have finished work at five the previous day. But like so much police work he could never plan a day with certainty. He had telephoned his wife, told her he would be late, how late he didn't know, yet somehow knowing that this one would drag on.

Sanchez blinked, rubbed his thumb and forefinger into his eyes, fighting the aching tiredness trying to take hold. He tried to concentrate, tried to think through the transcript of the taped conversation again in his mind, searching for clues, for something to point a way.

'How long before you get the information on Tsarkin's background?' Volkmann asked.

Sanchez looked up and shrugged. 'The office of immigration records does not open until 7 a.m. Then we can check Tsarkin's past. When he came to Paraguay and from where. But it may be a slow and difficult task, perhaps taking several days. Also, I will have Tsarkin's servants questioned again as soon as I can get another man. Perhaps they might know some things about their dead employer. Business acquaintances. Friends. People he socialised with.'

Sanchez looked at his watch. Almost four o'clock. He, too, remembered the words on the tape, the words the girl had transcribed.

'We leave Paraguay on the sixth.'

He pushed himself achingly up from the chair and stretched his arms. The smoky air in the office stung his eyes, yet he stubbed out his cigarette and lit another.

He crossed to the window and opened it some more. There was no rush of coolness; the darkness outside still and humid, the palm tree fronds limp below the window. Further down the street he could see the corner of the pink-domed Pantheon of the Plaza de Heros, the sombre monument to men killed in battles long ago, all lit up and with its perpetual guard of honour. The two soldiers standing stiffly to attention at the memorial must be tired. Almost as tired as he himself.

He sighed, tried to concentrate his mind again as he

smoked his cigarette silently and stared out onto the street. A distance away he saw a taxi draw up outside a hotel and four passengers climb out. Two middle-aged men and two young women. He watched them walk towards the hotel entrance, the men well dressed but a little unsteady on their feet, the girls smiling, wearing bright, skimpy dresses and high-heels.

Visiting businessmen, Sanchez guessed, returning after a late night out at a city nightclub. The women were probably hookers. Sanchez scratched his stubble as he watched the taxi pull away from the kerb. When he finally turned round after several minutes silence, he saw Volkmann and the girl stare at him.

Volkmann said, 'A problem?'

Sanchez slowly shook his head. 'No. A question. In the hotels Winter stayed at, he always hired a suite. You asked a question. Why does one person need to hire a suite?' Sanchez paused. 'To impress someone? A business contact, or a woman, perhaps?' Sanchez paused again. 'A suite, it is also big enough to hold a meeting, *si*?'

Sanchez raised his eyebrows questioningly. He looked at Volkmann and Erica Kranz.

'A hotel would also be a suitable place for someone to hire a room and try and listen to what was being said in another room nearby, would it not?' He looked down, plucked the list of hotels from the relevant file and shrugged heavily. 'Perhaps it is worth investigating. Just now it is all I can think of.'

Volkmann said tiredly, 'It's possible. But which hotel? Asunción's a big city.'

Sanchez briefly examined the list. 'The hotel Winter stayed in most often, your hotel, the Excelsior. Perhaps if we tried there first? Then the Hotel Guarani.'

The receptionist insisted on calling the night duty manager first. The man appeared minutes later, tall and immaculately dressed in a dark suit and crisp white shirt and grey silk tie, looking fresh and clean-shaven and alert despite the early hour.

177

Sanchez showed the man his identity card and repeated his request. The night duty manager offered no resistance, led them politely to his office around the corner from the lobby. The office was small, but uncluttered, several rows of metal filing cabinets neatly lining the walls.

The manager pulled up chairs for all of them and said to Sanchez, 'The date again?'

'November twenty-fifth.'

The manager crossed to one of the filing cabinets and rummaged through a drawer. He finally removed several thick wads of registration cards held together with elastic bands and brought them over to the desk and sat down.

'Is there a particular name you wish to check on?'

'Hernandez. Senor Rudi Hernandez. He may have been a guest here.'

'Information regarding guests is kept on computer. However, the original registration cards are kept in alphabetical order, so it should not be difficult to find.'

The manager riffled through the first block of cards he picked, flicking through them expertly. 'Hernandez . . . Hernandez . . . Yes.' He looked up at them. 'One Hernandez, but the first name is . . . ' He consulted the card again. 'Morites . . . Morites Hernandez.'

Sanchez held out his hand; the manager passed him the registration card. A commercial traveller, the card declared, from São Paulo.

Sanchez glanced at Erica's handbag and said in English, '*Senorita*, do you have any correspondence from Rudi with you?'

The girl hesitated for several moments. She glanced at Volkmann, then looked back at Sanchez and said, 'In my room . . . I have a letter in my suitcase.'

'Would you be so kind as to bring it to me, please?'

Erica Kranz nodded silently and left. When she returned five minutes later she handed the letter to Sanchez, unfolding the pages first, the manager looking on curiously as Sanchez compared the handwriting on the registration card to the handwritten letter he placed beside it on the desk.

The writing sloped different ways; the writing on the registration card cramped, secretive; the writing on the letter Rudi had sent to Erica large, stylish, the letters fat, generous.

Sanchez looked up. 'No. Not the Hernandez we are looking for.'

The manager appeared slightly relieved. Sanchez said, 'November twenty-fifth. How many people stayed at the hotel?'

The manager looked from Sanchez to Volkmann and Erica, this time switching to perfect English. 'It was a busy night, I remember. We were full. There was a convention and several functions . . .'

'How many?' repeated Sanchez.

'Perhaps three hundred guests.'

When Sanchez sighed, the manager shrugged. 'I'm sorry I haven't been able to help you.'

Sanchez looked determinedly at the manager. 'We will need to check all of these cards.'

The man stared at him in disbelief. '*All, senor?*'

'*Si*. All. And I will need a list, a computer list, of all the guests who stayed here on November twenty-fifth. Their names. Their passport numbers if they were foreigners. Who made their reservations. Who paid their bills.' Sanchez paused. 'Your computer. It has all this information?'

The manager nodded, dumbly.

'Then please see to it at once,' said Sanchez.

'*Senor*, you realise the hour? I have other duties to attend to. Perhaps when the day staff arrive . . .'

Sanchez interrupted sharply. 'I need this information now. It cannot wait. So please do as I ask. Otherwise I will be forced to contact your superior.' Sanchez' voice softened a little. 'I would be grateful for your co-operation, *senor*.'

Sanchez stared piercingly at the night manager through bloodshot eyes.

The man hesitated, then sighed. 'Very well. I will see what I can do.' He turned to go.

'One more thing,' Sanchez added.

'Yes . . .?'
'Could we have a pot of coffee? Strong coffee.'
The manager nodded abruptly and left.
Volkmann glanced at his watch. It was 5 a.m.

Chapter Seventeen

North-Eastern Chaco.
5.40 a.m.

The sounds of the jungle had woken him.

He rose from the bed, drew away the mosquito net and dressed slowly. As his eyes adjusted to the semi-darkness, he took in the room, bare now except for the bed and suitcases and the clothes hung on the back of the door where one of the Lima boys had left them, freshly washed and pressed for the journey. He thought of the boys now as he buttoned the soft cotton shirt. Their deaths had been necessary. Totally necessary to protect him.

When he had finished dressing, he went quietly downstairs to the kitchen. He found Kruger sitting at the pinewood table smoking a cigarette, a glass of water in his other hand. He looked as if he had slept badly, dark rings underneath his eyes.

'We burned the remaining provisions,' Kruger said, looking at him. 'If you wish to breakfast there's only some bottled water and dried nuts.'

The silver-haired man nodded. 'Just water, Hans.'

Kruger stubbed out his cigarette in an empty cigarette packet lying on the table, then crossed to the sink in the corner and unscrewed the cap off a plastic bottle of drinking water. He took one of the remaining glasses and rinsed it first with the tepid water before filling it almost to the brim and handing it across.

The silver-haired man took a sip, looked out beyond the open kitchen window, at the dark mass of jungle rising up to the distant rain-forest. Already the dark sky was streaked with an aching blue. It would soon be light. The unceasing sounds of the jungle throbbed outside. A bird flew past, a banana flit, its yellow plumage discernible even in the twilight. He looked back at Kruger and spoke quietly.

'The boys . . .?

'It's done,' Kruger responded. 'Schmidt made sure it was as quick and painless as possible. And that no one could identify them.' He paused, saw a look of pain cross the man's face.

'We decided to wait until first light to burn what's left in the house. Franz and his men should arrive in the next hour to pick up the vehicles. A few more items have to be loaded onto the truck. Half an hour's work, no more. Then we'll begin the final check and clean up.'

The tall, silver-haired man looked towards the corner of the old, small wooden outhouse. A place where he had spent solitary hours in childhood, serving his sentence alone.

He put down the unfinished glass of water on the pine table. 'I wish to take a walk before we leave, Hans. The men can stay here. I would prefer to be alone.'

The silver-haired man saw the look of alarm on Kruger's face, and he smiled gently as he placed a hand reassuringly on Kruger's shoulder.

'I will be perfectly safe, Hans. There is no danger, I promise you.'

'Of course. As you wish.'

The man crossed to the door and stepped outside.

Kruger watched him go, then glanced at his watch.

Six-ten.

Three more hours. Three more hours and they would finally all be quit of this hellish place.

He reached into his pocket for another cigarette.

Asunción.
5.55 a.m.

It took them almost an hour to find the hotel registration card.

It was Volkmann who found it, the three of them sitting

around the desk, a pile of registration cards and a page from Hernandez' letter in front of each of them. The signature on the card was in a different name, Roberto Ferres, but the style unmistakably the same: the sloped and dotted letters, the amplitude of the script matching Hernandez' writing exactly.

Once Volkmann had found the card, Sanchez had also requested a specific list of guests staying on the first and second floors. The information lay in front of him, as yet unexamined, several reams of folded computer printout sheets. Sanchez held the registration card in his hand now as he looked up at the harried manager. The coffee he had had brought was hardly touched.

'The room that Senor Ferres hired on the first floor. The bill was paid in advance?' The information was on the registration card, but Sanchez asked just the same. There was an amount included in the bill for a bottle of champagne and canapés. That had puzzled Sanchez.

'Yes, in cash,' the manager replied, glancing at the card in Sanchez' hand.

'The room key, was it returned?'

'There is no need for our guests to return keys. The locks are opened with plastic disposable key cards. For security the numbers are changed by computer each time a new guest checks in and a new plastic key card is issued. Each guest has his own individual code.'

Sanchez nodded.

'You wish to see the room where this gentleman stayed?' the manager asked. 'I believe it is unoccupied at present.'

'Perhaps later.' Sanchez knew it was pointless. By now the room would have been cleaned a dozen times. He looked at his watch. Six-fifteen.

Sanchez said, 'If there had been a disturbance in Senor Hernandez' . . . Senor Ferres' . . . room, it would have been reported?'

The manager looked slightly alarmed. 'What kind of disturbance?'

Sanchez shrugged. 'A fight. A disagreement. Excessive noise.'

The manager said, 'My staff are very diligent. If anything happened, they would have reported the matter and it would have been recorded.' He shrugged and smiled briefly. 'Sometimes it happens. Couples argue. Throw things. You think something happened in this gentleman's room?'

'Perhaps. Perhaps not.'

'I can check the day book for complaints on that floor if you wish?'

'I would appreciate it. Also, if this gentleman left anything behind in the room. Perhaps personal belongings. You can check?'

The manager nodded, then left them once more.

Sanchez rubbed his eyes and said to Volkmann and Erica, 'The champagne and food . . . I am puzzled. Why would Rudi want to order them?'

He picked up the ream of computer printout he had requested and unfolded the paper. The sequential list started with the first room number on Hernandez' floor. Slowly, carefully, he read through the printout, eyes scanning the information presented. Room number. Guest. Bill charges.

After a while he blinked several times, rubbed his bloodshot eyes, then looked up.

'At last, a light shines in the darkness.'

Volkmann and Erica Kranz stared at the fat detective.

'Someone booked a suite on the same floor as Rudi's room.' Sanchez smiled broadly for the first time. 'A Senor Nicolas Tsarkin.'

The manager returned moments later carrying a thick ledger, open in his hands. He informed Sanchez that nothing had been recorded as left in the room and no complaints had been made concerning the first floor on November 25th or in the early hours of the following morning. There had been two complaints only: one on the second floor concerning an overactive couple who had made considerable noise in their bedroom much to the annoyance of an elderly lady in the next room. The second had occurred earlier in the day on the third floor when a guest who had drunk too much had repeatedly propositioned one of the house maids. Sanchez asked if they could see the suite Tsarkin had hired.

'I'm sorry, it is occupied at present. But as soon as the guests check out this morning, I will arrange it.' The manager shrugged. 'I'm sorry I can be of no further help.'

Sanchez nodded. 'I am grateful for your assistance, *senor*.'

There was a knock on the door. Volkmann saw a man enter and speak quietly to Sanchez in Spanish. Sanchez asked to be excused and crossed to the man and they both stepped outside the office.

Volkmann looked at Erica. He realised neither of them had slept for more than a couple of hours in the past twenty-four. The girl's tiredness showed; she was restless, her eyes sleepy. A wisp of blonde hair fell across her face; she brushed it away, smiled briefly across at Volkmann.

Volkmann looked at her and said, 'If you want to go up to your room and rest, I'll call you if anything comes up.'

The girl shook her head. They both looked up as Sanchez came back into the room, talking to them directly, ignoring the manager's presence.

'That was Detective Cavales, the man I put onto Tsarkin's case. He managed to get a list of telephone calls made from Tsarkin's house in the last two weeks. There were two calls made to a radio-telephone link in the north-eastern Chaco . . .'

Sanchez paused, let the infomation sink in. They were both exhausted, Volkmann and the girl, but now they both looked intently at Sanchez.

'The radio-telephone link,' Sanchez went on. 'We've got a name, Karl Schmeltz. And an address. It's in an area up in the Indian country. Just north of the Salgado river near the border with Brazil. A desolate place with not many people. Jungle and scrubland. The kind of place where a man shoots himself for something to do.'

'How far?' Volkmann asked.

Sanchez shrugged. 'Four hundred kilometres, maybe more. It takes perhaps ten hours to reach by car. The roads are bad, very bad. Jungle roads.'

Volkmann checked his watch. Six-thirty. He needed sleep, to close his eyes, not travel along rutted jungle roads. And by then, by then perhaps it would be too late.

'By helicopter,' Sanchez said, 'it takes two hours. Maybe a little less.'

'You can arrange that?' Erica asked.

Sanchez nodded.

Asunción.
6.41 a.m.

Volkmann stared down through the helicopter's Plexiglass as the buildings of Asunción shrank below him.

It was cramped and warm in the cockpit, the sun ahead of them, the military pilot wearing sunglasses to shield his eyes. The muted noise of the blades as they chopped the warm air filled the cabin.

There were five of them in the Dauphin helicopter apart from the pilot. Erica and Volkmann, Sanchez and the detective, Cavales, and another detective named Moringo.

Sanchez' two detectives were each armed with standard-issue thirty-eight pistols and pump-action shotguns. Two military M-16 rifles lay beside Sanchez along with six spare clips of ammunition.

The second rifle was for Volkmann, Sanchez keeping the weapon by his side, but Volkmann knowing it was for him, if needed.

The Dauphin bumped a little as they climbed higher, not too high, because in the heat, Sanchez had explained, the blades couldn't grip the thin air. Volkmann saw the helicopter's altimeter rise to two thousand feet and settle.

They were over scrub forest and jungle already, *adobes* and huts of wood and straw and fields of sugar cane below, the landscape dotted with the ruins of old sugar mills. The Rio Paraguay flowed off to the right, a grey-green ribbon of water snaking through a patchwork of greens stretching as far as the distant horizon.

Volkmann could sense the tension in the cramped cabin. Tension and tiredness.

Finally, the radio crackled and a metallic Spanish voice came over the speaker. The pilot switched to earphones, the noise in the cockpit too loud. He spoke for a few moments, then turned to speak to Sanchez in Spanish. Sanchez nodded and said something briefly to the detective, Moringo, his voice almost a shout to drown out the noise, then turned to Volkmann and Erica.

'That was Asunción on the radio. I requested the local *policia* to meet us near the house. Their orders are to point us to the property and assist us if we need them.' He glanced at his watch. 'We will be in radio contact in just under an hour. Moringo here knows the region but not the exact place. He thinks it is very remote.'

Volkmann nodded. He sat back, his body aching now for sleep as he stared down, mesmerised by the vast emerald oasis of jungle below, the monotonous, rhythmic sound of the chopping blades overhead almost sending him to sleep.

He looked up from the hypnotic green towards Erica Kranz. Her face showed signs of strain and tiredness and she stared at him sleepily at the same moment, her face expressionless. Then she turned back to look down at the jungle below.

Volkmann looked at the pretty profile for several moments, then checked his watch.

It was 7 a.m.

North-Eastern Chaco.
8.25 a.m.

Kruger looked up at the sky as he stood on the veranda, scanning for the helicopter, for a glint of sun on Plexiglass, listening for the muted sound of the blades.

Nothing.

Franz Lieber had departed with his men an hour earlier, driving his own Mercedes back down the gravel path, each of the men he had brought with him driving one of the vehicles they had come to take to Asunción.

It was warm already, humid and hazy, clouds obscuring the sun. As he turned back towards the house he saw the man come out of the jungle fifty metres away, hands clasped behind his back as he stalked through the thin undergrowth that led to the narrow path down to the river.

Kruger walked to the end of the veranda, looked out towards the side of the house where the ashes of Schmidt's fire still smouldered faintly. Everything had been burned. Schmidt had done a good job. Kruger had checked the house and the outhouses himself. Nothing remained.

He ran a hand through his hair, was about to look up at the sky again when he heard the noise and turned round. The man had stepped onto the veranda, looked out towards the lush grounds.

As he came to stand beside Kruger a flock of tiny yellow birds flew past them.

'Franz came,' Kruger said, watching the streak of yellow disappear into the jungle. 'He sends his regards and says he looks forward to joining us later.'

The silver-haired man nodded silently, continued to stare out at some distant point, as if deep in thought. Moments later both men heard a faint sound. They looked up instinctively, but saw nothing. One of the men in the house must have heard it too, because he came out with a pair of powerful Zeiss binoculars, started to sweep the sky from left to right, right to left.

Kruger saw the man smile faintly as the sound in the distance increased; a faint throbbing now, growing perceptibly louder with each passing second. Kruger scanned the hazy sky again but saw nothing.

Then there was a brief glint of light off to the right, in the direction the man had pointed the binoculars, then seconds later another glint, as the sound became louder, more vibrant, an unmistakable chopping sound in the air.

Kruger glanced at his watch. Eight-forty. 'The helicopter,' he said calmly. 'It's early.'

The man nodded in reply and moved to the end of the veranda, as Schmidt and the other two men came out of the house to stare up at the sky. He took one last look over at the small outhouse, then at where Schmidt had burned the remaining papers, even the old things he had kept since childhood.

All gone now, black ashes, smouldering still. His eyes swept over the jade green of the jungle. One last, lingering look before he turned finally to Kruger as the sound of the helicopter grew louder.

'Tell Schmidt to check and douse the fire. Ensure everything has been thoroughly burned. Then get the men together with the suitcases.'

It was Volkmann who saw the vehicle first, rubbing his tired eyes to make sure, the blue and white of the police car a mere speck barely visible, waiting on the ribbon of desolate road in the distance. The roads here were primitive, brown-red strips of dirt cutting through the jungle, looking like tape stuck onto the lush green earth.

Volkmann tapped Sanchez on the shoulder and pointed downwards. Sanchez nodded as his eyes picked out the blue and white, pointed the direction for the pilot. The Dauphin banked sharply, turned towards where the speck of colour waited.

They had been in contact with the local *policia* on a special frequency for almost fifteen minutes, Sanchez translating the commentary for Volkmann, looking tired, so very tired, but coming awake now, staring out beyond the Plexiglass, talking rapidly into the microphone to the sergeant in the car, almost directly below them now, the helicopter moving fast.

Sanchez turned to Volkmann. 'The sergeant says the property is straight ahead along the road another kilometre. They will follow us there.'

There was a cry from the detective named Cavales as he pointed beyond the helicopter's Plexiglass. 'There. To the left.'

The pilot followed the line of his finger. The sky was hazy

with cloud, but even Volkmann could see the house now, less than a kilometre away. It stood alone in the midst of jungle, painted off-white, large, very large, one of the largest *haciendas* they had flown over in the last half-hour, a narrow private road leading up to a clearing in front of the property.

As the tension rose in the small cabin, the helicopter began to bank sharply to the left. The pilot shouted something to Sanchez. Sanchez nodded, turned to Volkmann.

'The pilot . . . he says maybe he can land in front of the *hacienda* if there is a big enough clearing.'

Volkmann glanced down, saw the blue and white car race below and behind them, moving fast along the narrow dirt road, plumes of russet dust in its wake. The helicopter suddenly slowed, hovered now, less than a quarter of a kilometre from the *hacienda*, the pilot shouting something to Sanchez.

'We go for the clearing, OK?' Sanchez said to Volkmann. 'But two sweeps over the *hacienda* first, just in case there's trouble waiting.'

Sanchez tapped the pilot on the shoulder and spoke rapidly. The helicopter began to move forward fast, dropping height, going in low, the pilot pushing forward on the control stick. Volkmann tensed. Sanchez clenched his teeth and grabbed one of the automatic rifles and three clips of ammunition. He handed them to Volkmann.

'For you, in case there's trouble. But make sure the girl stays in the chopper, *si*?'

Volkmann glanced up briefly at the hazy sky, saw something glinting in the far distance, a flash of white light and then it was gone. He tensed, checked the rifle, then looked down as the helicopter began its first sweep.

Volkmann knew after the first sweep that the white house was empty.

The pilot kept the helicopter in a steady angle of bank, circling the property in a perfect circuit, then sweeping out, coming in low again, barely clearing the surrounding jungle.

The place appeared deserted. There was a black stain on the landscape to the right side of the house, looking like an oil spillage from the distance at first, but on the second sweep Volkmann recognised the remains of a fire, the helicopter's blades causing the dark blot to lift and swirl, as small black flakes rose and billowed into the air, eddying into a scattered mess.

The veranda was empty, the windows of the house bare of curtains, and a clutter of outhouses stood at the rear, looking dilapidated and weathered, a small wooden outbuilding set off to the right of the house.

On the second sweep Volkmann glanced over at Sanchez. The man's fat unshaven jowls looked like hanging lumps of black rubber, disappointment on his face, but the eyes alert, awake, ready, but there was no need to be ready, Volkmann knew, seeing the blue and white police car coming up fast along the private gravel track that led up to the white *hacienda*.

As it came to a sudden halt four *policia* scrambled out, wrenching guns from holsters, crouching as the helicopter began to descend on a flat clearing to the right of the gravel driveway.

As soon as the helicopter landed, Sanchez stepped out, followed by his men, pistols and shotguns at the ready, Volkmann close behind carrying the rifle, Erica remaining with the pilot, who was closing down the engines.

The heat and humidity of the jungle hit them like a force as they crouched instinctively to keep their heads below the slowly dying blades. Then the swish of the metal died, and it seemed to Volkmann that there was only utter silence and wilting heat, until seconds later the clicking, shrieking sounds of the jungle erupted all around them.

Two uniformed *policia* from the car rushed forward, waving their guns, chattering loudly, pointing to the house.

Sanchez spoke to them briefly, then replaced his gun in his waist holster. He turned to Volkmann, the look of exhaustion on his face saying it all, knowing, as Volkmann knew, that they were too late.

He nodded towards the house. 'Come, *amigo*. Let's take a look inside.'

* * *

It became apparent to Volkmann that something was wrong.

No one left a house this empty, this bare. No one picked a house this clean, leaving it like a corpse stripped of its flesh after the vultures had been.

That is what the house, the property, suggested. A wooden skeleton. Echoing, hollow, the scrubbed floorboards inside creaking eerily underfoot, swept clean, swept of everything.

Erica joined them from the helicopter, only the pilot choosing to remain outside, indifferent, listening to a commercial radio station he had tuned into the communications receiver on board, oblivious to the heat as he stalked the area around the Dauphin, chewing gum.

The house was large inside, thirteen rooms, Volkmann counted, each sanitised, each bare, nothing covering the floorboards, not even a thread of carpet remaining. It seemed even the dust had been swept away.

Sanchez ordered all the *policia* and his own men to go through the house room by room, checking them for anything, for any clues. Then he went with Volkmann and Erica to look at the outhouses.

There were three of them. Two had been garages, they guessed, big enough to accommodate a large car each, but nothing, again, in either, except faded, oil-stained patches on the ground.

The last outbuilding to the right of the property was not much larger. It appeared to have been a store room, or a child's playhouse, built of wood. Again, nothing inside, only a number of very faint white paint marks on one of the walls. Volkmann and Sanchez moved closer, examined them. They had been painted a long time ago, and when they looked closely they saw the markings resembled faintly the pattern of a spider's web, as if someone had started painting the interior and then changed their mind, or a child had been playing with a paint brush.

None of them spoke as they examined the wooden outhouse, Sanchez smoking a cigarette, looking over the walls, the floors, until he seemed baffled and overcome by it all.

As they stepped out into the sunlight Volkmann saw the remains of the fire. The ashes had been scattered in small, irregular clusters by the wake of the helicopter's blades. He knelt down and touched the centre of the largest cluster. The ashes were soggy, as if water had been poured on them. He found a stick in a nearby thicket and poked the remains, until he had sifted through them all, all the black clusters the helicopter's blades had scattered.

Nothing.

The sun was out now from behind the clouds, the heat becoming unbearable. Volkmann looked at Erica, then at Sanchez. There were small beads of sweat glistening on the fat detective's brow.

'The local sergeant,' Volkmann said. 'Tell me what he told you.' Sanchez had told him already, but he wanted to hear it again.

'He said he has lived in the area most of his life. He never even knew the house existed.'

'How far to the nearest town?'

'He says twenty kilometres away. The nearest house ten kilometres.'

Volkmann kicked a cluster of ashes, paused, then looked at Sanchez and said slowly, 'What do you think, Vellares?' It was the first time Volkmann had addressed the man by his first name.

Sanchez wiped his brow with the back of his hand, looked at him, shrugged. 'The Indians in my country, they have a word . . .' Sanchez said the word, a long, unfathomable word, a bewildered look on his sagging face as he said it. 'It means . . . very strange. Very . . . *weird*.' He stared at Volkmann. 'You know what I'm saying?'

Volkmann nodded. In the house, in the house and the small outhouse, Volkmann had sensed something. He had shivered stepping into both of them. Shivered violently. Something inside him touched by something, Sanchez sensing it too, and the girl, Volkmann could tell.

A feeling none of them could put into words.

He turned to Erica. She was looking at him, this German girl who had hoped, who had travelled so far.

There was a noise behind them. Volkmann turned, saw the helicopter pilot call Sanchez over, talking in Spanish.

Volkmann and Erica looked back at the white house, neither of them speaking. They heard Sanchez' footsteps moments later and turned. The detective held something in his hand.

'The pilot,' Sanchez said to Volkmann. 'He found this lying in the bushes. The helicopter blades must have blown it from the fire.'

Sanchez handed him a piece of glossy paper. Volkmann saw that it was the remains of a very old black-and-white photograph. Half of it had been burned, the right side of the picture cracked and worn, but the image still discernible. The photograph was of a woman, a blonde young, pretty woman, smiling out at the camera, sky and snow-capped mountains behind her.

The young woman's right hand was linked through the arm of a companion, a man wearing some sort of uniform. Only the man's shoulder, his left arm and part of his torso were still visible. The rest of the photograph had been burned, its black edges ragged, flaking with cinder. But what caught Volkmann's eye was the conspicuous dark band around the man's arm: a black Nazi swastika set in a white circle.

Volkmann stared down at the photograph for a long time until Sanchez said, 'Turn it over.'

Volkmann did as the detective asked.

There was a date, in German, scrawled in the top right-hand corner in faded blue ink. *'Elfter Juli, 1931'*: 11th of July, 1931.

Volkmann looked up, shielded his eyes fron the strong sun. He saw Erica and Sanchez stare over at the white house before both turned back to look at him.

'What does it mean?' Sanchez asked.

Volkmann flicked over the half-burned photograph, looked down again at the blonde young woman in the picture, and wondered the same.

PART THREE

Chapter Eighteen

Genoa,
Italy.
December 9th

Franco Scali stood at the window of the harbour office and gripped the Zeiss binoculars tightly. She was two hours late, the *Maria Escobar*, and in those two long hours Franco thought he must have lost half a kilo in sweat. But now the ship was heading into the harbour. All twelve thousand tonnes of her. A beautiful sight.

'Franco . . .?'

Scali put down the binoculars and smiled at the pretty, dark-haired young secretary seated behind her desk.

'What is it, sweetie?'

He was glad of the distraction now that the ship had finally arrived. The girl wore black stockings and a short, thick black woollen skirt, a glimpse of stocking top visible when she crossed her legs. Franco knew she did it to tease him, an unhappily married man with three growing children. He sighed inwardly. Women were like that. Teasers.

The small office above the warehouse had a sweeping view of the old port. But it was a drafty cramped place and Franco wore a heavy woollen sweater. He felt hot, despite the fact that outside an icy wind whistled around the port. It was stress, Franco knew, because the temperature in the room was pretty low. The girl shivered, the single-bar electric heater on beside her throwing out hardly any heat.

'The *Maria Escobar* . . .' the girl said finally.

'What about her?'

'The ship's load sheet. Don't forget to give me the copy.'

'It's downstairs in the warehouse. Don't worry, I'll give it to you later, after the *Escobar*'s been unloaded.'

The load sheet contained the original and the carbon copies, all part of the one form so there could be no mistakes, no alterations, as far as the ship's cargo was concerned.

The girl gave Franco a wicked, flirting grin out of the side of her wide, sensual mouth. Franco grinned back, realising the double meaning he had inflected.

'Unless, sweetie, you want it *now*?' He grinned broadly, saw the girl try in vain to suppress a smile.

'Franco . . . you're a married man.'

'They're the best kind. Didn't your Mama ever tell you that?'

The girl giggled. 'The copy load sheet, Franco . . .'

'When I'm through with the ship.'

'Well, don't forget.'

She was only a junior secretary, Franco the senior clearance clerk, fifteen years older, but she talked to him like she was his boss. Franco liked it. The girl thought she had him by the balls, flashing her breasts and legs, teasing him, tempting him, wearing those short skirts and stockings, the tight blouses. But she hadn't: Franco was too clever for that, far too clever. She would be good for a discreet roll in the hay, but that was all. Besides, Franco Scali had other plans.

He turned his head away from the girl's black-stockinged legs, one swinging seductively as she crossed them and began to polish her crimson nails, his eyes going instead to watch the *Maria Escobar* as she crept into the harbour. There was no need for the binoculars now, because the ship was close, very close, only five minutes from docking, the sprawling old city of Genoa further off to her left, its maze of narrow streets climbing in jagged steps up the foothills of the Apennines.

Franco turned to look at the girl and grinned again. She responded, her generous lips curling into a sexy smile. Franco winked and put down the binoculars on the desk and turned towards the door.

'*Ciao*, sweetie, I've got work to do.'

*   *   *

He went down the stairs to the busy warehouse, picked up the paperwork from the tiny glass-fronted office at the entrance.

An icy wind blew in from the sea and he pulled on a reefer jacket and crossed the yard apron. He looked up at the crane cabin where Aldo Celli waited to operate the grab, gave the man a wave and then the thumbs-up sign. Seconds later he heard Aldo start up the crane's motor. Aldo the Hawk they called him. Because the man swooped down with the crane grab on the cargo containers like they were prey.

Franco looked out towards the harbour, the *Maria Escobar* slowing down, backwatering, turning just a touch to starboard before coming in stern first, the men on the deck and the docks moving fast to tie her up. He looked around for the customs officer, saw no sign of him, but he'd be here, for sure.

Sometimes customs just checked the seals, or broke the previous port seal and looked inside the big steel cargo containers to satisfy themselves, or just to show their authority. But they had never caught Franco yet. He was always careful, and this one was a peach. There would be enough from this one job to buy a new car and plenty left over to spend on the girls in the smart clubs near the Piazza della Vittoria, the ones who did it for almost a million lire a go, but were worth every lira. And he needed money. Everybody needed money these days, things were going so crazy. Even his old man had said it was worse than the old days.

Franco licked his dry lips. The cargo was well hidden, he told himself, relaxing a little. The *Maria Escobar* was almost in now, the guys getting ready with the ropes, Aldo up in the crane, itching to get going with the grab.

Franco ground out his cigarette on the apron's concrete and glanced left of the harbour. He felt a nervous flutter in his chest. Coming fast across the yard apron was the fat, waddling figure of Paulo Bonefacio, the customs officer. Paulo the Pest, *Il Peste*, for short, because he pestered you, hassled you, wanted to check every fucking container, every nook and cranny, like the man was looking for a medal from the

Italian Customs Service. What the fuck was he doing here? It should have been his day off. Vincenti was rostered on, not Bonefacio . . .

Il Peste came up to him, puffing and grunting.

'*Ciao*, Franco.'

'*Ciao*. What happened to Vincenti . . .?'

'He's sick,' answered Il Peste. 'Why, you expecting an easy time?'

Franco forced himself to smile back, the *Escobar* docking now, gangway coming down. He could feel the tension returning . . . *Jesus . . . of all people it has to be Il Peste checking the fucking containers . . .*

'Come on, Franco, let's see what we can find, eh?'

Franco swallowed, not too hard, and tried to keep smiling. 'Sure.'

The fat customs official grunted and started across the harbour apron, towards the place fifty metres away where Aldo would put the containers down before the conveyer took them further along the port.

Franco Scali followed, saying a silent prayer.

He watched Aldo Celli swing the crane grab round and pick up one of the heavy metal containers off the ship like they were lightweight cardboard boxes. The one he was waiting for, the blue container with the three grey-striped markings, hadn't come out of the hold yet. There were only five containers on the dockyard apron where Aldo had dropped them. Forty containers this load, and knowing Il Peste he'd want to check almost every fucking one.

Franco was moving around, trying to look like he was working, expending some energy to show for all that sweat he was pumping, helping the men manoeuvre the containers into place as Aldo lifted them up from the *Maria Escobar*'s hold and swung them round and down onto the apron. *Jesus . . . let's get this over with*, thought Franco.

He saw Il Peste examining the clipboard list of documents in his hands. The man was totally incorruptible, got a fucking erection when he found something not right on the ship's manifest, or contraband in the containers.

It didn't happen too often, but if Il Peste found anything like that your ass was in the slammer. And no one would dare retaliate: the man's brother, Stefano, was a Carabiniere inspector. Do that and you had every cop in Genoa crawling up your ass. Naturally, Franco tried to time it so that Il Peste wouldn't be around when he had something special coming in. Only it didn't always work out that way.

Like today.

Franco cursed under his breath now as another container came swinging out of the *Escobar*'s hold, Aldo enjoying himself up there in the crane's nest – twenty-five more to go – Franco sweating, moving and shouting like he was really working as the big metal boxes slapped down on the ground. Franco looked over at the customs official. The man was staring soberly at the neat line of containers laid out on the apron, waiting until the last one was out before starting work, like an athlete waiting for the crack of the starting pistol.

The wind whistled around the harbour. Franco watched as Aldo swung the crane grab up and into the hold again.

It was the last container. Blue, a band of three grey stripes around the sides. The one Franco was waiting for. Aldo lifted the bitch up, swung her across and down, landing her with a smack.

Jesus . . . take it fucking easy. What I got in there is worth a whole lot of fucking money, you Genoese asshole!

Franco heard the dying whirr of the crane's motor. There were shouts from the men as they finished working and removed their leather gloves, waiting for Il Peste to start.

He came up beside Franco, looking serious, looking like he was ready to do battle.

'Forty containers, right?'

'Yeah.'

'You got all the documents?'

Franco handed them over. All the containers were sealed individually with a stamped customs seal from the last port, or from the port of origin. Franco's job was to clear his cargo through customs as fast as he could. Do all the necessary paperwork, get the container in and out of the port with the minimum of hassle. In and out, time is money, as Franco's boss never stopped reminding him. Mostly the customs guys didn't delay you, took a perfunctory look to cover their asses.

But not Il Peste. He was meticulous. And sometimes he used the duster, a brass knuckle-duster, to tap the insides of the big steel boxes, listening for the sound as he tapped away, listening to the timbre of the returning sound, to make sure there were no false bottoms or walls. That was the one fear Franco had today: if Il Peste used the duster.

The fat official looked up from the documents. 'OK. Everything looks in order.'

'How many you want to do?' Franco asked. None, he hoped, but knew that was asking too much. One, two maybe. *But please, asshole, not the last, not number forty.*

Il Peste looked at his watch. 'I gotta finish early today. I got a christening to go to. Stefano, my brother, his wife had a baby boy. I'm an uncle again.'

'Congratulations!' Franco slapped Il Peste on the shoulder as he turned to the other men waiting nearby. 'Hey! What you think? Paulo is an uncle again. Stefano's wife just had a baby boy.'

The men muttered their congratulations. Il Peste smiled, apparently warmed by their mumbled good wishes. It was good, thought Franco, a good sign, a fucking good sign. Maybe his prayers had been answered. Maybe the man wasn't going to be too thorough today.

A chill wind whistled through the harbour as Franco smiled. 'You got time afterwards, I'd like to buy you a glass of *vino* to celebrate.'

'Some other time, Franco, I got to be at the church by three.'

'Sure, no problem.'

Il Peste consulted the documents on his clipboard. 'We just do . . . Let me see . . . Number three. The third one.'

Franco beamed. 'OK by me.'

'And then the last one. Number forty.'

Franco swallowed, trying hard not to show his apprehension, smiling and looking friendly, trying to stay cool, but feeling his legs begin to tremble.

'Sure . . .'

Il Peste turned towards the containers, laid out in aisles of ten, four deep, before looking back at Franco, staring into his face.

'What's wrong, Franco? You look pale. You feeling OK?'

Franco felt his bowels shiver, rubbed his stomach, grimaced weakly. 'My wife cooked *carbonara* for dinner last night. It didn't taste too good.'

Il Peste nodded, mildly sympathetic, then strode quickly towards where the rows of containers began.

Franco was sweating like a pig.

Come on, man, get it over with. Get the fucking thing over with.

Number three container done, and no problems. The contents tallying with the customs manifest.

They were outside the last container now, number forty, Franco trying to control his fear as he watched Il Peste break the lead customs seal before two of the men opened the container doors for him.

Whatever you do, don't use the knuckle-duster, man . . . don't use the fucking duster.

The official consulted the clipboard. 'What's the port of origin?'

'Casablanca.'

Il Peste looked at the documents, shook his head. 'No, it's not.'

Franco looked up, glanced at the documents over Il Peste's shoulder. 'Oh, sure . . . I forgot, it's . . .'

'Montevideo,' corrected Il Peste. 'Casablanca was first port of call.'

'Yeah, Montevideo.'

Containers from South America usually put the customs

guys on guard. Narcotics were the big thing. Franco, sweating, stepped a little into the container, twenty-six boxes inside, twenty-six big and small, but still room for more, the big container not full.

'What's the manifest say?' Il Peste asked, but not waiting for a reply, looking down at the document himself on the clipboard. 'Twenty-six boxes. All machine parts, except one box of medical supplies. OK, let's have a look.'

They stepped into the container and Franco saw him take a torch from his pocket. He flicked it on and counted the boxes, checking that none had been tampered with. Il Peste finally grunted his satisfaction, ticked off one of the entries on his customs form, then suddenly looked up and sniffed the air.

'You get a funny smell?'

Franco sniffed. 'No . . . I don't smell nothing.'

'The medical supplies . . . Which box?'

Franco moved several of the boxes aside, felt the sweat drip down his back, on his brow. He wiped his forehead with the back of his hand.

'I think I see it,' Franco said.

Il Peste moved to where the box lay on top of another and picked it up, sniffed it, then put the box of medical supplies aside. 'It's OK.'

Franco almost sighed out loud. But Il Peste didn't put his torch away. Franco saw the man's right hand go into his coat pocket, the gold-coloured knuckle-duster coming out. *No, man . . . not the fucking duster!* Franco watched, horrified, as the man fitted the chunky brass metal into his fat fingers.

He smiled at Franco. 'A couple of taps . . . For luck.'

Franco smiled back, tried not to betray his unease, watching nervously as Il Peste went around the container tapping the sides, stopping, then tapping again, listening carefully to the sound, comparing it to the previous one, as if he were a fucking piano-tuner.

When he began moving towards the right container wall, Franco felt his heart beat even faster, the pumping sound in his chest coming through his ears, through his whole body, feeling his pulse in the tips of his fingers.

Jesus . . . Not the fucking right wall . . .

The duster kept tapping . . .

Tap . . . Tap . . . Tap . . .

Tap . . . Tap . . . Tap . . .

Il Peste suddenly stopped.

Franco saw the man's head turn slightly to the right. *Jesus . . . he's found it . . . The fucking asshole has found it!* Franco wanted to weep, felt the blood drain out of his body as Il Peste hit the spot again.

Tap . . . Tap . . . Tap. . . . The brass knuckle-duster smacking against the right side wall, down near the back of the container, Franco listening, hearing the slight difference in sound, just a touch.

Tap . . . Tap . . . Tap . . .

Franco wanted to throw up. Il Peste was hitting a spot now less than a metre away from the hidden compartment and then another part of the container wall to his right, comparing the two echoing sounds. There was a slight but definite difference between the two sounds.

'Hey, Franco . . .'

Franco looked up, startled, his heart beating in his ears like hammer blows.

'Yeah . . .?' The question came out like a croak in his throat.

Il Peste looked up at him in the dim-lit back of the container, pointing the torch away. 'You got the right time?'

'What . . .?'

'The time . . . What's the time?'

Franco looked at his watch, hand trembling. 'Two . . . Two-thirty . . .'

'I've got to call my brother at the station. You mind I use your telephone?' Franco shook his head dumbly and swallowed. Had the torch been shining on Franco's face, Il Peste would have seen its paleness. 'Why . . . what's up . . .?' Franco said quietly.

Il Peste tapped at his own watch. 'My watch . . . It's stopped, that's what's up. I'm gonna be late for the christening. Let's wrap her up.'

Franco sighed audibly, the sigh sounding like a small breeze. Il Peste heard it, shone the torch in Franco's face.

'Hey . . . You look sick, Franco. You OK?'

Franco belched with fear and smiled innocently. 'It must have been the pasta.'

It was dark, almost six o'clock when he came out of the warehouse and crossed the harbour apron to where the containers still stood. He had the torch with him and the screwdriver and the other stuff he needed, the stuff he kept carefully hidden away in his locker.

The girl in the office had gone home an hour before, the men over two, leaving Franco alone. There was nothing due in this part of the docks until after midnight, no one about, and the men who shunted the containers further up the docks on the conveyor were at break. Franco had delayed the further movement of this load from the *Escobar* deliberately, so that he would have time to do what he had to do next.

He glanced back over his shoulder. Lights were on in the warehouse, the security man in the back somewhere reading a newspaper. Franco's own white Fiat was parked outside, ready and waiting. A hundred metres away to its right stood the two-storey customs building, the lights out but a faint flickering blue visible inside. The guys on the late shift watching television.

Over three hours had passed but Franco was still on edge. It had been close today, a real close thing.

He took one more look around the apron to make sure it was clear. Even the bitter, icy wind had stopped. He crossed quickly to where the container with the three grey stripes stood, knelt down at the right side end and flicked on the torch before placing it on the ground.

The three painted stripes ran in bands around the sides, each painted band roughly the width of Franco's wrist and about a quarter of a metre apart. Franco took a screwdriver from his pocket and placed it beside him then picked up the torch. He ran the light along the right-hand side and felt carefully with the tips of his fingers along the grey stripes of the corrugated metal where he knew the hidden compartment was located.

After a few moments he found what he was searching for. A small indent in the metal, the size of a thumbnail. This was Franco's marker. Ten centimetres to the left, but invisible even as he shone the torch on the spot, was the first screw. Four bevelled screws in all holding in the metal plate, all their heads recessed neatly beneath putty, painted over carefully the same colour grey paint as the stripes around the container. Pretty neat idea, Franco thought.

He picked up the screwdriver and the torch, scraped away the dried hard putty and quickly unscrewed all four screws, carefully placing them on the ground beside him, removing the half-metre high plate that meshed into the container's side.

A really neat job.

Even looking closely no one would have noticed that the plate was there. Franco gripped the metal and placed it flat on the ground beside him very gently, careful to make no sound.

A neat, recessed cubby-hole was now revealed. Franco shone the torch inside and saw the metal box held onto the container structure with two steel clamps. He unscrewed one of the clamps quickly, holding the box in place with his free hand.

He reached in and hefted it out. The box measured roughly a quarter of a metre by a quarter of a metre, not too deep, but it was so heavy Franco needed to arch his back for support. He placed it beside him.

It took him less than two minutes to replace the false side and screw in the four bevelled screws. Then from his pocket he took the things he had kept hidden in his locker, wrapped up in an oily cloth: a ball of soft putty, an artist's paintbrush and a tiny pot of grey paint. With the soft putty he filled in the screw holes. That done he took the paint brush and the small tin of grey paint and quickly but carefully painted over the putty.

He examined the result with the torch. *Perfect*.

The screw holes were invisible again now, the grey paint

Franco had used matching the grey of the stripes exactly. Satisfied, he gathered up his things and put them back in his pocket and switched off the torch.

He picked up the metal box again. *Jesus, heavy*. He wondered what it contained. Gold, must be, judging by the weight of it. Heavy, like all the others. But much smaller. And this time they'd used a different container.

But it wasn't any of his business what the Germans were smuggling. His business was to make sure he was paid.

Franco ran the palm of his hand over his brow. His forehead and hair were drenched in sweat. He glanced at his watch in the poor light. Ten minutes past six. Franco looked about the harbour again. Still quiet, still deserted. The finger of light from the *Lanterna*, the old lighthouse out in the harbour, probed the darkness.

He strode smartly back across the apron towards where his white Fiat stood parked outside the warehouse, carrying the heavy metal box.

It was raining on the Via Balbi when he finally parked his car across the street from the bar.

Franco saw the man as soon as he stepped inside. Blond and young, thin-lipped, sitting alone at the counter, maybe mid-twenties and wearing glasses, his mackintosh open to reveal a grey business suit. The man flicked a glance at Franco and removed his glasses and wiped them with a handkerchief.

Franco ordered a *vino rosso* and lit a cigarette. The blond man's action was his signal. The cigarette was Franco's: no problems, he had the box. The blond young man stood up, paid for his drink and left the bar, ignoring Franco as he passed him. Franco waited another couple of minutes, finishing his cigarette and wine, then paid the barkeeper and stepped outside.

He climbed into the Fiat and drove around the corner to the deserted parking lot opposite the Banco d'Italia.

A dark-coloured Fiat was already waiting. The blond young man sat in the front with a passenger, a man whose face was partly hidden in shadow. Franco rolled down the window and the blond man did likewise, the rain falling more softly now.

'You have the cargo?' the man said in good Italian.

'Sure. You got the money?'

The man handed across a large envelope to Franco. 'Count it, if you wish. As quickly as possible.'

Franco nodded and took the envelope in through the open window and flicked on the torch. Inside were fresh, ten-thousand-lire notes in thin wads. There were ten wads and Franco flicked through them all.

'The box,' the man said.

Franco leaned across the seat, pressed the button underneath the dashboard, the lid flicking open. His own secret cubby-hole; he had fitted it himself and it was virtually undetectable. The box just about fitted. He hefted it out and handed it across through the window gingerly. It was so damned heavy Franco had to support it on the car's window frame. The man handed it carefully to the passenger beside him.

The young man said to Franco, 'Don't forget our arrangement. Any problems, any inquiries, you contact us.'

Franco said, 'That was the last one?'

'Yes.'

'Good.'

The young man turned sharply towards Franco, sensing the tone in the Italian's voice. 'Why? . . . was there a problem?'

'No. But there could have been. The customs guy today . . . He looked hard, you know what I mean?'

There was a slight trace of panic in the young man's voice. 'But he found nothing. Suspected nothing?'

'You think I'd be here if they did?' Franco shook his head. 'No . . . I'm getting out of this smuggling business. No more contraband. From now on I just do my job. You ever want something else delivered, you don't call Franco, OK?'

The blond man said, 'I think that's a wise decision.'

Franco started the car, said it aloud as he pulled away in the white Fiat: 'So do I, *amico. Ciao.*'

Chapter Nineteen

Strasbourg.
Friday,
December 9th

The flight from Asunción to Madrid had been delayed and it was almost midday when Volkmann and the girl landed in Frankfurt.

When they arrived at Volkmann's apartment three hours later he left the girl and drove to the office and typed up a preliminary report. He put a copy in Ferguson's mailbox, with a note saying he'd be in the next morning before noon.

At five he had an early dinner with Erica in a small restaurant near the Quai Ernest and they walked back to his apartment. After he had unpacked he made up the spare bedroom and poured two brandies.

The girl looked exhausted. The afternoon before, Sanchez had driven them to a small cemetery on the outskirts of the city. The sky was cloudless, the heat unbearable, and Volkmann and the fat detective had waited under a jacaranda tree while the girl had said her prayer.

Later Sanchez had taken them to the house in La Chacarita where the bodies had been discovered and there had been brief interviews with Mendoza and Torres but neither man had been able to add to their statements. They had visited Tsarkin's residence in the late afternoon, and Volkmann had seen the manicured lawns, the paintings on the walls, the open safe behind the one in the study, cool marble floors that echoed as they walked through the mansion under glittering chandeliers. Sanchez' men had searched the rooms again, top to bottom, but found nothing of importance.

At the airport Sanchez had promised to get the report on

Tsarkin's background to Strasbourg as quickly as possible. His men were still digging through the files at the Immigration Office.

'I hope to have some information within the next twenty-four hours,' Sanchez had said as he led them to Departures. Erica Kranz had thanked him and the detective had smiled and said to Volkmann, 'Look after her, *amigo*. Take care, and good luck.'

On the flight back Erica had asked Volkmann why his people were really interested in Winter and when he told her she made no comment, simply nodded her head and turned away towards the window.

In the apartment she had been subdued and tired, exhaustion showing on her pretty face. He had explained that he wanted her in Strasbourg should Ferguson need to talk with her and she accepted his suggestion that she stay at his place rather than book into a hotel.

After she had gone to bed Volkmann poured himself another brandy. Darkness had fallen beyond the window, the spire of the Gothic cathedral illuminated in the distance. No heat here, just a cold chill wind rattling the windows.

As he sat there sipping the brandy, feeling the aching tiredness take hold, Joseph Volkmann heard the girl tossing restlessly in her sleep. He thought of the heat and the jungle of yesterday. Of the white house and the photograph of the woman taken a long time ago.

He wondered what Ferguson and Peters would make of it all.

The three men sat quietly in the warm office, Peters and Volkmann facing Ferguson's desk.

The tape machine beside Ferguson was on.

When it had finished playing through, Ferguson switched off the machine and shook his head.

He had replayed one sentence several times. *Sie werden alle umgebracht.* They will all be killed. Played it and replayed it to make sure there could be no mistake, heard the soft but distinctive voice of the speaker.

There were three photographic copies lying face up on Ferguson's desk, copies made by the police in Asunción, and he stared down at them with interest. Faces to go with the story. One was a shot of the men, Dieter Winter and the old man named Nicolas Tsarkin, taken with a telephoto lens. Another of Tsarkin himself, head and shoulders only, that looked like a copy from a passport. Hard eyes and a narrow mouth and a face that was thin and secretive. The third was a black-and-white copy photograph of the woman, her right hand linked through a man's arm. The Nazi armband was an interesting curiosity, Ferguson reflected.

He adjusted his glasses and picked up the copy photograph of the pretty blonde woman and stared at it again. There was a note made by Volkmann, paper-clipped to the copy snapshot, mentioning the date on the back of the original photograph. Ferguson had written the date in pencil at the end of Volkmann's report. July 11th, 1931.

He had also made small asterisk marks and questions in pencil in the margins of the report, points to be clarified by Volkmann when he arrived.

Now Ferguson scanned through the report once again. It had made interesting reading. Volkmann had spared no detail in describing the scene at the remote house in the Chaco. When Ferguson turned back moments later, he looked directly at Volkmann.

'The remains of the bonfire . . . you say they were analysed?'

Volkmann leaned forward in his chair. He appeared tired, but his eyes were alert. 'Sanchez' people did a preliminary analysis of the remains. They were papers and photographs mostly. And wood and cardboard. But also some food traces. Dried provisions. There was nothing in the house or outhouses. Every room had been stripped clean. For whatever reasons, whoever these people were, they wanted any trace of their presence completely destroyed.' Volkmann shook his head. 'I've never seen anything like it before, sir. It looked like the whole property had been sanitised. As if whoever had lived in the Chaco house had gone through it with a fine-tooth comb and then scrubbed it clean.'

Ferguson paused before speaking. He looked out towards the window, then back again.

'Leaving the question of the Chaco property aside for now, the question is, surely, where's the connection to Winter? What has all this got to do with Winter's death?'

Tom Peters leaned forward in his chair. 'Might I make a suggestion, sir?'

Ferguson half smiled. 'By all means do.'

'The report on the shooting in Berlin said the ammunition used was South American in origin. We know Winter was in South America. And not just once, but on at least eight occasions.'

'Go on,' Ferguson prompted.

'We know the ammunition used in both the Winter shooting and the killing of the businessmen in Hamburg a year ago was South American. We also know a lot of terrorist groups have been getting their supplies from there, since the Russians are no longer in the supply business.' Peters hesitated, glanced at Volkmann. 'And then there's the cargoes flown to Montevideo. There are countless possibilities, of course, sir. But it could have been weapons and munitions supplies. And it's a plausible reason why Winter would have been in South America.'

Ferguson sighed, then stood up and crossed to the window. 'Plausible, yes. But speculative. And I'm afraid it doesn't explain why Winter was killed in Berlin.' Ferguson turned and raised an eyebrow, looked at Volkmann.

'What do you think the cargoes might have contained, Joseph?'

Volkmann hesitated. 'It's difficult to say, sir. Weapons or narcotics seem likely. Or even precious metals. But if it was narcotics Rodriguez transported for these people, then the Chaco house wasn't used. The chemical agents used in the processing would have left behind trace elements.' Volkmann shook his head. 'But there were no chemical or narcotics traces on the property.' Volkmann glanced at Peters. 'What

Tom says is still possible, sir. But there wasn't any hard evidence to support it.'

'What about the land the property is on; was it checked?'

'Sanchez had the local police check the land within a three-kilometre radius. There was a field that looked like it could have been used as a temporary air strip about two kilometres from the house. There were deep tyre marks on the surface and some faint oil stains in the soil. Nothing much else. But it could have been the place Rodriguez landed.'

'Was the aircraft this man Rodriguez used examined for narcotics traces?'

'The DC4 was impounded at Asunción. Sanchez had his lab people go over it.'

'And?'

'There were minute cocaine traces in the aft cargo area.' Volkmann shook his head as he looked at Ferguson. 'But it proves nothing. According to Sanchez, Rodriguez could have made dozens of runs in between for other customers, ferrying narcotics.'

Ferguson sighed and crossed back slowly to pick up a file from his desk. Inside were the original and two copies of the faxed report he had received an hour before from Asunción. He had delayed showing it to the men seated opposite, wanting to discuss Volkmann's report first. Now he opened the file, removed the contents.

'I received a report from Paraguay an hour ago. It's in English. I think perhaps you had both better read it before we proceed further. There are copies for each of you. It rather deepens the mystery, I'm afraid, not clarifies it.'

Ferguson handed across the copies of the confidential report to Volkmann and Peters, the report Sanchez had promised. Volkmann took the three sheets of proffered paper and looked down at the report and read slowly.

To: Head, British DSE.
From: Captain Vellares Sanchez. Policia Civil, Paraguaya.
Subject: Visit of your officer, J. Volkmann, and his investigation.

Status: Highly Confidential.
After recent investigation the following can be reported:

(1) The Chaco property your officer visited occupies a tract of land some four hundred acres in size and was bought and registered in the name of Erhard Schmeltz in December 1931, one month after Senor Schmeltz and his wife, Inge, and their son Karl emigrated to Paraguay. Records reveal that Erhard Schmeltz was born in Hamburg in 1880, his wife one year later. According to his immigration records, Schmeltz served in the First World War in the German army. His financial status upon arrival in Paraguay was five thousand US dollars.

The Chaco property was one of several Senor Schmeltz purchased in Paraguay, beginning in December 1931, though the others were not in the same Chaco region. The Chaco property was used for the production of quebraco wood until 1949. Senor Erhard Schmeltz died in an automobile accident in Asunción in 1943.

Police file sources disclose that from December 1931 to January 1933, he was in receipt of considerable sums of money sent from Germany. From February 1933 onwards, money was sent to him in Asunción via the official German Reichsbank at exact six-monthly intervals, using bank drafts. Each draft was for the sum of five thousand US dollars. After his death Schmeltz's wife became the recipient. The drafts finally ceased in February 1945.

Despite inquiries, which will continue, we have no further information on the recent occupants of the Chaco property. Senor Schmeltz's wife died in 1949. The property register then recorded a change of ownership to the Schmeltz's son, Karl, born in Germany in July 1931. No specific town or city of birth was given in the immigration records and there are no photographs recorded in civil offices of Karl Schmeltz. His present whereabouts are unknown.

(2) Regarding Senor Nicolas Tsarkin, the following information has been confirmed:
Senor Nicolas Tsarkin arrived in Asunción from Rio de

Janeiro on November eight 1946, and applied for Paraguayan citizenship two days later.

His immigration application stated his place of birth as Riga, in Latvia, 1911. In his possession on arrival in Paraguay in 1946 he had the considerable sum of twenty thousand US dollars. Senor Tsarkin described himself on his application form as a war refugee and businessman. He was granted Paraguayan citizenship one week after his application.

For your information, the application forms of the time for citizenship were of two kinds: one for public records and one which was held in the files of the seguridad – the security police – which contained information of a more confidential nature. Many refugees came to South America from Europe after the war and the Paraguayan government of the time had pro-German sympathies: thus ex-Nazis were admitted, particularly those with foreign currency or gold in their possession. Depending on the subjects' influence and financial status, some were helped to arrange a new identity and residence within Paraguay.

In Senor Nicolas Tsarkin's case, a seguridad file exists. I have seen the file but am not permitted to transmit a copy. However, the following facts were recorded:

(a) Nicolas Tsarkin was born in Berlin, not Riga, in 1911.

(b) Tsarkin's real name was Heinrich Reimer.

(c) He was a major in the Leibstandarte (SS) Division when the war ended in 1945.

(d) According to then reliable sources named in the file, Tsarkin was responsible previously for a number of war crimes on the Russian and Allied fronts, and wanted by the Allied and the Russian authorities in this connection. It should be pointed out that at no time during his life in Paraguay was Tsarkin ever in trouble with the police. Nor were there any applications for his extradition, overt or otherwise. He apparently led an exemplary and successful business life and covered up his past successfully.

Tsarkin prospered in Paraguay, starting a number of

*businesses, importing farm machinery and mechanical parts.
He also purchased a number of farms in the hinterland for
cattle breeding and beef production. Tsarkin was unmarried.
No business connection has been discovered between Tsarkin
and the Schmeltz property. Tsarkin's holding company was
sold six months ago to a native-born Paraguyan citizen.*

*(3) Immigration returns from border stations are still being
thoroughly checked, but no additional immigration cards have
so far been found or registered for Senor Dieter Winter other
than those already discovered.*

*(4) One further interesting detail. A military radar instal-
lation at Bahia Negra north-east of the Chaco registered an
unfiled flight thought to be a light aircraft or helicopter, shortly
after our arrival at the Chaco property. The unidentified
aircraft was vectored proceeding north-east to the Brazilian
border towards Corumba and was then lost from radar contact.
This is being investigated further.*
ENDS.
Sanchez.

Volkmann looked up. He hadn't noticed Ferguson stand up
from behind his desk and cross to the window again.

Tom Peters had finished reading his copy and was shaking
his head.

Ferguson looked down at him. 'As I say, it rather deepens
the mystery, doesn't it?'

'You think there's a link to Winter's death in all this?'
Peters asked, looking from Volkmann to Ferguson. 'To the
photograph of the woman? To what happened to the journalist
and the young girl?'

'It's possible,' Ferguson replied noncommittally.

Volkmann said nothing, but looked out beyond the window.
The sky was grey and it was cold outside, cold enough for
snow. He looked back and saw Ferguson staring down at the
copy photographs, the one of the blonde young woman.

When Ferguson looked up he said to Volkmann, 'You say
Tsarkin was responsible for booking the hotel suite.'

'That and every hotel suite used by Winter in the last two years during his visits to Paraguay.' Volkmann shook his head. 'But that tells us nothing, sir. Except that maybe Reimer was some sort of organiser for these people.'

Ferguson made a steeple of his fingers. 'I'll have a copy of the taped voices sent to the language laboratory in Beaconsfield for analysis. Not that it can tell us much from the voice syntax and accents, apart from the approximate age of the speakers and their likely regional origins. But it may offer some clue. As of now we're in the dark completely.'

Ferguson paused, looked towards the window, then back again. 'However, there is one curious, but thin connecting strand, if either of you gentlemen have noticed?'

Ferguson saw both men stare at him. He held up the copy photograph of the young woman. 'This man Erhard Schmeltz, the one mentioned in the report. The money he received from Germany and the Nazi Reichsbank commenced the same year the photograph was taken, if the date on the reverse is to be believed.' Ferguson paused, a perplexed look on his sallow face, as he placed the copy photograph back on top of the file. 'Erhard Schmeltz seems a rather curious proposition. He arrives in Paraguay in 1931 from a depressed Germany with five thousand American dollars in his possession.'

Volkmann looked across at Ferguson. There was a line in the report from Sanchez that had troubled him, another connecting strand, between Tsarkin and Erica Kranz's father, and he guessed the others had noticed it also, but for now no one had commented.

'What did Hollrich say when you showed him the report?' Volkmann asked.

'I haven't,' Ferguson replied. 'With all the uncertainty about just now I'm not sure the Germans would pursue it with much vigour. The file might be left gathering dust. Besides, for now it's in our court.'

'So what do you want me to do, sir?'

Ferguson thought a moment. 'The shipment talked about on the tape. It may connect to the Italian mentioned in the conversation. It may be worth asking the Italian desk to double-check their port entries for consignments from Montevideo after the twenty-fifth. But as we can't be very specific, I doubt if we'll have much success.' Ferguson hesitated again. 'Do either of you have any other suggestions?'

Volkmann hesitated, then said, 'The girl, maybe she knew students who were close to Winter at Heidelberg. People at the same faculty who might have known him.'

'It's worth a try,' Ferguson replied.

'You want me to go it alone?' Volkmann asked.

'For the moment, yes. Take the girl along if she has no objections, she may be helpful, considering her contacts at the university. Bearing in mind her press connections you had better explain that this is still a security operation. And if you need any help, let me know.'

Volkmann stood up slowly. 'The photographs, sir . . . I'd like copies.'

'Of course. I'll have the lab organise it.'

'What about Erhard Schmeltz?'

Ferguson looked up. 'What about him?'

'Could we have his background checked? It may turn up something. The fact that he was receiving drafts from the German Reichsbank, it may tell us something about the occupants of the house.'

Ferguson nodded. 'Very well, I'll have Tom send a request to the American Documentation Centre in Berlin. Schmeltz would have left Germany before the Nazis came to power, of course. But who knows? Because of this Reichsbank business, he could have been a Nazi Party member, and the Document Centre may have him on file. I'll also request information on Reimer alias Tsarkin, to confirm the information from Asunción. If what this fellow Sanchez says is true, they ought to have his file. Leibstandarte SS. The same SS Division as the girl's father, if I remember from her file. Had you noticed?'

'Yes, sir.'

'Another curiosity. The girl, do you trust her?'

'In what way?'

'The fact that she knew this Winter at university. And that

her father and Reimer were in the same SS Division. One connection I could accept, but two I'd have doubts about. And there's a third.'

'What do you mean, sir?'

'She's been to South America and she knew the journalist. Do you think she's telling you everything she knows.'

Volkmann finally shook his head. 'I couldn't say, sir.'

Ferguson nodded to indicate the meeting was at an end.

'Very well, let's leave it at that for now. Good luck, Joseph. And keep in touch so I can keep you informed if anything comes in from Asunción.'

Ferguson watched as Volkmann rose and left the office. After the door had closed he looked at Peters.

'You think he'll be able to handle it?'

'Sir?'

'You know how Volkmann dislikes the Germans.'

Peters shrugged. 'Would you prefer me to cover it?'

'No. Volkmann has the language and the experience. I think for now we'll leave it in his hands. By the way, the girl is staying at his place.'

Peters raised his eyebrows. 'Who suggested that?'

'Volkmann took it upon himself.' Ferguson smiled. 'Either he's softened his attitude or he really doesn't trust the girl and wants to stick close to her.'

'You mean if she's covering something up? Not telling us the full story?'

'I imagine so. But it begs the question as to why she came to us in the first place. And why she insisted on dealing only with the DSE and not the *Bundespolizei*.' Ferguson hesitated. 'Something's not quite right, Tom. And I don't like it.' He looked at Peters. 'By the way, what's she like?'

'The girl? A bit of a stunner. A body you'd crawl over broken glass to get a look at.'

Ferguson smiled. 'That'll be all for now, Tom.'

'Right, sir.'

The Oriental Restaurant in Petite France was empty except for the two of them.

The girl's blonde hair fell loosely about her shoulders and she had put on make-up. She wore a pale blue sweater and a black skirt, legs smooth in sheer stockings.

A waiter hovered over them, serving them attentively. Crisp beef and vegetables. A bottle of Sauterne, ice-cold.

Volkmann had told her about the report from Sanchez, stipulating that it was confidential. He watched her face as he explained about Tsarkin's past and the owner of the Chaco property, and that his people were checking on the backgrounds of Schmeltz and Reimer. He saw the look of puzzlement and then Erica Kranz frowned.

'But the Reichsbank business with this man Erhard Schmeltz, it happened so long ago.'

'We still need to check it out. The fact that the date on the back of the photograph and the first drafts being sent to Schmeltz happened in the same year may have some connection. Besides, it may tell us something about Schmeltz's son. Because apart from his name, we've very little to go on.'

The girl looked at him and put down her glass. 'I don't understand – you mean records are kept going back that far?'

Volkmann explained that there were two ways that someone like Reimer's past could be verified. There were two agencies in Germany that kept records of former Nazis and SS personnel. The first was in Zehlendorf in Berlin and called the Berlin Document Centre. It was an American institution funded by the German government and was a repository of Nazi Party organisation documents. In 1945 American troops had captured almost the entire personal records of SS personnel and the Nazi Party and its organisations in various locations throughout Germany. These and other party records were later stored in Berlin in special underground vaults, to help in the prosecution of likely war criminals and to help determine which citizens of the Reich had been Nazi Party members during subsequent de-Nazification.

The second agency was was run solely by the German government. Known as the Z-Commission, and located in the small town of Ludwigsburg in Württemberg, its staff consisted of a small number of dedicated detectives and attorneys whose function it was to investigate, and prosecute if necessary, known war criminals. Whereas the Berlin Document Centre was a repository of Nazi organisation and SS documents, the Z-Commission had actually hunted down Nazis and SS guilty of war crimes and mass murder, and most of the documented files it kept were copies of the ones in Berlin. But because many of those wanted for war crimes were either dead or had been prosecuted, or most likely had long ago managed to cover up their pasts successfully, the staff had found its funds from the Federal Government gradually diminished, and the Z-Commission was gradually being wound down.

Volkmann looked at the girl. 'So the files and records of most former Nazis or SS will be in either Ludwigsburg or Berlin, but Berlin has all the original documents so that's our best bet. They may have no record of Erhard Schmeltz because he left Germany before the Nazis came to power in 1933, but it's worth a try.'

He saw the girl hesitate and turn away, then look back again. 'The aircraft in the area Sanchez mentioned in his report. Could Sanchez find out where it landed?'

Volkmann shrugged. 'If it was anywhere other than a regular airport I doubt it. It could have been another helicopter. In that case it could have landed anywhere there was a clearing big enough. And we're assuming it was the people from the Chaco house. It may not have been.'

The girl brushed her hair from her face. 'So we still have nothing really to go on?'

'Maybe not. What about Winter's old friends from the university?'

'What do you mean?'

'People Winter associated with,' Volkmann said. 'Did you know any of them at Heidelberg?'

'I moved in a different circle of people. But there were a couple of girls I knew in Winter's circle. Why?'

'Did you know anyone who was close to him at Heidelberg?'

He saw the girl hesitate a moment. 'There was a guy named Wolfgang Lubsch from Baden-Baden that Winter seemed pretty close to. I often used to see them drinking together in the old town.'

'Where's Lubsch now? Any idea?'

Erica shook her head. 'No. But I knew his girlfriend, Karen Holfeld. We roomed together for a couple of months. I think she's living in Mainz somewhere.'

'You think you could find her?'

'I could telephone some old girlfriends who might know. She may have lost contact with Lubsch. But if I do find her what do I say?'

Volkmann thought a moment. 'How about you tell her you're writing a piece with a colleague for one of your magazines. Heidelberg students then and now. Tell her you'd like to talk with Lubsch in confidence. You're doing the same with other former students. But keep it low-key. And if you can't find the girl through your own friends I'll put my people on to it.' Volkmann hesitated. 'Was there anyone else you remember who might have known Winter?'

The girl thought for several moments, then looked at him. 'There was another guy I remember. His name was Herman Borchardt. I think he and Winter were friends. But he didn't stay long at the university. His father was a wealthy businessman who owned a string of clubs up in one of the red-light districts in Hamburg. The St Pauli district, I think.'

'Why did Borchardt leave Heidelberg?'

'I think his father died and he dropped out to take over running the clubs.'

'You think you could find him?'

'I guess so.'

'Call him and see if he'll talk to me. Just say I'm a journalist friend of yours writing a story and would like to talk with him. Don't tell him any more unless you have to.'

Volkmann hesitated, looked about the room. For a long time he said nothing, then he turned to look back at Erica.

'I'd like to ask you a question. The house in the Chaco. Did you sense anything strange about it?'

'In what way strange?'

'Apart from the way the house had been left. A feeling. Like an atmosphere.'

The girl put down her fork and Volkmann saw the look on her face. 'I sensed something. But I'm not sure what. The small house, the one next to the *hacienda* . . . I remember I shivered when I stepped inside even though it was a hot day.' Erica Kranz shrugged, then hesitated. 'It was kind of like the feeling you get when you step into a house in which someone has died.' She looked directly at Volkmann. 'Is that what you mean?'

'Maybe. I'm not sure.'

'Is it important?'

Volkmann shrugged again and smiled. 'No. It's not important. Forget it.'

When the waiter had taken away the dishes, the girl reached across and touched Volkmann's hand.

'I would like to say thank you, Joe. Thank you for your help.'

Volkmann looked over at the blue eyes and the pretty face and wondered if she meant it or if she was just a good actress.

He was woken by the telephone ringing in the next room. It was dark in the bedroom, the window open, curtains lifting and falling in a soft breeze. He switched on the bedside lamp and looked at his watch. Midnight. He dressed and went into the living-room.

The girl was sitting by the telephone, a notepad open beside her. She looked tired.

'I've made a lot of calls. I got the number for one of Borchardt's clubs from a reporter I know in Hamburg. When I rang they said Borchardt wasn't there and I'd have to phone the office tomorrow. I told them it was urgent and they gave me the home number of Borchardt's secretary, so I rang her.'

'What did she say?'

'She was pretty annoyed about being called at home. She said Borchardt's in Munich on business and won't be back until the day after tomorrow. I told her I was a journalist and an acquaintance of Herman's from university. I explained a colleague needed to talk with him for a story he was working on and that it was important. She said he wouldn't be free during the day but he would be in one of his places on the Reeperbahn called the Baron Club after six if you wanted to try then. She said she'd pass on the message.'

'Did you manage to find out about Wolfgang Lubsch?'

Erica nodded. 'Through a friend of Karen's . . . A girl I knew in Heidelberg . . . She gave me Karen's phone number. But when I called, Karen seemed very wary, afraid to talk to me.'

'Why?'

'She said Lubsch is keeping a low profile. I got the feeling he's in hiding.'

'Did your friend say why?'

'No. She didn't offer to tell me, so I didn't ask.'

'Where's Lubsch now?'

'I don't know.'

'So how do we contact him?'

'I told Karen what you told me to say. I said I wouldn't use Lubsch's name, but that the article was very important to me. She told me she would phone Lubsch and ask him. She rang back just now and said it's OK.'

'So when do we get to meet him?'

'I've got the name of a bar. It's in an old wine town on the Rhine called Rüdesheim, about an hour's drive from Frankfurt. Tomorrow afternoon we're to be in a place called the Weisses Rossl at four o'clock. Karen asked me not to involve anyone else, apart from us. I assured her she could trust me.'

Volkmann waited until the girl had gone, watching the long shapely legs retreat into the spare bedroom, before he telephoned the night duty officer, Jan De Vries, and requested they check the files for information on Wolfgang

Lubsch of Baden-Baden, a graduate of Heidelberg. De Vries promised to get back to him by eight that morning.

After Volkmann replaced the receiver he crossed to the bookshelves. He found the *Times Atlas* and flicked the pages. He traced with a finger to the place on the border between Paraguay and Brazil named Bahia Negra, where Sanchez had said the radar had picked up the signal. From the map it looked like a small, insignificant town straddling the border on the banks of the river Paraguay. He wondered if Sanchez had made any further progress, but knew the man would make contact if he did.

He replaced the atlas on the shelves and a little later he went into the bedroom and found the Beretta nine-millimetre service pistol, removed it from the belt holster and checked the action. There was a full clip of shells and a spare magazine in the plastic pocket. He left the weapon and the spare magazine on the bedside locker and the holster on the dressing table. Then he went to sit by the window and read through the tape transcript again. When he finished he looked up. It was cold outside and raining now, fine needles scratching at the glass. He lit a cigarette, inhaling slowly.

Chapter Twenty

Rüdesheim.
December 10th,
3 p.m.

The town faced onto the Rhine waterfront, a maze of cosy inns and narrow cobbled streets.

In summer, the pretty wine town would have been flooded with visitors, the Rhine banks awash with the floating hotels and tourist barges that plied the river. But in winter the visitors trickled to a few hardy weekenders who drove from nearby cities and towns.

They had called at Erica's apartment first for her to check her mail and pack some clothes, then took the autobahn to Mainz before turning off for Rüdesheim and past the sleepy villages that peppered the Rhine valley, arriving a little after three.

Volkmann drove through the town to get his bearings then down towards the waterfront and parked the Ford near the railway station. He left the Beretta and his DSE identity card tucked under the driver's seat, and Facilities had provided him with a press ID card.

A couple of squat tourist ferries were tied up for the winter season. It didn't feel like Christmas, but decorations hung in shop windows and in the central Platz a giant pine had been erected, coloured lights winking in the darkening afternoon light.

They walked back uphill through the narrow cobbled alleyways towards the centre of the old town. Most of the *weinstuben* were closed but they found a café open and ordered coffee and pastries.

The girl wore a loose-fitting woollen sweater under a blue

oilskin, jeans and sneakers. Her blonde hair was tied back and she wore hardly any make-up, but her face was still strikingly pretty.

As she sipped her coffee, Volkmann said, 'You had better describe Lubsch to me.'

The girl shrugged. 'He wasn't the kind of guy most women would find attractive. Small. Thinly built. He wore glasses and had red hair. But he looked kind of vulnerable, and at the same time arrogant, if you know what I mean. A dreamer. But bright, very bright.' She paused. 'Does that help?'

Volkmann smiled, 'It's enough. Does your friend Karen still have a relationship with Lubsch?'

The girl hesitated before she spoke. 'I got the feeling she still saw him. She must do, if she was able to contact him.' She smiled. 'And Karen always liked sleeping with intelligent men. At Heidelberg, I think she thought that by sleeping with enough bright undergraduates she'd absorb what she needed to know through osmosis. Maybe she did, but she also got a reputation as a man-eater. Knowing Karen, she probably still sleeps with Lubsch, even though she's married now.'

'Tell me about her.'

'She and her husband run a business together. It's in the centre of Mainz. And her name's no longer Holfeld, but Gries.'

'What kind of business?'

Erica smiled. 'Leatherwear. They supply the sex-show scene and show-business people with stage outfits. Some of it's pretty daring, according to Karen, but business is booming.'

'Which faculty was she in?'

'Politics, the same as Lubsch.'

'Your friend sounds like she picked the wrong faculty.'

Erica smiled. 'Not really. Karen was always interested in politics. But she's also what you might call a very sexual animal. A lot of the guys on campus were glad to help her with her grades in return for bedroom favours.'

'Tell me about your time at the university. You said around the time Rudi visited there were groups who would have supported what Winter said.'

'You mean the remarks about immigrants? It wasn't an organised thing, if that's what you mean. Not so far as I know. Just groups of right-wing students who talked in the inns.'

'What did they talk about?'

Erica shrugged. 'The state of the country, mostly. How they thought Germany had become a half-breed race because of its five million immigrants. When they had drunk too much they usually passed remarks about those students nearby who might have come from immigrant stock.'

'What else do you remember?'

The girl looked away, then back again. 'When they were drunk, they had a rally call. "Germany for the Germans." And once or twice in the inns I saw a hand raised in the Nazi salute. But no one paid much attention. I think most students thought it was stupid, the kind of thing you'd expect from shaven-headed toughs who support the Republican Party.'

'Did it only happen in Heidelberg?'

'No, I believe in other universities also. But it wasn't always a blatant thing. More an undercurrent.'

'What did the university authorities do about it?'

'After there were complaints I think they must have had words with the people involved, because it stopped. And these people had little or no support. Besides, by their final year any support they had seemed to die out.'

'And afterwards?'

'What do you mean?'

'After these people graduated. Did you come across any of them? Did they express the same feelings?'

Erica shook her head. 'There was no one from my faculty involved that I knew of.' She smiled briefly. 'They were more interested in drugs and rock music and sex. Concerning the others I can't say.' She smiled briefly and looked down at the cup held in both hands. When she looked up again she said, 'You know what's strange?'

'Tell me.'

'You make me want to fill the silence by answering your questions. Even confide in you. I'm the journalist. And that's supposed to be my strategy. But with you it doesn't work. Also, it's rather absurd.'

'What is?'

'I spend the night in a man's apartment about whom I know nothing. It's not the kind of thing that usually happens, Joe.'

'And what does usually happen?'

The girl smiled. 'Nothing to write home about, I assure you. I have my work. I listen to my music. I go out with friends. But mainly my work. I'm afraid I'm not *hausfrau* material.'

'You have a boyfriend, Erica?'

She shook her head. 'There's no one special right now.' She looked across at him. 'Don't I get a chance to ask some personal questions?'

Volkmann smiled. 'What would you like to know?'

'Do you like your work, Joe?'

'It's what I'm trained to do.'

'You sound like a regular soldier answering a civilian who's just asked him the same question.' She smiled again. 'But do you really like your work?'

'Yes.'

He smiled back but looked away towards the window, as if to avoid further questions. Dusk falling. Lights coming on in the cobbled street outside.

When he turned back he said, 'There's something you ought to know before we meet Lubsch.'

'What?'

'He isn't the innocent intellectual you made him out to be. He's on the *Bundespolizei* wanted list. He's a known terrorist.'

She stared at him. 'What are you talking about?'

'I had Lubsch's background checked out. He's one of a group that operates from the Swiss border up to Frankfurt. An off-shoot of the Red Army Faction terror group, the RAF. The young man you knew at Heidelberg has dirtied his bib since then. He's been involved in at least two kidnappings and the murder of an industrialist in Freiburg. He also likes to make withdrawals from German banks, without having an account.'

There was a puzzled frown on the girl's face now, her blue eyes staring at him intently.

'I don't understand. You asked me to describe him to you . . .'

'I got my information over the telephone. There wasn't time to wait for a photograph from the *Bundespolizei*.'

He saw a flash of anger in the pretty face. 'Why didn't you tell me before now? If what you say about Lubsch is true, we could both be in danger meeting him.'

'Because there was a chance you might not have wanted to go through with this. And right now it's the only lead we have.'

The girl hesitated and the flash of anger left her face as quickly as it had appeared. 'If it means finding the people who killed Rudi, I'm not afraid to meet him.'

'Then there's no way Lubsch can know I'm with DSE, unless you tell him.' Volkmann produced his press ID card. 'It's genuine. So what you told Karen ought to hold up. And no matter what, stick to our cover story. Understand? If Lubsch learns who I am it could make things awkward.'

'How awkward?'

Volkmann smiled. 'He'd probably try to kill me.'

He saw the girl turn pale. She looked away a moment, then back again.

Volkmann said, 'Are you OK?'

'Yes, I'm OK.'

'It's not going to happen, Erica, if you do as I say, but if you think you can't go through with this, then say it now. Otherwise, one or both of us could end up floating in the Rhine. I didn't bring a weapon with me. If Lubsch is going to meet us, he'll check to see if I'm armed. You can count on it. So we're both taking a risk. But if you want me to help you find the people who killed Rudi, it's a risk you'll have to take.'

'What happens when we have to ask Lubsch about Winter?'

'Play it as it happens, but stick to our cover no matter what.'

He saw the girl hesitate, then nod her head. 'OK.'

'You're sure you can go through with it?'

'Yes.'

He watched her for several moments, searching her face, but he couldn't detect any real fear. Volkmann glanced at his watch and when he looked back he saw the girl's blue eyes looking at him intently before she turned away.

A few moments later he paid the waitress and asked for directions to the Weisses Rossl.

They reached the tavern five minutes later, back down towards the waterfront, an ancient *bierkeller* of dark wooden beams that smelled of smoked sausage and candle-wax.

They were the only customers and Volkmann chose a table at the back next to a fire exit and ordered two glasses of schnapps.

The girl who served them had hardly left their drinks when a clean-shaven, stocky, dark-haired young man came in wearing a grey plastic windcheater. He ordered a beer and sat at the bar as he unfolded a newspaper.

Five minutes passed and Volkmann became conscious of the young man observing them. Now and then he glanced out towards the street. Volkmann recalled Erica's description of Lubsch. The man seated at the bar in no way resembled the terrorist and Volkmann guessed that if he was one of Lubsch's men, he was going to check them out and would make his move soon.

When the girl behind the bar went into a tiny kitchen annexe, sure enough the young man stood up slowly and crossed to their table. One hand remained inside his pocket.

He looked at Erica and said sharply, 'Your name is Erica Kranz?'

'Yes.'

Volkmann saw the man's brown eyes study him. 'You're Volkmann?'

When Volkmann nodded, the young man hesitated, then said to Erica, 'Wolfgang wants me to check you both out.' He half smiled. 'You understand, it's simply a precaution.'

The man's eyes flicked momentarily towards the kitchen where the girl had gone.

'There's an alleyway behind here, directly to the right. Finish your drinks and meet me there in two minutes. When you approach me keep your hands out of your pockets and by your sides. All I want to see in your hands are identity papers. If you see anyone else approaching, pretend you know me and stop to talk. But don't attempt to put your hands in your pockets or do anything foolish. Do you understand?'

Erica began to speak but the man barely perceptibly raised his hand. 'Just do as I say. Otherwise the meeting's off.'

The man turned back towards the bar. He finished his drink and folded his newspaper, bade goodbye to the girl behind the counter as she came out of the kitchen. Volkmann saw him go out the front and veer right and disappear. Volkmann looked at the girl. There was no panic in her face as she stared at him.

'OK, finish your drink and let's do like the man says. You've got ID?'

Erica nodded, searched in her coat pocket, removed her driving licence.

'Keep it in your hand like he says.' They finished their drinks and Volkmann led the way.

The alleyway behind the *bierkeller* was long and narrow and poorly lit. They came out into a small cobbled yard, a light on somewhere overhead, flooding the area. Five metres away Volkmann saw another narrow alleyway leading to a street. The young man was waiting at the mouth of the second alleyway, hands in the pockets of his windcheater.

As they moved towards him he said quietly. 'To the right, please. Quickly. Hands up against the wall. And don't speak.'

He said to Erica, 'I'm going to have to search you too.'

The man's hands moved roughly but expertly over them, searching for concealed weapons. When he finished he told them to turn round.

'Your identity papers.'

They handed them over and the man scrutinised them, turning the photographs towards the light, looking from photographs to faces. He handed them back and looked at Volkmann.

'You came by car?'

'Yes.'

'Did you see anyone following you?'

'No.'

'You're certain?'

'I guess so.'

'I asked if you were certain, Volkmann.'

'So far as we could tell, no one did.'

The man hesitated, then said, 'OK. Follow me. And no questions.' He turned impatiently and led the way down the alleyway behind him.

As they stepped through into a narrow deserted street the young man looked left and right. Then he raised his hand and the dull growl of an engine filled the growing darkness.

A big grey Mercedes delivery van suddenly came out of nowhere and pulled up sharply across their path. A man with pock-marked skin and wearing green overalls sat behind the wheel, gunning the engine.

The side doors of the van opened with a roll of metallic thunder and two young men jumped out. One of them held a Walther pistol in his hand and gestured for Volkmann and Erica to get inside.

The men pushed them forward into the Mercedes and as they clambered in they were forced down roughly onto the floor and then the door banged shut.

'Put these on.'

One of the men thrust two black balaclavas at Volkmann and Erica. Each was eyeless, a small slit at the mouth to breathe through.

When Volkmann hesitated the man seemed to lose his patience and kicked out at him viciously, his boot slamming painfully into Volkmann's thigh.

'Do it! *Now!*'

As Volkmann pulled on the balaclava he saw Erica do the same and then the blackness took over as the young man spoke again.

'Try to move or talk, either of you, and you're both dead.'

The big diesel engine gave a deep noisy roar and the Mercedes lurched and moved forward.

Chapter Twenty-One

The Mercedes van turned off the mountain road and drove down into the heavily wooded valley.

Darkness had fallen and the headlights were on. Five minutes later the driver halted outside the mountain cabin. As he switched off the engine the side door of the Mercedes slid open and the two men in the back climbed out.

Volkmann felt a hand grip his arm and he was pulled out roughly. He could smell the woods, heavy and pine-scented, and hear the sounds of feet crunching on gravel. Seconds later he was being pushed in through a doorway.

Now the smells were different: dry must, rotting wood, rancid food. Wooden floorboards shook under his feet. Almost a minute passed before a hand yanked the eyeless balaclava from his head and in the sudden flood of light that followed he was momentarily blinded.

He blinked. Erica stood beside him. The balaclava was gone and her face was smudged with make-up. She glanced at him briefly before she looked over at a young man wearing wire-rimmed glasses who stood by a shattered window.

The man wore a dark padded windcheater, blue jeans and scuffed white sneakers. He was small and wiry and his face had several days' growth of red stubble. His red hair was untidy and he looked as if he hadn't slept for a week. His features didn't look German to Volkmann, except for the man's eyes, which were very blue and sharp, like the small eyes of a nervous animal, but with a hint of arrogance. His windcheater was unzipped and a Walther automatic pistol was tucked into his trouser belt.

Volkmann guessed from the look on the girl's face that she recognised him and that the man was Wolfgang Lubsch. The young man stared over at them but said nothing.

A portable gas lamp hung from a meathook embedded in a ceiling beam overhead. A second lamp stood on a wooden table in the centre of the filthy room, throwing shadows about the bare timber walls.

Volkmann guessed the room they were in was part of a mountain cabin. A traditional *Berghütte*. One of the many thousands that dotted the German hills and valleys, used by hunters and woodsmen and holidaying families, but this one was old and there was a faint smell of excrement and rot.

Thick wooden beams ran overhead and the only furniture was the ancient pine bench that stood in the centre, four wooden chairs set around it. Two doors led off to other rooms but the cabin looked and smelled like it hadn't been used for some time and it was icy cold.

Volkmann could see a bright moon through the broken window, and cold drafts of wind blew in through the shattered glass. A forest disappeared into blackness, and the dark forms of what looked like hills topped with snow were visible in the far distance.

They had been in the Mercedes for perhaps half an hour, the engine straining uphill for the last half of the journey, and Volkmann guessed they were somewhere in the Taunus mountains north of Rüdesheim, or in the hills that sloped up from the Rhine valley.

Now the young man standing by the window looked over at him. 'Don't even think about trying to make a run for it, Volkmann. You wouldn't get five metres.'

The two young men from the Mercedes stood nearby. One was tall and blond and carried a Kalashnikov AK47 slung over his shoulder. The second man was smaller and ruggedly built. His crooked nose looked as if it had been broken more than once and a jagged scar ran across his forehead. He looked like someone who relished physical contact and he held a stubbed leather truncheon in his right hand as if to prove it.

Volkmann's wallet lay on the table, the contents scattered. The photograph from the Chaco of the blonde young woman lay beside a clutter of paper money and his French driving licence and press ID, and the contents of Erica's handbag had been spilled out next to them.

The man with the truncheon pointed silently to the chairs.

When Volkmann and the girl sat, the young man wearing glasses stepped slowly forward. He looked down at the items scattered on the table before his fingers probed among the pile. He finally picked up Volkmann's driving licence and examined it for several moments, then threw it back down on the table.

He took a pack of cigarettes from the pocket of his windcheater and lit one with a Zippo lighter. As he inhaled, his nervous blue eyes settled on Erica.

The girl looked up at him but said nothing. The young man stared back at her.

'Erica Kranz. It's been a long time. You look as pretty as ever . . .'

'Wolfgang . . .'

'Forgive the dramatics in bringing you here like this, but I'm sure you realise someone in my situation has to tread carefully.' Lubsch paused to smile. 'But then I'm presuming you know why I've been cautious?'

Erica glanced over for a moment at the man brandishing the AK47, then back at Lubsch. 'Because you're a terrorist.'

'That's a question of perspective, surely?' Lubsch smiled again. He removed his glasses and rubbed his eyes. 'So, tell me. Why did you want to meet?'

'I told Karen the reason why.'

Lubsch replaced his glasses and shook his head as he smiled. 'Not for some prissy college article, surely?' Lubsch crossed back to the window and looked at Erica. 'There were others at Heidelberg far more suitable and accessible if that was the case. And besides, I was never destined to be a pillar of German society, now was I?' Lubsch stared at her. 'So let's dispense with any pretension. Tell me the real reason you wanted to meet me.'

Erica hesitated a moment, then said, 'Because we needed your help.'

'Why?'

The girl glanced at Volkmann, then looked back at Lubsch. 'Because we're working on a story together.'

'Karen told me. But what sort of story?' Lubsch smiled. 'Not the one you told Karen about.'

'A man was murdered in Berlin ten days ago. Someone you knew at Heidelberg.'

'Who?'

'Dieter Winter.'

Lubsch paused, but his face showed no reaction. 'I read about it in the papers. What's it got to do with me?'

'We're trying to find who killed Winter and why.'

'And why are you so interested in Winter's death?'

Erica Kranz hesitated. 'Because we think his death is connected to other murders.'

'Really. And what murders might these be?'

She told him about Rudi, Winter and the illegal cargoes. Lubsch inhaled on his cigarette, then shrugged. 'Someone's murdered on the other side of the world. So what's it got to do with me?'

'The police don't know who killed Winter or why. I remembered you knew Winter at Heidelberg. I thought you could help us. That maybe you knew people we could talk with who might know what Winter was involved in, or who his friends were. That's why we needed to meet with you.'

Lubsch looked away a moment, then back again. 'Do you know what these cargoes from South America were?'

'No.'

Lubsch stood there for several moments, not speaking, then looked at Volkmann.

'And what part do you play in all of this, Volkmann?'

'We're working on the story together.'

Lubsch looked down at the table. 'You carry a French driving licence, Volkmann. But you're not French, or German, are you? Your German is rather excellent, but your accent' – Lubsch shook his head as he looked back up – 'a vowel here and there betrays you.'

'I'm British.'

The small blue eyes stared down suspiciously at Volkmann.

'Is there any other reason you're both so interested in Winter, besides what you told me?'

'Should there be?'

'I asked the question, Volkmann. Answer it.'

'There's no other reason.'

For a second Lubsch hesitated, then suddenly he nodded his head, the merest of gestures.

The scar-faced man lifted a hand and the stubbed leather truncheon swished through the air like a blade and struck the left side of Volkmann's face. The force sent Volkmann flying backwards. The man with the truncheon caught the chair and pushed it back again. Erica screamed and a hand went over her mouth.

Volkmann felt the sharp, cutting sting the leather truncheon had left on his face and when his hand went to touch his jaw he felt the painful angry red welt where the weapon had struck flesh.

Lubsch suddenly gripped Volkmann's hair and yanked his head back.

'Are you sure there's no other reason, Volkmann?'

'I told you . . .'

Lubsch stared into Volkmann's eyes. 'Then listen to me, Volkmann. Listen to me both of you. Number one, I don't help smart reporters who set me up for a meeting on the pretext of some stupid story. Number two, I take a very poor view of people wasting my time and putting me at risk meeting them. Do you understand?'

Lubsch waited for an answer. When Volkmann didn't reply, the terrorist yanked Volkmann's hair back savagely.

'I asked you a question, Volkmann. Do you understand?'

'Yes.'

'Good.'

Lubsch released his grip and turned to Erica as the hand covering her mouth came away.

'And you. Don't try to contact Karen again. What Volkmann got was a friendly warning. Next time, there won't be one. For either of you. And there's something else I want you both to understand. You're on dangerous ground sniffing around

Winter's friends. If you want to stay alive, forget about him and your story.'

Lubsch nodded to the man with the truncheon, who turned and went outside. Moments later came the sound of the Mercedes starting up.

The man with the AK47 removed the lamp hanging from the meathook in the beam overhead, then slipped outside. Then came the rumble of the van door sliding open.

Lubsch picked up the second lamp and crossed to the door. He looked back at Volkmann and Erica.

'Remember what I said. And be grateful you're both still alive.'

Lubsch extinguished the lamp and the small cabin plunged into darkness. Footsteps crunched on the gravel outside and a door slammed shut.

The Mercedes moved off down the track. Its engine noise faded and there was only silence and darkness and the fetid smells of the cabin.

They followed the track through the forest and it took them half an hour to reach the village. The name on the sign as they entered said Kiedrich. It was pitch dark and, when Volkmann and the girl stepped into the first inn they saw open, the half-dozen customers inside looked at them warily.

The girl looked pale and her lips trembled. Their clothes were covered in mud after the walk through the woods and they tried to ignore the stares of the people in the inn. Volkmann went into the toilet and threw cold water on his face. The welt had swollen painfully and it hurt when the water touched his skin, but the flesh hadn't been cut.

When he came out Erica had ordered two brandies and Volkmann asked the innkeeper for some ice. He put a couple of ice cubes in a handkerchief the girl gave him and pressed it on the welt on his face.

According to the innkeeper they were twenty kilometres from Rüdesheim and there was a taxi service in the town but when Volkmann telephoned, he was told the only driver available had taken a local girl to hospital in Wiesbaden and it would be another half-hour before the taxi could pick them up.

The innkeeper asked Volkmann if he was all right or if he wanted to call a doctor but Volkmann told him no, and the man shrugged and inquired no further.

It was almost an hour before the taxi came and another half-hour by the time they arrived back in Rüdesheim. The Ford was still parked near the station and they drove back to the girl's apartment, arriving just after seven.

Erica looked at his swollen face and went into the kitchen. She came back with some ice cubes wrapped in a cloth and a bottle of schnapps. She poured two large measures and handed one to Volkmann after he had taken the cloth. She went to sit on the couch and looked over at him as he dabbed his face.

'Are you OK, Joe?'

Volkmann tried to smile and winced with pain. 'Sure.' He noticed the girl's hands were trembling as she sipped her drink. 'What about you?'

The girl shivered. 'I thought Lubsch was going to kill us. Do you think he meant what he said?'

'Yes, I do.'

'You think he knows something about Winter?'

Volkmann put down the cool cloth. He picked up his glass and looked at her.

'I think Lubsch has something to hide. If there was nothing to his relationship with Winter he would have told us and been done with it. And I doubt he would have threatened us.'

'Why do you think he wanted to warn us off?'

'I don't know, Erica. Only Lubsch can tell us that. I'd like to know why he wanted to know if we were interested in Winter for any other reason besides the one you gave him.'

'You're not going to try and contact him again, are you, Joe?'

He looked at the girl and shook his head before he sipped the warm schnapps and put down his glass. His mouth hurt when he swallowed.

'People like Lubsch don't give second warnings. If we try to contact him again he'll do as he said.'

'So what do we do now?'

Volkmann hesitated and thought a moment. 'I want you to drive down to my place in the morning and wait for me there. I'll give you a key. I think it's better after what's happened that you stay out of Frankfurt for now.' He looked at the girl. 'You've got a car?'

She nodded. 'Yes, it's down in the parking lot. You're sure? About staying in your place?'

'It's for your own safety, Erica. If Lubsch is in contact with Winter's friends, it's best this way. They may come looking for you or both of us.'

The girl was silent for several moments, then she stood up and said, 'Do you want me to get some more ice?'

Volkmann shook his head. 'No, but another drink wouldn't go amiss.'

She took the dripping cloth from him and poured him another full glass. He watched her as she went back into the kitchen. She seemed to have calmed down but she still looked pale. The incident with Lubsch had had its effect and the girl hadn't turned down his offer to stay at his place. She seemed genuinely afraid.

He stood and crossed to the window and pulled back the curtain. The wind had died and it was a clear calm night and the Rhine barges moved slowly back and forth on the water. Across the street by the river he saw a group of youths with shaven heads drinking from cans of beer as they strolled towards the Eisener Steg, their harsh, guttural voices carrying in the darkness.

She had made dinner for them and afterwards she turned on the radio, a Schubert violin concerto playing softly in the background. They sat on the couch and after she poured them another drink she looked over at him.

She hesitated before she spoke, brushed a strand of hair from her face. 'You're such a strange man, Joseph Volkmann.'

'In what way strange?'

'I get the feeling nothing frightens you. Me, I'm still trembling inside after meeting Lubsch. Doesn't anything frighten you?'

'The same things as most people.'

'Tell me about yourself, Joe.'

'What do you want to know?'

'Anything. Everything.' Erica hesitated and smiled. 'You're a stranger to me, and yet I feel safe with you.'

Volkmann picked up his glass. 'There isn't much to tell.'

'Are you married?'

'Divorced.'

'You had children?'

'No, no children, Erica.'

The girl looked at him. 'Tell me about your family. In your apartment there was a photograph. Of you as a small boy, I think. The couple were your parents?'

When Volkmann hesitated, Erica lifted her glass, held it in both hands. She was ignoring his reticence and Volkmann guessed maybe she was talking out of nervousness.

'You've heard of Cornwall?'

'Yes. It's in the south-west of England.'

'The photograph was taken there, by the sea. It's where my parents spent their summers when I was a child.'

'What did your father do?'

'He was a lecturer at a university.'

'Do you see him often?'

'He's dead. He died six months ago.'

'I'm sorry . . . ' Erica paused, then looked back at him. 'He looked very much like you. You never wished to follow in his footsteps?'

'For a time, yes. But after university I couldn't seem to fit into a teaching job, and office work bored me. So I took the King's shilling instead.'

'The King's shilling . . .?'

Volkmann smiled and his jaw hurt. 'It's an expression. It means to enlist. I joined the army as an officer cadet.'

'Was your father proud of you?'

'My father hated uniforms, Erica. He didn't particularly like the idea. But I had my mind made up.'

'How come you ended up in DSE?'

Volkmann half smiled. 'That's a long story. And probably

covered by the Official Secrets Act. Let's just say I was seconded.'

'Tell me more about your family, Joe. I'd like to hear.'

Volkmann looked away a few moments, then back again. 'My old lady used to be a concert pianist only she doesn't play professionally any more. Her fingers have become rusty with age, but you can't tell her that.' He smiled. 'She doesn't accept old age gracefully. My father used to say she was only ever happy sitting on a rostrum playing piano with a spotlight on her.'

Erica smiled back. 'She sounds like a *gnädige Frau.*' She paused. 'Were you like your father, Joe?'

'In some ways, yes.'

'He didn't look like an Englishman.'

'And how are Englishmen supposed to look?'

'I meant he looked more middle-European. Tall and dark.'

Volkmann was silent a moment, then he said, 'He was a refugee, Erica, he and my mother both. They went to England after the war. My mother was from Hungary, my father from the Sudetenland. You've heard of the Sudetenland?'

The girl hesitated. 'It was an area in Czechoslovakia that the Nazis claimed was German soil.'

'A minority of the people who lived there were of German origin. My father's family lived there, in a town called Smolna.'

'They came from Germany?'

'Yes, they came from Germany. They were Jews, German-speaking Jews. Volkmann isn't exclusively a Jewish name but that's what they were.' He saw a look of surprise on the girl's face and she blushed. 'That's how I learned my German. For a long time it was the only language my father spoke. He always spoke English badly.'

The girl said quietly, 'And your mother's family? They were Jewish also?'

'Hungarian and Catholic. So I guess that makes me half-Jewish.'

'Do you go to the synagogue?'

'No. My father's family weren't Orthodox Jews. They were

Jews in name only. When I was a child my father took me only once to the synagogue, just to show me what it looked like and satisfy my curiosity. But that was as far as he went in his religious commitment.'

Erica put down her glass. For a long time she was silent, then she said, 'The war must have been terrible for your father.'

Volkmann hesitated. 'He was in a camp, if that's what you mean. That's where he first met my mother. They were both sixteen. They used to meet at the wire separating the men's compound from the women's. When the camp was liberated, they lost each other. They met again in London after the war and married.'

'I don't understand. Why was your mother in a camp? She wasn't Jewish.'

'Not only Jews were sent to the camps. Intellectuals, homosexuals, vagrants, gypsies. Even respectable, middle-class ordinary people like my mother's family. Anyone whom the Nazis considered a threat to the Reich, however feeble the reasons. Surely you knew that?'

He saw the look on her face then and she turned away. When she looked back she said, 'It was a terrible time . . . For Jews, for Germany, for everyone. You must hate Germans?'

Volkmann stared at her for a long time and then he said, 'Not hate, but distrust. And not individuals. Just the whole collective psyche thing. How your countrymen could let it all happen. I worked in Berlin for three years. I used to wake nights, thinking of what had happened here in this country of yours. To my parents and people like them.'

The girl was silent for several moments, then she looked at him and said, 'There's something I don't understand.'

'What don't you understand?'

'You said your father hated uniforms. But you chose to wear a uniform. Why?'

He shrugged. 'Because maybe I always wanted to protect him.'

'From what?'

Volkmann hesitated, turned his face away. He heard the

Schubert die in the background, the soft strains of the violin washing away.

'From anyone who might try to hurt him again.'

When he turned back he saw the girl looking at him. Was it compassion and understanding in her eyes or something else?

Volkmann hesitated, then looked away again. 'How in God's name did we get into that?'

'I'm sorry, forgive me, Joe. I shouldn't have been so inquisitive.'

Volkmann stood up slowly. 'I think I need some coffee.'

He was standing over the sink rinsing a cup when she came in to him moments later.

'Joe . . .?'

He turned, saw the girl standing there, looking up into his eyes. She spoke softly.

'When you came to my apartment at first I thought you were distant. Maybe even rude and arrogant. And that you didn't like me. Maybe that feeling was even mutual. But in Asunción when I cried I felt you cared. I felt you knew what pain was.' The blue eyes looked into his face. 'Something terrible once happened to your Papa, didn't it, Joe?'

He did not reply but stood there, looking into her face.

She said, 'Would it sound terrible if I asked to kiss you, Joe?'

She was standing close to him. Her fingers gently touched his lips before she moved her body against his, Volkmann feeling the softness of the full, womanly figure, the warmth of her breasts comforting and full against his chest, her lips meeting his mouth softly at first, then more fiercely as they kissed and she pressed her body hard against his.

When they finally drew apart, she looked up at him and said, 'I think I've wanted to do that since Asunción.'

They could see the patina of sweat on Felder's fleshy face and almost smell the man's fear as they stood in the Grunewald. Spring was in the cold dawn air and as the yellow sunlight filtered through the canopy of trees overhead Volkmann remembered how absurd it was: the trees budding into life and Felder about to die.

The big East German had his hands tied behind his back and he was shaking as his eyes flicked nervously from Ivan Molke to Volkmann. They both trained the silenced Berettas on Felder and he had started to quake as soon as they had stepped from the car.

As they stepped into the clearing, Felder began to plead and Molke said quietly, 'Turn round and look away, Felder. It'll be easier.'

Suddenly Felder seemed to break, anger taking over. 'Anything I did was on orders, I swear it.'

Ivan Molke shook his head. 'You want to know something, Felder? Your people at Karlshorst will think we've done them a favour.'

There were beads of sweat on Felder's brow and he said, 'Yes, I killed two of your people. But I did it on orders. I swear.'

'That's not what your people are saying. They're saying you overstepped your authority.'

'It's a fucking lie.'

There was a sudden noise from behind and Molke and Volkmann turned. A pigeon flew out of the low branches, its wings beating furiously in the silence of the forest.

Volkmann heard the grunting noise from behind and as Volkmann turned back he saw Felder make a run for the trees.

Volkmann raised the Beretta and fired.

The first shot hit Felder in the back of the head, his body punched forward, the second hit him in the shoulder as he stumbled. The big man groaned and rolled over on his back, his eyes wide with pain. Molke ran forward and pumped another shot into Felder's barrel chest. As he lay on the ground, blood pumping from his wounds, a harsh gurgling sound came from his open mouth.

Molke looked at Volkmann and said hoarsely, 'Get the shovels from the car.'

When Volkmann hesitated, staring down at the body, Molke said again, 'Get the shovels from the car, Joe. We haven't got all bloody day.'

For a few moments more Volkmann said nothing, just stood there with the Beretta in his hand, staring down at Felder in his last moments of life, the smell of cordite mingling with the fresh smell of the woods around him. He had killed and seen men killed before, but never so close that he could hear their dying breath. Then he looked up and was aware of the cold sweat on his forehead and the feeling of nausea in the pit of his stomach as he walked back towards the car.

As he removed the shovels from the boot he heard the faint crack of Molke's Beretta.

He came back and Molke said, 'Are you OK?'

'Sure.'

Volkmann looked down at the body. There was a trickle of blood at Felder's right temple where Molke had given him the coup de grâce.

Volkmann suppressed the bile rising in his throat, looked instead at Molke and asked, 'What he said, was it true?'

Molke took one of the shovels and started digging two metres from where Felder lay.

'No way, Joe. When he wouldn't talk, we gave him scopalomine, the truth drug. Felder was an evil bastard. He got a kick out of torture. He was getting out of control. When our people broke into his flat off the Friedrichstrasse they found the usual stuff people like him are into.'

'What?'

'Pornographic books and video tapes. Pretty violent stuff. A real chamber of horrors. Kiddies being raped. Women being cut up. Felder was trash. One of our contacts in Karlshorst told us even the Stasi and KGB guys were shocked at what he did to our two men.'

Volkmann looked away and started to dig. The earth was soft and moist, the sweet humus of the forest rising up to their nostrils. A metre deep and then they would bury Felder.

'But they'll know what happened to him when he doesn't turn up.'

'Sure, and they'll put two and two together and be grateful. They'll know it was quid pro quo. *We'd expect the same if any of our people acted like Felder. There are unwritten rules,*

Joe, and Felder broke them.' There was a sharp crack as the shovel hit something hard and Ivan Molke suddenly stopped digging and stared down at the soil, a look of horror on his face.

'Jesus . . .'

It was then Volkmann saw the top of the muddied skull in the fresh soil and as Molke's shovel turned it over, there was another skull beneath.

Molke had turned pale and as he knelt down he took out his gloves and pulled one on, picked up the skull, placed it beside him, then the other, before he clawed at the earth with his gloved fingers. There was a tangle of bones, the remains of two bodies and it looked to Volkmann as if they had been there for a long time. There were neat holes drilled in the back of each skull. Molke turned away and vomited.

'Cover it up again.'

'But . . .'

Molke wiped his mouth with the back of his hand. 'Just do it. Cover it up, we'll bury Felder some place else.'

There was sweat now on Molke's face and brow and Volkmann remembered thinking it absurd that Molke could be so calm seeing Felder's bloodied corpse while the skeletal remains had deeply affected him.

As they drove back towards the city an hour later Molke was silent.

It had started to rain and ten minutes from the Kurfurstendamm Ivan Molke pulled up outside a café and filling station on the autobahn and switched off the engine.

'Let's have a drink.'

His hands were shaking and Volkmann followed him inside and they found a quiet table away from the groups of noisy truck drivers. Volkmann ordered a coffee and Molke asked for a double schnapps and turned to look silently beyond the window at the early-morning traffic. When the waiter had left, Volkmann looked at his colleague. The older man swallowed half his schnapps then looked away again, his mind preoccupied as his hand gently massaged his neck.

'What do we do about the remains we found?'

Molke looked at Volkmann and said quietly, 'Nothing. Whoever they were they've been dead a long time. I just didn't want a bastard like Felder buried beside them.'

'I don't understand.'

Molke looked at him. 'The bodies, they've been there since the war.'

'How can you be so sure?'

'Joe, I was born in Berlin. My father too. The Sicherheitsdienst *and SS used to take people out to the Grunewald and put a bullet in the back of their skulls. Communists. Socialists. Jews. People they didn't want to bother sending to the camps or to prison. They simply took them out into the woods and shot them.' He considered a moment, the irony striking him. 'Just like we did with Felder. Except these people were not like him. They were just ordinary people.'*

'How can you know for sure?'

'About the bodies? My old man was in Flossenberg.'

Volkmann looked at him. 'He was Jewish?'

'No, he was a socialist. He managed to hide out until forty-four. Then one night the Sicherheitsdienst *raided the house where he was in hiding. They took him away, and the people who had hidden him. My uncle, his wife, their two young boys, they took to the Grunewald. My old man they sent to the camps. Ravensbrück first, then Flossenberg.'*

'Your father died there?'

Molke shook his head. 'He survived. He lived in Hamburg in an old folk's home until his death five years ago. I guess Berlin had too many memories for him.' Molke looked away, towards the window and the cold spring morning and the passing traffic. 'When he came home after the war he was in limbo. Nothing mattered. Flossenberg finished him. He was never the same. My old lady and him split up. She said she couldn't live with a ghost. That's what he was, a ghost.'

There was a look of grief on Molke's face and then he said, 'You know what the strange thing was? The day he died one of the old SS camp guards at Flossenberg was in a Munich courtroom. They'd been waiting fifteen years to bring the bastard to trial. But because he had such a good defence attorney he'd managed to hold off the case with legal wrangling. The guy must have been nearly eighty. He'd killed men with his bare hands. But the jury took pity on him because he was an old man and near death and gave him a suspended sentence. One year.' Molke gritted his teeth. 'A week after I buried my father there was a picture in the Münchner Post *of the old SS guy coming out of court with a smile on his face and waving to his friends and family. He didn't look near death to me. I'd like to have put a bullet in the bastard's head. You know what his defence attorney said? "Justice has been done." ' Molke shook his head. 'The longer I live in this world the more I realise there's no such thing as justice. Not real justice. There's an old saying. Every sin has its own Avenging Angel. But it never works out that way. You know what I mean?' Molke hesitated, looked at Volkmann. 'What about your old man? He's alive, Joe?'*

'Yes.'

'You see him much?'

Volkmann looked away towards the window, wanting to tell Molke, but hesitating. Not then, not there. Another time.

'Sure.'

'You're lucky, Joe. Sons need fathers as much as fathers need sons.'

Chapter Twenty-Two

It's a long drive from Frankfurt to Hamburg and it took Volkmann most of the following day.

He left the girl that morning at ten, watched as she put her suitcase in the white Volkswagen he had seen parked in the front lot of the apartment block, before she set off for Strasbourg.

The weather was crisp and clear and Volkmann took the autobahn north to Kassel and then on to Hanover, past the sprawling carpet of Lüneburg Heath. It was almost five when he drove over the Elbe river, heading west into the area of Neustadt, until he came to the glittering ribbon of the Reeperbahn in the St Pauli district. The centre of Hamburg was brilliant with Christmas decorations and St Pauli's infamous red-light area was ablaze with neon and busy with customers.

He found the Baron Club off the Holstenstrasse and parked the Ford in one of the side-streets and walked back.

It was Sunday and only six in the evening but the blue neon sign outside flashed in the cold evening air and loud rock music came from inside. The club was small and clean but the soft red lighting gave it a dingy appearance. There was a tiny stage off to the left and fake-leather couches and easy chairs were set out in front and around the walls. A couple of girls sat around smoking and chatting with two middle-aged men who looked like the only customers. The stage was lit with a spotlight and a beautiful Filipino-looking girl was dancing to the rock music. She wore only a tiny pair of black briefs and above her a video screen showed a blue movie.

He gave his name to the girl behind the bar and asked if he could speak with Herman Borchardt. The girl told him to wait and came back a little later followed by a man.

He was tall and blond with a thin moustache. He was very good- looking and wore an expensive pale grey suit but had a seedy air about him and Volkmann found it hard to imagine him as a Heidelberg student. He carried a portable phone in his hand and when Volkmann had introduced himself, Borchardt led the way to a vacant table.

Volkmann asked all the relevant questions and the young man listened quietly, but by the time Volkmann had finished it was apparent that Borchardt had little if nothing to say and his disinterest was obvious. Every now and then he kept looking around the club or glancing at his watch.

He showed no interest in the fact or circumstances of Winter's murder and claimed he had not really known him well at Heidelberg. As to Winter's friends he could not recall any of them. He admitted to meeting Winter occasionally at parties or on campus, but he had never heard of Kesser and did not remember Winter ever discussing politics.

The only time Borchardt showed any mild interest was when Volkmann asked him if Winter had done drugs.

Borchardt smiled. 'Everyone did drugs on campus, Volkmann. Hard and soft. Has Winter's death got to do with drugs?'

'I don't know, Herr Borchardt.'

Borchardt shrugged. 'Sorry I can't help you, Volkmann. But I only spent a year on campus and that was long enough. I hardly remember Winter.'

Volkmann watched the young man's eyes, but he seemed to be telling the truth.

'You remember Erica?'

Borchardt grinned. 'Who wouldn't? She was a great looker. All the guys had the hots for her.' Borchardt picked up his portable phone as if to signal the end of the conversation.

As Volkmann stood, Borchardt smiled and said, 'When you see her, send her my love.'

It was almost seven but Volkmann decided to make the long drive back to Frankfurt rather than stay the night in Hamburg.

It took him over five hours to cover the drive south with only a brief stop for a meal outside Kassel, and when he reached Frankfurt it was almost 1 a.m.

He removed the Beretta from under the driver's seat and slipped it into his pocket before he went up to the girl's apartment.

His body ached with tiredness and he made himself a coffee. He sat on the couch for ten minutes resting his eyes and then he went to look around the apartment, starting with the living-room. He didn't know what he was looking for and he disliked having to search through the girl's personal belongings but he knew it had to be done.

Beside the computer terminal there was a neat stack of papers and a small wooden filing cabinet. He searched through the papers first. They were mostly rough drafts of magazine articles and correspondence related to her work; magazine and newspaper cuttings high-lighted in marker pen and some copies of her own articles cut from popular German magazines. The filing cabinet was unlocked and he looked through it. There were more magazine articles under indexed headings and lots of filed correspondence from editors.

He was aware of the scent of the girl's perfume as he went through the cupboards and drawers in her bedroom. Her clothes and underwear were put away neatly in the drawers and under some panties and stockings he found a bundle of old letters addressed to her with Paraguayan stamps. They were all in Spanish, except for a couple of greetings in German, and they were all signed by Rudi Hernandez. He replaced them and looked through the other drawers. There was another stack of letters, from an old boyfriend, he guessed, with a Darmstadt postal marking, stamped the year before.

He checked under the mattress and found two old diaries, but many of the pages were illegible and most of the entries were simply shopping lists or reminders of meetings with girlfriends. He saw no references to Karen Holfeld or Gries but the pages containing addresses at the back of both diaries had been torn out.

There were two slim photograph albums on the top shelf in the mirrored sliding wardrobe. One of them contained mostly photographs from the girl's childhood and there were pictures of Erica and her mother and sister that appeared to have been taken in Argentina; some on the beach and others in what looked like the grounds of a spacious villa, crimson bougainvillaea against white walls in the background. In a couple the girl wore a bikini, the skimpy swimsuit showing off her long legs and full breasts.

He flicked through the cellophaned leaves and at the end of the album he saw an old black-and-white photograph of a group of men and women standing around the pool sipping drinks with the blonde woman, Erica's mother. The shot was slightly out of focus and the faces were blurred, but the men looked European rather than Latin. The second album contained mostly photographs of the girl in her teens and twenties, taken with friends at Heidelberg, and a couple with Rudi Hernandez, one of them a copy of the same photograph he had seen in Hernandez' apartment.

He put the albums back on the shelf. There were some boxes containing old jewellery and trinkets and a stack of old records and tapes on the wardrobe floor and he looked through them all carefully.

He checked through the rails of clothes, searching in pockets but found nothing of interest. When he had made sure everything was back in its place he checked the bathroom. Perfumes and make-up and some pills and herbals in plastic bottles.

He crossed back into the kitchen and washed the coffee cup and replaced it on the hook, then went into the living-room and sat on the couch. He knew that because Borchardt had proved a dead-end there was really no other way he could go but to make contact with Lubsch again. He sat there for five minutes before he stood up and picked up the commercial directory by the telephone and found the name and address in Mainz.

He wrote down the address and then went to the bookshelves and took down the Rhine-Palatinate *Länd* map. There was a street map of Mainz and he found the street near the cathedral where Karen Gries had her shop.

Stockholm,
Sweden.
December 12th,
7.30 p.m.

The restaurant was ten kilometres from Stockholm along the north coast, an intimate place of log fires and pine tables near Saltsjöbaden. There were only half a dozen other customers in the place, and with typical Scandinavian respect for privacy they ignored Shaeffer and his companion.

The food was really rather excellent, Shaeffer thought, as he chewed a delicious mouthful of fried Baltic herring then washed it down with a sip of ice-cold beer. It was a pity about the company.

The Turk had hardly spoken. He was tall and thin, with a haunted look in his dark brown eyes. In his late twenties, his prematurely thinning black hair was brushed back off his face and he wore a cheap, ill-fitting suit. He had a permanent frown on his handsome face, though the man's eyes regarded Shaeffer with wary detachment, and when he did speak he spoke good German. Shaeffer noticed the thick pink scars on the backs of the man's hands.

Shaeffer looked across the table. 'I take it the meal is to your satisfaction?'

Kefir Ozalid sipped his mineral water and spoke quietly. 'Yes, thank you.'

Polite but distant. As if the man disliked Shaeffer. The Turk had irritated him from the beginning of the meeting. Had it not been for the excellent *smörgåsbord*, Shaeffer considered, the evening would have been thoroughly boring.

It was almost an hour later, after the near-silent meal and the post-prandial drinks – the Turk drank only mineral water throughout – that the waiter returned with their overcoats and Shaeffer and his companion stepped out onto the cold, snowy street.

A wooden promenade overlooked the glassy, freezing sea across the street, a small desolate harbour nearby. He could understand why the Turk had chosen such a place, obviously a summer resort of some sort, Shaeffer reflected, never having been here before; but in winter it was deserted and eerie, the harbour town in the grip of a desolate hibernation. The road out from Stockholm had been almost empty of traffic. A following vehicle would have been easy to spot.

He watched now as the young man pulled up the collar of his frayed overcoat and tugged on his woollen gloves, then gestured for Shaeffer to follow him across to the promenade.

They walked along the hollow boardwalk for several minutes, the Turk silent, their breaths foggy in the chilled Baltic air and Shaeffer's teeth chattered in the freezing cold after the warmth of the restaurant's log fires. It was a clear December night and to the south the lights of the archipelago that was Stockholm winked in the darkness.

Shaeffer could see the young man's dark, handsome face when he stopped under a boardwalk streetlamp to look out towards the glassy sea. The face was expressionless: it was time to talk.

'There have been no changes to the plan?' Ozalid asked finally.

'None.'

Shaeffer hesitated as the man took a cigarette from a crumpled packet inside his overcoat pocket and lit it. The Turk blew a ring of pungent-smelling smoke into the frosty air and continued to stare out at the freezing Baltic waters, a haunted look on his face.

Shaeffer said, 'And you, there are no last-minute doubts?'

The young man shook his head. 'None.' There was a finality in the Turk's reply and he looked at Shaeffer. 'Your people will keep to their agreement?'

'Of course,' Shaeffer replied. 'Concerning the financial arrangements . . . I have been authorised to transfer the money to the Swiss account once your part of the bargain has been kept.'

The Turk looked away, a haunted look on his face, as if the money was of no importance. As he stared out at the cold, dark sea Shaeffer removed an envelope from his pocket, handed it across.

'All the necessary details are inside. Destroy them once you have memorised them. The airline ticket is in the name on your false passport. I suggest you pay careful attention to the passport photograph. You should appear as in the photograph you sat for. Also, the clothes you wear should reflect your alias. I have made a list and the money in the envelope should more than cover your expenses.'

'There is no change concerning my identity?'

Shaeffer shook his head. 'None. You are a businessman trading with a Berlin electronics company. Should there be any problems with immigration, the telephone number of the company in the envelope can be given to confirm that.' Shaeffer paused. 'You know what to do. But I suggest you familiarise yourself with the surroundings first. The boat will be left by the lake as we agreed. Also, use public transport, not taxis. There is less chance of you being remembered. Do you have any questions?'

The Turk shook his head and Shaeffer said, 'If there is anything you feel needs further explanation, you may contact me at any time using the usual precautions.'

The Turk placed the envelope in his pocket.

Shaeffer added, 'Once you reach the safe house, our people will give you safe passage to Switzerland. From then on you are on your own.'

The Turk flashed a rare smile, but no humour there, a resigned look on his face.

'Presuming I live, of course?'

Shaeffer smiled back. 'I'm sure you will.'

'*Allaha ismarladik.*'

Shaeffer gave the expected reply, before the Turk turned abruptly and walked back across the snowy street.

Snow was falling as the Turk entered the drab apartment building near Stockholm's Södertälje district.

He went up in the creaking lift to the eighth floor. Graffiti on the walls in languages he didn't understand; the noisy, overcrowded apartment block bursting at the seams with immigrants. Ethnic music blared its discordant strains on every floor the lift passed, and children cried out in incomprehensible tongues.

The Tower of Babel, the tenants called it. Africans. Arabs. Vietnamese. Turks. Kurds. Refugees who had dreamed of a better life and found they had traded their dignity for a nightmare.

Despite the shabbiness of the building the apartment offered a panoramic view of Stockholm. He switched on the lights, removed his overcoat and went to pour himself a mineral water. He took a sip and went to stand by the window. The lights in the city and harbour winked beyond the thick fall of snow. Like the snow that fell on the blue mountains in Izmir in winter. Only thicker, more incessant, and for a brief moment it made him think of home and Layla.

He tried to ignore the thought as he took the envelope from his pocket, ripped it open and studied the contents carefully. Half an hour later he put the contents back in the envelope and replaced them in his pocket, then lit a cigarette from a packet of Turkish he kept on the scratched pine coffee table.

Something bothered him about the meeting. Something bothered him about the whole thing. Something not quite right. He had sensed it from the start.

He didn't feel comfortable. Not about what he intended doing, but about the people and the plan. A doubt in the back of his head like a throbbing that wouldn't go away.

Yet he had accepted it knowingly; he so wanted to kill the man who had allowed his life to be flooded with grief. And if his own life was forfeit, then so be it. He had resigned himself to that.

For Layla.

Allah was with him, he sensed it in his bones. He glanced down at the thick pink scars that ran in puckered, unsightly waves along his hands and arms. He thought again of Layla.

Of the big, dark brown eyes lifting to his face, the skin white as milk, the sweet clean smell of her hair and the taste of her breath like honey on his lips, seeing her for the first time all those years ago in his father's village in the mountains. A young, innocent girl in bare feet. Far too beautiful for him.

He looked up at the photograph of her above the unlit fireplace and still he wanted to cry, no matter how long ago the pain. *Smiling Layla. Beautiful Layla.*

He finished drinking the water and put down the glass, tried to push away the thoughts creeping in on him: the fire consuming flesh, the sadistic grins on the faces of the men with shaven heads, laughing as fires raged around their victims. And Layla, beautiful Layla, her body bloated with their love, unable to move.

Hate made him want to do this. Hate made him want to kill.

A fleck of cigarette ash fell on his shabby suit, distracting him; he brushed it away fastidiously, then stubbed out the cigarette, before the salt tears came.

Minutes later, he had unrolled the bright blue woollen prayer mat, placed it facing the window.

When he had said his prayers, when he had prayed for Layla, he rolled up the prayer mat and kissed it as if he were kissing her again, then placed the mat on the shelf beside the fire.

Chapter Twenty-Three

Mainz

Volkmann took the A66 autobahn to Wiesbaden and across the Rhine into Mainz, arriving just after ten.

He parked the Ford in a twenty-four-hour underground car park near the cathedral and walked to Karen Gries's address.

The MarktPlatz was busy with Christmas shoppers. A maze of alleyways and shopping malls branched off from the street proper and Karen Gries's shop was on the first floor above a modern art gallery. Volkmann spent half an hour walking up and down the street, referencing the layout of the minor roads and side-streets to the tourist map he had studied in Erica's apartment.

It was cold and the sky overcast and as he walked up and down the street near the cathedral he tried to figure out the plan in his mind.

There was a bar almost directly opposite, and the name overhead said Zum Dortmunder. Maybe seventy metres away was a shopping mall. On the mall's first floor was a smart Konditorei whose panoramic window looked down onto the street, and Volkmann reckoned there was a clear view back to Karen Gries's premises.

He bought a copy of the *Frankfurter Zeitung* and went up to the café, sat by the window and ordered a coffee. As he sat there smoking a cigarette he watched the street below. The view either side was unobstructed and he could see Karen Gries's place clearly, about fifty metres to the left, on the opposite side of the street.

When the waitress came with his coffee, he asked her what time the Konditorei stayed open to and the girl told him they stopped serving fifteen minutes before the mall closed, at eight.

Volkmann sat there for another twenty minutes. When he had familiarised himself with the layout of the street he folded his newspaper and tucked it in his pocket. He went downstairs to the mall and crossed the road.

There were two alleyways nearby within twenty metres of each other on the same side as Karen Gries's shop. One led to the back of a bakery shop and then on to a public car park. On the opposite side he knew there were three alleyways before the street ended, because he had already checked them and two hadn't been noted on the map. For the plan to work so much depended on luck and timing, even assuming Karen Gries would take the bait.

A narrow flight of stairs led up to a landing and a glass-fronted door. There was red carpet on the stairs and the sign on the frosted glass said, *Lederwaren bei Bruno & Karen Gries*.

Rails of leather clothes lined both sides, covered in sheets of plastic, and when Volkmann stepped inside the sweet smell of leather was almost overwhelming. He saw a balding, middle-aged man showing a woman a skirt on one of the racks.

Behind the man was a glass-fronted office and beyond the glass a young, pretty woman with tight-cropped blonde hair and wearing a leather jumpsuit sat talking with an oriental woman. Volkmann guessed the young woman with the cropped blonde hair was Karen Gries and the middle-aged man was probably her husband.

Volkmann went to look around and a few moments later he heard voices behind him and saw the blonde woman walk to the door with the oriental. The blonde kissed the woman on the cheek and handed her a plastic shopping bag and when the woman had gone, she came over to Volkmann.

'Can I help you?'

She was smiling at him and her figure was a little too ample for the tight leather outfit she had on. She had a very sexy face but up close Volkmann saw she was attractive rather than pretty and she wore too much make-up.

Her lips and nails were the same bright red and she wore a couple of heavy gold bangles on her wrists and an expensive gold chain around her neck. The zipper of her leather jumpsuit was open a little at the top, exposing her large breasts, and whatever her looks close up, the girl certainly had the figure. The overall effect gave her the look of a woman made for the bedroom. Volkmann thought she didn't look like the kind who might be attracted to someone like Lubsch, unless the danger of it gave her a kick, but from the way her eyes wandered quickly over him Volkmann could tell she liked men.

'Karen Gries?'

'Yes.'

'My name is Volkmann, Frau Gries. I'm a colleague of Erica Kranz's.'

The woman's smile faded instantly and at that moment the door opened and a couple entered the shop. As they began to browse among the racks Karen Gries looked over at them and forced a smile as they waved to her, then turned back to Volkmann. The smile vanished again as she looked at him.

'What the hell do you want?'

'I'd like to talk with you about Wolfgang Lubsch. Is there somewhere quiet we can talk, Frau Gries?'

'What did you say your name was?'

'Volkmann. Joseph Volkmann.' Volkmann flashed the press ID and the girl looked at it.

'Why did you come here?'

'Your friend Lubsch had a talk with Erica and me yesterday. Only it wasn't very helpful. I need to talk with Lubsch again.'

Karen Gries's face flushed with anger. 'You're wasting your time coming here, Herr Volkmann. And Lubsch is not a friend, he's someone I knew a long time ago. Erica asked if I could help her find him because she needed to talk with him. But that's as far as I was prepared to go. So if you don't mind, Herr Volkmann . . .' The young woman turned away impatiently and looked towards the balding man who was finishing a sale. He noticed her look over at him and he half smiled and stared at Volkmann warily before turning back to his customer.

Volkmann said, 'Frau Gries, I need Lubsch's help. You're the only way I can get in touch with him.'

'I told you, you're wasting your time. I can't help you. And whatever your problem is I don't want to know. Now, goodbye, Herr Volkmann.'

As the girl turned to go, Volkmann said, 'We can do this one of two ways, Frau Gries.'

The girl hesitated. 'What do you mean?'

'Either you listen to me and do as I ask or I call the police and tell them what a bad girl you've been. I'm sure they'd be interested to know you're associating with a wanted terrorist. Before you know it the anti-terrorist squad will be crawling all over this place and questioning you and your husband. And I'm quite sure your customers will read about it in the papers. Do you understand me, Frau Gries?'

The woman's eyes blazed at Volkmann. 'Are you threatening me, Volkmann?'

'I'm asking for your help. I could also tell your husband you're still screwing Wolfgang Lubsch.'

Karen Gries stared at Volkmann. Her mouth tightened and her neck flushed red with rage.

'Who the hell do you think you are making an accusation like that?'

'You do still see him, don't you?'

The balding man went to open the door for his customer. Volkmann saw him stare over before he came to join them, as if he sensed something was wrong, ignoring the other two customers in the shop.

'Is everything all right, Karen? Can I be of any assistance?'

Karen Gries turned to him quickly and said, 'Bruno, this is Herr Volkmann. He's a colleague of a friend of mine. I'd like to talk in private. Can you be a sweet and look after things here?'

The man shook Volkmann's hand. 'Glad to meet you, Herr Volkmann.' He looked at his wife and his hand touched her waist. 'You're sure everything's OK?'

'Of course, Bruno.' Karen Gries smiled. 'You better look after the customers.' She turned back to Volkmann and said in a businesslike manner, 'We'll use the office, Herr Volkmann.'

Volkmann followed her. The small office they entered was cluttered and decorated with fashion shots of leather-clad models. There were signed photographs on the walls of nightclub acts and singers. The office desk that dominated the room was covered with fashion magazines and paperwork.

When she had closed the door Karen Gries sat stiffly behind the desk and glared at Volkmann. Beyond the glass he saw her husband talking to the two other customers.

'What the hell do you mean by coming here?'

The girl looked at him coldly and her breasts heaved under the zipper.

'Have you spoken to Lubsch since you arranged the meeting in Rüdesheim, Frau Gries?'

'No. I already told you, this has nothing to do with me. You're making a mistake.'

Volkmann looked at her face and knew she was lying.

'Lubsch wasn't very helpful.' He saw Karen Gries look back at him impatiently, as if she knew already. 'Do you know where he is, Frau Gries?'

'No, I don't.'

'But you can get in touch with him.'

Karen Gries leaned forward, placed her manicured hands on the desk. 'Listen to me. Lubsch isn't the kind you play around with. Do you realise the trouble you could find yourself in by coming here and threatening me? You could get hurt, Volkmann. Badly hurt.' She looked at his face. 'And I'm not just talking about a bruised jaw. That goes for Erica as well as you. You call the police and Lubsch won't take it lightly. Do you understand me?'

'I want you to contact Lubsch. Tell him to meet me again.'

'Are you crazy? Go to hell, Volkmann, get out of here . . .'

As Karen Gries stood up, Volkmann looked at his watch.

'It's eleven-fifteen, Frau Gries. I want Lubsch to meet me at seven this evening. That ought to give you enough time to get in touch with him. Otherwise I make my call.'

'Volkmann, you're crazy. I want you to leave. Now, this minute.'

'You want to know how crazy I am?' Volkmann picked up the phone on the desk and punched in a number as the girl stared at him.

They both heard the line click and Volkmann said, '*Polizei* . . .?'

He looked at the girl's face and saw her eyes open wide and then her hand reached across and slammed down hard on the cradle.

Karen Gries said, 'I never should have listened to Erica.'

Volkmann put down the receiver. 'Seven o'clock. If Lubsch is a minute late I make my call.'

The girl's face flushed red. 'Where?'

'Across the street in the bar called Zum Dortmunder. Tell him to meet me inside at seven exactly. Tell him I want to talk with him alone. Just talk. There's no need for any rough stuff, do you understand? And don't try to contact Erica, she's no longer in the country.'

'I hope you realise what kind of fire you're playing with, Volkmann.'

'Let me worry about that.'

Volkmann turned and went out of the door.

He walked back to the underground car park and drove over the Rhine bridge to Wiesbaden.

He still had almost eight hours to kill and he drove through Wiesbaden taking the minor road north, up into the hills behind the Rhine. When he reached the picturesque spa town of Bad Schwalbach he forked east and drove into the big Rhine-Taunus Nature Park. The journey took him under forty minutes.

In summer the big park would have been busy with tourists and campers but in winter it was a vast, desolate place, wind whipping through the banks of pine and fir trees that rose and fell in undulating hills. It was bitter cold and fifteen minutes beyond Bad Schwalbach he saw a sign that pointed towards the lake.

He drove off the track and he was fifty metres into the forest before he saw the sign for the lake. He climbed out of the car and locked the door and walked along the track through the trees. Five minutes later he reached the small lake.

The area was deserted and the water was choppy and a bitter wind blew across the sweep of water. Nearby stood a narrow wooden boardwalk jutting ten metres out into the cold grey lake, and at two-metre intervals were wooden tie beams for the small boats in season.

The water was deep at the end of the walkway and Volkmann stood there looking at the scene, smoking a cigarette, as he went over the possible scenarios in his mind. Five minutes later he stubbed out the cigarette and walked back to the Ford and climbed in and started the engine.

If his plan worked out, the lake was remote enough and quiet enough for him not to be disturbed.

If the plan worked.

He drove back into Wiesbaden and found a hardware store on the outskirts. He purchased a twenty-metre length of orange-coloured nylon rope and a rubber-wrapped torch and four spare batteries. He put his purchases in the glove compartment then drove back to the apartment in Frankfurt.

When he went up, the windows in the front room were closed but the air smelled of fresh lavender and he poured himself a scotch from the bottle in the kitchen, then went to lie on the couch.

He checked his watch. Two-fifteen. He would try to sleep for a couple of hours before driving back into Mainz.

He woke at four and drove back into Mainz, arriving a little after five.

He didn't know whether he would need the Ford or not, and it depended on how many men Lubsch would have with him and what kind of transport they had. He had no doubt Lubsch would make an appearance but he guessed he wouldn't come alone and the terrorist would certainly be armed.

He had dealt with people like Lubsch before and they wouldn't think twice of shooting in a crowded street and

Volkmann knew that for his plan to work he'd have to act quickly.

He decided to use the same twenty-four-hour underground car park again. It was only a block from Karen Gries's place but not as close as he would have liked if the car was needed, but the street where Karen Gries had her shop had double lines and he didn't want to risk being towed away. He checked the Beretta before he got out of the car. He made sure the safety was on and cocked the weapon and slipped it into his right pocket. He placed the torch and spare batteries in his other pocket and slipped the nylon rope in the pouch inside his overcoat.

It was just after five and darkness had fallen but there were Christmas lights strung across the streets and above the buildings. He walked up and down the illuminated one-way street where the shop stood, mingling with the shoppers. If he guessed right, Lubsch and his people would arrive early. He thought maybe an hour but just to be certain ninety minutes. He guessed Lubsch would send a runner to the bar first, rather than appear himself, and he'd have someone watch it long before Volkmann was due. Lubsch or his people wouldn't expect him to be armed and they wouldn't expect him to go on the offensive.

He bought a newspaper and walked back to the Konditorei where he had sat that morning and had to wait for ten minutes at the door before a seat by the window came free. He ordered coffee and unfolded his newspaper, but he kept his eyes on the road outside, looking up only to check his watch.

It was five-thirty-one.

It wasn't the Mercedes van this time but a dark blue Opel saloon.

He saw the car come down the one-way street half an hour later, then disappear round the corner. It did the same thing three times before it pulled up fifty metres away on the same side of the street as Karen Gries's premises. There were three men in the car: two in front and one in the back.

Volkmann recognised Lubsch sitting in the driver's seat, his face illuminated by a string of coloured Christmas lights above the street. The little red-haired man wore the same padded dark windcheater and his face was clearly visible but Volkmann couldn't see the faces of the other two men from where he sat.

Five minutes later the man in the rear of the Opel stepped out and closed his door and walked towards Karen Gries's shop. There was a chemist's shop beside the art gallery, its neon sign on overhead, and the man went to stand in the alcove. He pulled out a newspaper and began to browse through it. Volkmann recognised him as one of the men from the Mercedes. He was going to watch the bar from across the street and Volkmann guessed the man had a walkie-talkie.

He knew he had to move quickly and he was aware of his heart pounding in his chest and the sweat on the palms of his hands. The street below was still crowded with shoppers and it would give him cover but it was also open and vulnerable and dangerous. If Lubsch or his men started firing there was a real danger someone in the crowded street could get shot.

Volkmann rechecked his watch. There was still forty minutes to go before the meeting and he knew he had to make his move quickly, before Lubsch left the car or drove around the block again.

The man in the passenger seat beside Lubsch would be a problem and so much depended on timing and on whether the man who was watching the Zum Dortmunder had left the rear door of the car unlocked. Volkmann wasn't worried about the people in the street seeing anything because their eyes would be on the shop windows.

He saw Lubsch's face peer out through the glass and then look away again impatiently. The third terrorist standing in the alcove looked over at the bar from behind his newspaper every few moments. There was a Christmas tree in the chemist's window, its lights winking on and off; the lurid colours illuminated the man's face and fogging breath as he stared across at the Zum Dortmunder.

Volkmann felt the stress tensing the muscles of his neck.

He folded his newspaper and paid for his coffee.

It was time to go.

*   *   *

He stepped out onto the street and crossed over. He was ten metres behind the Opel and as he walked towards it he strained his eyes to see if the door lock in the rear was up. Five metres from the car he saw that it was.

The man sitting in the passenger seat was wiping the side window with the sleeve of his coat and Volkmann got a glimpse of his profile. It was the same man who had wielded the truncheon and he was grinning as he spoke with Lubsch and tapping his fingers impatiently on the steering wheel.

Volkmann turned and went back down the street. The alleyway behind the bakery shop was empty and as he entered it he unfolded his newspaper and slipped the Beretta under the fold in the pages and flicked off the safety.

As he went back out onto the crowded street he looked towards the blue Opel. The man in the passenger seat was still tapping the wheel impatiently and Volkmann saw the man standing in the alcove glance back towards the Opel then step back out of view.

Volkmann came up alongside the car from behind and wrenched open the door and clambered into the back seat, the Beretta already out and the safety off. The two men in the front turned round and Volkmann saw the surprise on their faces as Lubsch said, 'What the fuck . . .?'

And then Lubsch was reaching frantically in his jacket and the passenger was doing the same.

Volkmann's fist smacked twice into the passenger's face very hard and the man's head cracked against the window.

As Lubsch struggled to remove his gun, Volkmann pressed the Beretta hard into the terrorist's neck.

'Don't.'

Lubsch's face had turned chalk white and Volkmann said, 'Slip the gun out of your pocket. Hand it back to me, very slowly, grip first. You try anything and I take your head off.'

Lubsch said palely, 'Volkmann, you're dead . . .'

'Do it.'

Lubsch slowly removed a Beretta from his jacket and handed it over, his fingers round the barrel.

Volkmann said, 'Turn round. Face front. Keep your mouth shut and start the car. Drive straight to the end of the street and turn right. Keep going until I tell you. And don't try anything as we go past your friend.'

'Volkmann, when this is over . . .'

Volkmann reached over and yanked Lubsch's collar hard and pulled him back, pressing the Beretta harder into the terrorist's neck.

'Behave yourself and you and your friend here walk away from this alive. You don't and I drop you. Understand? Now start the car. Drive.'

Volkmann let go of Lubsch and the young man leaned forward and started the Opel. As he did so Volkmann's free hand was already moving over the passenger. The man was out cold and he found a Walther PPK in the terrorist's right pocket and a CEL walkie-talkie in the other. Volkmann put them on the floor beside Lubsch's weapon.

As the Opel pulled out from the kerb and picked up speed Volkmann kept the Beretta aimed at Lubsch.

He saw Lubsch's man in the alcove stare at the Opel in disbelief as it went past the chemist's shop, and then suddenly the man dropped his newspaper and was running after them.

Volkmann said to Lubsch, 'Keep driving. Move it.'

As the Opel picked up speed the third man caught up beside them, running fast. Volkmann put down the door locks just as the terrorist reached the car and began frantically wrenching at the door handles. The man's scarred face was up against the window, and when he couldn't open the doors his fists hammered madly on the glass, his face convulsed in confusion and anger.

Volkmann pressed the Beretta into Lubsch's neck and said, 'What's your friend's name?'

Lubsch answered through clenched teeth. 'Hartig.'

Volkmann smiled out at the running man.

'Happy Christmas, Hartig.'

And then the car picked up speed and rounded the corner and the man's face was gone from the window.

Chapter Twenty-Four

Thirty minutes later they turned into the town of Bad Schwalbach and Volkmann told Lubsch to take the turn-off for the Taunus Nature Park.

As the headlights of an oncoming car swished by in the darkness, the passenger beside Lubsch started to come round. Volkmann slid his thumb into the concavity behind the man's left ear where his jaw met his skull, his other four fingers sliding round the man's neck and locking in a vice. He applied the pressure quickly and heard a small cry.

Lubsch's eyes flicked angrily at Volkmann who kept the Beretta aimed at the terrorist and said, 'Keep your eyes on the road.'

He knew exactly how much pressure to apply to the point behind the ear and seconds later he felt the man's body sag. Hard pressure would have killed within a couple of minutes, but the amount of pressure Volkmann had applied would keep him out for no more than a couple of hours.

As the body slumped back in the seat he heard the man's breathing, heavy at first, then slow and regular. Volkmann slipped his thumb and forefinger around the limp wrist and felt the pulse. It was a little slow but Volkmann reckoned there wasn't a problem. There was a stream of blood on the man's mouth and chin, but the flow had stopped. From the crack of bone when he had hit the man, Volkmann guessed he had broken the man's nose or fractured his jaw.

Lubsch said, 'Who the fuck are you, Volkmann . . .?'

'Keep driving and shut up.'

When they reached the forest road ten minutes later Volkmann told the terrorist to turn off onto the narrow track that led down to the lake. There was a half-moon but the night sky was patchy with black clouds. Twenty metres from the lakeshore Volkmann told Lubsch to stop and switch off the engine and get out of the car. When the car halted Volkmann reached over and removed the keys from the ignition.

The trees at the edge of the forest tossed furiously in the wind and as Volkmann stepped out he flicked on the torch and told Lubsch to move down to the boardwalk. The patchy moon illuminated the choppy lake with faint silver streaks, and Volkmann shone the torch ahead of the terrorist as he followed him down to the water.

They were a couple of metres from the boardwalk when Lubsch suddenly made a run for it. He veered sharply right and started to run frantically towards a bank of trees. Volkmann sprinted after him and when he caught up he dropped the torch and gripped the terrorist's shoulder. As Lubsch spun round his small wiry frame crashed into Volkmann in the darkness and then his fists were pounding into Volkmann's body.

The terrorist grappled for the weapon in Volkmann's hand and tried to wrench it free. Lubsch was strong but Volkmann was stronger and his free arm came round and locked the little man's neck in a vice. Volkmann heard the terrorist gurgle as he fought for breath but he kept up the pressure on the man's throat. Moments later he felt Lubsch's body sag and slide to the ground.

Volkmann went back to retrieve the torch and shone it in Lubsch's face. He wasn't unconscious but his eyes were dilated from lack of oxygen and as his hands massaged his neck he started to cough up his lungs on the grass.

As he gasped for breath he looked up at Volkmann. 'When this is through, you're dead, Volkmann . . . Dead.'

The terrorist's voice was hoarse with pain and as he lay there Volkmann pointed the Beretta.

'Get up, Lubsch. Walk down to the boardwalk.'

Lubsch struggled to stand and when they came down to the water, Volkmann said, 'Now tie your shoelaces together.'

'What?'

'You heard me. Do it.'

Volkmann pointed the gun and watched as Lubsch tied his laces together. When he had finished Volkmann flashed the torch and checked them. He told Lubsch to take off his trouser belt and then lie down on the boardwalk on his stomach. When Lubsch hesitated Volkmann forced him down. Once the terrorist had removed his belt Volkmann used it to tie the man's hands behind his back. He pulled Lubsch up into a sitting position. It was bitter cold and the wind coming in off the black water clawed at their faces.

Volkmann said, 'We can do this the easy way or the hard way, Lubsch. The easy way is you tell me what I need to know. The hard way is I deliver you and your friend to the nearest police station.'

There was anger in Lubsch's face as he looked up at the harsh light. 'You think you'll get away with it, Volkmann? My men would hunt you down and find you. Who the fuck are you, Volkmann? *Polizei?*'

Volkmann ignored the question and said, 'Think about it. A high-security prison for maybe twenty years. And that's if the judge is in a good mood. Guards watching your every movement. No visits, except from your lawyer, if you were lucky enough to find one who'd take your case.' Volkmann slipped the Beretta into his pocket and removed the nylon rope and held it in front of Lubsch's face. 'So what's it to be? I wrap you and your friend up like a Christmas present and drop you outside the nearest police station, or you talk?'

Volkmann shone the torch in Lubsch's face and the terrorist blinked and looked away. The wind blowing across the black waters in the darkness was icy cold and the only sounds were the lapping water and the wind sweeping through the trees in ragged, harsh gusts.

Lubsch sat there on the freezing boardwalk, not moving, as if considering his predicament. When he looked back he shivered and his face looked red from the cold.

'And if I talk, what's in it for me?'

'I let you and your friend go.'

'What the fuck do you want to know, Volkmann?'

'What I wanted to know the last time we met. About Dieter Winter and his friends.'

'How do I know you'll keep your word and let us go?'

'You'll have to trust me, Lubsch. But if you don't tell me the truth, or I find out you lied to me or didn't tell me everything, your friend Karen gets a visit from the police.'

Lubsch's voice sounded thick with anger and his small blue eyes squinted as he looked up at the white beam and grimaced. 'You really are fucking crazy, aren't you, Volkmann? Just like Karen said you were. But if you think you can get away with this . . .'

Before the terrorist could finish his sentence Volkmann reached over and gripped the collar of Lubsch's windcheater and dragged him over to the edge of the boardwalk. He gripped a handful of Lubsch's red hair and pushed the terrorist's face down into the freezing cold water. Lubsch fought to get free and his body bucked and squirmed and his legs kicked wildly in the air.

Volkmann saw the air bubbles rise as he counted to ten. Then he pulled Lubsch's head back in again. The terrorist gulped in deep breaths as his lungs fought for air.

'Your last chance, Lubsch. Are you going to talk?'

When Lubsch didn't reply, Volkmann grabbed the man's collar again and went to push his head down again.

Lubsch coughed up water and said, 'For Christ's sake, Volkmann . . . OK, OK, I'll tell you.'

Volkmann dragged him back into the middle of the board-walk and waited until Lubsch had caught his breath. His hair was plastered over his forehead. Water dripped from his face and he shivered violently.

Volkmann said, 'I want to hear it from the beginning, Lubsch. From how you met Winter. Leave nothing out. Nothing. Do you understand?'

Lubsch coughed again and spat on the boardwalk. For several moments he sat there, his chest heaving as he took deep breaths. When his breathing had returned to normal he looked up at Volkmann for a moment, then turned his face away before he spoke.

'I first met Winter at Heidelberg. He was in the history faculty.'

'You were friends?'

'No, Volkmann. We weren't friends. Just acquaintances. We used to meet sometimes in the student inns to drink and talk.'

'Tell me about Winter.'

Lubsch sniffed, then spat out into the water. 'What do you want to know?'

'I told you. Everything.'

'Winter and I, we were on different sides of the fence, politically. He was a right-wing bigot, and me, I leaned to the left. But Winter was always a convincing speaker. For a time, he even managed to convince me that we both had something in common.'

'Tell me.'

Lubsch looked up at Volkmann, then turned his head away again. 'The future of Germany.'

'What do you mean?'

'It was a pet topic with Winter. He and his friends had this idea that they could change the country.'

'And who were his friends?'

'Fellow students. Others who shared his views.'

'Tell me about his friends, Lubsch.'

Lubsch hesitated, then said, 'What's this got to do with, Volkmann? The murders you spoke about, or something else?'

'Just carry on talking until I tell you to stop. What about his friends?'

Lubsch hesitated, looked away again towards the cold lake. His neck was lost in his wet padded windcheater and as he sat on the boardwalk his thin body shook with the cold. His eyes snapped shut, then opened again.

'Six months into our second year on campus I'd gotten to know Winter pretty well. Whenever we'd drink beer together we'd argue about politics. Winter was a drinker and a talker, but our talk was never violent, just heated discussion because we both had opposing views. Then one day he asked me to join him and a group of them for a weekend on Lüneburg Heath. There were to be seven of us. Some were students, but only Winter and I were from the Heidelberg campus. The others came from different parts of Germany and from different backgrounds, most of them working class. Toughs, a couple of them, and out of their depth intellectually, but Winter had asked them along. We stayed in a rented house in the forest and drank in the local inns. We walked and talked day and night. About politics. Philosophy. History.'

'And the others, they all knew Winter?'

Lubsch looked up a moment. 'Sure. It was like a fraternity. Like they all knew each other pretty well.'

When Lubsch paused, Volkmann said, 'Who were these friends of Winter's?'

'I told you, Volkmann. Winter had asked them along. I'd never met them before.'

'I want names, Lubsch.'

Lubsch hesitated. 'I only remember one. A science student. His name was Kesser. Lothar Kesser. He was about my age and he came from Bavaria.'

'Where in Bavaria?'

Lubsch shook his head. 'Some small hick town, I don't remember where.'

'You said the group was like a fraternity. What did you mean?'

Lubsch shrugged. 'It was like they had some bond between them. It was kind of weird. Like a secret society. Don't ask me to explain it, Volkmann, because I can't. But it was like I was outside the circle, not one of them. I was only there because Winter had asked me.'

'Go on.'

'One night after everyone's gone to bed this guy Kesser suggests we go for a walk in the forest. Just him and me. It's dark and gloomy outside, and we've had a few drinks. But I agreed, because I got the feeling Kesser wanted to talk with me in private.

'So we walked together for maybe an hour. Kesser kept talking about Germany's past. Not the bad things. The good things. How Germany had always come through times in her history of great suffering and upheaval. Overcome all obstacles. Created order out of chaos. That sort of shit.

Like Kesser was giving me some sort of political speech. He said that Germany would go through a phase of disorder again. There were definitely going to be problems in the future. Not only in Germany, but in all of Europe. Politically. Economically. Socially. But that there were also going to be opportunities. And that we were all Germans together and that when that time came we should strive together to seize the opportunity to create a better Fatherland. I was pretty drunk, but I thought Kesser was talking foolishly. I told him it all sounded like undergraduate, idealist shit to me.'

'What did Kesser say?'

'He got annoyed and said that when the right time came he and the others who supported his beliefs would have financial support for their cause. When I asked him to explain, he wouldn't elaborate. But he said he knew I was involved with an off-shoot of the Red Army Faction. Kesser said he and Winter didn't see me and my friends as terrorists, merely disenchanted Germans who sought a different Germany. He said we could join him if we wished.'

'And what did you say?'

'I said it was kind of him, but he was wrong. I wasn't involved with any group. I was drunk, Volkmann, but I was careful. Besides, I thought Kesser was playing some kind of trick. Maybe Winter and Kesser were *Bundespolizei* plants. They do that, you know. Send their brightest cadets into German universities to spy on extremist undergraduates. Lead them along and then trap them.'

'What was Kesser's reaction when you refused?'

Lubsch shrugged. 'He said I was making a grave mistake. He didn't say any more, and that was the end of our conversation. But after that, Winter kept away from me on campus. He rarely talked to me and whenever we met he'd keep his distance.'

The wind gusted across the lake and Lubsch shivered.

Volkmann said, 'Did you see Kesser again?'

Lubsch said nothing for several moments. He looked out at the water, then back again. 'Two years ago. I met him again.'

'Tell me.'

'A friend of mine gets a call one night. The guy wouldn't say who he was. But he wanted to pass on a message to me. He said Lothar Kesser wanted to meet me. That he had an important proposition that would interest me. He gave a number and a time to call back and asked my friend to pass on the message. So I called the number. Winter answered. He sounded pretty friendly and when I asked him what it was about he said he and Kesser wanted to meet me again and what they had to talk about couldn't be discussed over the phone. But he said it was very important. He said if I didn't trust him I could bring a couple of my men along, just to be sure. And I could decide where we met.'

'So what happened?'

'I was curious, so I agreed to meet outside a small town in the Black Forest. I took along a couple of men to check out the location first. But Winter and Kesser were there alone. We drove up into the mountains and the three of us went for a walk. When I asked them what it was about Kesser did all the talking. He said he had a proposition for me. Me and my group.'

'What sort of proposition?'

'He said he could offer us everything the Russians had supplied us with in the past.'

'What do you mean?'

'Weapons. Explosives. Whatever we needed.'

Volkmann paused. 'Did Kesser say where he got the supplies from?'

'No, he didn't say.'

'You asked him?'

'Sure. But he simply said it was none of my business. That the offer was genuine and I could take it or leave it. It was up to me and my people.'

'And what did you think, about this proposition?'

Lubsch smiled grimly. 'I thought it was crazy, Volkmann. A right-wing radical supplying a left-wing terror group with weapons. There was no sense to it.'

'You didn't accept?'

Lubsch half smiled. 'Of course I did, eventually. I might

have thought Kesser was crazy, but I wasn't. Our weapons dumps were pretty depleted. There wasn't much coming from the Soviets. And after the Wall came down they did a turnabout face.'

'What kind of weapons did Kesser's people deliver?'

When Lubsch hesitated, Volkmann said, 'What kind of weapons, Lubsch?'

'Small arms and explosives mostly. Machine-pistols, assault rifles, hand-guns. Grenades and Semtex. And once a rocket-launcher we needed to take out a politician's car.'

Volkmann looked down at the terrorist and hesitated a moment. 'What about conditions, did Kesser make any?'

'My people had to pay for the weapons. But it was a token payment. To cover costs.'

'Didn't your people question Winter's motives?'

Lubsch shook his head and laughed quietly. 'Volkmann, we would have taken weapons from the devil himself, as long as they were reliable and shot straight. We were just grateful for the supplies.'

'How long did Winter and his people supply you?'

'About eighteen months.'

'Why? What happened?'

Lubsch turned to look at him and Volkmann played the torch beam away from his face. 'There was one other condition Kesser made.'

'Tell me.'

'Every time we'd get a supply, we'd get a request. A favour to do in return. They'd suggest we hit certain targets.'

'What sort of targets?'

'Banks. Financial institutions. State property. Those Allied bases that still remained on German soil. Some of the hits suited us. They fitted in with our scheme of things and we were happy to oblige. But some didn't. When they didn't, we still did it because we needed the supplies.'

'So why did Winter and Kesser stop supplying you?'

Lubsch paused. 'About six months ago Kesser's demands started to become more outrageous. He wanted us to start bombing immigrant hostels. That wasn't our style. And he wanted us to hit some people. He gave me three names he said he wanted dead.'

'Did Kesser say why he wanted these people killed?'

'No. He didn't. Just that they were part of the deal.'

'So who were the people?'

'Two of them I'd never heard of before. But one of the names on the list I knew, and I wouldn't go along with.'

'Go on.'

'He was a liberal politician in Berlin. I told Kesser it wasn't our style. We'd hit politicians or businessmen who suited us. But we wouldn't do the names on the list.'

'What did Kesser say?'

'He just smiled and said he'd handle it himself. But after that things were strained between us. We were due one more delivery a month later but it never came. And Kesser or Winter didn't contact me again.'

'Who were the people Kesser wanted dead?'

Lubsch paused. 'A guy in East Berlin. His name was Rauscher, Herbert Rauscher. Another was a woman in Friedrichshafen, near the Swiss border.'

'Her name?'

'I can't remember.'

'Think, Lubsch.'

'Hedda something. Pohl or Puhl. I'm not sure.'

'Who was she?'

'A nobody. The widow of a businessman.'

'And the man in East Berlin, Rauscher?'

'A small-time businessman. Another nobody.'

'Your people checked their backgrounds?'

'Of course. We weren't going to kill just for the sake of it, Volkmann. That's not our style. We only hit selected targets we think deserve to be hit. Big businessmen who corrupt this country. Politicians who support them. The police and the armed forces.'

'And Winter or Kesser didn't tell you why they wanted these people killed?'

'No, I told you, Volkmann. Just that it was part of the deal.'

'Who was the politician in Berlin?'

'His name's Walter Massow.' Lubsch looked out at the cold lake and shivered violently, his lips trembling with cold. 'He's not a political animal, just a good and honest man trying to do his best for the downtrodden in this country. That's why I told Kesser, no way. We weren't racists and we wouldn't go along with his fascist ideals. I also told him if Massow was hit I'd take it personally.' The terrorist looked back. 'And after that, I told you, the supplies halted.'

Volkmann thought a moment, then said, 'Did you ask Winter or Kesser why they wanted you to carry out the attacks on the immigrant hostels?'

'Sure. Kesser said some of the immigrant groups in Germany had set up their own terror groups and were hitting right-wing supporters. Kesser said he was going to hit back. But Kesser was a right-wing bigot. It was the sort of thing you'd expect someone of his pedigree to use as an excuse for his action.'

'What do you mean?'

'That time on Lüneburg Heath, I overheard him talk about his father. He was some bigshot SS man during the war. I heard him say the old man had helped draft the Brandenburg Testament for Adolf Hitler, whatever that was. But Kesser said it like a boast, as if it were proof enough of his pedigree.'

Volkmann looked away, then back again. 'The politician, Massow, what happened to him?'

Lubsch shook his head. 'Nothing. He was left alone.'

'And the others?'

'I don't know. Dead, I guess.'

Lubsch shivered violently as a gust of icy wind blew in off the lake.

Volkmann said, 'Why do you think Massow wasn't killed?'

Lubsch shrugged. 'Maybe Winter thought it more tactful to let Massow live after he understood my views. I don't know, Volkmann. Either way, Kesser or Winter didn't contact us again. Besides, they had others to do their dirty work for them.'

'What do you mean? What others?'

'We learned that Kesser and Winter were supplying other groups, not just ours.'

'You mean terrorist groups?'

Lubsch half smiled and his lips trembled with cold. 'It's a question of perspective, isn't it, Volkmann? But yes, let us say terrorist groups in your idiom.'

'Which ones?'

'Pretty nearly all you could mention. Those of significance anyhow. He did the same deal for them. Weapons in return for hitting the kinds of targets I told you about.'

Volkmann hesitated. He stepped down to the edge of the boardwalk, felt the icy wind slash at his face.

He looked back at Lubsch and said, 'What you've told me, none of it makes any sense, Lubsch. What was Winter's angle? What was in it for him and his friends? Why did Winter want you to kill these people? Why didn't they do it themselves? They had the weapons.'

Lubsch smiled bitterly. 'I don't know, Volkmann. None of our people understood it. I had a theory. Some of it made sense, some of it didn't.'

'Tell me.'

'Maybe the plan was to spread anarchy. Winter and his people supplied weapons. Had those weapons used on certain targets they wanted eliminated. Businessmen. State and private institutions. Soft-line military personnel. But people blame the red terrorists for hits like that, and the right-wing gain more support.'

When Volkmann said nothing, Lubsch turned to face him. 'You think I'm crazy, don't you, Volkmann?'

'You said some of your theory didn't make sense. What part?'

Lubsch shrugged. 'The people Kesser wanted killed, besides Massow. And something else. Whoever was behind Winter, they must have had money and good organisation to buy and ship arms and supplies in such quantities. Maybe a right-wing group within the police or army. Or a cabal of wealthy business people could do it. People with something at stake.'

'Where did the weapons Winter and Kesser supplied come from?'

Lubsch shrugged. 'I don't know.'

'Winter's death. Was that your people?'

'No.'

'So who killed him?'

'I don't know, Volkmann. Winter lived on a knife-edge. He dealt with groups like mine. He also had a big mouth. And when he was drunk he liked to talk.' Lubsch shrugged. 'You play with fire, you get burned. So maybe one of them burned him.'

'When was the last time you saw him?'

'Six months ago, when I met Kesser.'

'How do I find Kesser?'

The terrorist looked up and his face was blue from the freezing cold. 'I don't know, Volkmann. But I'll give you some advice. The advice I gave you before. If you're wise you'll keep away from him and his friends. Unless you and the girl want to end up dead.'

'The names Karl Schmeltz or Nicolas Tsarkin. Did either Winter or Kesser ever mention those names?'

'No.'

'You're sure?'

'Kesser or Winter never mentioned names. Never. Apart from the names on the list I told you about.' Lubsch's teeth chattered and he looked up. 'Are you going to untie me now, Volkmann? Or am I going to sit here all fucking night and freeze to death? I've told you everything I know.'

Volkmann shone the torch slightly to the right so it didn't shine in the terrorist's eyes, but so that he could still see the man's reaction clearly.

'One more question. Erica Kranz.'

'What about her?'

'How well did she know Winter at Heidelberg?'

'What are you asking me for, Volkmann? Ask her yourself.'

'Just answer the question, Lubsch.'

Lubsch shrugged. 'A couple of times I saw them talking together at parties.' The terrorists's face looked frozen as he stared up at Volkmann. 'I thought she was a friend of yours?'

Volkmann ignored the question and stood up. 'I enjoyed our talk.'

'Fuck you.'

He saw the look of rage in Lubsch's eyes. As Volkmann moved away, he hesitated and turned back, shone the torch in Lubsch's face.

'I did you a favour tonight, Lubsch. By right you ought to be behind bars for the rest of your life. Only I'm keeping my word. But if I learn you've been lying to me, or you try to come after me, the police will pay your friend Karen a visit. And one more thing. Keep away from Erica Kranz.'

Volkmann flicked off the torch and the walkway plunged into darkness.

'You'll find the car somewhere near Karen's place. I'll leave your friend behind to keep you company.'

As he walked back towards the Opel he heard the wind raging across the lake in the freezing darkness, and Lubsch grunting as he struggled with the belt on the boardwalk.

Chapter Twenty-Five

When he let himself into the apartment it was almost midnight and the girl was asleep in the spare bedroom.

He telephoned Peters' home number. When Peters had activated the scrambler Volkmann told him what had happened with Lubsch.

'Christ, Joe, you took a risk. You want me to pass on the girl's name to the BfV?'

'No. Let's see what happens. If Lubsch tries to come back at me we'll do it then.'

'You think Lubsch told you the truth?'

'Your guess is as good as mine, Tom. I'd say yes, but I'll have to check it out.'

'What do you want to do? Ferguson's going to be away for a couple of days.'

'I'll carry on.'

'OK. But if you need help, let me know. About Erhard Schmeltz, we got some information from the Documentation Centre in Berlin.'

'What did they say?'

'They've got records of the Nazi Party going back to 1925, when the party really started to officially document their membership. There's an Erhard Johann Schmeltz born in Hamburg, and listed as party number six-eight-nine-six-four. His party application was made in Munich in late November 1927 and his year of birth is the same as in Sanchez' report. Considering the date he applied and the fact that the party had over ten million members in Germany at its peak, Schmeltz would have joined pretty much at the start.'

'What else did they say?'

'They have his original application and his record file and

photograph from the master files of the Nazi Party Headquarters in Munich. He was also a registered member of the Brownshirt SA, the *Sturmabteilung*. And Schmeltz didn't quit the Nazi Party when he went to South America. His party dues were paid until his death in 1944. He arranged payment *in absentia*.'

'How can they know that for certain?'

'The Nazis had something called the *Gau Ausland*. The best way to describe it is as a department that dealt with party members in foreign regions, people who had left Germany but still kept up their party membership. Committed Nazis. Schmeltz was registered with the *Gau Ausland* from November 1931.' There was a pause before Peters spoke again. 'There's something else, Joe. The Documentation Centre said Erhard Schmeltz's party application had a recommendation attached to his application.'

'What do you mean?'

'Apparently, every application for party membership had to have the application recommended and endorsed, usually by the local party group leader for the region in which he applied. But in Schmeltz's case there was a letter sent from Prinz-Albrecht Strasse in Berlin, the SS headquarters, at the time Schmeltz applied, which was pretty unusual, apparently. The letter was signed by Heinrich Himmler and it recommended Schmeltz's immediate acceptance. It suggests maybe Schmeltz was a close or trusted acquaintance of Himmler's, or had contacts pretty high up in the party.'

Volkmann paused, let the information sink in. 'Anything else?'

'The information on Reimer. The Document Centre had him on their list of personnel files on SS officers. Apparently, they've got pretty good records of SS officers that the Americans captured at the end of the war. But there's really nothing much in there that could help us. I'll have the copies of the information on Schmeltz and Reimer on your desk tomorrow, the stuff Berlin sent from their files. What about you, you need anything else?'

'Lothar Kesser, science student, from Bavaria. I want him

checked out. It's not much to go on but you may get lucky. And I'll need a return ticket to Zurich, first available flight tomorrow morning.'

'Why Zurich?'

'Remember Ted Birken?'

Peters laughed. 'I thought they put the old fox out to grass years ago?'

'They did. But he still has contacts and he may be able to help.'

'OK. I'll organise the ticket with Facilities right away. Keep in touch. Goodnight, Joe.'

'Night.'

When he put down the telephone Volkmann heard a sound and looked round. Erica Kranz stood in the doorway. She wore a dressing-gown and the blue eyes looked over at him, a hint of anger there.

'I heard you talking on the phone. You said you wouldn't contact Lubsch or Karen. Is that where you went today, to Karen's place . . .?'

Volkmann said nothing and the blue eyes continued to look at him accusingly. 'You know what kind of man Lubsch is. You know what he's capable of. Why did you do it, Joe? Why have you put us both in danger?'

'He won't bother you, Erica. I've made sure of that. If he does I tell the police about Karen. You've nothing to worry about, believe me.'

The girl hesitated. 'I think there's something that worries me more, Joe.'

'What?'

'That you didn't trust me enough to tell me what you were going to do.'

When Volkmann didn't reply, the girl sat down. She looked up at him. 'Tell me what Lubsch said.'

He told her and the girl watched his face. 'Do you trust him?'

'Trust him, no. Believe him, yes.'

Erica Kranz shook her head. 'Don't you think he could have been trying to mislead you? Winter's people, why would they want to kill these people? Why would they want Lubsch to carry out racist attacks on immigrants? To attack state institutions. The targets seem so diverse. There isn't any sense to it.'

'Maybe. But I don't think Wolfgang Lubsch lied, Erica. I think he told me the truth.'

'And what if he and Winter's people are still doing business together, despite what Lubsch said? If that's the case, then Lubsch will tell them about you and me.'

'It's a risk we'll have to take.' He looked at her. 'You want to find the people who killed Rudi, Erica. Getting Lubsch to talk was the only way.'

The girl said nothing and looked away. The anger had subsided but she didn't speak. Volkmann crossed to the window. When he looked back at her, he said, 'Do you have access to any newspaper libraries?'

The girl hesitated. 'The one at the *Frankfurter Zeitung*.'

'How about you check through the files there. The people Lubsch talked about that Kesser and Winter wanted killed. Rauscher, and the woman Hedda Pohl or Puhl. See what you come up with.'

'What are you looking for exactly?'

'If they were killed, or attacked. If they've been in the news for any reason. Anything at all.'

'Your people can't check on that?'

'It would mean going through the German Desk at DSE. And I'd rather we kept it to ourselves for now. The less I have to use them the better, until we know what's going on.' Volkmann paused. 'And the politician in Berlin, Massow, that Lubsch spoke about. See if you can contact his office and arrange a meeting. I can fly up there and talk with him if he agrees.'

'What do you want to talk with him about?'

'If what Lubsch said is true, there must have been a reason Winter's people wanted Massow dead. Maybe Massow knows why. I'll give you a number where you can reach me if anything turns up. If I'm not there you can contact Peters or leave a message.'

'You won't be in Strasbourg?'

Volkmann shook his head. 'The information Sanchez sent, about the money transferred from the Reichsbank to Schmeltz in Paraguay before and during the last war. There's someone I'd like to talk to in Zurich. Someone who may be able to help.'

He told her the news Peters had given him about Erhard Schmeltz. There was a puzzled look on the girl's face.

'You think Schmeltz's past has something to do with what Lubsch said was happening, as well as the murders?'

'I don't know, Erica. We know almost nothing about Erhard Schmeltz, or his son, apart from the fact they were the registered owners of the Chaco property and the information the Berlin Document Centre had on him. Let's wait and see what I can turn up in Zurich tomorrow.'

'This man Kesser. Lothar Kesser. Your people can find him?'

'If there's a file on him, yes.'

As she stood up, she said, 'What time are you leaving for Zurich, Joe?'

'Before nine, I guess. Why?'

The girl said, 'Then I better let you get some sleep.'

As she turned to go, Volkmann said, 'How well did you know Winter at university?'

The girl shook her head. 'Not well. I used to see him on the campus and met him at a couple of parties. Why?'

'What about your other friends on campus. Were any of them friendly with him?'

'No. I told you. The only students I remembered who seemed to know him were Wolfgang Lubsch and Herman Borchardt.'

The girl looked at him for a long time. She hesitated, as if about to speak, and then changed her mind. She turned and Volkmann watched her go into the bedroom.

Chapter Twenty-Six

He had made the telephone call to Ted Birken early that morning and Peters had arranged a ticket for the first flight out of Strasbourg to Zurich.

The plane was full and when it landed Volkmann took a taxi out to the house overlooking Zurichsee. It was bitter cold but the sky was clear and in the distance he could see the snow-capped mountains beyond the lake.

The house was small compared to some of the lakeside villas nearby but it was pretty and neat and set in its own tidy gardens twenty metres back off the shore road. The window boxes were full with colourful winter flowers and as he stepped from the taxi Volkmann saw Ted Birken come out to the front door and wave a greeting.

His shoulders were hunched beneath a loose-fitting cardigan and he looked older than his seventy-odd years. Volkmann realised it had been almost ten years since they had last met, when Birken had lectured at the house in Devon.

The blue eyes twinkled as he shook Volkmann's hand. 'Good to see you again, Joe. Come inside.'

Volkmann paid the driver and followed the tall, grey-haired man inside. The house was warm and in the study Birken had set out a small wooden tray with glasses and a bottle of cherry kirsch. A fire blazed in the hearth and the wide study window looked out onto the lake. A couple of sailing boats tossed in the gentle swell and Birken glanced at them as he lit his meerschaum pipe before turning back to

Volkmann, brushing aside his apology for the short notice of the meeting.

Ted Birken had been an intelligence officer for most of his adult life. A Jewish refugee from Germany, he and his family had escaped to Switzerland in 1940 when Birken was eighteen. The son of a once prominent and wealthy banker, he soon grew tired of sitting on the sidelines and within a year had left his family and the safe comfort of a neutral country behind him and made his way to Nice with forged papers. From there began a hazardous journey to Lisbon and then England where he attempted to join the British army. Interned ignominiously on the Isle of Man for the rest of the war because of his doubtful and uncorroborated background, he had to wait until the summer of 1945 to offer his services. By then the war was over but the officer who interviewed him realised that Birken's unique talents – he spoke German fluently and had connections through his father with many major Swiss banks – could be put to better use and passed him on to the intelligence service.

Thus began a career that for four years saw Birken tracking down and interrogating senior Nazis and SS who had secretly helped to dispose of many millions in gold and currency from the Nazi Reichsbank and death-camps in the last months of the war. When his work came to an end, Birken had become a British citizen and joined SIS, in later years becoming a senior intelligence figure before retiring to Switzerland.

Volkmann saw the elderly man puff on his meerschaum and fill the two glasses with kirsch before the sparkling blue eyes swivelled to look at him. Volkmann had explained on the telephone his reasons for wanting to see him and Birken was a businesslike man. As the blue, intelligent eyes looked at Volkmann, Birken got straight down to business.

'You had three questions, one about the money that was sent to South America by the Nazi Reichsbank. The other concerning these men, Schmeltz and Reimer, and the Leibstandarte SS. Let's start with the first, shall we?' He took a sip of his drink, then sat back, puffed on his pipe before speaking.

'First, perhaps I had better explain the background behind

Nazi funds, that way it may help you get a fix on things. At the end of the war, in May 1945, the equivalent of almost two billion in today's terms had gone missing. That included lots of valuable art objects too, but mainly gold and silver bullion, the so-called property of the Reichsbank. Some of it – quite a lot actually – had been plundered from invaded countries.' Birken paused to smile. 'There was enough to equip another German army, and I think that was the loose intention of the Nazis, especially Himmler, when the plans to hide the caches were first mooted. But of course as the war situation became more hopeless, that idea was quickly forgotten and many of the people whose job it was to hide the caches actually started working for themselves.'

Volkmann sipped his drink, then said, 'So what happened to the bullion and money, Ted?'

'Some of it we located. The British and the Americans. But a lot of it went missing. It ended up in Switzerland or South America, and some in the Arab countries that had been favourably disposed towards Hitler. A few unscrupulous Americans helped themselves to some of the gold or did deals with the Nazis they apprehended, but it was small-scale and to be expected. Quite a of number of Nazis escaped to South America, as I'm sure you know. And quite a lot of the bullion and currency went with them. The people involved ranged from lowly privates up to high-ranking SS and Gestapo. They slipped out of ports all over Europe, but mainly Italy. We tried tracking both them and the caches down in South America but it proved a rather hopeless exercise. Most of the South American countries still had pro-Nazi sympathies at the time and did nothing to help us.'

'What were the reasons behind taking the gold and currency to South America?'

Birken smiled indulgently. 'It was considered a relatively safe and distant place. Some countries there had been openly supportive of the Nazis, and those with large German colonies especially so. Paraguay is a good example. General Stroesser was the military dictator there for quite some time. He was part German himself and pro-Nazi. And there were many other countries in the region with the same sympathies. Most of the bullion and currency that ended up in South America lined private pockets, though a considerable portion of it was controlled by *Die Spinne* – the Spider – the secret organisation of former SS who set up down there. Otherwise known as the *Kameradenwerk*, and before that Odessa. There was a rather loose plan to regroup and eventually finance another Nazi party in Germany when the time was ripe once again, but of course it came to naught.'

Birken paused and the watery blue eyes looked at Volkmann. 'Die Spinne, you're familiar with its original function?'

'No.'

'Well, it had quite a number of functions, actually. But the primary ones were to protect former SS men from prosecution and to help establish those same former Nazis and their families in commerce and industry. And, of course, to continue to propagandise the ideals of the Third Reich.'

Volkmann looked out towards the grey, choppy lake for several moments. When he looked back at Ted Birken he said, 'Did you ever hear of funds being sent back to Germany with that purpose in mind, Ted?'

'In what respect?'

'To finance extremists. Neo-Nazis.'

Birken relit his pipe and said, 'Mossad had a theory that some of the neo-Nazi resurges in Germany over the last thirty years were financed in part from Die Spinne funds, but there was never any evidence of that. Of course, Die Spinne was notoriously secretive, and defied any attempts to infiltrate it. The Israelis tried it on a number of occasions, but their people involved on such missions usually disappeared, never to be heard of again.' The blue eyes regarded Volkmann keenly. 'I presume this has something to do with these men Schmeltz and Reimer you asked me to check on?' When Volkmann nodded, Birken said, 'Do you mind me asking why? Of course, if you'd rather not talk, I quite understand.'

Volkmann told him the story. It took him almost ten minutes to outline what had happened and Birken sat there quietly smoking his pipe, pausing only to refill the meerschaum. When Volkmann had finished, Birken leaned forward.

'Do you have the photograph of the young woman with you?'

Volkmann removed the photograph from his wallet and handed it across. Birken looked at it for a long time, then handed it back as he shook his head.

'I'm afraid I don't recognise her. Of course, that date would have been before my time. And of course the young woman could have been anyone. A public figure or simply an anonymous girlfriend of some Nazi officer.'

'What about Schmeltz and Reimer?'

Birken nodded. 'After you telephoned this morning I had a look back through my notes and diaries. I kept copious notes when I was tracking down the missing Reichsbank funds. As I told you once many years ago the team I was involved with at the end of the war had to go right back through the books, back to '33, to try and figure out where most of the money and bullion had come from. What part was party funds, what part belonged to the German people, what part had been spoils of war, and so on.' Birken smiled. 'I had hoped to write a book one day, but somehow I never seemed to get around to it. That's the reason I kept copies of almost all the major accounts serviced over the twelve years of the Nazi regime.'

Volkmann nodded. 'That's why I contacted you, Ted.'

'Well, I'm afraid I found nothing on this man Reimer, alias Tsarkin. He wasn't one of the people we were chasing. The ten thousand American dollars you say he had in his possession when he arrived in Paraguay could have been a little nest egg he had stashed away during the years of the war, or it quite possibly could have been paid to him from Die Spinne funds.'

When Birken hesitated, Volkmann said, 'What about Erhard Schmeltz?'

Birken again shook his head. 'I found no record of money being sent to any Schmeltz in Paraguay. Not that I expected to. That's not to say, of course, that the Reichsbank didn't send him the funds you spoke of. Such an account could have been serviced secretly, and most likely was. But the amounts sent to Schmeltz's account would have been small beer by comparison to some of the others the Reichsbank serviced abroad, both before and during the war. Those were mainly for espionage work, for propaganda purposes, and secret accounts that high-ranking Nazis could rely on if things went wrong. The amounts to Schmeltz were considerable, but still relatively small. The real question is, why was Schmeltz sent money before the war? And why did the money continue to be sent to his wife after his death?'

'Do you have any ideas, Ted?'

Birken smiled at Volkmann. 'God only knows. It could have been for anything. Some Nazis set up slush funds through German immigrants in South America in the belief, I suppose, that one day they'd need them. As I recall, there were always quite a number of German colonies in Paraguay, and most of them were fervently pro-Nazi.' Birken shrugged. 'Maybe the Schmeltz couple were simply playing bank manager for someone.'

'What about the fact that Schmeltz's Nazi membership was endorsed by Himmler himself?'

Birken smiled again. 'Now that *is* interesting. But I'm afraid I still can't give you an answer. It suggests that Schmeltz was a close personal friend or acquaintance of Himmler's or some high-ranking Nazi, obviously.' Birken shrugged. 'But if Himmler or someone at the top of the Nazi Party was using this man Schmeltz as a channel for siphoning away a secret money hoard for the future I'm sure the amounts would have been much, much larger.' Birken paused. 'Perhaps Schmeltz did someone a favour or kindness. Perhaps he was being repaid a stipend for it. It's the only explanation I can think of when one considers that Schmeltz retained his party membership despite being thousands of miles away. Either that or Schmeltz was being used to set up a slush fund for someone in the party. Blackmail is another possible reason for the drafts, of course. But it's unlikely that Schmeltz would have remained in the party if that were the case, although you never know. And I can only assume that the reason the monies ceased in February of '45 was because by then the Reichsbank was finding it increasingly difficult to transfer funds out of Germany, even through its Swiss accounts.'

'What was the bullion that made its way to Die Spinne actually used for?'

Birken looked out towards the view beyond the window a few moments, then turned back to face Volkmann.

'I think I'd have to agree with the Mossad's theory, at least in part. I'm sure some of it was used to finance neo-Nazi and right-wing movements over the years. And not only in Germany, but all over Europe and in America and South Africa in particular. But until now Germany's been too prosperous a country to have its keel unsettled by that kind of thing.' Birken shrugged. 'I imagine a lot of the money's still in South America, keeping a certain number of very elderly Nazis and their sibling families in considerable comfort.'

'Are we talking millions here, Ted, or what?'

'Oh, much more than that, my boy. Probably as much as a quarter of the original amount that went missing. Especially when you consider that the original capital would have been put to work.'

'How?'

'In business ventures mainly, and land purchase. Much of it in South America.' Birken paused. 'That's where your last question comes in. What do you know about the Leibstandarte SS Division?'

Volkmann shook his head. 'Very little. Just that they were an élite within the SS. And that Hitler's personal bodyguard was drawn from its ranks.'

Birken nodded. 'They were the élite of the *Waffen*, or armed, SS, all right. And principally Hitler's bodyguard. First formed after the Night of the Long Knives when the SA leadership was destroyed by Hitler because he saw them as a threat to his own future and survival. Sepp Dietrich, a fanatical and dedicated Nazi officer and a close friend of Hitler's, decided to set up a special SS unit to act as Hitler's bodyguard in any future crisis. The men were all hand-picked and hardened Nazis and fanatically loyal supporters of Hitler. The unit later grew to become a division. They were also instrumental in setting up Die Spinne and helping to get much of the Nazi gold to South America.' Birken paused and smiled. 'It's interesting, but there is a slim connection between this fellow Erhard Schmeltz and Reimer.'

'What kind of connection?'

'Reimer was Leibstandarte SS. Erhard Schmeltz was SA. A Brownshirt.'

When Volkmann nodded, Birken went on, 'Well, the Brownshirt SA were initially set up as Hitler's bodyguard. But after the Night of the Long Knives in 1934 when they were purged, some of their members, the ones ardently loyal to Hitler, were inducted into the ranks of the Leibstandarte SS.' Birken shrugged. 'It's a small connection, but a connection nonetheless.'

'What happened to Sepp Dietrich?'

'He survived the war and was sent to trial, but served only about ten years for war crimes. He died in Germany during the seventies.'

Volkmann glanced at his watch, then at the telephone on the study desk. 'I'm booked on the twelve-thirty flight back, Ted. Do you mind if I use your telephone to call a taxi?'

'Not at all. Let me do it for you.'

It was ten minutes later when they saw the taxi pull up on the gravel path outside. Volkmann finished his drink and Birken stood up shakily.

'One last question, Ted. Did you ever hear of something called the Brandenburg Testament?'

The old man thought a moment, scratched his chin. Finally he said, 'No, I'm afraid not. What is it?'

Volkmann shook his head, smiled. 'I'm afraid I've no idea, but probably nothing important. Thanks for your help, Ted.'

'Sorry I couldn't be more useful.' Birken paused, then said, 'About Schmeltz, there is something I could do, it may be worth a try if you're trying to get a fix on him.'

'What?'

'So many of the old Nazis are dead, of course. But there are still a few of them alive. I have a contact in the German Federal Archives Office in Koblenz. I could ask him to check and see if he can come up with some numbers close to Schmeltz's party membership number and check them with the WASt.'

'What's that?'

'It's an acronym for the *Wehrmacht Auskunft Stelle*. That's the German army information agency. It's in Reinickendorf in north Berlin and it's one of the main German military personnel records offices. The WASt keeps information on all former German army personnel, going back to before the last war. That includes SS, which was actually part of the army. Whenever former German military personnel wanted to claim state or federal pensions, either because they were war invalids or they had reached retirement age, they had to apply through the WASt. Only when the WASt had confirmed their military service records could the pensions be paid.'

'You mean former members of the SS are paid pensions?'

'Dreadful as that seems, yes.'

'How can the WASt help?'

'Well, if we can get a list of Nazi Party membership numbers and names that were close to Schmeltz's, and those people served in the German military or SS during the war and are still alive, they ought to be receiving pensions. The WASt will have a record of their addresses when they applied.'

'You think that will help?'

'Well, it's a long shot and there can't be too many of the old boys still around, especially those whose party numbers were close to Schmeltz's number. And even if they knew of Schmeltz they may have long forgotten him or not even want to talk. But it's the only hope you've got.'

'What if these people have changed their addresses in the meantime?'

Birken smiled. 'That's where German thoroughness comes in. Until a couple of years ago it used to be the law that whenever any German citizen changed their address they had to inform an office called the *Einwohnermeldeamt*. It was a special registration office run by the police. So finding addresses for these people isn't really a problem. Your real problem is the fact that so many of them will probably be dead by now. But leave it with me for now, and I'll see what I can come up with.'

'Thanks, Ted. I appreciate your help.'

'Not at all, my boy.' Birken's wrinkled hand went to his forehead. 'Come to think of it, there's someone who may be able to help you with the photograph of the girl. That's assuming the other figure in the photograph was a reasonably high-ranking Nazi or even Leibstandarte SS.'

'Who?'

'An American named Erdberg. Cole Erdberg. He used to work for the CIA but they kicked him out some years back. He's also a Nazi and SS buff. Especially SS.'

'Where can I find him, do you know?'

'He runs a small antiques shop in Amsterdam, but his real business is selling Nazi memorabilia to collectors.' Birken smiled and the watery blue eyes twinkled. 'I'm not quite sure if Erdberg's bread is fully baked – he's a bit of a fruitcake. But he just may be able to help. He's got a prodigious memory. So if he's seen the girl before in any photographs, he ought to remember her.'

'He's in the Amsterdam phonebook?'

'I would imagine so. His place is on the Herengracht. Tell him I sent you and that I thought he might be able to help.'

'Thanks, Ted.'

'Not at all, my boy. A pleasure.'

Birken led him to the front door and the blue eyes sparkled as he gripped Volkmann's hand. 'I'll be in touch if anything turns up.' He smiled. 'Do call again some time. It's so seldom one gets visitors these days.'

It was almost noon when the taxi pulled up outside the Departures terminal and as Volkmann paid the driver he noticed the dark green Citroën pull up across from the terminal. He had noticed the car in the rear-view mirror on the way in from the lake road.

It was too far away for him to get a good look at the two passengers inside without making it obvious, but when he went to check in he noticed the blond young man with the newspaper standing by the Hertz desk. He wore a long, dark winter overcoat and his hair was cropped close to his skull.

Volkmann thought there was something familiar about him until he felt certain he remembered that he had seen him that morning at the airport, standing by the courtesy desk as he came out of Arrivals.

When he was handed back his boarding card Volkmann looked round. There was no sign of the young man with the newspaper.

Volkmann walked back out to the Departure entrance and stepped outside. The green Citroën had disappeared and the blond man wasn't among the crowd on the concourse.

Volkmann waited another ten minutes, going through the old routines, but he noticed no one watching him and he was certain he wasn't followed as he walked back towards the boarding gate.

Chapter Twenty-Seven

Volkmann arrived back at DSE Headquarters at three. He telephoned Peters' office and was told by his secretary that he had left early. There was a message for Volkmann from the duty officer and when he was put through, Jan De Vries came on the line.

'There was an unclassified signal came through the Italian Desk,' the Dutchman said. 'They say they're rechecking all sea-port cargo manifests that arrived from South America within the last month. If they come across anything they'll get back to you.' De Vries paused. 'There's also a voice-analysis report that just came in from your place in Beaconsfield. You want me to pass it on to Peters, Joe?'

'I'll pick it up myself, Jan. Thanks.'

When he replaced the receiver he lit a cigarette and went to stand by the window. There was some correspondence on his desk but he ignored it for now. He felt certain the blond young man at the airport in Zurich had been watching him, and that the two men in the green Citroën had followed him out from the Zurichsee. But why? And who were the men? Had he seen the blond man outside the departures terminal he would have turned the tail around, only that hadn't happened. The business at the airport made him feel uneasy. Apart from Facilities and Peters, only the girl had known he was travelling to Zurich. He remembered she had asked him what time his flight left. Or had she asked him simply when he was leaving? He couldn't remember the words exactly, but the thought bothered him.

He signed for the Beaconsfield report then went back up to his office and read the two-page flimsy.

The report had determined three voices on the tape, all male.

The first was approximately aged in his late forties, and the diphthong and syntax analyses had regionalised the accent to within the Munich area, most likely the western city region. The man was a non-smoker and his build suggested as medium to heavy and the social class determined as middle.

The two other voices, the report stated, had proven more difficult. In both cases the German they spoke was a softer version of *plattdeutsch*. But it was not a native-spoken dialect and the analysis suggested that both men were bilingual, their voices softened by a Latinate tongue, most likely Spanish. Class in both cases impossible to determine exactly but possibly middle.

Of the other two voices one was of a speaker aged roughly in his middle-thirties, a smoker, likely stocky build. And the third voice was of a man aged in his early to middle sixties. Possibly thin to medium build, and a non-smoker.

The German they spoke was regionalised to non-ethnic German colonies within either Paraguay or Argentina, but again difficult to determine which exactly and the report suggested it could be a border region straddling both territories.

Volkmann read through the report several times and then made two copies and left one each marked for the attention of Ferguson and Peters.

When he went through the correspondence on his desk, he found a large envelope from Peters containing the photocopied material from the American Document Centre in Berlin. He opened it and slid out the contents.

There were two manila folders inside, each containing a sheaf of photocopied pages. There was a note paperclipped to the front of one of the folders. It explained that one set of copies was from Heinrich Reimer's file and the second from Erhard Schmeltz's, and they were copies of the original documents held at the Berlin Document Centre.

Volkmann picked Reimer's first.

All the relevant information was in the file. SS number, Nazi Party number, and application forms for each, filled out and signed by Reimer himself. There were notes concerning his education, medical check, his officer training courses, his transfers and promotions, up to October 1944. The space for his marital status said he was single and there were blank spaces to record the names or births of any children Reimer had fathered. There was also a four-page copy of Reimer's family tree, dating back to 1800, to show the Aryan purity of his background.

Three of the pages were copies of a typed questionnaire, called a *Fragebogen*. According to the notes from the Document Centre, this was standard practice for SS officers. The replies were neatly written in Reimer's own handwriting. Reimer's age at the time was given as twenty-five and his place of birth as Lübars in Berlin.

There was a handwritten, one-page personal biography. Reimer started with his date and place of birth and went on to describe his education and family background, the son of a bakery worker, his involvement on the fringes of the Nazi Party in his late teens in 1929, to his joining the party in 1930; his entrance into the Leibstandarte SS in July 1934. Most of the information was unremarkable and described his involvment in helping at party rallies and his attendance at party education seminars and it was all written in a stilted fashion, the last paragraph a gushing statement of Reimer's dedication to Adolf Hitler and the Nazi Party. It was signed by Reimer and his rank given as *SS Untersturmführer*, lieutenant.

The third page contained three black-and-white photographs of Reimer. Two were head-and-shoulders shots; one front and one side profile. The third was a full-length photograph of Reimer in the black uniform of Untersturmführer SS, taken against a white background. His hands were clasped in front of him and he wore polished, high black boots and wing trousers. His SS rune flashes were visible on his collar. On the left sleeve of his officer's uniform was a swastika armband and above the sleeve cuff another armband that said, 'Adolf Hitler'.

All three photographs were of a solemn-looking young man

with cropped blond hair and a sharp face and bore little resemblance to the photograph Sanchez had shown him. There were the same thin lips and high forehead, but that was where the similarity ended.

Reimer's promotions from his entry into the ranks of the SS officers corps in 1934 to 1945 when he had attained the rank of *Sturmbannführer*, Major, were all recorded. He had seen service in Austria, Poland, Russia, France and the Balkans. His last posting was recorded in October 1944, when he was transferred to a Leibstandarte SS training school in Berlin's Lichterfelde district.

Volkmann put Reimer's file aside and opened the folder on Erhard Schmeltz.

There were four pages inside and one was a copy of Schmeltz's original Nazi Party application form. At the top of the application it read: *Nationalsozialistische Deutsche Arbeiterpartei*, and underneath: *München Braunes Haus*, the address of the Nazi Party Headquarters in Munich. Below the header was the application proper.

There was a line for the applicant's signature and it contained Erhard Schmeltz's, the letters firm and bold. For Profession or Occupation, the words *Fabrik Werkmeister*, Factory Foreman, were written in Schmeltz's handwriting. The place and date of birth were given as Hamburg, March 6th, 1880. In a box in the top right-hand corner was stamped the number 68964.

Schmeltz's address was given as 23 Brennerallee in Schwabbing and the date of application was November 6th, 1927. Underneath the official's scrawl were the words *Verweisung: Hauptquartier*. Refer to headquarters.

Volkmann guessed it referred to the endorsement concerning Schmeltz's application Peters had told him about, and when he looked at the next page he saw a copy of a letter headed Prinz-Albrecht Strasse, Berlin, the headquarters of the Reichsführer SS.

The letter was dated three days before Schmeltz had applied for party membership and addressed to Gau: München. There was a terse message that simply said. '*I recommend immediate acceptance of party applicant Erhard Johann Schmeltz into Gau Munich. Any queries contact me personally.*' The letter was signed *H. Himmler, Der Reichsführer SS*, and the signature below the letter bore an official stamp.

The other two photocopies were front and back shots of Schmeltz's original Master File Card from Nazi Party records.

Schmeltz's card contained very little information; name and address, party membership number, date of entry into the party and the Nazi Gau and Ortsgruppe to which he belonged. There was a head-and-shoulders photograph of Schmeltz on the reverse side in a black bordered frame.

The face in the photograph showed a plain, middle-aged man with a broad, rural face and a thick, bullish neck. His dark hair had partly receded on top and what remained was oiled and combed over his scalp. He wore a dark, ill-fitting suit that looked tight under a stocky, muscular body and an old-style wing collar and tie. The eyes were narrow slits, but bright and piercing, and his bushy dark eyebrows were knit together as if he were trying to concentrate as he stared at the camera.

Volkmann stared down at the photograph for a long time, wondering again what had made Schmeltz leave Germany and travel to South America with his wife and child. And why he had received such large sums of money. There was nothing in his file to suggest why, and the only thing unusual was Himmler's letter, but Volkmann guessed many party applicants had asked senior ranking Nazis to look favourably on their application.

It was almost half an hour later before he finally put the folders containing the copied pages back in the envelope.

He checked with the international operator and got an address and phone number for Cole Erdberg on Amsterdam's Herengracht. When he phoned, a female voice answered.

She sounded young and Volkmann asked if he could speak with Erdberg.

'He's not here, he's away on business. Can I help?'

'I'm afraid not. Can you tell me when he'll be back?'

'Tomorrow morning.'

Volkmann thanked the woman but didn't leave his name and said he'd call back, then phoned Facilities and had them book him on the first available flight to Amsterdam the next morning. When they confirmed he had a seat on the 8 a.m. flight he tidied his desk and left the office and drove to his apartment.

It was after five and dark when he let himself in and he saw the girl had set the table for dinner. She told him she had gone shopping in Petite France and bought fresh fish and vegetables and two bottles of Sauterne and intended cooking dinner for both of them.

She looked good in jeans and a tight sweater that showed off her figure and her hair was down and fell about her shoulders. Over the meal he told her about the voice analyses report and his visit to Zurich but he made no mention of the man at the airport who had followed him.

'Did your friend in Zurich have any idea why Erhard Schmeltz received the money from the Reichsbank?'

He told her what Ted Birken had said, then shook his head. 'But he was just speculating, Erica. So anything is possible. Even blackmail could have been the reason Schmeltz received the money. What about you, did you turn up anything?'

'I spent the day at the *Frankfurter Zeitung* office, going through the library cuttings.'

'And?'

The girl hesitated. 'Lubsch must have told you the truth. At least about the two people Kesser wanted him to kill.'

'Why?'

'There was a man named Herbert Rauscher murdered in East Berlin five months ago. It's got to be the same man. The Berlin papers ran stories and they were picked up by the major dailies.'

'Tell me.'

'The reports said Rauscher was shot at his apartment near the Pergamon Museum. Two bullet wounds in the head. He died immediately. According to the newspapers there were no witnesses and the Berlin police had no leads. I telephoned the Berlin homicide department but they wouldn't give me any information, other than that the case is still under investigation and no one has been arrested and charged with the murder.'

Volkmann looked across at the girl. 'What about the woman?'

'Her name was Hedda Pohl and she was murdered too.'

'Where?'

'Not far from Friedrichshafen in southern Germany, where she came from. It's near the Swiss border, beside Lake Konstanz. The murder happened a week before Herbert Rauscher was killed. All the Munich papers ran stories but I rang the local one in Friedrichshafen.'

'What did they say?'

'I spoke to one of the reporters. She said the woman was murdered between midnight and 2 a.m. in a wood outside the town. She was shot three times in the head and back. The reporter knew very little except that the case was still open. She just gave me what details she could. Hedda Pohl was in her early sixties, the widow of a businessman, with two grown children. She seemed pretty highly regarded in the town. There was no motive for the murder and the police didn't seem to be making much progress.'

'Did you contact the local police in Friedrichshafen?'

The girl shook her head. 'No, I thought you'd want to do that. But I've put a file together with all the newspaper cuttings I could get on the murders.'

'What about Rauscher's background? Did the newspaper reports say?'

'Just that he was a businessman, that's all.'

Volkmann sighed and thought a moment. 'What about the politician, Massow?'

The girl brushed a strand of blonde hair from her face. 'Still very much alive. He's got an office in the Kreutzberg district in Berlin. It's a place where mostly poor immigrants live. I telephoned and his secretary said Massow was away for several days at a convention in Paris, but she pencilled you in for an appointment in two days' time. 10 a.m. in Massow's Kreuzberg office.'

He wondered whether to mention the man at Zurich airport,

but decided not to. He told her he would be gone the next morning for a day or two at most but he did not tell her where and she didn't ask him. The blue eyes were looking back at him and he smiled across at her as he cleared away the dinner table. 'Now, how about some coffee?'

She had opened another bottle of Sauterne and he spent a half-hour reading through the file she had made from the newspaper cuttings on the murders. There was very little detailed information in the articles apart from what Erica had told him but when he finished reading the cuttings on Herbert Rauscher he decided he needed to talk with Jakob Fischer in Berlin. Fischer was a detective in the Berlin KriminalAmt whom he knew well and the only contact he could think of who might help him keep his inquiry into Rauscher's murder unofficial. He knew no one in Friedrichshafen and there it would be a matter of figuring out how to get the information on Hedda Pohl's death from the local police.

Several times he had gone to the window when the girl wasn't in the room and looked down at the parking lot and the street opposite but he saw nothing suspicious and if he was being watched then whoever was doing the watching was good. He had left the Beretta in his overcoat pocket so the girl wouldn't see it and become alarmed.

As she came to sit beside him on the couch Volkmann saw the soft nape of her neck as she leaned forward to refill their glasses. He thought she looked very beautiful. Her skin was tanned and flawless and she wore no bra underneath the simple white cotton top. As she leaned forward he saw the cleft between her full breasts and the dark rise of her nipples under the thin cotton.

When she sat back she noticed him staring at her.

'What are you looking at, Joe?'

'You.'

She didn't blush but turned away. When she looked back, Volkmann said, 'Did you love Rudi?'

There was a look like pain on her face and she closed

her eyes and opened them again before she answered the question.

'Yes, I loved him. But not in the way you might mean. He was good to me. He always made me laugh. And there were times in my life when Rudi was the only person I could turn to. There were certain things I had to face up to, unpleasant things, and he was there when I needed to talk. Even if only on the telephone.'

'You think he loved you too?'

She hesitated, then said, 'Yes. I think he did.'

'What were the times you say he was the only one you could turn to?'

She hesitated again. 'Why do you want to know?'

'For the same reason you wanted to know about me.'

She looked over at him and then turned away. When she finally spoke her voice was almost a whisper.

'There was a time when I felt ashamed. Ashamed of certain things in my family's past.'

She hesitated, bit her lip and Volkmann knew she wouldn't go on. He said quietly, 'You mean about your father?'

The blue eyes turned to him again but this time he saw the startled look on her face as she blushed.

'How did you know?'

'Erica, the German police keep files on most of your country's citizens, you must know that.'

'You mean especially on the children of war criminals?'

Volkmann nodded. 'It's your government, Erica. And it's been so for almost fifty years.'

The girl said nothing for a long time. When she looked back she said, 'Tell me what you know.'

He didn't repeat all the details in the file but there was no need to. 'Your father served in the Leibstandarte SS Division. The same Division as Heinrich Reimer.'

'What else do you know?'

'At the end of the war he escaped to South America. The war crimes people tracked him down to Buenos Aires but he died before he could be extradited.'

The girl said nothing for several moments, then finally

she said, 'The first day I met you, did you know about my father?'

'Yes.' He looked at the girl as she spoke.

'That first time we met I sensed you found it difficult being near me. It was in your manner, in the way you looked at me. That maybe you hated me a little. Did you hate me a little, Joe?'

He shook his head. 'No, I didn't hate you, Erica. Hate's too strong a word. Distrust, maybe.'

'Because I was the daughter of an SS officer? Because of what happened to your parents? And now you must distrust me even more because my father was in the same SS Division as this man Reimer.'

He did not speak and the girl looked at his face. 'Was that the reason why you didn't want to sleep with me, Joe? Because of who my father was?'

'Yes.'

She shook her head. 'You know, it is a terrible thing that hate or distrust can be carried from one generation to another, Joe. That it can be passed from father to son. Because if that is so then there is no hope for any of us, not ever. Don't you see? You are blaming me for my father's sins also.'

Volkmann hesitated, then shook his head. 'I'm not blaming you for anything, Erica.'

'Oh, but you are, Joe, you are. Even though maybe you don't want to. I want to tell you something. When I was a little girl my father was everything to me. But I didn't know what he had done. Killed people in cold blood. Men, women, children. I didn't know that the hands I had held had inflicted so much suffering and death. I trusted him. And when he died I felt I had lost someone that I had looked up to. I was sixteen when I first heard the rumours. And it was a year later before my mother finally told me the truth. From that moment on, he was no longer the Papa I had loved but a beast. He had let me love him and trust him when he didn't deserve my trust or love. But no, your files will never tell you that. They will never tell you the pain and suffering and the humiliation of the families and children of these people who shamed Germany so. Do you think every child of every Nazi is proud of his parents' past? Do you, Joe? Some, maybe, but they are sick people. Decent people, ordinary people, they suffered because of what their parents did. I carry a scar around as much as you.'

'Tell me.'

She looked at him for a long time and then she said, 'I can only tell you how I felt after I learned the truth about my father. I used to wash myself – my hands, my body – a dozen times a day just to try and rid myself of him, the places he had touched me, kissed me. I had no choice in who my father was. But I could never trust a man again. Except maybe Rudi.'

The blue eyes looked at him intently. 'We are both victims. You a victim of your father's past and I of mine. But you cannot see that, Joe. You think all Germans are untrustworthy and barbarians.'

'I never said that.'

'You don't have to. It's in your eyes. In the way you distance yourself. Just like now. You still don't trust me, do you, Joe?'

Volkmann said nothing. Finally he looked at the girl's face. 'I was followed in Zurich today.'

'What do you mean?'

'The man I went to meet in Zurich. Two men in a green Citroën followed me from his home to the airport.'

'What are you saying?'

'Apart from my office, you were the only one who knew I'd be in Zurich.'

Volkmann saw the girl's face turn red, and her eyes blazed back at him.

'What are you saying? You think I told someone?' When Volkmann didn't reply the girl said, 'Who could I have told, Joe?'

'I don't know, Erica.'

She looked at him for a long time before she shook her head. 'You really still don't trust me, do you, Joe? Because you can't trust anyone. I won't even dignify your question by telling you what I think of it.'

He saw the wet eyes and the struggle on her face to keep

back the tears and he wondered if she was genuine. She didn't cry but sat there looking at him, her lips quivering.

As she stood up slowly, she said, 'And now I am tired. I will say goodnight, Joe.'

He watched her leave the room and he sat there, not knowing what to say or whether to believe her.

He called Facilities again to have them change his ticket and book a connecting flight from Amsterdam to Berlin the next morning. He would have to speak with Jakob Fischer in Berlin about Rauscher's case and he made a note in his diary to call the detective at the Berlin KriminalAmt the next day.

He went to bed just after eleven but slept fitfully and woke at two. He crossed to the window and lit a cigarette and then pulled back the curtains.

It had stopped raining and in the distance he could see the lights of Germany. The door to his bedroom was open and he stubbed out his cigarette and crossed to the hallway and opened the door to the girl's room. The bedside lamp was still on but Erica was asleep. He could see her bare tanned shoulders and her blonde hair lay strewn about the pillow. For a long time he stood there, looking down at her, and he thought how beautiful she looked.

The girl was right: he trusted no one. He wondered if he had been too harsh with her and too distrustful. And what she had said about him not sleeping with her had been true. He felt attracted to her physically and in a strange sort of way emotionally, though his distrust had held him back. And he knew it was really the thought of what men like her father had once done to his Papa. But how could it not be so? He had loved the man and had there been any way to cancel out his father's pain or repay the people who had caused him so much suffering he would have done it a long time ago.

A car hooted in the distance and distracted him. He looked at the girl's sleeping face one last time before he flicked off the bedside lamp and crossed over to the window and pulled back the curtain. The window looked out towards Strasbourg and the lights of the city peppered the darkness. He thought briefly of the report from Beaconsfield. Three voices. Three men. A little more substance to go with the shadow but still things moving too slowly.

Sie werden alle umgebracht. They will all be killed.

He went through the taped conversation again in his mind, trying to unravel what he had learned in the last few days, trying to find threads that connected, pieces of the puzzle to fit into a shape or pattern. There were two separate but perhaps parallel lines: what was happening now and what had happened in the past. The people from the Chaco house and what they were doing now. And Tsarkin and the man Schmeltz and his past and the photograph of the young girl, and how they related to the present.

How and why did they connect?

He wondered if Sanchez had made any progress. The two disparate dialects on the tape had confirmed that there was a link between Paraguay and Europe. But what was the link? And what Lubsch had said had disturbed him more than he let the girl know. Yet still he was floundering.

He heard the soft rustle of sheets and turned round, saw Erica sit up and look at him sleepily in the light washing through the window. She startled a moment before she spoke:

'Joe . . .?'

'It's me. Go back to sleep.'

She looked very young and very innocent just then, like a child woken from sleep. And as she sat there looking at him in the pale light that washed through the window he realised how much he wanted her.

'Some of the things I said . . . I'm sorry, Joe. Can you forgive me?'

Her voice was husky with tiredness and he could smell the scent of her body as he went to sit on the edge of the bed and looked at her.

'Maybe it was my fault too. Maybe you were right in what you said.'

'Then will you do something for me?'

'What?'

'Try to trust me, Joe.' He placed a hand on her face. She

pushed her cheek into his open palm and then kissed his fingers.

It seemed to happen so naturally and as she pulled him towards her he found her mouth and kissed her. His hand cupped one of her breasts and as he moved onto the bed beside her she was already pulling him on top of her urgently, kissing his neck and face and lips, her nails raking the sensitive flesh of his back and tearing at his clothes.

There was a savagery to their love-making that surprised Volkmann. As if both of them were in the grip of some uncontrollable frenzy and when they finally spent themselves their bodies were drenched in sweat.

For a long time afterwards they both lay there, the girl's head on Volkmann's chest.

Her voice came to him out of the darkness. 'Tell me about your father, Joe. Tell me what happened to him.'

'Why do you want to know?'

'Because I want to know everything about you.'

He looked away then, towards darkness, towards nothingness, and when he spoke his voice was soft.

'When the Germans came to the Sudetenland my father's family moved to Poland, to a village near Cracow. My father and his parents and his two young sisters. Then the war came and it wasn't safe any more. The *Einsatzgruppen* were moving through the villages, rounding up and killing Jews. They were the special groups of mobile killing squads the Nazis used before they organised the extermination camps. One day my father's parents went out to get some food. They never came back and my father never saw them again.

'My father was fourteen. The two little girls were eight and ten. On the fifth day when his parents didn't come back he knew something had happened. He learned in the village one of the *Einsatzgruppen* had come and taken them away. He decided to try and make it over the Tatra mountains to reach Budapest where his mother had relatives. He got some food and wrapped up the little girls in warm clothes and they set off.

'On the third day they reached the border. One of the killing squads caught up with them. They took them into a forest clearing with a group of other Jews and made them stand in front of a shallow pit. My father knew what was going to happen. Everybody did. His sisters were trembling and crying and so was he. My father begged one of the guards to spare the little girls.

'The guards pulled my father aside and called him a filthy Jew and made him watch while they stripped the small girls. They raped them in front of his eyes. Then they threw the girls into the pit and shot them.

'Then they made my father kneel down in front of the pit. The guards were drunk. The one who shot my father in the face wounded him but didn't kill him. My father lay in the pit with the bodies of his sisters, pretending to be dead. When the Germans had finished their work they just covered all the bodies with clay and left.

'My father lay there, bleeding, too shocked to move, and barely able to breathe. When it was dark he managed to free himself from the pit and the tangle of corpses. He buried his sisters in a shallow grave and wandered the mountains for days with a bullet in his face. This time he made it to Budapest and his relatives.

'Then the Germans came again. His relatives were taken away. My father was caught in a round-up and they sent him to Dachau, then Belsen. The others were sent to the ovens. My father survived, but he could never forget what had happened to his two young sisters.'

He lay there silent in the darkness and he could hear the girl breathing. He couldn't tell if she was crying and he didn't speak or make a sound. It was such a long-ago pain that he couldn't cry, and all he could do was think of his father.

It seemed the silence went on forever in the darkness, and it was a long time before her hand came to touch his face. But the girl said nothing. There was nothing to say.

PART FOUR

Chapter Twenty-Eight

Asunción.
Sunday,
December 18th,
2.45 p.m.

Thick, juicy steaks and fat sausages sizzled on the charcoal barbeque and sunlight washed the garden.

Vellares Sanchez gazed down at one of the slabs of meat with no appetite as he speared it with a fork, turned it over to reveal the pink and bloodied rare underneath. Many things bothering him. Many things but all connected to one thing.

The face of Rudi Hernandez flashed before his eyes. Lying on the morgue slab. White sheet pulled back, wounds uncovered.

Sanchez grimaced and looked away from the sizzling, unappetising meat towards the sunlit garden. Clusters of neighbours and friends and relatives stood chatting, drinks in hand. A special day. Maria, his youngest daughter, had made her Communion.

Innocent girls in white Communion frocks and boys in ill-fitting suits sipped lemonade and ate chocolate cake and traipsed about the lawn, bored now the ceremony was over. Not that Sanchez necessarily wanted to be here this day himself. But family duty was family duty. He saw Maria catch his eye and wave at him and smile. He waved and smiled back.

The girl was pretty. Very pretty. A tribute to her mother's good looks. One day the boys would be falling over themselves to catch her eye. But not yet. Innocence was to be savoured.

The girl came up to him, flouncing her white frock.

'Is the food ready yet, Papa? I'm hungry.'

Sanchez patted her head of dark, curled hair. 'Not yet, my sweet.' He saw his wife Rosario coming towards him from the patio. She had gone inside the house earlier, to freshen up, Sanchez had thought, but now she had a frown on her face.

He tapped his daughter's shoulder. 'Do Papa a favour, precious. Go see if everyone is OK for drinks.'

The girl nodded and skipped away.

Rosario came up beside him, still frowning.

'I thought this was your day off?'

'It is.'

'Is everything OK?'

He nodded. 'The food's almost ready.'

'I didn't mean the food.' She saw him look at her with sleepy, curious eyes and she said, 'Detective Cavales is inside. He said he was passing and decided to call. I asked him to join us but he said no. He'd rather speak to you in private.'

'Where is he now?'

'In your study.'

'Then I had better see him. Do me a favour. Take care of the steaks.'

As he turned to go his wife said, 'And I thought you were going to be free today.'

He shrugged. 'So did I.' He kissed her cheek as she frowned. 'A policeman's lot is not a happy one.'

'Nor his wife's. But you should have told me that before you asked me to marry you.'

Sanchez smiled. 'And risked losing such a beautiful woman?'

She frowned in mockery then smiled back at him, picked up two cans of beer from the buffet table and handed them to her husband.

'Take one in to Cavales. He looks as though he could do with a drink.'

'He looks that bad?'

'He looks thirsty.'

He took the beers, crossed to the patio and stepped inside. The house was cool after the garden. Plants and flowers everywhere. Why had women such an obsession with flora, he wondered? It was a mystery he had never been able to solve.

He found Cavales standing by the study window, examining a hardy yucca plant. Hardy because it had been able to withstand the fumes from Sanchez' untipped cigarettes and thrive. Sanchez closed the door and crossed to where the detective stood and handed him the beer.

'Compliments of Rosario. She said you looked like you needed one.'

Cavales nodded. 'It's hot.' He looked towards the scene on the lawn outside. 'Nice day for a barbeque.'

'Maria's Communion,' Sanchez explained. Cavales was single. No ties. No responsibilities. But a good cop. Ambitious, in a quiet way. And thorough.

'So,' Sanchez said finally, 'what brings you to this neck of the woods on my one day off. It's not a social call?'

Cavales shook his head. He appeared tired. Like Sanchez, he had been working hard. Too hard. Days and late evenings working on the case. And others besides. Manpower was limited right now. People on summer leave. Sanchez gazed out of the window and sipped the cold beer.

'Tell me.'

'I've been over at Tsarkin's house again.'

Sanchez turned to look at his colleague. 'Go on.'

'I know we searched it three, maybe four times and found nothing.'

Sanchez smiled. 'But you wanted to pick over the bones?'

Cavales nodded. 'Something like that.'

'So what did you find that the rest of us couldn't find?'

'What makes you think I found something?'

'You see enough of my face at the office. And I'm not such an attractive man.'

Cavales smiled. 'You're right.'

'That I'm not such an attractive man or I was right?'

'The second.'

'Good. For a moment I thought you were going to hurt my feelings.' Sanchez half smiled, sipped his beer, blinked. 'So, tell me.'

'I went through all the rooms again. Top to bottom. Just in case we missed something.' Cavales paused. 'We did.'

Sanchez raised his eyes. 'And what did we miss?'

'Photographs.'

Sanchez blinked. 'Explain.'

'Photographs. Everybody keeps them. Albums. Of friends. Acquaintances. Relatives.'

Sanchez shook his head. 'There were none. I remember. Except one. A photograph of Tsarkin himself. On a dressing table in his bedroom.'

'That's what I mean. There were no other photographs other than the one in the bedroom,' Cavales said quietly. 'Old people. They always got photographs.'

Sanchez smiled. The man had a perceptive mind. 'Go on.'

'I spoke to Tsarkin's butler about it. He was very uncomfortable when I mentioned the photographs. Even more than when we spoke to him before. Like he had something to hide.'

'And did he?'

Cavales nodded. He put down his beer and lit a cigarette, offered one to Sanchez, who accepted.

'You bet.' Cavales glanced towards the scene beyond the window, then back at Sanchez again. 'I told him if there was anything he knew and hadn't told us, he could be in big trouble. I told him I wanted him to come down to the station. The old guy got upset. Said he hadn't done anything wrong.'

'But what *had* he done?'

'He said the day after Tsarkin committed suicide, and before we thoroughly searched the property, a man came to the house. An acquaintance of Tsarkin's who occasionally visited. A businessman, the butler thought. He asked what the police had done. Wanted to know if there were any papers left behind by Tsarkin. When the butler said no, he said he wanted to look just in case. When the butler protested, the man persuaded him it might be better if he co-operated.'

'This man threatened him?'

Cavales shrugged. 'Implied, rather than verbal.'

'Continue.'

'The man searched the house thoroughly. He took away some photograph albums Tsarkin kept.'

'And?'

'That's it. He also told the butler to tell no one he had been there, or that anything was missing.'

Sanchez sighed, blew out smoke. He sat on the edge of the chair by the window. 'The visitor. Did you get a name?'

Cavales smiled and nodded. 'After a little friendly persuasion.'

'The name?'

'Franz Lieber.'

'Who is he?'

'All I know right now is that he was an acquaintance of Tsarkin's. But the name is obviously German.'

Sanchez glanced out of the window towards the sunlit gardens and the cheerful knots of visitors. Maria was comparing dresses with another little girl. His wife stood among a circle of female friends, laughing. He loved that woman, loved her to distraction. Many times he wished he wasn't a cop, had chosen a different vocation so that he could spend more time with her and Maria.

He turned to Cavales. 'Give me an hour. I'll meet you at the office. I want Lieber's address. Information on his background.'

'I'm checking already. Two of the day shift are working on it.'

Sanchez nodded. 'An hour then.'

When Cavales had left quietly without finishing his beer, Sanchez moved closer to the window.

Sunshine swamped the lawn. The sound of laughter reached him. A day to enjoy. Rosario wouldn't like it if he left, but he had work to do. He checked his watch; half an hour, then he'd drive to the office.

He stubbed out his cigarette and went to rejoin his guests.

4.35 p.m.

The brothel was near the railway station and the Plaza Urguaya.

Despite its shabby exterior, inside the decor was sumptuous. Coral blue stucco walls, expensive cotton print drapes. Silk-sheeted beds. Saunas and steaming showers for clients to cleanse their sweaty, sated bodies. Private rooms decorated with panache and with an eye for the discerning client.

The girls were equally attractive. Reputedly the prettiest in Asunción. And the most expensive.

Lieber had picked a girl no more than fifteen. His companion had preferred a more mature woman. Large-busted, thirty, voluptuous hips. Two bottles of champagne had been brought.

When they had been drunk and the sex was over, Lieber found his wallet and peeled off some notes and handed them to the girls as they threw on flimsy gowns. The second man still lay on the bed, a glass of champagne in his hand, a grin on his weasel face.

'Take it,' Lieber said to the girls. 'A bonus.'

As the girls went to leave, Lieber said to the older of the two, 'My friend and I have some business to discuss. Tell Rosa to make sure we're not disturbed.'

The girl nodded and left with her friend, Lieber watching the pair of pale, retreating buttocks through her flimsy gown with diminishing pleasure.

He took two fresh glasses and a half-finished bottle of champagne from a nearby table and turned to the still naked man sitting on the bed.

'Well, Pablo . . . You're satisfied?'

The man opposite Lieber was small and wiry. His name was Pablo Arcades. For ten of his thirty-five years he had been a *seguridad* officer. An invaluable acquaintance of Lieber's. Especially since the man had two universal vices. Money and women. As vices they were weaknesses to be exploited.

The man grinned as he pulled on his trousers. 'You know me. I could fuck all day.' He zipped his pants and slipped on his shirt. 'You brought the money?'

'Afterwards. First, let's talk.'

6.02 p.m.

Lieber drove back through the darkening Asunción streets.

He had made the call on the mobile phone ten minutes before, to verify the girl, remembering her name from the list, the names in the web. She would have to be contacted as a matter of urgency, of that much Lieber was certain, to confirm what had happened, the ramifications of any further progress made clear to her.

The rest of Arcades' information he would pass on. It would have to be acted on, quickly. The men would have to be dealt with. Volkmann. Sanchez. But Volkmann's part he couldn't understand; a *British* DSE officer, and not German. If anything, it should have been German. Lieber shook his head in confusion; the girl would be able to explain. He didn't understand why she hadn't been contacted before now. What was the bitch up to?

His mind was preoccupied as he went through a check list of what had to be done. First contact security, then Kruger in Mexico City. They were there for another forty-eight hours. There was business to be discussed with old Halder and the Brazilian, Ernesto. And there would be visitors, old faces calling to pay their respects, and offering their advice for the days ahead.

Arcades' information would have to be discussed, decisions made; the girl's position clarified; take her out of the web or keep her in.

Lieber turned the Mercedes into the driveway of his house, going fast, tyres burning on gravel.

Out of the corner of his eye he caught sight of two men standing behind the open gates. Lieber, startled by their presence, was already fifteen metres beyond them, about to slam on the brakes and look back when his eyes caught sight of a second irregularity.

The lights were on in the porch and another two men

stood there, an unfamiliar white car parked directly outside the front door.

Panic gripped Lieber but there was no time. Already he had reached the top of the gravel path and come to a sharp halt in front of the car.

Lieber climbed out warily, as the two men came quickly forward.

'What's going on . . .? Who are you . . .?' Lieber demanded.

One of the two men spoke. He was short and fat and pale; his grubby suit hung loosely on his flabby body.

'Senor Lieber, I presume?'

Lieber said nothing.

The fat man smiled thinly as he looked up. 'My name is Sanchez. Captain Vellares Sanchez.'

Chapter Twenty-Nine

Asunción.
6.32 p.m.

Every light inside the house appeared to be on, the *mestizo* butler nowhere to be seen.

They were in the study. The two detectives and Lieber. The fat detective smoked a cigarette as his companion sifted through the contents of Lieber's polished walnut desk. The locks had been forced; papers and documents lay scattered on the floor and on top of the polished wood.

Lieber looked at the fat detective palely.

'You have no right . . .'

'*Senor*, I have every right.'

'May I remind you that I am a personal friend of the Police Commissioner's . . .'

'And might I remind you that my search warrant is in order.'

Lieber had seen the warrant, signed by a magistrate.

'There is no need to subject me to such treatment. If you would only tell me what it is you are looking for . . .?'

'I told you already.'

'I don't know what photographs you're talking about. All I know is my property has been damaged. And that this is a flagrant abuse of . . .'

'Please, *senor*. Spare me.' The hooded, sleepy eyes regarded Lieber carefully. 'If you simply told us where the photograph albums are, it would help matters.'

'I really don't know what you are talking about.'

Sanchez ignored the gaping look of acted innocence on Lieber's face. 'As I explained already, they were taken from the house of a friend of yours the day after he killed himself.

335

Tsarkin's butler already told us. Really, *senor*, you are wasting my time.'

Lieber swallowed. 'I refuse to speak until I have contacted my lawyer.'

'As you wish. You have a safe in the house?'

'A safe?'

'A safe for personal belongings. Businessmen usually have. And you own several businesses in Asunción, *senor*. An import-export agency. A property development company. A plush office on the Calle Palma.' Sanchez paused, letting Lieber know he'd done his homework, saw the man's eyebrows rise. 'So, do you have a safe here in the house?'

'That is none of your business.'

'*Senor*, you can be agreeable and co-operate. To do otherwise will certainly not help your situation.'

'And what is my situation?'

The fat man scratched his ear. 'If I am unsatisfied with your replies, you may find yourself under suspicion of being an accessory to the murder of one Rudi Hernandez, journalist. And two other murders, also.'

'That is quite ridiculous,' Lieber said hoarsely. 'I don't know what you are talking about.'

The detective ignored Lieber's words. 'You haven't answered my question. You have a safe?'

Lieber thought a moment, then slowly took a set of keys from his pocket, handed them to the fat detective. 'In the bedroom upstairs facing onto the driveway you will find a painting. A Vermeer copy. Behind it you will . . .'

Sanchez took the keys. 'I know.'

He spoke quietly to the two detectives for several moments before handing one of them the keys. The men left. Lieber heard their footsteps quickly climb the stairs.

Left alone with the fat man, Lieber glanced round, then said amicably, '*Amigo*, there must be some mistake. You know, I have friends in high places, people who could . . .'

The detective raised his pudgy hand to silence Lieber's words.

'Please. Spare me.' He sat down and produced a cigarette,

lit it. 'My men will search the rest of the house again. To be certain. This may take a little time.'

'My lawyer . . .'

Sanchez waved his hand dismissively once again and drew on his cigarette, blew smoke out into the warm air. 'I suggest you remain silent.' The fat face smiled thinly. 'I'm sure you are quite happy to do that.'

Lieber pursed his lips and said nothing.

It took almost an hour of waiting as Lieber sweated. Sweated but felt strangely confident. There was nothing in the house to incriminate him. Nothing to connect him to what had happened to the journalist and the girl. Not a shred.

He saw the two detectives come into the room as he sipped a scotch. One of them carried an album of photographs. Lieber frowned. It was an old album he kept in his bedroom. It hadn't been added to in years.

He saw the man Sanchez take it in both hands and examine it, begin to flick through the cellophaned leaves. After a time he pursed his lips and looked up, walked over to where Lieber stood.

Sanchez held up the album. 'This is yours?'

Lieber hesitated, then said, 'Yes, it belongs to me.'

Sanchez leaned forward, pointed to a photograph in the album. Lieber swallowed.

'This snapshot,' Sanchez asked. 'Where was it taken?'

The picture was of a white house. Three men together, Lieber one of them. Jungle flora cutting in on the right of the frame.

'I can't remember,' Lieber said hoarsely.

'*Think*. In the Chaco perhaps?'

'I told you. I can't remember. It's an old photograph.'

The detective saw the look on Lieber's fleshy face and pointed again to the photograph. 'The man on the left is you. The other two men . . . Who are they?'

Lieber shook his head as he saw the detective's pudgy finger point out the two men in the photograph, taken many years before; one stocky and dark-haired and young, the other older, tall, silver-haired, handsome.

'I told you. It was taken a long time ago. I don't recall.'

Lieber saw the detective stare at him, frustration on his fat face. The man was unsure of himself, Lieber could tell. Searching. But lost.

'Senor Lieber. On the evening of November 25th and the early morning of November 26th, can you recall where you were?'

Lieber frowned and said, 'I was at home.'

'Alone?'

'Apart from one of my staff, yes.'

'How can you be so certain?'

'I had important paperwork to attend to.'

'No doubt your member of staff will attest to this if necessary?'

'No doubt, yes.'

Sanchez glared at the man, saw the confidence in his hard eyes. The answer had been too sure, too certain.

The detective to whom Sanchez had given the keys to the safe returned, shook his head as he handed them back. Sanchez grimaced, placed the keys on the coffee table in front of Lieber.

Lieber said, 'Have your men finished?'

The detective hesitated, then said, 'For now. *Si.*' He turned to the other man and gestured for him to leave them.

'You intend arresting me?'

'No.'

Lieber suppressed the sigh that almost came to his lips. 'Then I want you and your people off my property.' He stood to his full height, towering over the little man. 'Your Commissioner will hear about this intrusion of my privacy. Now leave. At once.'

Sanchez put down the photograph album on the study desk. For a long time he said nothing, simply stood there, staring up at Lieber's big bulk towering over him. When he spoke his voice was low, but threatening.

'*Senor*, I will be back. Again, and again, if necessary. I wish to assure you of that.'

'That's harassment.'

'No, *senor*,' Sanchez smiled grimly. 'I prefer to call it thoroughness. It is a terrible trait of mine. You must have patience with me.'

Lieber felt the anger rise in him. 'Be assured, your Commissioner will hear from me.'

Sanchez' smile broadened. 'Yes, I'm certain he will.' The detective hesitated, then said, 'But you see, *senor*, there is a certain matter of a tape. A tape recording of a conversation in a certain hotel. I'm sure you know what I'm talking about. So be assured, Senor Lieber, you will see me again.'

Lieber's smugness vanished. Perplexed, he felt the blood rise uncontrollably to his cheeks, saw the fat detective's hooded eyes stare up at him, search for a reaction.

Lieber checked himself, then said hoarsely, 'Go.'

He watched as the fat detective turned and left.

Forty minutes later Lieber was on the Plaza del Heros. He parked the Mercedes outside and checked the street. He had checked the rear-view mirror on the way and so far as he could tell he had not been followed, deciding to use a public phone in case the scrambler wasn't safe, or the telephones in his house were bugged.

In a hotel near the Plaza he got change in the bar and crossed to the telephone kiosks near the toilets. He made the two calls he needed to make, listened to the incredulous voices as he sweated in the tiny hot kiosk. He kept the conversations as short as possible, all the time his eyes searching the hotel lobby to make sure he wasn't being watched. He told them his plans and received their immediate approval.

The third call he made to an unlisted number on the outskirts of the city. Lieber told the man what he wanted done then put down the telephone and lit a cigarette and waited for the reply call.

It came less than five minutes later. Lieber listened to the voice and noted the instructions. Less than a minute later he replaced the receiver and stepped from the hotel and walked back towards his car. His eyes scanned the busy streets for anyone following him.

No one did.

Sanchez stood at the office window looking down at the fronds of the palm trees along the Calle, a mug of steaming coffee in one hand, a cigarette in the other.

Almost 9 p.m. Traffic streaked below, the blue and whites pulling up outside every now and then, disgorging their nightly cargo. Hookers. Pimps. Thieves.

He heard the door open loudly and turned. Cavales came in, closed the door.

Sanchez said, 'Well?'

'You want to know everything?'

'Everything.'

'It was just like you said, he went to make a call. I had four teams following him. Twenty minutes after we left he drove to the Plaza del Heros and went into a small hotel, the Riva. We think he just made a couple of telephone calls, but we can't be sure. The girl watching him said he was pretty uncomfortable so she didn't push it.'

'Go on.'

'He drove back home, stayed half an hour. Then he left and had the manservant drive him to the outskirts. He walked for five minutes then hailed a taxi. He changed taxis twice. The second took him to the airport. He picked up a suitcase at the airport baggage desk. We tailed the servant too. He drove to the airport after he dropped Lieber off and stashed the suitcase in the left luggage, where Lieber picked it up.'

'You managed to check the suitcase?'

Cavales nodded. 'It contained a couple of shirts and a suit. Underwear and toiletries. The usual stuff. Nothing interesting.' Cavales paused. 'There's something else.'

Sanchez raised his eyebrows but said nothing, waited for Cavales to speak.

'He picked up a package at the information desk, along with

the ticket for his luggage. Two of our people followed him to the departure area.'

'They didn't stop him?'

'There was something much more interesting to consider.'

'Tell me.'

'He had a passport in a different name and checked onto a flight for São Paulo, with the first connection to Mexico City tomorrow night. I guess the passport was the package he picked up. He must be running scared.'

'The name he used?'

'Monck. Julio Monck.'

Sanchez sighed.

Cavales said, 'You want me to get the immigration boys in São Paulo to pick him up?' He checked his watch. 'The flight doesn't land for over another hour. Possession of an illegal passport is one thing. Using it is another. On that alone he's got some questions to answer.'

Sanchez sat down with a heavy sigh. He said nothing, his eyebrows knitted closely together, as if the act of thinking was painful.

After a long time he looked up.

'Bring me the map from the wall.'

Cavales crossed to the facing wall and unhooked the large hanging map of South America, placed it on Sanchez' desk.

The fat detective stared down at the multicoloured patterns on the laminated, nicotine-stained cardboard, then began to trace a pudgy finger from the north-east, Chaco, to the Brazilian border.

After a few minutes' silence he looked up again.

'The report from the radar people at Bahia Negra. They said the flight they vectored disappeared towards Corumba, over the Brazilian border.'

'*Si.*'

Sanchez' finger traced a line on the map. 'It's only a short distance from there to Campo Grande.'

Cavales scratched his chin. 'I guess so.'

'There's an airport at Campo Grande. With a shuttle service to São Paulo, I believe.'

341

Cavales frowned. 'I don't see the point?'

'*Think* about it. From Paulo there's a connecting flight to Mexico City. Lieber's destination. The people from the Chaco house. Maybe they took that route. Maybe they went to Mexico City also. Now Lieber's worried. He needs to talk to them. In person.'

Cavales smiled. Sanchez said, 'It's possible, no?'

'*Si*. Either that or Lieber's running for good.'

Sanchez shook his head. 'I doubt it. People like Lieber have too many connections. No. He's scared about something. We frightened him tonight. You saw the look on his face when I mentioned the taped conversation? It really worried him.' Sanchez thought a moment, then said, 'Get on to Chief Inspector Eduardo Gonzales in Mexico City. Inform him of Lieber's likely arrival there in the name of Monck. And have our people check the passenger lists on flights from São Paulo to Mexico City in the last ten days. If the name Karl Schmeltz turns up, let me know. I doubt that it will, considering our friend Lieber used a false passport, Schmeltz could have done the same. But no harm in checking.'

'This Gonzales in Mexico City . . . He's a friend of yours?'

Sanchez nodded. 'We met at a police conference in Caracas. Have a copy photograph of Lieber wired to him. Lieber's connecting tickets are in the name of Monck, so just in case Lieber has another passport they should be able to identify him from the photograph. And get on to São Paulo too. Ask them to watch Lieber when he arrives there, make sure he makes the connecting flight he has booked. If he uses a hotel, ask them to observe his movements. I want to know of anyone he meets. But also ask them to be very discreet. Ask them to use their best undercover people. It's top priority. I don't want it blown.'

'You want this Gonzales to pick up Lieber?'

'No. Simply followed. I want to know where he goes. Who he meets.'

Cavales nodded, went to leave.

'And Cavales . . .'

'*Si?*'

'The first available connecting flight to Mexico City. Book two seats.' Sanchez smiled thinly. 'But not the same route as Lieber, obviously.'

Cavales smiled back, nodded and left.

Sanchez opened his wallet and stared down at the photograph. It was the one of three men he had removed from the album in Lieber's house. He had removed it deftly. Theft, but justifiable. He doubted Lieber had noticed, the man had been too distracted.

Now he placed it on his desk and blinked. He stared at the two men flanking Lieber in the picture. One young and dark-haired and stocky; the other tall and handsome and silver-haired. From the cut of the clothes, he guessed Lieber hadn't lied when he said the photograph was taken a long time ago. Ten years, maybe, but difficult to say. There was a veranda behind the three men. Painted white. Like the house in the Chaco jungle. And every sense told him it *was* the house in the Chaco.

He scanned the photograph again. He would have the faces of the two men flanking Lieber checked out. Perhaps the files would turn up something.

He sighed now as he thought of the work ahead, ran a hand through his thinning, greasy hair. He would telephone his wife and tell her of his plans. No more than a day or two in Mexico City, if he was lucky. He stared down at the photograph of the three men once more as he picked up the receiver and went to dial his home number.

Rosario would understand.

This one was for Rudi Hernandez.

This one was personal.

Chapter Thirty

Volkmann took the early KLM flight to Amsterdam and left his overnight bag at the left-luggage desk at Schipol.

In the arrivals area he telephoned Jakob Fischer at the Berlin KriminalAmt, but the policeman who answered said Fischer wasn't in his office and wouldn't be back until late that afternoon. Volkmann left a message that he had called and would ring back later.

This time he checked when he left the terminal at Schipol and he was certain he wasn't being followed. He took a taxi to the Raadhuisstraat and walked back through the narrow cobbled streets to the canal until he found the address on the Herengracht.

The antiques shop was on the ground floor of one of the old narrow four-storeyed Dutch buildings, near a corner between a sex shop and a small hotel. The sign on the front of the shop said Classic Antiques and when Volkmann pushed the door a bell sounded overhead.

A young blonde-haired girl no more than twenty sat curled up on a red sofa in a corner, a grey Persian cat on her lap. Volkmann guessed she was the one he had spoken to on the phone. The girl wore tight jeans and a red track suit top and sneakers and her brown eyes looked at Volkmann as she uncurled and stood up. The cat brushed around Volkmann's legs and the girl came forward and picked it up again as she looked up.

'Hi!'

The small shop was cluttered with restored antique furniture. A long glass show case served as a counter and inside were old sepia photographs in silver frames and bric-a-brac. Volkmann saw a green curtain covering a doorway he presumed led in to the back. The girl looked at Volkmann

and he guessed by her English she thought he was a
tourist.

'If you want to look around, it's OK. Or can I help you?'

Volkmann smiled. 'I'm looking for Cole Erdberg.'

'Are you a cop?'

Volkmann smiled again. 'Now why do you ask that?'

'Because you look like one.'

The girl didn't smile back and the narrow green eyes of the
Persian looked up at him.

'Is Cole here?'

The girl hesitated and said, 'Why you want to see Cole?'

There was a trace of an accent in the girl's English but
Volkmann guessed she wasn't Dutch. She hugged the cat
closer and her brown eyes watched Volkmann's face.

'Tell him a friend of Ted Birken's wants to see him.'

'Who?'

'Ted Birken.'

'And what's your name?'

'Volkmann. Joe Volkmann.'

The young girl hesitated again and pursed her lips as if
trying to decide.

'You wait here.'

Then she turned and went in through the green curtain,
carrying the grey Persian against her shoulder. She was
pretty and had a good body and the tight jeans hugged her
full figure. Volkmann glimpsed a door beyond and heard the
girl open it and she was gone.

Volkmann looked around the cluttered shop. On a wall near
the glass-fronted window was an ancient bracketed flintlock
rifle and two flint pistols underneath. On another wall were
some original paintings of eighteenth-century Dutch scenes.
The shop smelled of must and cats and the pungent stale odour
of marijuana. Volkmann heard the door open behind him.

A man stepped through the curtain. He was tall and thin
and he had several days' growth of grey beard. He was almost
bald and the straggle of dyed black hair at the back of his
head was tied in a pony tail with an elastic band. He held
a pair of wire-framed glasses in his hand. He slipped them

on and peered over. He was in his middle to late fifties, Volkmann guessed, and he was wearing a pair of long khaki shorts and sneakers without socks. His black cotton shirt was open to reveal a gold medallion lost in a tuft of grey chest hair.

He looked up at Volkmann and the accent was southern American states.

'I know you?'

'Cole Erdberg?'

'That's me.'

'My name's Volkmann. Joe Volkmann.'

'Misha told me you were a friend of Ted Birken's. What can I do for you?'

'Ted said you might be able to help me.'

'Are you with the outfit?'

Volkmann smiled. 'No, I'm not with the CIA, Mr Erdberg.'

'Who you with?'

Volkmann showed his ID and Erdberg peered at it. He looked back up at Volkmann and smiled. 'How's old Ted doing? Still living alone in the Alps with those fucking boring Swiss cheeses?'

Volkmann smiled back and Erdberg said, 'He ought to find himself a nice young girl, make the most of the few years he's got left.'

Erdberg's eyes had a glazed look, like he was still slightly high on dope.

'So what can I do for you, Joe?'

'Ted said you're expert on the SS. That you might be able to help me identify someone in a photograph.'

The curtain moved behind Erdberg and the blonde-haired girl came through carrying the Persian. Erdberg looked at her.

'Misha, how about a cup of coffee for me and Joe here? You want coffee, Joe?'

'Thanks.'

'Two coffees, Misha. And try to keep that fucking grey thing out of my room while I'm working. OK, honey?'

The young girl pouted and made a face and as she

left Erdberg slapped her bottom playfully and said, 'I love you too.'

He looked at Volkmann. 'Come in back here, Joe.'

They stepped in through the green curtain. The room was a storage area and repair shop and cluttered with musty furniture in various states of repair. There were the same stale smells but this time mixed with the smell of shellac and wood polish. Tools were scattered about a long table cluttered with pieces of a chair. There was a poster on one of the white-painted walls of a man wearing a cowboy hat and boots sitting on a toilet. Underneath it said, '*I'm proud to be an asshole from El Paso.*'

Erdberg led the way to another door at the end of the room and unlocked it with a key from his pocket and switched on the light. As with all the buildings in Amsterdam it was deep rather than broad. The room they stepped into was maybe twenty metres long and when it flooded with light Volkmann saw what looked like a miniature museum.

On each side of the long room were deep glass show cases up to the ceiling. Inside were selections of uniforms and medals and insignia from the Third Reich. Ceremonial Nazi swords and daggers and a couple of weapons; a dozen rifles and automatics and one MP40 machine pistol, the barrel plugged. There was a big polished walnut desk at the end of the room and on top stood an impressive silvered desk lamp. On its square base was the raised relief of a Nazi eagle, a swastika gripped in its talons.

The room was cold and Erdberg shivered and lit a cigarette.

'So how can I help you, Joe?' He saw Volkmann look around the room and Erdberg said, 'Impressive, huh?'

Volkmann went to stand in front of a glass case containing a selection of Nazi daggers and swords and a silver gorget of the Nazi *Feldgendarmerie*.

Volkmann said, 'Do you mind if I ask what you do with all this, Mr Erdberg?'

'Call me Cole. What I do with it? I sell the fucking stuff. And collect it.'

'Sell it to who?'

'Collectors. Nazi memorabilia freaks. Anyone who's interested. Lots of people are. You'd be surprised. I hire out to film companies when they want something genuine and special. I've got a storeroom out the back. Uniforms. Flashes. Medals. I guess you could say I act like a kind of consultant.'

Volkmann looked around the glass cases. 'It doesn't . . . disturb you?'

'Disturb me? It only disturbs me if no one's interested. But that don't happen. I do good business. The shop out front pays the rent. This pays for drinks and girls and everything else a guy needs to sustain himself.'

The door opened and the girl came through with two cups of coffee.

'This disturb you, Misha?' Erdberg gestured to the glass cases.

The girl handed them the cups and shrugged. 'No.'

Erdberg said, 'Misha, meet Joe Volkmann. Joe, Misha.' Erdberg smiled. 'Misha is Jewish.'

The girl smiled at Volkmann. She looked like one of the blonde sabra you saw in the Kibbutz with her light hair and brown eyes and her good figure.

Erdberg turned back to Volkmann and said, 'I ain't no neo-Nazi, just in case you wondered. But the whole Third Reich thing blows my mind. What about you, Joe?'

'I can't say that it does.'

The girl left them and Volkmann ran his hand over the walnut desk. Erdberg looked at him.

'You know who that desk belonged to?'

'Tell me.'

'Ernst Kaltenbrunner. Number two in the SS after Heydrich got stiffed in Czechoslovakia by the resistance. Kaltenbrunner. One of the biggest fucking maniacs in the SS. He used to sit at that desk drunk out of his little mind, signing death warrants. For Jews and resistance fighters and anyone else he took a care to.' Erdberg moved closer to the desk, smiled, ran a hand over the polished wood lovingly as if it were a woman's thigh. 'Kind of creepy, ain't it?'

Volkmann said, 'You're familiar with the Leibstandarte SS Division?'

'Like I know every hair on my ass. Cream of the SS. Officially formed by arch-Nazi Sepp Dietrich, 1934. Better known as Hitler's bodyguard. Originally comprised one hundred and twenty hand-picked men, but later expanded to become a Division. Each man took a blood oath of allegiance to Adolf Hitler. Served as a motorised division in Poland in '39. Campaigns in Greece and Russia, '41 to '44. Responsible for the Malmedy massacre in Belgium in '44, and countless others in Russia that if I told you about I'd be here all fucking night. Last division to fight in Hungary and Austria in '45. You want more? I'm just getting warmed up. That what you come about, the Leibstandarte SS?'

'You're familiar with most of the top people?'

'I guess.'

'What about their wives, girlfriends, mistresses?'

'Some, why?'

Volkmann removed the copy photograph of the blonde young woman and handed it across.

'Do you recognise this woman, Cole?'

Erdberg looked at the photograph. He hesitated, then removed his glasses before searching for a magnifying glass in one of the drawers of a nearby desk. He held it over the photograph. After a long time he looked up.

'Who was she?'

'That's what I need to know. I hoped you might have been able to help me.'

Erdberg shook his head. 'She doesn't look familiar. Not to me.'

'You're sure?'

'Sure.'

'The Nazi armband you see in the photograph. Is there anything special about that?'

Erdberg examined the photograph again, then looked up. 'No, I can't say there is. Standard Nazi swastika armband. Why?'

'What about the uniform sleeve?'

Erdberg looked at the photograph again and shrugged. 'It's hard to say. The shot's pretty grainy. And there's not enough of it showing.'

'Leibstandarte SS?'

'Sure, they wore armbands like that, on their left sleeve. But so did a lot of other SS and Nazis. But with Leibstandarte you'd also see a flash in silver and grey on the left sleeve saying *Adolf Hitler*. That's how you knew they were Leibstandarte. It still could be SS, only I'd need to see more of the uniform in the photograph to give you a definite answer to that question.' Erdberg smiled. 'Only I guess that ain't possible?'

When Volkmann shook his head, Erdberg waved the photograph. 'So where'd you get this?'

'South America.'

Erdberg smiled. 'What's the story? You hunting some old Nazi? I didn't think there were any of those guys left worth talking about.'

Volkmann shook his head. 'No. I'm trying to trace a man. His father emigrated to Paraguay before the war. The photograph may be a clue.'

'What year we talking about here?'

'1931.'

The American frowned. 'So what's the Leibstandarte SS got to do with it?'

'The man's father, he was a Brownshirt, SA. Ted Birken told me some of the Brownshirts later became Leibstandarte SS.'

'That's right.' Erdberg paused and shrugged. 'But sorry, I can't help you.'

'You know anyone else who could?'

'With the photograph? Hey, it could be anyone.' Erdberg shrugged again. 'If you think she was some high-ranking officer's girlfriend or wife, then maybe a good historian. Someone who specialises in the thirties pre-war period. I don't know any offhand, but even if I did I doubt whether they could help. The girl, I mean, she could be no one important. And besides, apart from Eva Braun and Magda Goebbels, who remembers any of the top Nazi's women? And the girl in your photograph, she sure ain't either of those two sweet ladies.'

'One more thing, Cole. Did you ever hear of something called the Brandenburg Testament?'

The American thought a moment, then shrugged. 'Can't say that I have. What is that?'

Volkmann smiled. 'Maybe nothing important. Thanks for your time.'

'No problem.'

Volkmann took the photograph from Erdberg and replaced it in his wallet, then took one last look around at the glass cases.

Erdberg said, 'I've got some great pieces. Iron crosses with diamonds and oak leaves. Himmler's ceremonial sword. A party badge that belonged to Martin Bormann. Now there's a guy could have ended up in South America. You got time, I could show you some.'

'I've got a flight to catch, but thanks just the same.'

'You see Ted, you tell him from me to find himself a nice little woman. Twenty. Big tits. Firm ass. Do it before it's too late.'

Volkmann smiled. 'I'll tell him. I'll find my own way out.'

At the door, Volkmann hesitated. 'You mind if I ask you a personal question, Cole?'

'Why not?'

'Ted said you were with the CIA.'

'Twelve years.'

'Why did they kick you out?'

Erdberg smiled. 'You kidding? Wouldn't you have?'

He managed to get a seat on the two o'clock KLM flight to Berlin. He had spent two hours waiting at Schipol but he hadn't seen anyone following him. It was after four and growing dark when he landed at Tegel and he booked the Hotel Schweizerhof at the tourist desk. He went through the same routines as at Schipol then took a taxi to the hotel on the Budapesterstrasse and it was half an hour later before he made the call to Jakob Fischer. He had to wait five minutes before Fischer came on the line and the old detective was apologetic for keeping him waiting.

'It's been a long time, Joe. How are you, my friend?'

'Good. And you?'

'Six months from retirement and I can't wait to throw off the harness. What can I do for you, Joe?'

'You got my message?'

'This morning.'

'I need to ask you a favour, Jakob.'

Volkmann explained about Herbert Rauscher and when he had finished Jakob Fischer said, 'Is this official, Joe?'

Volkmann told him he wanted to keep it unofficial and low-key for now and Fischer said, 'You better tell me what you want.'

'I'd like to know what your people have on Rauscher's death. And whatever background information you've got on him.'

'You say this Rauscher lived over on the East side. It's off my patch, Joe. Our people handle the eastern side of the city now, of course, and I'm KriminalAmt. But the homicide boys may get suspicious if I ask them to look at the file. You know if this Rauscher was involved in any criminal activity?'

'I don't know, Jakob.'

'OK. I'll try to get a look at the file anyway and see what happens. We keep most stuff on computer and I may be able to get access.'

'I'd appreciate it, Jakob.'

'You had better give me some of the details so I'll be prepared.'

Volkmann told Fischer what he knew on Rauscher from the newspaper cuttings and the old detective said, 'Where are you staying?'

'The Schweizerhof on Budapesterstrasse.'

'OK. Give me an hour and I'll call you back.'

'Thanks, Jakob.'

It was almost two hours later when Jakob Fischer rang back.

'I'm afraid I only got limited access to the file on the computer, Joe, and there wasn't much there. So I decided to call the guy who handled the case but it turns out he's on leave. I spoke to one of the other detectives at the same station and he told me what he could. It wasn't much but it may help you.'

'You want to tell me over the line?'

'I think it's best we meet, Joe.'

'Say where.'

'How about your hotel. We can have a beer and I'll fill you in.'

'When?'

'About an hour, in the bar. There are a couple of things I still need to check.'

'An hour's fine.'

'Talk to you then.'

The main bar in the Schweizerhof was empty except for a couple of men in business suits talking at the bar. Volkmann was sitting near the door an hour later when he saw Jakob Fischer appear. The detective looked much older and he seemed to walk with a stoop but he was still sprightly. His blue eyes looked tired and the full dark head of hair he had always been proud of was flecked with grey. He shook hands with Volkmann and slumped into one of the big armchairs opposite.

Volkmann asked him if he'd eaten but Fischer settled for a club sandwich and a glass of Weizenbier. They spent five minutes talking about old times and when Fischer finished his sandwich he wiped his mouth with a serviette and said, 'This case, what's it about, Joe, do you want to tell me?'

Volkmann told him the bare facts and Fischer said, 'Sounds like a lot of trouble. So why are your people handling it and not ours?'

When Volkmann told him, Fischer nodded and said, 'OK, you want to hear what I've got?'

'Tell me.'

'Background first, just to fill you in. Herbert Rauscher was born in Leipzig. Forty-nine years of age last birthday. Moved to Berlin twenty-eight years ago. Single, never married. Worked in a small publishing firm as a manager until the Wall came down and he lost his job. After that he was registered as unemployed for about three months before he started his own business. The Stasi KriminalAmt people had a file on him. What was in it I don't know for sure because a lot of the files disappeared or were destroyed after the Wall came down. Rauscher's file vanished too. Our people managed to get a few details from former Stasi personnel after Rauscher was murdered, though not much. But apparently Rauscher wasn't the upstanding DDR citizen he once appeared to be.'

'In what way?'

'He ran a small publishing business on the side. Pornography. Glossy girlie magazine stuff but pretty hot. The same kind of business he started up after he lost his job. And after reunification and publishing restrictions were lifted business started to pick up. He also started to dabble with drugs after the Wall came down, but small-scale dealing. He bought himself a second-hand Merc and moved to a better apartment, but still on the East side. Then six months ago someone hit him. It happened late at night, about eleven. Two shots to the head. According to the detective I spoke to there were powder burns on the skull, so it was a close hit.'

'What did forensic say about the ammo or the weapon?'

'They think a Beretta was used, with a silencer. But I've no info on the ammo, except that it was nine-millimetre.'

'Where was he killed?'

'At his apartment. It's near the Pergamon Museum. His girlfriend came home and found him. According to the file she was checked out but she came up clean.'

'Where's the girl now, any idea?'

'I'm trying to find out, Joe, because I reckoned maybe you'd want to talk with her, but no luck so far. Her name's Monika Worch. That's all I know.' Fischer smiled. 'Apart from the fact that she used to pose in the buff for some of Rauscher's magazines.'

'What about Rauscher's death, did your people turn up anything?'

The detective shook his grey head. 'Nothing, Joe. They tried the usual angles. People in the same business, but they didn't turn up anything, according to the detective I spoke to. But Rauscher must have known who his killer was because there was no sign of anyone breaking into his apartment and it happened in the front room. One of the janitors who was on duty in the building said he heard nothing and saw nothing. Same with the neighbours. The feeling is, maybe Rauscher crossed someone. Tried to expand too quickly and stepped on someone's toes. Since the Wall came down the crime rate is way up on the eastern side. Everyone's going into business for themselves and trying to be a successful little capitalist and make a bundle. So maybe Rauscher got on the wrong side of someone by moving in on their territory. It's the only angle that makes sense. But our people still came up against a brick wall with that avenue.'

'Was Rauscher political?'

Fischer frowned and shook his head. 'Not that our people know of. And from the type of guy Rauscher was, I'd say probably no. He seemed more interested in making money than in politics. Why, you think Rauscher's death was political?'

Volkmann hesitated. 'I don't know, Jakob.' Volkmann looked towards the window. The late-evening traffic streaked by and a couple of people passed the window, collars up against the cold. Volkmann looked back at the detective.

'What about Rauscher's girl?'

'What about her?'

'You think you could find her for me?'

Jakob Fischer shrugged. 'Sure, if she's still in Berlin. But it may take time. My guess is she's still in the business. I'll ask around.'

Volkmann said, 'Is Rauscher's apartment still unoccupied?'

'I believe so.'

'Can I take a look?'

Fischer smiled. 'I guessed you'd want to. My car's outside.

Finish your beer and then I'll drive you over. We'll see if my ID can get us in.'

It was after nine when they pulled up outside the apartment block near the Pergamon Museum.

It was one of the luxury modern apartment blocks the Soviets had built for their liaison personnel in East Berlin over thirty years before. It was still well kept and there were neat, well-kept gardens either side of the entrance. There were eight storeys and according to Jakob Fischer, the apartment was on the top floor.

There was a porch light on in the entrance and a double glass entrance door. Fischer ignored the intercom system and banged authoritatively on the glass doors like a true policeman. A couple of minutes later a stooped, middle-aged man appeared, dressed in a shabby blue suit.

He was the night block porter and Fischer flashed his ID and told the man he wanted to see Herbert Rauscher's apartment. The man seemed intimidated by the authority of Fischer's voice and badge and once he'd led them inside he scurried off to find the keys.

When he came back five minutes later, Fischer told him they'd go up in the lift by themselves. The man handed over the keys and Volkmann and Fischer took the creaking lift to the penthouse apartment on the top floor.

There was a sign pasted to the front door by the Berlin homicide police forbidding anyone to enter the apartment and they had fitted a third lock on the door. Fischer had to go back down in the lift to his car and it took him almost half an hour to open the third lock with a filed key from the big set he had on a metal ring.

When they stepped inside, Volkmann was surprised by the lavishness of the apartment. There was a panoramic view of the granite facade of the Pergamon, and in the distance they could see the illuminated top of the Brandenburg Gate and the narrow cobbled streets of the old eastern quarter softly lit by yellow street lamps.

The apartment smelled of dry air and must and it was

expensively furnished with black hide furniture. There was a Sony TV and video in a corner and an expensive Bang and Olufsen hi-fi by the window, a selection of rock and jazz tapes and discs. There were a couple of dozen pornographic videos in a glass cabinet and some books on the shelf above them.

There was a marble chessboard with silvered set pieces on the glass coffee table and the carpets were all plush pile and cream-coloured. But when Volkmann stepped towards the window he saw the dark red bloodstain near the coffee table. It was a big dark patch and it looked like someone had once spilled red wine there. The police hadn't left the rooms in disarray and Volkmann had a look around the two bedrooms and the rest of the apartment.

The wardrobe rails were full of expensive suits but there were no women's clothes and Volkmann guessed Rauscher's girlfriend had cleared out all her belongings.

There was a small selection of pornographic magazines in one of the bedrooms, the pages open where the detectives had browsed, but the rest of the apartment looked as if it had been tidied and the drawers in the bedrooms were empty of any personal belongings except for some underwear and monogrammed silk shirts.

There was nothing in the apartment to hint that Rauscher had any involvement in politics and the only books on the shelf were glossy coffee-table books, and a couple of erotic novels.

It was eleven when Jakob Fischer drove him back to the Schweizerhof and the detective told him he'd get back to him as soon as he had any news on Rauscher's girlfriend. Volkmann told him to leave a message where he could contact him if he wasn't there and Fischer said he'd do that.

Chapter Thirty-One

He took a taxi to Walter Massow's office in Kreuzberg the next morning.

It was in a drab, pre-war building just off the Blücherstrasse, right in the middle of a block of neglected tenements that teemed with Turkish and Asian immigrants, in the old, still war-scarred suburb in the south-east of the city. The front of the building had been daubed with painted slogans which someone had painted over again and the windows on the lower two floors were boarded up.

It was ten when Volkmann arrived and there was a young man seated behind a desk on the ground floor. He looked up cautiously as Volkmann entered. When he had checked Volkmann's identity card he pressed a button under his desk and a door sprang open that led upstairs.

Four flights up a young secretary sat typing in an outer office and she asked Volkmann to wait while she went to fetch Massow. She returned moments later followed by a man about fifty. Big, powerfully built, wearing glasses, and whose gentle manner and soft voice belied his physique.

'Herr Volkmann, I'm Walter Massow.'

He shook Volkmann's hand firmly and led the way down a corridor into a large cluttered office.

Bright winter sunlight filtered through a large window and there were metal filing cabinets against the peeling walls. There was a half-eaten sandwich in paper wrapping on the cluttered desk by the window. The office overlooked a small park below and there was a clear view to several blocks of dilapidated flats opposite. Washing hung on nearby balconies and here and there immigrant women leaned from windows.

The young secretary brought them coffee and when she had left them, Massow sat back in his chair. He selected a toothpick from a tray on the desk and played it around in his mouth as he looked across.

'May I ask what this is about, Herr Volkmann?'

It took Volkmann several minutes to explain the reasons for his visit. He kept his information to a minimum and explained to Massow that he was investigating the murder of a man named Dieter Winter and that the investigation had revealed that Massow's name had been mentioned in connection with an attempt on the politician's life. Volkmann spoke briefly about Winter's background and the circumstances of his death, but he didn't elaborate.

Massow didn't seem unduly surprised or perturbed, but simply sat there, listening calmly. When Volkmann had finished, the politician sipped his coffee and sat back further in his chair and it creaked under his weight.

'May I ask why a British DSE officer is investigating this case? Surely it would be an internal matter for our police, Herr Volkmann?'

Volkmann explained that the weapon used to kill Winter had been used before in the shooting of a British-born businessman in Hamburg and when Massow nodded his understanding, Volkmann said, 'Have you ever heard of Dieter Winter before, Herr Massow?'

The big man shook his head firmly. 'No, I haven't.'

Volkmann looked across at the politician and said, 'Do you have any idea, Herr Massow, why this man Winter might have wanted you killed?'

Massow smiled as he chewed on the toothpick. 'You say this Winter was a right-wing extremist.'

'It would seem so.'

Massow shook his head and smiled ruefully. 'Herr Volkmann, if I had a Deutschmark for every death threat or hate letter I received from people like that, I would be a wealthy man by now.' Massow suddenly stood up. 'Let me show you something.'

The politician crossed to a filing cabinet and removed a file. He flicked through a thick sheaf of papers and crossed back to his desk and sat down again. He pushed his unfinished sandwich aside and spread the papers on his desk.

'Letters,' explained Massow, 'rather unpleasant letters. These are copies, the police have the originals, not that it means much. They never find these people.'

Massow selected one and handed it across. The single-sheet copy page had been constructed from cut-out newspaper headline type.

Across the top of the page a single line said: *JEW LOVER. WE'RE WATCHING YOU.*

When Volkmann had looked at it, Massow handed across another.

This time it was another single page but in writing, the letters big and bold and threatening.

IMMIGRANTS OUT! MASSOW YOU ARE DEAD!

Massow said, 'Those are some of the milder threats. There are others much worse.' He smiled. 'It comes with the territory, as they say.'

The politician sat back again and gestured to the window.

'This area I represent, Herr Volkmann, the people here are mainly of immigrant stock, as you are probably aware. Turks. Poles. Slavs. Asians. Greeks. People from the African countries. I do my best for them. But there are those, as there are in every country, who think people like my constituents should be sent back to wherever they or their parents came from. No matter that they have perhaps been born here and are as good a citizen as the next.' Massow shook his head. 'It happens in every country you care to mention, Herr Volkmann. France. Germany. England. Italy. And no doubt, if the extremists and racists had the chance they would send people like me back with them.' Massow shrugged his big shoulders. 'Now and then the thugs who call themselves Germans throw a petrol-bomb or deface our building. But we've become used to it. And my staff are dedicated, diligent people. I'm not saying such things don't worry us, but we go about our work, nonetheless.'

Volkmann gestured to the letters and said, 'Who are the people who send you these?'

'People like your friend Winter, I should imagine. Extremists. Neo-Nazis. Immigrant-haters. People-haters. Lunatics.' Massow shrugged, smiled. 'I think I've covered all the possibilities.'

Volkmann said, 'Have you ever heard of a man called Wolfgang Lubsch?'

Massow frowned. 'The terrorist?'

'Yes.'

'Yes, I've heard of him.'

'How well do you know him?'

Massow raised his eyebrows, then smiled and said guardedly, 'Herr Volkmann, the man is a wanted terrorist. Many years ago when he was a student I met him briefly at a political rally in Hamburg. He is not a friend, if that's what you are implying. And on that subject I say no more.'

'And the death threat I spoke about?'

'What about it?'

'Do you have any idea who might have been behind it?'

'No, Herr Volkmann, I don't. Except the kind of lunatic fringe I just talked about. Like I said, I receive so many threats.' Massow smiled. 'In fact, if they stopped, I might get worried that the racists and bigots have come to like me. And that would *really* frighten me.'

'Why would such people want you dead?'

'Because to the extremists and the racists, people like me are a thorn in their side.'

'Tell me.'

Massow stood up, took a step closer to the window. The bright winter sunshine pouring through the window washed the big man's face, made him squint. He looked down at Volkmann. In the harsh light Massow's clothes looked shabby and his big, kindly face was creased with worry lines and he looked serious.

'Do you have any idea how immigrants are treated in this country, Herr Volkmann? There are five million people of immigrant stock in Germany. In France, in Italy, there is a similar problem, but my real concern is Germany. Many of them came here in the years after the war when there was a labour shortage and ordinary Germans had become too affluent and proud to do menial work. They came as labourers and did the dirty work most Germans refused. They settled and had families and made a life for themselves in this country. Now they are almost seven per cent of the population, a figure greater than the Jews before the last war. But unlike the majority of Jews of that time, many are caught in a poverty trap. There was a time when these people were needed. Now we have Germans from the former East bloc along with immigrant ethnic Germans who are quite willing to take their jobs.

'The German employment laws demand that every worker be treated equally but the reality is somewhat different. Wages among immigrants are lower than average and unemployment runs at twenty-five per cent. So they live in ghettos and immigrant hostels. The problem, then, is real and troubling. But even more troubling is Germany's response. When the racists and neo-Nazis provoked violence it caused not only indignation but also calls for a limit to the number of foreigners entering this country. As if the victims were at fault and not those people persecuting them.'

Massow frowned. 'Now, when there is terror, the politicians say they don't have enough police. Yet when the terrorists rack this country they manage to guard almost every important businessman and executive in the land.'

Massow looked out at the bright sunlight then back at Volkmann. 'When you leave this office, Herr Volkmann, take a walk through the streets. Look at the living conditions. Look at the faces of the people living in this neighbourhood. *Really look*. They are frightened people. Frightened of the shaven-headed toughs who attack their homes. Frightened of the future. What you see outside, Herr Volkmann, is a tinderbox waiting to be ignited. Because some day these people are going to raise their voices and organise themselves and fight back. And then you will have big trouble. The whole damned country will be set ablaze.'

Massow shook his head ruefully. 'Sometimes I wonder if things have really changed in this country in over fifty years.'

'What do you mean, Herr Massow?'

Massow selected a fresh toothpick, hesitated before popping it in his mouth.

'Before the last war, the rally call of the Nazis was *Juden-frei*. Free of Jews. These days it's *Ausländer-frei*: Free of foreigners. Today, there are hardly any Jews left in Germany. But there are immigrants who might become the nation's scapegoats again. And the same feelings are there. The same undercurrents. Because these people are not Aryans with blond hair and blue eyes they are not considered Germans.' Massow sat forward. 'Let me give you an example. The ultra-right Deutsche Volksunion Party alone once used a simple anti-immigrant slogan in the state of Bremen during the elections there. "The Boat is Full," they said. And for that they gained six more seats in parliament.'

Massow sat down again slowly and said, 'Forgive me, Herr Volkmann. This is not what you came here to talk about. You asked about this man Winter and I end up giving you a lecture on what's wrong with Germany.'

Volkmann said, 'Herr Massow, you're certain you never heard of Dieter Winter?'

Massow shook his head. 'Never.'

As Volkmann stood, Massow offered his hand and said, 'I wish you luck with your investigation. Good day, Herr Volkmann.'

He walked back through the streets to the U-Bahn Station.

The winter sun was still shining and the air clear and cold. The suburb was a busy maze of thoroughfares and as he walked back he did what Massow had suggested. Massow's claims seemed slightly histrionic as befitted a politician but Kreuzberg had always been a working-class area since before the last war and the immigrant tenements he passed were derelict and shabby.

Near the station he bought a bratwurst from a Turkish vendor and as he stood eating and waiting for the train he noticed the station walls daubed with racist slogans and here and there the hastily painted swastikas.

The people on the platform had the same dark haunted brown eyes of his father and for a moment Volkmann thought of the faces in the old black-and-white photographs of the ghettos at Warsaw and Cracow.

He pushed the thought from his mind as the train pulled into the station and the doors opened and he stepped on board.

There was a message for him when he got back to the hotel at noon to say that Jakob Fischer had rung ten minutes before and there was a number to reach him. When he called he heard Fischer's voice.

'I found the girl, Joe.'

'Where is she?'

'Still in Berlin, but she's a Westie now. I got an address for her from one of the detectives in Vice. She's living with some director guy who makes dirty movies.'

'You've got a telephone number, Jakob?'

'Sure. I rang her a little while ago. She said she didn't want to talk about Rauscher's murder. I told her I didn't want to have her brought to the station and go through all that routine and that I wouldn't take up much of her time. Just a quick friendly chat.'

'What did she say?'

'She'll talk to us. She'll be at home about eight, and her boyfriend's out of town tonight. Can I pick you up about eight-thirty?'

'Sure. I'll be in the foyer.'

The apartment was south of the city in Friedenau and when they came out of the lift on the third floor Fischer rang the buzzer.

She was about thirty with long blonde hair and very good-looking. She wore tight black ski pants and flat shoes and her white T-shirt was tucked tightly into her pants to show off her breasts. She was a big girl and Volkmann watched her as she closed the door and led them into the living-room.

The apartment was done in a modern style and the lighting was soft. There were framed modern paintings on the walls and a couple of charcoal nude drawings in expensive metal frames.

Jakob Fischer showed the girl his ID but she didn't pay much attention to it and she hardly looked at Volkmann.

'I told you on the telephone: I told your people everything I know.'

'I understand that, Frau Worch, but my colleague would like to ask you a few questions. We won't take up much of your time.'

Volkmann looked at the girl and she looked back at him indifferently.

'How long did you know Herbert Rauscher, Frau Worch?'

'Two years.'

Volkmann looked at the girl's eyes. 'Did you ever hear of a man named Dieter Winter?'

'No.'

'Are you sure Herbert Rauscher didn't know of anyone with that name?'

The girl shrugged. 'I don't know.'

Volkmann went through the other names but the girl just shook her head indifferently. 'I didn't know any of his business acquaintances or friends. The only people I knew that he was friendly with were a couple of the photographers he used.'

'And you never heard him mention any of those names?'

'No.'

'Please think hard, Frau Worch'.

'I did. I never heard of those names.'

The girl looked back at him steadily and he guessed she was telling the truth.

'Was Rauscher involved with any political group?'

The girl looked at him. 'What do you mean?'

'Did he ever express any political opinions to you?'

The girl frowned, then shrugged. 'He used to say how shitty it used to be living under the Soviets. Is that what you mean?'

'Anything else?'

The girl half smiled, then the smile left her face. 'Mostly he talked about sex. Or how much money he was going to make. Or what kind of car he was going to buy next. That's all.'

'Was he ever racist in his remarks?'

'I don't understand.'

'Did he ever say how he felt about the immigrants in this country?'

The girl looked at Fischer. 'What is this?'

'Please just answer the questions, Frau Worch.'

The girl looked back at Volkmann. 'No.'

'Did he have any right- or left-wing acquaintances, or friends or enemies?'

'What do you mean?'

'Extremists. Neo-Nazis. Terrorists.'

The girl laughed and her breasts heaved under the flimsy cotton. 'Is this some kind of joke?'

Jakob Fischer said, 'Please just answer the question.'

'Herbert didn't mix with anyone like that.'

'What about his background?'

'What about it?'

'Did he ever talk about his past? His parents? His family?'

The girl shrugged. 'Once or twice, sure. But he didn't say much.'

'Tell me what he did say.'

'His mother died when he was twenty. His father he never knew.'

'Why?'

The girl shrugged again. 'He died in some camp.'

'A concentration camp?'

The girl grinned. 'No. One of those places in Siberia the Russians sent our soldiers to after the war.'

'Why was Rauscher's father sent there?'

'He was a Nazi. Some kind of officer. I don't know what. Herbert only mentioned it once. When he was drunk.'

'What did he say?'

'That his father had been wounded in Berlin at the end of the war and had been captured by the Russians and sent to one of their camps in Siberia. That he was a Nazi officer.'

'Do you remember anything else he said about his father?'

'No. Just what I told you. He didn't really talk about his past.'

'But you're sure his father was a Nazi officer?'

'That's what Herbert said.' The girl sighed impatiently and looked at Volkmann. 'Look, is this going to take much longer?'

'One more question. Do you have any idea why your boyfriend was murdered?'

The girl shook her head and said impatiently, 'No, I don't. And I told your people that a hundred times already.'

Volkmann looked at Jakob Fischer and nodded. Fischer stood up and said, 'Thanks for your time, Frau Worch.'

He had one drink in the Schweizerhof bar with Jakob Fischer. He thanked the detective for his time and help and when they had finished their drinks he walked with Fischer to the foyer.

'What about Rauscher's father, Joe? You going to check up on his background?'

'There's not much point, Jakob. I could try the Russians but I doubt if they'll be much help. And I don't have a rank or any background information for the Documentation Centre to be of much use. They'd need a date of birth and a Christian name at least. There could have been hundreds of officers named Rauscher.'

'Anyhow, let me know how it works out.'

'Sure. I'll call you. And thanks again for all your help, Jakob.'

'It's been good seeing you again, Joe. Take care.'

He watched Fischer go and then he went up to his room and poured himself a scotch. He went and opened the window and stood at the cold balcony.

None of it made any sense to him. If what Monika Worch had said was true about Rauscher's father being a Nazi officer, then Rauscher would have been the least likely target for Winter's people. But there was nothing in the man's background to suggest that he was involved with either right- or left-wing groups. And besides, Herbert

Rauscher would have been a small child when his father had been captured by the Russians and might never have known the man.

He wondered if the fact that Rauscher's father had been a Nazi was a mere coincidence. So many people of Rauscher's age had had parents in the German army and he guessed maybe it was irrelevant and there was another angle to it.

He phoned the girl at the apartment before he undressed for bed.

He told her about his meeting with Walter Massow and what he had learned about Rauscher.

He heard the frustrated sigh and then Erica said, 'What about the woman, Hedda Pohl?'

'We can drive down to Lake Konstanz, see if we can turn up anything.'

'When will you be back, Joe?'

'I'm taking the first flight back tomorrow.'

There was a pause, then Erica said, 'Joe . . .?'

'Yes?'

'I miss you.'

'I miss you too.'

Chapter Thirty-Two

Volkmann could see the snow-capped mountains of Switzerland across Lake Konstanz as they drove into the pretty lakeside town of Friedrichshafen. There was a light fall of snow as they pulled up on the lake promenade in the late afternoon and Volkmann parked the Ford and they walked back along the lake. There were Christmas trees in the windows of the old Bavarian-style houses and the whole town was lit up with coloured lights.

He and Erica had lunch in one of the pretty restaurants that overlooked the lake and Volkmann decided that the best approach was to visit the police station in the town. He couldn't use his DSE identity card without arousing the suspicion of the local police but he still had the press ID Facilities had issued him and he decided to use that. He left Erica in the car and walked back to the station near the lake front.

There were two officers on duty at the desk and Volkmann showed his ID and asked to speak with one of the senior detectives on duty. He had to wait for ten minutes before a middle-aged man appeared from one of the offices. He was big and ruddy-faced and heavily built, his beer belly protruding over his belted trousers. He introduced himself as Detective Heinz Steiner. When Volkmann showed him the press ID and asked to speak in private, Steiner shrugged and led him back to a small office down the hall. When they were seated the detective looked at Volkmann.

'What can I do for you, Herr Volkmann . . .?'

Volkmann told the detective that he was a freelance journalist writing a series of articles on unsolved homicides for a popular German magazine and wanted to talk with him about the murder of a local woman named Hedda Pohl five months before. When the detective raised his eyebrows and queried Volkmann's interest further, Volkmann told him he had picked up Hedda Pohl's case from the Munich dailies and thought it would interest his readers. Steiner's eyes flickered with interest but he didn't move in his chair.

'What do you want to know exactly, Herr Volkmann?'

Volkmann smiled. 'About the woman's background, Herr Steiner. The newspapers didn't go into much detail at the time. And if you have any idea why she was killed or by whom I'd be grateful for your help.'

Steiner shook his head and his tone became less formal. 'We have no idea why she was killed or by whom, Volkmann. But the case is still open, I assure you.'

Volkmann took his notebook and pen from his pocket. 'Can you tell me how the woman was murdered?'

Steiner lit a slim cigar and blew smoke up to the ceiling. 'Three shots, one in the chest, two to the back of the head at close range. Thirty-eight-calibre slugs. She went out one night in her car and told her son she was going for a walk on the promenade. But she didn't go to the promenade so far as we know. And she didn't come back. Her body was found by a hiker two days later in a forest, about two kilometres inland. Her handbag had been rifled through and her purse had been stolen.' Steiner frowned and his ruddy face creased with lines. 'But the murder, it was very strange.'

'In what way strange, Herr Steiner?'

'You're a journalist, Volkmann. You ought to know that that kind of crime isn't prevalent in this area.'

'Of course, but I thought you meant something about the case.'

'That too. Hedda Pohl, she's not your typical victim for that kind of death.'

'Tell me.'

'Lots of reasons why. The style of murder was more like a gangland killing. Hedda Pohl was sixty-two. A widow. Well off, but not rich. No vices. Absolutely no criminal past or convictions. The woman hadn't ever been given a parking ticket in fact. A very upstanding lady who was involved in the community and church.' Steiner hesitated and drew on his slim cigar. 'And there was something else. We found her car nearby in the forest. It was like she went to meet someone she knew. But her family knew of no prearranged meeting.'

Volkmann scribbled a few notes in his pad and said, 'Was she active politically?'

Steiner's eyebrows rose. 'No, definitely not. Why do you ask that?'

'No reason, just trying to get a fix on the lady. How well did you know her, Herr Steiner?'

Volkmann thought for a moment that the detective was going to say something, but instead Steiner leaned back in his chair.

'Quite well.'

'Is there anything else about her background you think might help me?'

Steiner shrugged. 'Her husband used to be a respected businessman. He's dead maybe ten years.'

'What about him, did he have any criminal background?'

Steiner laughed and shook his head. 'He was as clean-living as a Lutheran minister. A good man. Very upstanding.'

'How did he die?'

'Heart attack, so far as I recall.'

'What about her family?'

'All upstanding. And as I said, she was a good woman and well liked locally.' Steiner shrugged. 'As to the murder, the only scenario we can think of that makes sense is that she picked up a hitch-hiker. Some crazy who decided to rob her and kill her. It's the only theory that makes some kind of sense.'

'What about clues?'

Steiner puffed on his cigar and shook his head. 'Nothing. No fingerprints. No clues. Whoever did it must have been very careful. A professional criminal, perhaps. Or someone who had killed before. And we checked every usual angle. Family, friends, acquaintances. But nothing that gave off a whiff of suspicion.'

Volkmann looked at his watch, then said, 'Thanks for your help, Herr Steiner. I'm sure you're a very busy man, so I won't take up any more of your valuable time.'

'You're welcome, Volkmann. You'll send me a copy of your article?'

'I'll do that, certainly.'

The snow had stopped and a cold, fresh breeze blew in off the lake as they walked along the promenade.

The girl slipped her arm through his and when they sat on one of the benches that faced out towards the water, she said, 'The woman, there's no obvious reason why Winter's people would want to kill her. She had no terrorist connections. No criminal past.'

'There has to be a connection somewhere between Rauscher, Hedda Pohl and Massow, Erica. We just can't see it.'

'So what happens now?'

Volkmann shook his head. 'I wish I knew.'

He saw the girl purse her lips, as if she were about to say something, then she seemed to change her mind. She shivered. Volkmann looked at her.

'What's the matter?'

She shook her head. 'Nothing.'

'Sure?'

The blue eyes smiled up at him. 'I'm just cold. Take me back to the car, Joe.'

As Volkmann stood he looked out at the grey choppy waters of Lake Konstanz. There was a small boat with a blue sail tossing in the swell and as it tried to hug the shore further along the lake, the image seemed oddly fitting. He felt hopelessly lost and there and then he made up his mind to talk with Werner Bargel of the Landesamt in Berlin.

The Landesamt was the German equivalent of MI5 and the section responsible for keeping track of terrorist and extremist organisations in all categories, and Volkmann knew it was the only hope he had of turning up more information on Kesser and Winter. If there was anything of significance in either man's past then the Landesamt would have it in their files. There was a danger Bargel would see his inquiry as official, but he had gone too far and was so adrift that he reckoned it was the only course open to him.

As he looked out at the choppy waters he wondered if Sanchez had made any progress. Probably not. The man would have made contact, he was certain of that. He turned back and joined Erica and she leaned in close as they walked back to the car.

Mexico City.
1.02 a.m.

Kruger stood beside the shimmering turquoise water of the swimming pool in the darkness as he smoked a cigarette, thinking of the telephone call from Asunción. He ran a hand through his dark hair and sighed.

Disturbing. Most disturbing.

So close.

And now this.

He would have to wait until Lieber arrived to hear the full story, but what he had heard had unsettled him. Had unsettled all of them. Halder said Brandt had left saying they would be back for the meeting with Lieber. The others had gone to bed, leaving Kruger alone.

He stubbed out the cigarette in the ashtray on the poolside table then walked through the villa to the rear gardens.

Five rooms through to the kitchen, then he stepped outside onto the back lawn. He checked his watch, noted the time, and then began to walk across the moonlit grass at a smart pace.

Balmy. The sound of crickets and the smell of eucalyptus. But Kruger's mind was on other things. Contingencies. Once Lieber arrived in Mexico City he would have him checked thoroughly for tails before he brought him here. That went without saying. But better still to be prepared.

Kruger reached the clump of trees at the end of the back

lawn and checked his watch again, holding the face up to the moonlight.

Two minutes exactly.

He had already timed how long it took to cross the expansive rear lawn to the old concrete garage behind the clump of trees, but he wanted to be certain. He had passed one of the armed guards halfway across, acknowledging the man's nod.

When he reached the old building he opened the door and stepped inside the garage. Darkness. The smell of grease and oil. The large double wooden doors were bolted.

He crossed to the doors in the darkness, past the dark form of the vehicle, and pulled back the bolt, swung the doors out and open. The overgrown path outside veered immediately left, barely discernible in the moonlight.

Halder had told him about the old garage and the hidden rear exit the first day at the villa. Unlikely that an emergency exit would be needed, but old Halder understood the need for such contingencies. The garage stood a hundred metres from the villa proper, half hidden behind a clump of eucalyptus trees, and the beauty of its existence was that the narrow back alley it led onto gave way to another which cut down to the labyrinthine backroads of Chapultepec. Unlit. Unknown almost, the narrow roadway partly overgrown with sward and overhanging branches. But plenty of room for the car to pass. An ideal emergency exit.

The rear exit proper at the far side of the garden could easily be sealed off if someone chose to. But this narrow road was almost invisible from the outside.

Perfect if it was needed but Kruger doubted it. Still, such precautions were his domain. He had driven with Schmidt to the safe house half a dozen times using two routes, so that both men could be familiar with the plan, if necessary.

He moved back inside the garage, bolted the doors again, then crossed back to the far wall and flicked the switch. A blaze of light flooded the room and the dark, anonymous Ford stood waiting in the centre of the garage.

A full tank of petrol and a fresh battery. He had had Schmidt take the car for a daily run since they had arrived. Again, all part of the contingency plan.

Kruger took one last look about the room then switched off the light, closed the door, and walked back across the lawn towards the villa, counting his steps.

Chapter Thirty-Three

Mexico City.
Tuesday,
December 20th,
3.15 p.m.

Chief Inspector Eduardo Gonzales was a thin, energetic man of fifty. He had the gnarled face of a tough street-fighter, an appearance that belied his sharp intelligence.

And despite his pugilistic appearance he was unhealthy: he had managed to smoke his way through three packs of cigarettes a day for the past thirty years. As a result he spoke hoarsely and coughed with almost every sentence he spoke. His fingers were stained brown with nicotine, yet his pale grey uniform with red epaulettes was crisply ironed, the crease marks sharp as blades, the only outward sign of his own fastidiousness.

His office overlooked the Plaza de San Fernando and had an excellent view of Mexico City; the sprawling, ragged metropolis part of which was his dominion. The office itself was functional and tidy, the only suggestion of untidiness being overflowing ashtrays, strategically placed about the room to accommodate his habit: one by the panoramic window, another on top of a metal filing cabinet near the door. Two on the desk, one of them of functional glass, the other a beautiful, ornate affair of quebraco wood in the shape of a half-cut coconut shell, carved by the Indians in Paraguay's Chaco, on a base that was a sparkling slice of jagged quartz. A present from his friend, Captain Vellares Sanchez.

The dark wood had a pungent aroma that could still be smelled faintly despite the years of stale cigarette ash and, despite its appearance, was a work of art. Ugly, brooding

379

mulatto faces with closed eyelids were cut in the dark, granite-hard wood, the receptacle clasped and cupped by a perfectly carved wooden hand; the firm hand so in contrast to the ugly carved faces that it resembled on first sight some hedonistic chalice; the wooden faces looking like the shrunken heads of Amazonians one saw in the museums. But not frightening. Rather they served to remind that evil had to be controlled by good; a strong hand holding evil in check. Beauty and order controlling evil and ugliness.

According to the Indians.

So Sanchez had told him when he presented the gift in Caracas years before, but with a smile on his face that suggested the story might be apocryphal.

The explanation appealed to Gonzales' quirky humour, despite the fact that experience had taught him such was not always the case. In a crazy, oxygen-thin city of over twenty million grubbing souls, anarchy and chaos ruled every waking day. Nevertheless, the gift from Vellares Sanchez took pride of place on his desk. When people remarked on it, Gonzales told them the story with a smile.

Now strong December sunlight poured into the office. Hot, despite the season. A freakish warm front in from the Gulf of Mexico. An air-conditioning vent in a wall below the ceiling blew out a faint, ineffective stream of chilled air.

A metal tray cluttered with bottles of sparkling water and a jug of fresh, iced lime juice and four glasses lay on Gonzales' desk. Despite the heat they had remained untouched since a young *policia* had brought them fifteen minutes before.

The four men sat around the desk. Gonzales and his senior detective named Juales, a rugged, short-necked man with a squat body and bushy eyebrows, sat on one side; Sanchez and Cavales on the other.

Eduardo Gonzales inhaled on a cigarette, coughed throatily, blew thick smoke out into the warm air. He tapped ash into the dark-wood ashtray and then looked across at his two visitors seated opposite. Both men were tired, their eyes red-raw after their long journey. And the high altitude of the city must be making them dizzy, Gonzales thought.

It took the tourists and visitors at least forty-eight hours to accustom their lungs to the rarefied oxygen, and the two men seated before him had been in Mexico City less than an hour. A police car had taken them directly from the airport, siren blaring, lights flashing. Their lungs must be on fire, Gonzales thought, their minds fogged and hurting from altitude sickness. But neither visitor complained.

The formalities had been dispensed with, the greetings and well-wishings over. Sanchez had briefly explained his reasons for wanting Franz Lieber, alias Julius Monck, followed.

Gonzales had listened attentively, his brow furrowed in concentration while Sanchez had spoken. Now it was Gonzales' turn. He coughed. 'OK. Let's take it from the beginning. OK with you?'

Sanchez and Cavales nodded. Gonzales nodded in turn to his senior detective, Juales. The man leaned forward. His voice was thin, but his Spanish had an educated timbre. He wore a shirt and tie and a portable phone was clipped to his trouser-belt, on the opposite side to his holstered, blunt-nosed Smith and Wesson thirty-eight. He spoke slowly, glancing up at Sanchez and Cavales every few moments as he read from written notes.

'The subject, Julius Monck, alias Franz Lieber, arrived in Mexico City two hours ago. One-sixteen local. I had six men watching him in the Arrivals terminal, another two on the airport ramp dressed as airport staff to identify him as soon as he stepped off the plane. We got an ID, no problem, from the photograph you sent.' Juales glanced at Sanchez, then back at his notes.

'As soon as he collected his luggage, he went straight through the green channel. I had briefed one of the customs men to stop him and he checked the luggage thoroughly. Nothing of interest. There's a list of the contents of the single suitcase, if you want it?'

Sanchez waved his hand in reply. 'Later, please go on.'

Juales looked down at his notes again.

'The subject made one telephone call at one-forty-seven in the Arrivals terminal after passing through customs and then he went to a change bureau. He changed US dollars into Pesos and got some small change. The officers watching him couldn't get close enough to see the numbers dialled, because the subject was blocking their view. The call lasted just under one minute. Lieber seemed anxious. Soon as he finished the call he went to a taco stand outside the terminal and bought a glass of fresh fruit juice, drank it, then went to the taxi rank at one-fifty-six. One-fifty-seven he took a taxi to the City Sheraton, arrived there at two-thirty-nine, and booked in straight away under the name of Julius Monck.' Juales looked up from his notes. 'He was still there as of fifteen minutes ago. Room two-one-five.'

'And now?' Sanchez asked.

Juales tapped the portable phone clipped onto his trouser-belt. 'I've got six undercover men at the Sheraton. If Lieber goes in or out or anybody visits him or he makes a call, my men will let me know.'

Gonzales interrupted. 'The call Lieber made, you've got something on that yet?'

Juales shook his head. 'Not yet. I've assigned one of my men to check it with our technical people.' He turned to Sanchez and Cavales. 'I ought to explain. After Lieber made the call at the airport, I had one of my men wait by the telephone until a colleague from technical division came with a tape-recorder. They hit the re-dial button and recorded the digital dialling pips. They can play it back and decode it in the tech lab and find out the number. Then we can trace to wherever it was called.' Juales glanced at his wristwatch. 'We ought to have that soon.'

Sanchez nodded, saw Gonzales smile through stained-yellow teeth.

'Technology,' said Gonzales, waving his cigarette. 'It's beyond an old policeman like me. These young boys in the basement lab are like Einsteins. They play with computers all day. Me, I'd go crazy down there.' Gonzales smiled.

Sanchez nodded his head and smiled faintly. His bones ached to the marrow and his chest hurt when he breathed, brain fogging with a deep, throbbing pain. He glanced at

Cavales. The detective stared ahead, blankly a few moments, then rubbed his raw eyes. He must be feeling the same, Sanchez thought. A bed would be welcome; a cold shower first, then sleep. But there was no time for that. Not yet. His mouth felt dry and the iced fruit juice looked tempting, but he ignored it.

He turned to look at Juales and Gonzales. 'The passport Lieber used. Did he ever use it to visit Mexico before?'

Gonzales went into a fit of coughing, pounded his chest with his fist before he replied. 'I had that checked, too, Vellares. The answer's no. Never. No Julius Monck with that number on the passport.'

Sanchez looked at Juales. 'How many nights did Lieber book at the Sheraton?'

'He told the desk-clerk one, possibly two. He couldn't be certain.'

'And the hotel people. They are being co-operative?'

'We spoke with the manager,' Juales replied. 'No problem. He's been very discreet. Even gave us a room two doors away. We've got two men there. If Lieber comes out we've got a copy key card. We can plant a bug in his room, no problem, just in case he entertains visitors.'

'What about his telephone?'

Juales said, 'We've got that covered already. We're going to wire into the hotel telephone system. The manager wanted to see our permission first. Chief Inspector Gonzales has organised it.' Juales glanced at his watch. 'Our technical people are on their way and should be patched into Lieber's telephone within the next half-hour.'

Sanchez looked at Gonzales, inclined his head gratefully. 'You're being more than helpful, Eduardo. My thanks.'

Gonzales shrugged, coughed again, waved his hands dismissively and looked at the carved ashtray as he ground out his cigarette, the dark, ghoulish, blank-eyed faces staring up at him. He smiled across at Sanchez. 'It's the only way we beat the devils of this world. No?'

Sanchez smiled back, faintly.

Gonzales stood up, hitched his grey cotton trousers further

up his thin waist, glanced at the liquid refreshments still untouched on his desk. The atmosphere in the office felt charged. Expectant. Like worried fathers outside a maternity ward. Not a place to relax.

Gonzales said, 'There's nothing more we can do until Lieber makes a move. We've got a rest room for visitors down the hall. Why don't we all go down there? I'll have some tacos and fresh drinks sent up and you can rest yourselves. Juales here will come with us. If a call comes through from any of his men, we'll get it there.' He looked down at Sanchez and smiled. 'Besides, it will give us a chance to catch up on gossip since Caracas. OK?'

4.40 p.m.

Franz Lieber stood at the window on the fifth floor of the Sheraton. He swallowed his second scotch and soda, gripped the empty glass tightly in his big hand as he stared down at the city below. The air-conditioning was on, the hum distracting.

Tiredness racked his body, pains arcing intermittently across his broad chest in spasms, like tiny jolts of electricity. Rivulets of sweat ran down his back and temples, despite the coolness of the room.

Stress.

Lieber ran the back of his hand across his forehead.

The flights had been bad enough. Asunción to São Paulo. An overnight in Paulo, then the long haul to Mexico City. The worry of his information throughout his long journey gnawing like a rodent inside his skull, eating away brain tissue, making his head ache. Even now. Not just the altitude.

He took a deep breath, let it out slowly. Did the same again, three times, trying to relax, but knew it was useless.

Mexico City out there and beyond, a ragged, noisy, dirty sprawl of human ants on a high-altitude dungpile. Cities like this drained him. Claustrophobic, chaotic, orderless. They made his headache worse.

A woman would help relieve the tensions. But Kruger had expressly forbidden visitors or phone calls.

Just wait. For the return call.

The hotel would be checked first. To make sure he had no tails, no one watching him. Lieber had tried to tell Kruger it was OK when he had phoned him from the airport, that he had been careful, but Kruger had refused to accept his assurance.

'Just stay in your room. I'll get back to you.'

'How long?'

'As long as it takes; just wait for my call,' came the curt reply, before Kruger hung up.

Lieber shook his head and swore to himself, felt the trickles of sweat tickling his spine. The waiting wasn't helping his stress.

How long before they checked him out? He'd been in the room almost two hours now; the tension of waiting unsettling him. As he went towards the mini-bar to pour himself another scotch, the telephone rang. Lieber, startled, felt as if a shock of electricity had jolted his body.

He hesitated, but only for a moment, put down the glass and wiped his brow again, then went to pick up the receiver.

Sanchez sat quietly in the small hospitality room. White walls. Thick, deep-pile carpet the same grey-blue colour as Gonzales' uniform. Pine and canvas director's chairs, old but comfortable. Ink drawings of the old city on the walls. *Adobes.* Street vendors. Carnival. An Aztec temple. A coffee-machine percolated in a corner, the fresh-ground smell stimulating. A water cooler beside it. A wide window offering a panoramic view of the city. In the distance the imposing spires of the Cathedral Metropolitana dominating the Zocalo, its volcanic rock mottled black from pollution.

For ten minutes he and Gonzales had spoken, until the tiredness had overcome Sanchez. Now he sat, sipping freshly-squeezed orange juice from a paper cup. A half-eaten taco and a hot chili sauce dip lay in front of him on a paper plate, beside it a dish full of grilled *charals*. Hunger was in his stomach but not on his mind. He had eaten some of the taco out of courtesy, the hot chili sauce burning his tongue, until he had washed the tang away with two glasses of iced orange juice.

The others sat and talked. Mainly Gonzales. Cavales listened out of courtesy to the older man's rank. Stories about the old days in Mexico City, the problems, the interesting cases.

Juales sat there nodding occasionally at his boss, his neck lost in his shirt so that it looked like he had no neck at all. Sanchez guessed he was very capable. A thorough man. His boss had chosen well. The narrow, careful eyes flicked to Sanchez as Juales smiled briefly and turned away.

'You think Asunción's bad,' Gonzales was saying to Cavales, both men puffing on cigarettes, 'you ought to try a month here. Twenty-three million people, *amigo*. Like a cross between a zoo and a lunatic asylum. But without walls.'

Sanchez closed his eyes tightly, eyelids aching; opened them again. The view beyond the panoramic window was stupendous, as far as the high Sierras surrounding the city. He wondered how Gonzales and his people managed to cope. Lots of crime, lots of crooks. The organisation itself must be a headache like no other.

His own head throbbed. The high altitude had a dizzying effect, tightening his chest, dulling his mind, making the effort of thinking and talking a slow process. As if the thin oxygen slowed your body clock, made you wind down.

The plane journey – Asunción to Lima, Lima to Colombia, then to Mexico City – had totally drained him. Couple that with lack of sleep in the last two weeks and you had a lethal cocktail. He felt chest pains; small tinglings in his sternum.

But something was happening.

He could sense it.

The next move was Lieber's.

He wondered what it would be?

He looked up absentmindedly as a lull in the men's conversation distracted him; heard a soft click as the door behind opened. Sanchez turned, saw a good-looking young man in a cream-coloured linen suit standing in the open doorway. He clutched a sheaf of papers in one hand, smiled warily at the two visitors and Gonzales before his eyes shifted to Juales.

'Captain . . . may I speak with you?'

Juales stood up, crossed to the man and they stepped out into the hallway together. Gonzales stood and hitched his trousers, puffed on a cigarette as he frowned and looked at the two men in the hallway huddled in conversation. Juales returned after a brief interlude holding a single sheet of paper.

'We traced the call made at the airport.'

'And?' Gonzales prompted.

'It was to an address in Lomas de Chapultepec.'

'An expensive area,' commented Gonzales. 'Did you get the name of the occupant?'

Juales shook his head. 'No, not yet. But my man did a little quick checking. The property is owned by a company called Cancun Enterprises. It's run by a man named Josef Halder. He's a businessman. Old guy. Very wealthy.'

'I know who he is,' Gonzales said quickly. He looked at Sanchez and Cavales. Both men had stood up, faces staring at him expectantly.

Gonzales drew on his cigarette, blew out thick smoke. 'Halder is German-born. Rich. A retired businessman. Owns a lot of property in the city.' Gonzales coughed and smiled. 'Maybe this fits in with what you told me about this other old guy . . .'

'Tsarkin?'

'*Si.*'

'Tell me.'

Gonzales sighed. 'Halder came here from Brazil maybe forty years ago. Started in business in the city. He must be in his eighties now. But well known, lots of powerful friends. I remember him because there was a problem with an extradition warrant from France when I worked in headquarters. The French said Halder was wanted for war crimes he had committed there. Claimed Halder was in the Gestapo. Long time ago I know, but Halder must have greased a lot of palms because the charges were refuted by our people. At that stage Halder was tied into the business life in the city. Lots of businesses, lots of employees. And more importantly, lots of powerful political friends. The French persisted for a while but eventually Halder swore an affidavit of innocence and that was the end of it.' Gonzales smiled. 'Simple when you have money, *si*?'

Sanchez nodded. 'And this is one of his properties?'

'It would appear so,' said Gonzales. 'It's in a pretty wealthy area up in the Chapultepec Hills. A long way from the working-class *colonias*. It's a very beautiful place. Hilly, forested ground. Huge mansions and villas in the middle of landscaped parks and rocky ravines. Very *chic*. Where only the very rich live.' He smiled. 'And maybe a few corrupt police chiefs and judges as well.'

'Can you make a check on the occupants?'

'I could, but that would mean going through Halder's company people. Like waving a red flag.' Gonzales shook his head. 'Better that I get some people over there straight away. Undercover. Have them watch the place, see how the land lies, who comes and who goes. How does that sound?'

Sanchez nodded. 'I would appreciate that, Eduardo.'

'No problem, *amigo*. Juales will organise it straight away.'

A shrill sound startled them as Juales' portable buzzed. The man unclipped it, flicked it on and listened.

Sanchez heard nothing, only Juales' sharp replies as he frowned.

'When? You got the number? Put out an all-cars alert. But tell them don't approach. Just observe and report their position. Understood?'

Juales let his hand fall, looked at Gonzales.

'Lieber got a call in his room three minutes ago.'

Gonzales smiled. 'Our men were tapped into his phone?'

Juales shook his head. 'No. The technicians were still working on it. They missed the call. By the time they got on to the operator, Lieber had put down the phone.'

'*Shit!*'

'That's not all. Lieber left the Sheraton two minutes ago. Went down to the lobby and crossed the street and bought a newspaper. A car came by and Lieber climbed in and the car moved off like a bat out of hell.'

'The car was a taxi?'

'Not a taxi. A civvy. Volkswagen Beetle.'

'Our men followed?'

'*Si.*'

'And?'

Juales swallowed. 'As of just twenty seconds ago we lost him.'

Chapter Thirty-Four

5.14 p.m.

Lieber sat in the front seat of the white Volkswagen as it wove through the chaos of traffic.

Lunatic Mexican drivers, chili and pepper smells, and all the time the pressing, claustrophobic sensation of sweaty bodies. Everywhere. Millions of the Dago bastards.

His head ached. Sweat still poured through his shirt, a fresh one he had hastily dragged on before he left the hotel after the call. He was clear, according to Kruger. Two of Halder's men had checked out the hotel and lobby for almost two hours. Waited and watched. No *policia* or plainclothes so far as they could tell.

If he had been watched then the watchers were very good. But Lieber doubted that. He had moved too quickly, too carefully. Besides, Dagos were notoriously inefficient. Except the women. Hour-glass bodies of curvacious flesh made for pleasure. And the cop, Sanchez, was not one to underestimate. But still a cretin. All Dagos were when it really came down to it.

The cramped whining Volkswagen felt claustrophobic, despite the windows being down. The man in the driver's seat was one of Halder's people. He wore a sweat-shirt and tennis shorts and his forehead was creased as he concentrated on the traffic.

Outside the windows of the tiny Volkswagen darkness fell, lights coming on, the traffic thickening – if it could get any thicker – a scene of utter chaos. But the driver knew the city, wove down side-streets and alleyways, ignoring the irate screams and cries of street vendors whose barrows got in the way, until now the small white Volkswagen was climbing up into the hills, the streets becoming cleaner, less cluttered, the air fresher, cooler. But still skull-crushing pressure as the whiny-engined Volkswagen strained ever upwards. The car had been well chosen. Mexico City thronged with Volkswagens.

Now whitewashed *adobes* and filthy *colonias* were replaced by middle-class homes, were replaced by splendid villas with walled gardens. Armed, uniformed guards, some with leashed guard dogs, stood behind gates, carefully watching the roads.

Lieber had been in the city many years before: the lava ravines and soaring rocky outcrops of the Chapultepec landscape familiar to him; flowered walks and tiny lakes dotted with clumps of *camelotes*. Narrow winding streets with unobtrusive but guarded entrances that often belied the sumptuous properties beyond. A place for the very rich and élite.

Suddenly the Volkswagen turned into a quiet avenue and halted outside a double wrought-iron gate. In the semi-darkness a man appeared beyond the gate and peered into the car. Moments later he opened the gates manually and let them through.

The Volkswagen strained up a winding gravel road, a white villa waiting in the distance, set amidst lush gardens. Jacaranda trees and thick-clumped flower beds of poinsettias and *zempoazuchitl*. The flower of death, old Halder had once told him it was called.

Sulphur yellow light washed over the vast lawns dotted with palm trees, and lights blazed in windows. The villa was the acme of luxury. Sumptuous decor. Lights on everywhere outside. A big place. Impressive. Private. Secure.

Now the road swung round so that Lieber could see the swimming pool, a kidney-shaped shimmering of turquoise light. He saw the patio and the french windows at the side of the house. And then he saw the guards, Werner and Rotman. They wore shorts and sneakers and light rainproof jogger jackets as they patrolled the gardens, carrying Heckler and Koch MP 5K machine-pistols.

He glimpsed big Schmidt, away from the other two men, a pistol in a shoulder harness across his chest, no sign of the big sheathed Bowie knife but Lieber knowing the man went nowhere without it.

Inside the windows the lights were on and he could see the figures waiting for him. There were four men present. The tall, silver-haired man and Kruger standing; old Halder seated in a comfortable armchair, lost in the leather, an inhaler clutched in one of his hands. Wrinkled, wheezy old Halder, face like a dried prune: thin lips, emaciated features, looking like an old buzzard. They said he had killed men with his bare hands in the old days; strangled them, gouged out eyes, raped. But to look at him now he could have been a grumpy, harmless old grandfather near the end of his days. But still important. Still part of the web.

The fourth man, Lieber knew, was Ernesto Brandt. A *mischling*. German father, Brazilian mother. Brown thinning hair, brown eyes, tanned skin, metal-framed glasses with thick lenses and a high forehead that made him look like some humanoid or eccentric professor. Maybe fifty, but youthful-looking. An unusual physical combination. But the man was important, had been one of the vital keys to the plan.

Lieber looked round as the Volkswagen came to a sudden halt in front of the porch.

They were there.

5.20 p.m.

In the growing darkness, the traffic was bumper to bumper.

Sanchez' body seemed to ooze sweat. With tension, heat, altitude sickness.

As the unmarked police car inched forward in the heavy traffic, Gonzales, sitting in the front passenger seat, said, 'To hell with this, *amigos*,' as he hefted out the blue light and reached out and up through the rolled-down window, clamped it on top, flicked a switch on the dashboard.

393

The piercing scream of the flashing siren tore into the growing darkness like a banshee. Traffic separated, horns honked, and then they were through.

'Take the next left,' Gonzales commanded.

Juales swung the car down a one-way street of two-lane traffic. He let out an uncharacteristic whoop as he nudged onto the pavement, the car tilting, driving for thirty metres like this, children and passers-by staring. And then they were through onto another street. The siren wailed on as they picked up speed, lanes of traffic separating to allow them to pass.

'The only way to travel,' Gonzales remarked with a smile.

The news had come over the mobile radio five minutes before, and Juales had repeated it aloud, a look of triumph on his face. *'They caught sight of the Volkswagen, heading up to the Chapultepec Hills. We're in luck.'*

Now Sanchez said, 'What happens when we get there?'

Gonzales swivelled round to face him and Cavales. 'We look and watch.' He paused. 'There's a couple of Browning pump-actions in the back in case we need them. You both know how to shoot those damned things? I don't want my ass ending up like a colander.'

Sanchez and Cavales smiled, said yes, they knew how to use the Brownings. The traffic suddenly thinned and the car began to climb, the streets becoming less crowded, the houses less shabby, the air slightly cooler. Gonzales switched off and removed the siren.

Juales' phone buzzed on his lap and he picked it up. He listened for several moments and then said, 'Good. Wait there. We'll be with you in ten minutes.'

Then he turned to the others and said, 'The Volkswagen just turned in through the front gates of the address in Chapultepec. There's a guard at the gate. No way of getting past him. My men are parked and waiting with the others a hundred metres down the street.'

Gonzales smiled. He turned to Sanchez and said, 'The people you want. You think they'll be at this place waiting for Lieber?'

'I hope so.'

'You understand, Vellares, I can't go in without a warrant. And this place, it's full of rich people. The rich, they protect themselves. And someone like Halder's got lots of friends in high places, you can count on it. So we better do it strictly by the book.'

'What do you suggest?'

'Well, we need a search warrant, to protect my ass.' Gonzales hesitated. 'There's a judge named Manza. He often helps me. Law and order type, straight down the line. I think he's my best bet.'

'What about the periphery of the property?'

'The area is all hills and narrow winding streets. Difficult sometimes to know where one property begins and another ends. But I'll have one of the other cars take a quick run round. Have a look for rear exits and try to find a good vantage point where we can observe the place. But let's talk to the judge first.'

Gonzales picked up the mobile. 'Control. This is Chief Inspector Gonzales here. I want you to patch me through to Judge Ricardo Manza . . .'

The avenue was well lit and Juales had moved the car in the shadows between two street lamps on a hill overlooking the villa, under a copse of sweet-smelling eucalyptus. The place was a perfect vantage point in the bright moonlight: the property lay almost two hundred metres below and, beyond them, the walled perimeter, the gates, the path leading up to the villa itself clearly visible, obscured only in places by occasional clumps of trees.

The windows of the car were rolled down, the air cool. The smell of eucalyptus and poinsettias. Big houses all around.

Sanchez had listened while Gonzales had spoken with the judge for at least five minutes, arguing his case. The conversation had been heated; but the judge finally gave in. He would agree to sign the search warrant.

'*Don't compromise me, Gonzi. Don't fuck me up*,' Sanchez heard the judge say over the mobile.

395

'*You have my word on it,*' Gonzales had replied, then said his polite goodbye, turned to the others after he had put through a second call.

'One of my men is picking up the warrant. He should be here in ten minutes.'

'What happens then, Eduardo?'

Gonzales looked back at Sanchez. 'If we go up to the gate with the warrant and demand entry, whoever's at the gate can stall us and let whoever's up at the villa know we're coming. So it's best one of my men goes over the wall just before Juales hits the guy on the gate with the warrant. With one of our men inside, he'll make sure the guard doesn't have time to alert the villa. It's risky, I know. They could have armed guards patrolling the grounds and they might start shooting in any confusion. But it's the only way we're going to surprise them. Let's just pray they don't have guard dogs loose on the lawns or an electrified perimeter. Whoever goes over the wall could get chewed or crisped.'

'What then?'

'Our man lets us through the gate and we drive up to the house, quick as we can. One of the other men can take over from Juales and we move in with another car behind us, go up the driveway fast as hell. We put the sirens and lights on at the last moment. That way there can be no mistake. They'll know it's police, but they won't have time to think. And if they run, they run like scared rabbits.' Gonzales paused. 'But leave any talking to me once we're inside, OK? After I've done the preliminaries, you can have Lieber and whoever else you want for questioning.'

Cavales said, 'The people inside, they may be heavily armed.'

Gonzales shrugged. 'Up here in Chapultepec, everyone's heavily armed, *amigo*. They're probably legally held weapons. But once they know we're police, they'd be crazy to open fire. Unless they want to get out of that place pretty bad.'

There was a tap on the roof on Juales' side and everyone started. A man stood outside and Sanchez realised it was one of the plainclothes policemen.

'What's the problem?' Juales said.

'There's some movement round by the side of the villa. A group of men just came out onto the patio. They're sitting at a table by the pool. Looks like they're having a meeting.' The man paused and held up a night-finder. 'You want to take a look, sir? You can see them pretty well if you move up the rise.'

Juales took the night-finder and handed it across to Gonzales, who said to the man, 'You've found the rear entrance?'

'I believe so, sir. I've got a car there, with three men.'

'Good. You've got another night-finder?'

'Yes, sir, Barca has one.'

'Then we'll hold onto this one. Thanks, Madera.'

The man turned and walked away into the shadows.

Juales looked across at Gonzales. 'You want to try and see the men by the pool?'

When Gonzales nodded, Juales started the car and shifted into first gear. He drove up the rise for twenty metres and halted. They could see the side of the villa now, the faint turquoise shape in the distance that was the swimming pool. Gonzales stepped out of the car and looked through the night-finder across the narrow valley, then handed it to Sanchez.

'You can't see too good, Vellares. Just a bunch of people. No faces, just blurry green blobs.'

Sanchez got out and peered through the night-finder. The swimming pool looked bright green and when he swung the finder a little to the left he saw a group of static figures seated at a white table beside the pool. But too far to get a clear view, the images hazy.

There was a sound behind him moments later and the same detective who had given them the night-finder handed Gonzales a folded sheet of paper, explaining it was the authorised warrant. Gonzales took it, flicked on the interior light, scrutinised the sheet.

When he looked back up Gonzales considered a moment, then said to the detective, 'The pool at the side, can it be reached directly from the driveway?'

The man shook his head. 'The driveway cuts only to the left, past the pool. But you could maybe make it across the lawn. There's some trees in the way, but you could cut round them, drive straight over towards the pool area.'

'Thanks, Madera.'

Gonzales went to dismiss the man, but before he did he explained he wanted him to go over the wall just before Juales served the warrant. The man looked unhappy about the arrangement, but didn't argue.

'You got a pair of thick gloves in the car?'

'No, sir.'

'Well, get a pair from one of the others. And quick. Someone's got to have a pair. Try one of the uniforms. Put them on before you go over the wall, because if you don't and that wall's electrified you end up with stumps. And tell the others to prepare to move, but wait for my call.'

Madera moved off at a jogging pace.

As they sat there in the darkness, Gonzales said, 'OK, we've got five cars. Three men to each car, except this one. Sixteen men in total. Six uniformed.' Gonzales paused, lit a cigarette, blew out smoke. 'The three other cars stay outside, two covering the front and one the rear. So that leaves us and one more car to go through the gates. Any questions before we go?'

Nobody spoke.

Gonzales turned and peered through the night-finder quickly, then handed it to Sanchez. The images through the lens were grainy, eye-straining green, but Sanchez could still see the figures by the pool. Very little movement: a figure shaking its head, another leaning forward.

Sanchez put down the night-finder.

Gonzales said to Juales, 'The pump-actions, you want to hand them out?'

Juales went to the back and unlocked the boot, came back with two pump-action Browning shotguns and two boxes of cartridges. He handed a weapon each to Sanchez and Cavales, and a box each of cartridges.

They stepped out and loaded the weapons, then climbed

into the back seat again. Gonzales took the night-finder once more, one last check on the figures by the pool, then he turned round in his seat.

He looked at Sanchez. 'There are a couple of guys wandering around the lawns. But it's difficult to see them clearly.'

'They look like they're armed?'

Gonzales shrugged. 'I can't tell, Vellares. But we'll have to risk it. Everyone ready?'

They nodded.

Gonzales slid his own Smith and Wesson pistol from its holster and placed it on his lap, then picked up the mobile and pressed the transmit button.

'One to Nightwatch units . . .'

6.02 p.m.

On Gonzales' command, Juales stepped quickly from the car and unholstered his gun and began to move down the hill at a jogging pace. Sanchez saw him raise his Smith and Wesson to chest height as he moved.

They saw the detective, Madera, come out of the shadows where the other police car was parked twenty metres away.

The man wore a pair of white gloves and when Gonzales saw him he smiled and said, 'Jesus . . .'

As Gonzales slipped across into the driver's seat, Sanchez' eyes moved back to watch Juales, outside on the street, ten metres from the gates, slowing now, the gun held down by his side, the white warrant sheet visible in his hand. A couple of metres from the gates, Juales halted, pushed himself back against the wall and waited.

The detective named Madera joined him moments later. Juales lay down the gun and warrant and cupped his hands and Madera slid in his foot. Juales lifted him up. It took three attempts before Madera gripped the ridge of the wal!. He pulled himself up warily and seconds later they saw him hesitate, then disappear over the top.

Juales retrieved his gun and warrant and began to move towards the gate. Sanchez noticed a police car a hundred metres down the street begin to move slowly out of shadows, ready to follow Gonzales' car through the gates.

Eyes went back to Juales as he waited with his back to the wall.

There was a sudden loud explosion, a gun discharging, followed by another shot, and Gonzales said, '*Fuck . . .*'

Everyone in the car tensed and they saw Juales race to the gate, his weapon raised and clutched in both hands. Then the gate swung open and Madera appeared.

Gonzales let out a deep sigh as they saw Juales slip inside, his gun raised in his right hand, his other hand with the warrant waving at them frantically, but not looking at them as he moved in.

At that moment, Gonzales said, 'OK, *amigos*. Let's go . . .'

He hit the accelerator and the unmarked police car scudded quickly down the hill and raced towards the entrance gates.

The five men sat around the poolside table.

Turquoise water shimmered under lights. Two butlers had served them drinks, then left them alone. They had moved out to the pool at Halder's request, the villa humid, his wheezy old chest unable to stand the cloying air.

Lieber had told his story while the others remained silent. Told his story and waited for the reaction.

Old Halder coughed and sucked on his inhaler, took a deep breath. Everyone around the table looked at him. Very slowly he rose from his sunken position in the chair. He was a small man, smaller still with the weight of years on his buckled old shoulders.

There was spittle on his lips as he spoke to Lieber. 'How, Franz? How could there have been another tape?' Halder's voice sounded like a whispered, throaty death rattle.

Lieber sighed deeply. 'Either we destroyed the wrong tape, or there were two tapes. There's no other explanation.'

There was a long silence at the table. Halder's wrinkled

claw of a hand went to his brow, massaged the flesh there. Thinking. Thinking hard.

'Is your *seguridad* source absolutely certain about the information?'

'Certain.'

After a long time, Halder said, 'Let us reconsider the situation, shall we?'

Halder glanced quickly at the silver-haired man, saw him nod his head for permission to continue.

Halder turned back slowly, his watery eyes taking in everyone at the table, before he looked directly at Kruger.

'Brandenburg . . . was it discussed in completion at the hotel? The full implications of the plan?'

Kruger shook his head. 'We went over the latter stages. But . . .'

'*Details*, Hans. I want details. Tell me *exactly* what was discussed,' said Halder quickly.

When Kruger told him, Halder said, 'Can the girl be contacted?'

'I can have Meyer see to it.'

Halder paused, then looked at the expectant faces. 'The problem is not insurmountable. Kruger can arrange with Meyer what must be done. There are four days remaining. We know what lies ahead.'

The old man hesitated. He looked across at Ernesto Brandt, then at the silver-haired man. Halder was about to speak further when they all heard the crack of a gunshot somewhere in the distance, then another.

Kruger sat bolt upright, then jumped to his feet, his eyes fixed on something over Halder's shoulder. Halder turned, saw one of the guards come running across the lawns, machine-pistol in his hand, the big man's body pounding hard across the grass.

Kruger was already moving towards the man, meeting him on the lawn ten metres away. The man spoke rapidly and Kruger turned and raced back just as everyone around the table heard the whine of car engines straining in the distance.

Kruger reached them, his face deathly pale, urgency in his voice. 'We've got company. Two cars just came in through the gates.' He turned back smartly, called out to the guards. '*Rotman . . . Werner . . . cover us!*'

Just as Kruger wrenched the Walther from its shoulder holster, there was a sudden shriek of sirens, a ghostly flashing of blue light visible through the shrubbery and trees, and then the growling nose of a car screamed around the gravel driveway and bumped onto the lawn. Sixty metres away, heading straight towards the poolside, lights blazing.

'Everyone! . . . Inside!' Kruger screamed at the top of his voice, and as they moved towards the patio he turned, saw the first car, then the second, racing towards them out of the darkness, blue lights flashing, sirens wailing.

The guards were already reacting. Werner raised his machine-pistol and the weapon chattered in his hands, flame leaping from the barrel.

Kruger saw the windscreen of the first car shatter, heard the thumping report of lead ripping through metal. The car careened across the lawn and scudded into a tree, its blue light suddenly dying, its siren fading like a dying wheeze.

The second car, thirty metres away now, weapons prickling from its windows. A blaze of fire erupted from the vehicle, shotguns exploding in the darkness. Werner was blasted in the chest, his big body flung backwards.

Kruger swore, reached the patio doors just as a blast of lead pellet peppered the wall to his right. He saw the look of alarm on the faces of the others as they moved into the villa through the french windows, saw the sudden paleness on the face of the silver-haired man as he called out to Kruger, 'The back way, Hans. Quickly now!'

Schmidt had already torn the Magnum from its holster, and now he aimed at the oncoming car, squeezed the trigger twice.

The explosions rang around the lawns, echoed about the patio.

Kruger roared, '*Inside!*'

He pushed them in through the patio doors, hesitated long

enough to see Rotman fire a long burst at the second car: the chattering weapon puncturing the vehicle, screams erupting into the night, windscreen shattering, figures inside trying to shield their faces as the driver was hit in the chest and the car wove aimlessly across the lawn, shot halfway across the turquoise pool and nosed into the water.

As the guard fumbled for a fresh magazine, Kruger roared: 'Keep us covered, Rotman!'

The guard didn't even look behind, simply raised his hand as he went to slam another magazine into the Heckler and Koch and moved for cover.

Suddenly, Kruger glimpsed a movement to the left of the first car, saw a figure crawl out of the wreckage where it had hit the tree.

Kruger raised the Walther, aimed, fired three quick shots, then turned and disappeared into the villa.

Chapter Thirty-Five

6.07 p.m.

Sanchez lay on the grass, sweat pumping from every pore as he glimpsed the man disappear into the house.

The car had come to a halt in a thicket of shrubbery, the left side of the vehicle embedded in the trunk of a eucalyptus tree. When Sanchez tried to move, he felt a jolt of pain shoot down his right leg.

He had flung himself from the car at the last moment, landed hard on the grass. Now his right hip was on fire, excruciating when he moved. The car was five metres away. He couldn't see inside, the windscreen shattered and frosted, riddled with bullet holes.

Sanchez still had the shotgun, gripped in both hands, and he ignored the pain in his hip, grimaced as he called out, 'Gonzales! Cavales!'

There were a few seconds of silence and then he heard a groan before an answer came back – Gonzales' voice – pain in the reply.

'Over here . . .!'

Before Sanchez could reply he heard a movement off to the right and turned. A man crouched near the pool, a machine-pistol in his hands. At that moment a blaze of light erupted from his weapon and a rake of fire razed the grass beside him.

Sanchez rolled right, into shrubbery, then aimed at the moving figure. The pump-action exploded in his hands and the recoil shook his body, but the man by the pool had moved out of sight and into the shadows of a clump of palm trees.

Rear guard. To slow them, Sanchez guessed.

The shrubbery Sanchez found himself in was poor cover,

but better than nothing. Twenty metres away the second car sank in the turquoise pool, its blue light still flashing, but no sound from the siren, oxygen bubbles rising like froth, crimson patches here and there in the pale water. The left rear passenger door was open and riddled with holes, one of the bodies of the men hanging half in, half out. Sanchez could make out a head thrown back in the driver's seat, mouth open in death.

He suddenly thought of Cavales and Juales. Dead or still alive?

He heard Gonzales swear from behind the wreckage of the car by the tree.

Sanchez called out, 'Stay where you are.'

Suddenly another burst erupted from near the pool, fire raging across the grass, raking the car, then the firing stopped. Gonzales swore again. The rear guard.

Sanchez whispered, 'Are you OK?'

'I'm alive,' came the reply. 'Can you see the bastard with the machine gun?'

'Thirty metres away, by the pool. Can you cover me?'

'I'll try. But take it easy, *amigo*.'

Sanchez turned, rolled deeper into the shrubbery, ignoring the pains that shot through his hip, conscious of the passing seconds, of the urgency to move into the villa after the men. He crawled quickly on his belly through the thorny undergrowth, the pain making him wince. He came out ten metres away, at the base of another eucalyptus tree, eyes trying to pick out any movement in the darkness where the figure had darted.

Nothing.

If he was going to pursue Lieber and his people he would have to move quickly.

Suddenly a movement off to the left caught his eye and he heard a faint rustling of bushes. He strained his eyes, then saw the man crouched low among the shrubbery, caught in a shaft of moonlight. The man was waiting, hesitating, like he was trying to decide whether to take the risk and move across the lawn. Sanchez inched forward slowly, came to within a dozen metres of the man before he saw him turn, a startled look on his face as he saw Sanchez.

The pump-action in Sanchez' hands rose and exploded. The blast hit the man in the chest, a muted cry as the man's body was hurled back into the shrubbery.

At that moment Sanchez heard sirens wailing in the distance. He turned, moved quickly back to Gonzales, ignoring the terrible pain in his own hip as he knelt down beside him. In the wash of light from the side of the house he could see the sweat glistening on Gonzales' brow, the man's face contorted in pain. A patch of dark below the right elbow where a bullet had penetrated flesh.

'Your arm . . .'

'It's nothing. Just a flesh wound. We're getting too old for this, *amigo*. Let's stick to conferences. You got the bastard?'

Sanchez nodded as he quickly examined Gonzales' forearm. A bullet had rutted the flesh, chipped bone. Nothing serious, but painful.

As Gonzales tried to push himself up, he said, 'The others . . .?'

Sanchez looked back into the silent, bullet-riddled car, saw the frosted glass and ruptured metal where lead had punctured neat holes, aware of his heart beating wildly in his chest as he moved forward to look. Bile in his stomach, anger in his head like a wild thing, knowing what to expect.

Even in the poor light he could see the bodies clearly. Juales in the front passenger seat, his head to one side, mouth open, a slash of red across his chest in a rising angle, blood everywhere below the torso and waist. Sanchez put a hand to the man's mouth. A faint breath. He moved as quickly as he could to the rear, unable to ignore the excruciating pain in his hip.

In Cavales' case there was no doubt: the top of the man's skull had been torn apart, a gaping hole in the lower cheek where the handsome face had once been, dark treacle spilling out, running down his jacket. A sickening mess. Sanchez took a deep, angry breath, wanted to vomit, held it, fury welling up inside him, almost taking over, wanting to rush into the villa after Lieber's people, blow them away.

He heard a sound behind him, looked round. Gonzales had stood up, a hand on the front wing of the car, as he stared at the scene inside.

Sanchez said, 'Juales, he's barely alive, see if you can help him.'

'Where are you going, Vellares . . .?'

But Sanchez wasn't listening. As he moved away, towards the villa, the shotgun gripped in both hands, he was aware faintly of the police cars straining up the driveway, the wail of sirens coming closer. He looked back at Gonzales.

'I'm going in after them, Eduardo. Tell your men.'

He heard Gonzales' voice call out after him. 'Are you crazy? Wait . . . Vellares . . . my men are coming . . .'

Sanchez didn't reply. His eyes were fixed on the patio door and the darkened room beyond, cocking the pump-action as he moved towards the villa.

6.08 p.m.

As they moved through the rooms, Kruger was in control, covering the rear.

Sweat dripped from every pore in his body, the emergency plan clear in his mind: move to the garage as quickly as possible, across the open space of the lawn first – a problem, of course, too vulnerable – then drive down the narrow private road through the warren-like park to the safe house. Speed vital.

Keep moving.

Five rooms to the exit that led to the lawn and the escape route. They were in the third room. No more than two minutes to the garage. But already things not going according to plan. Kruger swore. Old Halder was the problem. The old man moving slowly, joints buckled and gnarled.

He ordered Lieber and Brandt to carry old Halder between

them, and now the six men moved through the house more quickly, little old Halder, feet dangling in mid-air between Lieber and Brandt.

Schmidt held the Magnum .357 in his right hand, eyes watchful. The house was lit up like a Christmas tree. *Too much light*. Kruger extinguished each light as they left each room. It would slow anyone who followed.

Suddenly up ahead a butler appeared, stepping out of a room to the right, face pale, eyes wide. Everyone startled.

Before the man had a chance to move Schmidt raised his Magnum and fired. The explosion reported throughout the house, the force of the bullet sending the man sprawling backwards against a wall, blood erupting on his white jacket.

Kruger swore. The noise of the big Magnum would alert anyone coming after them.

They stepped aside, passed the crumpled body.

Up ahead now Schmidt opened another door, moved quickly inside, weapon at the ready. Another door. Then they were through into the deserted kitchen. Stainless steel, copper, dark wood. The door at the end led outside, to the garden, darkness beyond, and Kruger saw through the windows the vast stretch of silvered lawn.

Vulnerable. Too open. Sixty seconds to cross it at a trot. More because of the others. Maybe ninety. He heard old Halder moan and ignored it. Almost there. They could make it.

Keep moving.

Schmidt moved to the kitchen back door, opened it slowly, peered left, right, ahead, towards the vast silvered lawn, then turned back and nodded the all-clear.

Schmidt stepped out, the others following, old Halder wheezing and groaning now. Kruger swore again. He ought to put a bullet in the old bastard, he was slowing them up as they moved across the lawn.

Kruger was the last to step out, and as he did so he saw the light switch by the door and hesitated.

He heard a noise behind him, faint, but distinguishable, coming from somewhere back in the house. A door opening?

This time he left the light on, then followed after the others.

He was moving backwards across the lawn ten seconds later, still covering the rear, the Walther ready in his hand, when he saw the kitchen door move. Barely discernible, yet he saw it, every sense alert, his body drenched in sweat as he narrowed his eyes.

They were perhaps twenty metres across the grass, moving fast – as fast as old Halder would allow – Lieber and Brandt grunting under the weight of the old bastard as they carried him between them, another forty metres to go, breaths gasping, hearts pounding.

Kruger had left the kitchen light on deliberately, knowing that if anyone came through they would be at an immediate disadvantage: light looking into dark.

But Kruger would be able to see. Able to see and respond.

And Kruger *definitely* saw the movement. Seconds later the door burst open, a figure appearing, but only a glimpse and then the figure disappeared from view.

Kruger swore, went to fire, but knew the shot would be wasted. He swore again . . . heard the panting and groaning of breaths of the others behind him.

'*Keep moving!*'

He hesitated, knelt, raised the Walther, aimed towards the lighted kitchen, waiting to see the figure move again, judging the distance – a difficult shot . . . eyes scanning the room for movement, counting the seconds . . . two, three, four, five, six, seven . . . and then a shotgun blast erupted and the kitchen light went out.

Fuck!

The bastard was clever, knocking out the light, guessing strategy. Dark looking into light so easy, dark into dark difficult, evening the odds.

Kruger waited . . . eyes narrowing, straining desperately to see into the silvery darkness, counting . . . eight . . . nine . . . ten . . . eleven . . .

A faint movement, to the left?

Kruger fired off three rapid shots . . . heard the thud of lead smacking into glass, plaster, heard the kitchen window to the left shatter.

Then nothing.

A shout from behind him. 'Kruger!' Lieber's voice. 'It's Halder! Something's wrong!'

'*Keep moving!*' Kruger shouted back, not turning. *Fuck Halder*.

But he heard Halder's wheezing gasps and Kruger's eyes darted back; the others still moving, almost at the garage, but Lieber and Brandt slowing, holding the sagging, ancient body of Halder between them, something up with the old man, his heart probably, not able to take the strain. Kruger wiped sweat from his brow, tried to control his breathing as his eyes went back to the kitchen.

A movement. To the right.

Kruger fired three more quick shots in a short arc, heard the reciprocated smacks as the lead hit glass, then concrete, wood, concrete.

And then suddenly he saw the figure.

Moving towards them out of shadow: a short fat figure in a light suit moving quickly out onto the silvered lawn like a spectre, long barrel of a weapon at waist height visible as the man advanced steadily towards them.

'*Alto!*'

Kruger heard the voice call out in Spanish. He aimed and fired, three quick shots at the ghostly figure, saw the man buck and then spin.

Kruger went to fire again, but the hammer clicked. Empty. He tore out the spent magazine, slammed home a fresh one from his pocket.

He focused on the man. The bastard was still coming, his body listing to one side.

'*Alto!*'

The voice louder now, firmer.

Kruger brought up the Walther, aimed at the centre of the target, squeezed off one round, was about to squeeze the trigger again when at almost the same moment he saw

411

the man's hands swing up the shotgun, the weapon exploding and a blast of air whistling past Kruger's left, like a hurricane, then another, and another . . .

Jesus . . .

Screams erupted in the night, something stung Kruger's left shoulder and he was spun round, the Walther wrenched from his hand, and as he spun Brandt and Lieber punched back onto the grass, hands flailing, old Halder collapsed between them.

Kruger searched frantically on the grass for the pistol, but couldn't find it . . . a numbing, prickling pain in his left forearm and hand . . . heard a groan from the tangle of bodies on the grass, then silence.

Forget the weapon . . . The man fifteen metres away . . . halting, loading again in the darkness, calmly . . . like it was no big fucking deal.

Kruger saw the moment and seized it.

He scrambled backwards on his hands, past the pile of bodies – Lieber, Brandt, old Halder – oblivious to his pain, not caring whether the three men on the grass were dead or alive, as he ran towards the garage where the others had entered.

As he ran, gulping deep mouthfuls of air, he waited for the shotgun blast to hit him in the back.

It never came.

Panting, he reached the garage door and stepped into darkness.

Sanchez stood in the middle of the lawn reloading the shotgun.

He saw the man run towards the building at the end of the lawn, half hidden behind a clump of trees. Too far away now to get a good shot.

There was a numbing, prickling sensation in his right shoulder where two bullets had hit him with the force of sledgehammers, sending him reeling. No pain there, not yet, but it would come.

He loaded five shells and cocked the pump, stepped

forward, started to trot, pain shooting through his thigh and hip like fire.

The man on the lawn had given him no choice but to fire. To not have done so would have meant death. He had fired, but missed, the shotgun exploding in his hands, firing right, hitting the group of men instead as they moved with their backs to him across the lawn.

Shit.

These were the men; these were the people. No doubt in his mind.

And he had wanted them alive, hoped they still were.

As he approached the bodies on the grass, he held the shotgun at the ready. He saw Franz Lieber's face clearly in the moonlight, contorted, twisted. The blast from the pump-action had hit him in the back. Lieber wasn't moving. Sanchez grimaced; he had wanted Lieber alive, and now this.

He heard a groan, halted, looked down. Another body, arms twisted either side. A man with glasses, big forehead. This one was still alive. A gurgling sound came now from the man's throat, his eyes closed, face screwed up with pain. There was a dark patch of blood on his left arm and shoulder.

Sanchez saw a third figure between the two men, lying face down. There were bloodstains on the back of the pale suit where the shot had blasted the man's body. Sanchez bent, turned him over. A small, wizened old man. It was the pale suit he had seen on the dark lawn, and aimed towards it. One of the old man's claw-like hands was raised as if in supplication. Sanchez stared at the face. Not one of the faces in Lieber's photograph. Nor the man lying on the grass near him, the one still alive. The man groaned again. Sanchez ignored him. Gonzales' men would deal with him.

Behind him suddenly came muted, distant noises. He turned sharply, saw no one. Gonzales' men, somewhere in the house behind him. Sanchez ignored the noises and turned back, towards the building. The man who had escaped had gone inside after the others and he knew the only real hope lay in finding them.

413

He began to step towards the building behind the clump of trees.

Sweat pumped from his forehead, drenched the back of his neck, images burning in his skull. Rudi Hernandez and the young girl, the savage wounds inflicted on their bodies. The body of Cavales, face blown away. Gonzales' men: Juales and the men whose car had been raked with fire and driven into the pool.

The images drove him on, made him oblivious to his own safety, wanting the men who had escaped, wanting them badly, ignoring pain.

The bodies on the grass behind him: he had seen how the man had ignored them, unconcerned about his comrades, concerned only for his own safety. A coward. Ruthless.

He stepped closer to the building, no longer aware of the ache in his hip and leg, the pump-action held firmly in both hands.

Ten metres from the building he saw the door, silver light washing on wood. He approached the door cautiously and raised the shotgun. He squeezed the trigger twice: the blasts shattering silence, fragmenting wood, sending what remained of the frame smacking back against the inside wall as it bounced and shuddered off concrete, then settled on creaking hinges, as the peppering lead rattled against metal somewhere inside the building.

Then the noise died.

Darkness inside, beckoning. Sanchez pressed himself against the outside wall. There was a crack where the door had abutted the frame. He peered in, listened. No sound. But if the men were inside they could be waiting. He stepped round warily, the pump-action at the ready, eyes narrowing, concentrating on the darkness facing him, trying to discern shape, form.

The smell of oil. And petrol. A garage? He peered again, could make out the faint shape of a big car parked in the centre of the building, a dull glint of polished metal, a sheen of glass reflected. Now that he looked closely he saw another door, ajar, at the end of the building, a thin crack of silver moonlight shining through. Had the men escaped? Or were they waiting for him? If they were waiting, this time he would have to wound, not kill. Difficult with the pump-action. He would have to be careful.

He listened.

Still nothing.

He couldn't wait forever.

He took a deep breath, felt the sweat coursing down his face as he levelled the shotgun, swung round from the wall, moved inside.

And then . . .

A light went on suddenly overhead and blinded him.

Sanchez barely heard the barked command: '*Schmidt!*'

In the sudden, blinding light he saw the huge form of a man lunge at him from behind the car – big, blond, a crazy look on his face like a wild animal, the glint of jagged metal in his hand.

Sanchez swung the pump-action up and round and squeezed the trigger. The deafening roar that followed raged through the garage like a sonic boom.

Sanchez saw the look on the man's face: ugly, animal, his body like some boulder of granite bearing down on him, as the shotgun exploded half a metre from the man's chest.

The force of the blast halted his body in mid-air – his chest and belly exploding, a cavernous hole appearing in the centre of his huge torso, gut spilling out and a wave of gushing blood, the animal look on the man's face becoming a look of horror.

The man collapsed on top of Sanchez, pinned him against the wooden wall cladding, the crushing weight knocking his breath out, his face up against Sanchez' own, eyes open wide.

Sanchez smelled the wheezing, foul breath against his face. *The man was still alive.*

Sanchez' fingers tried frantically to unpin the shotgun, struggled to push the man off, but the weapon was wedged between them. The terrible weight pressing down on him, making him helpless.

Two other men were visible now out of the corner of his eye: a young dark-haired man carrying a big Magnum pistol, and another man, older, tall, silver-haired, coming towards him out of nowhere, Sanchez recognising the faces from the photograph in Lieber's house.

Sanchez made a supreme effort, pushed with all his strength. The blond man moved and his huge hand swung up. Sanchez saw the blade of the Bowie knife arc in his hand. Sanchez found the pump-grip, reloaded, pulled the trigger just as the jagged knife thrust into his shoulder, cut through bone and flesh, pinned him to the wall.

Sanchez screamed in pain and the shotgun exploded again. This time the man's face and head disintegrated, flesh peeling from bone, his body flung backwards, another wave of blood drenching Sanchez as shotgun pellets deflected back, prickled his body.

And then everything seemed to happen at once.

The two men came forward.

The younger man held the big Magnum pistol in his hand, rage on his face, Sanchez realising that the dead man had been expendable, a diversion. The man pointed the gun at Sanchez' temple, his other hand reaching to grasp the pump-action, wrench it away.

The silver-haired man stepped quickly forward. His tall frame towered over Sanchez. Kind, soft blue eyes but something in the eyes Sanchez couldn't fathom.

Did it matter now?

The man's voice whispered something to his companion but Sanchez didn't hear. Voices – Gonzales' men – coming from outside now, distant, too distant to save him, muted, carrying across the lawn.

The distant voices had decided his fate.

The man holding the Magnum pressed the big pistol hard against Sanchez' head.

It exploded.

Sanchez had always believed that you never heard the gun-shot that killed you, up close, in the head. That lights simply extinguished, all senses sterile. That you felt nothing, no pain.

A lie.

He heard it.

A cracking, deafening boom.

And he felt it.

A hot, terrible pain imploding in his brain.

And he saw.

And still sensed. Even in the last seconds of primary pain after the second bullet entered his forehead, skewered up, tore into his cerebral cortex, came out through the top of his skull.

But everything in slow, slow motion; body and brain winding down. Sanchez just glimpsing the two darkening figures as they moved towards the car and the faint sound of an engine roaring before vision blanked out.

6.20 p.m.

The silvered lawns seemed awash with uniforms in the moonlight. Grey uniforms and flashing blue lights.

Ambulances came and went. A little later a detective took a dazed Gonzales to the old garage, past the bodies on the grass.

When they showed him the body of Sanchez he wanted to weep but didn't.

He looked at the corpse for a long time; the pitiful lifeless corpse pinned against the wall, the jagged blade driven through his shoulder into wooden cladding, the powder-burned hole drilled through his forehead, the floor awash with blood.

Then he looked at the body of the big blond man. What was left of it. There was a pervading smell of human excrement. Both bodies had defecated after death. Normal.

Sanchez had got four of the bastards. It was little consolation. None really. Besides, there was no pistol near the body of the blond man; someone else had done this. A detective had already told him roadblocks were being set up around the perimeter of Chapultepec. But it was a big area. Some hope.

When he finally stepped outside, he threw up on the lawn. In the silver light someone lit him a cigarette and he took it, wiped his mouth, inhaled deeply.

Another detective stood beside him now. After several moments of silence Gonzales gripped the man's arm.

'Juales . . . did he make it?'

The detective shook his head. 'Dead before they got him to the ambulance.'

Gonzales closed his eyes in grief, opened them slowly again, said in a dazed voice, 'How many others dead?'

The detective's eyes were glazed over with incomprehension, not that Gonzales noticed; he himself stared into nothingness.

'Four of our own men. The two friends of yours from Asunción. Six from the villa. That includes Halder and their man on the gate who got it from Madera when he tried to pull a gun.' The man paused. 'I'm having roadblocks set up all the way to the city. Every possible route. A rookie says he thought he heard a car move off just after he heard the last gunshot. But in the confusion and noise, he's not exactly sure. Difficult to smell exhaust fumes with the smell of cordite and shit in there.' The detective swallowed. 'But the garage doors were open. Some traces of dark paint on the garage doors but we'll have to wait for forensic.' He nodded back towards Halder's villa. 'It's possible some of them got away.'

'The roadblocks, I want them tight. You understand?' Gonzales sighed, said impatiently, 'Only trouble is, we don't know who or what we're looking for. What about the man you found alive on the lawn?'

'He's wounded, not badly, but he's lost a lot of blood. Two of our men went with him in the ambulance. We'll make him talk just as soon as he's patched up.'

'What about staff from the villa? Anyone alive?'

'A butler. One of two. We found him hiding in the basement. The other's dead. I forgot about him: we found him in the house. Shot in the chest. He must have got in the way of their escape. That makes thirteen dead in all. But the butler who's alive is throwing up and shitting himself, too shocked to make sense. He took some pills to calm down.'

Gonzales jabbed a finger at the detective. '*Make* him make sense. Have him and the one from the back lawn brought to the *Central*. Find out how many people were here. Get descriptions, names.' Gonzales shook his head. 'Thirteen men dead . . . I don't believe it.' He drew on his cigarette; his hands trembled.

He spat out bile on the lawn and said hoarsely, 'And they're allowed no calls, understand? To hell with procedures, I want answers first.'

The man nodded and walked away.

Gonzales looked back towards the scene of the carnage – all for what? Who *were* these people? What the fuck was going on?

The sound of an ambulance wailing up the driveway distracted him. Too late now. Far too late. Sanchez never had a chance. To do what he did was *loco*. Stupid. He must have wanted these people from the villa badly.

Another sound distracted him; this time footsteps, a soft voice saying, 'Sir . . .?'

He turned, in a daze.

A young *policia* stood there, awkwardly. 'Sir, there's a man out front who says his name's Cortes. Judge Felipe Cortes.' The young man put the emphasis on *judge*, hesitated, looked pleadingly at Gonzales.

'What does he want?'

'He says he wants to talk to the officer in charge. He seems pretty angry. Wants an explanation for all the noise and shooting. He asked if we knew where we were.' The *policia* swallowed nervously. 'He said this was Lomas de Chapultepec, a respectable area, and not some tin and cardboard *barrio*.'

Gonzales grimaced. He knew the judge: a fat and pompous bastard. He lived not far from here. Big Chapultepec house with servants and a fat wife. Corrupt as many of his neighbourhood friends.

'Did he?' Gonzales was barely able to contain his rising anger. 'Tell him I'm busy.'

'Sir, I told him. He refuses to listen.'

'Then' – Gonzales said it slowly, but frustration in his voice – 'tell him to go fuck himself. And if he's not careful I'll have him arrested for hampering the police in the course of their duty.'

He saw the young *policia*'s eyes open wide; at the disrespect, the anger.

Gonzales stubbed out his cigarette on the lawn. 'Don't worry, I'll tell him myself.'

He turned and left the young man standing there, walked slowly back up towards the villa, each step an agony.

PART FIVE

PART FIVE

Chapter Thirty-Six

Berlin

Werner Bargel sat in his office in the building on the corner of Auf dem Grat and Clay Allee in Berlin's Dahlem district, and waved to the chair opposite for Joseph Volkmann to join him.

At forty-two, Bargel was one of the youngest men ever to hold the position of Assistant Director of the *Landesamt für Verfassungsschutz* in Berlin, the State Office for the Protection of the Constitution, otherwise known as LfV.

The function of the LfV is similar to British M15, in that its brief is to gather intelligence on terrorists, extremist organisations and espionage networks that are a threat to security, except that in the case of the Landesamt, its responsibilities usually only concern the city and state of which it is a part, and generally not the country as a whole.

For unlike M15, the German intelligence service is far more bureaucratic and regionalised.

Its offices are divided up into nineteen state departments, each called a Landesamt, or State Department, with each Landesamt responsible for intelligence-gathering within the state to which it belongs. However, all Landesamt offices come under the umbrella of the central Federal office in Cologne, called the *Bundesamt für Verfassungsschutz*, or the Federal Office for the Protection of the Constitution, and while each Landesamt is autonomous, it is ultimately responsible to the Cologne main office.

The beige-painted two-storey Landesamt building in the leafy Berlin suburb of Dahlem looks unremarkable to the passer-by, but its offices house almost a hundred staff who are daily engaged in gathering vital intelligence information –

on terrorism, extremist organisations, and those engaged in espionage against the state of Berlin, and it keeps comprehensive files on anyone who is or was engaged in such activities in the past. Overlooking a neat park, the site of the long, low building is unknown to most Berliners, and just two doors away is the home of the CIA Head of Station in Berlin.

Like all Landesamt in Germany, the Director or Head is a political appointment, and can change with each election. But the Assistant Director and next in line is always a senior, professional intelligence officer, and it is he who bears responsibility for the day-to-day running of the department.

Tall, thin, and boyishly fresh-faced, Werner Bargel looked more like a young, bespectacled accountant than a senior intelligence officer.

'Well, Joe, what brings you to Berlin?' He looked across at Volkmann and smiled. 'It must be at least a couple of years since we last met?'

'More like three.'

'So what can I do for you?'

'I'd like to pick your brains, Werner. And ask you a favour.'

Bargel raised his eyebrows. 'Is this something you're working on that directly concerns my people?'

'It's too early to say.'

'What kind of information are you looking for?'

'Have you been getting much trouble from the extremist groups recently?'

Werner Bargel sat back in his seat, placed his hands behind his neck. 'Whenever you get a recession, you always get an upsurge in left- and right-wing activity, you know that, Joe. You get our monthly and annual reports from Cologne?'

'Sure.'

'As I recall, there's a piece in this month's report about a percentage rise.'

'What about the right wing, any new groups?'

'A couple, but none that have caused us much grief. But the old ones have been pretty active of late. The usual stuff. Last month in Hoyerswerda another refugee centre was evacuated after a three-day siege by right-wing gangs. Two black street-traders stabbed in Leipzig a week later. A Turkish boy was tossed from a second-floor window in Essen and died from his injuries the same day. I could go on. But it's all in the report I told you about.'

'Are your people worried?'

Bargel smiled thinly. 'That kind of thing always worries us, Joe. We try to keep it under control. But there's always going to be that fringe element in every country, isn't there?'

'What about the immigrant extremist groups?'

'What about them?'

'Are they hitting back?'

'At who?'

'The right wing, the neo-Nazis.'

Bargel shrugged. 'There are a few organised gangs who hit back after right-wing attacks. But it's small-scale, Joe. They're mainly defensive groups, not offensive.'

Volkmann looked out beyond the window. There was a small cobbled courtyard below, a half-dozen cars parked there. When he looked back he saw Bargel was staring at him.

'Is that the real reason for your visit, Joe? All that stuff you can get in our reports you receive.'

'I need a favour, Werner.'

'What sort of favour?'

'About a month ago a young man named Dieter Winter was shot to death in Berlin. You recall the case?'

Bargel frowned, thought a moment. 'The incident at the Zoo Station?'

'That's the one.'

'What about it?'

'I'd like to know if you kept a file on Winter. I saw a BP report on him but there was very little in there.'

Bargel smiled. 'They don't plumb to the same depths as we do, naturally. I can have it checked. Anything else?'

'I'm flying to Munich tomorrow. Winter had an address there but the BP had no record of it. I'd like you to contact the Landesamt people in Munich. I need to take a look at Winter's

place if they know where it is. Also, a guy named Lothar
Kesser. Comes from somewhere in Bavaria. Graduated from
Munich University about four years ago in computer science.
If you've got a file on him and a photograph I'd like to see
them too.'

'That'll probably be Munich, but it shouldn't be a problem.
If they or any of the Landesamt offices have a file on him,
they can wire us a copy within minutes. Was Winter involved
with a right-wing group?'

'That's what I'm trying to find out. The weapon used in
the Zoo Station shooting was used on a British industrialist
in Hamburg a year ago, that's why Ferguson is interested.'

'What about this guy Kesser?'

Volkmann hesitated. 'I'm only fishing at this stage, Werner.
There may be no connection.'

'You think some immigrant extremist group could have hit
Winter?'

Volkmann shook his head and smiled. 'You're way ahead
of me, Werner. I really don't know.'

'But you'll keep me informed if anything comes up we ought
to look into?'

'Sure.'

'I'll get you a copy of last month's report as well. And a
preview of the month's to come.' Bargel stood up.

'I'd appreciate that, Werner.'

'You're staying in Berlin tonight?'

'At the Schweizerhof.'

'I can have my secretary book a table for us at Le Bou Bou
if that's OK with you?'

'Why not. We can have a chat about old times.'

The restaurant on the Kurfürstendamm was almost empty
but the service superb as always.

Bargel had brought along the reports and the files that
Volkmann had requested but he did not discuss them,
except to say that he had arranged for Volkmann to be
met in Munich by a Landesamt man and taken to Winter's
last known address, an apartment in Haidhausen, and that

the Munich contact would fill him in when he arrived. They spent almost two hours talking about the old days in Berlin and when they had finished their meal Bargel walked with Volkmann back to the hotel.

As they strolled back along the Kurfürstendamm towards the Budapester Strasse, Bargel said, 'Do you ever see Ivan Molke now, Joe?'

Volkmann shook his head and said, 'I hear he's in Munich.'

Bargel nodded. 'He took early retirement. Maybe you ought to give him a call when you go south? I can phone you his number before you go.'

'Sure. Why not?'

'You and he were pretty close.'

'Close enough, I guess.'

'Can I ask you a personal question, Joe?'

'Sure.'

'What did you and Ivan do with Felder.'

'I thought you knew?' When he saw Bargel shake his head, Volkmann said, 'We took him out to the Grunewald.'

'I always wondered. The bastard deserved what he got.' He looked at Volkmann and said, 'It was a lousy business in those days. But somebody had to do it.'

'Your people've still got the boys who do the dirty work?'

'You mean the killing?'

'Yes.'

'No way, Joe. In those days it was the Stasi and the KGB we were up against. Our group who looked after that kind of thing was disbanded after the Wall came down.'

'For sure?'

'For sure, Molke will tell you so himself.' Bargel smiled. 'Nowadays we're clean as green.'

Volkmann hesitated, then said, 'Are your police and armed forces partisan when it comes to right-wing activity?'

Bargel shrugged. 'They're apolitical, or supposed to be. What they think personally, of course, is quite another matter. But sure, I guess there are some who might sympathise with fascist groups. But there's nothing we can do about that, so long as it doesn't interfere with their work.' The

427

intelligent eyes regarded Volkmann carefully. 'Why do you ask, Joe?'

'The number of right-wing attacks is increasing. But your people don't seem to be having much success.'

Bargel said, 'It's a difficult area, you must know that, Joe. You've got the usual calls to put all these extremists away. But if you started doing that you'd get the bleeding-heart liberals who oppose them saying we're becoming a police state again, putting people in concentration camps. And for us Germans, that's a touchy subject.' Bargel shook his head. 'There's no easy solution. Some of the right-wing groups have been proscribed. It's damped it down a bit, but not entirely. But then you only have to read the papers to know that.'

'Do these people have much support?'

'You mean the right-wing groups, the neo-Nazis?'

'Yes.'

'Some, but their extreme policies wouldn't appeal to the majority of Germans, that goes without saying.'

'What kind of numbers are we taking about?'

'In Germany? A conservative figure would be sixty thousand.'

'Hard-line?'

'Pretty much hard-line. You could probably treble that figure with softer supporters.'

'That's a lot of support, Werner.'

The intelligent eyes looked at Volkmann. 'What you're really wondering is, could it happen over again? Could a political party like the Nazi Party ever come to power again in Germany. Are you asking me that, Joe?'

'If I remember my history, the Nazis had less than five thousand supporters when Hitler led the beer-hall putsch in 1923. When he started his campaign to be Chancellor of Germany, the Nazi Party had less than a quarter of a million members.'

Bargel shook his head fiercely. 'It couldn't happen again, Joe. Politically and legally, it's enshrined in our constitution, surely you know that? Only those parties that conform to the constitution are admitted to the political system. Which is why the communists and neo-Nazis were banned from political office in the past. And then there is the five per cent barrier. In simple terms that means that any party polling less than five per cent of the vote in an election cannot enter the Bundestag, which excludes effectively extremists and independents from entering our parliament. But besides all that, people are wiser, Germany would never tolerate another Nazi Party or anything like it.

'Sure, we have a problem with neo-Nazi extremists. A neo-Nazi riot in the streets of a German city and the world's press print banner headlines that suggest the Fourth Reich is imminent. But in Germany, these groups have never had great support. And the people who do support them are cranks and misfits. Not responsible Germans. The shaven-headed thugs who beat up immigrants and desecrate Jewish graves are not organised. It's a fringe element. And the ones who are organised are small-scale and we keep them under control as best we can.'

Volkmann looked across at Bargel. 'But there are similarities, Werner. The street riots. Immigrants being attacked instead of Jews. The call to have foreigners expelled. All the social and economic problems you had in the past when the Nazis came to power.'

Bargel nodded. 'Of course, you can draw parallels in any situation. But another Nazi Party in power? Joe, it's not possible. Germans would not allow it. You may say they allowed it in '33. But that was different then. Germany was different. The circumstances may appear the same, and in some ways they are, but they are intrinsically different. And besides, every day we Germans see reminders, on television, in the press, of the sins committed in our name, and the vast majority of us have no wish to repeat those sins.' Bargel shook his head vigorously. 'That another Nazi Party would ever come to power in Germany? Joe, for that to happen it would have to be presented to the German people as a *fait accompli*. And that, I could never envisage happening. I admit there are problems and some of them appear to be getting worse. But the problems will be resolved, believe me.'

'How?'

'You know of Konrad Weber?'

'The Vice-Chancellor? Sure.'

'He's also the Interior Minister, responsible for Federal security. He's a good man, Joe. Tough, conservative, but responsible. Weber's already banned some of the more extreme groups. And he's been making more noises lately about the level of extremist activity. Says it's still unacceptable. Between you and me I hear he wants to bring in some tough changes in the law to put a brake on these people for good.'

'What's he going to do?'

Bargel smiled. 'Even if I knew I couldn't tell you that, Joe. But my ears in the Interior Ministry tell me Weber's going to crack the whip pretty hard and put a stop to it once and for all.'

'When's it going to happen?'

Bargel smiled again. 'Weber's people are hinting he wants a special meeting of the Cabinet. Soon, but I can't tell you more than that.'

They had reached the hotel and Bargel handed across the large envelope containing the files and reports.

'You'll destroy the file copies when you're through with them?'

'Of course.'

He shook Volkmann's hand. 'If there's anything else you need, give me a call.'

'Thanks, Werner.'

As Bargel turned to go, he touched Volkmann's arm and the sharp eyes looked at him.

'And don't forget, Joe, if anything comes up that concerns me, let me know.'

He read the reports in the hotel room of the Schweizerhof.

There was very little new in Winter's file except that he had been brought up in a Catholic orphanage near Baden-Baden but there was no mention of his parents' past. Judging from his institutional background, Winter was a classic joiner; a loner who needed to identify with a cause. There was also a report going back three years stating that Winter had taken part in a right-wing march in Leipzig in which two policemen had been seriously injured. But there was no further evidence of his involvement with such groups.

Kesser's file was a précis that contained very little: a head-and-shoulders photograph of a young, handsome young man with thinning fair hair and high cheekbones. Graduating from Munich University the same year as Winter, he had worked as a programmer for an unnamed Government research establishment on a year's contract before moving to a commercial bank in Nuremberg. Volkmann guessed the unnamed research organisation was military.

There was no mention of Kesser ever having being a member of any right-wing party and his address was given off the Leopoldstrasse in Munich's Swabbing district. There was no indication given of his present employment. Volkmann guessed the file had been kept deliberately brief because of Kesser's involvement in military research and the file was probably classified, hence the précis.

The monthly reports Werner Bargel had included mentioned an eighteen per cent rise in the rate of right-wing incidents and attacks and the preliminary report for the present month estimated a further three per cent rise but noted that with seasonal unemployment taken into account such rises should be expected. There were several more incidents noted, including an attack by right-wing extremists on an apartment building in Hamburg four days previously in which two Turks had been badly wounded. And in Leipzig, neo-Nazis had attacked and stabbed two Asian immigrants. There were two incidents noted in which immigrant gangs had attacked known right-wing supporters: in Rostock a Greek immigrant had petrol-bombed a bar frequented by neo-Nazis, and in the Hamburg red-light district a group of Asians had attacked a right-wing gang on the rampage in St Pauli. The report concluded that further incidents were expected over the coming months and that two new neo-Nazi cells had sprung up, one in

Regensburg and the second in Cottbus, near the Polish border.

When Volkmann had finished reading the files and reports he replaced them in the envelope and poured himself a scotch from the mini-bar. He opened the window and stood by the cold balcony, wondering what Erica was doing at that moment.

As darkness fell across the bare winter landscape of the Tiergarten, he could see the Brandenburg Gate illuminated by sulphur yellow light and the winged statue on the gilded Victory Column was lit up so clearly it could be seen for miles.

He remembered the news pictures that had flashed across the world the night the Wall came down, and the happy crowds waving the colours of the Bundesrepublik; the young men climbing on top of the Brandenburg Gate in a rush of fervent nationalism, the looks of joy and energy on their faces that night as he watched in his apartment in Charlottenburg, hearing the passionate voices singing *Deutschland über alles*, and Volkmann wondering if the character of a nation had really changed that much in fifty years.

The distant roar of a lion in the Zoo distracted him and as he closed the window he took one last look at the Brandenburg Gate and the Reichstag building standing close together in the distance, their colonnaded pillars and granite facades illuminated by yellow arc lamps, then he locked the window and went to bed.

Munich was bitterly cold and it was almost ten when the Landesamt man delegated to meet him at the airport pulled up outside Winter's address in Haidhausen.

It was a modest apartment building and Winter's rooms were on the second floor.

When the man unlocked the door and stepped inside he handed Volkmann the key and told him he'd wait outside in the car until Volkmann had finished.

The studio apartment smelled musty and unused and a colony of spiders dangled on silken threads from webs in the ceiling-rose. The studio consisted of three rooms – bathroom, bedroom, kitchen – and there was a collection of records neatly stacked on the floor by the bed and a hi-fi unit on a writing table next to it. German ballad collections mostly, and some brass-band music.

The tiny kitchen was filthy and in the press under the sink were three empty Bushmills whiskey bottles and a couple of unopened cans of Dutch beer. There was an electric hotplate and some unwashed cutlery on the draining board and some canned meat on one of the shelves. The plastic garbage bin in the corner had been emptied but there was still a smell of rancid food. A film of grime covered all the surfaces and the place didn't look like Winter had spent much time cooking gourmet meals.

Two bookshelves ran along the far wall above the bed. The bed had been tossed and Volkmann guessed the police had searched the place thoroughly. Among the books were several copies of Spengler's works and Volkmann noticed a tattered copy of *Mein Kampf*, the Zentner edition, which was standard reading for German history students like Winter, but apart from those the rest were paperback thrillers. There were no photographs on the shelves and no inscriptions in any of the books.

The driver had told Volkmann on the journey in from the airport that after Winter's death they had received a request to go over the apartment but it had looked as though someone had beaten them to it. Most of Winter's belongings appeared to have been taken and several drawers had been emptied in the writing table. It had been a professional job and the police hadn't found anything of interest and hadn't wasted their time taking prints.

Volkmann spent half an hour looking through the apartment before closing the door and stepping down into the cold street to join the driver.

He had booked a room at the Penta on the Hochstrasse and after he had been dropped off he checked into his room and telephoned the number Bargel had given him for Ivan Molke.

The woman who answered was Molke's sister and she told Volkmann that her brother was in Vienna on business and wouldn't be back until late that afternoon. He thanked the woman and said he would phone back in the evening.

Fifteen minutes later he had showered and unpacked his overnight case and telephoned the Hertz office on the Hochstrasse to hire a car.

It was just after midday when he parked the Opel round the corner from Lothar Kesser's apartment and walked back.

The address off the Leopoldstrasse in Swabbing turned out to be a fairly prosperous-looking block and Volkmann found Kesser's name on the intercom outside.

It had started to rain as he walked back down the street. He found an office supplies shop in a mall around the corner and bought a plastic clipboard and large notepad. When he walked back to the apartment block he wrote the names of all the residents on the intercom on his open pad and then pressed all the intercom buttons except Kesser's. During the barrage of questions that followed the door lock buzzed and sprang open. Someone expecting someone.

As he stepped inside an elderly woman appeared and looked at him quizzically, her eyes going to the clipboard.

Volkmann smiled and said, 'Block management. A problem with the plumbing.'

The woman nodded and went back into her apartment.

He climbed the stairs to the second floor, knocked on Kesser's door and when there was no reply the second time he removed the filed penknife from his pocket and probed the lock. It took him less time than he thought and he stepped into Kesser's apartment and closed the door after him.

The one-bedroom apartment was neatly and tastefully furnished and there was a TV and video recorder in one corner and an expensive hi-fi nearby.

He checked the bedroom first and looked through the mirrored clothes cupboards. There was a suitcase containing old clothes and a pair of worn-looking climbing boots. A half-dozen pairs of mens' and womens' shoes were neatly stored on the cupboard floor and a stack of old records was packed in plastic shopping bags. Marching band music and a complete collection of Wagner's operas. In one of the drawers he found several parcels of new baby clothes still in their cellophane wrappers. He checked under the bed and mattress and then looked in the kitchen and bathroom.

He left the living-room until last. There was a photograph of Kesser and a pretty young blonde girl on the windowsill.

There were a couple of dozen books on the shelves, computer programming books mostly, and Volkmann came across a recent Bundeswehr signal operations codebook marked '*Geheim*', Secret, and some books on Ada, the military programming language. An album on one of the shelves contained photographs from Kesser's youth and university days and in one of them Volkmann saw a picture of Kesser and Winter together, taken in a beer-hall, the two young men smiling out at the camera.

When Volkmann leafed back towards the front of the album he saw a photograph of an older man who slightly resembled Kesser. But it was a snapshot taken long ago in black-and-white and the man was in the uniform of a Leibstandarte SS General, as he posed beside a burned-out Russian tank. He looked young for a general and there was a written inscription at the bottom of the photograph: '*To Hildegard with love. Manfred. October 1943.*'

On one of the pages there was another picture of the same man, but this time in colour, and the man much older, sitting outside a house somewhere in the mountains, a young boy on his knee, and Volkmann guessed from the resemblance that the boy was Lothar Kesser as a child, the features unmistakably similar. There was a date written in the bottom right-hand corner: April 4th, 1977.

He heard the faint sound of a car pulling up in the parking lot below. Volkmann closed the album and replaced it on the shelf. He crossed to the window. A young man had stepped out of a grey Volkswagen and as he locked the door, a blonde attractive girl in her early twenties, and looking obviously pregnant, stepped out of the passenger side, her stomach bulging under a floral maternity smock.

Volkmann recognised Kesser and the girl from the album photographs.

He took a note of the telephone number and then he stepped out into the hallway and closed the door. He passed Kesser and the girl on the first-floor landing, the couple ignoring him as they carried flimsy plastic bags of groceries. The girl looked much prettier close up and Volkmann noticed that neither Kesser nor the girl wore wedding rings.

In the parking lot he took the registration number of Kesser's Volkswagen and five minutes later he drove back to the Penta.

He poured himself a scotch from the mini-bar and went to stand at the window looking down on the rain-lashed Hochstrasse. The sky was grey and dismal and as he stared at the rain-streaked glass he thought of the photograph in Kesser's apartment of the man in uniform. The Leibstandarte SS General could have been Kesser's father, for the family resemblance was unmistakable. He finished his scotch and undressed and climbed into bed.

He slept until six and after he had eaten he went to make the call to Ivan Molke.

Chapter Thirty-Seven

Munich

It took him an hour to walk to the Victualan Markt and another ten minutes to find the *bierkeller*.

The tables and chairs at the front were full and when he stepped down into the warm bar a group of young people were singing in a corner. He had almost forgotten it was less than a week away from Christmas and then he saw Ivan Molke sitting alone at the end of the bar hunched over a beer.

He looked older, his hair greying at the temples, and he wore a grey business suit instead of the casual clothes he always used to favour. He recognised Volkmann at once and waved his hand for him to join him.

'It's good to see you, Joe,' Molke said as he shook his hand firmly.

He looked younger when he smiled and then he said, 'There's a room in the back where we can talk.'

He ordered a beer for Volkmann and when it came he led the way into the small room. There were two trestle tables laid out end to end, thick pine benches both sides, and the dark, oak-beamed ceiling gave the room a traditional look. A holiday poster of Bavaria was stapled on one wall and the place had a musty, unused air. Molke explained that the owner was a friend and he thought the room would be more private.

They sat facing each other and Molke looked at Volkmann and said, 'I heard about your father, Joe. I was sorry to hear of his death.' There was a pause while Volkmann nodded and then Molke added, 'I presumed when you rang me that this wasn't going to be a social call. So maybe you better tell me what it's about.'

'I need your help, Ivan.'

'What's it got to do with? DSE?'

Volkmann nodded and said, 'You're still in the business?'

Molke half smiled. 'You know what they say: once in, never out. I quit officially two years ago and came south. But then you would have heard.' Molke paused to sip his drink. 'I'm in partnership in an agency in the city. Countering industrial espionage.' He smiled. 'Not as exciting as the old days in Berlin but it pays the bills.'

'But you're still in?'

'The State Interior Ministry here calls me in on a consultancy basis maybe once or twice a year.' Molke paused. 'How did you get my number?'

'From Werner Bargel.'

Molke nodded and said, 'So tell me what it's about, Joe.'

It took Volkmann almost fifteen minutes to fill Molke in and when he had finished and shown him the copy of the black-and-white photograph of the woman they had found in the Chaco, Molke stared at it a while before frowning and handing it back.

'Interesting. But what's the connection between the past and the present? Between South America and Germany?'

'That's what I need to find out, Ivan. That's why I need your help.'

'Can you find out who the young woman in the photograph might be?'

Volkmann shook his head. 'I haven't had any luck, Ivan. Besides, it was such a long time ago. And the girl may have been no one important, not even related to Schmeltz. But the man in the photograph, he may be a clue.'

Molke thought a moment. 'Back over twenty years ago, when Willy Brandt got tough on our institutions in Germany responsible for hunting down wanted Nazis, they used to use some experts during the investigations, to verify identities from photographs. The people they used were mostly academics who specialised in the Nazi period, and some ex-Nazis themselves. I can ask around if you like? If the girl in the photograph was somebody important, they may be able to help identify her.'

'Thanks, Ivan.'

Molke smiled. 'I'm not saying you'll get lucky, but no harm in trying. This guy Kesser whose apartment you checked. What do you intend doing?'

'I'd like to tag him for a few days. Maybe it'll turn up something. If you agree to come in on it, I'll see you get paid consultancy rates.'

Molke smiled and waved his hand dismissively. 'We're old friends, Joe. Let's call it a favour. When do you want to start?'

'Tonight, if that suits you?'

Molke checked his watch. 'OK, but I'll have to cancel a dinner engagement. It's nothing special, just an old friend. If we're held over I can call the office in the morning.' He stood up. 'OK. I'd better make the call. Where are you staying?'

'I'm at the Penta. Room one-two-eight.'

'I can meet you there in an hour.'

'I appreciate it, Ivan.'

'No sweat, Joe. You want to use two cars or one?'

'Two.'

'I'll bring along a couple of talkies in case we need them, that way we can keep in touch. They're long-range. The latest stuff.'

Volkmann nodded.

As Molke rose, he said, 'I'll go make the call.'

It was eight-thirty when they pulled up in their cars round the corner from Kesser's apartment and they walked back. It had stopped raining and the light was on in Kesser's living-room and the Volkswagen was in the lot out front.

They walked back and drove Molke's green BMW back round and parked across the street by the park where they could see Kesser's apartment block. Molke gave Volkmann one of the two-way radios and Volkmann showed him the head-and-shoulders photograph of Kesser.

They sat in the BMW until well after midnight when the lights in Kesser's apartment went out. A little after one they decided to call it a night and arranged to meet back at the park at 5.30 a.m.

Volkmann slept until five then showered and shaved.

As he pulled up outside the park half an hour later it was still pitch dark but Molke's BMW was already there. The light was on in Kesser's living-room and Volkmann could see a shadow move back and forth across the room.

As he climbed in beside Molke, the older man said, 'The light went on ten minutes ago, just after I got here. Looks like he's getting ready to move. You want to do first tag?'

'Sure.'

'Don't forget to keep the radio on. We can change tag every ten minutes. The traffic's going to be pretty thin while he's driving.'

'OK, Ivan.'

As Volkmann climbed out of the BMW, Molke grinned and said, 'Let's hope Kesser's not just taking an early-morning jog in the park, my friend. I'd hate to have got up this early for nothing.'

Volkmann smiled and walked back to his car.

Kesser came out of the apartment block half an hour later wearing a blue rainproof anorak and carrying a briefcase.

It had started to rain heavily and when Kesser's Volkswagen pulled out of the parking lot Volkmann gave him a fifty-metre start before following, seeing Molke's lights behind him.

Fifteen minutes later the Volkswagen pulled up at a filling station-restaurant on the Munich ring road and Kesser took half an hour over breakfast and read a newspaper before filling his car and taking the road south to Bad Tolz.

The traffic was already busy by seven-thirty and it was over an hour later when Kesser turned off from the Tergen See road and the Volkswagen began to climb into the mountains. The traffic was light and several times both Molke and Volkmann had to drop back until they saw the grey Volkswagen turn off to the right and climb up a steep, narrow mountain track.

Volkmann halted the Opel a hundred metres beyond the track. The narrow mountain road Kesser had taken wasn't signposted but a sign said the property beyond that point was private and trespassers would be prosecuted. When Volkmann looked up he saw a steep rocky outcrop patchy with snow rise above a thick forest of pines, the top of the mountain smothered in a halo of low rain cloud.

Molke pulled up and climbed out of the BMW and moments later he slid in beside Volkmann. He rubbed the fogged window and stared up at the pine slopes.

'What do you think, Joe? You want to risk going up after him?'

Volkmann hesitated. 'The mountain, you know what's it called?'

'I saw a sign a kilometre back that said the Kaalberg was this way.' Molke smiled. 'There's got to be something up that mountain for Kesser to drive all this way. You want to risk playing lost tourist? The last town we passed through had a hunting shop. I could go and get us a couple of walking canes and waterproofs. A little exercise might do us both good.'

'Sure, why not?'

Molke smiled and as he climbed out of the Opel into the drizzle, he said, 'If Kesser appears again, give me a buzz on the radio. I'll be as quick as I can.'

Volkmann moved the Opel into a lay-by fifty metres beyond. There was a steep tier of pines leading up to the mountain and below and to his left lay a deep wooded valley. The quaint wooden houses of a Tyrolean village were barely visible in the distance through the thin membrane of rain.

As he sat there smoking a cigarette and listening to the radio he saw the green BMW return almost an hour later. Ivan Molke climbed out carrying two sturdy mountain walking sticks and olive-green waterproof capes. He removed a pair of powerful Zeiss binoculars from the boot before joining Volkmann.

They decided to keep off the dirt track Kesser had taken and instead climbed up through the thick pines. There were patches of snow in the clearings and the rain had softened to a light drizzle. On the two occasions they crossed the dirt track they saw that it had been covered with a surface of cracked pebble and when they had gone a hundred metres into the forest on the far side, Ivan Molke tapped Volkmann's arm and pointed through the trees.

With the powerful Zeiss Volkmann could make out a narrow wooden sentry hut and two men standing outside. To the right of the hut a grey-painted metal barrier gate was lowered in place. Both men wore civilian clothes and had Heckler and Kochs draped across their chests and one of the men was smoking a cigarette. Past the barrier Volkmann could make out a narrow road leading up.

Beyond the cover of the trees they could see the sloped, grey-slated high roof of a large traditional Berghaus, but the view was too obscured for them to see the big house entirely and the top of the mountain that rose above and behind it was still covered in low cloud. Volkmann thought he saw what looked like a low-walled balcony jutting out from the back of the Berghaus, but he couldn't be certain. Beyond the house stood what appeared to be the top of a big, square drab-looking concrete or metal building, maybe twenty metres square, but it was difficult to judge from the distance. To the right of it were what looked like two old, traditional wooden barns with sloped roofs.

Fifteen minutes later they had moved back down through the forest and were sitting in Ivan Molke's BMW.

Molke lit cigarettes for both of them and as he handed one to Volkmann he said, 'What do you make of it, Joe?'

Volkmann shook his head. 'Have the Government got any covert research establishments in this part of Germany?'

'Why do you ask?'

'Kesser worked for a Government research unit a couple of years back. And those guys at the sentry box wore no uniforms but they carried Heckler and Kochs.'

'There's a couple of hush-hush places in Bavaria, sure. But where, I couldn't say. You want me to try and check it out for you?'

Volkmann thought a moment before replying. 'It'll have to be done discreetly, Ivan. I don't want Berlin or London coming down on Ferguson for playing off pitch.'

'OK, I'll check it out. But if it gets too hairy I'll back off quietly. You want to call it a day?'

Volkmann nodded. 'But I'd like Kesser watched for the next couple of days. A record of his movements kept. Who he talks to, who he visits.'

'You want me to do it?'

'I'd appreciate it, Ivan. I want to keep it low-key. Otherwise I'll have to call in my own people and that may cause problems with the German Desk. By the time they're briefed, we'd have lost a few days.'

Molke nodded. 'I'll get a couple of the men from my agency, it shouldn't be a problem.' Molke paused. 'What about a bug on Kesser's phone?'

'You think you could do that?'

Molke shrugged. 'If his girl stays out of the way long enough, it might be possible.'

'You better warn your people to be careful, in case Kesser is armed. Can I contact you at home?'

'Sure. And if I'm not there leave a message. I'll start the watch tonight.'

Volkmann had checked out of the hotel and returned the hire car and it was two hours later when they came off the Brienner Strasse and turned right for the airport.

As they passed the signpost for Dachauer Strasse, a white-and-green tour bus was turning off towards the concentration camp road.

The old camp at Dachau had been preserved after the war and lay a couple of kilometres to the north, a place the tourists and the curious came to see and one of the few remaining legacies of the Third Reich preserved for posterity. He had visited it once before, after his last term at Cambridge; stood on the infamous Appellplatz where his father would have stood on cold winter mornings, waiting for the five o'clock roll call, the barbed-wire perimeter and the watch-towers and the gas chamber and the ovens all grim and tangible reminders of his father's nightmare.

Beyond the rain-streaked glass of the tour bus he could see the faces of the passengers. Young faces pressing sombrely against the damp glass. Volkmann saw that several of them wore Jewish skull caps, and a sign against the glass proclaimed that they were a student tour group from Tel Aviv University.

As they overtook the bus, Volkmann saw the grim look on Ivan Molke's face but neither man spoke.

It was almost seven when he arrived back in Strasbourg but he drove to the office and checked his desk. There were no messages and neither Peters nor Ferguson were in their offices. There were two Italian officers still on duty and they stood by the coffee machine talking with Jan De Vries. Volkmann lingered with them for ten minutes before he telephoned Erica and drove over to the apartment.

She seemed glad to see him and Volkmann realised he had missed the girl in the past forty-eight hours. He booked a restaurant in Petite France and over dinner she asked him what he had been doing in the last two days. He didn't go into detail and he didn't tell her what had happened with Kesser, just that he had got more information on him and Winter but that for now it was classified. She didn't question him and she didn't ask him what the information was, although he could see the curiosity in her eyes.

After dinner they walked back through Petite France. The old town with its pretty period houses and its narrow cobbled streets and babbling river was deserted, and at one of the weirs Volkmann stopped to look down at the water. He was aware of her looking at him and when he turned to look back he saw the blue eyes linger on his face.

Before he could speak she had stepped closer and as her lips brushed his cheek he could smell her perfume.

She slid her arm through his and they turned and walked back through the empty cobbled steets.

He looked back twice but could see nobody following them.

Chapter Thirty-Eight

Mexico City.
December 21st,
00.10 a.m.

It was warm in the basement interview room. The atmosphere charged with tension.

Tension and frustration.

The grey walls were awash with bright light and Gonzales gritted his teeth as he stared down at the Brazilian, Ernesto Brandt, seated behind the table. The man's left shoulder and arm were bandaged, his arm in a sling, and he looked to be in pain. The hospital had taken care of his wounds and given him a shot of painkiller but that was hours ago and the drug seemed to be wearing off. Brandt's face was pale and now and then he grimaced with discomfort and clenched his teeth.

Gonzales himself had been attended to by a paramedic at the villa; the man had given him a couple of yellow pills and told him to see a doctor urgently. The throbbing in Gonzales' arm wouldn't go away but the doctor would have to wait; there was too much to do, too little time.

He stared down at the Brazilian.

The man had thinning brown hair and wore metal-framed glasses with thick lenses. His high forehead made him look like a professor or some sort of academic. He sat there, impassively, except when his face showed his pain, but silent throughout the one-sided conversation that had gone on for almost three hours.

Gonzales had put his two best interrogators on the job and they had questioned Brandt for an hour before Gonzales himself arrived. Now he glanced at his watch. After midnight.

The interpreter, a shy young bespectacled man, sat opposite, his presence a waste of time because Brandt was saying nothing.

He had been read his rights, in Portuguese, by the translator. Gonzales spoke a little Portuguese himself; not much, but enough to get by, enough to be understood. No lawyer until Brandt spoke. No food, no water, no painkillers. Nothing. Extreme, for this was an extreme situation. But hours had gone by now and Gonzales might as well have been talking to a mute.

When he had first come into the room, after speaking to the Mexico City Commissioner of Police – a heated discussion that had left Gonzales angry and drained – Brandt had already been interviewed by the two senior detectives using the translator.

Gonzales had spoken briefly to one of the detectives outside in the hallway before entering the interview room, had the man called outside, saw the look of frustration on his face.

'I'm talking to myself,' the detective had said.

'Tell me,' Gonzales almost spat.

'His name's Ernesto Brandt.'

'He told you?'

The detective shook his head. 'He told us nothing. He hasn't spoken a single word. Just sits there. When we searched him we found a key card for the Conrad Hotel. I had a man go over and check out the room.'

'And?'

'Our dumb friend checked in two days ago off a flight from Rio. Our man went through his luggage. The usual garbage. But also a Brazilian passport in the name of Ernesto Brandt with our friend's photograph. Aged fifty, born in Rio. The passport looks good.'

Gonzales had raised his eyebrows. 'You checked it out with the Brazilian Embassy?'

The detective nodded. 'They're checking with Brasilia. They'll get back to us as soon as they have anything.'

Gonzales had sighed. The detective had said, 'The roadblocks, any luck?'

Gonzales had shaken his head. No luck. But then, they didn't know what they were looking for. An immediate disadvantage in a city of over twenty million. Brandt would know how many people had been in the villa and who they were. Or what type of car the person or persons who had murdered Sanchez had escaped in.

The only people at the villa that had any sort of identification were Lieber – the false passport in the name of Monck – and the two butlers.

The second butler, who had survived, had been able to tell them nothing. They had learned from the contents of his wallet he worked for a hire-in catering company often used by Halder. But the butler had been in a chronic, advanced state of shock. Two months before he had come out of a mental institution after a breakdown. Immediately after the shooting at the villa the man had swallowed a hundred and fifty milligrams of Largactil and twenty milligrams of Serenace. A strong cocktail of calmers. Now he was muttering dazedly, sometimes catatonic, tranquillised to the eyeballs in the psychiatric unit of the Valparaise Hospital on Calle Ciudad. A zombie.

The psychiatrist attending him said maybe in twenty-four hours the police could talk with him, but right now, the drugs were in control. 'You might as well talk to the wall,' the doctor had said. The shooting and the blood and the bodies had sent the man back over the edge again. A detective was beside the man's bed, in case he became coherent. But it was unlikely, not at least for many hours.

And time was one thing Gonzales did not have.

He had learned that the old man named Halder wasn't quite dead when the shooting stopped. He'd suffered a heart-attack. The wrinkled little old bastard had died as they stretchered him to the ambulance, just like Juales. He could have been useful, said something, given them some clue.

The detective had nodded back towards the interview room and said, 'You want to try with Brandt? Personally I think you'd get more response from a chimp at the city zoo. The guy has got glue on his lips.'

Gonzales scowled and nodded towards the interview room. 'OK. Let me talk to him.'

The man had watched him entering the room. Watched and said nothing. Gonzales felt the vexation rise in him, wanted to lash out, beat the silence out of Brandt, pummel him with angry fists. Juales dead. Cavales dead. Sanchez dead. And eleven others.

Thirteen bodies. A bloodbath.

And yet this man said nothing. No sign of fear on his face. Calm. Controlled, despite his pain. Hours of frustrated questioning, threats, pounding the table in front of him had produced nothing.

Gonzales tried again. 'Your name?'

Silence.

'Why were you at the villa?'

Brandt continued to look straight ahead at the far wall. Gonzales gritted his teeth.

'Tell me the names of the men who were with you at the villa.'

Brandt showed no reaction.

'Talk!'

Brandt licked his upper lip, but his eyes didn't move or flicker.

Gonzales took a deep breath, let it out. The man's silence irritated Gonzales to a near fever. He wanted to hit the cocky bastard, on the face, crush bones, feel skin and muscle rupture beneath his fist. Wanted to scream, but checked it.

Instead, Gonzales said, 'One last time, I'll tell you. You can make this easy or you can make it difficult. The charges against you are serious. Complicity in the murder of six police officers. Resisting arrest. Attempting to flee the scene of a crime. I could go on but I'm losing my patience. You realise that?' Gonzales' fist pounded the table. 'So talk! Why were you at the villa? Who were the men meeting Lieber?'

Silence.

'Talk!'

Brandt continued to look ahead, blank-faced, not responding.

Anger got the better of Gonzales. 'You fucking bastard! Talk! Do you hear me? Talk!'

Brandt said nothing.

Gonzales reached over, wrenched Brandt from his seat by the lapel nearest his wounded arm, then jerked back his right hand, the fist already clenched into a tight, angry ball.

For once Brandt reacted. He screamed in agony.

Gonzales let fly.

The fist halted a hair's breadth from the man's face. Gonzales let out a deep sigh of frustration. Out of character, this behaviour, but born of frustration. Out of the corner of his eye he saw the detectives and the interpreter stare at him. Slowly, he let go of the Brazilian's lapel.

Brandt's face was contorted in pain. Slowly he sat down. He stared up at Gonzales a moment but remained silent. No sign of fear, but a little anxious now. Close, so close, his face a split second from being smashed into his skull.

Gonzales took a step backwards and clenched his teeth, felt the sweat drench his face and shirt.

In all his years as a policeman he had never come across such stubbornness. Even the hardened criminals talked, eventually. You knew it by their attitude; hard recalcitrance at first, but always the slight edge of fear, the knowing look in the eyes that told you they would talk; not then, maybe, but later. Sometime. But with Brandt, he knew he was talking to a brick wall.

Calmly now, controlled again, Gonzales said quietly, 'I want you to listen to me, Brandt, or whoever the hell you are. Listen well. Thirteen men are dead. Some of them were policemen, close personal friends of mine. Good friends. Good men. Men who cared.'

Gonzales hesitated, took a deep breath, let it out, then went on, 'The charges you face are serious. But if you can help me, with names, descriptions, the number of people in the house, anything, no matter how small, I will make certain that your help is considered by the court, you understand?'

Gonzales left the words hanging; waited for a response. In the silence that followed, he could hear his own breathing; the breathing of the others in the room. The bright lights blazing on grey walls giving him a headache.

Finally, after what seemed like an age, there was a brief flicker in Brandt's eyes. He looked up at Gonzales, stared at him.

Gonzales watched the man's face. *He's going to talk*, thought Gonzales.

Then Brandt opened his mouth and the words came out in Spanish, as he stared at Gonzales, contempt in the Brazilian's face.

'I have nothing to say. *Nothing*. Except that I want to speak with a lawyer.'

Gonzales exhaled with a terrible frustration.

For a brief second he meant to rush forward and lash out again, but this time he was going to beat the shit out of Brandt; crush bone, rupture flesh, destroy the face staring up at him so impassively. But there was a sudden knock on the door and a young detective entered.

Gonzales looked at the young man angrily, rage in his voice, and screamed, 'Out!'

The detective flinched, his embarrassment evident. Then Gonzales heard the raised voices in the hallway beyond the open door before the young detective spoke nervously.

'Sir, I think you had better come outside . . .'

The fishing village lay three hundred kilometres north-east of Mexico City, along the Caribbean coast.

The large villa stood alone, on a hill overlooking the sea, surrounded by a two-metre-high wall. A white-painted place of lush gardens, the wall protecting it from the curious eyes in the village below the hill.

It was the rear entrance the rusted old delivery van halted outside. The men climbed out of the van wearily. A rotting, fetid stench of fish filled the air, rose up from the harbour village below and even the sweet-smelling gardens couldn't overcome the prevailing aroma.

The men wore the traditional *peon* blanket, their heads covered with straw hats, looking like workmen after a hard day in the fields as they stepped from the rusted van.

A guard came out of the shadows and quickly unlocked the gate. The men stepped into the garden and the gate was locked after them. The smells of hyacinths and poinsettias.

Another man came towards them out of the villa. Thin, middle-aged, wearing a white linen suit and shirt and tie. He smiled, like it was an honour to have these men dressed as peasants on his property.

The three men walked towards the villa. The stench of fish was gone now, the scent of flora almost overwhelming. The gardens were illuminated as they approached the house.

Kruger said, 'Everything has been organised?'

The villa-owner nodded. 'The ship is ready and waiting. We thought it better than an aircraft. In this region aircraft are more thoroughly checked and thus vulnerable. The passports are prepared. Once you reach Vera Cruz the transport onwards has been arranged. A chartered plane to Miami. I anticipate no problems.'

The tall, silver-haired man placed a hand gently on the villa-owner's shoulder. 'We need to make an urgent call, Frederick.'

The villa-owner looked up at the handsome face with nothing short of adulation.

'Of course. Follow me.'

The villa-owner led the way through the garden towards the house and the telephone.

The man was tall and grey-haired and wore an expensive well-tailored suit. His face was tanned and handsome.

They sat in Gonzales' office, the two of them alone. The lights of the city sprawled and winked beyond the window.

In his left hand Gonzales held the embossed personal card the man had handed him in the basement hallway minutes before. Now Gonzales stared down at it again. Serif type in gold with raised lettering. Gonzales ran a finger across its shiny rough-smoothness.

First Secretary to His Excellency, the Ambassador of Brazil. The man's name below his title.

The man said in perfect, cultured Spanish as Gonzales looked up, 'Perhaps you had better explain the situation to me.'

Gonzales ignored the niceties. Told it straight. What had happened at the villa. Thirteen people dead.

The diplomat had showed no reaction until Gonzales mentioned the body count. He raised an eyebrow, faintly, and sighed.

When Gonzales had finished, there was a long pause, then the diplomat said, 'After your detective phoned the embassy, we contacted police headquarters in Brasilia. The passport this man Brandt carried is legitimate. And concerning Brandt, I believe our Chief of Police in Brasilia will be contacting his opposite number here in Mexico City to discuss the matter.'

The man hesitated and Gonzales saw the perspiration on his upper lip. Like the man was scared. Worried. When Gonzales had met him in the hallway he had asked to see Brandt, see him but not talk with him. The diplomat had looked at Brandt silently for a long time. The diplomat's face had turned pale, then he had nodded to Gonzales before being led upstairs to the office.

'Go on,' prompted Gonzales.

The diplomat paused again, as if uncertain, then said, 'This is a rather . . . sensitive matter. I believe I ought to speak with your Commissioner first.'

Gonzales frowned, took a deep, angry breath, then let it out and looked the man in the eye.

'I am in charge of this case. You talk only to me. Thirteen people are dead and your countryman downstairs is implicated in some way. I want answers, and fucking fast. Who's Brandt? Why are you people so interested that the First Secretary himself comes here? Tell me, and tell me quickly.'

The diplomat's face flushed red with anger. Not used to being talked to in this way. *Fuck you*, thought Gonzales, and to hell with protocol, a firmness in his voice that told the diplomat he wasn't going to take shit.

The man looked across at him. He removed a silver cigarette case from his pocket, selected one. For a long time the man said nothing, the tanned face looking sullen as he smoked his cigarette, as if Gonzales' lack of respect had offended him deeply. A picture of upper-class privilege. But still looking worried. Perspiration still glistening on his upper lip and brow.

Gonzales said impatiently, 'I haven't got all day, *senor*. So talk.'

He wanted to add '*you asshole*', but bit back the temptation.

For a second or two the diplomat glared at him, the curtness of Gonzales' tone and manner an affront. He inhaled deeply on his cigarette, then his tone changed, became almost familiar.

'Very well, Chief Inspector. But your own superior will no doubt confirm this once our Chief of Police has spoken with him. However, I will tell you myself. What you are about to hear is highly classified and sensitive information . . .'

1.02 a.m.

The Gulf waters were smooth as glass, the air balmy, as the ship moved out of the harbour and navigated an easterly course.

An hour out from the port, the silver-haired man stepped out under the green hue of the port light and moved towards the stern. The sky above starry, clear. He wore fresh clothes: a windcheater and heavy cotton pants, a warm woollen sweater underneath the coat. A quick, steaming shower, to rid himself of the foul smell of fish that pervaded the air during the drive down to the harbour from the villa, had invigorated his tired body.

He regarded the retreating waters, the churning white of

the wake waves bubbling and frothing at the stern as if some great furnace were beneath the water.

The call had been made. The information passed on. Priority.

Close. So close.

Almost all their plans had come to naught.

But he had survived. Schmidt's death had been regrettable, but it had served a purpose.

And Halder. An old comrade. But not much life in him. Death only a whisper away. But his advice would have been very useful in the days ahead.

The *mischling*, Brandt, of course, had served his purpose. The cargo had safely arrived. The cargo, one of the vital keys to the plan.

The ship bobbed, settled. His stomach churned. He held onto the rail.

Of two things he was certain.

One, the plans went ahead.

Two, the people responsible for what had happened in Mexico City would die. Those and any others who posed a threat. His call would make it imperative.

The girl, of course, was another matter. She was one of their own. Part of the web. Like her father. Her information would be vital. And it was time now to pull her into the web. Meyer would see to it.

He looked up at the sky.

The future lies not in our stars but in ourselves.

A paraphrase, but both were true. Our stars and ourselves.

He looked out at the sea one last time, then turned and stepped back towards the green hue of the port light.

It took the diplomat less than five minutes to explain.

Gonzales listened in silence, not interrupting. But now and then he stared at the man in pale horror; the enormity of what the diplomat was saying making him understand Brandt's reluctance to talk.

When the diplomat had finished, Gonzales was silent for a

long time, and when he was satisfied the man had told him everything Gonzales thanked him and led him to the door, then crossed quickly back to his desk.

The call from the Commissioner came immediately.

The conversation lasted almost two minutes, then Gonzales tapped the receiver and made the necessary phone calls immediately. All border posts, all air and sea ports on twenty-four hour alert.

Then he tried the number of the Central Police Office in Asunción himself but the lines were busy. He called the operator on the ground floor, gave him the number and told him to keep trying until he got through. He checked his watch. In a little while he would have to drive out to Tacubaya and tell Juales' widow of her husband's death. An unpleasant thought and deed. The man had been a good and competent policeman and a close friend.

His head ached. He stood, lit a cigarette, and inhaled deeply as he crossed to the window. His arm still throbbed painfully, but he tried to ignore the discomfort of the tight dressing the paramedic had applied around his shoulder and arm.

Beyond the glass, stardust lights stretched to the Chapultepec Hills and the Sierra de las Cruces. A big city. So many places to hide in a city of over twenty million souls; so many routes of escape. He didn't hold out much hope.

Gonzales inhaled deeply on his cigarette. People like Halder had connections, and there were other Halders. What did they call it in the old days? *Die Spinne*. The Spider. He remembered hearing the stories told to him by the old detectives when he was a young rookie. The *gringos* who had come to Mexico with gold and money after the war and bought the big villas in the Chapultepec Hills and down along the coast. And their organisation – the Spider – that was secretive and efficient in the extreme.

The chances of catching the men were slim. But still, he would try. Without question he would try, dig out the old dusty files, make telephone calls to the retired men who had worked on the old cases, but something telling him the men from the villa were already gone. It was going to be a difficult, tiring, frustrating day. Still, he had to do it. For Juales and his men; for a dead Sanchez and his dead compatriot lying now in the police morgue.

The telephone buzzed. He turned, startled.

Asunción, he hoped. His call to Paraguay.

They would need to know about Sanchez and Cavales; how they had died. And much as importantly, why.

And now he knew himself, he shook his head in disbelief. No wonder the men had been so desperate to escape the villa. He crossed back to his desk, stubbed out his cigarette and picked up the receiver.

Chapter Thirty-Nine

Genoa.
Monday,
December 19th

It was the night shift, Franco told himself. Working nights messed up your metabolism, all the guys at the docks knew that.

The half-litre of wine he had lingered over in the bar off the Palazzo San Giorgio before coming to work hadn't helped either; had upset his stomach.

He felt lousy.

But then Il Peste didn't look too good either. Franco saw the fat man waddle towards him out of the darkness as he stood outside the warehouse entrance, gulping air, trying to ease the sickness in his stomach. Il Peste looked like he was hassled, something on his mind. If the asshole *had* a mind. Man, you just programmed him, pointed him in the right direction . . .

'*Buona notte!*' said Franco.

'What's so good about it?'

'What's the matter . . .? You got a problem?'

'No, *amico*. It's *you* got the problem.'

This was all Franco needed. Problems. The official was in a sour mood; working nights had that effect on everyone. Franco tried to smile but found it an effort. The man irritated him, especially now, this minute, Franco's stomach churning. He saw Il Peste look at him sharply.

'I need to see some of your load sheets.'

'You saw them when the ship came in from Piraeus two hours ago . . .'

'Not those. The ones from last week. The ones from the *Maria Escobar*.'

'What d'you mean?'

'Just what I said. The *Maria Escobar* . . . the load sheets. I want to see them again.'

'What for?'

'Don't mess with me, Franco,' Il Peste said impatiently. 'I've got a busy night ahead.'

'I don't understand . . .' Franco said. There was a sudden aggressiveness in the custom official's tone that made him feel uneasy.

'Look, just do as I ask. Where's the paperwork?'

'Upstairs, in the office.'

Franco swallowed, something telling him this was trouble, something in the back of his head sending warning signals coursing through his body like electricity.

Il Peste said impatiently, 'The Carabinieri want us to double- check the load sheets for all ships from South America. Everything that came in within the last month. I've done all the others. Only one left is the *Maria Escobar*. And I can't find all my copies. Now, *amico*, do as I tell you. I'm tired . . .'

Franco felt tired, too. And a little frightened. The blood drained from his face; his legs beginning to tremble.

'I'll get the keys to the office,' Franco said quietly.

'I'd appreciate that.'

As they climbed the stairs, Franco felt his legs weaken. With effort, he looked behind him, down at Il Peste.

'So why are the Carabinieri interested?'

'Don't ask me. I'm not the Commissioner of Police,' the customs official said moodily. 'I got to recheck the load sheets, the invoices, the customs declaration forms, make sure they tally.'

Franco almost sighed. 'That's all?'

'It's enough. I got three ships coming in in the next two hours. So let's get it over with.'

Franco felt better almost immediately. He had nothing to

worry about. The box hadn't even been on the declaration forms.

He halted on the landing, found the spare keys on the ledge and unlocked the office door. Once inside he flicked on the light and crossed to the filing cabinet.

He unlocked and pulled open one of the drawers and sifted through the files, found the folder he was looking for and handed it across.

Il Peste took the folder for the *Maria Escobar*, crossed to the desk and sat down, taking a notebook and pen and several crumpled forms from his pocket.

Franco stood there, wondering. What were the Carabinieri looking for? The box he had given the men? Or something else? It had to be the box, something important in there. The cops hardly ever bothered you unless there was something major wrong. His fear returned as he looked down at the fat official. He was writing something in his notebook, a list of figures, a puzzled frown on his flabby face as he checked through the paperwork. When he finished writing, he chewed the end of his pen thoughtfully.

'What's the matter?' Franco asked.

Il Peste looked up, frowning. 'One of the containers from the *Maria Escobar*, the weight doesn't tally with the paperwork.'

'By how much?'

'Twenty kilos.'

Franco shrugged and said amicably, 'Hey, that's nothing. What's twenty kilos?' Il Peste knew that, it was all part of his job. What the fuck was going on? Customs didn't start to get suspicious unless the tally was out by at least fifty kilos.

'Hey . . . Come on, Paulo . . . I'm up to my ass in work,' Franco protested.

Il Peste ignored him, stabbed a fat finger at one of the documents. 'This container . . . I checked it, didn't I?'

Franco looked down, saw the plump finger point to a number on the customs form. The number of the container with the hidden compartment. He felt his stomach churn.

'I don't remember,' Franco lied.

'Sure you do. I used the 'duster. I had to leave early to go to the christening of Stefano's kid. Remember now?'

'Yeah, I remember now . . . Sure.'

Franco saw Il Peste hesitate, thinking, the fat wrinkles of flesh on his forehead creasing.

'Twenty kilos . . .' the fat official muttered, staring down at the paperwork.

The difference was negligible, Franco knew.

'It's nothing,' he said. 'A discrepancy like that happens every day.'

'I agree. Every day you get a container weight that doesn't tally. The weight isn't always the same as declared . . . The paperwork doesn't add up . . .' The fat man in the baggy uniform looked up. 'Only that shouldn't happen . . .'

'People make mistakes . . . A few kilos here or there . . .' Franco offered.

'Sure. Or weighing machines don't work right or people don't read them properly.' Il Peste grimaced. 'But if people did their damned jobs right, used accurate weighing equipment, there shouldn't be no discrepancy. People did that they'd make my job a lot easier.'

'Sure.' Franco said agreeably. 'But what's the problem?'

The fat official scratched his nose. 'The problem is, *amico*, the Carabinieri . . . Any discrepancy in any cargo arriving in Genoa from Montevideo, they want to be informed . . . The *Maria Escobar* has been the only ship from there the past month.'

That was all Franco needed. Cops swarming all over the docks with four-legged sniffers and light probes. Climbing up his ass.

Franco spoke slowly, forcing himself to look calm. 'Hey, what are they looking for, anyway?'

'Who knows? Could be anything. But South America, it's white powder country.' The fat official gathered up his papers and closed the file and handed it back to Franco. 'It's probably too late now anyhow. If anything was smuggled here in that container, it's long gone. We ought to use that weighing bridge more often . . . It ought to be mandatory.'

Franco feigned a look of concern. 'I agree, man . . . Too lax.'

Il Peste pushed his fat bulk from the chair, turned towards the window, looked out at the light of the arc lamps spilling onto the apron across the way. Something on his mind, Franco thought, something troubling him.

'Can I lock up now?'

Il Peste turned towards him slowly, ignoring the question. 'That last container, from the *Maria Escobar*, I checked it good, didn't I?'

Franco forced a weak smile. 'Sure you did, I remember.'

'I tapped it with the 'duster.'

'Yeah.' Franco suddenly began to feel weak again. 'Why?'

'My daughter, Bianca . . . she plays the piano, real good. She says I got a good ear for music. I know when music's good, when it's bad . . .'

Franco smiling now, difficult, but doing it. 'Really . . .?'

'Yeah. I can't read a word of the stuff . . . But if a note's not right, I know it's not right. You know what I mean?'

'Yeah, sure.' The smile on Franco's face gradually folding, falling away, forcing the facial muscles now . . . *Smile*. Franco smiled.

'That container . . .' said Il Peste, letting the sentence hang in mid-air, his eyes far away, not on Franco, not on anything in particular. Vacant.

'What about it?' Franco asked nervously.

'The day I tapped it with the 'duster, the notes weren't right. I remember now. Something was out of tune.'

Franco shrugged, felt sweat on his neck, on the palms of his hands. 'Hey, man, I'm just a clerk, you know. I leave that kind of thing to you guys. Me, I just do my job.'

Il Peste was staring at him. Franco held the stare, every muscle in his body tensing, concentrating, forcing himself to stay calm.

Slowly, Il Peste turned away, stared out of the window. 'Only that day I remember I didn't have time. If I had, maybe I would have taken a closer look.' He paused. 'I've got the container number. According to our paperwork, it ought to be due back here; booked out on a freighter to Piraeus in a few days' time. Maybe I'll check it out if I got time.' Il Peste moved towards the door and was gone.

Franco stood there in the middle of the office, shaking, hearing the man's footsteps go down the stairs. He sighed, a deep troubled sigh, rubbed the back of his neck. He felt lousy. Really lousy. And worried. Man, really worried.

What the fuck was happening? If Il Peste found that cubby-hole he'd know something was up. Only the cargo was gone. And Franco could play dumb. They had nothing on him. *Nothing*. And with nothing in the cubby-hole, they had nothing on Franco.

He wiped sweat from his brow. *You're safe, man. Safe. Nothing to worry about. Relax.*

He took a deep breath, let it out slowly. Took another couple of deep breaths, felt the cold air reach the pit of his lungs.

Suddenly, his stomach and bowels shuddered in a series of violent spasms. He flicked out the office lights and closed the door and went downstairs quickly to use the toilet.

Chapter Forty

On Tuesday morning Volkmann had gone into the office at ten and there were two telephone messages on his desk. One was from Ted Birken in Zurich to ring him back and the second was a call from Ivan Molke, who had left an urgent message for him to contact his Munich office.

He tried Ivan Molke's number first but the secretary who answered said he was at a meeting and would have him return Volkmann's call.

When he telephoned Ted Birken's number in Zurich the line was answered promptly and he heard the polite, cheerful voice of Birken reply.

'I've made a little headway, Joe. Have you got a pen and paper ready?'

Volkmann reached for a pad and pen. 'Is it good news?'

'Difficult to say, but it's better than I expected. My contact at the Federal Archives office in Koblenz was transferred but he passed the request on to a friend, the Director of the Berlin Document Centre, a chap named Maxwell. He asked him to check back through the early Nazi Party numbers and try to come up with a list of those whose membership was close to this Erhard Schmeltz.

'Maxwell knew about the request from your people for information on Schmeltz and he rang me, wanted to know what it was about. I told him the story, that you had asked me to help, and that we needed to find anyone still living who had had a number close to Schmeltz's. After he had me checked, he got back to me and agreed to have his people

463

go through the files of fifty numbers, twenty-five numbers above Schmeltz's party number and twenty-five below.

'Then I checked with the WASt and the relevant authorities. Out of the fifty names only four were still alive, and two of those are living in South America. Both of the other two are registered as living in Germany. The first is a man named Otto Klagen, and his party number was six-eight-nine-four-eight. Born in Berlin, 1910. He was a fairly young man when he joined the party. His membership application was dated November 1st, 1927.'

'Where's Klagen now?'

Volkmann heard Ted Birken sigh at the other end. 'That's the problem. His last address was in an old folks' home in Düsseldorf. I telephoned the home and they said Klagen had a stroke about two months ago and was still in pretty bad shape and hardly able to talk. He's now in the city hospital on Graülingerstrasse. His mind's not the best, apparently, and he's not very coherent, so I doubt if Klagen's going to be much use to you, even if he had heard of this fellow Erhard Schmeltz. You can try him if you wish but I wouldn't bet on getting anywhere. Besides, Maxwell said the German authorities investigated Klagen twenty years ago. He was a diehard SS man. The war crimes people wanted to nail him on atrocities they said he committed in Poland during the war but the prosecution didn't have enough evidence and had to let the case drop. All a long time ago, of course, but a leopard doesn't change its spots.'

Volkmann took a note of the hospital and said, 'What about the second man?'

'Wilhelm Busch. Party number six-eight-nine-seven-eight. Like Schmeltz, the place of application was given as Munich.'

'Have you got an address?'

Ted Birken gave Volkmann an address in Munich's northern suburb of Dachau.

'The man will be in his early eighties now. I hope he's in better shape than Klagen. Otherwise you'll be completely wasting your time.'

'Have you got a telephone number for Busch?'

'No telephone number, I'm afraid. I checked with the operator for the number but it's unlisted. But then you'd probably be best just calling cold and catching him unawares, otherwise he might not even consider talking to you.'

'What was his war record like, Ted, any idea?'

'According to Maxwell, Busch ended up in military intelligence – the *Abwehr*. One of Admiral Canaris' people. He wasn't wanted for any war crimes, and his last rank in '45 was *Hauptmann* – captain. Surprising, really. Usually those who joined the Nazis before 1930 were considered the party aristocrats. Busch really ought to have risen higher in rank considering his *Abwehr* background, unless maybe he dirtied his bib along the way.'

'What's his background after '45, any idea?'

'Maxwell had a quiet word off the record with the Berlin CIA station, who had Busch's background checked. Busch spent ten years in the Gehlen organisation, the forerunner of the German security services. It was riddled with ex-Nazis, as you probably know, so his credentials would have served him a treat. He retired from that outfit over thirty years ago and went into private security. But he's a very old man now, long retired and living on his pension.'

'Thanks, Ted, I appreciate your help.'

'Not at all, my boy. And if you need any more help from the Document Centre in Berlin, you can contact this chap direct. Just ask for Ed Maxwell and mention my name. It's been good talking with you.'

It was noon when the telephone buzzed on Volkmann's desk. It was Ivan Molke returning his call.

'We need to meet and talk, Joe.'

There was an urgency in Molke's voice and Volkmann said, 'Is there a problem, Ivan?'

'I think you could say that. I've pulled my men off watching Kesser.'

'What's the problem?'

'I'd rather not talk about this over the line, Joe. Can we meet? There's something I think you ought to see.'

'I could drive down to Munich, be there about three.'

'Let's make it we meet in Augsburg. It'll shorten your journey and besides, I need to get out of the office. You know where the Hauptbahnhof is in Augsburg?'

'No, but I'll find it.'

'I'll be there by two-thirty, in the main bar. One last thing. Do me a favour.'

'What?'

'When you drive down, check your tail.'

Volkmann frowned. 'What's up, Ivan?'

'I'll tell you when I see you, but just do as I ask,' answered Molke, and then the line clicked dead.

It was almost two-thirty when Volkmann stepped into the Hauptbahnhof. He had parked in an underground lot near the railway station and walked back.

On the drive down to Augsburg he had watched in the rear-view mirror and taken note of the cars behind, but none were tailing him and he had stopped at half a dozen filling stations en route to be certain.

He saw Ivan Molke sitting over a cup of coffee and smoking a cigarette in a corner of the bar. He appeared tired and his face looked tense. He nodded for Volkmann to join him and when he had ordered a beer and sat down, Volkmann saw the dark rings under Ivan Molke's eyes.

'No tails on the way down?'

'Clear all the way. What's the problem, Ivan?'

Molke stubbed out his cigarette. 'You came clean to me on Lothar Kessser, Joe? You told me everything I needed to know?'

'Of course, why?'

Molke looked across at Volkmann. 'I put two of my men on Kesser the day before yesterday. One of them managed to get into Kesser's apartment yesterday evening. His girl's been there most of the time and she left only once with Kesser to visit a local doctor. The girl's name is Ingrid and she's Kesser's live-in girlfriend. By the look of her she's about six months pregnant.'

'So what's the problem?'

'My man had maybe ten minutes in the place before Kesser drives back alone. The second man tagged Kesser back from the doctor's surgery. The guy at the apartment hadn't much time but he managed to find a notebook belonging to Kesser and a spare set of keys to the apartment. He didn't have time to plant a bug on Kesser's phone but he photographed a couple of pages from the notebook and got out just before Kesser came up the stairs. My men made their report to me last night about nine and gave me a mould of the keys and the photo prints they took of the pages in Kesser's notebook.'

Molke sighed, quickly lit another cigarette and inhaled. 'In the middle of the night I get two calls within the space of ten minutes. It's the two guys I put on Kesser. One of them says his wife wakes up about 3 a.m. and goes downstairs for a glass of water. She sees the door to the study is open. She flicks on the light and there's this guy searching through her husband's briefcase. She screams. The guy pulls a gun and points it at her like he's going to blow her head off. By the time her husband gets down the stairs the intruder's gone and his wife's fainted on the floor.'

Molke saw the look on Volkmann's face. He paused before he went on. 'The next time the phone rings it's Pieber, the second man. He's at his girlfriend's place and he leaves late. He notices he's being followed home. Two guys in a dark-coloured Volkswagen but he didn't get the number because the licence plate was muddied. When he gets to his apartment he goes to his bedroom and switches off the lights and checks the window but sees no one below. But half an hour later he hears whispered voices outside the apartment door. He puts on the hi-fi, walks around the apartment, making noise, like he's very much awake, then he telephones me. I get there ten minutes later but there's no one outside the apartment. But someone's been at the door lock, no question.'

For a long time Volkmann was silent, then he looked over at Molke.

'You're certain this has something to do with watching Kesser?'

Molke said, 'Joe, there's nothing my men are working on at present that would bring that kind of flak. And certainly nothing that would involve guns.'

'What do you propose to do?'

'My men are off Kesser since last night. Your people have official authority and they carry weapons. My boys can't and it's getting too dangerous.' Molke shook his head vigorously and crushed his cigarette in the ashtray. 'I just can't risk them getting hurt, Joe; you understand?'

Volkmann nodded. 'You think Kesser knew your men had been in his apartment?'

'That's the funny thing. I asked them the very same question. They said they were sure Kesser suspected nothing, didn't know he was being watched.'

'And they didn't see anyone else watching Kesser's place?'

'Not that they were aware of, but I guess they were too busy watching Kesser to take much notice.'

'What about Kesser's movements in the past two days?'

Ivan Molke removed a notebook from his pocket, flicked it open. 'Twice he's driven up to the mountain. It's called the Kaalberg all right. Yesterday and the day before, he drove up there again early, about seven in the morning, and left about noon.'

'Did your men see any other movement up there?'

'No one came or left apart from Kesser, and the armed guards are still there.'

'What about checking out the place like I asked?'

'You mean if it's a Government research place?'

'Yes.'

'I talked with a few people I know at the ministry. They confirmed that there's maybe a dozen places in Bavaria used for hush-hush lab work. Military communications mainly and a couple of Government-funded weapons and missile research labs. But I got the feeling they didn't want to talk, so I backed off, tried another tack. I went back to the village where I bought the mountain gear and asked around.'

'And?'

'Nobody I spoke with seemed to know anything except

there's a lot of private land up there. Maybe a couple of square kilometres. Pretty rocky, forested ground. The solid rock outcrop that tops it off – that's the Kaalberg. Unsuitable for skiing or pretty much else. There's a big mountain house up there, the one we saw. A couple of wooden barns and a flat concrete building directly behind the house that could be a laboratory, but no other buildings apart from the sentry hut on the road leading up. The mountain and all the land around used to belong to a private sanatorium but it closed down maybe ten years ago. Someone bought the site a couple of years back but none of the locals seem to know who it belongs to now or what goes on up there. They think the government owns the place but they're not sure. They say the site's been marked off with "Entrance Forbidden" and "Private" signs all over the place.'

Volkmann sighed and looked away towards the crowds on the railway platforms, then back again. 'What do you think, Ivan?'

Molke shrugged. 'It could be a Government research place. You said there were some books in Kesser's place, military communications stuff, so it's possible Kesser might be involved on some hush project up there when you consider his background. And after what happened to my two men I'd say it's likely. It sounds like a Landesamt job. They keep watch on their boffins and if they're being followed or something suspicious happens to them they investigate. Only in my business, Joe, I don't need that kind of heat. I could have my licence pulled and I'd be out of a job. That's why I think it's best to back off and let your people handle it.'

Volkmann thought a moment, then said, 'If Kesser was working for the Government and I asked the Landesamt to see his file, I doubt if they'd let me.'

There was a puzzled frown on Ivan Molke's face. 'What do you mean?'

'Werner Bargel let me see a précis of Kesser's file. Government research personnel files usually have restricted access. So it doesn't make sense that Bargel would let me see Kesser's.'

Molke shrugged. 'Not unless Bargel suspected your people were on to something that might involve Kesser. And if Kesser is still involved in Government research work that way it might make sense. Did Bargel ask you to get back to him if you came up with anything?'

'Yes.'

'Then maybe that's it.'

'Maybe. What about you, you have any doubts?'

Molke hesitated. 'Something doesn't make sense. The pages in the notebook my men found in Kesser's apartment. According to Pieber, there were maybe a couple of dozen pages of lists of names and what looked like some pages of diagrams of some sort. But Pieber only had time to photograph two pages.'

The girl serving behind the bar came to replace the ashtray with a fresh one and wipe the table and, when she had gone, Ivan Molke reached into his pocket and took out an envelope. He slid it across to Volkmann.

'Maybe you ought to take a look at the photographs.'

Volkmann opened the envelope and slid out the contents. Inside were two photographic enlargements of narrow, faint-ruled pages. One of the pages had a list of three names with an X marked beside each.

The second page contained what appeared to be a roughly drawn map of some sort of building. Beside it was another map, this time giving directions, and underlined were the names of several towns. On closer examination Volkmann saw what looked like the word 'KLOSTER' circled in ink above the drawing. The German word for monastery. Volkmann looked at the names again.

Horst Klee.

Jurgen Trautman.

Frederick Henkle.

He looked up at Molke. 'Any idea who they are?'

'None. And like I said, there were lots more names. Dozens. My man only had time to shoot one of the pages with names on it.'

'What about the map?'

'I checked it out this morning.'

'And?'

'The directions were clear enough. It's an old deserted monastery off the main autobahn to Salzburg, an hour's drive from Munich. It hasn't been used in years. Looks in pretty good shape but there's no one there, you can check yourself. I've drawn a proper map for you with directions on how to get there.' Molke took an envelope from his inside pocket.

As Volkmann took the envelope, he said, 'Who owns the monastery; do you know?'

'After the religious order moved out over twenty years ago, the German Government bought it, but it hasn't been put to any use since.' Molke shrugged. 'If Kesser's still working for the Government, it could be some place they're going to set up and use. So I'd tread carefully if I were you, Joe. The ministry people responsible for special projects are pretty sensitive about security.'

Volkmann hesitated, then tapped the photographs of the two pages from Kesser's notebook. 'You mind if I keep these, Ivan?'

'On one condition.'

'What's that?'

'If the Landesamt come knocking on my door I want your word you'll explain that what my men did was sanctioned officially. That I was working for you.'

'You have it, Ivan.'

Molke reached into his pocket, slid across a set of keys. 'They're for Kesser's apartment. I had them made from the moulds. In case you still wanted to take it further. But I'm out, Joe. From now on your people will have to handle it. And you didn't get the keys from me.'

Volkmann nodded and slipped the keys into his pocket. Molke finished his coffee and put down the cup.

'I also think it would be best if I had something on paper, Joe. Just in case.'

'I understand. I'll have Ferguson sort out your expenses and I'll write up a letter personally. Thanks for your help, Ivan.'

471

'One more thing. The photograph of the girl. The one you found in the Chaco.'

'What about it?'

'I checked up on the specialist people our Government used during the Nazi trials I told you about.' Molke paused. 'There was a woman, a historian. She specialised in the Nazi period and pretty much knew all the players. She just may be able to help with the photograph, or maybe know someone who can.' Molke shrugged. 'It's all I can come up with, Joe.'

'What's her name?'

'Hanah Richter. She was in the history faculty of Stuttgart University. But that was over twenty years ago and she wasn't young even then, so I'd say she's well retired by now. And I'm assuming she's still alive.'

'OK, I'll have my people check on her.'

Volkmann walked back to the underground car park and went through the routines to make sure he wasn't being followed.

The streets were crowded with Christmas shoppers but no one was tailing him and when he reached the car he climbed in, lit a cigarette and sat there for ten minutes, thinking over what Ivan Molke had told him about Kesser. None of it made any sense, none of it at all, and he wondered if he had been mistaken about Lothar Kesser.

Apart from Wolfgang Lubsch's word and the two photographs in the apartment – one of the men in uniform he assumed was Kesser's father, and the photograph of Kesser and Winter together – there was little to implicate him. And all the clues seemed to suggest that Kesser was still involved in Government research work. He stubbed out his cigarette and lit another, trying to figure out what to do next.

He decided the best thing to do was to concentrate on the information he had: the two names Ted Birken had come up with whose Nazi Party numbers had been close to Schmeltz's, Otto Klagen and Wilhelm Busch, and the sketch Ivan Molke had given him from Kesser's notebook. He could phone the duty officer later and have him check the three names on the list in Kesser's place. It occurred to him they could be research people Kesser worked with and if that was the case he would have to back off. He shook his head in confusion and frustration before he crushed out the cigarette in the ashtray and started the Ford.

He drove out of the car park and took the road to Friedberg that led him back onto the E11 and south to Munich. In Friedberg he stopped at the first hotel he saw and used one of the phone booths in the lobby.

He got the number for the hospital in Düsseldorf where Klagen was a patient from the North Rhine Westphalia directory.

He told the girl who answered that he was a relative of Otto Klagen's and asked if the old man was still a patient. The girl checked the patient register while he held on and when she told him Otto Klagen was still in the hospital, he asked to speak to a doctor on duty who was familiar with Klagen's case.

He had to hold on for another ten minutes before a female doctor came on the line. He told her he was Otto Klagen's nephew and he was phoning from Bavaria and inquiring about his uncle's case. He wondered if it was possible to visit and speak with him.

'You weren't told about his condition?'

'I'm afraid I've been abroad and just heard the news. Is my uncle that bad, doctor?'

'I'm sorry to say he's had a cerebral stroke, Herr Klagen. He's paralysed down his right side and his speech is still virtually incoherent. He couldn't really communicate if you visited, but of course you're welcome to see him.'

'When do you think he'll be able to talk again?'

'That depends on his progress and therapy, Herr Klagen, but at this stage the prognosis isn't good and he isn't making much progress. And at his age, I'm afraid . . . you understand?'

Volkmann said he did and that he'd call again to check on his uncle's condition. He thanked the woman and hung up.

The next call he made was to his apartment. When Erica answered, he told her where he was and explained about Ted

Birken's information and what had happened with Klagen but he made no mention of what Ivan Molke had told him. When she heard him sigh she said, 'What about the second man, Busch?'

'It's an hour from here to Dachau, so I'll carry on. I just hope I have better luck than with Klagen.'

'When will you be back?'

'That depends on whether I can locate Busch or not. And even if I do he may not even want to talk. But probably tomorrow. You're sure you'll be OK on your own?'

'I'm going to take a long walk in the Orangerie and then come back and drink your wine and watch television. Isn't there anything I can do?'

Volkmann smiled. 'Keep the bed warm. And keep your fingers crossed Busch is in better health than Otto Klagen. Talk to you soon.'

It was almost four when he reached the old town of Dachau, turning off the main E11 autobahn for Obroth and taking the minor road that came in north of Munich.

Dominated by an ancient castle, the pretty Bavarian town looked a picture of rural charm. But it seemed somehow absurd to Volkmann that the place that had once lent its name to the infamous concentration camp should be lit up with glittering seasonal lights, and in the small park near the S-Bahn station a Christmas tree winked in the fading afternoon light.

He found the address Ted Birken had given him in a street of drab pre-war detached houses, a ten-minute walk from the road that led down to the old concentration camp. There was a Christmas tree in the window of the house but when Volkmann walked up the concrete footpath and rang the doorbell several times, no one answered.

As he stood there wondering what to do next, a young woman pulled up outside the house in a white Volkswagen and stepped out. She looked to be in her late twenties and as she carried several bags of shopping to the front door, Volkmann went to help her.

'*Danke schön.*'

The young woman smiled as she reached in her purse for her key. Then she looked at Volkmann more warily and said, 'I'm sorry, I don't think we've met before . . .?'

Volkmann saw she wore no wedding ring. 'I'm looking for Wilhelm Busch. I believe he lives here.'

'Are you a friend of my grandfather's?'

'No, we've never met.' Volkmann produced his ID and the girl stared at it a few moments.

The woman turned suddenly pale. 'Are you with the police? My grandfather isn't in any sort of trouble, is he?'

Volkmann smiled. 'No trouble at all, I assure you. May I speak with him?'

'I'm afraid he's not here.'

'Can you tell me where I can find him?'

'My boyfriend's driven him to Salzburg to visit a relative. My grandfather's sister hasn't been well.'

'When will your grandfather be back?'

'Sometime tomorrow. Perhaps if you can call back. Can I tell him what this is about?'

'It's a private matter, Frau Busch. I'd really rather discuss it with him.'

The woman shrugged. 'Very well, I'll tell him you called.'

And with that she turned the key in the door and stepped inside.

He found a small hotel opposite the park near the S-Bahn Station and checked in for one night.

He did not like the waiting but there was nothing else he could do. He had no change of clothes with him, just an empty travel bag he had kept in the boot. Near the *Rathaus* he found a chemist's and bought some disposable razors and a can of shaving foam, and on the way back to the hotel he bought a pair of socks and underwear and a fresh shirt in a shop in one of the old cobbled streets.

The room overlooked the small park facing the station and when he had shaved and showered he went down to the hotel bar and had one beer. He had dinner in a restaurant at the end of the street and then he decided to drive back up to Busch's house just to check if the old man had come back early, but there was still only the white Volkswagen in the driveway and the light was on downstairs, the Christmas tree winking in the window.

At the end of the street he turned left to come back into the town and he saw the road that led up to the camp. He skirted back to the town and when he had parked the car in the hotel's back lot he went up to his room and phoned the duty officer in Strasbourg.

It was one of the young French officers named Delon who came on the line and Volkmann explained that he wanted a list of three names checked. He read out the list of names from Kesser's notebook and spelt them phonetically.

'You've got addresses or descriptions?'

'I'm afraid not, André.'

'That's going to make it difficult. What are you looking for, Joseph. Anything in particular?'

'Just if those names come up on our files and if there's any connection between the three men.'

'Which area – criminal?'

'I don't know, André, so you better leave it open. But the main thing is to try and link them.'

The young Frenchman sighed. 'If you're trying to link them, that means we will have to do a random check on the names first. It may take some time.'

'I'm aware of that, but it's priority. If you have no luck with our computer, ask the German Desk to help. It's more than likely their territory, anyway, judging by the names. But there's a chance the three are Government research employees, so if the German Desk tells you their files are restricted, just back off and don't explain. So see what we can come up with first.'

He gave the Frenchman the details on the woman, Hanah Richter, that Ivan Molke had given him and asked Delon to do what he could to locate her.

'OK. This ought to keep me busy for the shift. Where can I contact you?'

'If I'm not in the office, leave a message at my apartment. If a girl answers, just say you rang, or whoever's on duty.'

'A girl? You want to tell me what she looks like?'

'Pretty, very pretty. Be good, André.'

He took a walk through the town to get some air, aware of his restlessness.

The old castle on the hill was lit up with yellow lights and Volkmann realised that there was nothing to suggest to the casual visitor unaware of the town's past and the nearby camp of the brutality and murder that had happened here.

A small town in Germany like so many others, with young people in good spirits filling the streets and inns in the days before Christmas. He looked at them as he passed the crowded bars, their glasses raised and their voices loud and harsh and full of confidence.

It was almost midnight when he got back to the hotel. He ordered a drink from the night porter and sipped the double scotch to help him sleep.

As he lay in the bed in the darkness he could hear the voices in the street below as the bars emptied. They carried up to his window, some of them shouting as only Germans can shout. The voices faded and a little after midnight a train rumbled past in the station across the street.

Chapter Forty-One

He woke at eight the next morning and after breakfast checked out of the hotel and drove by Wilhelm Busch's house again.

It was unlikely the old man would be back that early but he had wanted to try just to be certain. The white Volkswagen wasn't there and when he rang the doorbell there was no reply.

He drove back into town and walked through the streets for almost an hour, still with the feeling of restlessness.

He spent a frustrating hour in the park outside the S-Bahn Station, reading the *Frankfurter Zeitung*. There was snow forecast in the next twenty-four hours and he decided that if Busch hadn't appeared by the middle of the afternoon, he would drive down to the old monastery off the Salzburg road before the weather turned bad and return to Dachau later.

There was nothing to do but wait and his mind was restless. He walked back to the Ford and drove up the hill at the end of the town and when he had descended the far side and crossed the Amper river he saw the sign that said Niebelungenstrasse.

When he reached the old camp five minutes later, the parking lot reserved for the tourist buses was empty. He parked the Ford near the new entrance and walked up to the gate. The railway tracks were no longer there, but the old moat was, its trough overgrown in places with dockweed and bramble, and he could see the guard towers that still stood along the perimeter.

The gate was open but a sign on the wire fence said the camp was closed to visitors. He saw a truck with building materials parked inside but when he couldn't see anyone he decided to step through.

The camp remained much as it had looked during the war, but cleaned up and prettied. The *Blockhaus*, the U-shaped barrack house that had once served as the stores and administration building, was now a museum and cinema. To the right were the cells that had housed the maximum security prisoners, kept in isolation by the SS.

The camp was still ringed by the original slatted concrete walls and barbed-wire perimeter, but the only testament to the rows of prison huts that had once stood were two solitary wooden replicas, reconstructed to show visitors how the prisoners had existed in the squalidness of the camp. Facing the *Blockhaus* building was the Appellplatz, where the prisoners had assembled each morning. At right angles ran the Lagerstrasse, the long street down the centre of the camp, once flanked either side by the crowded wooden prison huts.

The original gates to the camp, still bearing the words '*Arbeit Macht Frei*', were off to the left, set in the centre of the concrete guardhouse that had controlled the entrance into Dachau. Volkmann could see a red-bricked chimney through a clump of fir trees in the distance, where the old crematorium still stood.

There was a sign on the wall outside the modernised annexe to the left of the *Blockhaus* that said: *Verwaltungsgebäude*; Administration Building.

Volkmann opened the door and found himself in a large, empty office. There were rows of metal shelves stacked with books and a sign on the wall in German said 'Reference Library'. Another door led off to the right and another sign said 'Museum'.

He opened the door. The *Blockhaus* museum was long and wide. Someone had left the lights on overhead and there were windows in the thick walls at two-metre intervals, pale, watery winter sunlight pouring in, dust motes rising in the air.

Blown-up photographs were hung from the walls and there were several exhibits in glass cases. A tangled mound of spectacles in one, looking like some grotesque work of art;

a tattered striped prison uniform in another, a ragged yellow Star of David sewn on its sleeve. In the middle of the long room stood a grim reminder of the brutality inflicted in the camp: a wooden whipping block, used by the SS guards.

On the wall to the left was a series of photographs: victims of the camp experiments, a cattle train loaded with corpses, lines of emaciated flesh that had once been men, women, children, laid out in the sun. In one a frail young woman, wide-eyed in death and clutching a dead little girl with matchstick legs, was propped up against the wall of a barrack building, as a grinning SS officer stood looking down at their bodies, his hands on his hips.

He did not know why he had come here but for a long time he stared at the pictures until he was overcome by the images of brutality and torture.

There was a noise behind him and Volkmann looked round. A woman stood in the doorway, carrying a sheaf of papers.

Volkmann guessed she was one of the administration staff and she seemed startled by his presence.

'Are you with the building repair people?'

When Volkmann shook his head, the woman said, 'The camp is closed to visitors right now. Didn't you see the sign outside on the gate?'

He walked past the woman but said nothing and went outside.

As he drove out of the parking lot minutes later he was thinking of his father and he never noticed the dark green Volkswagen pull out a hundred metres behind him.

When he drove by Busch's house again, there was still no car in the driveway, but he decided to stop and try just the same.

When he rang the bell the second time he saw the shadow behind the frosted glass and then the door was opened by a man. Despite his obvious age he was big and burly and he looked fit and tanned. He wore tinted, thick-lensed glasses and a heavy grey woollen cardigan, and his head of snow-white hair was swept back off his deeply wrinkled face.

He peered at Volkmann sternly.

'Yes?'

The voice was sharp and aggressive and when Volkmann looked closely he saw the man's skin was a pale yellow, and the colour wasn't from sun but ill-health.

'Herr Walter Busch?'

'Yes, I'm Walter Busch. What do you want?'

'Herr Busch, I wonder if I might speak with you?'

'About what? Who are you?'

Volkmann produced his identity card. The old man held out a wrinkled yellow hand and took it, stared at the ID for several moments before looking back at Volkmann.

'You're the fellow who called yesterday. My granddaughter told me. What do you want?'

There was a bullish tone in the old man's voice as he handed Volkmann back the ID card.

'I was hoping you might be able to help me, Herr Busch. I'd like to ask you a few questions.'

'Questions about what?' the old man demanded.

'Could we talk inside?'

Busch went to reply but broke into a sudden fit of coughing. He removed a handkerchief from his pocket and covered his mouth. Volkmann heard the wheezing breath. When he had recovered from the fit of coughing, Busch wiped his mouth with the handkerchief and said brusquely, 'You better come in.'

The old man led him into the hallway. As soon as they stepped through, Busch broke into another fit of coughing. He took out the handkerchief again and coughed into it, then pointed to a door on the right. 'Wait in there, in the conservatory,' he said gruffly.

The old man left him, opened a door into another room and Volkmann did as Busch said.

The living-room he stepped into was long and wide and at the end of it steps led down to a sunken floor that formed part of a conservatory. Strong winter sunlight poured in through the glass and the room was very warm. There was cane furniture and cushions in pastel colours and the place looked comfortable. A half-open door led out from the conservatory to a big garden and in the middle of the lawn four sturdy wooden chairs were set around a wooden picnic table. There were vegetable beds and bare fruit trees and a slatted garden shed at the end.

The framed photographs hanging on the living-room walls were of Busch's extended family, he guessed, and Volkmann saw an old one in black-and-white of Busch in officer's uniform.

Volkmann went to sit in a cane chair.

Busch came into the room moments later. He was still good on his feet considering his age but when he sat opposite, he placed a hand on his chest as he looked at Volkmann. 'The consequences of old age and too many cigarettes, Herr Volkmann. The medicine helps for a while. Now, what is this about?'

There was still a gruffness in the man's voice that irritated Volkmann and it suggested he was the type used to giving orders. The images on the walls of the camp museum were still fresh in Volkmann's mind and when he glanced at the photograph of Busch in uniform he felt a flush of anger. He looked at Busch and his tone was businesslike.

'You're familiar with DSE, Herr Busch?'

'I've heard about it, yes.'

'You were with the Gehlen Organisation after the war. You were an intelligence officer.'

'That is correct, yes. But what's this got to do with . . .?'

'During the war you were also an officer in the *Abwehr* . . .'

Busch's watery blue eyes became suddenly wary. 'That was a long time ago. Perhaps if you tell me what this is about?'

'A case I'm working on, I hoped you might be able to help me.'

Busch hesitated, and his tone seemed to mellow slightly. He half smiled. 'Herr Volkmann, I retired from intelligence work many years ago. I am no longer involved, even indirectly. So I don't understand why you would want my help.'

Volkmann explained about Hernandez' murder and the

story the journalist was working on. When he told Busch about the house in the Chaco and the man who owned it, Volkmann saw the confused frown still on Busch's face and said, 'Herr Busch, the man who owned the house joined the Nazi Party in Munich in 1927. His party number was six-eight-nine-six-four. Twelve numbers away from yours.'

The look on Busch's face went from puzzlement to understanding and then the old man said, 'I see.'

He looked away for several moments, then back at Volkmann. 'And how did you find me, Herr Volkmann?'

'You know of the Berlin Document Centre?'

'Of course.'

'I had the Nazi Party membership files checked and cross-referenced with the WASt for a recent address, where your military records were confirmed before you received your State pension. There were only two men still alive in Germany who had party numbers relatively close to the number of the man I spoke of. You were one of them.'

Volkmann explained about Otto Klagen and Busch simply nodded. The old man looked away towards the garden a few moments. The heat that lingered in the conservatory had become stifling and Busch shifted uncomfortably in his chair.

'You said this man in Paraguay was dead. I don't understand: what relevance has he to the murder of the journalist you spoke of?'

'None, obviously, Herr Busch, but he originally owned the house and property where we found the photograph, and his past is very unclear. There was someone living in the house related to him and who may be implicated in the murder. It might help if I knew more about this man whose number was close to yours. It may help fill in some gaps in the investigation.' Volkmann paused. 'I also learned that while living in Paraguay, the man who had owned the property had received large sums of money from Germany, both before and during the war. I don't know why. Your party number was close to his. I was hoping you might remember him, and shed some light on the matter.' Volkmann paused again and looked at Busch. 'I realise it's unlikely, Herr Busch, but you are the only connection I have.'

Busch half smiled and shook his head. 'Herr Volkmann, we're talking about a long, long time ago . . .'

'I realise that. All I ask is that you just look at the photograph, and tell me if you recognise the man.'

Before Busch could reply Volkmann removed the photograph of Erhard Schmeltz from his wallet and handed it across.

The old man sighed, then slowly took the photograph. He looked down at it, then back up at Volkmann and shook his head.

'The face . . . I'm sorry, I can't remember. Besides, my eyes are not what they used to be. I'm sorry you've wasted your time.' He looked at Volkmann as he went to hand back the photograph. 'The man, what was his name?'

'Erhard Schmeltz. He came from Hamburg. But like I said, he joined the party in Munich.'

Something flickered in the old man's watery eyes and he stared down at the photograph again. When he finally looked up, Volkmann saw the look of disbelief on the wrinkled face.

Volkmann said, 'You remember him?'

Busch said slowly, 'Yes, I remember him.'

'You're certain?'

Busch's yellow skin had turned pale. 'I met him many times.' Busch paused a moment. 'And the name, yes . . . I remember. Erhard Schmeltz. From Hamburg.'

Volkmann said, 'Can you tell me about him?'

Busch hesitated, then looked out at the garden; he suddenly looked very uncomfortable. He turned back to Volkmann and his tone softened.

'Would you mind if we stepped out into the garden, Herr Volkmann? The heat . . . I need some air.'

When Volkmann nodded, the old man stood up shakily and led the way to the door.

They sat facing each other on the wooden chairs at the picnic table. Busch still held the photograph of Erhard Schmeltz in his hand and he looked down at it. His voice sounded shaky, and when he looked back up again he didn't look at Volkmann but towards the bare fruit trees at the end of the lawn.

'Erhard Schmeltz, from Hamburg. Yes, Herr Volkmann, I knew him.'

'Can you tell me about him?'

'What do you wish to know?'

'What sort of man he was, how you met him. Anything at all may help.'

Busch looked back as if he were still lost in a reverie.

'He knew my father. That was how I first met Erhard Schmeltz. He had served in the First War, so he was much older than me. He and my father worked together for a time. The kind of man Schmeltz was? Physically, he was a big man. Tough and dependable. But a peasant, not an intellectual. The type who takes orders, not gives them.'

'How did you meet him?'

Busch hesitated. 'It was the winter of 1927, just before I joined the party. In those days the Nazi movement was gaining ground. Germany had come out of a war with nothing.' Busch stared at Volkmann. 'People say things are bad now, but in the old days it was worse, believe me. Do you know what it's like to see a man wheeling a barrow full of banknotes to the bakery shop to buy a loaf of bread, Herr Volkmann? Crazy. But that's how it was in the 'twenties.

'Every day there were riots and protest marches and armed anarchists roaming the streets. Germany was in a state of chaos. No one could find decent work. And when people saw university professors reduced to selling trinkets and matches on street corners, they knew they were lost.' Busch removed his glasses, rubbed his eyes. 'My father had been a soldier in the First War, like Schmeltz. And when he returned after the armistice there was nothing for him but a long list of menial, badly paid jobs. We went from lodging-house to lodging-house, barely eking out an existence, never enough bread in the house to feed a hungry family.

'And then came the Nazis. They promised prosperity. They promised work. They promised hope. They promised to make

Germany great again. Drowning men will grasp at straws, and we Germans then were drowning, believe me. There was a price to be paid, of course, but that came much later.'

Busch stopped rubbing his eyes and stared at Volkmann.

'You might ask what has all this got to do with Erhard Schmeltz? Nothing, except that I want you to understand the background and how we came to meet.'

Volkmann said quietly, 'Tell me about him.'

'Schmeltz worked in the same factory as my father in Munich. One day in the early winter of 1927 the factory closed down. That evening my father and his colleagues went out to get drunk to forget their sorrows, and later my father took some of them home to meet my family.'

Busch paused. 'My father and his friends were very drunk and very despondent. One of the men present was Erhard Schmeltz. They all sat around the table in our kitchen having soup and bread. They talked of Germany's hopelessness. I sat with them. Schmeltz, I remember, was a quiet man. He had been a factory foreman. Diligent and trustworthy. The loss of his position had upset him completely. At the table he brought up the subject of the Nazis. Most of the other men present were communist or socialist party supporters. My father was apolitical. But Schmeltz declared that he was going to support the Nazis and become a party member. He said they were the only hope for Germany and suggested my father and the others do likewise. When they declined, Schmeltz tried to interest me. I was a youth and easily impressed by Schmeltz's enthusiasm, and the fact that Schmeltz said that he knew Hitler and had served in the First War with him and some of the other top Nazis. A week later I applied for membership and was accepted.'

'How often did you meet Schmeltz?'

Busch shook his head. 'After that night I didn't see Erhard Schmeltz again for at least another year. I joined the party without Schmeltz's help or recommendation. He and I were not close friends – he was much older than I, but I got to know him.'

'You say he knew some of the top Nazis personally. Who did he know?'

Busch paused a moment, looked out at the bare winter trees. 'Himmler, Goering, Bormann. And he and Hitler were old comrades. They had served in the same regiment. I later heard that Heinrich Himmler himself had proposed his Nazi Party application. But that's all I know. I didn't hear Schmeltz mention his connections again after that night. He was really a very private man. But it gave him a certain amount of status in the party.'

'What was Schmeltz's function in the party?'

Busch shrugged. 'Nothing important. He was just a party functionary. He helped at elections and played bodyguard. Many times I saw him at party rallies or in the Munich beerhalls, with some of the bigwigs. Especially Bormann and Himmler. But he wasn't the type who would have made it to the top himself. He came from simple peasant stock. He had been a farmer until the Weimar depression ruined him and he came south to Munich with his sister. He was more brawn than brain, but a loyal and trusted party man.'

'Did Schmeltz wear a uniform?'

Busch nodded. 'Yes, he wore a uniform. Black jackboots and kepi and brownshirt. Standard SA uniform.'

'Did you know Schmeltz emigrated to South America, Herr Busch?'

'No, I didn't know he went to South America. And by telling me you solved an old mystery.'

'How?'

'Sometime in 1931, Erhard Schmeltz disappeared. No one knew where he had gone. But if what you say is true, now I know.'

Volkmann paused, looked at the garden, then back again. 'Do you know of any reason why Schmeltz might have gone to Paraguay? If he was the loyal Nazi Party member you say he was, why did he leave Germany?'

Busch turned back. The old man regarded Volkmann solemnly.

'Why is this so important, Herr Volkmann? All this happened over sixty years ago. What relevance has it to now, to the present?'

'I don't know why exactly, but I believe it has. Do you know why Schmeltz ended up in Paraguay, Herr Busch?'

Busch paused, then slowly shook his head. 'No, I don't. But I do remember there were rumours after he disappeared.'

'What rumours?'

'That he had fallen foul of someone high up in the party and been killed.' Busch shrugged. 'But there were so many rumours. That he had been sent away on a mission. That he had got into someone's bad books and been forced to leave the country. But which story is true I cannot say. All I know is that one day he was there, the next he was gone. And so much was happening within the party at the time, a man like Schmeltz was soon forgotten.' Busch hesitated. 'You said there was a photograph . . . of a woman?'

'Yes.'

'May I see it?'

Volkmann removed the photograph from his pocket and handed it across. Busch squinted down at the image.

Volkmann said, 'Do you recall ever having seen that woman before, Herr Busch?'

The old man looked up. 'Herr Volkmann, at my age, faces are difficult to remember. The girl could be anyone. And my eyes . . . they're not the best, I'm afraid. You know the young woman's name?'

Volkmann shook his head. 'No. There was just a date on the back of the original photograph. July 11th, 1931.'

'That's all?'

'Yes, that's all.'

Busch peered intently at the image once again, then shook his head. 'The girl . . . I'm afraid she is not familiar to me.'

'Could she have been a relative of Erhard Schmeltz?'

Busch thought a moment, looked again at the photograph more closely, then shrugged, handed back the photograph.

'Perhaps. It's possible. I thought perhaps his sister. I met her many times, but it's not her.'

'What about his wife or a girlfriend?'

Busch shook his head firmly and smiled, 'No, definitely not. Most definitely not. Schmeltz wasn't a womaniser. He was a big awkward countryman who always appeared ill at ease around women.' Busch paused. He went to say something, then appeared to change his mind.

Then as Volkmann replaced the photograph in his pocket, Busch said, 'You're not telling me everything, are you, Herr Volkmann?'

The light was fading to grey now, the sun gone behind clouds, the air turning chilly as a faint gust of wind rustled the dead leaves at the bottom of the garden.

Volkmann said, 'Erhard Schmeltz emigrated to Paraguay in November 1931. According to records in Asunción, he had with him his wife, Inge, and their child, a boy named Karl. Schmeltz also had five thousand American dollars in his possession. Two months later he received a bank draft from Germany for another five thousand American dollars. At exactly six-monthly intervals afterwards he received further drafts of five thousand American dollars each. At first, the drafts were sent privately. But after the Nazis came to power they were sanctioned and sent secretly by the Reichsbank, right up until Schmeltz died in Asunción in 1943. After that his wife received the money, until February 1945, when the drafts ceased.' Volkmann paused. 'I'd like to know why Schmeltz received that money, Herr Busch. It may or may not have relevance to the case I'm working on, but I'd like to know. It's part of the puzzle.'

Even in the fading light he saw that the old man had turned pale again and he stared into Volkmann's face. He opened his mouth to speak, then closed it.

Volkmann said, 'Is something the matter?'

Busch hesitated, shook his head slowly. 'No.'

'Something I said, did it surprise you?'

Busch was silent, then he said, 'Everything you have said so far about Erhard Schmeltz has surprised me.' Busch looked away, stared out into the fading light, then back again. His face was still white as chalk.

'Do you know who sent the money Schmeltz received from Germany?'

'I've no idea. But someone with authority. It had to be, once the Reichsbank was involved.'

'May I ask you a question, Herr Volkmann?'

'Of course.'

'Why do *you* think the money was sent?'

Volkmann shook his head. 'I've no idea.' He looked at Busch. 'But it surprises you that Erhard Schmeltz was sent such large sums?'

'Of course. He wasn't a wealthy man. At least not while I knew him. And I can't think of a reason why he would have received such amounts.'

'You think it's possible Schmeltz was playing banker for someone, helping them to put away money secretly. Someone high up in the party?'

Busch thought a moment, then shrugged his shoulders. 'It's possible. When I worked in the Gehlen Organisation after the war, certainly information like that came to light. Germans abroad helped Nazis set up secret bank accounts. But that happened mostly towards the end of the war, when everyone knew defeat was inevitable. Not before. And most of those accounts were kept in Switzerland.'

'Did you ever hear of Erhard Schmeltz mentioned in that regard?'

'No, Herr Volkmann, I didn't.'

Volkmann looked at the old man. Something seemed to be troubling him but he remained silent, his brow furrowed.

Finally, Volkmann said, 'One last question, Herr Busch.'

Busch looked round absentmindedly and Volkmann said, 'When you were an intelligence officer in the Abwehr, were you familiar with any of the officers in the Leibstandarte SS Division?'

'Some, yes.'

'The names Heinrich Reimer or Lothar Kesser, do they mean anything to you?'

'They were Leibstandarte officers?'

'Both of them. The first held the rank of Major in '44. The second was a General.'

Busch thought a moment. 'The name Heinrich Reimer is not familiar to me. I don't recall any Leibstandarte officer of that name. But Lothar Kesser, I believe, I may have heard of. But only in passing. I don't believe I ever met the man.'

'Did you ever hear of something called the Brandenburg Testament?'

Busch's wrinkled face came up sharply to stare at Volkmann.

'Has this got something to do with what we're discussing?'

'Let's just say it came up in conversation. Why, you've heard of it?'

'Yes, I've heard of it.'

'Tell me what it was.'

'Just old Nazi propaganda, Herr Volkmann.'

'What do you mean?'

'In late February 1945, two months before the war ended, a meeting was said to have been held in Berlin in Hitler's bunker, in the Reich Chancellery grounds near the Brandenburg Gate. It was supposed to be top secret but we heard rumours about it afterwards in the Abwehr. Hitler's most loyal SS were said to have been present at the meeting. Mostly Leibstandarte SS, his bodyguard. The people he thought he could most trust. Even they knew defeat was imminent by then, but none would dare admit it publicly. Instead, they talked about regrouping to carry on the war. The Testament was said to have been a legacy proposed by Heinrich Himmler, and sanctioned by Hitler.'

'What kind of legacy?'

'Herr Volkmann, it was really only propaganda nonsense, I assure you.'

'Tell me anyhow.'

'In the event of the Reich being defeated, gold and bullion held by the Reichsbank and SS were to be both secretly shipped to South America and also hidden in parts of Germany. The belief was that, when the time was right again, the party would be resurrected. You could say it was a blueprint to secretly re-establish the Nazi Party.' Busch paused. 'When we heard about the plan in the Abwehr, we laughed. As with so much that was promised at the end of the war, we knew it was an empty promise. The foolish hope of desperate men, Herr Volkmann. Like Goebbels' Werewolves, the underground army that was supposed to destabilise Germany after the Allies had occupied this country.' Busch looked at Volkmann. 'Besides, the Testament, it came to nothing. Certainly gold and other bullion made its way to South America after the war. But most of it was used for no other purpose but to keep a chosen few in comfort and security for the rest of their lives. But the amounts of money you say Schmeltz received and when he received it, that would eliminate him from any connection, surely?'

Volkmann nodded.

For a long time Busch was silent. It was growing cold in the garden and he finally looked at his watch and stood up slowly.

'I'm afraid I must take my leave of you. I have things to attend to.'

Volkmann stood up and said, 'Thank you for your help.'

Busch led him inside and when they reached the front door, he said, 'The smuggling operation you spoke of, Herr Volkmann, you think it's gold?'

'I really don't know, Herr Busch.'

Busch half smiled and the blue eyes looked at Volkmann keenly. 'I really wouldn't place any credence in the Testament you asked about, Herr Volkmann, believe me.'

Volkmann nodded. Busch seemed about to say something, but hesitated.

'There is one more thing. Something perhaps you should know. I don't know if it's relevant and I meant to say it earlier, but our discussion was somehow deflected.' The old man paused as Volkmann looked at him. 'Erhard Schmeltz. You say he went to South America with his wife and child.'

'That's what the records in Asunción say.'

'The boy's name again?'

'Karl.'

'And when was the boy born?'

'The records say four months before Schmeltz arrived in Paraguay.'

Busch shook his head vigorously. 'Herr Volkmann, it couldn't have been Erhard Schmeltz's wife and it couldn't have been his son.'

Volkmann stared back at the old man in confusion.

'Why?'

'Because Erhard Schmeltz never married, Herr Volkmann. At least not in Germany. Nor did he have any children that I knew of. And the woman who emigrated to South America with him would have been his sister. I thought perhaps it was her in the photograph you showed me, but it wasn't. Her name was Inge, I remember. She was a rather unattractive, awkward countrywoman who had never married or had children. She lived with her brother as his housekeeper and she disappeared at the same time as Erhard Schmeltz.' Busch paused and shook his grey head. 'So whoever the boy was you say they took with them to Paraguay, he wasn't their child.'

Chapter Forty-Two

It was almost five-thirty when Volkmann reached Schliersee. Twenty minutes later he had already left Hundham behind him and the Ford was climbing easily up the gentle slopes where the Wendelstein begins.

He consulted Ivan Molke's drawing. There was a minor road that led to Hundham and Molke's map had placed the monastery eight kilometres from the town going south-east towards the Wendelstein, on the road for Waldweg.

There was snow on the distant hills and the road was still busy with returning traffic from the city. For another ten minutes there was traffic behind him until he turned off the narrow road and found the road sign that said Waldweg.

It led down an unlit, desolate winding road and Volkmann followed it until he came to the end. The road appeared unused and was lined either side by tall fir trees. As the headlights of the Ford swept around a corner the roadway came to an end and he saw a narrow granite bridge, and beyond it the two massive wooden doors of the monastery entrance, set in high sandbrick walls.

He left the headlights on and as he climbed out of the car some instinct told him to take the Beretta. He flicked open the glove compartment and slipped the pistol into his pocket and took the torch and the spare batteries.

The sandstone brickwork was cracked in places and the pointwork crumbling, but the solid walls that appeared to ring the old monastery were still standing and unbreached. There was a metal crucifix high over the ancient wooden gates, its iron rusted and flaking, a brown rust stain running down the pale sandstone. A judas gate was set in the middle of the gates and Volkmann flicked on the torch before he doused the headlights.

As he stood there in the silence that followed he shone the light towards the judas gate. When he pushed it the gate swung open on creaking hinges and he stepped inside.

He found himself in a broad, cobbled courtyard. As he played the torch about the shadows he saw the arched cloisters that ran along the sides. With the torchbeam he picked out an ancient rusted handcart and mounds of debris littered about the cobble. His footsteps echoed in the darkness as he walked towards the centre of the cobbled square.

Beyond the courtyard he saw what appeared to be a building of some sort, its roof pitched higher than the cloister and beside it stood what looked like a belfry tower.

He stepped into the arched cloister to his left.

It smelt of excrement and the plaster had crumbled in places and here and there were several doors leading off. One of them hung on broken hinges and Volkmann stepped inside. He was in what appeared to have been an office of some sort. There were the remnants of old furniture, an ancient broken chair and a heavy wooden desk and the wood smelled of decomposition. For a few moments he stood there, the rotting stench filling his nostrils, until he found it overwhelming and stepped outside into the cloister again.

A sandbrick archway led into another open space. Here and there was a scattering of withered fruit trees and cracked paving ran round what had once been a tiny garden. An old fountain stood in the centre, its stone bowl filled with rainwater. As Volkmann stood there in the moonlight he shone the torch about until the shaft of light caught the building and the tower again at the end of the garden.

It was a small church consisting of belfry and nave and tiny chancel. A vestry door stood half open, the arched doorway covered with bare, overgrown withered ivy, the parched twists of wood gnarled and brittle in the torchlight. When Volkmann pushed open the nave door the sound cracked inside like a roll of thunder. There were broken stained-glass windows set high in the walls, watery moonlight filtering through, the tracery shattered in places, and here and there an ancient pew rested on its side.

The place smelled of must and decay and as Volkmann went to step outside again he hesitated. The wash from the torch caught a shadow on the wall to his left. He shone the torch on the spot and saw the shadow was the entrance to a stairway. Stone steps led down into darkness. Volkmann played the torch over the walls and stairwell but could see nothing beyond.

He followed the steps down warily, until he found himself in the cellars beneath the church. At the end of the stairs was an ancient, solid wooden door. Volkmann gripped the rusted ball knob and twisted. The door gave in easily but its rusted hinges yawned with a jarring screech.

He found himself in a large storeroom.

Bags of plaster and cement were stacked against the walls and cans of paint piled neatly in a corner. Volkmann knelt and examined the materials. They appeared fresh and unused and there was a considerable supply. As he stood up again he heard the noise.

He froze.

Footsteps echoed from somewhere above.

He slid the Beretta from his pocket and flicked off the safety. The noise sounded as if it came from the church.

He moved back towards the door and crossed to the end of the stairwell, only dousing the torch when he had reached the first step. When he arrived at the top he peered out into the shadowy moonlight of the church, but saw and heard nothing.

Moments later he heard a noise again, off to the right, where he had entered the vestry, and it sounded like the click of a shoe.

He raised the Beretta and moved out into the darkness. When he reached the entrance to the vestry he halted and listened. The doorway was open a crack and there was a faint scraping noise coming from somewhere inside.

He felt the sweat rise on his brow as he crossed silently

to the door. He heard another scraping sound and then more footsteps.

Volkmann levelled the Beretta and flicked on the torch, moving quickly into the room, playing the torchlight on the walls as he tried to find a target.

The room was silent and empty.

Another door led out. As he stepped through he found himself in another garden, much larger this time. There were three arched cloisters, the fourth leading out to open space and darkness beyond, and he could make out the dark tilted forms of ancient headstones in the watery moonlight.

He heard the footsteps again, but this time they were slow and echoing.

He flicked on the torch, played it about the archways and then he saw a shadowy figure dart back towards the garden behind him. As the figure vanished into the shadows, he heard the footsteps echoing hard on the cobblestones.

Volkmann raced back towards the first garden that led to the main gates, the Beretta at the ready, and as he came round into the courtyard he saw the figure move between the cloisters.

At that precise moment the figure halted, turned, fired twice, all in one fluid movement. The bullets cracked into the wall above him and Volkmann pulled back into the shadows for cover.

The Beretta came up fast and he fired off three quick shots into the dark cloister, heard the bullets smack into sandstone and ring about the courtyard, but the figure had already vanished and as the echo of the firing died he heard the footsteps racing away.

Suddenly Volkmann heard the roar of a car engine and then two more shots. Moments later came the sound of a car door slam and the screech of tyres.

He was already moving towards the monastery gates and as he stepped through the judas he saw the tail lights of a car disappear down the roadway. Some instinct told him to check the Ford and when he raced towards it he saw the two front tyres had been shot through.

He swore out loud and when he looked up again he could just make out the red of the tail lights, fading through the trees before they disappeared into the darkness.

It took him almost an hour to reach the service station on the autobahn, driving on one flat tyre after fitting the spare wheel. It took another half-hour to have two new tyres fitted and give a ten-mark tip to the grumbling station assistant. By then it was almost nine and he drove back to the monastery to take another look around, this time leaving the car half a kilometre from the Waldweg road and walking back, taking the torch and spare batteries with him.

There were marks on the gravel where the fleeing car had burned rubber, but apart from that he had found nothing unusual as he walked the perimeter before venturing inside again. At the stone bridge he had stopped and shone the torch and saw a stream that ran in a moat around the perimeter.

He estimated the property stood on several acres, walled with sandstone and, despite its years, was still in solid condition, but there was nothing in the monastery or the outhouses or the gardens that suggested anything unusual and he wondered again what significance it had to be drawn in Kesser's notebook.

He shone the torch under the cloisters where the fleeing figure had fired but there were no spent cartridge shells. Whoever had fired at him had used a revolver and not an automatic weapon.

He walked back up to the old cemetery and flashed the torch between the rows of headstones. Most of the graves dated from before the war and the most recent headstone bore an inscription dated twenty years before, and he guessed that the cemetery was a private one and had belonged to the cloister. There was no evidence of any freshly dug soil and none of the graves appeared to have been disturbed.

He drove back on the Augsburg road, stopping twice for coffee and to check if he was being followed but no one was tailing him; at that hour on the autobahn the traffic was thin and he would have noticed.

He wondered about the men in the car. Kesser's people or Landesamt? If the men were Landesamt he guessed they would have handled it differently and not shot at him or shot up his tyres. That only left Kesser's people. He had checked his rear-view mirror all the way down from Strasbourg to Augsburg and he definitely hadn't been tailed. And he realised the girl was the only one who knew he was driving down to Dachau.

He had been too preoccupied to check if he was being followed when he left there and he should have heeded Ivan Molke's advice.

It was almost three in the morning when he let himself into the apartment. The girl was asleep in his bed and the bedside lamp was on, her blonde hair strewn about the pillow. He stood there for several moments looking down at her face, thinking about what had happened, wondering if he had been reckless in trusting her.

When he finally turned off the light and closed the door, he went into the kitchen and poured himself a scotch and drank half of it in one swallow. When he came back he saw the note by the telephone.

'André rang. He said to phone him.'

He made the call to the duty office and the Frenchman answered sleepily.

'Any luck with the names?'

'Depends what you mean by luck, Joseph. The three names you gave me, Henkle, Trautman, Klee, they didn't turn up on our computer. There was a Franz Henkle, but it turns out he's Dutch, and wanted for narcotics smuggling. I tried every area I could but nothing came up for any of them. So I passed it on to the German Desk like you said.'

'And?'

'They came back pretty quick. They wanted to know if we had anything on the names and what the story was. I told them I didn't know, just that I got a list of names to check, and if we came up with anything I'd come back to them.'

'So what did the German Desk say?'

'If they're the same people, they turned up as homicides in the past six months.'

'How did they die?'

'Henkle was a hit-and-run victim, but suspected homicide. That happened six months ago. Klee was shot, Trautman the same. The Klee killing happened four months back; Trautman, five. In each case none of the victims had any criminal background. Middle-aged, middle-class men with no records worth talking of. No witnesses, no suspects arrested or charged. That's why the Germans were so interested to know if we had anything.' The Frenchman paused. 'What are you on to, Joe?'

'I don't know, André.' He wrote down the details on the pad beside the phone. 'Anything else I ought to know?'

'I just got the bare details. Henkle and Trautman came from Essen, Klee from Rostock. Henkle was a career army officer, *Bundeswehr*, rank of Major, fifty-two years of age, married, two grown children. Trautman was a businessman, a year older. Divorced. Klee was a senior civil servant who was posted to Eastern Germany after the Wall came down. Married, no kids. Forty-eight years of age. That's about it. If you want to see the homicide reports you'll have to request them through the BP.'

'What about a connection, André?'

'I specified that when I asked the German Desk. Apart from the homicide link, there's no connection that they know of between the three men, but they'd be very interested to know if there is. Does any of that help?'

'I don't know, André. But it's something. What about the woman, Hanah Richter?'

'The university is closed for the holidays. But I got the home number for the Dean of Stuttgart from the BP headquarters in Altstadt and called him. He remembered the woman. She retired about ten years ago, went back to Nicolassee in Berlin where her family came from. He had an address in an old diary but no number so I had the operator check. She's listed. I got the number and the address. You want to take them down?'

Volkmann wrote down the number and address. 'Thanks for your help, André.'

'Any time. And send my love to the girl. She sounds OK.'

He sat on the couch sipping the scotch, thinking over the information the Frenchman had given him.

There was a connection to Kesser now, no question, and he wondered what the reason was for the deaths of the three men. The names in Kesser's notebook meant even if Kesser was working for the Government he was implicated by having the list and he figured the next step was to pull Kesser in, but to do that he'd have to go through the German Desk.

But there was still no pattern to the puzzle. All the men, Henkle, Trautman, Klee, were middle-class with professional or business backgrounds. Like Rauscher and the woman, Hedda Pohl. All were middle-aged and the only connection Volkmann could see apart from their class backgrounds was that they would all have been born while the Nazis were in power, but that told him little if nothing.

As he lay back on the couch he thought again of the shadowy figure in the monastery courtyard. The car could have followed him on the main autobahn and then tracked him at a distance down the Waldweg road with its lights off, and he guessed that was what had happened.

He found the tape in his briefcase and slipped it into the cassette player. He sat on the couch for a long time in the silence, smoking a cigarette, before putting on the headphones and switching on the play button.

He listened to the tape play through a half-dozen times, listened to the voices in the darkness, knowing the words before they came, knowing each inflection.

'The shipment . . .?'

'The cargo will be picked up from Genoa as arranged.'

'And the Italian?'

'He will be eliminated, but I want to be certain we don't

arouse suspicion concerning the cargo. It would be prudent to wait until Brandenburg becomes operational. Then he will be dealt with along with the others.'

Pause.

'Those who have pledged their loyalty . . . we must be certain of them.'

'I have had their assurances confirmed. And their pedigree is without question.'

'And the Turk?'

'I foresee no problems.'

'The girl . . . you're absolutely certain we can rely on her?'

'She will not fail us, I assure you.' Pause. *'There are no changes to the names on the list . . .?'*

'They will all be killed.'

When tiredness finally overcame him he turned off the cassette player and removed the headphones.

He stood and crossed to the front window and peered down into the courtyard. There was no movement below and no unknown cars in the driveway and as he turned back he heard the girl stir in her sleep then fall silent again.

It was warm in the front room and he decided to sleep on the couch, too tired to move into the spare bedroom. He didn't want to wake the girl and he didn't want to talk with her just then, his mind too troubled and confused.

His head throbbed and as he lay back he massaged his temples and closed his eyes and tried to empty his mind, but the voices on the tape came in on him again. What was the shipment? Who was the Italian? The Turk? And who were the people to be killed? The people on the lists in Kesser's notebook?

And who was the girl? Erica's father had been a Leibstandarte officer, like Tsarkin, like Kesser's father. And she had known Winter at Heidelberg. Volkmann shook his head; he wanted to believe the girl, wanted to believe what she had told him, but there was a doubt still in the back of his mind and it would not go away.

The lamp on the coffee table was still on and as he lay there on the edge of sleep, he thought of the images on the *Blockhaus* walls at Dachau; the white bodies lying out in rows under the sun and the big dark lifeless eyes of the woman clutching her dead little girl to her breast and the grinning face of the SS man looking down at her.

He closed his eyes as if to erase the images from his mind.

But the last thought on his mind as he lay on the edge of sleep was a line on the tape.

It came like a click in the back of his head.

So obvious he wondered why it hadn't come to him before now.

He was aware of his heart racing in his chest and his mind was wide awake. There was something he hadn't thought of checking, something so obvious and it made him restless now. It was too late to do anything about it and he would have to wait until morning to check with Berlin. But he wondered if it might be a glimmer of light in the darkness.

Chapter Forty-Three

He woke three hours later, showered and shaved and drove over to the office. The girl was still sleeping and he left a note saying he'd be back by noon.

The hours of business of government agencies in Germany are normally eight to four and when he made the telephone call to the Berlin Document Centre it was 8 a.m. exactly.

He asked to speak with Maxwell and the voice that finally came on the line was soft and American.

Volkmann explained that Ted Birken had told him to contact Maxwell personally if he needed any information from the Centre. Maxwell seemed mildly put out when Volkmann gave him the list of names and requested the information he needed.

'What the hell's up with DSE that you're checking all these names, Volkmann? We've had a couple of requests from your people in Strasbourg apart from the one you routed through Birken.'

'I'm afraid it's classified right now, Mr Maxwell, but you think you could check the areas I asked you about?'

Maxwell sighed. 'Well, I guess . . . but it may take a little time.'

'How long?'

'Maybe a day or two. We're pretty understaffed, you know. And it's Christmas. We're winding down. Won't it do after the holidays?'

'I realise I'm asking a lot, but it is important. I need the information today. You think it can be done?'

Maxwell sighed again, a deep sigh. 'It depends how lucky I get. It means a lot of checking. So what you're looking for is a connection in regard to these names, right? Where they were stationed in the period you specified.

And, if they had any children, their names and dates of birth.'

'That's it.'

Maxwell blew out air over the line. 'It's going to mean going right back through a whole bunch of files to find the right ones, if they exist. You realise that? All you've given me is names. No dates of birth, no rank.'

'I realise that, Mr Maxwell. But as I say, it's important.'

Maxwell seemed to hesitate before he said, 'OK, you better leave it with me. I'll see what I can do. But I can't promise I'll get through them all.'

Volkmann thanked the man and clicked the cradle and punched in the number for Hanah Richter in Berlin's Nicolassee.

When a woman's voice answered she told Volkmann that Frau Richter was not at home and wasn't expected back until later that morning. Volkmann left his name and number and asked the woman to have Hanah Richter phone him back.

The return call came an hour later. A woman's voice, deep and commanding. She introduced herself as Hanah Richter.

'What's this about, Herr Volkmann?'

Volkmann explained he was with DSE and how he had got her name. He had heard she had once worked for the German Government during the Nazi trials of the 'sixties and was an expert on the Nazi period. He explained he was working on a case and had a favour to ask; would she take a look at a photograph, a photograph of a young woman taken during the 1930s? He explained about the Nazi armband in the photograph. Perhaps she might be able to identify the woman or know someone who could help.

'Is this something official?'

'Yes.'

'Are you trying to track some Nazi?'

'No, Frau Richter.' He told her he couldn't explain any more but that he would appreciate her help.

'You're going back a long time, Herr Volkmann. A very long time indeed.'

He asked if he could call on her in Berlin the next day and the woman said that wasn't possible.

'You've caught me at a very bad time. I'm going to Leipzig early tomorrow to stay with friends. I won't be returning until after the holidays. And besides, I stopped doing that kind of work a long time ago, Herr Volkmann.'

'I realise this might be an inconvenience, Frau Richter, but what if I flew to Berlin this evening?'

'Is this really that important?'

'It's important. And I'd greatly appreciate your help.'

'This young woman . . . you've no idea who she might be?'

'Perhaps the wife or girlfriend of a senior SS officer or Nazi official. But I'm only guessing. The photograph was taken in 1931.'

He heard a deep sigh at the other end. 'Herr Volkmann, you may have been told I was an expert on the Nazi period but my depth of knowledge does not extend to every friend of every Nazi. And you're talking about two years before the Nazis came to power, you realise that?'

'I appreciate that, Frau Richter,' Volkmann persisted. 'But if you could just take a look at the photograph . . .'

There was a long silence at the other end of the line and then finally the woman gave another deep sigh.

'Very well, Herr Volkmann, I had better give you directions to my home.'

He organised a return ticket to Berlin with Facilities. The flights out of Frankfurt were full, but there were plenty of seats on the six o'clock shuttle out of Stuttgart, over an hour's drive away. It was almost two when he got the return call from Maxwell.

He listened as the Director of the Document Centre gave him the information, jotting the details in his notebook, and when the American had finished, he said to Volkmann, 'You still there?'

'Yes, I'm still here.'

'The information, does it help any?'

Volkmann smiled, 'I think you could say that.'

'Now would you care to tell me what this is about, or is it still classified?'

'I still need to do some checking with the WASt, but as soon as I know for certain myself, I'll let you know. One more thing, Mr Maxwell . . .'

'What?'

'Happy Christmas.'

'Same to you.'

Volkmann put down the receiver, looked down at the information in his notebook, and started to make the phone calls.

It took him less than a half-hour to get the information he needed and when he had finished making the calls he could feel the sweat running down the back of his shirt.

He was aware of his heart pounding in his chest as he drove to the apartment. The girl wasn't there but she had left a note to say she had gone for a walk in the park.

He drove down to the Orangerie and parked the car. He found her walking by the lake and they went to sit on one of the benches.

He told her everything that had happened the previous day and he saw the look of surprise on her face when he told her about Busch and what had happened at the monastery.

'Whoever shot at me, I don't think they meant to kill me. I was an easy target, but they fired high. And there's something else that's strange.'

'What?'

'I had a feeling about the place. As if I'd been there before. Not there exactly, but somewhere like it.'

'What do you mean, Joe?'

'I can't explain it. Like a feeling of *déjà vu*.'

She raised a hand to touch his face. 'Tell me you'll be careful. It frightens me. What happened to Ivan Molke's men? You think the two things are connected? You think it's the same people?'

'Maybe.'

'The Landesamt?'

'If Kesser is still working for the Government on some research project, it could be one of their specialist units.'

'You think they're protecting him?'

'It's possible, but I'm not so sure.'

He told her he was flying to Berlin that evening to see the woman named Hanah Richter, and explained who she was. 'She may be able to help identify the woman in the photograph. Or if she can't, she may know someone who can.'

'The old man, Busch, was he certain about Erhard Schmeltz and what he said about the boy? About the child not belonging to either Schmeltz or his sister?'

'Busch was adamant. And just like you said, the woman would have been too old to have had a child. The question is, who did the boy belong to if he wasn't the Schmeltzes' child?'

'What Busch told you about this Brandenburg Testament, do you think it's of any significance?'

Volkmann looked at her. 'Yes.'

The girl frowned. 'But how can you be so certain, Joe?'

He looked into the blue eyes and the pretty face. He had wondered whether to tell her and now he decided to.

'Because, Erica, I had the Document Centre in Berlin do some checking for me. Let's take Lothar Kesser first. The records say he was an SS General. Leibstandarte SS. He was stationed in Berlin at the time Busch said this Testament would have been pledged by the Leibstandarte SS. So what Lubsch heard Kesser boast about is in all probability true.' He looked at the girl's face. 'I also asked for seven other names to be checked.'

'What names?'

'The names in Kesser's notebook. Trautman, Klee, Henkle. And the other names, the people Lubsch was asked to kill. Massow, Hedda Pohl and Rauscher . . .'

'But why ask the Document Centre to check those names? You said only Rauscher's father was a Nazi officer.'

'There was a word on the tape. Lubsch used the same word when he spoke of Kesser. Pedigree. That was the first thing. But what made it click into place was the Chaco photograph. The Nazi armband on the man's arm.' Volkmann paused. 'It was the only connection I could think of that was possible, apart from middle-aged, middle-class backgrounds.

And the information they came up with at the Document Centre, it makes a connection between all of the names. Massow, Rauscher, Pohl, Trautman, Klee, Henkle.'

'What connection? None of these people were Nazis, Joe. They were too young to have served during the war.'

'I'm not talking about them, I'm talking about their fathers. Each of their fathers were Leibstandarte SS officers. And every one of them was stationed in Berlin before the war ended. The time the Testament was signed.'

'But how do you know for certain?'

'The three people Kesser wanted killed, Massow, Rauscher and Pohl. There were three Leibstandarte officers with those names, Erica. All of them with the rank of *Standartenführer*; Major. The same applies to the three names found in Kesser's apartment: Trautman, Klee, Henkle. There were three Leibstandarte officers with those names, with the rank of Major or above. And they were each stationed in or near Berlin at the time Busch spoke of. My guess is, they could have been signatories to the Testament. And the people who were killed were children of those officers.'

'But there could have been hundreds of officers with those names? How can you be certain that these people are the same children?'

'Every SS officer's file stated if he was married and had children. The names and dates of birth of the wife and children were recorded in his file. And the three people Kesser wanted killed, Massow, Rauscher, Pohl, their births were all recorded in their fathers' files. After I got the information I telephoned Walter Massow in Berlin. His father was a Leibstandarte officer, prosecuted and imprisoned for war crimes. Maybe that's why he's a liberal politician and helping the people he's helping, trying to do penance for his father's sins. I also called the detective in Friedrichshaften. He confirmed that Hedda Pohl's father had been a Leibstandarte officer.'

'And Herbert Rauscher?'

'The Document Centre had a file on one Wilhelm Rauscher, a Leibstandarte major. When I checked his name with the WASt the information they had was that he was captured by the Russians in the battle for Berlin in April 1945. He was sent to a German prisoner-of-war camp in Siberia. They believe he died there. It just has to be the same Rauscher. The family address was in Leipzig, where Herbert Rauscher was born.'

Volkmann let the information sink in, saw the girl hesitate before she looked at him.

'I don't understand. Why would Kesser want these people killed? Kesser is a fascist, a neo-Nazi. Why would he want to kill Massow, Rauscher, Pohl – and the others? Why would he want to kill the children of former SS officers?'

Volkmann shook his head. 'I'm only certain of one thing. We're not only talking about the deaths of Rudi and the others. This is something that goes much deeper. Something that goes back a long time. To the last months of the war in Berlin when these people swore their allegiance to Hitler. There's a reason these people were killed. Maybe they know something they shouldn't. Maybe there's a secret someone still wants to hide. Something damaging enough to kill for. And we're not only talking about six people. There were other names in Kesser's notebook. For all I know they could be dead. Or they're going to die. Maybe that's what the voice on the tape was talking about when it said the names on the list would all be killed. The question is, why? What was it the children of these officers were involved in or knew that Kesser wanted them dead?'

'Massow wasn't killed. Did you question him, ask him if he knew the others?'

Volkmann nodded. 'I told him everything I could. He seemed totally baffled by the whole thing. No one approached him, hardly anyone knew about his father's past and that's the way he wanted to keep it. He knew none of the other people. He didn't know of any secrets his father was privy to and his father died in prison over twenty years ago.'

'Are you going to talk with Ferguson about all this?'

'Not until I find out why these people were killed. Whatever's happening it has to do with the Leibstandarte SS and their senior officers. With the pledge Busch said they made in the last months of the war. The people who were killed, the children of those officers, are somehow tied into it. That's how I see it. Maybe it has to do with the cargoes being smuggled.'

'You think Rodriguez was smuggling gold?'

'Maybe. But I've got a feeling there's another angle to it, not just a smuggling operation. We'll have to pull Kesser in and have a talk with him.'

The girl hesitated. 'You said there were seven names you checked besides Lothar Kesser's. You mentioned only six. What was the other name?'

He had been waiting for the question and he looked at her, searched her eyes. 'Your father's. He was stationed in Berlin at the same time as all the others. He was posted to an SS training school in the district of Lichterfelde in January 1945.'

There was a long silence and the girl looked away, towards the park, then back again.

He saw the look on her face and heard the defensiveness in her voice. 'Why did you check on my father?'

'Because he was an officer, the same as the others. Because he could have been one of the people Busch told me about.'

'That's not the truth completely, is it, Joe? It was because you didn't trust me and you wanted to see my reaction when you told me. And you still don't trust me, do you? Even though you're telling me all this? You look into my eyes and I know you're searching for answers. You're searching to see if I'm telling the truth or lying.'

'I want to believe you, Erica.'

The girl said nothing for a long time, then she looked at him. 'If I was one of Kesser's people, then why would I have come to your people in the first place? Why would I have wanted you to investigate Rudi's death? Why, Joe? Why would I have done these things?'

He had no answer and he knew it.

'Joe, I hardly knew my father. I never believed in his ideals. I'm not one of Kesser's right-wing extremists. You must believe this. You must trust me. The fact that my father was in Berlin at the same time as the others, that he could have even signed this Testament, I never knew any of this until you told me.'

He looked at the blue eyes watching his and remembered the warm body and the hands touching him in the darkness and how close he had felt to her. Looking at her now he wondered how he could doubt her.

Her hand came up to his face and touched his cheek and her voice was soft, almost pleading.

'Prove that you trust me, Joe. Please.'

'How?'

'Just believe me. And don't leave me on my own. I think I'm going to go crazy cooped up in your apartment all day. Take me to Berlin with you. After what happened to you and Ivan Molke's men, I'd feel safer.'

When he hesitated, Erica said, 'When is your flight to Berlin?'

'Six.'

'Will you take me with you, Joe?'

He still hesitated, aware of her watching him. Finally, he said, 'I'll have Facilities organise a ticket.'

'Do you have to go back to the office?'

'Why?'

'We won't have to leave for another hour. There's something else I want you to do for me.'

'What?'

'Take me to bed. I've missed you.'

The blue eyes looked into his face and as she smiled again he stood up and took her hand in his.

She leaned into his shoulder as they strolled back through the park.

Neither of them noticed the two men sitting in the parked car in the distance, observing them through the bare winter trees.

Chapter Forty-Four

Bavaria.
December 22nd,
11.58 p.m.

Meyer saw the lights of the small Tyrolean villages in the valley below as the big, blunt-nosed Mercedes growled up the steep mountain road to the Kaalberg.

There was a sprinkling of snow on the thickly forested slopes and as he came round the bend in the forest track the road ahead levelled off, the headlights of the Mercedes picking out the thick cluster of evergreens that ran in a half-circle about the small plateau. The closed metal barrier gate was off to the right, a sign attached, the words *'Eintritt Verboten!'* in bold red lettering, and the narrow road beyond it ran through thick forest.

Meyer halted the car on the clearing and switched off the engine. He flashed the headlights three times before dousing them completely, then pressed the button to roll down the electric window.

The heavy scent of pine-gum wafted into the car on the crisp, cold air and he heard a sound off to the right, saw one of the guards come out from behind the thick pine trees where the small wooden guard hut was hidden from sight.

The man had a Heckler and Koch MP 5K machine-pistol draped across his chest and as he approached the car the electric torch in his hand came on suddenly. He flashed the light at Meyer and around the inside of the Mercedes and after several moments nodded for Meyer to proceed.

As the guard moved back towards the trees, Meyer flicked on the car's headlights. Another man appeared and unlocked the barrier gate and waved Meyer towards him.

Meyer started the Mercedes and the car moved slowly forward.

Kesser and Meyer crossed the gravel driveway together to the flat concrete building. Kesser opened the double dead-locks on the the grey-painted steel door with the bunch of keys from his pocket. Once inside, he flicked the switch and the big room flooded with light.

The interior of the building was icy cold but the contrast with the bland, functional exterior was stunning.

The wedge-shaped steel gantry stood in the centre of the room. A metal launch pad cradled in the gantry held the oblong grey-painted warhead at a forty-five-degree angle. Below the gantry was a concrete pit measuring three metres by three metres, the bottom and sides of the concrete lined with matted asbestos sheeting and Meyer knew it was to damp the launch burn-off.

Two metal sliding doors were set in the flat roof and the building walls were painted military grey. To the right of the gantry stood the IBM computer mainframe, its chassis a metre wide and a metre deep. A console screen and a standard keyboard stood on top, two rotatable chairs set in front. A galvanised alloy conduit ran from the base of the console to the bottom of the gantry, carrying the cables that would control the missile and gantry movement and launch.

There was a grey telephone on top of a wooden desk beside the mainframe and Kesser's briefcase was open, a screed of computer print out paper unfolded, notes scribbled on the paper where Kesser had written. A thermos flask beside the briefcase, its plastic cup half filled with black coffee.

Kesser led the way past the gantry to the computer and sat in one of the chairs facing the computer screen. He flicked a switch on the fascia and the screen flickered and turned blue, lights flashing on the panels.

Kesser said, 'I ran the program. It's fine. No bugs.'

'Is it safe?'

'Of course.'

Meyer looked on alarmed, but Kesser shook his head.

'The warhead hasn't been activated.' He pointed to the computer. 'The program's simply loading up. It takes about a minute.'

Meyer saw the computer screen blank, then become blue again, as a series of unintelligible figures and characters began scrolling rapidly on the screen. Finally, the scrolling stopped, and a white cursor blinked on the screen's top left corner.

'Now the program's loaded,' said Kesser. He pointed to the screen. 'Watch.'

He tapped in a series of commands and the screen blanked again, but this time it threw up a graphic computer picture in white against a blue background. Meyer saw the grid outline map of Germany, and this time there were grey lines criss-crossing on the blue screen.

When Kesser hit another key, Meyer heard a sound like muted thunder overhead. The metal doors set in the concrete roof began to roll open on their steel runners. An icy blast of air gusted into the building and Meyer shivered as the night sky came into view, stars glittering in the cold heavens.

When Kesser tapped the keyboard once more, the electric whirr of the stepping motor filled the room. Meyer saw the grey-painted missile twitch in the gantry until it assumed its programmed angle, and then the whirr of the stepping motor died and there was silence again.

Kesser said, 'Now look at the screen.'

Meyer saw a white image in the shape of a tiny circle appear on the grid in the area around Berlin. The white circle winked for several seconds, then stopped, but it remained on the blue screen.

Kesser said, 'Locked on target. The middle of the circle is the epicentre. I can expand the scale if you want to see the exact point in Berlin, but you know how it works. Right now the target centre is between the Brandenburg Gate and the southern side of the Reichstag building.'

Meyer took a deep breath. The air in the dark concrete building had become incredibly chilled, the metal doors above wide open. As he pulled up the collar of his loden coat he felt a shiver run through him. Cold or fear? He couldn't tell which.

Kesser said, 'Of course, it will never come to a confrontation. They will all back off. The Americans, the British, the others, once we tell them our intentions, won't they?'

Meyer did not reply, but moved away towards the grey metal gantry.

There was a long silence and then suddenly the telephone by the console buzzed, the shrill noise echoing throughout the building. Kesser leaned across and lifted the receiver, listened, spoke briefly, then turned to Meyer.

'There's a call for you. Priority.'

The flight to Berlin that evening was delayed and it was just after eight when they landed at Tegel.

They took a taxi from the airport and Volkmann told the driver to wait while they checked into the small hotel off the Kurfurstendamm. The reception clerk gave them a room facing the Wilhelmskirche and it was half an hour later when they pulled up outside the lakeshore house.

It was one of the old, pre-war wooden properties that ring the Nicolassee shore, painted brown and white, the clapboarded windows shut to keep out the freezing blasts of Baltic wind that race across the lake in winter. Dark clouds wafted across the moonlit sky.

It was bitterly cold as they stepped from the taxi and Volkmann asked the driver to wait. They saw the porch light come on and a middle-aged woman appear behind the glass ante-door. She looked to be in her late sixties but very sprightly and she wore a blue, heavy-quilted coat. She rubbed her hands to combat the cold and when they came up the path she waited until the last moment before opening the door.

'It's kind of you to see us so late, Frau Richter.'

The woman smiled at them both. 'Please, come in, Herr Volkmann.'

The house was warm and she led them into a study that Volkmann guessed overlooked the lake. Pleasant in summer, but in winter the shutters were firmly closed. A neat, tidy desk stood facing the window. On the desk was an ashtray with half a dozen cigarette ends. The study walls were lined with shelves of books and Volkmann noticed that most of them were on the subject of the Third Reich. There was a framed, signed black-and-white picture of Konrad Adenauer, the first president of the post-war German State, on the wall by the window.

He introduced Erica and the woman shook their hands and told them to sit down.

Hanah Richter was tall, with a face that was more handsome than pretty, her greying hair tied back, emphasising her high forehead. But her eyes were bright Nordic blue, and they sparkled in her face, giving her the appearance of someone who lived life with much enthusiasm.

Moments later a very old woman came into the room carrying a tray with three steaming cups.

'Some hot chocolate,' Hanah Richter explained. 'It's my nightly ritual. I thought it might warm you both before your journey back. A small compensation should your journey have been wasted. This is Hildegard. She has been a housekeeper with my family since I was a child.'

They thanked the old woman and she smiled and bade them goodnight and left.

Hanah Richter sipped her chocolate and looked at both of them, keen eyes searching their faces as she lit a cigarette between nicotine-stained fingers. She inhaled on her cigarette and stared at Volkmann. 'So what's so special about this photograph, Herr Volkmann?'

'It may be no one important, but we need to be certain. It's of a young woman, taken on July 11th, 1931 . . .'

Hanah Richter interrupted gently. 'Perhaps you ought to simply show me the photograph.'

Volkmann removed his wallet and handed the photograph across; the photograph of the blonde young woman, smiling out at the camera, the mountains behind her, the sun in her eyes, the unseen hand linking hers. Hanah Richter put down her cup and took the picture, held it in both her hands. She stared down at the image and after a brief moment she looked up.

'You said the photograph was taken on July 11th, 1931?'

'That's what it said on the back of the original. But I'm afraid we've no way of knowing for certain if the date is correct.' Volkmann paused. 'Why?'

Hanah Richter shook her head as if dismissively, then squinted down at the image once more as she reached into her pocket and removed a pair of reading glasses, placed them carefully on the tip of her nose.

There was a blank expression on her face as she stared intently at the photograph for a long time. The wind gusted and whistled outside, lightly shook the clapboarded windows, but the historian didn't look up.

Volkmann said finally, 'The girl in the photograph. Do you recognise her?'

When she looked up, Hanah Richter said, 'Yes.'

PART SIX

Chapter Forty-Five

Nicolassee,
Berlin

'Her name was Angela Raubal.'

Hanah Richter looked down at the photograph again as a gust of wind rattled the clapboarded window. The fire crackled and flickered in the hearth, casting dark shadows about the room.

When the historian looked up again, Volkmann said, 'Who was she?'

'She was Adolf Hitler's niece. The daughter of Hitler's half-sister, also named Angela Raubal. But the young girl was called Geli, to distinguish her from her mother.'

Volkmann said intently, 'You're absolutely certain about her identity?'

'Quite certain. I've seen her picture many times before. Although never this one, not in any of the history books.'

Volkmann stared at the historian seated opposite. 'And there's no doubt in your mind that it's the same girl?'

Hanah Richter shook her head as she looked at Volkmann. 'Absolutely none whatsoever. During my academic career, I wrote several papers on the period from 1929 to '31 and how it influenced Hitler's personal life. The girl – Geli Raubal – figured largely in that period. I researched her background as thoroughly as possible. It was a very difficult time for Hitler. He was beset by all sorts of problems, personal and otherwise. And this young woman was one of them.' Hanah Richter pointed at the photograph, then put it down. She looked at Volkmann. 'May I ask where you got this photograph?'

'From South America.'

He saw the woman raise her eyebrows a moment. He thought she was going to question him further but then she seemed to change her mind.

'You don't look very convinced, Herr Volkmann? About the identity of the young woman, I mean.'

Volkmann glanced at Erica. The girl said nothing, but she looked at him silently a few moments then over at the photograph. Volkmann turned back to Hanah Richter.

'It's a question of certainty. We need to be absolutely sure.'

'If you won't take my word for it, I can show you several other photographs of the same girl. Then you can compare them and come to your own conclusion. Would that help?'

'That would help greatly, Frau Richter.'

'Please, call me Hanah.'

The woman stood up, crossed to a bookshelf and put on her glasses again. She searched along a shelf and finally selected two books, came back to where Volkmann and Erica sat.

She laid the two books side by side, then placed one under the reading lamp. Slips of yellow paper, reference markers, stuck out between the covers.

'These are fairly standard books dealing with the period. This first is Toland's biography of Adolf Hitler. The man's an absolute expert on the subject. I met him at a Harvard lecture once. Fascinating man. This second book I wrote myself.' She smiled. 'My one brief moment of literary glory.'

Volkmann looked down at the blue-bound cover she had placed a hand on and she smiled and said, 'I'm sure you'll find copies in the second-hand book stores if you care to look. I'm afraid the book had a rather limited academic interest.'

She opened the first book, leafed through the plates of black- and-white photographs inside and finally found what she was looking for.

Her finger pointed to a snapshot of a young, dark-haired girl standing against a black Daimler car. Behind her sloped a blurred forest. From the look of the car Volkmann guessed it was a mid-1920s model. The girl stood with one foot on the Daimler's running board, one hand on her hip. She wore a pale sleeveless summer blouse and a darker skirt to knee length.

'This particular photograph was taken sometime in the summer of 1930.'

Volkmann and Erica examined the image closely. The girl was dark-haired and pretty; her face square-jawed but attractive. A light-hearted girl trying to look serious for the camera. There was a faint likeness to the girl in Volkmann's photograph, but not a very noticeable one.

Volkmann looked at Hanah Richter and said, 'She's not blonde?'

The elderly woman smiled and glanced at Erica a moment before looking back at Volkmann.

'It was common practice then as much as now for girls to dye their hair. Peroxide may change appearances but the facial structure remains the same. The girl often changed her hair colour. In some photographs she's blonde, in others dark-haired. But if you look closely you'll see it's definitely the same girl.'

Hanah Richter opened a drawer in the study desk and took out a magnifying glass, handed it to Volkmann. 'Please, be my guest.'

Volkmann held the glass over the image and focused. The basic facial structure of the girl in Hanah Richter's photograph was without doubt the same: square-faced, high cheekbones, pensive eyes, thin, wide mouth.

'You see a resemblance?'

When Volkmann nodded, Hanah Richter said, 'But you're still not convinced, are you? Perhaps it's the colour of the girl's hair?'

'That and her figure.'

The historian smiled. 'True, in this photograph the girl looks much thinner. In yours she appears quite plump. Let me show you another, taken in the spring of 1931.'

Hanah Richter opened the second book. Midway through was a collection of photographs and again she leafed through and found the one she was looking for and pointed to it.

The scene was a Bavarian restaurant. Four people sat at

a table; two men, two women. Both women were blonde, one young, one middle-aged. The younger of the two women definitely resembled the young woman in Volkmann's photograph. Her features were fuller and remarkably similar, her hair blonde and done in plaits in the style of young German girls. She wore a traditional Bavarian costume with lace collar. She smiled out at the camera, as if someone had just made a joke.

Two of the people seated with her around the table Volkmann recognised at once. To her left Adolf Hitler, his arms folded, a trace of a smile on his thin lips. Opposite sat the diminutive, grinning Joseph Goebbels, the Nazi propaganda minister. The older blonde woman seated next to him had her arm linked through his.

Hanah Richter said, 'The girl with Hitler is Geli Raubal. This time with blonde hair. The woman with Joseph Goebbels is his wife, Gerda. And in this photograph there's something much more interesting. A clue that relates to your photograph. Pass me the magnifier, if you would be so kind.'

Volkmann did so and Hanah Richter placed Volkmann's photograph beside the photograph in the book.

'Now look closely, please.'

She positioned the glass over the new photograph and Volkmann held it. The focus swam and settled. Erica leaned in closer and Hanah Richter said, 'If you both look at the girl's right wrist, I think you'll see something interesting.'

On the girl's wrist was a faintly glinting bracelet. Hanah Richter shifted the glass to Volkmann's photograph. Again, clearly visible, was a metal bracelet on the girl's right wrist.

Hanah Richter said, 'The bracelet was a gift from Hitler to his niece, in October 1929 when he took her to a Nazi Party rally in Nuremberg. It was made of solid white gold, with rubies and sapphires. Hitler mentioned it in a letter he wrote to a close friend. A white gold bracelet which Geli Raubal later always wore on her right wrist.' Hanah Richter looked up at them over her glasses. 'Even besides all that, the facial features of the girl in your photograph are unmistakable, I assure you. It's definitely the same girl.'

Volkmann took the magnifying glass again, held it over the photograph as Erica stood beside him, comparing the two photographs. The same wide, thin lips. The same cheekbones. The same eyes. The same shaped face. He looked at Erica, but she said nothing. She stared at him blankly before she looked back at Hanah Richter.

'I realise the hour, Hanah, but can you tell us about the girl's background? You said she was one of Hitler's problems. How was she a problem?'

'Because she committed suicide.'

'When?'

'Almost two months after your photograph was taken. After a blazing row with Hitler in his Munich apartment, the girl shot herself through the heart. You see, the two were lovers for a long time.'

When Volkmann and Erica stared at her in disbelief, Hanah Richter looked at them both and said, 'I'm afraid you've aroused my curiosity. Is this very important?'

Volkmann said, 'It may be.'

'Would you care to tell me why?'

Volkmann hesitated. 'It has to do with a criminal investigation, Hanah. I'm afraid I can't tell you more than that.'

There was a puzzled look on the historian's face, and then she said, 'When you say a criminal investigation, what do you mean? To do with the girl?'

Volkmann said, 'Not the girl. Someone else.'

'But what has the girl got to do with it? Her death happened such a long time ago.'

'I'm sorry, Hanah. I can't tell you any more than that.'

Hanah Richter frowned slightly at Volkmann, her disappointment evident, then she sat back and said, 'Very well, what is it you wish to know about Geli Raubal?'

Volkmann said, 'Everything you can tell us.'

Hanah Richter offered round cigarettes, and lit each of them in turn.

Volkmann sat forward. 'You said the girl and Hitler were lovers. Can you tell us about that?'

The elderly historian drew on her cigarette and sat back in her chair. 'Certainly there was a relationship between them. One that went far deeper than a normal uncle-niece relationship. You see, the girl lived in the same house as Hitler for a time, and they had become very close. In 1927, when Hitler moved to his *Berghaus* in the mountains at Berchtesgaden, his step-sister moved in with him to act as his housekeeper. Hitler distrusted many of those around him, so his half-sister was an obvious choice. She tended to his housekeeping needs, organised his meals, his clothes. And with her came her daughters, Friedl and Geli.'

Volkmann said, 'What about their father?'

'He had died when Geli was quite young. Perhaps that was part of the girl's attraction to Hitler. Very early on he became a kind of father figure. She was a very high-spirited girl. Flighty, if one is to believe the history books.' Hanah Richter smiled. 'She was born in Vienna, so perhaps it was her Viennese charm. Of course, Eva Braun took centre stage as far as Hitler's private life is concerned. She was the mistress the history books all record. But before her came Geli Raubal. She was Adolf Hitler's first real romantic attachment – I won't say love because the man was incapable of human love. But let us say it was a romantic attachment that was reciprocated. She adored her uncle, and he her.

'For a time they went everywhere together and when Hitler moved from Berchtesgaden to an apartment in Munich, Geli Raubal joined him. She was studying medicine at Munich University at the time, so the move was convenient, but close friends knew that the arrangement was more than simple convenience, that it was an excuse for both of them to remain together.'

'What do you mean?'

The historian half smiled as she looked at Volkmann and Erica. 'Think about it. It was rather a strange relationship. Just the two of them, uncle and niece living in the same apartment together. And Geli was only twenty-three when she died. Naturally, tongues wagged in the Nazi Party about the arrangement. Hitler had always had a preference for young, fresh-faced girls – the younger the better – because he couldn't relate to women of his own age. And besides, young girls were more easily manipulated, and fell easily under his spell. Of the seven women with whom we can be reasonably sure he had intimate relationships, most of them were young. And of the seven, six committed suicide or made serious attempts to do so. So Geli Raubal wasn't alone in that regard.

'Hitler seemed to have had a mesmeric effect on women. The ones he was successful with intimately as much as the mass of German women he was to appeal to when he became Führer.

'And like a lot of women in Germany at the time, Geli Raubal found his personality magnetic. She would have done anything for him. She most certainly wanted to marry him despite the circumstance of their being related. And for a time Hitler plainly acted like a suitor. He hinted to some of his close party friends he might actually marry the girl.'

Hanah Richter looked at Volkmann and Erica. 'Repugnant as that might seem, one must remember that this was before Hitler's true brutality began to show. His career was on the rise and he had started to make a name for himself politically. He seemed to many destined to lead Germany. Geli Raubal would have gladly married her uncle, despite their age difference of nineteen years and despite the near incestuous connotations it would imply. So she flirted wildly with him, seduced him, if you like.'

The wind rattled at the clapboards again, the fire embers flickered. Volkmann stared at the flaring coals a moment, then looked back at Hanah Richter as the woman started to speak again.

'It was an absurd situation, of course, and it couldn't last. The people close to Hitler in the Nazi Party who knew what was going on were horrified: middle-aged uncle who intended marrying his very young niece. In their public lives most Nazis were outwardly moral, but inwardly we know they were vipers. And they were against it all the more because Hitler was preparing to take part in the presidential campaign.

It was a decisive time. A Nazi victory was absolutely vital. It was everything the party had struggled for. Geli Raubal was Hitler's niece and half his age. So marriage or the hint of a scandal would have been disastrous for the party. One must remember the morals of the period. Such a thing certainly wouldn't have helped Hitler's image in his public life. But in the end I think he just led the poor girl a pretty dance until he got tired of her and moved on to Eva Braun.'

Volkmann glanced over at the photograph lying on the table. 'So why did Geli Raubal kill herself?'

Hanah Richter looked away a moment, then back again. 'If we're to believe the history books, the girl was going through some kind of emotional disturbance. Probably because she realised Hitler was slowly but surely withdrawing himself from their relationship. On the 17th of September, 1931, the two had a heated argument in Hitler's Munich apartment on the Prinzregentenplatz. When Hitler was leaving, Geli Raubal calmly said goodbye to him, then went up to her room and locked herself in. The next morning she was found dead, shot through the heart at close range. There was a small-calibre pistol lying on the bedroom floor next to her. The Bavarian police determined that she had died sometime in the early hours of the 18th.

'Hitler was in Nuremberg when he heard the news of her death. Outwardly, he appeared devastated, but some of those close to him in the party thought he was actually relieved that the girl was out of his life. And of course, there were the rumours. The press at the time went wild and printed all kinds of stories.'

'What kind of rumours?'

Hanah Richter smiled at Volkmann. 'They ranged from the slightly believable to the utterly ridiculous.'

'Tell me.'

'That Hitler had the girl killed in a fit of jealousy because she was seeing someone else. Certainly he was prone to violent fits of jealousy. On one occasion it was said he broke her nose during a row. It's possible he *had* her killed, of course. He would have been quite capable of that, and just as possible his associates in the Nazi Party killed her because they saw the relationship with the girl as a threat of scandal that might ruin their hopes of power. But it's more likely the girl killed herself out of some sort of desperation. If you want my opinion I'd have to say a combination of accident and desperation – the fact that she realised Hitler was never going to marry her and wanted to end their relationship and some kind of depression. But then we shall never really know the true story.'

'What else did the newspapers say?'

Hanah Richter smiled. 'There were so many rumours, not all of them credible. The most scandalous suggested Hitler had his niece killed because the affair had got out of hand and threatened his public image. The police were called in to investigate because of the suicide and the very same rumour, but nothing came of it, and no charges were brought. There were allegations that the Minister for Justice at the time, Herr Gürtner, had the file of evidence destroyed. Certainly it disappeared and whatever evidence there was against Hitler was never found.

'After Hitler came to power, Herr Gürtner rose very quickly within the ranks of the Nazi Party, so perhaps that speaks for itself and deepens the mystery. Perhaps he did help Hitler in some way to hide the real truth, whatever it may be.' Hanah Richter shrugged. 'Certainly there was some mystery about the girl's death, but most people close to the girl thought the suicide was simply a dramatic accident that happened when she was at a low ebb, emotionally. That she was playing theatre with the gun when it went off. And I'm inclined to agree.'

Volkmann stared down at the girl's image in the Chaco photograph, the mountains in the background, the unseen hand linking hers and the Nazi swastika emblazoned on the armband.

He said quietly, 'Who do you think the other person in the photograph might be?'

'Possibly Hitler. They were still seeing each other at that time, though for a period before that Hitler tried to extricate himself from the relationship because of pressure from the party. The girl decided to make him jealous and started seeing Hitler's chauffeur, Emil Maurice. She even got secretly engaged to Maurice. When Hitler found out he flew into a rage and dismissed his chauffeur. Then Hitler started seeing the girl again secretly, until her death.'

Volkmann hesitated, then said, 'The 11th of July 1931. Can you recall anything special happening on that date?'

'You mean special for Geli Raubal?'

'Yes.'

Hanah Richter thought a moment. 'The girl died on September 18th, so your photograph would have been taken over seven weeks before her death. She had been in hospital for a minor problem a week before your date, during her semester from medical school. And about two weeks later, I believe, she stayed with some friends in Freiburg. In between she saw Hitler a number of times, but he was busy with the presidential campaign and didn't have much time for the girl.' Hanah Richter thought again, her brow furrowed in concentration, then finally said, 'No, I'm sorry. The date you mention is not one that sticks in my mind. Believe me, if it was, I'd remember.'

'One more question. Did the girl ever visit South America?'

The elderly woman shook her head. 'No, definitely not. She only ever travelled in Germany and Austria.' She looked from Erica to Volkmann. 'Has your question got something to do with how you came to have the photograph?'

Volkmann nodded and said, 'The name Erhard Schmeltz, does it mean anything to you?'

'In what connection?'

'In connection with Geli Raubal.'

The historian frowned. 'Who was Erhard Schmeltz?'

'A Nazi Party member. Someone Hitler knew when he served in the First War.'

The historian shook her head slowly. 'Well, whoever he was, he mustn't have been very important. I don't recall having heard the name in connection with either Hitler or the girl. Not ever.'

'Have you any idea, Hanah, how a photograph such as this could have ended up in South America?'

'You're absolutely certain it was an original and not a copy?'

'Yes.'

'So many Germans emigrated to South America at the end of the war. The photograph could have been taken there by someone close to Hitler or the girl.' Hanah Richter shrugged. 'As to who, I haven't the faintest idea. People like Eichmann and Mengele never knew her. And Bormann, well, he would have known her, certainly met her often socially, but the possibility of him having survived the war and escaping to South America has been well and truly eliminated. Possibly a close friend, or a high-ranking Nazi official or trusted SS. But who, I'm afraid, I couldn't possibly suggest.' The historian paused, looked pointedly at her watch and said, 'Does that answer all your questions?'

Volkmann stared down at the photograph in his hand then looked up at the woman and nodded. 'Thank you for your time, Hanah. Our apologies for keeping you up so late.'

'That's quite all right.' The woman smiled and stood up.

As Volkmann replaced the photograph in his wallet, Hanah Richter said, 'I would appreciate a copy of that for my files, if you could send me one?'

'Of course.'

Hanah Richter shook both their hands and led them to the door. The taxi was still outside and as they stood in the open porch, Volkmann turned to the woman.

'Geli Raubal, do you know where she was buried?'

'In Vienna. The old Central Cemetery.'

'Is the grave still there?'

Hanah Richter shook her head. 'I'm afraid the Nazi authorities in Vienna had that part of the cemetery destroyed in 1941. The grave and all others around it were completely razed.'

'Why?'

'Heaven knows. It seems most strange. No one I ever spoke to about the matter knew who issued the order. I suppose it only added to the whole mystery of the girl's death.'

'Do you think the Nazis wanted to cover something up?'

'You mean about the girl's death? It's possible, considering the circumstances of her death were never fully explained. But then we've no way of ever knowing.'

Volkmann hesitated. 'There is one last thing, Hanah.'

'Yes?'

'Geli Raubal – you said she was a hospital patient. When?'

'In late June 1931. She spent a few days in a private nursing home in Garmisch-Partenkirchen.'

'What was she being treated for?'

'Some said depression, because Hitler had spurned her and was secretly seeing his new mistress, Eva Braun. Others said she went in for minor surgery. I have no way of knowing. And certainly you won't find any hospital records. They would have been long ago lost or destroyed, I'm sure. Why do you ask?'

Volkmann felt the biting wind coming in across the lake waters, glimpsed the waiting taxi-driver in his cab, drumming his fingers impatiently against the steering wheel as he stared at them through the glass.

Volkmann turned back, saw Erica pull up her coat collar against the icy wind. Hanah Richter waited, shivering, for the question to be answered.

For a long time Volkmann seemed to hesitate, then he said, 'This proposition may seem absurd, Hanah. But could Geli Raubal have been pregnant?'

Hanah Richter raised her eyebrows and looked at him.

'Actually, that supposition was suggested as one of the reasons why the girl might have been murdered by Hitler or his people. But it was never proven. A journalist at the time, a man named Fritz Gerlich, claimed the girl was pregnant and Hitler had her killed for that reason. But the story was never published.'

'What happened to Gerlich?'

'He was arrested and later murdered in Dachau. But really his information was never proven. And there were other reasons the Nazis would have wanted Gerlich dead, besides that story.'

'What reasons, Hanah?'

'Gerlich owned the newspaper he wrote for. The paper was strongly anti-Nazi. Many of its articles and editorials had condemned Hitler before he came to power.' Hanah Richter paused. 'But why do you ask?'

Volkmann hesitated. 'What if Geli Raubal already had a child?'

'You mean by Hitler?'

'Yes.'

Volkmann saw the woman's expression change. She stood in the doorway, open-mouthed, the question totally unexpected, a look of utter amazement on her face. Erica looked at him too, a white stricken look that for a moment made her look ill.

Then Hanah Richter stared at Volkmann and said incredulously, 'Really, Herr Volkmann, something like that would *never* have escaped the history books.'

He saw the woman's expression of amazement become disbelief. Then suddenly the disbelief turned to irritation as she hunched her shoulders against the biting cold and shivered.

'You can't *possibly* be serious?'

Volkmann said quietly. 'No, of course not, Hanah. You've been most kind. Thank you for your help.'

Chapter Forty-Six

They hadn't spoken during the entire journey in the taxi back from the lakeshore house. Volkmann stared out at the lights of Berlin from the cab window, but said nothing.

When they pulled up outside the hotel off the Kurfürstendamm, the girl had looked at him, a troubled look on her face, the after- shock of the question he had posed the historian half an hour before still evident on her face.

As soon as they had stepped into their room, Volkmann went to pour them both a drink. He saw Erica stare at him as he handed her a half-tumbler of scotch. She took it and crossed to the window before she looked back at him palely.

'What you said to Hanah Richter, you really meant it, didn't you, Joe? That the girl could have been pregnant? That she could have had a child by Adolf Hitler?'

'Yes.'

'But Joe, that's absurd.'

There was tension in Volkmann's voice as he put down the glass and said, 'Erica, it fits the jigsaw. It fits everything we know and don't know about the identity of Karl Schmeltz. And you heard what Hanah Richter said. The girl could have been pregnant. It was also a likely reason she might have been killed or committed suicide. Everything Hanah Richter told us tonight explains the puzzle about Karl Schmeltz. Surely you see that?'

Erica Kranz stared back at him. 'I can accept that the girl could have been pregnant. But that she actually had a child? Joe, how could it be possible? As Hanah Richter said, such a thing could *never* have escaped the history books. If Hitler had fathered a child, it could *never* have been kept a secret all these years?'

Volkmann heard the strain of incredulity in the girl's voice.

She ignored her drink but Volkmann quickly swallowed his scotch and put down the glass.

'It sounds crazy, Erica, I know, but it also makes some kind of sense. Just *think* about it. Erhard Schmeltz and his sister emigrate to South America from Germany in mysterious circumstances in late 1931 two months after Geli Raubal's death. They take with them a boy who's obviously not their son. Remember what Wilhelm Busch said about Schmeltz? He didn't have any children and had never married. As for Schmeltz's sister, she was older than her brother, most likely too old to have a child that young. So that discounts either of them.'

The girl looked at him. 'But the child *could* have belonged to one of them, Joe. It's not impossible to imagine. Either of them could still have been the child's natural parent.'

'If the child belonged to one of them, then why did they leave Germany so mysteriously? Why suddenly disappear? And I told you what Busch said about the rumours that went around when Schmeltz and his sister vanished. One of them was that Schmeltz had been sent away secretly. The circumstances suggest the boy most likely wasn't theirs. So who did he belong to?'

There was a mounting excitement in Volkmann's voice as he looked at her. 'Erhard Schmeltz was a loyal and close friend of Adolf Hitler. And his party membership application was recommended by Himmler which suggests he was on good terms with those at the top of the party. People he had served with in the First War. People he knew as friends and who accepted his loyalty. Now consider what Hanah Richter said: Hitler had been having an affair with Geli Raubal, an affair that was well known among Hitler's friends and close acquaintances.'

Volkmann crossed to the window, turned back to look at Erica. 'According to Hanah Richter, two months before Geli Raubal was found dead in her uncle's apartment, she was a patient in a private nursing home. When she comes out she's under stress, something troubling her. It must have been something significant, because two months later the girl supposedly kills herself. Whether Hitler had her killed or she committed suicide isn't relevant.

'But what *is* relevant is what could have been troubling her. The girl's in love with Hitler. She wants to marry him. So why did she kill herself? Hanah Richter said Hitler had spurned the girl. That he was preparing for the presidential elections and it was vital for him to win or at least gain ground for the Nazi Party. The last thing he needed at that time was the kind of scandal his relationship with the girl might have caused . . .'

'But Joe, that the girl could have had a child. It's just not possible.'

'Why isn't it possible? You admitted the girl could have been pregnant. What if she *was* expecting a child by Hitler? According to Hanah Richter, the two were lovers. What if the reason the girl went into hospital in Garmisch-Partenkirchen was because she was expecting a child by her uncle? Hitler knows or learns about it, realises the whole affair could ruin his career. *Think* about it. If the girl *had* been pregnant, if that kind of news had got out, Hitler would have been ruined, politically and every other way. Just like Hanah Richter said: He may have dragged the Nazi Party down with him because of the scandal. So he, or those closest to him, come up with a plan. Send the child away, somewhere a long way from Germany. And with someone Hitler could trust. A couple like the Schmeltzes would have been ideal. Erhard Schmeltz was a loyal, trustworthy Nazi and a close friend of Hitler's. And the place they emigrated to with the child couldn't have been more remote, a jungle region in Paraguay, so the secret is safe.'

He saw Erica look at him palely, and he stared down at her. 'That scenario would explain three things, Erica. Three very important things. One, the amount of money Schmeltz had when he arrived in Paraguay. Two, the fact of his sudden emigration just before Hitler prepares for the presidential election. Three, the drafts from the Nazi Reichsbank sent to Paraguay right up until 1945. Someone high up had to sanction such large sums of money. And only someone high up would have the authority to keep it secret and unrecorded.

'If we're to believe what Wilhelm Busch said, Erhard Schmeltz wasn't a rich man. And a man who had fallen foul of the Nazi Party doesn't receive money from the Reichsbank. Nor does he keep his party membership *in absentia*. And blackmail's out because if that was the case then Schmeltz wouldn't have had the child *with* him.' Volkmann looked intently at Erica. 'That still leaves the question of whether Schmeltz was hoarding the money for someone else. I don't believe he was. The money he received was sent through the Reichsbank, and no Nazi would have done that. They would have used some anonymous Swiss bank. Only Hitler or a very high-ranking Nazi would have had the kind of authority to use the Reichsbank. So that suggests only one remaining possibility. The money was sent to Schmeltz to support him and his sister and the boy. Geli Raubal's and Hitler's son.

'The very fact that we found the girl's photograph at the house in the Chaco confirms the link between Erhard Schmeltz and Geli Raubal. And you heard what Hanah Richter said about the girl's relationship with Hitler. If she had an affair with him, why couldn't it be possible she had a child by him?'

He saw Erica shake her head. 'But if what you're saying is true, then why didn't Hitler have her abort the pregnancy?'

'Maybe the girl didn't tell him until it was too late. Maybe she wanted the child and didn't want to tell him until that solution wasn't possible. And even if the girl *did* commit suicide she must have been desperate over something. Something very emotional was hanging over her. She also could have been depressed after the birth. And if Hitler had refused to marry her or acknowledge the child and wanted the whole affair covered up by sending the boy away, it might have been enough to send the girl over the edge.'

'But there must have been people who knew? People who would have talked about such a thing. It couldn't have been kept secret after all these years. It just *couldn't*.'

'Geli Raubal was a medical student, Erica. She could have got help from friends or contacts in the profession, people who would have helped her keep her secret. Medical people who could have helped her with the birth. Isn't that possible? And you heard what Hanah Richter said about the journalist who was sent to Dachau. What if he had heard the truth? What if *that* was the reason he was killed?'

He saw Erica stare at him, hesitate, then shake her head. 'Joe, there are too many ifs. Believe me, part of me wants to accept what you're saying, because it does make some kind of sense. But another part of me is saying it's crazy.'

Volkmann looked at her intently. 'Then consider this. Why did the Nazis destroy the part of the cemetery in Vienna where the girl was buried? Why did they want to destroy Geli Raubal's grave? There could only be one reason. There was a secret someone wanted to hide. Geli Raubal's secret. A post mortem could have determined if the girl had given birth. Destroying the grave meant destroying the evidence.'

He saw the look on Erica's face. She was pale and her eyes looked away vacantly. As if she had given up trying to dissuade him. He heard his own laboured breathing, the thought of what he had said dizzying. He saw Erica stare up at him.

'Then answer me this, Joe. Why didn't whoever wanted to keep the secret simply get rid of the girl's body? Why didn't they destroy the evidence that way?'

'Maybe they did.'

'I don't understand?'

'By removing the girl's body and destroying the graves around it, it would have made it impossible for anyone to know whether the girl's corpse had been removed from the grave or not. All that remained would have been a tangle of unidentifiable bones. That way any subsequent forensic examination could never have determined identities.'

There were beads of perspiration on his brow as he looked at the girl. 'Consider everything I've said and how it connects to the present, to everything that's been happening. To Rudi's death, to the other deaths. Why sanitise a house in a remote jungle? Why destroy all traces of occupation in the Chaco property? Why be so obsessive about secrecy? What had those people in the Chaco *really* got to hide, Erica? Not a simple smuggling operation. Not simply a connection to Rudi's death and the others. But something that goes far deeper. Not only about the present, but the past. You sensed something at the Chaco house, remember? We all did.'

'Joe . . .' The girl opened her mouth to speak, but she broke off.

He saw the tension in her face, her mouth set grimly, before the blue eyes looked away. There was a hopeless look on her face that said it all, as if she had tried hard to convince him he was wrong and failed.

He knew what he was suggesting was unreal, but it had a strange kind of truth and the thought made him shiver violently as he looked at her, his voice thick with emotion.

'There's only one possible answer that can explain Karl Schmeltz's identity, Erica. *Karl Schmeltz is Adolf Hitler's son.*'

The girl's face had drained of colour, and as she stood there Volkmann saw a look of utter distress in her eyes, as if she were still trying to decide something.

For a long time neither of them spoke, as if the awesome possibility that had joined them in the stillness of the room lingered like a living thing. Then Erica's voice came to him, suddenly hoarse and distant.

'What are you going to do, Joe?'

There was no emotion in her voice as she spoke and he looked back at her. 'Tell Ferguson and Peters, and just hope they believe everything I've said.'

'You think they will?'

'When they hear the evidence, yes, I think they will.'

The girl said flatly. 'And then?'

'Find Karl Schmeltz. Because he's part of what's happening, Erica. He's part of everything that's happened and is about to happen.'

He looked at her, held her stare. He spoke quietly, and for the first time he heard a real fear in his own voice.

'The voices on the tape Rudi recorded. The voices on the tape and what Busch said was promised in Hitler's bunker. They're talking about the same thing, Erica. The voices on the tape are talking about the same Brandenburg. What happened over sixty years ago in Germany when the Nazis came to power.' Volkmann paused, looked into her face. 'I think it's going to happen all over again.'

Stockholm.
December 23rd,
6.15 a.m.

The girl behind the SAS check-in desk at Stockholm's Arlanda airport watched as the swarthy-looking young man approached.

He wore an expensive camel-haired overcoat and a pale grey Armani suit that complemented his dark complexion. Good-looking, maybe thirty, good figure, but sad eyes.

The girl smiled. 'Good morning, sir.'

The man nodded silently and handed across his first-class tickets.

The girl typed in the details on the computer, Stockholm to Amsterdam, noticed the man had an onward connection to Berlin. As she checked in the man's leather suitcase, she smiled up at him. He smiled back; a shy smile. It was a pity he couldn't see her long legs tucked behind the desk; maybe she could have coaxed a date.

She completed the details on the computer and handed the man back his tickets and boarding card, noticing the name on the first-class ticket. As the man took them she noticed his hands. Strong hands, but criss-crossed with a web of thick pink scars that made her shudder inside. A definite turn-off.

'You may board straight away, Mr Kemal.'

'Thank you.'

She forced a smile. 'Are you travelling on business or pleasure, Mr Kemal?'

'Business.'

'I hope you have a nice trip.'

The man turned, unsmiling, and walked towards the boarding area.

Chapter Forty-Four

Genoa.
Thursday,
December 22nd,
11.57 p.m.

'Franco . . .?'

The voice came to him out of the darkness.

Franco Scali turned over sleepily in the warm bed and muttered, 'What . . .?'

A finger prodded him. 'Franco, there's someone at the door.'

Franco opened his eyes. The bedroom was pitch black.

'What time is it?' he called out to his wife.

'Midnight.'

Franco moaned as he heard the buzzing doorbell in the distance. He blinked, looked over at the bedroom window. The curtains were closed, but through a chink he could see the sky black beyond. He and Rosa had gone to bed early after spending the day Christmas shopping at the Loggia dei Mercanti; the kids had been dispatched to his parents for the night while he and his wife wrapped the presents. Afterwards, they had had supper and gone to bed early, totally exhausted. Now he felt Rosa's hand on his shoulder, shaking him.

'Franco . . .?'

'I heard you, woman.'

Franco threw back the sheets and dragged himself from the warm bed, felt the chill of the room. He flicked on the bedside lamp, blinked as the harsh light flooded the bedroom. He turned and heard Rosa moan as she pulled back the bedcover, Franco catching a glimpse of her pale, fleshy legs as the bell rang again downstairs, a couple of short, urgent bursts.

545

'Who the hell is it at this hour?' Franco grumbled.

'I think it's Aldo Celli. When I heard the bell I got up and thought I saw his car outside.'

'Then why didn't you answer the door?' Franco moaned.

'It might not be him,' his wife answered sharply. 'I said I *think* it's him. I'm not sure.' She moaned and turned over again, dragging the covers with her.

Franco sighed. *Lazy bitch*.

Aldo. Aldo the Eagle. The craneman at the docks. What the fuck did he want at this hour? Franco dragged on his dressing gown and went downstairs. When he unlocked and opened the front door he saw big Aldo standing under the porch light, his collar pulled up against the cold. Franco shivered as a blast of chilled air came in the open door.

'What the hell is this, Aldo? You know what time it is?'

'Can I come in, Franco?'

Franco hesitated, then sighed and led the big man into the sitting-room. He turned on the light first, then dragged up a chair for Aldo.

Franco said, 'What the fuck's up?'

Aldo's big, fleshy face showed concern. 'One of the juggernauts, it brought in a container in the evening, about eight o'clock. Il Peste was on the late shift. After I dropped the container, Il Peste came down and looked at the number. Then he had us open the container and he started using the duster and sniffing around.'

'So?'

Aldo blinked as he looked at Franco. 'I asked him what was up. He said it was a container that came in from South America twelve days ago. One he wanted to recheck.'

Franco's stomach churned.

'He found something, Franco,' Aldo went on.

Franco raised his eyes in mock surprise. 'What do you mean?'

'The side of the container, there was a hidden compartment held in by some screws. Pretty neat job, you never would have thought it was there. But Il Peste kept tapping away until he found it.'

Franco tried to hide his fear. An effort. Already he felt the sweat on his palms but he pretended surprise.

'Why you telling me?'

'The cops came. They seemed pretty interested. They took all our fingerprints, said they want us to stay back after our shift if necessary, in case they needed to talk with us. Something about the container . . .'

Franco felt his legs begin to go from under him. 'Go on . . .'

'Then Il Peste wanted to know when you were rostered on again. I told him you had a couple of days off for Christmas. I heard him mention your name to one of the cops. A detective named Orsati. Then I heard one of them say they'd call on you sometime this morning.'

Franco felt his stomach churn, tried not to throw up all over Aldo's shoes.

The big craneman stood up. 'I just thought I'd slip out and tell you, seeing you're the boss. Give you some idea what's happening. I got a feeling there's going to be trouble, Franco. The cops and customs, they're swarming all over the place like fucking ants.'

Franco nodded, managed a faint smile. 'You did right, coming here, I mean. If there's going to be trouble, I'll need to be prepared.'

'That's what I thought.' The craneman glanced at his watch. 'I'd better be getting back. The cops might get suspicious if I'm away for long.'

Franco felt his legs suddenly buckle under him as he pushed himself up from the chair. He braced himself, made a supreme effort. *Jesus Maria* . . .

'There's something else . . .' said Aldo, moving towards the door, then hesitating, still looking worried.

'What?' Franco almost croaked. It couldn't be anything worse.

'They want to check everybody's personal locker. They started an hour ago. A couple of guys said no.' Aldo swallowed. 'Maybe they got stuff in there, you know? Stuff they shouldn't have. But the cops, they made them open them

547

. . .' Aldo paused. 'They'll want to do the same with yours, Franco.'

Franco swallowed. 'Did they find anything? The ones they checked?'

'Nothing worth talking about. There's only yours and four of the other guys still left to check.'

Franco nodded. There was sweat on his back now, he could feel it, damp beneath his pyjamas, his legs still trembling. He managed to follow Aldo towards the door, saw him open it, ready to let himself out.

Then Franco said, in a low voice, almost a whisper. 'Aldo . . . I got to ask you something . . .'

'What?'

'The cops . . . where are they? On the apron?'

'There and everywhere. Looking, sniffing. They even got their four-legged friends in. Some Christmas present from Il Peste, huh?'

Franco chewed his lower lip, then said, 'My locker . . . you think you could get near it without the cops seeing you?'

Aldo went to say something, then hesitated. In the darkness of the porch Franco couldn't see the man's face clearly. He didn't want to. Yet he knew; knew this was why the big man had *really* come. An unspoken code among the men. Trouble for one meant trouble for all.

Aldo hesitated, then said, 'Franco, I don't want to get in no trouble with the cops . . .'

'Aldo, it's nothing big. Nothing important. Just something personal.'

Aldo thought for a long time, then he shrugged. 'OK, what do you want me to do?'

'There's an old tin biscuit box on the top shelf. Get rid of it for me.'

'What's in there?'

'Just some stuff. Bits and pieces.'

'Franco, the place is crawling with customs and cops . . .'

'Aldo, *please*, man, just do as I ask.'

'I don't want no trouble, *amico* . . .'

'No trouble, I promise. Just take out the box and throw it

in the water. But not near the apron.' He paused, put a hand lightly on the craneman's big shoulder. 'You do this for me, I owe you.'

Aldo hesitated, considering the proposition, then finally he said, 'I'll need a key, Franco. A key to your locker.'

'There's a spare one in the filing cabinet upstairs in my office, bottom drawer. If anyone's around, just tell them you gotta check some paperwork. There won't be no problem.'

'You're sure?'

'Sure. I swear.'

Aldo swallowed before he nodded. 'OK. I'll do it.'

Franco beamed. 'Thanks, Aldo.' He let his hand fall, shook his head. 'Hey, man, I won't forget this, really I won't.'

Franco went back to the bedroom, threw off his dressing gown and dragged on his clothes, feeling ill, feeling like he wanted to die.

Rosa came awake. 'What's wrong?'

Franco said, 'Nothing. Go back to sleep.'

She sat up, slowly. 'Who was at the door?'

'No one. You must have been dreaming, woman.'

'I heard the bell, voices downstairs.'

'You heard nothing. I gotta go out for ten minutes. Get some air. You got me up, now I can't sleep.'

Rosa protested, but Franco wasn't listening. It took him less than three minutes to dress and get down the stairs, lock the front door and reach the Fiat. He had told Rosa not to answer the door if anyone called. The woman knew better than to argue.

He drove to the Piazza della Vittoria, found an international kiosk and inserted one of the plastic cards he always kept in the glove compartment and punched in the number from the slip of paper in his wallet.

The Piazza wasn't deserted, people still coming out of the restaurants and the late-night bars in festive spirit. Their cheerful voices seemed to depress him even more. A couple of car horns hooted and suddenly a flock of sleeping pigeons rose off the statue on the square, the sudden eruption of noise causing Franco's heart to jump, beat even faster.

The number rang. It took a couple of seconds of fearful, crushing silence before the receiver was lifted and Franco heard the voice at the other end.

'*Ja?*'

Franco didn't speak German. For a moment he hesitated, flustered, his legs shaking as he panicked.

Again, the voice said, '*Ja?*'

Franco said, 'You speak Italian?'

A pause. The voice said, '*Si.*'

Franco sighed, a big, long sigh and said, 'Then listen, *amico*. We've got us a problem . . .'

Strasbourg.
December 23rd

They managed to get seats on the 7 a.m. shuttle from Berlin and they landed in Frankfurt just after eight.

Volkmann had left the Ford in the airport car park and they drove down to Strasbourg, reaching the DSE office by eleven-thirty.

He had telephoned Peters' secretary on the way from the airport, telling her he'd be back in Strasbourg before noon and requesting an urgent meeting with Peters and Ferguson. The girl said she'd make sure Peters got the message.

Volkmann parked the Ford in the underground lot and when they went up he left Erica waiting in his office while he went in search of Peters.

He found him in his office, talking with Ferguson's secretary, and as Volkmann entered, Peters came towards him.

'Joe, I'm glad you made it back, something's come up . . .'

'We need to talk, Tom. *Urgently*. Didn't you get my message?'

'I got it.' Peters saw the look on Volkmann's face and said, 'Is everything OK?'

'Where's Ferguson?'

'Gone to an early seasonal lunch with the Section Heads.'

Peters saw the look of frustration on Volkmann's face and turned to the secretary behind him and smiled as he said, 'Can you leave us, Marion?'

When the girl had gone, Peters said, 'What's this about, Joe?'

'I'd rather wait until Ferguson's here, Tom. I'd rather discuss it with both of you present.'

Peters recognised the urgency in Volkmann's voice but said, 'I'm afraid it'll have to wait. Something's come up, something important maybe. And Ferguson won't be back until the afternoon.'

'What's come up?'

'You're going to love this, old son. I got a call from the Carabinieri Headquarters in Genoa. They think their people have found something that fits in with our request to the Italian Desk. They want us to take a look at a container that came in on a ship called the *Maria Escobar* on the ninth of this month.'

'Where from?'

Peters smiled. 'Montevideo. I told them you'd be on the next available plane.'

'How long have I got?'

'There's an Al Italia flight from Frankfurt in under two hours. A return flight tonight at nine. You're booked both ways, pick up the tickets at the airport. You ought to just make it back unless something develops. I've already arranged a private charter from Strasbourg to Frankfurt-Main. It's waiting at the airport now.'

'What about our meeting?'

'I'll set it up for this evening at Ferguson's place. Phone me the minute you get back.'

Volkmann said, 'Do me a favour, Tom. While I'm gone, stay with the girl.'

Peters frowned. 'Any particular reason?'

'I just think she'd feel safer.'

He spoke with Erica before he left for the airport. He told her not to talk with Peters or Ferguson about anything concerning the case until he returned, that it was a matter of protocol.

A few moments later Peters came into the office and he introduced them.

Peters said charmingly, 'How about I take the young lady to lunch, Joe? Then I can drive her back to your place.' He smiled. 'Pretty much everyone's finishing early for the holidays. I'll leave a note on Ferguson's desk about the meeting, tell him it's imperative we talk.'

Five minutes later Volkmann left them.

As he drove to the airport, there was a knot of tension in his stomach like a ball of steel.

Chapter Forty-Eight

Strasbourg.
December 23rd,
3.02 p.m.

It had started to snow as Peters drove up outside the apartment on the Quai Ernest.

He parked in the courtyard and he and the girl went up. She had been subdued during their lunch in Petite France and Peters guessed something was troubling her, but he hadn't pressed her to talk.

When they stepped into Volkmann's apartment, he could see that she had made herself at home and had tidied the rooms, here and there small items rearranged since he had last visited and he began to sense that there was something between Volkmann and the girl.

A little later he excused himself as she made coffee and he went to the bathroom. On the way back he paused in the hallway and stepped into Volkmann's bedroom. The bed was made but he could smell the lingering scent of the girl's perfume. Her clothes were in Volkmann's open wardrobe and her make-up bag lay by the bed.

He stepped outside into the hallway again and opened the door to the second bedroom. The bed was made but the air in the room was odourless, the room tidy but unused.

As he stepped back into the living-room she came out of the kitchen. 'I never asked if you take sugar and milk?'

Peters smiled. 'Both. Two spoonfuls.'

She went back into the kitchen and Peters lit a cigarette and went to stand at the window. Flakes of snow drifted against the glass and Peters stood there, smoking, reflecting on the situation. It was really none of his business, Volkmann and the girl. He had been too long in the game to think that human nature could be suppressed, even in a situation like this, Volkmann's and the girl's backgrounds being so disparate. Ferguson might frown on it because it was unprofessional, but even those at the top knew that it sometimes happened, especially when the female case you were minding was young and pretty and intelligent.

But in Volkmann's case it came as a surprise. What Peters knew of the man, it wasn't his style. He had always kept to the straight and narrow and getting involved wasn't one of his weaknesses. Especially with a German girl. And especially with this one, as Peters recalled the line he had read in her personal file.

As he moved away from the window and went to flick on the remote control for the television, the girl came back in holding two mugs of steaming coffee. Peters took his and sat down, flicking a mote of cigarette ash from his white shirt.

As he leaned forward to pick up his coffee again he saw her stare at his waist. He looked down. The holstered Beretta was visible, clipped to his trouser belt. He looked up and saw the girl stare briefly at him before turning away. Without another word he stood and unclipped the weapon from his belt and placed it on his overcoat, then he sat back down again.

The Mercedes drove up and down the Quai four times and then halted outside the apartment block. Snow brushed against the car's windows and the wipers were on.

The passenger checked the address again and then nodded to the driver before he pulled up the collar of his raincoat and stepped out into the snow.

As the man disappeared into the courtyard the driver sat there, tapping his hand on the steering wheel, the engine still running, his eyes scanning the Quai. The traffic was thin as occasional amber headlamps swished past in the growing darkness, and besides, in the poor weather the man knew that people took less notice of what was happening around them, concentrating on the road ahead.

Three minutes later the passenger returned and climbed

back into the car, his hair and raincoat flecked with snow. The driver turned the heater up further and the passenger wiped his wet face with a big hand.

The passenger said, in German, 'It's the right apartment. Volkmann's name's on the doorbell. There's a window at the back. Two people inside. A man and a woman.'

The driver checked his watch. 'OK. Once more around the block, then we come back.'

As the Mercedes pulled out from the kerb the passenger reached under his seat and took out the two silenced pistols.

Genoa.
3.15 p.m.

Franco Scali stood at the entrance to the warehouse as the unmarked police car drew up and the detectives climbed out, holstered guns visible beneath their open winter overcoats.

When the guy in the back seat climbed out too, and Franco heard him talk briefly with one of the detectives in English, he was glad he had made the phone call. The whole thing was going to be big trouble. Franco sensed it.

He felt lousy, exhausted, unable to sleep after making the call, fear racking his body. He felt stressed, tingling pains arcing across his chest, was surprised he was still able to stand, his legs like rubber.

They had called to his home at eight that morning, two cops, told him they wanted to take him to the warehouse, see his paperwork on the container, ask him some questions. Franco had tried to play it like it was no big deal. *Sure, no problem*. But those guys could smell if you were shit-scared, they had a nose for it, and Franco guessed they sensed his apprehension.

They had taken his fingerprints first in the office upstairs, sent a cop away with the prints to police headquarters. He wasn't worried about that, he'd worn gloves when he had removed the box from the compartment. Then the cops had asked him some questions about the container. When one of them had asked him if he had anything he wanted to tell him, Franco shrugged, said no, of course not.

And they had nothing to nail him with. Even the stuff in his locker was gone, Aldo had seen to that. Good old Aldo; he owed him one.

Besides, the men he had dealt with had said they would help. Exactly how, Franco hadn't a fucking clue. But it better happen *fast*. He was buying time, that was all. Trying to think things through, find a crack of light in the blackness as exhaustion flooded in on him. When the cops finished, Franco had asked if he could go.

'We've got to wait,' the cop said. 'Some other people want to ask you some questions.'

'What people? What questions?' Franco had asked.

'Just wait. It won't be long,' the cop had merely said.

Franco had gone outside the warehouse for a smoke, tried to eat a little pizza one of the guys had brought him. He had to force himself. Appetite he hadn't got but he wanted to appear normal. For over seven hours now it had been an effort. Darkness slowly falling, the hours passing like years, his stomach so full of stinging acid Franco felt he would pass out with the nausea. When he had complained about his detention, the Carabinieri had ignored him.

And then the car had drawn up and the men climbed out. Then Franco had really begun to sweat.

Now Franco forced himself to smile as an Italian detective with a bushy moustache introduced himself – Orsati – and then the other man.

'*Signore* Volkmann, meet Franco Scali.'

Franco shook the man's hand firmly, so he wouldn't feel his own hand shaking. The men watched him with the eyes of hawks.

'*Ciao*,' Franco said.

The detective said, 'Let's start with the container.'

Franco forced himself to smile. 'Sure.'

The detective led the way.

3.35 p.m.

The Fiat carrying Beck and Kleins drove into the dockyard and came to a halt a hundred metres from the warehouse. There had been so many police cars on the apron no one had bothered to stop them.

As Beck switched off the engine, Kleins looked at his watch, then looked back up at the cars parked outside the warehouse. A hundred metres away on the apron the knot of men stood gathered around the big blue container.

Kleins reached behind him for the powerful Zeiss binoculars and focused on the men.

Volkmann stood on the dock apron, a soft breeze blowing in off the sea beyond the harbour end. The Klieg lights were on overhead, the powerful light flooding the area and the Carabinieri had sealed off part of the apron with rolls of yellow plastic ribbon.

A customs official, whom Orsati explained to Volkmann had discovered the compartment, came up and talked rapidly with the detective, then the fat official led them across the apron to the blue container with the three grey-striped markings.

Volkmann saw that a plate had been removed from the side and it lay on the ground, perfectly matching the gaping, quarter-metre-wide hole it had covered. The fat customs official beamed over at them.

Volkmann said to the detective, 'How did he find it?'

'He tapped the insides with a knuckle-duster. There was a slight difference in the metal sound towards the right end wall. But he knows of this container. Last time it was on the docks he suspected it, but didn't have time to do a thorough check.'

Orsati knelt beside the container, stared in at the small chamber within the gaping hole. Then he looked up at Volkmann and said, 'You want to take a look?'

Volkmann nodded and Orsati handed across a slim pencil

torch. Volkmann knelt down and flicked on the torch, probed inside the empty chamber. He saw the twin brackets welded onto the inner metal frame, left and right sides, maybe one-quarter of a metre apart. The chamber smelled of paint and rust. He stood and turned to glance at Scali. The clerk looked at him uncertainly.

Volkmann said to Orsati, 'Does Scali speak English?'

The detective turned to the clerk and asked him a question. Scali shrugged, said something in reply.

Orsati said, 'He says he doesn't speak English.'

'What do you think? You think he knows something?'

The detective smiled. 'Yes, I think he knows something. Whoever used the chamber, they may have needed inside help. Someone like Scali would be a good choice.'

'Did you find his prints in the chamber?'

'No. But I found something else. I've got a little surprise in store for him.'

When Volkmann asked what, the detective explained. Volkmann nodded and glanced back towards the clerk. The man looked worried, no question, but trying to hide it and failing.

'There's an office in the warehouse,' the detective said. 'But let me talk with him first. When I'm finished, believe me, Franco Scali will tell us everything he knows.'

'You want me to wait outside?'

The detective shrugged. 'Sure, why not. When Franco's sung his aria, I'll call you in.'

Kleins saw the knot of people around the container move away towards the warehouse. He picked out Scali with the Zeiss. He nodded to Beck who reached behind on the seat for the two briefcases.

It took less than a minute to assemble the two Heckler and Koch MP 5K machine-pistols and slam home the magazines. When they looked up they saw the knot of people reach the warehouse.

Kleins pulled back the cocking handle of his weapon, flicked his safety catch to off, and Beck did likewise.

Strasbourg.
3.55 p.m.

Ferguson sat in the office, snow falling outside. He had arrived back late from lunch with the Section Heads and saw the note from Peters about the meeting with Volkmann, Peters stressing it was urgent. There was a postscript to the note saying Peters was at Volkmann's apartment with the girl. He wondered what it was about, guessed it had something to do with Volkmann's investigation, and was about to telephone Volkmann's apartment when the telephone rang and he picked up the receiver.

Jan De Vries came on the line and told him a classified communication had arrived from Asunción for his attention, marked urgent, and he was delivering it to him personally.

Three minutes later De Vries arrived. He appeared subdued and Ferguson had waited until the man had left the office before breaking the waxed seal and opening the envelope.

Inside he found the signal and he read it slowly. And as he read his face drained of colour. Ferguson put down the signal and stood and crossed to the window, ashen-faced. He stood there for a full minute, in silence, in disbelief, oblivious to the snow brushing against the glass, then he crossed back to the desk and picked up the signal and read it again.

When he had finished this time, he hesitated, but only briefly, before picking up the telephone and quickly punching in the numbers. When the line clicked and rang out and he got no reply, Ferguson clicked the cradle with his free hand and thought a moment, his brow furrowed intensely in concentration, then he hit the receiver cradle smartly again and began to punch in numbers once more.

Had he stayed at the window he would have seen the black Mercedes draw up in front of the building and the two rain-coated men climb out, one of them carrying a briefcase.

They entered the building ten seconds later, showed their identity cards at the security desk, then crossed the lobby and moved towards the lift.

*   *   *

A kilometre away on the Quai Ernest another two men stepped out of their parked Mercedes into falling snow.

They walked purposefully across the white courtyard and climbed the steps. When they halted outside Volkmann's apartment, the driver of the car nodded to his partner. Both men opened their raincoats and withdrew silenced pistols.

While the driver scanned the courtyard below, the second man took a heavy bunch of keys from his pocket.

He selected one and tried it in the lock.

Chapter Forty-Nine

Genoa.
3.55 p.m.

The office on the warehouse ground floor was airless and claustrophobic, even though it had a clear view of the dock apron and beyond the warehouse through two wide, panoramic windows.

As soon as Franco was led inside he felt the panic coming on. He glanced briefly at the detective, Orsati, and the man stared back.

Franco swallowed, sensing what was coming, but knowing he had to act this one out. A real performance; otherwise he was finished.

There was a table that served as a desk and a couple of chairs. Someone had cleared the desk and Orsati told Franco to sit.

The second detective was young, in his late twenties, his black hair cropped short. He and Il Peste remained standing while Orsati produced a notebook and pen, like he was going to take notes. Il Peste was there, Franco guessed, because he wanted a fucking medal from the Italian customs service. *Fuck you*, Franco thought. *I'll deny everything.*

Orsati pulled back his coat and put his hands on his hips, showed the butt of his holstered pistol, a smile on the man's face now, perfect white teeth showing as he spoke.

'I'd like to ask you some questions, Franco. I want to help you, so I'd like you to think hard before you answer. It's easy to tell lies, *amico*. But lies only get you deep in trouble. And I don't think you want that, do you?'

The detective smiled more broadly. Franco said nothing.

561

The detective stopped smiling, and said, 'Tell me again what you know about the blue container outside.'

'I told you already, I just move the damned things in and out of here. I don't know nothing about no hidden compartment.'

'You did the paperwork when the *Maria Escobar* arrived from Montevideo?'

'Sure.'

'But you know nothing about the compartment we found?'

'It's the truth. I swear it.'

'You don't want to change your mind?'

Franco looked up guardedly, then said, 'Why would I want to do that? Hey, look, I told you . . .'

Orsati raised his hand for Franco to be silent. He stared down at him for several moments, then turned to his partner and nodded.

The other detective moved to the door and immediately Franco sensed something was wrong. The man opened the door and crooked a finger as if to beckon someone inside.

Big Aldo Celli stepped warily into the office. Franco put a hand out to hold onto the desk. Man, he was going under, his body on fire, throat dry as he swallowed hard.

Aldo stood there awkwardly, head bowed as he wrung his huge hands. When he finally plucked up courage he glanced up briefly at Franco.

'I'm sorry, Franco. They made me tell them about the stuff in the locker.'

Franco moved his lips, opened his mouth to talk, but no words came. Instead, he shook his head helplessly as Orsati dismissed the crane driver and the door was closed again.

Orsati said, 'If you like, I could call Aldo back and have him tell us again about the favour he did for you.' The detective put two fingers to the side of his mouth, scratched his moustache. 'You see, someone saw him dump the stuff from your locker. We're having a couple of divers sent over. They ought to be here soon. It shouldn't take them long to find the box Aldo threw in the harbour. You want to tell me what was in there, Franco?' Orsati glanced at his watch, then back up at Franco.

'You can save us a lot of time and trouble. Do you want to talk? Save everyone this embarrassment?'

Franco looked over and saw the smirk on Il Peste's fat face and wanted to throw up.

He glanced out at the harbour apron beyond the panoramic window, saw the wind blowing litter on the asphalt in eccentric whorls, saw the ghostly silver finger of light from the lighthouse out in the harbour probe the growing twilight. Far distant, towards the harbour end, he saw the shadowy figure of a man step out of a car, caught for a second in the silver shaft of light, but Franco's mind was too preoccupied to take much notice and he didn't see the Heckler and Koch machine-pistol gripped in the man's hands.

Franco turned back. His body was drenched in sweat and he tried not to look at the detective as the man pulled up a chair and turned it round and sat facing him.

'I think,' Orsati said firmly, 'you had better tell me everything.'

A cold breeze swept in from the sea, and it washed Volkmann's face. As he stepped out onto the apron from the warehouse entrance, he searched in his pockets for a cigarette. Finding none, he realised he must have left them in his overcoat in the unmarked police car.

As he reached the parked car ten metres away, he looked up, saw the figure of a man move towards the warehouse from the harbour end in the growing darkness, caught for a moment in the sweep of silver light from the lighthouse out in the bay. The man was fifty metres away, maybe less, a dark Fiat car obscured behind him.

Volkmann saw the machine-pistol in his hands and for a brief moment he thought the man was one of the Carabinieri, but the man moved at a trot and he wore no uniform.

Volkmann froze, a sixth sense telling him something was wrong. The man's stride was too purposeful, too determined, the weapon in his hands held across his chest at the ready.

For a second or two Volkmann turned and glanced back at the warehouse. Lights on in the tiny office where the Italian detectives and the customs man had taken Scali, looking like characters in some drama beyond the lit glass, Scali's lips moving, the others listening. Easy targets.

Volkmann felt the sweat beginning as he looked back again towards the man. Forty metres from the warehouse now, moving fast. As he passed under a Klieg light on the apron Volkmann saw the burnished glint of the Heckler and Koch in his hands.

Volkmann went to reach for his Beretta, suddenly realised he hadn't taken the weapon with him on the flight to Genoa.

He swore, moved rapidly back towards the unmarked police car, yanked open the driver's door and searched frantically in the glove compartment for a weapon. He realised the man with the machine-pistol had a clear line of fire towards the warehouse, realised Scali was the target, the voices on the tape echoing like an alarm bell in his head as he tried to find a weapon.

'*And the Italian?*'

'*He will be eliminated.*'

Volkmann swore. Apart from papers, the glove compartment was empty. He tried to think. Detectives always carried weapons in an unmarked car, Italian cops no different. But where? Sometimes in the boot; sometimes overhead in a zipped roof compartment. Volkmann felt along the coarse vinyl. No zip. No weapons compartment. He felt under the seats.

Nothing.

He checked for the keys in the ignition.

None.

Volkmann swore again as his right hand shot down to the side of the driver's seat, felt for a boot latch, found one, pulled it hard. Cold sweat beginning as he looked back out through the rear window, seeing the man twenty metres away now, as the boot yawned open and up.

Volkmann swung the driver's door open and clambered out, crouching low, praying there was a weapon in the boot.

As Kleins moved at a trot across the apron he could see the

knot of men standing in the lighted office window, see the faces plainly beyond glass, two men standing, two sitting, one of them looking like he was talking while the others listened.

Scali.

Fifteen metres to go now and still the men in the office hadn't seen Kleins.

He had left Beck sitting in the parked Fiat, watching his back, ready for the getaway; the second car parked in a side-street four blocks from the harbour entrance, ready for their escape to the safe house.

But a difficult hit. Not impossible, but too many people, too many things to go wrong, but the kill imperative according to Meyer.

The adrenalin racing in Kleins' veins now, his body on fire.

So close . . .

Twelve metres from the warehouse window and still the men beyond the glass hadn't noticed him. His finger slid around the trigger as he ducked under the line of yellow tape.

Ten metres from where the apron ended and the parking space in front of the warehouse began, Kleins hesitated, animal instinct telling him something was wrong. He saw a movement out of the corner of his right eye. As he looked right, the boot of the unmarked police car yawned open. Kleins glimpsed the figure of a man, crouching as he moved quickly towards the rear, his hand reaching inside the boot, searching frantically for something. Kleins couldn't see the man's face, but in those split seconds he knew the man was marked for death.

Kleins swung the Heckler and Koch round and fired in one swift motion. The apron erupted with a thunderous volley of sound as the man darted back for cover, a hail of lead ripping into the police car, shattering glass, puncturing metal.

Kleins swung the weapon back towards the warehouse window, saw the men behind the glass react to the sound of gunfire, mouths open as they froze in disbelief and stared out at Kleins.

Kleins squeezed the trigger.

The office window shattered, glass fragmenting, lead hitting concrete and wood and flesh as the Heckler and Koch's deathly chatter sprayed the tiny room, the figures beyond the window dancing like crazed puppets as Kleins kept the pressure hard on the trigger and discharged one long, sustained burst.

Click.

The magazine emptied. Kleins tore it out, slammed home a fresh one from his pocket, cocked the Heckler again.

Suddenly he glimpsed the figure move out again from behind the car, his hand coming round to pull something from the boot.

Kleins swung the Heckler and Koch round and levelled it and squeezed the trigger again.

Volkmann had crouched helplessly behind the car, eyes flicking from the man to the open car boot, to the shattering office window and the figures caught in the deadly burst of fire from the Heckler and Koch.

As the man concentrated on the targets beyond the window Volkmann had seen the opportunity, crouching low again as he moved forward once more towards the boot, hand reaching frantically inside, fingers probing, feeling for metal, for the hard form of a shotgun, a machine-pistol.

Nothing.

Then the cold metal of a wheel brace.

Then . . .

Something hard in his fingers, an L clamp, then another, then the outline of a weapon, fingers touching the hilt of an Uzi, grasping the comfort of cold hard metal.

Volkmann heard the deathly chatter of the Heckler and Koch suddenly stop, saw the man tear out the magazine, slam home a fresh one.

Volkmann swung round and up, saw the Uzi held in the L clamps with two rubber stays, tore them off, wrenched out the weapon, praying it was loaded.

The volley of gunfire that came just as he grasped the Uzi

sent him reeling back behind the car and he hit the ground, hearing the jack-hammer crack of bullets as they ripped into the car's metal. As he fell back and rolled along the side of the car the fingers of one hand fumbled wildly for the safety catch, found it, then the cocking handle.

He flicked the Uzi onto automatic fire with his thumb, bullets cracking into the ground around him.

The man with the Heckler and Koch moved forward, firing wildly; Volkmann rolled right on the asphalt and on the third roll aimed and squeezed the trigger.

The Uzi exploded in his hands.

The hail of bullets ripped into the man's chest, his body lurching, whirling in an obscene dance of death, hammered back onto the ground as Volkmann kept the pressure on the trigger.

Click.

The magazine emptied.

Silence.

Volkmann dropped the Uzi, stood and looked back towards the warehouse window. He saw no movement beyond the shattered glass, but he heard the moans of pain and the cries for help.

At that moment he heard the roar of a car engine, and saw the headlights of a car flick on to his left.

Beck saw everything happen from where he sat in the parked car.

He swore. Everything going wrong, just when it looked good, just when it looked like it was going to work. He saw Kleins fall under the hail of fire, saw the man drop his weapon and stand and move out from behind the shattered police car.

Beck gunned the Fiat's engine and flicked on the headlights.

As he reached for the Heckler and Koch on the seat beside him, he hit the accelerator hard and the Fiat lurched forward.

*   *   *

Volkmann heard the screech of tyres and saw the blinding beams of light race towards him out of the twilight.

Eighty metres.

Seventy.

Sixty.

He crouched as a burst of fire suddenly raked the ground to his left, chips of stone flying as lead cracked into asphalt.

Fifty metres.

Forty.

The Fiat growling towards him out of the fading grey light, headlights like the glaring eyes of some crazed wild animal; blinding him.

The empty Uzi lay five metres away, Volkmann's mind working feverishly, his body drenched in sweat.

He raised his hand to shield his eyes from the piercing lights, glimpsed the Heckler and Koch beside the man's pulped body; raced towards it, flung himself down and rolled the last five metres, his hands scrabbling wildly for the weapon as another burst of fire raked the ground to his left, the Fiat changing course, veering towards him.

Thirty metres.

Twenty.

Volkmann grasped the Heckler and Koch, rolled right, aimed, squeezed the trigger just as the Fiat appeared under the wash of the apron's Klieg lights.

The burst from the Heckler and Koch shattered the left headlight and the left side of the windscreen, turned it white under the Klieg lights, but the car kept coming, weaving crazily. Volkmann glimpsing the face of the driver beyond the half-shattered glass, the barrel of his weapon spitting flame.

At the last moment Volkmann released the pressure on the trigger, rolled right again, squeezed the trigger hard, felt the weapon chatter madly in his hands as the bullets ripped in through the shattered windscreen.

The second burst decapitated the driver, sent his severed head flying back hard against the headrest as the Fiat veered left, wildly out of control, screaming past Volkmann with a rush of air. There was a grinding screech of metal hitting metal as it smashed into the unmarked police car and then came a sharp crack as the petrol tank exploded and a geyser of orange flame erupted into the grey twilight.

Volkmann shielded his eyes as a wave of intense heat rolled towards him. He pushed himself up and raced back towards the warehouse, the tangled metal behind him engulfed in a pall of flame and acrid smoke.

The light was still on in the tiny shattered office, but no sign of life.

And then he saw a figure stand up unsteadily. Orsati – blood streaming down his face, his hand covering a head wound as he tried to steady himself against a wall.

Suddenly the harbour came alive. A siren screamed, and seconds later a ghostly blue light swirled in the grey twilight as a police car raced out of nowhere and screeched to a halt.

Volkmann flicked on the Hecker and Koch's safety and dropped the weapon and it clattered to the ground.

Two Carabinieri stepped warily from their car, pistols at the ready. As they crouched and aimed their weapons at Volkmann, they flicked disbelieving looks at the shattered warehouse office, then at the tangle of blazing metal.

As the men rushed forward, unsure of their enemy, Volkmann slowly raised his hands in an arc and placed them over his head.

And then another police car wailed into view and halted, and then another. More cops jumping from cars, unholstering guns, until finally all the sirens died and were replaced by babbling and screaming voices, the grey twilight streaked by the corona of revolving blue lights and the shadows of cops everywhere.

Strasbourg.
4.03 p.m.

The two men stepped out of the lift into the empty corridor.

The one carrying the briefcase led the way. It took them

less than twenty seconds to find the office, the name on the plaque on the door.

Ferguson was on the telephone and clutching a sheet of paper when the door burst in. He saw the two men and the silenced pistols in their hands and went to open his mouth to speak.

Four times he was hit in the chest, twice in the head, the force of the bullets sending him flying backwards and up, dragging the telephone and papers with him, his body hurled back against the wall.

The receiver was still clutched in his hands as he lay there, eyes open in death, blood pumping from his wounds, when the man with the briefcase stepped forward and coldly fired another two shots into Ferguson's head.

The two men remained in the office no more than another twenty seconds, one of them searching through the unlocked cabinets and desk drawers, the other opening the briefcase he carried, setting the timer on the bomb, then closing the briefcase again and placing it under Ferguson's desk.

Neither man noticed the classified report from Asunción lying on the floor, the page streaked with blood.

They checked the hallway, saw that it was clear and stepped outside, closing the door after them.

Erica sat alone in the bedroom.

Peters had started probing her with a few gentle questions so she had excused herself, saying she was tired.

A gust of wind rattled the glass, and a flurry of snow brushed against it. She started. As she went to draw the curtains she heard the noise. It came from the hallway: a sudden rush of heavy footsteps.

She moved quickly across the room. As she opened the bedroom door she heard the television on, saw Peters rising quickly from his chair, staring at some point towards the hallway, saw the colour drain from his face.

Peters said, 'What the . . .!'

And as he went to reach for the pistol lying on his coat Erica saw the two men with guns in their hands rush forward towards Peters, saw the backs of their pale raincoats.

As Peters reached for his pistol there was a strange whistling sound and then another and another as both men fired rapidly into Peters' body, blossoms of red erupting on his chest and face as he was flung back against the chair.

Erica screamed.

The Mercedes halted on the Quai Aperge and the man in the passenger seat checked his watch.

Fifteen seconds later both men heard the blast in the distance as the air ruptured with the sound of the explosion. The man nodded and the driver pulled out from the kerb.

Minutes later they heard the wail of sirens behind them in the distance but neither man looked back.

And neither saw the dark-coloured saloon car that pulled out quietly twenty metres behind them.

Chapter Fifty

Bonn.
Friday,
December 23rd,
9.30 a.m.

Chancellor Franz Dollman grimaced as he sat in the back of the black Mercedes. Beyond the bullet-proof windows of the stretched limousine a police escort guided the car through the streets of Bonn.

As the car passed the Münster Platz, Dollman looked up from his paperwork. The lights of a Christmas tree winked on the Platz. The thought of Christmas approaching normally depressed him, but this time he looked forward to a few relaxing days away from his gruelling State duties. Already his Cabinet were a week behind the scheduled Christmas recess, so many problems still remained to be dealt with.

Dollman sighed as he sat back. He had flown in from Munich that morning, after a late-night meeting with the Bavarian Prime Minister, had been up since six, assembling his paperwork, then breakfast followed by a quick glass of schnapps to help brace himself for the day ahead and the emergency Cabinet meeting.

The Wednesday morning meetings in Bonn's Villa Schaumburg were always the same of late, had been for the last year. An utter shambles. Dollman expected the same of this one, wondered how the country had managed to survive, put it down to the resolute, hard-working nature of the German people. They had seen adversity before and were certainly seeing it now.

As the car sped past the Markt Platz, Dollman glimpsed the broken shop windows, the littered glass, the paint daubed on walls. All the hallmarks of another riot. He turned to Ritter, his personal bodyguard, sitting beside him. The man was disrespectfully chewing gum.

Dollman nodded gravely towards the scene beyond the glass. 'What happened?'

Ritter's jaws moved slowly as he chewed. 'It started off as a protest march about unemployment. Then the right-wing groups joined in. Before long it was a riot.'

Dollman sighed. 'Anyone killed?'

Ritter shook his head. 'Not this time. The riot squad moved in after midnight and cracked a few skulls, that's all. But I hear there's another scheduled to start tonight from the Rathaus. A protest march by immigrants.' Ritter's jaws tightened. 'If you ask me, these demonstrators ought to be locked up.'

It was getting out of control, Dollman reflected, as the Mercedes turned towards the Hofgarten and headed southwards towards the Rhine and the Villa Schaumberg. There were more shattered windows along the route. Pavement slabs had been torn up, shopfronts vandalised.

Dollman didn't bother replying to Ritter's remark. The man was an excellent bodyguard, tough and discreet and reliable, but had a limited intelligence and so Dollman always kept their conversations to a minimum. If Ritter had his way, half the world would be behind bars.

It was the same everywhere these days. Riots. Marches. Protests. The immigrant problem. The French Interior Minister had complained of the same to him only last week.

'Lock the lot up and throw away the keys. That's the answer,' Ritter added.

If only it were possible, Dollman reflected. He personally would start with half his bickering Cabinet.

The stretched Mercedes had turned slowly into the courtyard of the Villa Schaumburg and come quietly to a halt outside the imposing entrance. His wife would be in their residence on the grounds. There would just be time to see her after the Cabinet meeting before he left for the Charlottenburg Palace in Berlin. Another boring function to attend, before Weber's special security meeting the next morning. Still,

Weber's meeting suited perfectly. He would spend the night in Wannsee and that at least Dollman looked forward to. The thought briefly lifted his spirits as the chauffeur stepped out smartly and opened the rear door. Dollman gathered up his papers, closed his briefcase and handed it to Ritter.

As Dollman climbed out he saw Eckart, the Finance Minister, waiting in the doorway to greet him. The man looked as glum and depressing as the dark brooding sky over Bonn. No doubt there was more depressing financial news even before the Cabinet meeting began.

Dollman sighed and strode grimly towards the Villa entrance.

The meeting had gone on for almost two hours.

It was no different this morning as Dollman observed the drawn faces of the men seated at the large oval table.

There had been riots the previous night in Berlin, Munich, Bonn and Frankfurt, and even in Dollman's own beloved Mannheim. The latest financial news was depressing. Eckart had wrung his hands in despair when he imparted the details.

Dollman removed a fresh white handkerchief from his pocket and dabbed his brow; the Cabinet room was hot, the heating full on to counter the chill outside. Beyond the bulletproof windows he glimpsed a harsh wind whipping the trees.

A tall, distinguished-looking man in his early sixties, Dollman's thinning grey hair was swept back off his fleshy face. He had been Chancellor for eighteen months. Eighteen hard, difficult, trying months. He would gladly have resigned; indeed, had considered such a course of action on two occasions at least, but knew that he was the only one in the room capable of a semblance of leadership in these pressing times.

He looked up now from the reports lying in front of him on the polished oval table and replaced the handkerchief in his breast pocket. All of the Ministers were present except Weber, the Vice-Chancellor. The man was expected later. A fresh outbreak of rioting in Leipzig had demanded his presence. He didn't envy the man. Weber had requested the portfolio, his temperament suited it because he brooked no nonsense, but a security brief was just asking for nothing short of a permanent blinding headache. Still, that was Weber's problem.

Eighteen men at the big oval table, including himself.

Dollman heard a cough and turned his head to see Eckart trying to catch his attention.

'The economics reports, Chancellor. Do you wish me to start?'

Dollman glanced at his watch. 'What's remaining?'

'Just the economics reports, and, of course, the report on Federal security. But we're still waiting for Vice-Chancellor Weber to arrive. If he is further delayed I fear we shall have to reconvene after lunch.'

Dollman sighed. 'Very well, Eckart, you may begin.'

Dollman sat back. He knew what was coming as Eckart's dry, monotonous voice called the Ministers to attention, before he launched into the report proper.

Dollman's mind was elsewhere. On the house in Wannsee. There would be time to call on the way to Charlottenburg, then back after the civic function. He had telephoned the night before, said he would stay over. Even the thought of the voice and the voluptuous body sent him into spasms of sexual anticipation. The woman was a politician's dream. Discreet, beautiful, undemanding, lustful and willing in bed. He always found her company invigorating.

Dollman surpressed the smile of contentment that threatened to cross his lips, Eckart's depressing monologue interrupting his thoughts.

'. . . The treasury reports difficulty in maintaining current welfare payments . . . Contributions to the Community are overdue by three months . . . Fangel requests that international loan repayments be reduced by negotiation . . . Bundesbank reports further imminent reduction in the value of the mark against all major currencies in the light of our balance of payments . . . The State of Hesse is requesting financial aid, as is Bavaria . . .'

Eckart's monotonous voice droned on. Dollman saw the assembled Ministers stare ahead or look towards the windows. He should have read the report himself if only to avoid Eckart's tedious delivery.

He had gone past trying to make sense of the chaos. At that moment all he hoped was that he could make it to Berlin by evening. He looked up as at last Eckart's boring monotone was coming to an end.

'. . . And that concludes the economics reports. Thank you, Ministers, for your attention.'

What attention? thought Dollman. Half of them were sleeping, or trying to, or bored to death. There was a sudden eruption of coughing, and then a hushed silence. Dollman looked at the faces around the table. Minister Franks raised his hand.

'Yes, Franks?'

'What does the Chancellor propose to do about the situation in Hesse and Bavaria?'

'I'm glad you asked that question, Franks. I'm sure Minister Eckart will have some proposals for discussion at our next scheduled meet. Until then, I ask you to be patient.'

A politician's answer. Dollman avoided Franks' stare, saw the look on Eckart's drawn face.

'Any further questions?'

There was a murmur from some of the Ministers at the back. He saw Streicher raise his hand, no doubt to probe Dollman's glib reply. But that was how he felt this morning. Glib and depressed. Dollman deflected any further questions by looking pointedly at his watch.

'Gentlemen, I suggest we reconvene after lunch to hear the Vice-Chancellor's report. As Interior Minister, I believe he has some important points to discuss.'

As Dollman finished speaking he heard the door to the Cabinet room open and saw Konrad Weber step into the room. He carried a thick folder in one hand, his briefcase in the other. He was a tall, grim-looking man, a law-and-order type who brooked no nonsense. Weber's drawn, pallid face looked serious, as always. But a good Vice-Chancellor. One who took his responsibilities seriously. Perhaps too seriously. Had Weber had his way, the extremists would be off the streets and behind bars. Dollman was glad to have him on his side, but from the strained look on his thin, Prussian face Konrad Weber looked as if he were about to impart doom.

'Chancellor, gentlemen, my apologies for being late . . .'

'Take a seat, Weber. You are ready to read your special report?'

Dollman looked up at him, glad of the interruption, but dreading Weber's reports. At least it saved him from further questions. Now Weber could take some of the flak.

The Vice-Chancellor nodded to Dollman as he moved to his place at the oval table but remained standing. He placed his briefcase on the floor beside him and opened the folder. As Weber placed his papers in front of him, Dollman saw that several of them bore official red BfV stamps. *Highly Confidential*.

Dollman sat back and sighed quietly; the meeting had gone badly enough without further depressing news. Weber had already informed him privately on the phone the night before that the news would be serious, and the Vice-Chancellor's stance and demeanour looked grave. From the look on Weber's and the Cabinet's faces, his security reports would send them all rushing towards the windows.

Dollman tried hard to relax, wondered where it would all end. He thought of Lisl, lying naked in bed in the house at Wannsee, and the image of her full, luscious body sent a delicious, erotic shiver down his spine.

If it wasn't for the girl, he felt certain he would have rushed towards the windows himself long ago.

Chapter Fifty-One

Genoa.
5.30 p.m.

Volkmann waited his turn to speak as he sat in the Commissioner's office on the Plaza di Fortunesca.

The tension in the room as thick as the cigarette smoke that rose like a grey cloud to the white ceiling. The detective, Orsati, sat in the centre of the brightly lit office, a broad strip of flesh-coloured plaster ran from just below his left eye to the middle of his cheek. Around his head a white bandage where a bullet had nicked and rutted flesh.

He had smiled at Volkmann nervously after the doctor and nurse had attended him on the dock apron, cleansed and dressed the wounds, given him the painkilling shots, but he had brushed aside their request to come with them in the ambulance.

'A flesh wound. Nothing to worry about,' he had said to Volkmann, white teeth flashing behind his moustache, but the man looked badly shaken.

Now tiny beads of perspiration stood out on Orsati's forehead and his face looked tense and pale as he waited for the conversation to finish.

Apart from Volkmann and Orsati there were two other men present in the room. One was the Genoese Police Commissioner. A bespectacled, handsome man, he wore civilian clothes. A smart grey business suit with a pale blue tie and handkerchief. A touch of flamboyance but the man totally in control, professional, brown eyes peering sharply from behind his metal-rimmed glasses.

The fourth man present was the Chief of Detectives, tall, parchment-white skin, with an aquiline nose and brooding intelligent eyes and flecked, steel-grey hair. He wore casual clothes, a black leather jacket, grey slacks, a white sweater, the casualness of his dress evidence that he had come to his superior's office hurriedly and at short notice, from a pre-Christmas party in a hotel on the Via Piaggio.

Orsati had explained that Scali had talked before the bullets had ripped into the clerk's body. One small box, the last consignment. A heavy box, concealed in the false side of the container. Several other consignments over the past year. Weapons, Scali had guessed, or maybe even gold. The last consignment a heavy box. But the little man had not been sure, the contents of all the consignments a mystery.

Orsati had explained that the forensic people were still conducting tests. The Commissioner sat behind the desk, chewing an unlit cigar, rolling it round grimly in his mouth, listening.

The only one talking now was the Chief of Detectives. Talking animatedly and chain-smoking. Strong cigarettes that gave off pungent wisps of bitter smoke.

Volkmann watched him, listening, but only understanding a word here and there, and waiting for the man to finish talking to his Commissioner, waiting for the man to translate. He spoke good English, the Commissioner only a little.

The man had been speaking for almost five minutes now, uninterrupted. Volkmann had told his story in English, corroborated by the detective.

As far as the Commissioner was concerned it came down to four bodies and two badly wounded men on life supports in Santo Giorgio Hospital. His own two men had escaped with minor flesh wounds. One of the dead was an official of the Italian Customs Service, Paulo Bonefacio, the other Scali, and the two armed men on the apron.

The assassins' clothing was of German manufacture. But they carried no identification papers of any sort.

'Like a suicide squad,' Orsati had remarked of the men's action. 'Crazy.'

Now Volkmann looked up as the Chief of Detectives stopped talking.

He turned to Volkmann and said, 'I have explained every-thing to the Commissioner. As you and Detective Orsati told it to me. However, there are some things that need clarification. Do you have any idea why the two men on the dock apron wanted to kill Franco Scali?'

Volkmann looked away, towards the window, darkness outside, black sky, no stars. He looked back again and said, 'I can only tell you what you know already. We received information about a cargo from South America, with Genoa as the possible destination. We passed that on to your people in DSE. We requested that a thorough check be made on all cargoes from South America, in particular from Montevideo and São Paulo.' Volkmann stared at the man. 'I gave you the name and telephone number in Strasbourg. I suggest the Commissioner contact Ferguson urgently and tell him what's happened.'

The man sighed. 'Signore Volkmann, we are trying to make contact with your superior. But in the meantime your help in this matter would be greatly appreciated. Naturally, I doubt if any charges will be brought against you. You were acting in self-defence. But I must point out that co-operation is vital. You understand?'

The man paused, stared at Volkmann. 'There is nothing else you can tell us?'

'Nothing.'

The man sighed again, impatiently. 'You must understand our predicament.' He glanced over at Orsati, then back at Volkmann. 'I think we have been more than co-operative. Now, it is your turn. Four men are dead and we don't know why. I want to know why.'

Volkmann recognised the frustration in the man's tone. But he would need permission from Ferguson before going further. It wasn't a question of non-co-operation, merely approval from Ferguson. He or Peters would have to be the arbiters of how much he could tell the Italians.

Volkmann said, 'I need clearance.'

The man's face showed his frustration. 'Then what has happened goes much deeper?'

Volkmann nodded.

The Chief of Detectives looked at him. 'We've tried to contact your headquarters, but have been unable to get through. The operator thought there was a line fault but the exchange knew nothing.'

There was a knock on the door and a detective entered. He looked at the Chief of Detectives and asked to speak in private. Both men stepped outside a moment into the hallway, their heads bowed in whispered conversation. Moments later the Chief came back into the room, his face pale. He looked at Orsati, then the Commissioner, went to speak but hesitated and looked at Volkmann instead.

'We contacted one of our liaison officers in Strasbourg at his home number . . .' The man paused. 'He said there has been an explosion at your Headquarters. Our officer knows nothing concerning casualties, only that all his own people are accounted for.'

The man hesitated, flicked a glance at the others before he looked back, saw Volkmann's face drain to white.

'There is also something else, Signore Volkmann. Something important, I believe. Our forensic people at the harbour, one of the tests they carried out on the container . . . they used a Geiger meter. It registered a high reading.' The man paused. 'It suggests perhaps that the cargo Scali removed, it contained radioactive material.'

Wannsee,
Berlin.
December 23rd

The stretched black Mercedes turned into the large private grounds of the house in Wannsee just after six.

Set twenty metres back off the lakeshore road and surrounded by high poplar trees, the property was not overlooked front or rear by any of the big old pre-war houses that ringed the lake.

Ritter stepped from the car and led Dollman to the front

door, the two other bodyguards in front of the Mercedes remaining in their seats.

The beautiful young woman who opened the door greeted Dollman with a smile but ignored Ritter. Once the two men were inside Ritter was consigned as usual to the comfortable front study on the ground floor, while Dollman and the young woman waited a respectful five minutes in the sitting-room at the back of the house before they repaired upstairs.

Fifteen minutes later Chancellor Franz Dollman lay naked on pink satin sheets in the master bedroom. The girl had slid the disc into the hi-fi, the strains of Wagner filling the room. His favourite music to relax by. He held a glass of champagne in one hand as he stared up at the reflection in the mirrored ceiling.

There was an expression of pure pleasure on his face as he watched the image of the girl's naked, full-figured body sending pleasure shocks through his flesh.

Her blonde hair lay strewn about his stomach, her long nails stroking the insides of his thighs, sending exquisite waves between his loins. She was a rare specimen indeed, his Lisl; helped him dissipate all those tensions that came with high office. And there had been many of those of late.

Until he had met her almost a year before there had been a physical void in his life: he and his wife hardly ever did it together. There were public expressions of endearment, for the television cameras, for the newspapers, but his Karin was not a sexual woman, a trifle dowdy, yet an ideal Chancellor's wife: loyal, moral, conservative.

But Lisl.

Twenty-three and a body made for pleasure.

She ran two pink-nailed fingers slowly across his chest and pouted her perfect cupid lips. Moments later her hand went down to stroke him in an unhurried rhythm.

'Good?'

'Exquisite,' Dollman replied.

A tiny, sensual sigh and then Lisl said, 'Would you like me to dress up for you?'

Dollman said, 'Something nice.'

'What if you're late for the Palace?'

'To hell with them.'

The girl smiled and stopped stroking him, raised herself gently from the bed onto all fours, displaying her well-rounded buttocks.

Dollman watched as she stepped slowly from the bed, swaying her hips and bottom as she crossed to the chest of drawers. She opened the top one, removed a pair of coral-pink silk stockings, ran the sheer material sensually through her hands.

Next came the suspender belt, pink and flimsy. She clasped it around her hips and Dollman watched as she dressed slowly, seductively, sliding the sheer stockings onto her long, shapely legs. He suppressed the urge to reach out and take her there and then, prolonging the torturous but delectable pleasure.

When she had stepped into a pair of coral-pink stiletto high heels, she turned to face him.

Dollman said urgently, 'Come to me . . .'

'No, I want to tease you first.'

She was playing with him, something she liked to do now and then, the feline in her, and Dollman tried hard to control his urgency. She came and lay next to him on the bed. Pink fingernails scraped along his legs, sending tiny sensuous shivers up his spine.

The thought of spending Christmas in a boring house, with a boring family, when he could have this, the body of the woman he truly adored and loved.

Another woman would have bitched about the important times when a family came first. Lisl, as ever, hadn't complained. 'I understand, *liebchen*. That's where you should be at Christmas.'

She was purring now, and as she began stroking him again Dollman relaxed and enjoyed the erotic pleasure.

He had managed to keep her out of the limelight with no great effort. Besides, it was a tacit understanding among Cabinet members: one's private life was just that, private. Unless the press got hold of it. In which case you swam with denials or sank ignominiously. Much depended on the woman in question and her tacit understanding; in Lisl's case, her desire for secrecy had been on a par with his own. It was the answer to a prayer.

'Tell me about your meeting.'

The fingers that gripped his hard flesh suddenly slowed. *Keep going*, he wanted to scream. *Don't stop*. The throbbing in his loins unbearable now.

'As usual Weber sees extremists under every bed. He's scheduled an emergency security meeting for tomorrow morning.'

'In Bonn?'

Dollman smiled and shook his head. 'The Reichstag.'

The girl frowned. 'Is it serious?'

'Weber seems to think so.'

Dollman didn't elaborate. Federal Security was not a subject to be discussed with a mistress. Besides, the girl would hardly be interested. He didn't tell her Weber was putting the finishing touches to an emergency decree that very night, to resolve finally the extremist problem, and wanted full Cabinet approval. Weber's plans for internment of all extremists would put the final nail in the coffin.

The meeting in the Reichstag was to be held in room 4-North, the secret room. The room always intrigued Dollman, a place few Germans knew about. Specially designed to counter any possibility of bugging or electronic eavesdropping, suspended in mid-air on eight steel wires from each corner, so that no part of it touched walls or floors.

He felt her fingers on his thighs and saw her smile.

'That means you've no excuse not to stay tonight.'

Dollman smiled. The function at the Palace would be finished by midnight, no later. Then he could spend the night with Lisl before the Christmas holiday and family beckoned.

She turned her magnificent breasts towards him and purred. He cupped one in his hand as she spoke.

'I'll cook supper. Just the two of us, alone.'

Dollman glanced towards the curtained window. Even as they spoke he knew there were three armed men stationed strategically in the two cars outside in the driveway, another three positioned along the cold street in an unmarked car. Ritter, as always, in the study below. In the brains department, the man might be lacking, but his loyalty and discretion were beyond question.

The tiny transmitter Dollman himself carried everywhere was on the bedside locker. The nine-milimetre pistol he was supposed to carry he had left in the Mercedes. The thing troubled him, made him think of violent death. A necessary precaution, the weapon, but a precaution he often disregarded.

She continued stroking him, her plump breasts swaying.

My God, what a body! It was like a pain in him, wanting her.

She smiled. 'You're going to be late for the Palace.'

Dollman smiled back, looked at his sixty-year-old body as he lay back on the bed, noticing the wrinkled flesh of his legs and stomach, the greying chest hair, the aging, out-of-condition body. He was still hard, though, and not many men could keep it that way for long at his age. But then again, not many men had the benefit of a woman like this. What was a boring civic function at Charlottenburg with the Mayor of Berlin compared to this?

He feasted his eyes on her cream-skinned thighs, her breasts proud, the tantalising sight of the flesh at the top of her pink stockings exciting him.

'Lisl, come here . . .'

She stopped stroking him. Dollman reached across and gently kneaded a breast.

Lisl said, 'What time will you be back?'

'A little after midnight. No later.'

'You promise?'

Dollman let his eyes wander over her magnificent body, the triangle of golden hair between her legs. At that moment he would have promised her the Vice-Chancellorship.

'I promise.'

In the darkened study below, Ritter relaxed on the couch with his feet up. The portable phone was in his pocket and he had turned down the volume on the walkie-talkie that lay on the coffee table in front of him; his holstered nine-millimetre Sig and Sauer P6 pistol draped over the end of the couch.

He heard the moans of sexual pleasure coming from the bedroom above, rising above the faint strains of Wagner, and he smiled to himself.

Chapter Fifty-Two

Strasbourg

It was after seven when the Lear private jet touched down.

Volkmann telephoned his apartment from a call-box in the terminal and let the number ring out until it clicked dead. When he tried the office numbers the same happened. He guessed the lines had been damaged and he wondered if Peters had heard the news and had taken the girl with him to the building.

He picked up the Ford from the airport parking lot and twenty minutes later he was standing at the corner of the Orangerie. Lights blazed from the fire-tenders in the winter darkness. In the lobby temporary lighting had been rigged up and he heard the whine of a mobile electric generator, but most of the building was still in darkness.

The snow had stopped and the streets were covered in grey slush. A half-dozen gendarmerie cars stood outside, their blue lights flashing. Two fire-tenders were parked nearby, the brigade men talking among themselves and smoking, others reeling in hoses. A couple of forensic men in dark overalls were still sifting through the debris that lay littered about the Platz.

On the third floor shadows moved in and out of the rigged lights and Volkmann guessed they were more forensic people. The third floor appeared to have taken most of the damage and Ferguson's window was blown out, revealing a black cavity where the office had been. Where windows had been shattered, black traces of soot from the blast and the flames had stained the external walls.

As he stood in the shadows he saw several faces he recognised in the crowd but he saw no sign of Erica or Peters. His heart raced and his mind was in turmoil. One of the German officers, tieless and wearing casual clothes, stood chatting to one of the gendarmes, smoking a cigarette, and Volkmann thought of approaching him, but some instinct made him hesitate.

He stood there for five minutes before he turned and walked back along the street, wondering what to do next. He decided to try calling the duty-officer once more. He walked to a call-box at the end of the street and this time he got through on a crackling line.

He heard the voice of the young French officer, Delon, answer, and Volkmann gave his name.

Delon said urgently, 'Where the hell are you, Joe?'

Volkmann ignored the question and said quickly, 'Tell me what happened.'

There was a deep sigh at the other end and then Delon said, 'Ferguson is dead, Joe. A bomb went off in his office two hours ago. I was on duty in the basement. As soon as the blaze was out we found him. What's left of him is in the gendarmerie morgue. Jan De Vries is in the Civil Hospital with severe concussion. He was in one of the offices on the second floor when the bomb went off. I've taken over as duty officer.'

'How did it happen?'

'The guy on the front desk admitted two men fifteen minutes before the blast. They had Belgian Section IDs that looked bona fide. They took the lift up to the third floor but never came down. We found a fire-escape door on the first floor open. They must have left that way.' Delon paused and then Volkmann heard the panic in the young man's voice. 'All hell's broken loose, Joe. No one knows what's going on.'

'Are you the only one on duty?'

'No, Reauld from the Belgian Section's with me. He's duty officer on the next shift. He's in the next room talking to his people in Brussels about the IDs. But no names so far.'

'Who was on the front desk when it happened?'

'One of our guys from the French Desk. He's been with us only three months. I'm going to recommend he's transferred back to where he came from. The dumb son of a bitch never even got them to sign in.'

'Did Lamont get descriptions of the men?'

'I questioned him earlier. It was snowing outside and the men wore overcoats with their collars up. Both tall, fair-haired, mid-thirties, but that's about it. They didn't speak, just showed their IDs. According to Lamont they seemed familiar with the layout of the building and knew where they were going.'

'What time does Reauld take over?'

'Half an hour from now. He heard the blast from his apartment and came in early to see if there was anything he could do.' Delon paused. 'I've been trying to contact Peters, but there's no reply from his number. The same with yours. There was a security signal for Ferguson. It came in just before the blast.'

'From where?'

'South America. De Vries delivered it to Ferguson just before the place went up.' Delon paused again. 'I think either Peters or you should see it, Joe. It's important. Not something I want to discuss over the phone. I've got a copy in the signals room basement safe.'

'Is there anyone from the German Desk in the building?'

'One or two.' Delon paused. 'Why?'

'You don't show the signal to anyone, André. Not until I've seen it. Do you understand?'

'Of course.'

'My place is on the Quai Ernest. Meet me there as soon as you come off duty. Come alone and tell no one where you're going. And bring the signal copy.'

'What the hell's up, Joe?'

'Just do as I tell you, André.' He gave Delon the address, then said, 'When did you last see Peters?'

'This afternoon. He left early with some girl. Why?' Volkmann heard the pause and then the young Frenchman said, 'Is everything OK?'

'For now just do as I say. I'll talk to you later.'

It took Volkmann two minutes to drive to the Quai Ernest. Peters' Volvo was parked in the courtyard and caked in snow and as he went up the steps he saw the smudged footprints in the slush leading down to the courtyard.

At the top of the balcony he hesitated. The front door to the apartment was closed and there were faint noises coming from inside. The light in the small bedroom was on beyond the curtained window and he rang the bell before he went to insert the key. When no one came to the door he hesitated, then retraced his steps down to the Ford.

He found the Beretta under the driver's seat, closed the door again and flicked off the safety catch and cocked the weapon. He walked round the side of the courtyard to the small garden at the rear of the apartment building and looked up at the window. The light was on in the front room but he saw no movement, just the blue flicker beyond the curtained glass that told him the TV was on. The bedroom window next to it was lit by the sulphur-coloured light from the bedside lamp. His heart was pounding as he walked back round and climbed the courtyard steps once more.

He unlocked the front door warily and stepped inside, the Beretta at arm's length, aware immediately of the stench of lingering cordite as he went through the drill of checking the rooms, his heart pounding wildly in his chest.

He saw Peters' body lying across the breadth of the settee chair and the room in disarray. He felt a jolt of fear, then caution, replaced by anger, felt the blood drain from him as his eyes flicked constantly from the bloodied corpse to take in the rest of the room. The air smelled of cordite and there was blood on the carpet; blood clotted and caked on Peters' face and neck and clothes. There was a bullet wound above Peters' right eye and two more in his chest cavity. A trickle of dried blood had congealed in the eye-socket and the other eye stared open in death. He touched Peters' left wrist. Rigor was beginning to set in and the man's flesh was ice cold.

It took him ten seconds more to check the apartment and by then his body was drenched in a cold sweat. He saw the splintered wood of the bedroom door and the telephone off its cradle and one of the girl's shoes by the door. When he didn't find her body he felt relief and then fear and then a terrible anger took over.

For a long time he simply stood in the centre of the living-room staring at the bloody scene. He thought of what might have happened to the girl and felt his hands tremble with rage and his heartbeat race and he was aware of an overwhelming need to act; knowing Kesser's people had been responsible for what had happened, knowing they had taken Erica.

It took several minutes before his self-control returned and he took deep breaths as he tried to control the overpowering need for revenge that threatened to engulf him.

Then he flicked on the safety catch of the Beretta and found a towel in the bathroom and placed it over Peters' face and went to sit in the chair by the door.

He waited for Delon to arrive.

Volkmann removed the bloodied towel briefly and then replaced it.

The Frenchman's face had turned pale and his fists were clenched tight by his sides as he stared at Peters' body with disbelief.

'*Jesus* . . .'

As Delon shook his head from side to side and looked about the room, Volkmann said, 'He's been dead maybe a couple of hours.'

'Who did this, Joe . . .?'

'The same people who killed Ferguson.'

The young Frenchman looked so badly shaken Volkmann thought he might collapse. Then suddenly the sharp blue eyes regarded him with detachment and his professionalism took over.

'Joe, I think you had better tell me what is happening here.'

Volkmann ignored the question and said, 'You brought the signal copy with you?'

Delon hesitated, then slowly took an envelope from inside his overcoat pocket and opened it and handed it across.

The Frenchman said, 'You think this information has something to do with what happened tonight? Because if you do,

591

you had better tell me what's going on. I was the acting duty officer. This is my concern also.'

Volkmann glanced at Delon before he took the flimsy and read it slowly.

> TO: *Head, British DSE*.
> FROM: *Chief, Seguridad Paraguaya, Asunción*.
> *The following information is classified and urgent:*

(1) Regret to inform the deaths of Captain Vellares Sanchez and officer Eduardo Cavales in Mexico City, approx 20:00 hours local time, Dec. 20. Deaths occurred in the course of police raid on residential property in suburb of Chapultepec, during attempted arrest of one Franz Lieber, travelling on alias passport of Julio Monck, from Asunción. Lieber – alias Monck – also confirmed dead. Lieber known aquaintance of Nicolas Tsarkin. In course of raid two occupants thought to have escaped. Both male Caucasian. One believed named Karl Schmeltz. Second escapee believed named Hans Kruger. Chief Inspector Gonzales in charge of case in Mexico City. Gonzales mounted immediate search but suggests that the two may have already fled Mexico. The Chapultepec property owned by one Josef Halder, naturalised Mexican citizen, but formerly wanted for war-crimes. Halder also died in course of raid. Investigation proceeding. Will contact if further information from Gonzales, Mexico City.

(2) Priority and highly classified: Confirmed to us by Gonzales, Mexico City, that one of the men arrested at above residence identified as Ernesto Brandt, Brazilian passport holder. Subject refuses to co-operate, but it has been confirmed by First Secretary, Brazilian Embassy, that Brandt employed by Brazilian Government civil nuclear research establishment and suspected of involvement in disappearance of 12 kilos – REPEAT 12 KILOS – weapons-grade PLUTONIUM. Investigation proceeding. ENDS.

Volkmann hesitated before he looked up and as Delon saw the look on his face he said, 'This has something to do with what happened?'

'Yes.'

Delon said solemnly, 'Then this goes beyond just you and me, Joe. You must know that.'

'Has anyone else seen the signal apart from you and me?'

'Only De Vries.'

'Then before you contact anyone I want you to listen to me. The people who did this to Peters – the people who killed Ferguson – they've taken someone else.'

'Who?'

'A German girl. The girl you saw Peters leave the building with. She was the one staying here and Peters was playing minder.'

Delon frowned and said, 'Who is she?'

'A journalist. She put us on to this.' Volkmann held up the signal. 'That's why she was taken tonight. Whoever's behind it, they want to find out what she knows; who she told her story to. And it's probably why Ferguson and Peters were killed. The two men who were killed in Mexico City, Sanchez and Cavales, were involved in the case.'

The Frenchman saw the look of anger on Volkmann's face, then shook his head and said, 'Joe, you're telling me very little.' He glanced uncomfortably at Peters' body. 'Who are the people who did this?'

'They're neo-Nazis, André.' Volkmann saw the look of confusion on Delon's face. 'The German names I had you check. The same people who took the girl were responsible for their deaths. Why they were killed I don't know, but it's tied in somehow with what's happening.'

Delon said hoarsely, 'What are you saying: the people who killed Peters have this plutonium?'

'They've been taking it into Germany in small consignments from South America over the past year. The last one came through Genoa port a couple of weeks ago.' Volkmann told Delon what had happened in Genoa, saw the man turn paler still.

When Volkmann explained about the tape, Delon said angrily, 'This group . . . Why weren't we informed? The French? The others?'

'Because until you showed me that signal I didn't know what the cargoes were. We thought it was weapons being smuggled. Maybe even gold. Not nuclear weapons material. Until now the pieces of the puzzle didn't fit together.'

The Frenchman shook his head. 'Then this isn't something that solely concerns the British Desk. I will have to inform my superiors.'

'André, I need time before the alarm bells start ringing. If these people learn that we know about the material, then God knows what they might do.'

Delon looked at Peters' body then back again. 'What do you mean? How could they know?'

'Because they're planning a coup. A *putsch*.'

The Frenchman's face was ghostly pale. His head shook slowly as if not daring to believe what he had heard. His eyes stared into Volkmann's face as he spoke, his voice almost a hoarse whisper.

'How do you know this?'

'Trust me, André. It's going to happen. The signal confirms it. And the people behind it, they have sympathisers and supporters in the German police. In the German army. They must do if they intend to succeed. And if you tell the German Desk there's a chance word will get to these people.'

Delon looked at him doubtfully. 'I don't understand, why the plutonium?'

'To stop others interfering. It's the only answer that makes sense. Germany has never had a strategic nuclear arsenal of its own. And with nuclear weapons these people might be capable of anything. And my guess is that's what they have.'

Delon moved slowly across the room and let his body slump onto the couch. It was an act of indecision and it showed on his face, his brow furrowed in deep concentration and his big hands clenched and unclenched. A hand went up to his face and cupped his brow.

Volkmann watched him. Telling him about Schmeltz would totally bewilder him and Volkmann decided not to. For a long time Delon just sat there as if in deep shock. When he looked up and saw the grim look on Volkmann's face he seemed to finally realise he was being told the truth. He sat forward suddenly and shook his head.

'What you ask, I can't do it, Joe. I can't take the chance. It's too much to ask.' The Frenchman's blue eyes regarded Volkmann keenly.

'The girl . . . you're close to her?'

'Yes.'

'Then emotion is clouding your judgement. You must realise that?'

Volkmann shook his head. 'You're wrong, André. Believe me.'

'Then I have a question. These people, how much support have they got?'

'I don't know, André, but with the material they've got they don't need it. They simply hold the country to ransom.'

Delon thought a moment. 'You say you need time, but what do you propose to do?'

'There's one of their people in Munich named Kesser. He may know where they have the material. You give me eight hours. If I can find out I'll call you. In the meantime you contact your people. You contact every Section Head personally. But stay clear of the German Desk. Tell the others what I told you. There are people in Berlin I'd trust but I'd want to talk with them personally. The first thing to do is to locate the material. Point our people to it. You have the signal from Asunción. Show your people, and the others. Tell them what I intend doing.'

'And this *putsch*, when is it going to happen?'

'My guess is soon. It's Christmas, every army in Europe will have most of its personnel on leave. No one would be expecting something like this.'

Delon looked at Volkmann anxiously. 'And what if I don't hear from you within eight hours?'

'Then it's up to our governments. If it means crossing German borders to stop these people, I hope they're capable of making that decision.'

Delon sighed deeply and wiped his brow and Volkmann knew the Frenchman had given in.

Volkmann said, 'Can I keep the signal copy?'

'Yes. The original's still in the basement safe.'

'Give me a number where I can contact you, André.'

The Frenchman wrote a number on a piece of paper and handed it to Volkmann. 'You know the security-desk number and the others. I'll stay at headquarters. But that's my own private line, in case you can't get through. The lines were damaged by the blast but we patched up the emergency ones just before you rang. I'll call the Section Heads on a secure line as soon as I get back. I just hope they believe me.' The young man looked at him. 'You're sure you don't want any back-up?'

Volkmann shook his head. 'There isn't time, André.' He saw the beads of sweat on the young Frenchman's face as he looked at him.

'You think you're doing the right thing doing it this way, Joe?'

'It's the only way, André, believe me.'

'Then good luck, my friend.'

Volkmann took the road to Kehl. He estimated it would take over three hours to drive to Munich, sticking to the main autobahn and avoiding the road through the Black Forest to Herrenberg.

As he turned onto the autobahn to Ulm it started to snow and by the time he reached Augsburg almost two hours later it was coming down heavy, the fields of Württemberg already ghostly white.

The traffic was thin and as he passed Augsburg a column of twelve German army personnel carriers and six supply trucks lumbered in single file in the slow lane, heading towards Munich.

Volkmann's heart pounded as he overtook the army trucks slowly, trying to glimpse the stencilled divisional markings, but the vehicles were caked with snow and mud. Fifteen minutes later he pulled into the next filling station and made a call from the kiosk. The conversation lasted less than a minute.

As he climbed quickly back into the car he checked his watch before he turned back onto the Munich road. It read ten-fifteen.

Chapter Fifty-Three

Berlin.
8.15 p.m.

Kefir Ozalid stepped out of the crowded S-Bahn Station at Wannsee.

He carried the briefcase and wore his overcoat, scarf and woollen gloves and walked across the street towards the lake and stepped into the shadows between two street lamps. From where he stood he could see the dark jetties and the tourist boats tied up for the winter. The wind coming in off the choppy water was biting cold but he was immune to the icy blasts, adrenalin pumping through his veins.

He had hesitated at the station exit to make sure he hadn't been followed and now he checked again, pausing for several moments to light a cigarette, his breath fogging in the chilled air as he looked across at the lake in darkness then back over his shoulder.

He saw no one following him, only workers and Christmas shoppers coming out of the station, returning late from the city, but no one remotely interested in him. He waited a few moments, then turned towards the narrow road that led down to the lakeshore. It took him ten minutes to reach the house.

There were lights on downstairs and a Christmas tree stood in the window and as he walked past he saw the porch light was off, as it should be. He took the narrow footpath that led round the back and found the gate he had seen earlier. He flicked up the wooden latch and led himself in, eyes alert and watching. The houses nearby were bordered with high evergreens and their privacy ensured no one could see him.

There were no lights on at the rear of the house but he could see the open basement window and walked smartly across the lawn and knelt down. There was enough room for him to squeeze through and moments later he was standing in the basement.

He closed the window and made sure the latch was firmly locked in place before he removed the pencil torch from his pocket and shone the beam around the room.

The walls were painted lime green and there were five wooden boxes stacked against the wall furthest from the window. There was an old frayed ottoman covered in crushed red velvet below and to the right of the window. He saw the bare wooden stairs that led up. He placed the briefcase on the floor and crossed the room and climbed the stairs carefully, keeping to the side so the wood didn't creak.

When he had reached the top he gripped the door handle. As he opened the door a crack, faint music came from somewhere in the house. A pleasant wave of heat wafted against his face and he saw the stairs leading up to the bedrooms. He couldn't hear the girl but he knew she was there, somewhere in the house, a faint scent of perfume in the hallway.

He closed the door and descended the basement stairs, then crossed back to the ottoman. He lifted the lid and played the torch inside, smelled the musty smell and saw the jumble of discarded women's clothes: sweaters, coloured ski-pants and crumpled lace underwear. He closed the lid and sat down on the ottoman before picking up the briefcase and flicking open the locks. When he had removed the Beretta pistol and the silencer and the two loaded magazines, he closed the briefcase again and placed it beside him.

It took him less than twenty seconds to screw on the French-made Unique silencer and slide a magazine into the pistol butt. When he felt it gently click home he slipped the second magazine into his left pocket. He left the Beretta's safety catch on, but held the weapon lightly on his lap.

That morning after checking into the small hotel off the Witzleben he had taken the S-Bahn out to Wannsee, had walked by the house twice before taking the narrow side path that came out at the rear of the property, quickly examining the layout of the house and the grounds, relating the reality of his surroundings to the map and the photographs the German had given him in Stockholm. He had spent an hour walking through the narrow streets and footpaths that bordered the lake, getting his bearings. He rode back on the train to the S-Bahn Station on Witzleben and an hour later as he sat in his hotel room the knock came on the door.

The blond young man who stood there had looked him over silently before handing him the brown-wrappered parcel. Ozalid had waited until the man had gone before he unwrapped the parcel and removed the freshly oiled Beretta and the silencer and the two fully loaded magazines of nine-millimetre shells inside the clear plastic bag.

The same pistol he had been given ten solid hours of instruction with in the woods outside Stockholm. Solid-form targets at ten paces. Surprisingly, he had proven an expert shot. But Ozalid guessed it had more to do with unremitting motive than any latent talent.

He had checked the action of the blue-metal weapon and examined the silencer and magazines and then placed them carefully in the cut-out foam in the briefcase. Then he had lain on the bed and smoked four cigarettes. When he closed his eyes and tried to sleep the adrenalin was still racing through his veins and he swung his legs down and went to the bathroom and shaved and ran a hot bath. He lay silently in the steaming hot water for almost an hour, his mind going over the plan until his head ached. Then he had towelled himself dry and put on fresh clothes. The suitcase he would leave behind.

He had not taken the blue prayer mat with him, but there was a small red foot carpet by the bed and he carefully turned it round to face the wall before he knelt down. He said one final prayer for Layla before he touched the rug gently with his lips and stood up. Five minutes later he had locked the room after him and stepped down into the street and he walked towards the S-Bahn Station.

Now, sitting in the cold basement, he checked his watch: eight-forty-five.

Four more hours.

Four more hours and Dollman would be dead and Layla would be avenged.

He flicked off the torch and sat waiting patiently in the darkness, aware only of the faint sounds of his own breathing and the distant strains of the music coming from above.

Munich

It was ten-forty-five exactly when Volkmann pulled up outside the house in the Starnberg district.

Ivan Molke came out to stand under the porch light in the lightly falling snow as the Ford halted in the driveway. The older man didn't waste any time but quickly led Volkmann into a panelled study where a fire blazed in the grate.

When they were seated, Molke said seriously, 'Your phone call was very brief, Joe. Has this got something to do with what happened in Strasbourg? I heard it on the news.'

For a long time Volkmann looked at Molke, saying nothing. When Volkmann finally spoke his voice was thick with emotion. It took him almost five minutes to explain all that had happened and he saw the reaction on Molke's face as he spoke, disbelief mixed with fear, and when Volkmann had finished, Molke stared at him with wide, incredulous eyes.

'Is this some kind of absurd joke?'

'No joke, Ivan. You know me better.'

Molke shook his head from side to side, seeing the strained look on Volkmann's face. He reached across for a pack of cigarettes on the study desk, took one and lit it with trembling hands.

'*Jesus* . . .' he breathed. His face had turned chalk white and his voice trembled as he said, 'You're certain about the girl in the photograph?'

'Hanah Richter identified her, no question. The other part's guesswork, Ivan, but it makes some kind of sense. All the pieces of the puzzle fit together when you consider everything that's happened.'

'Karl Schmeltz is Adolf Hitler's son?' Molke shook his head and as he stood up he said, 'It sounds crazy, Joe.' His face was deathly pale. 'A neo-Nazi *putsch* I can imagine as possible, yes. But not another Hitler, Joe. Never that. No way.'

As Molke continued to shake his head, Volkmann took out the signal copy from Asunción and placed it on the study desk. Molke read the flimsy. After a time he looked up as if in a daze and walked back across the room and stared into the fire, then looked back at Volkmann.

'Tell me this isn't true, Joe. Tell me it isn't. Tell me I'm dreaming and this is a nightmare.'

'I wish I could.'

'The people who tailed my men, you think they were Kesser's people?'

'I don't know, Ivan. But it's possible. Has anyone been watching your house or tailing you since we last spoke?'

Molke shook his head grimly. 'Not that I'm aware of. And I've been careful, Joe, believe me. After what happened with my guys I've been extra vigilant.' Molke slipped his right hand into his trouser pocket and removed a slim automatic Browning, weighed it in his palm. 'I haven't been taking any chances. I keep this with me.' Molke swallowed hard as he placed the pistol on the study desk. 'Do you have any idea where the girl is now?'

'Assuming she's still alive, Kesser's people probably have her.'

'Where's Schmeltz, do you know?'

Volkmann shook his head. 'After what happened in Mexico City my guess is he's already in Germany. If not he will be soon.'

For a long time Molke looked at Volkmann blankly, then he said, 'What do you want me to do?'

'Do you know someone with authority in the State Ministry? Someone you'd trust your life with.'

Molke said palely, 'I don't know if I'd go that far with those guys. They're career types. But there's a politician in the upper house named Grinzing I'm on first-name terms with. He's the only one I can think of right now who might listen to me.'

'Then I want you to deliver a letter to him by hand, tonight. See that he reads it. In the letter will be everything that I've told you, everything I suspect, except what I told you about Karl Schmeltz. Because no doubt Grinzing will want to ask you a few questions about me.' Volkmann paused. 'Like if I'm crazy. If the letter is some kind of joke. The contents he'll have to judge for himself. Regarding me, I want you to be honest. Just tell him my background. Make him believe that he can trust me.' He looked directly at Molke. 'We worked together in Berlin for four years, Ivan. You know my character. You know I can be trusted. Simply tell him that when he asks. But above all tell him it's vital he acts on the letter. Tell him the signal from Asunción can be verified by Strasbourg. His own State Security people can make contact there directly.'

'Why don't you want me to tell him about Schmeltz?'

Volkmann shook his head. 'He'd never believe it, Ivan, you must know that. And explanations will only waste time. I don't know how long we've got before these people start to move but I can guess from what's happened it's going to be soon.'

'And if Grinzing doesn't believe me, what then?'

'You still know people in Berlin. Contact them. The same with the Landesamt here. Tell them what's going to happen, everything you're going to tell Grinzing.'

'You honestly think they'll believe me?'

Volkmann shook his head. 'I don't know. But you're the only hope I have, Ivan.'

'What are you going to do?'

'Drive over to Kesser's place. If he's not at the apartment, his girlfriend may be. One of them's got to know something. If neither of them are there I'll drive up to the place at Kaalberg.'

'And do what?'

'Find Kesser. He'll know what's going to happen and who's supporting them.'

Molke shook his head vigorously. 'Joe, you saw the armed guards up there. It's too dangerous. Let me call a couple of my people in as back-up.'

'There's no time to lose, Ivan, and it would complicate things further. Just deliver the letter.'

Molke sighed. For a while he said nothing, simply looked at Volkmann solemnly, sweat glistening on his forehead. Finally he shook his head.

'You know, I never thought this would ever happen again in Germany. Not in my lifetime. Sure, there's always been the crazy, extremist groups like the ones who burn down immigrant hostels or cause unrest. The shaven heads with swastikas who march and give the Nazi salute at the Brandenburg Gate every anniversary of Hitler's birth.' Molke shook his head again and crushed his cigarette fiercely into the ashtray. 'But not this. *Never this.*'

He tried not to think of the girl, but her face kept coming into his mind, and she was still in his thoughts when he reached Kesser's apartment off the Leopoldstrasse twenty minutes later. The snow had stopped falling and he tried to check his anger as he stepped out of the car, forcing himself to figure out how to handle Kesser or his girlfriend.

There were Christmas candles burning in the windows of apartments and nearby houses, and here and there the lights of a Christmas tree winked on and off. The lights were off in Kesser's apartment and as he walked towards the block entrance he saw no sign of the grey Volkswagen in the parking lot. His heart skipped a beat when he thought Kesser or his girlfriend might not be at home.

He had the Beretta in his pocket, and the safety catch was on. This time he used the copy keys Ivan Molke had given him and he let himself in the front entrance and went up to the second floor.

He hesitated before knocking on the apartment door, but when he knocked three times and there was no reply he let himself in, the key offering a little resistance before it turned in the lock.

The apartment was in complete darkness and as he flicked on the light nothing happened and then suddenly he was caught in the glare of a powerful beam of torchlight. As he wrenched

603

the Beretta frantically from his pocket he felt the hard stinging blow on the back of his neck. Then there was only a blinding pain and whiteness as he heard the muffled voices and felt the fists hammer painfully into his body and then something sharp jab his left arm.

He was barely conscious but still fighting blindly as he was carried back down the stairs and out into the cold air and then there was only the distant far-off sounds of car doors opening as he was bundled into a narrow space.

After that the blinding whiteness took over and it seemed to smother him.

When he came awake he saw the snow falling beyond the windscreen wipers as the car's headlights probed the way ahead. He felt a stab of excruciating pain behind his eyes and when he tried to move his head he started to go under again. He was faintly aware of the lights of the city far below him and beyond the falling snow and he heard the engine whine as the car moved up a steep hill. As he strained to look again another stab of pain arced across his forehead.

The last thing he saw before he started to go under again was the pistol in the hand of the man seated beside him.

Chapter Fifty-Four

It was almost eleven-forty when Ivan Molke saw the black
BMW pull into the driveway of the house in Bogenhausen,
the exclusive inner suburb across the Isar.

He had telephoned only to be told that Johann Grinzing was
unavailable and had gone to a Ministry Christmas party at the
Steigenberger Hotel on the Hofplatz.

Molke had telephoned the hotel and had Grinzing paged.
After several checks a colleague had come to the telephone
and said Grinzing had left early.

Molke had driven back across the Isar at high speed and
parked outside Grinzing's residence. There was a uniformed
policeman on duty in the hut that stood inside the gates and
Molke showed his ID and the man phoned through. Grinzing
still wasn't at home and Molke had told the policeman that
he would wait. The man had regarded him warily and twice
afterwards he had appeared at the gate, walking down from
the house to watch Molke's car, until another plain-clothes
man had come out from the house to join them and, recognising
Molke, walked over to the car.

'What's this all about, Ivan?'

'I'm waiting for Grinzing. Private business.'

'You've no appointment?'

'No.'

'I can't let you wait inside, Ivan. Grinzing will have to give
me clearance first.'

When Molke saw the lights sweep up the snowy tree-lined
avenue moments later, he waited until the car had entered
the driveway and then the BP bodyguard telephoned through
and one minute later Molke found himself in Grinzing's study.
The panelled room was cold and the walls were lined with
expensive, leather-bound tomes.

Johann Grinzing was forty-two, tall, with blond, thinning hair and a high forehead. An ambitious man who exuded an air of confidence, he wore his expensively tailored suits well. His face was rugged rather than handsome and his slim hands were perfectly manicured. If he had left the party early Molke considered that Grinzing had probably spent the rest of the evening with one of the pretty young secretaries from the Ministry pool. A minor weakness with the man was women, yet he was still one of those in the Ministry whom Molke felt he could trust.

Grinzing lit a cigarette and sat behind his study desk, gesturing for Molke to be seated opposite.

He glanced at his watch and regarded Molke with raised eyes. 'So, what brings you here, Ivan? Is there a problem?'

Molke nodded. 'I need your help, Johann.'

'Tell me.' Grinzing glanced at his watch again impatiently. 'But please make it quick. I have to be up quite early and I must get my beauty sleep.' White teeth flashed a smile but when Molke didn't smile back, Grinzing said simply, 'How can I help you?'

Molke reached inside his overcoat pocket and took out the buff-coloured envelope. He saw Grinzing stare at it and before Molke handed it across he said, 'I want you to do two things for me, Johann. First, I want you to listen to what I have to say, then I want you to read the contents of this envelope.'

Grinzing said impatiently, 'What's this, Ivan?'

'A friend asked me to give it to someone I trusted in the State Ministry. Someone with influence. Once he had told me what it was about I chose you.'

'I'm flattered, but go on.'

'The man's name is Volkmann. Joseph Volkmann. He works for the DSE in Strasbourg.'

Grinzing raised his eyebrows perceptibly. 'This has something to do with security?'

'Yes.'

'Bavarian or national?'

'Both. I could have gone to the State Interior Minister,

Kaindel, or even contacted Weber myself, but I don't know either personally.'

Grinzing hesitated, then lifted the cigarette to his mouth, drew on it slowly as if considering something, before he blew out smoke.

'So, tell me.'

'Before you read what's in the envelope I want you to know two things. One, there was a bomb planted at the DSE offices this afternoon.'

Grinzing nodded solemnly. 'I heard it on the news in the car. Has this got something to do with it?'

Molke nodded back. 'Then you may also have heard that the Head of the British DSE was killed. Plus another man. Also British.'

'I thought it was two missing? That's what the last report said.'

'That's Volkmann. He hasn't contacted his people in London.'

Grinzing raised his eyes again, and said, 'Go on, please.'

'Number two, Volkmann is totally trustworthy. I worked with him in Berlin. He's one of the few people I'd trust with my life.'

'Why are you telling me all this?'

'Because after you read the letter, probably the first question you're going to ask me is, do I trust him? I want that clear from the start. I do. Implicitly.'

Grinzing said a little impatiently, 'You're finished with the preamble?'

'Yes.'

'May I see this letter?'

Ivan Molke handed it across. As Grinzing leaned over to take it Molke saw that there were small beads of perspiration on the man's forehead. He scented trouble in the wind, and from the look on his face he was mildly excited. Grinzing opened the unsealed envelope and plucked out the contents, unfolded the pages promptly and read.

Molke watched Grinzing's tanned face become waxen and then he looked up. 'Is this Volkmann serious?'

'Perfectly.'

'And you really trust him?' There was a tone of incredulity in Grinzing's question.

'I told you already, Johann. Please believe what you read.'

Grinzing shook his head slowly, his voice only a whisper. 'It's almost beyond comprehension.' He looked down at the pages again and then up at Molke. 'You really expect me to go to the State Prime Minister with this? That a group of neo-Nazis are planning to take over the country? That they may have a nuclear weapon?'

'If you don't then I will. There isn't much time. A matter of hours, perhaps.'

'And where's this Volkmann now?'

'In Munich.'

Grinzing put down the letter. 'I'd be laughed at. You must realise this.'

Molke said grimly, 'And you must realise that if these people carry out what they intend, this entire country is in danger of stepping back over fifty years.'

'I find that difficult to believe. And even if what you said were true, a democracy like Germany cannot be dismantled overnight by such people. It's absurd.'

Molke looked pointedly at his watch, then back at Grinzing determinedly.

'They'll have supporters. In parliament. In the armed forces. In the police. They have to have because it's the only way they can stand a chance of succeeding. And it only takes a small number to lend their support to this act of madness for the whole country to be plunged into chaos and for the nightmare that happened in Germany to be repeated again.'

Grinzing shook his head, but his face was pale and his voice hoarse. 'I really can't believe that, Ivan. It's not possible.'

Molke sighed deeply. 'Very well. May I have the letter back? I'll take it to the Minister myself, even if I have to kick down his bedroom door.'

Grinzing hesitated. For a long time he looked at the letter in his hand and then he looked up at Molke slowly, as if reconsidering. Molke saw the beads of perspiration on the man's forehead glistening in the light from over-head.

Grinzing said, 'What if the Minister believes you? What do you expect him to do?'

'Alert Berlin and Bonn. The BfV federal office in Cologne will have a list of loyal army and police officers the country can rely on. Every sensible democracy takes that precaution to counter such a situation as this. A coup that might threaten its existence.'

'And if the Minister doesn't believe you?'

'I think he will. But if he doesn't I still have friends in Berlin who might listen.' Molke's voice became strained. 'My God, Grinzing, we have to do *something*.'

There was an uncharacteristic anger in Molke's voice and Grinzing hesitated, looking as if a great weight were pressing down on him. Finally, he stared directly at Molke.

'I want you to do something for me.'

'What?'

'Give me five minutes alone to think this through. You must understand my position. Such a decision cannot be taken lightly.'

Molke looked at his watch, saw the anxiety on Grinzing's face.

Molke nodded. 'OK.'

Grinzing stood, clutching the pages. 'I'll leave you here alone. You'll have my answer within five minutes.'

As the door closed softly after Grinzing, Ivan Molke let out a deep sigh.

At least the man was beginning to take him seriously.

Johann Grinzing stepped out into the hallway, past the guard sitting in the chair reading a newspaper under the portrait of Grinzing's father.

The guard went to rise out of respect, but Grinzing gestured for him to remain seated. He crossed out through the kitchen and stepped towards the back door, opened it softly and moved outside.

The gardens were white and the air crisp and cold, the

branches of the bare apple and pear trees at the end of the garden covered in fingers of snow and the house behind him eerily quiet. His wife had gone to her mother's in Bodensee with their two daughters for the holidays and even the servants were on leave. His brow was aflame with fever and he hesitated briefly before he lit another cigarette.

It had stopped snowing, but only for a time, Grinzing knew. Not that the weather was his preoccupation but the cool had a mildly calming effect. And he needed calming. What he had just heard from Molke disturbed him greatly.

As he stood there, reflecting on the situation, Grinzing dabbed his brow with a handkerchief.

For eighteen years he had been a public servant. For all those years he had never been faced with a decision as grave as this one. He stared down at the pages in his hand, legible in the harsh wash of light from the security floodlight on the back wall of the house. What Molke had said was true. There *was* a list of people loyal to the Government. They could be activated quickly, if necessary. Cover all the major cities and ports; air and sea.

He thought of making a call first to seek advice but reconsidered. He was on his own. It was his decision to expedite the matter if he chose. Any delay would be on his shoulders.

He would have to inform his superiors and urgently. But he would extract the most from it, of course. If he came out of it well, there was opportunity here.

But how to approach it? How to resolve it? His mind began working feverishly, yet he was aware of the passing minutes.

Three minutes later he had figured out what to do, sweat pumping from his brow. He dabbed it once more and replaced the handkerchief in his pocket. He stepped back inside and closed the door after him but forgot to wipe his feet, went through the kitchen and out into the hallway again. This time the BP man didn't rise but simply gave a respectful nod and went back to reading his paper. Late-night visitors were common in Grinzing's household.

For a few brief seconds Grinzing glanced up at the painting of his father. The blue-suited man stood erect, behind him in the portrait the distant image of the Munich Rathaus, the State and Federal flags flying above the clock tower. A loyal Bavarian to the core. It was strangely appropriate, Grinzing reflected. The man had been dead some twenty-five years. The portrait's blue eyes stared down and seemed to warn him. What he was about to do could ruin him if it went wrong. Already there were doubts in his mind. Yet he knew he had to go through with it. His future could hang on this. And the future of the Fatherland.

His father's eyes looked on just as he remembered them. Blue. Honest. True. A fanatically loyal servant to his Fatherland and State. Only the blue business-suit looked out of place.

All that was missing, Grinzing reflected – recalling the old photographs he had kept since childhood – was the black uniform of the Leibstandarte SS.

Molke turned as Grinzing stepped back into the study and closed the door after him. When the man had crossed the room and sat behind the desk again, Molke said, 'You've reached a decision?'

'Yes.'

'Which is it?'

'There are a few matters I wish to discuss first.'

Molke saw Grinzing's hand reach over slowly behind the desk. In an instant the drawer was opened and the Walther pistol was cocked and pointing at Molke's chest.

Molke stared over and went to speak but no words came.

Grinzing said, 'I want you to listen to me very carefully, Molke. What I have to say and how you react may determine whether you live or die in the next few minutes.'

Molke still said nothing, simply stared at the man and then at the Walther again, his mouth open in disbelief.

Grinzing said calmly, 'You're surprised, Molke, I can see that. I have a confession to make but one which by now you've undoubtedly guessed. The people you are in so much fear of, I belong to that group. I and many, many others.'

Molke said, simply, 'Why?'

There was a grim, nervous smile on Grinzing's thin lips. 'Why? I'll tell you why. Because for the first time in years this country has a chance to be truly strong again. To re-instil the old virtues we once prided ourselves on. To stop apologising for our past. To cleanse our country of all the filthy, stupid imported breeds our politicians had the mendacity to invite here. To reawaken a sense of pride in being German. And I wish to be part of that change that is about to take place. It offers a great future for someone like me, I think you'll agree.'

'You're a fool, Grinzing. You'll rot in prison for the rest of your days when this is over. It can't succeed.'

'On the contrary, it can. Too much planning has gone into it for it not to succeed. It can't fail and it won't.

'Dollman and the Cabinet would never sit back and allow this country to be dragged into the gutter again by you and your friends.'

'Dollman won't be alive to obstruct us. As for the Cabinet . . .' Grinzing hesitated and smiled. 'I think I've said enough already. Suffice it to say that they won't be able to hinder our plans.'

'You're crazy, Grinzing. That's an act of madness. The German people would never support the murder of the Chancellor. Never. You'd be signing your own death warrants.'

'But they will, Molke. It has all been worked out. Our strategy will ensure the people will rally behind us. And once they see that we are capable of elevating this country to its former greatness, building a new and prosperous and powerful Reich that will stand tall and proud and strong again, one day they will thank us. It can and will be done, I assure you, and that's all you need to know. Doesn't the prospect excite you just a little?'

Molke ignored the question and looked at Grinzing. 'It all sounds like a nice little speech, Grinzing. Did it take you long to rehearse it?'

Grinzing's thin smile widened. 'If you're trying to anger me, Molke, trying to deflect me in an attempt to make a run for it, forget it. You'd have a bullet in you before you'd gone one pace. And believe me, I'm a capable marksman. But you can take your chances if you wish. It would be my word against the word of a dead man. A dead man who had already waited anxiously outside my home for my return. Rather suspicious, don't you think? One of the guards even asked me if I wanted him to be present. He said you looked troubled, Molke. And troubled men are capable of strange behaviour. Like attempting to murder a State politician.' Grinzing smiled again nervously. 'I'm certain I could come up with a plausible reason as to why you tried to kill me and how I defended myself.'

Molke said grimly, 'I want to hear your reasons.'

Grinzing raised his eyebrows before he spoke. 'You just heard them.'

'And the nuclear material? Tell me why.'

'I would have thought that was obvious, Molke. There is a warhead. It will give us the leverage to seize NATO nuclear missiles on German soil and foil any attempt by outside powers to interfere. If any of the world powers attempt to stop our progress they face the possibility of a holocaust. And Germany still has the largest army in Western Europe, Molke, don't forget that.' Grinzing paused. 'There's nothing more to say, except that after the *putsch* happens – and it will happen, Molke, it's happening already, even as we speak – there will be a reckoning. Those with us, those against us. Those against will be dealt with harshly, I assure you.'

'No doubt, Grinzing, you're going to start building concentration camps again.'

Grinzing smiled again. 'I'm sure that will be on the agenda if these imported breeds refuse to leave our country. A necessary evil, I'm afraid, to rid us of unacceptable elements.' Grinzing paused. 'You're a sensible fellow, Molke. I've always thought you so. You have an option now. There's a door off to my right. It leads eventually to the garage. I can phone through to the guard and tell him we're leaving. You come with me quietly and sensibly. If you make no fuss, by noon tomorrow I promise I shall make those who will be in power aware of your . . . shall we say, silent compliance. You'll be a free man.'

Molke glanced towards the door, then looked back. 'I'm a free man now.'

Grinzing smiled. 'Of course you are. Except I have a gun pointed at your chest and won't hesitate to use it if you try to call the guards or escape.'

For a long time Molke hesitated as he looked blankly towards the far wall, then he turned back to stare at Grinzing.

'I want to tell you something, Grinzing. And also ask your advice. But first, may I have a cigarette?'

Grinzing hesitated, then nervously took a cigarette from the pack on the table, lit it, handed it across carefully, the Walther still trained on Molke's chest.

Grinzing flicked a glance at his watch. 'Tell me what you wanted to say.'

Molke drew hard on the cigarette and stared across at the man seated opposite. 'It concerns my father.' Molke saw the frown on Grinzing's forehead and then went on, 'I'm sure you understand father-son relationships, don't you? The portrait on the wall outside. Is it of your father?'

'Yes.'

Molke nodded. 'I thought as much. So you were close. He influenced you.'

'Get on with it, Molke, I'm losing patience.'

'If you told me he was a Nazi Party member, I doubt if it would surprise me.'

'Both Nazi and SS. Leibstandarte SS.'

Molke saw the look of pride on Grinzing's face as he spoke.

'Do you know anything about that organisation, Molke?'

'They were murderers.'

'On the contrary. They were the best, most loyal soldiers this country ever had. The cream of Germany. The chosen few. And their officers were the élite of the SS. The most fanatical, unswerving men the Reich had. Let me tell you something, Molke. My father and many others like him took an oath to Adolf Hitler and the Reich. To perpetuate the ideals they fought for and made sacrifices for. To serve their Fatherland with every gram of their being. And the only people who have the given right to lead this country to greatness again are their children and their children's children. I am one of them. We've waited a long time for the right moment and now it's come. Look at what's happening in this country, Molke. Not only on the streets. Even ordinary Germans are saying the Reich had its merits. Why? Because they know it's time to clean this country up, Molke. Time to wake up and be Germans again. Time to shake off that stupid mantel of pious remorse for the past. To purify this country and clean up its mess. And yes, you were right, there are people, many in positions of power, people like me, men and women who have waited a long time for this moment. They are bound in blood to fulfil their fathers' pledges. And believe me, Molke, when the time comes, and it will come within the next hours, they will do their duty.'

Molke looked at Grinzing palely. 'I can't believe you think that every German thinks like that, Grinzing. If you do you ought to be certified. Or that every son and daughter of every SS officer will support this madness.'

Grinzing half smiled. 'Those who don't will be dealt with. Some already have been. They disgraced their father's testimony by refusing to help us in the days ahead. But those with us will help mould the future, will help create an even greater Germany. I'm talking about a formidable force, Molke, not some half-baked group of anarchists. Do you understand what I'm saying?'

Molke said nothing for several moments. There was an almost manic look on Grinzing's face. Finally Molke said, 'Then I think you're going to appreciate what I have to say, because it's going to affect the outcome of this situation.'

'How?'

Ivan Molke hesitated. When he spoke, his voice was calm, almost without emotion. 'In 1935 my father was a young man of twenty with a young wife and a baby. He was a socialist and lived in Berlin. After the Nazis came to power they began to purge the socialists and communists, but doubtless you know that . . .'

'I'm growing tired of this conversation already, Molke, I think you had better finish rather quickly.'

'Bear with me. Because after I tell you I want to ask your advice.' Molke paused a second, saw Grinzing stare at him quizzically. 'My father was called on one night by the Gestapo. They took him to Spandau and beat him to within a breath of his life. Why? Because he was a socialist. Because he had dared to join a party other than the Nazi Party. Because, in the words of the Nazi propaganda writers, he was "an anti-social element". For that privilege he spent twelve years in concentration camps. At Flossenberg he broke and carried rocks and was treated worse than a pack mule. He was beaten, humiliated, starved. He was treated as less than human. He was whipped on the whipping block until he couldn't walk and that for simply losing a button on his camp uniform. All these things, the endless beatings, the humiliations, the erosion of his privilege as a human being, they affected him deeply. He saw men being killed on the whim of a guard. Men being killed for no reason other than the sadistic pleasure of a camp commandant. He saw boys of no more than fourteen being hung from gibbets because the SS guards wanted some fun to liven up their dull afternoons; place a bet on who would wriggle the longest before death.'

'You're trying my patience, Molke . . .'

'I'm almost finished. My father survived the camps. But he wasn't my father any more. He was dead.' Molke raised a finger, put it to his head. 'Up here he was dead. A ghost walking in our house. A father we could never get close to because his pain was like a wall around him.' He looked intently at Grinzing. 'There are no Jews worth talking of in Germany, Grinzing. Not any more. But there are Turks and Serbs and Poles and others who no doubt your neo-Nazi comrades would class as racially inferior. Scapegoats to blame. Impurities to cleanse. Will they be the new Jews? Will they go to the ovens too?'

There were tears in Molke's eyes and very slowly he leaned a little forward towards Grinzing. He saw Grinzing move back slightly in his chair and raise the Walther.

'So I have a question for you, Grinzing. What would you do in my situation? If your father had been an inmate at Flossenberg would you keep your mouth shut and believe in someone like you? Or even in this man Schmeltz? This man you believe to be Hitler's son. Would you, Grinzing? Or would you take your chances?'

There was a brief, quizzical smile on Grinzing's lips and then his mouth opened in alarm as he heard Ivan Molke's words.

Molke shifted his hand quickly to his right pocket and shifted left just as the Walther in Grinzing's right hand exploded.

The first shot clipped Molke's right shoulder blade, shattered bone, the force of the nine-millimetre bullet jacking his body backwards, the second bullet nicking the aorta above his heart.

But the third shot was from Molke's own Browning automatic he carried in his right pocket. One shot before the weapon jammed on the reciprocating load.

The bullet hit Johann Grinzing square in the face, drilling a neat hole through the bridge of the man's nose and exiting the middle of the cranium, sending thick, viscous spurts of crimson in both directions. A jet of blood hit Molke in the face as he slid off the chair before collapsing onto the floor.

As his head thudded against the carpet there were screams and shouts from outside and then the study door burst in and the cries and rushing feet rent the air. Hands gripped Molke, shook him, wrenched his hand from his pocket.

As consciousness went from him, he heard voices swearing, saw hands moving about Grinzing, whose body had been flung backwards and hit the wall, then slid down and listed to the right before collapsing on the floor behind the desk, his shattered face lying directly across from Molke's.

They stared at each other in death.

The last thing Ivan Molke saw before he closed his eyes and death swept in was the look of utter surprise on Grinzing's dead face.

Chapter Fifty-Five

As the car jerked to a halt, Volkmann became conscious again.

The headlights were extinguished and the car doors opened. He saw the secluded house directly in front of the driveway. There was a garage off to the left and the front door of the house was open.

A row of pine trees ran up along the sloped driveway and he could see the lights of the city beyond the trees and the thinly falling snow. He thought he saw the lights of other houses through the pines and he guessed they were somewhere in the mountains near Munich. When he looked back he saw the figure of Wolfgang Lubsch step out of a lighted doorway into the falling snow. He wore a heavy parka and his spectacles glinted under the light.

There was an arc light on overhead somewhere and as the terrorist stood watching, Volkmann was dragged from the car and moments later they were in a warm comfortable living-room. Glass doors led to a balcony and all the lights were on. On a table were a half-bottle of schnapps and some glasses.

Lubsch kicked forward a chair. 'Sit down, Volkmann.'

When Volkmann ignored the command, the terrorist said, 'Under normal circumstances I'd have no hesitation putting a bullet in your head. You're not a journalist, are you, Volkmann?'

Volkmann stared back at Lubsch. The icy blasts of air that hit him as he was dragged from the car had brought him quickly awake, but he was still fighting to regain his senses.

Lubsch lit a cigarette and looked at him. 'It wasn't difficult to discover who you are, Volkmann. People like you and me, we scent each other like cat and dog. After our talk at the lake, you worried me. Who were you? Why were you so interested in Winter's death? So interested that you'd risk coming after me, despite my warning.'

Volkmann spoke slowly as he stared at the young man's face. 'The airport in Zurich, those were your people?'

Lubsch blew smoke out into the air. 'Every move you and the girl have made since the day at the lake, we've been watching you both. You don't know how close you came to losing your life at the monastery, Volkmann.'

'How?'

Lubsch sat down. 'How did we follow you? The girl was easy. But you . . .' Lubsch reached into his pocket, removed a small electronic device with a pin-like aerial, held it between two fingers. 'A simple transmitter attached to your car. That way we couldn't lose you. The same with your friend Molke and his men. You see, you confounded us, Volkmann. Everything about this business confounded us. Until now.'

'You're not with Kesser and his people?'

'Give me some credit, Volkmann. We accepted his help, but that was of necessity.'

'Where are we?'

'Somewhere quiet where we won't be disturbed.'

Volkmann looked round the room. Two of Lubsch's men stood in front of the door that led out. One held a Walther in his hand. Volkmann recognised both of them. One was the man named Hartig he had seen at the car window; the other the scar-faced young man who had wielded the truncheon. Both looked over at him, their faces expressionless. Volkmann turned back to face Lubsch.

'Why have you brought me here? To let your friends settle old scores?'

'Hardly. We have matters to discuss.'

'What have we got to discuss?'

'Something of importance to both of us.' Lubsch paused. 'You must forgive the behaviour of my men, Volkmann. But you see, we thought Kesser's people would turn up looking for their missing friend. Instead, you showed. It was quite a surprise.'

Volkmann looked at the terrorist's face. 'Where's Kesser, do you have him?'

Lubsch ignored the question and stood. He crossed to the window and turned back to face Volkmann.

'We Germans, we have a certain drama about us. We can be loud, aggressive, unfeeling. But we are not all beasts, Volkmann. Even us so-called terrorists. And we don't all want another Reich.'

'You know what Kesser's people intend?'

'Yes, Volkmann, I know.'

'Did Kesser tell you?'

'Hardly. He's dead.'

Volkmann went to speak, but Lubsch interrupted. 'Two of my men were waiting for him outside his apartment. My instructions were to take Kesser alive. I had hoped he would tell us what we needed to know. Kesser came out and drove to the mountain. Halfway there my men overtook his car and blocked the road. When Kesser realised what was happening he pulled a gun and shot one of my men. They fired back. One of them hit Kesser in the head. He was still alive when they took him to one of our safe houses. But by the time I got there, he was dead.'

Volkmann took a deep breath in anger, let it out. 'Do you know what you've done, Lubsch . . .?'

'The world's a better place without him, believe me, Volkmann.'

'Did you kill Winter too?'

'That was Kesser's own people.'

'Why?'

'I told you at the lake, Volkmann. Winter was a braggart. And especially when he was drunk. He liked to talk about the new order he and his friends were going to create. The new Germany. The closer it got, the more Winter talked. So Kesser used him less and less, because he'd started to drink too much and talk too much. Until Kesser gets a call from one of their people in Berlin to say Winter's in a bar and drunk and shooting his mouth off about things he shouldn't. For that, Kesser had him hit. And they hit him near the Zoo Station so maybe the cops will think there's a drugs connection and Winter's been killed because of that.'

Volkmann looked away, towards the lights of the city beyond the glass doors, then back again.

'Why did you want to take Kesser?'

'The same reason as you. To find out what his people intend. Two of my men were watching your apartment in Strasbourg. They saw the girl being taken by two men in a black Mercedes. They heard an explosion and decided to keep tailing the Mercedes. They managed to follow the car as far as Augsburg, but lost it in the bad weather. We guessed Kesser's people were behind what happened, so we decided it was time to pay him a visit.'

There was sweat on Volkmann's face as he stared at Lubsch. 'Do you know where the girl is?'

'At the place you followed Kesser to, the Kaalberg.'

'She's alive?'

'I've no idea, Volkmann.'

'How do you know she's at the mountain?'

'The same way I learned about Winter. After what happened to Kesser, we went back for his girl. Once we showed her Kesser's body, the rest was easy. She's involved, only her loyalty didn't extend to losing her own life. Taking the girl in Strasbourg was part of a plan Kesser's people had. To find out how much she and your people knew.'

'What else did Kesser's girlfriend tell you?'

Lubsch looked steadily at Volkmann. 'The people behind it. What they intend. Everything she knew.'

'Tell me.'

Lubsch hesitated, reached for the bottle of schnapps and one of the glasses. He filled the glass quickly and handed it to Volkmann.

Volkmann pushed it away. 'I don't want a drink, Lubsch. I want to know what the girl told you.'

'Take it, Volkmann. You're going to need it when I tell you. And then, my friend, I'll tell you what we're going to do.'

Snow flew against the windows. Volkmann had emptied the

glass and replaced it on the table. Lubsch poured himself a drink and went to stand by the fire.

'They've got a missile sited at the Kaalberg. The nuke variety, not a conventional warhead. They've got neo-Nazi cells in the army and police, and politicians who are supporting them. The man you asked me about at the lake, Schmeltz. He's there, at the mountain, he's the one who's pulling the strings. They're trying to repeat history with a *putsch*, just like the Nazis tried in '23. Only this time there's a missile as a deterrent. If any outside power tries to march over German borders and interfere, they risk a calamity.'

Lubsch swallowed the liquid in one gulp. 'The girl wasn't privileged enough to know everything. But she knew enough. To start with, they're going to kill Dollman and his Cabinet.' Lubsch saw the look on Volkmann's face.

'How?'

'There's a house in Berlin's Wannsee where Dollman keeps his mistress. Her name's Lisl Henning. She's one of Kesser's people. Dollman's due there sometime after midnight. There's a Turk named Kefir Ozalid waiting to put a bullet in his head . . .'

'And the Cabinet . . .?'

'The girl didn't know. Only that it happens after Dollman gets hit. They'll all be killed.'

Volkmann hesitated, the voices on the tape suddenly clear. There were beads of sweat on his face as he spoke. 'Why Ozalid, why not one of Kesser's own people?'

'Because they've been very clever, Volkmann. As soon as Ozalid pulls the trigger and the Cabinet get hit, the streets are going to be full of righteous Germans baying for immigrant blood. Kesser's friends have set it up perfectly. They blame the deaths of Dollman and the Cabinet on immigrant extremists. They pit German against immigrant and in the chaos make their *putsch* a walkover.' Lubsch put down his glass. 'They've got everything worked out down to the last detail. The monastery you went to see. You know what it's for? It's to be a detention centre . . . for undesirables. Immigrants and others. Another Dachau, no doubt. And it's not the only one.

Kesser had a long list of such places to fill once their people take over. And they'll have most of the country on their side after Dollman and his Cabinet are killed.'

For a long time Volkmann looked towards the windows, saying nothing, then he looked back at Lubsch.

'Tell me what you intend doing?'

'The only thing we can do. We can't reach Berlin, but the Kaalberg is half an hour from here. My men and I are going to try and take out the missile. Neutralise it.'

'You're making a mistake, Lubsch. There's no way you'll succeed on your own. Let me call Berlin. They'll send in their people . . .'

Lubsch shook his head. 'How long's it going to take you to convince them, Volkmann? And by then it may be too late.'

'What makes you think you and your men can succeed?'

'Volkmann, in this weather, we'll be lucky just to make it up the mountain. But if we do we stand some chance. By simply informing Berlin we have none. The girl didn't know how Kesser's friends are going to hit the Cabinet, but someone up there will. If Dollman's killed, this country can still pull together and stop what's happening. Without a government, there isn't a chance in hell and Kesser's friends can do what they want.

'According to the girl, there's never more than a half-dozen armed guards on the property. I have three men with me, with you and me that makes five in all, so the odds are pretty even.'

'You'll need weapons.'

'We have them. Machine-pistols, grenades.' Lubsch half smiled. 'Most of them supplied by Kesser's people. Ironic, don't you think?' Lubsch hesitated. 'So what do you say, Volkmann? Are you with us?'

Volkmann looked out beyond the window, at the lights discernible beyond the mist of slanting white. He turned back to Lubsch. His eyes searched the terrorist's face. 'Why are you doing this, Lubsch? Why are you helping me?'

'For the reason I told you, Volkmann. I don't want another Reich or anything like it. To you, I'm simply a terrorist. But

I believe in a better future for my country. That future may not be to your liking, and it may be idealist. But of one thing I'm certain. Kesser's type don't belong in it. I don't want the mistakes of the past repeated. Because if that happens, there would never be another Germany. Not ever.' Lubsch smiled grimly. 'Absurd, I know, you and I joining forces, but there you have it.' Lubsch stared at Volkmann. 'So are you with us?'

Volkmann hesitated. 'There are two things I want to make clear.'

'What?'

'I make my call to Berlin.'

Lubsch considered a moment, then said, 'And the second?'

'The man . . . Schmeltz.'

'What about him?'

Volkmann looked away, towards the window and the falling snow, then back at the terrorist's face. 'If we make it up the mountain, he's mine.'

Lubsch said nothing for several moments. 'It's not only because of the girl, is it, Volkmann? Not only because of Erica Kranz?'

'There's something the girl didn't tell you about Schmeltz.'

The terrorist shook his head and his voice was suddenly strained.

'She told us, Volkmann. I didn't mention it because I thought you'd think I'd lost my reason.' Lubsch shook his head as if in disbelief. 'Part of me wants to believe what she said, and yet another part of me is questioning my sanity. And yet I know she didn't lie. Not now, not after you've told me. They say that history repeats itself. Only in this case, who would have believed it?' He paused. 'What do you want, Volkmann? A chance to speak for the dead?'

Chapter Fifty-Six

The Mercedes braked to a halt on the gravel driveway.

The porch light was on outside the house and as Ritter opened the car door for Dollman, the Chancellor slid out of the warm limousine.

The girl was waiting in the hallway and she hesitated while Ritter disappeared as usual into the study before she closed the front door and led Dollman inside.

On the dining-room table supper was laid: a bottle of Dom Perignon stood in a silver bucket of crushed ice, beside it a selection of cold dishes. There were fresh flowers and two lighted candles. The girl had drawn the curtains to stop the prying eyes of the bodyguards and as Dollman crumpled into a leather armchair by the fire the girl smiled and went to stand behind him.

She massaged his shoulders and Dollman groaned with pleasure. Moments later she felt his hand grasp her arm and he pulled her round. She saw the wolfish smile on his face and knew it of old, his eyes feasting on the firm breasts beneath the tight blouse.

She saw the look of impatience on his face and said, 'Let's eat first.'

Dollman's hand went to slide along her thigh but she smiled and took his hand and led him to the table.

Dollman wolfed down his food and drank three glasses of champagne. When it came to dessert the girl stood and came round to serve him with chocolate mousse. He looked longingly again at the firm breasts, his eyes moving greedily over her full, inviting hips and the long legs and the sheer black stockings she wore. He let his hand slide down the curve of her thigh, felt the slight, uneven bump of the suspender belt beneath.

The girl smiled down at him. 'What about dessert?'

The Chancellor grinned. 'I'd much rather have you, my sweet.'

She smiled back and Dollman stood and took her by the hand and led her upstairs to the bedroom.

Five minutes later, as Dollman undressed, he watched as Lisl slid a disc into the hi-fi and listened as the strains of Wagner filled the room.

The girl undressed slowly and came to lie beside him on the pink silk sheets. For several moments Dollman's eyes feasted on the perfect body, and then he took her hungrily, grinding his hips into hers. Five minutes later his body shuddered as he spent his frustration.

He kissed her shoulder, the scent of her perfume mingling with the musky smell of sex, but when his hand moved to satisfy her minutes later, she gently pushed it away.

'Sleep, *liebchen*. You're tired.'

Dollman murmured, grateful for the reprieve, and turned over.

The girl waited several minutes before she slid off the bed and crossed to the window and peered out through a chink in the curtain. She could see the three cars parked below: one in the street, the others in the driveway, but no movement. But they were out there, Ritter's men. And Ritter himself downstairs in the study, as usual.

As the curtain fell back into place she heard Dollman begin to snore, his big naked body rumbling under the covers. She checked her watch before she crossed to the hi-fi again. She lowered the volume to near silence, waiting for the second hand to sweep past for one minute exactly, aware of her heart beating furiously, then she raised the volume again gradually until the music resumed its former pitch. She pulled on her silk nightgown and went to sit at the dressing table. She lit a cigarette, the fear and excitement causing her stomach to flutter, her hands trembling as she stared down at her watch again.

One-ten.

In another ten minutes it would all be over.

In the basement room, Ozalid tensed as he heard the strains of Wagner die and flicked on the pencil torch. He watched the second hand sweep round; one minute and then the music rose again in pitch.

He had heard the cars pulling into the driveway; heard the sounds of footsteps on the stairs as the man and the woman moved up to the bedroom. But nothing this last half-hour. Until now.

He tensed. His watch read one-ten. He flicked off the torch and stood in the darkness, a knot of tension in his stomach, a spasm of fear shuddering through his bowels, but every sense alert, adrenalin coursing through his veins.

His heart beat in hammer blows and his limbs ached from lack of circulation. He laid the Beretta on the ground beside the ottoman and for several minutes he massaged his legs.

Then he sat down again, shifted nervously and took a deep breath as he picked up the weapon once more.

Five minutes, just to be certain.

Then he would move.

12.46 a.m.

Christian Bauer was Director of the Berlin Landesamt, a tall, lean man in his mid-fifties with grey sleeked hair and a handsome face. He wore a dressing gown over blue crumpled cotton pyjamas but even so the man had the well-groomed look of the diplomat about him.

He had made coffee but Werner Bargel ignored the steaming black liquid. When he heard the strains of his wife's snoring coming from upstairs, Bauer smiled apologetically but Bargel didn't smile back. Bargel had telephoned him five minutes before to say he was coming over. That it was urgent.

It was strictly business and Bauer saw that his assistant's face was deathly pale, but Bauer spoke calmly, as if he were used to emergency calls to his home in the early hours.

'Tell me what's so urgent, Werner.'

Bargel took a deep breath before he spoke. 'I got two telephone calls just before I rang you, sir. Both from Munich. The first was from a man named Volkmann. He's with DSE but he worked here in Berlin with British SIS.'

'Go on.'

Bargel said quickly, 'Volkmann said that a man named Kefir Ozalid was going to assassinate Chancellor Dollman.' Bargel paused briefly, saw the look of alarm on Bauer's face. 'He also said the entire Cabinet is going to be killed . . .'

Bauer's mouth was open. 'When?'

'Tonight. Now. How the Cabinet are going to be assassinated, he didn't know, only that it's going to happen after the attempt on Dollman's life.' Bargel swallowed. 'All the Cabinet are staying in Berlin, sir, for Weber's security meeting in the Reichstag this morning.'

Bauer put down his cup and raised his eyebrows, his face draining of colour.

His Assistant Director flicked a glance at his watch, as if for emphasis. 'Before I came here I asked the security desk to run Ozalid's name through the computer. We're also trying to locate the Chancellor.'

Bauer hesitated, despite his alarm, not a man to rush into things, the cautious eyes searching Bargel's face. 'What did the computer say?'

'There's a Kefir Ozalid listed under security-risk category two. He's Turkish. Emigrated to Germany in his teens. Twenty-seven years old.'

Bauer stood up anxiously. 'OK, so we've got a file on him, but what about motive? Why would he want to assassinate Dollman?'

'Two years ago Ozalid spent three months in prison for

seriously assaulting an Interior Ministry official in Bonn. The sentence would have been longer only the court took into account extenuating circumstances.'

Bauer's eyebrows rose. 'What extenuating circumstances?'

'According to his file, he and his wife were the victims of a group of right-wing thugs on the rampage in Essen. Ozalid suffered second-degree burns when the thugs firebombed an immigrant hostel he and his wife were visiting. His wife died from her injuries. She was also pregnant. The thugs involved were never apprehended.' Bargel paused. 'Chancellor Dollman was Interior Minister at the time, responsible for Federal Security. Apparently, Ozalid wrote to him on a number of occasions, accusing him of not having the thugs found and brought to justice. He accused Dollman of being personally responsible. The official Ozalid attacked in Bonn was one of Dollman's staff.'

'Oh my God . . .' Bauer breathed. He looked down at Bargel sharply. 'Did the computer say anything about Ozalid's whereabouts?'

'He left Germany a year ago, last known address in Stockholm. But he could have slipped back into Germany on a false passport . . .'

Bauer thought a moment. 'This Volkmann, do you trust him?'

'Yes.'

'Where is he in Munich, can we speak with him?'

Bargel shook his head, sweat dripping from his brow, aware of the passing seconds. 'He just made the call to my home number, pressed on me the absolute urgency of the situation and gave me the information. Then he rang off.' Bargel paused. 'But there's something else, sir, tied in with Volkmann's information. Something very disturbing.'

Bauer's sharp blue eyes stared piercingly at his assistant's face.

'What?'

Bargel took a deep breath. 'According to Volkmann, the threats to Dollman and the Cabinet are only part of it. There's going to be an attempted *putsch*.'

Christian Bauer looked at Bargel disbelievingly. 'By whom?'

When Bargel told him, Bauer shook his head slowly and said, 'Jesus Christ.'

Bargel did not stop; he told Bauer about the missile and its location and for a moment he thought his superior was going to crumble under the strain.

Bargel caught his breath nervously, drew in a deep lungful of air, saw Bauer's face white as a sheet.

The Director of the Landesamt then said quickly, 'Where's Dollman now?'

'With his girlfriend.'

'Which one?'

'Security think it's the blonde. Lisl Henning. But they're not sure, they've to get back to me.' Bargel swallowed. 'Volkmann said she was involved.'

'He mentioned her by name?'

'Yes, sir. I ordered security to contact Dollman's personal bodyguard Ritter as a precaution and inform him what's happening. However, because of the complexity of the situation and the protocol involved, the other orders I gave await your confirmation.'

'What orders did you give?'

'I gave the duty officer a list of senior military officers and security personnel to contact. On your command they're to come here immediately. There's a twenty-man team assembled and already on it's way to the girl's house in Wannsee – I took the precautionary liberty of issuing the order as soon as I heard from Volkmann.' Bargel quickly checked his watch. 'They should be arriving within the next few minutes. Another team is making ready in Munich to move to the Kaalberg. We can do the co-ordinating from here over a secure line.' Bargel paused. 'You may, of course, countermand my orders, sir.'

'What about the Cabinet?'

'I've already ordered that their personal security be trebled and put on alert.'

Bargel looked at his superior expectantly. There were beads of sweat on Christian Bauer's face, the tension showing. He nodded quickly.

'OK. We act on this. Confirm your orders, with my approval.'

'What about the Interior Minister, sir? He'll have to be informed.'

There was a strict hierarchy in German Federal Security and Bauer couldn't neglect his duty. The Interior Minister and Vice-Chancellor, Weber, was top of the pyramid.

Bauer was under pressure and he spewed out his words. 'I'll contact Weber myself. But for God's sake, get on to Ritter.'

At that moment the portable buzzed in Bargel's hand. He listened for several moments and then covered the mouthpiece quickly and looked up at Bauer and said, 'Dollman and his security people are definitely at the girl's house in Wannsee.' There was a brief pause as Bargel listened again on the phone, before he spoke sharply into the receiver. *'Keep trying! For God's sake keep trying!'*

As Bargel covered the mouthpiece again and looked up, there was sweat coursing down his temples, a deathly grey pallor on his face.

Bauer said urgently, 'What is it?'

Bargel shook his head. 'It's Ritter, sir – Dollman's bodyguard – we're getting no reply from his phone . . .'

Karl Schmeltz stepped out onto the snow-swept balcony and buttoned up the green loden coat to the collar. He crossed to the end of the low wall and stared out at the snowy darkness.

Ghosts.

Ghosts everywhere.

An icy wind gusted up the valley, eddying the snowflakes. He looked down again at the obscured view; snow falling thinly in the valley below.

He had been here before, in these mountains, listening to the *Föhn*, knew it with certainly. Osmosis. Absorbed in his bone jelly. The memory ached there now like a soft, pleasant pain.

For the first time it felt like . . . like what? Home? Where he *belonged*. His destiny. Melancholic, he knew, and always he tried to suppress such thoughts but on this occasion he permitted himself the pleasure.

Flakes of icy snow brushed against his cold cheeks. Chilled, invigorating.

Bone-cracking coldness.

He sucked in a deep breath, felt the chilled air probe lungs like icy fingers.

Good.

Twice, in youth, he had been taken here, to the south, remembering faces and names before his journey began: *Bormann, Mengele, Eichmann.* Secret trips and safe houses and furtive meetings. *Yes, here's the boy. Take a good look at him. Some day, not in your lifetime, perhaps, but some day . . . when the time is right, when the opportunity presents itself.*

The Prussian snapping of heads, the firm shaking of hands, the pledges of allegiance. Old faces and new faces, faces that kept the torch burning.

Who would have thought it would have taken so long?

An icy blast blew across the balcony. He sucked in another deep breath of the chilled air through gritted teeth.

So close, so very close.

He heard a noise and turned towards the french windows. He saw Meyer step out onto the balcony, his footsteps crunching on snow as he came to join him.

Schmeltz looked at him expectantly. Meyer said, 'The girl's here.' Schmeltz nodded and both men strode back towards the french windows.

Ozalid flicked on the pencil torch.

One-fourteen.

Four minutes had passed. Four minutes in which he had heard his own every heartbeat, every sound within the house; every movement outside in the cold dark garden beyond the small window where the guards moved at intervals.

He flicked off the torch again.

In the darkness he took a quiet, deep breath. Impatience setting in. Wanting it to happen. To be over.

He thought of Layla.

Of her beautiful dark face and her smile and what the men had done to her, a strange lightness in his head now, knowing the moment was near.

Do it.

No time to think about it.

Just do it.

He listened for any sound coming from outside in the garden, and hearing none he stood, flicked on the torch again, used it to guide him to the foot of the basement stairs, felt his legs shaking as he moved.

He took several deep breaths, let them out slowly, willed himself to remain calm. When he felt his legs stop shaking, he began to climb the steps very slowly.

When he reached the top, he flicked off the Beretta's safety, switched off the torch and slid it into his left pocket, then gripped the door handle lightly.

He opened the door a crack. The table lamp was on in the hallway, the study door closed, and he could see no light under the door where the guard would be resting.

He stepped out smartly into the hallway.

Above him, the landing was in darkness, but he could hear the music coming softly from the bedroom. He crossed towards the stairs, every sense alert, suddenly feeling no fear now, but aware of a brief sensation of lightness before his whole body seemed to relax, knowing the moment he had waited for was near.

He climbed the stairs slowly.

When he reached the landing he hesitated, the music louder now. The bedroom door was open a crack, a thin shaft of light breaking through the gap.

Ozalid took a deep breath, let it out quietly as he raised the silenced Beretta.

He stepped towards the light.

In the study darkness Ritter heard the buzz of the portable and came awake with a start.

He had lain back on the couch and flicked off the table lamp, tired after a hectic schedule with Dollman, resting his eyes but falling asleep in the process, listening to the soothing strains of Wagner.

Now he fumbled for the portable in the darkness, found it, said sleepily, 'Ritter.'

'Ritter, this is Werner Bargel. Where the hell have you been? Are you with the Chancellor?'

Ritter found the table lamp and switched it on, almost knocking it over as the voice crackled its urgent response.

'Why? What's up?'

'There's no time to explain, just listen, Ritter, and listen carefully. There's going to be an attempt on the Chancellor's life. Stay close by him. Do you hear? Stay close! Don't let him out of your sight. There's a support team on its way. They'll be with you in minutes. *But stay with Dollman!*'

Ritter dropped the portable and swung his legs round and stood up, every sense alert. He grasped the walkie-talkie on the table and spoke into it rapidly, heart pounding, not waiting for a reply from the men in the cars outside.

'*Watch units . . . Alert Red! . . . Repeat Alert Red! Watch units . . .!*' Ritter shouted into the mouthpiece, his voice strained. '*Cover entrances and exits, now!*'

Ritter turned and reached the door in one big stride, stepped frantically out into the hallway, the Sig and Sauer P6 nine-millimetre pistol already out and raised in his free hand, eyes scanning the ground floor, left and right. Music, but other sounds, too, doors opening outside in the driveway, the other men responding to his call.

As Ritter moved towards the stairs he glimpsed the open door leading down to the basement. His heart skipped a beat, every sense signalling danger. He hesitated, but only for a split second; his thought processes racing, mind on fire. The door hadn't been open earlier, he was certain, and if it was open now then someone must have . . .

Jesus.

He could hear the men moving frantically about outside, but he ignored the sounds now as he turned and raced up the stairs.

Heart pounding, pistol at the ready and taking three steps at a time, he bounded up towards the landing.

As Ozalid stepped into the bedroom he saw the man sleeping in the pink-covered bed, the beautiful young woman wearing the nightgown sitting by the dressing table, smoking a cigarette.

She stared over at him silently, not making a sound, but fear in her eyes.

There was something surreal about the scene, the opera music playing on, and for an instant Ozalid hesitated as he stared back at the young woman.

He recognised the beautiful face he had seen in the photographs. Their eyes met and as she looked at the silenced Beretta raised in Ozalid's hand she seemed overcome with fear. Then her stare shifted nervously to the figure lying on the bed, as if pointing out the target.

Ozalid saw Dollman's body half covered by the pink bedclothes, his white shoulders and his back and part of his torso visible, the grey chest hair and the plump pot of his belly rising and falling as he breathed.

Ozalid felt a wave of hate overcome him. As he stepped forward and lowered the Beretta and went to aim he heard the noise coming from the stairs, a slight pitch above the music.

Racing footsteps.

Then other sounds from below the landing, wood splintering, a door crashing in . . .

Ozalid turned instantly as the bedroom door burst in and the bodyguard appeared, a pistol in his hand.

Ozalid knew death now that he faced it, welcomed it. But this last thing to do . . .

The bodyguard saw the gun in Ozalid's hand swing round, Ritter's face registering his shock and his disadvantage.

As Ritter rolled suddenly right, Ozalid fired two quick shots, one of them clipping Ritter's left shoulder. The bodyguard screamed in pain as the bullet cracked into bone, but the Turk past caring now as he turned back to face his target.

He aimed smartly as Dollman came suddenly awake, a

startled look on his shocked face, the big body rising from the covers.

Ozalid fired twice before the Chancellor could speak.

He saw the red blossom on Dollman's left cheek just below the eye-socket as the first bullet hit him in the face, then Dollman was flung back in the bed as the second shot punctured his chest.

As Ozalid went to fire a third time, out of the corner of his eye he saw the bodyguard raise his pistol.

Before Ozalid could turn back to aim at Dollman again he heard the explosion and felt the piercing hot lead enter his right side. And then he was punched sideways by a quick series of shots, lead tearing into his flesh as the bodyguard emptied the P6.

Ozalid reeled back, glimpsing the woman in the pink night-gown, hearing her screams.

As he was spun round by the force of another bullet the gun went off in his hand. The shot tore into the woman's throat, and she was flung back against the wall, her hands flailing as she gasped for breath, her pretty face contorted, eyes wide open in pain.

As the last burst of lead hammered into Ozalid's body he pitched forward violently onto the soft pink covers on top of Dollman, not aware of the rush of feet on the stairs or the sounds of the men bursting into the room, or the harsh voices screaming frantically, but dimly conscious of the hands tearing at his body, pulling him off the Chancellor.

And as he closed his eyes for the last time, the only thought on his mind was of Layla.

It was forty seconds later, one-sixteen exactly, when Konrad Weber got the call in his suite on the sixth floor of the Kempinski Hotel on Berlin's Kurfürstendamm. He had received the message from the Berlin Landesamt on his portable phone, requesting him to stand by for an urgent call.

Despite the hour, Weber was still dressed and reading through his papers and he sat up expectantly and placed his leather briefcase on the bed beside him. When the call was patched through ten seconds later, Konrad Weber listened in stunned silence as Christian Bauer told him what had happened to the Chancellor in Wannsee and outlined the scenario as Bargel had told him.

When Bauer had finished giving him the available details, there was a brief silence and then Weber said, 'Oh, my God.'

The two men spoke for another six minutes exactly.

As is customary in German politics, on the death or incapacitation of a Chancellor due to ill-health, the Vice-Chancellor assumes the position of head of the German Government until a new Chancellor is nominated and elected.

Konrad Weber, a pragmatic and precise man, who normally responded calmly under pressure, was clear about his responsibilities and duties as Vice-Chancellor despite the shock news of Dollman's death, and left Christian Bauer in no doubt as to what had to be done to protect the security and integrity of the German Federal State. Weber would assume the position of Chancellor immediately and convene an emergency Cabinet meeting within the next hour.

The threat to the lives of the Cabinet was a grave and real one and Weber agreed with Bauer's extra security measures. Reichstag security officers were already contacting Ministers staying at hotels throughout the city; the Intercontinental, the Schweizerhof, the Steigenberger. Security at the Reichstag was to be stepped up in case of an attack on the building itself or the Ministers during the coming hours.

A state of emergency would be declared by Weber and enacted at once. Those in the army and police whose loyalty was without question would be contacted immediately and both forces put on instant alert and borders sealed.

Weber ordered Christian Bauer to confirm the location of the site in Bavaria but to hold off any confrontation or any attempt to seize the missile until Weber had informed the Cabinet and considered a course of action. He was quite adamant about that, and despite Bauer's protests Konrad Weber said he wasn't going to risk the decimation of Germany and its people until he had all the facts concerning the *putsch* and who the plotters were, and ordered Bauer to stand by until he had consulted with the Cabinet, and to keep him informed of any further news.

The next minutes and hours were of grave importance and Bauer was to answer only to him and no one else, no matter what their position or authority. Weber would assume control of the armed forces and police and all significant requests for their use were to be routed through him.

When he finally terminated the phone conversation in his suite at the Kempinski, Konrad Weber, caretaker Chancellor of Germany, a normally composed and restrained man, was covered in a lather of sweat and his hands were trembling almost uncontrollably.

He was acutely aware of the terrible weight of responsibility pressing down on him as he looked over at his brown leather briefcase on the bed beside him, certain he had everything he needed for the emergency Cabinet meeting he was about to convene at the Reichstag parliament building, and convinced that his intentions and actions were for the good of the German people. The future of Germany depended on him and almost him alone.

Pausing only to wipe the perspiration from his brow with the back of his trembling hand, he began making the phone call to his bodyguard and driver asleep in the suite next door.

Chapter Fifty-Seven

The driver had pulled in under a clump of trees on the mountain road. He switched off the engine and doused the headlights, and the five men climbed out of the cramped Opel. There was a sudden burst of activity, the car boot opening, weapons being dispensed in the snowy darkness.

One of the terrorists thrust a Kalashnikov into Volkmann's hands. He took the weapon and checked the safety was on, made sure the magazine was loaded. Lubsch had returned his Beretta and he slipped the automatic into his pocket.

He looked up towards the mountain. The weather had turned worse, the snow coming down heavily now. A thick clump of pine trees faded into a mist of snowy whiteness, the visibility down to no more than ten metres, the mountain invisible beyond a curtain of snow. They had made it up the steep road with difficulty, the engines straining up the sharp incline before they halted on the main road, fifty metres from the private track that led up to the Kaalberg. The driver had kept the engine revs low for the last two hundred metres, to mute the noise of their approach.

The thought of what might have happened to the girl kept coming into Volkmann's mind and he tried to push it away, tried to concentrate on the climb ahead. Flakes of snow stung his face and as his eyes became accustomed to the poor light, he looked over at Lubsch. He was talking to the man named Hartig and then Volkmann saw the man nod his head before Lubsch tapped him on the shoulder and the man disappeared into the swirl of snow, a Kalashnikov draped across his chest.

Lubsch came to stand beside him. 'You and me go up through the trees. As soon as we get close enough I use this.' Lubsch held up a CEL transceiver. 'When the men below get the order they start firing on the men on the plateau. If they can't eliminate them they'll try to keep them pinned down. Hartig has gone to try and find the telephone and power line junction boxes. If he can do that, he'll cut them. That way Kesser's friends will be cut off from the outside world. It might give us some advantage in case they try to call in help. If we need to use the telephone line, Hartig can reconnect us. If the worst happens, there's a call-box a kilometre from the main road.'

'Why the power lines? They may have an emergency generator.'

'No doubt they will. But Hartig's the expert and he says to cut them. If an emergency generator kicks in, Hartig says the supply will only be connected to the lighting circuits and power sockets. But nothing heavy duty, like electrical motors, because the emergency circuit wouldn't take a heavy load. That way, the missile will be out of the equation.' Lubsch smiled. 'But let's not count on it, Volkmann.'

Lubsch took a deep breath and exhaled, the air around him fogging in the icy coldness. 'We'll have to play the cards as they fall. But we have the advantage of surprise, so let's just hope the bastards on the plateau barrier don't hear my men coming.' Lubsch glanced up towards the trees and the blanket of white. 'Let's not waste any more time, Volkmann. And watch out for trip wires, just in case their security is better than the girl told us.'

Lubsch checked his watch and called the rest of the men together. Two minutes later he had gone over the plan again and had the others synchronise their watches.

The Reichstag parliament building on the Platz der Republik was as busy as an ant hill, inside and out, and lit up like a Christmas tree.

Werner Bargel had never seen so much activity. Not since the Wall had come down and the crowds had swarmed over towards the Reichstag building from the Brandenburg Gate, two hundred metres away. That was a night to remember.

So was this.

Bargel stood on the steps outside the double glass doors on the southern entrance on the Scheidemannstrasse, his breath fogging in the December air as he paced the concrete nervously, the shock of Dollman's death still on his mind.

On everybody's mind.

The massive, imposing granite building had borne witness to history in the past. The Reichstag Fire. The storming of Berlin by the Russians. The Berlin Wall going up and coming down. And it was witnessing history in the making again right now.

It seemed like half the cops in Berlin were swarming around the Reichstag.

At least sixty green-and-white Volks, the same number of police Mercedes vans, green-and-whites with riot squad police inside and out, dressed in full riot gear, some with leashed Alsatians, white helmets and Perspex shields and gas guns, at least four helicopters hovering overhead, their noisy rotors throbbing in the darkness swept by the blue lights on top of the police cars.

Green uniformed cops milled around in nervous clusters, talking, worried looks on their faces; other groups racing off into the trees in the small park opposite, flashlights flaring and sweeping in the darkness, dogs barking, voices calling out, walkie-talkies and car mobiles crackling. Everywhere frantic activity. Like World War Three was about to begin.

Jesus.

Bargel shook his throbbing head, felt his own legs tremble.

The threat of the missile was daunting enough, without the threat to the Cabinet's lives to have to worry about.

He checked his watch.

Two-ten.

Three of the Ministers had already arrived without incident. Grim-faced all of them as they nervously climbed the stone steps on Scheidemannstrasse, flanked by a deep wall of anti-terrorist police as they entered the Reichstag. Dollman's death had shattered them all. No doubt the threat to their own lives wasn't helping their nerves. Streicher looked like a corpse already. Eckart like someone had a gun at his back.

Bargel looked out towards the waves of green uniforms and plain-clothes. All of them wore yellow discs on their lapels, marking them out as part of the security teams. But a yellow disc meant nothing. Anyone out there in the street could be waiting for the right moment, including someone in uniform. Bargel scanned some of the faces of the cops, chatting nervously in groups, some of them watching the entrance.

Any one or more.

Who to trust?

Jesus.

But Bargel doubted anyone in their right mind would risk an assault on the Cabinet now. If they did, it would be suicide. Security at the Reichstag tight as a duck's ass.

No one allowed in or out without the personal permission of the Berlin Chief of Police, except Cabinet Ministers and the Reichstag security force, and Bargel himself on Bauer's instructions. The Chief of Police stood outside on the cold street, ten metres away, his face looking like someone had cut his arteries and he was slowly bleeding to death, as he talked with a beefy dark-haired young man in his early thirties, Axel Wiglinski, the Head of Reichstag Security, both men's eyes darting nervously every now and then to survey the crowds.

No one looked sure of anything, despite the precautions. Wiglinski's teams had already scoured the Reichstag building three times with police sniffer dogs in tow, checking all the rooms and every cranny, the basement, every floor, every wing of the building, north, south, east, west.

Nothing.

No one there who shouldn't be there, no bombs or explosives.

Bargel had talked with the Chief of Police, discussed what would happen next. As the Cabinet arrived, they were to be led to a lift that would take them to the third floor and the north wing of the building, to the room designated 4-North. The route was two minutes' walking distance from the Scheidemannstrasse entrance. When Weber arrived accompanied by his bodyguards, Bargel and Axel Wiglinski would lead him there personally.

The room called 4-North had another name in the Reichstag. The Wire Room, they called it. Used only in emergencies and for high-security meetings.

Not so much a room as a big sound-proofed box with one double-door entrance, the room suspended on eight thick steel wires above the floors of the Reichstag. Ten metres by ten metres. No way to bug it because the walls, ceiling and floor touched nothing. No telephones. No communication. Only one way in and out, sealed by oak doors with bullet- and bomb-proof sheeting. And that entrance would be heavily guarded, even with the Reichstag police and anti-terrorist squad in the hallway outside the room.

Bargel glanced over at faces in the swarms of cops, picking out several in the crowds, thinking again about what Volkmann had said. Any one of them could be an assassin, waiting for the moment to strike.

But that was too risky, too unlikely.

It had to be a bomb, Bargel thought. But the building had been thoroughly checked, even room 4-North, even the security staff's own personal lockers. Nothing. Clean. Not a trace of explosive. Unless Wiglinksi's men had missed something. He doubted that, too. The man was thorough in the extreme and the bomb-squad boys had used three teams, going over the same ground, one after the other, working fast, but efficiently.

So if not a bomb, how?

Bargel had listened to the Chief of Police, gone over the security measures, saw the grim look on the man's face, noticed the vein on the man's right temple twitching nervously from stress.

Then the man left him, went to talk with his men and Axel Wiglinski again.

There was a sudden scream of sirens and Bargel's heart jumped. A cavalcade of Mercedes and motorcycle cops swept round onto the Scheidemannstrasse. More Ministers arriving, worried faces stepping out of black limos, fogging breaths, cops surrounding the cars, helicopters hovering lower overhead, radios crackling.

Three of the Cabinet climbed the steps smartly in single file and Axel Wiglinski greeted them at the door, eighteen of his armed men waiting inside, one assigned to guide each of the Ministers to room 4-North along with one of their bodyguards.

More wailing sirens, blue lights. Four more ministerial Mercs, then another two.

The next Merc was Konrad Weber's.

There was a buzz of activity as faces strained to see Weber arrive, a rush of men from the anti-terrorist squads as they surrounded the car to protect him, like they didn't even trust their uniformed colleagues in green.

Bargel prayed that none of the A-T squad were there to kill Weber.

They jostled four deep and as Weber approached the steps, Bargel deftly unbuttoned the jacket under his raincoat where the Sig and Sauer P6 pistol was clipped to his belt, ready just in case but somehow knowing nothing would happen here. He waited at the double glass doors until Weber had climbed the steps, the man's long dark winter overcoat flapping about his legs, a grim look on his white face, the two bodyguards flanking him trusting nobody, not even the Berlin Chief of Police leading the way.

Once inside the glass doors, Weber nodded solemnly to Bargel.

Bargel gestured towards the long hallway that led towards the lift and room 4-North. He let out a quiet sigh. With Weber inside the Reichstag he felt safer.

For a moment, Bargel hesitated. What did he call Weber now? Vice-Chancellor, or Chancellor? Stick with the safe one.

'This way, sir,' he said gravely.

Bargel led the way across the polished hall and Weber and his bodyguards and Axel Wiglinski followed.

Meyer had left the house and walked across the lit snowy driveway to the concrete building.

As he stepped in he flicked the switch and the light flooded the cold room. He closed the door after him and crossed to the console and the telephone, his eyes flicking to the grey gantry standing in the centre of the building as he picked up the receiver, aware of his heightened anxiety.

He had tried calling Brenner, the Head of Security, from the house but the line had gone dead. The same from the phone upstairs.

Brenner had called twenty minutes before, relaying the news from Berlin. Not only Dollman dead. Meyer had heard the alarm in Brenner's voice and as he listened his face drained.

Grinzing dead too.

Kesser and his girlfriend gone, the apartment in disarray.

Brenner had said he would call back within ten minutes, his men were searching Kesser's apartment, hoping to find some clue, trying to get further news on Grinzing.

But still no call now.

The lines dead.

Meyer swore now as he tried the only other line, aware of the beads of sweat on his face, of the others waiting in the house for him to return before Kruger went down to the barrier to find out if anything was wrong.

Dead.

He tapped the cradle a half-dozen times just to be certain, but still nothing. He slammed down the receiver just as he heard the far-off sound, a welter of crackling gunfire . . .

For several seconds he paused to listen, hardly breathing, like an animal scenting the wind, his heart skipping a beat, then beating in hammer blows as the crackling gunfire raged in the distance, before he pulled himself together and hurried towards the door.

Snow fell incessantly as Volkmann and Lubsch came out of the bank of trees to the right of the driveway.

There were floodlights on overhead, white light flooding the snowed-under driveway, tyre marks on the white carpet, empty except for two Mercedes, their bodies caked in snow.

Off to the right the roof of the flat concrete building was covered in white. They moved quietly towards it and crouched low behind the rear of one of the Mercedes.

Volkmann looked over at the house through the falling snow. There were lights on but beyond the veil of white they saw no movement in the windows.

Volkmann turned to Lubsch. The terrorist nodded and flicked on the CEL, spoke quickly, then turned to Volkmann.

'Hartig cut the telephone lines. Let's hope he can find the power lines. You ready?'

Volkmann nodded.

Lubsch barked a command into the CEL.

Seconds later came the distant crackle of small explosions, as the woods and valley below seemed to echo with a welter of gunfire.

Volkmann moved forward across the snow-covered gravel towards the Berghaus, Lubsch after him, just as they heard the door open behind them.

As he stepped out into the falling snow, Meyer saw the two men standing there, a surprised look on their faces. Both pointed their Kalashnikovs at him.

Meyer froze in shock, icy flakes brushing against his cheeks.

The dark-haired man put his a finger to his lips, said quietly, 'Not a word, not a whisper. Keep your hands by your side.' He took a step towards Meyer. 'Schmeltz and the girl, where are they?'

For a moment, Meyer hesitated. The man pointed the barrel of the weapon directly at Meyer's head.

Meyer's legs began to buckle as he swallowed. The man stepped closer, grazed the cold tip of the Kalashnikov against Meyer's forehead.

'*Answer!*'

'Inside the house.'

'Your name?'

'Meyer.'

The man with the Kalashnikov flicked a glance back towards

the grey concrete building, light spilling out from the open steel door. 'Move back inside, Meyer.'

Meyer hesitated, his mind in turmoil. He flicked a look at the second man; young, in his twenties, the light from the flood lamps overhead reflecting off his glasses. The welter of gunfire rose in pitch to a thunderous volley and Meyer wondered why the others hadn't heard it and come out of the house.

The cold tip of the Kalashnikov's barrel pushed painfully hard into his head and Meyer faltered.

'Move or I blow your head off.'

Anger in the man's eyes, a kind of madness, but controlled; he would squeeze the trigger, no question.

Meyer went to move into the building.

There was a faint noise from behind and a split second later Kruger came running out of the house, the Walther in his hand, a look of alarm on his face.

There was the briefest second of indecision as Kruger took in the scene before he raised the Walther in one swift movement.

Before Volkmann could swing the Kalashnikov round the man fired wildly.

Meyer's body was punched back and the Kalashnikov was wrenched from Volkmann's grasp as a bullet pierced his hand.

A hail of lead ripped through the frozen air, a scream from behind as Lubsch took the brunt of Kruger's fire, bullets cracking into concrete and flesh.

As Volkmann crouched and rolled right in the snow he felt another round hammer into his right arm, glimpsed Kruger moving back frantically towards the house, still firing wildly.

Volkmann gripped the Kalashnikov in his left hand and brought it up and fired in one fluid movement, just as Kruger reached the door.

As the Kalashnikov bucked wildly the hail of bullets tore into Kruger's left side and he spun violently.

Volkmann squeezed the trigger again.

The second burst caught Kruger in the neck, almost decapitating him, and his body arched and fell.

The gunfire echoed and died.

Volkmann stood, suddenly aware of a numbing sensation in his arm as he stared down at his wounds. A bullet had pierced his right hand, exiting through the palm and blood oozed from the gaping wound; a second bullet shattering bone just below the elbow, thick rivulets of warm dark red trickling down under his sleeve. No pain, not yet, just a dull sensation, but pain would come soon enough.

The bodies of Lubsch and Meyer lay on the snow. Meyer's eyes were open in death and there was a gaping hole in Lubsch's face, his glasses lying in the white powder.

From far below Volkmann could hear the faint, drifting sounds of sustained gunfire. Lubsch's men, meeting stiff resistance by the sound of it, but it seemed far away, as if happening in another time, another place.

There was a timelessness to everything but he was aware of his heart pounding wildly, aware of the ticking seconds, aware of the terrible pain now flooding into his arm and hand.

Suddenly he was plunged into darkness, every light extinguished. Volkmann stood there in the dark void, feeling cold snow on his face, his heart pounding.

Seconds later the area flooded with white intense light, blazing through the falling snow as the flood lamps came on again.

Hartig had cut the power lines, the emergency generator kicking in now.

The porch light of the house and the flood lights overhead flickered a couple of times, then settled, their glow diminished, then came bright again as the generator settled.

Volkmann turned, looked back at the concrete building. The door still open but inside in darkness.

If Hartig was wrong . . .

The sound of gunfire rose; raging, eddying, dying, rising again.

Then a sudden, awesome silence that seemed to fill the snowy darkness like a force as the firing died abruptly.

He turned back towards the house, light spilling out from the hallway, dropped the heavy Kalashnikov, fumbled as he wrenched the Beretta from his pocket with bloodied fingers, felt a sudden weakness engulf him, his mind fogging, and he closed his eyes as a terrible pain began to flood into his wounds.

He opened his eyes again, inhaled a deep lungful of chilled air, tried desperately to remain conscious.

He crossed quickly to the door past Kruger's body and stepped into the house.

Chapter Fifty-Eight

A log fire blazed, french windows leading to a balcony. Salt-and-pepper darkness beyond, white flakes dashing against glass.

The man stood by the fire. A surprised look on his face, but no fear. Erica stood beside him. As Volkmann came into the room, she saw the Beretta, went to speak.

Volkmann said, 'Nobody move.'

He held the weapon at arm's length, took a deep breath, tried to take in the scene. Erica and the man, standing close together. As if they knew each other. The girl looked at him palely, shock on her face, and Volkmann felt the confusion. Blood draining from his shattered arm, senses bluring.

He stared over at the man. Fit-looking. Tanned skin, fine wrinkles around the soft eyes. Handsome. Silver hair. Schmeltz, no question. Volkmann watched him as his eyes flicked to the Beretta, then back at him.

Erica went to move towards him, and the man made no move to stop her.

'Joe . . .'

Volkmann swung the Beretta to point at her, said hoarsely, 'I said nobody move. Just do as I say.'

The girl froze, her face white.

Volkmann aimed at the man's head, gestured towards the table.

'Move away from the girl. Slowly.'

Schmeltz hesitated, then did as he was told. The lights suddenly flickered overhead, then settled. Schmeltz glanced up a moment.

Volkmann said, 'Sit down. At the table. Keep your hands on top.'

The man hesitated, then moved slowly to the table, placed

his slim hands on the polished wood as he looked over at Volkmann impassively.

Schmeltz said calmly, 'Who are you?'

'My name is Volkmann.'

For several seconds Schmeltz stared at him, the blue eyes becoming hard; then he looked towards the floor between Volkmann's feet.

Volkmann glanced down. Blood trickled onto the carpet. Red spots. Life draining from him. His face burned and there was sweat dripping from his forehead.

He looked back up as the girl said, 'Joe, listen to me, please.'

Concern in her voice. Or was it his imagination? Volkmann felt his senses slipping away, his vision going. An unreality about the scene.

He blinked, tried to focus. The girl went to move towards him again, slowly this time. He swung the Beretta round sharply. The girl hesitated, then stood still, stared at him in astonishment.

'I told you. Don't move. Don't speak.'

Schmeltz said suddenly, 'If you came here to stop what's happening, you can't.' He shook his head, the knowing eyes watching Volkmann. 'You really can't stop it.'

'Why not?'

'It has gone too far. If you kill me this moment it would make no difference. Do you intend killing me, Joseph?'

Volkmann ignored the question, tried to keep his eyes focused, fight the void threatening to engulf him as he stared down at Schmeltz.

'There are people in Berlin who know. They can stop what's happening.'

Schmeltz looked towards the french windows. Snow dashing against glass. A look on his face as if nothing mattered. When he turned back he shook his head slowly.

'It hardly matters. Dollman is already dead, believe me, Joseph.'

'And the others. What do you intend for them?'

Schmeltz's eyes opened wide as he reacted to the words.

His face turned pale as he glanced over at the girl, then back at Volkmann. When he spoke, his voice was almost a whisper.

'How did you know?'

'Just answer the question. What's going to happen to the Cabinet?'

'That hardly matters now. It's too late to stop it, believe me.'

Volkmann's finger tightened on the trigger. 'It matters if you want to stay alive.'

Schmeltz paused, as if considering. 'You didn't come alone, did you?' He looked over at the telephone. 'Your people, they cut the lines?'

Volkmann nodded faintly.

Schmeltz looked back. 'That was stupid. The telephone would have been your only chance of warning Berlin. But now it's too late. And whether I live or die is really not important. Because there is nothing that can be done to stop what is about to happen, Joseph.'

Volkmann moved closer. The tip of the barrel touched Schmeltz's forehead. The man's head jerked back in alarm and his eyes opened wide in fear, but Volkmann kept up the pressure, pushing the Beretta hard into the man's flesh.

'Tell me, and tell me quickly. Or so help me I'll squeeze the trigger.'

Konrad Weber looked at the faces seated around the table in room 4-North.

In the harsh neon lights every face looked like death.

The doors had been locked and the meeting had begun. Weber was on his feet. He had spoken for almost a full two minutes uninterrupted, outlining the situation to the Cabinet of Ministers. Now he paused for breath, saw the stunned looks on the white faces around the table.

He carried on, addressing the seventeen men.

'Gentlemen, I have several proposals to counter this unprecedented emergency. Extreme courses of action that must be taken.' Weber's voice was firm and resolute, but tiny beads of sweat glistened on his brow and upper lip.

'I hope to have your full co-operation in each and every one of these proposals. The President has been informed of the situation. Those senior officers in the army and police force whose loyalty we can absolutely depend on are already at their posts. All the forces at the disposal of the Federal Republic are ready to act. What happened to Chancellor Dollman and what may be about to happen are outrageous, alarming acts that threaten the Republic's existence. Those responsible must be swiftly dealt with. I need hardly remind you that all our lives may be in danger, not only the lives of the Republic's citizens.'

Weber cleared his throat, saw heads nod in solemn agreement.

'Firstly, a State of Emergency will be immediately declared. Secondly, a decree for the protection of the people and the Federal State will be enacted. It will dispense with all civic and constitutional rights until the State has been purged of those elements that threaten democracy. Thirdly, I want every known neo-Nazi and every extremist irrespective of political leanings rounded up and interned at once. This will be co-ordinated with the Landesamt offices and the BfV.'

Weber paused, wiped the sweat from his brow with a handkerchief from his pocket. 'The problem of the missile is a grave and alarming one. As soon as Bauer and the BfV have more information on the organisers behind this outrage, and what measures can be taken to neutralise the threat, we shall act immediately. To do otherwise and without proper information would be folly. Gentlemen, I must ask for your complete co-operation in all these measures.'

Weber felt the sweat dripping under his arms, saw the deathly faces and frightened nods. He knew the pressure and apprehension was telling on his face. In the silence that followed, Weber heard a faint ticking noise and looked down, alarmed. The sound grew louder. Weber looked up, realised the noise came from the electric clock on the wall, the second hand ticking away. He let out a small sigh, recognised his paranoia, looked at the faces at the table.

'Gentlemen,' he said firmly, 'I must telephone the President out of protocol before we enact these proposals and any others we deem necessary. So let us proceed. Are we all agreed on these measures?'

Weber look at the sober faces around the room and quickly asked each Minister by name in turn, as protocol demanded.

Every one of them agreed.

Snow dashed in flurries against the french windows and the log fire crackled.

Volkmann kept the Beretta pointed at Schmeltz's head. He felt the faintness begin to sweep in again, the butt of the weapon sticky with red, blood dripping onto the floor. Eyes losing focus, images fading. He blinked, sucked air deep into his lungs, tried to clear his head. He heard the girl, panic in her voice, but it seemed to come from far away.

'Joe . . . let me help you.'

If she came closer, she could distract him, allow Schmeltz to make a move. He forced himself to ignore the voice.

Suddenly a surge of pain flooded his entire body and he faltered, slumped back in the chair. He snapped open his eyes, kept the pistol pointed at Schmeltz as the girl spoke again.

'Joe, please.'

Volkmann said, without looking at her, 'You move again and I shoot.'

He saw Schmeltz lean forward in his chair, heard him speak softly.

'You'll bleed to death, Joseph. Listen to what the girl says.'

'Just tell me what's going to happen.'

'You're a remarkable man, Joseph, do you know that?'

'Tell me.'

'To have unravelled what is happening. To have found me. I admire your ability, your tenacity. Your courage.' Schmeltz paused. 'Your name is German, but you are not German, are you, Joseph. You're British.'

'Tell me, Schmeltz. Whoever the hell you are.'

'You know who I am, Joseph. Just as I know who you are. Just as I know about your father.'

There was a flash of anger in Volkmann's face. He looked

at the girl as she said, 'Joe, he made me tell him everything.'

He saw what looked like pain in her face. Truth or lie? A few minutes ago he had wanted to ask her what she had told them, wanted to know why, but somehow it didn't matter now, all that mattered was Schmeltz, speaking now, staring back at him. The man's face went in and out of focus a few moments, then came back.

Schmeltz leaned closer. 'Forgive me. But I wanted to explain. The mistakes of the past, they won't be repeated. What happened to your father, it won't happen again, Joseph. Not ever.'

'I don't believe that, Schmeltz. And neither do you. It may not happen to Jews, but it will to others. Your time's up. No more talk. Tell me what's going to happen in Berlin or I kill you, right now.'

Schmeltz hesitated, looked towards the telephone, sat back in the chair, the soft blue eyes more confident.

'You have no way of stopping what is about to happen. No way of informing Berlin or the Cabinet.'

'Tell me, *quickly*.' Volkmann's finger tightened, went to squeeze. 'TELL ME!'

Volkmann's scream rang around the room. Schmeltz's eyes dilated as he swallowed, his Adam's apple bobbing in his throat. He spoke hoarsely.

'The Cabinet, they're meeting in the Reichstag. Weber has assumed Dollman's position. He is proposing measures to stop what is happening. But the meeting is a charade.'

'Why?'

'Because once Weber has made his proposals he will excuse himself. Leave the room. Go to his office.'

Schmeltz hesitated. Volkmann looked at his face, tightened his finger on the trigger again.

'Keep talking.'

'Weber will have left his briefcase behind. When he reaches his office he will detonate a device in the briefcase. A bomb will explode, killing only those inside the room where the Cabinet is meeting. The structure of the room makes it impossible for anyone to survive. The Cabinet will all be killed. Weber will have assumed complete control.'

Schmeltz paused. There was a long silence and Volkmann looked away, towards the girl.

There was a pleading look on her face, tears at the corners of her eyes. He wanted to trust her. Wanted her to help stop his pain. But the doubt in the back of his mind wouldn't go away.

His mind began to fog again, pain rolling in. He felt the sweat course down his temples as he looked back at Schmeltz.

'And where do you figure in this?'

'Weber's position will be temporary.' Schmeltz looked directly at the Beretta. 'But my part is not important. Not now.' His eyes shifted back to Volkmann. 'Even if you kill me, Joseph, it would make no difference. The seeds have been sown. There is no going back once the Cabinet are dead. Only Weber can hold Germany together. Weber and others like him. Men and women who will uphold their father's testimony.' Schmeltz leaned forward. 'And they will do it, Joseph, believe me, they will.'

There was a hint of excitement in Schmeltz's voice. Volkmann stood up, Schmeltz's face clouding in front of him.

He looked away, tried to focus, couldn't. When he looked back Schmeltz's features were a blur.

Volkmann said, 'Is she one of your people too?'

He was faintly aware of Schmeltz glancing at the girl, a thin smile on his face. 'No.'

Truth or lie? Volkmann flicked a look at the girl, her features hazy, like seeing her through frosted glass. He filled his lungs with air, short deep bursts, blinked hard, cleared the fog. He wanted to believe in her. But nothing was clear, not even the images in front of him. He tried to concentrate on Schmeltz's face.

'Not all Germans are Nazi supporters. Not all of them will support this.'

'Enough will. You think we haven't planned this to the last detail?'

'How?'

'Weber will denounce the murders as a treasonable act by immigrant extremists to destabilise the Fatherland. There will be a surge of nationalist fervour that has not been seen in fifty years.' Schmeltz paused, looked at him. 'Listen to me, Joseph. Do as I say and you won't be harmed. You can walk away from here. You have my word. The Austrian border is –'

'Stand up.'

Schmeltz stood up slowly, his tall frame towering above Volkmann, his eyes cautious. 'What are you going to do?'

'It's what you're going to do. You're going to walk to the car outside with the girl. If any of your people are left to try and stop us, I'll put one in your head.'

Schmeltz licked his lips nervously. 'If you're trying to reach a telephone you're wasting your time. And others will come here because they cannot get through. You won't get far.'

'Move.'

As Volkmann flicked the Beretta, blood dripped onto the carpet from his wound. He started to feel himself go under, gripped the back of the chair.

'Joe, for God's sake . . . you'll bleed to death.'

Volkmann stared at Erica, saw the tears at the edges of her eyes.

He didn't see Schmeltz's hand move until the last moment. It came up smartly and gripped the Beretta, twisted, pointed the weapon towards Volkmann.

The pistol exploded.

Erica screamed.

Volkmann felt hot lead crack his skull, a sudden blast inside his head like a sonic boom.

As Schmeltz grasped the Beretta, Volkmann gripped his arm blindly with both hands, clung to it, oblivious to pain, oblivious to the agony in his own arm and hand, to the nauseous ringing inside his skull. Schmeltz tried to wrench himself free. Volkmann pulled down hard, heard the sharp crack as the bone broke and Schmeltz screamed in agony as he squeezed the trigger.

The weapon exploded again.

The bullet tore into the girl's side and Volkmann saw with horror as she was slammed back against the wall.

As Schmeltz struggled to release himself, Volkmann pushed with all his weight into the man's body; both men tumbling back, shattering glass and wood as they crashed out through the french windows, the weapon flung from Schmeltz's grasp as they rolled across the breadth of the balcony, snow and shattered glass crunching under their entangled bodies.

Volkmann smacked against the concrete balcony, the force knocking him breathless, Schmeltz's weight crushing into him a fraction of a second later.

Icy blasts of wind, flurrying snow.

Pain. Piercing cold.

Cold keeping him conscious, his chest on fire, pain flooding into his head where the bullet had cracked bone.

As he struggled to move, Volkmann felt Schmeltz's weight come off him. He closed his eyes, opened them again, the image of Schmeltz swam before him, crawling back across the balcony, scrabbling wildly in the snow, breath rising in hot panting bursts like a laboured animal's.

Volkmann forced himself to stand, saw Schmeltz's hand reach out for something.

Volkmann lunged.

He landed on Schmeltz's back and the man exhaled air like a bellows.

Volkmann clambered over him, fingers groping in the snow, eyes searching frantically for the weapon.

And then Schmeltz's arm came out of nowhere and his weight landed on Volkmann's back, knocking him breathless, arms locking around Volkmann's throat, strangling him, knuckles digging into his windpipe, crushing throat muscle.

Volkmann felt himself go under as he fought for breath, tried to grasp Schmeltz's arm, the effort painful, impossible.

He wrenched with a supreme effort, with all the strength he could muster, twisted and shrugged and the man's body came off him.

Schmeltz's body rose, suspended in mid-air, then tumbled over Volkmann's, crashed into snow.

Volkmann glimpsed the dark metal against white, a metre away, turned towards where the pistol lay, fingers scrabbling in the snow, cold, so cold, difficult to discern metal, difficult to move.

Please God.

Something hard, still warm.

He found the handle of the weapon, gripped it in his left hand.

He turned, saw Schmeltz crawling back towards the balcony.

Volkmann held the pistol at arm's length, aimed at the back of Schmeltz's head, trying to judge distance, two metres, less.

'*Don't move.*' The words gurgled, painful.

Schmeltz ignored the command, stood up, chest heaving as he fought for breath, blood streaming down his face from the shattered bridge of his nose, eyes wide and staring.

'*I said don't move.*'

There was a timelessness to everything.

Snow swirling. Silence except for both men's laboured breathing and the gusting flurries of snow.

'*Listen to me, Joseph –*'

Volkmann stood, panting, looking into Schmeltz's face, fought the nausea sweeping over him, stabbing pains in his temple where the bullet had cracked bone and ruptured flesh. A cold sweat drenching his body.

He glanced back in past the shattered french windows, saw Erica's body crumpled against the wall and a surge of anger gripped him.

And then there was a sudden throbbing of helicopter blades from somewhere in the swirl of snow above. Volkmann heard it and glanced up. The sound coming closer, coming in fast. More than one craft. Swishing of blades as they cut the icy air.

Bargel's people.

Or Schmeltz's.

Volkmann aimed the pistol at the centre of Schmeltz's forehead.

Schmeltz's eyes open wide.

A voice screamed inside Volkmann's head.

Do it.

He took a deep breath, tried to control the urge.

Wait, for justice.

Justice is here. Now.

He thought of the pictures hanging on white walls. A dead woman clutching the lifeless body of her child. The grinning SS man standing over her.

His father's pain.

A deep breath now, sweat dripping down his face, eyes narrowing into slits.

Do it.

Schmeltz's voice, coming to him faintly.

'Joseph, listen.'

Schmeltz moving closer.

Volkmann felt himself start to go under again, eyes beginning to cloud. His body winding down, a terrible, excruciating wave of pain almost suffocating him. He gritted teeth, fought the pain. A chill going through him, making him shiver. Death coming? He took a deep breath.

Let it out.

Slowly.

Schmeltz moved closer.

'Don't fucking move.'

Schmeltz stopped.

Volkmann aimed between Schmeltz's eyes.

The dull chopping noise of blades coming closer. Schmeltz's eyes flicked up to the swirling heavens, then came back to Volkmann.

Volkmann wanting to scream the words aloud, but instead saying them softly.

'They say every sin has its own avenging angel, do you believe that?'

Volkmann looked at Schmeltz's face.

He didn't wait for the reply.

The Beretta exploded.

*   *   *

When he came to he was lying on a stretcher.

He was aware of the ghostly swirl of flashing red and blue lights in the thinly falling snow and he heard the wailing sirens, and there was a harsh metallic clatter of blades somewhere overhead. There was a babble of loud and desperate voices fading in and out, guttural orders being shouted and carried on the icy wind.

When he tried to look round he saw ghostly figures in white Arctic fatigues appearing out of nowhere, weapons at the ready, but then they began to blur and he lay back again.

A rugged-faced man in white fatigues and a Heckler and Koch machine-pistol draped around his neck loomed over him suddenly, looked down into his face.

He smiled briefly and his hand touched Volkmann's shoulder as if to reassure him. Volkmann tried to speak, tried to tell him about Weber, tried to tell him to contact Berlin, tried to tell him about the girl, but when he went to speak the words would not come.

The man looked away. There was a voice, telling him something, then a burst of gunfire from somewhere out in the whiteness, and then the man turned away grimly and barked an order and there was a rush of feet crunching on snow and he was gone.

And then all life seemed to go from Volkmann again. He saw only a hazy nimbus above, a feeling of lightness in his head, washing in on him, as moments later he felt the stretcher lifted, or so it seemed, and he was suspended in mid-air.

And then a tidal wave of intense pain washed in and smothered him.

He drowned in darkness.

It took Konrad Weber three minutes to walk to his private office on the third floor of the Reichstag.

Werner Bargel and Axel Wiglinski accompanied Weber and his two bodyguards.

When they reached the Vice-Chancellor's office, Weber unlocked the door and stepped inside, then locked it again, leaving the two men outside in the hallway.

In the oak-panelled room he crossed to his desk and sat down.

His palms were drenched in sweat and his hands were shaking as he opened the drawer and removed the remote-control transmitter, placed it in the palm of his left hand.

As he clenched the fingers of his free hand, he took a deep breath.

The portable buzzed in Werner Bargel's hand.

Bauer's voice, frantic. *'Where are you Bargel?'*

'Outside the Vice-Chancellor's office.'

'Jesus, Bargel, listen to me, for God's sake . . .'

Konrad Weber heard the frantic voices in the hallway, heard the crash of splintering wood as the door burst in, saw the Sig and Sauer pistol in Bargel's hand.

As Bargel raised the pistol to aim, Weber touched the button.

The distant explosion, when it came a split second later, cracked through the Reichstag like a clap of thunder.

Epilogue

Volkmann came awake in the private ward in Munich General Hospital a little after 10 a.m. two days later.

He heard a radio on somewhere, music beyond the closed door. *Tannenbaum*. The carol that had always made his father cry and he wanted to cry too, not because of the music but because he was breathing, alive.

He was connected to tubes and there were probes wired to his arms and chest and linked to a machine. His heart beating in tandem with white blips on a green screen. There was a tightness still around his head, not a band of steel but something soft. He touched the cotton dressing. Another on his numbed right hand. A hard crust of white plaster around his right arm.

Werner Bargel was seated at the end of the bed. A nurse appeared out of nowhere and then there was a sudden rush of activity.

He heard Bargel's voice.

'How do you feel?'

His lips stuck together, an effort to part them.

'Lousy.'

It was another twenty minutes before Bargel spoke again, until after the doctors had been called and examined him, after the nurse had attended him, sips of cold water to wet his cracked, parched lips. A couple of yellow pills to swallow. A damp cotton cloth dabbed on his face and neck. Refreshing. Cool.

He saw Bargel talk with the doctors out of hearing range and then the room emptied and the door closed and he and Bargel were alone.

Bargel sat in the chair beside the bed.

'The doctors assure me you'll make a speedy recovery. But for a while there it was touch and go.'

Volkmann raised himself, then slumped back in pain. The throbbing in his right temple became a blinding ache.

'Take it easy, Joe. They've given you something to ease the pain, so it should take effect soon. The fact is, you're damned lucky to be alive. Apart from your other wounds a bullet chipped a piece out of your skull. You've had severe concussion.' Bargel leaned closer in his chair. 'The gods must have been smiling on you, my friend. Another couple of millimetres into that head of yours and heaven would have had another lyre player. For now it's best you just relax. You're not going anywhere.'

Volkmann said, 'Erica . . .?'

Bargel sat forward. 'She's in a private room a floor below us. The medical team got to her in time. Don't worry, Joe, she's going to be all right.'

He saw Bargel smile faintly and Volkmann turned his head and tried to take in the room but there was a fuzzy quality to everything. He looked back slowly.

Bargel said, 'She thought you'd gone over the edge when you confronted her and Schmeltz at the mountain.' Bargel hesitated. 'But when you stepped into that room you still didn't know if you could trust her, did you, Joe?'

Volkmann shook his head slowly. 'I didn't know what to think.'

Bargel nodded. 'You'd lost a lot of blood. I'm surprised you were able to remain conscious. And the girl had been through her own ordeal. They'd pumped her full of the truth drug, scopalomine, to make her talk.' Bargel shook his head firmly. 'But she was never one of their people.'

'She told you about Schmeltz?'

Bargel nodded and his face looked pale and serious. 'She told us everything she knew. The rest we were able to piece together.'

'How long have I been unconscious?'

'Two days.'

'Tell me what happened.'

It took Bargel ten minutes to explain. Dollman and the Cabinet were dead, except Weber, who was in a high-security cell in Moabit Prison. The President had taken over the duties of Chancellor and a caretaker government had been formed. They had found a list of conspirators in the safe in Grinzing's study. They were keeping Weber company in Moabit. All known extremist neo-Nazis and their supporters had been arrested. One of Lubsch's men had been killed in the assault, the others had escaped into the mountains before the all-weather choppers had landed.

When he mentioned Ivan Molke, Bargel saw the look of pain on Volkmann's face.

'Ivan was a good man, Joe. And a good German.'

Volkmann looked away, towards the white wall. Bargel's voice brought him back.

'What Lubsch and his men tried to do was remarkable. It gives me some faith in the future of this country.'

Bargel leaned forward. 'When the girl told me about Schmeltz, at first I didn't believe her. It sounded so damned crazy. I thought she had cracked after her ordeal. It sounded so impossible, so unbelievable.'

'What made you believe her?'

'One of the people on Grinzing's list talked. An army officer named Braun. Everything you deduced, everything the girl told us, it's true. Geli Raubal had a son. The Schmeltz couple took him to South America in '31. He lived with them as their child until Die Spinne took over as his protector.'

'What about the body?'

'It's been disposed of, secretly.'

'Where?'

Bargel shook his head. 'Even I can't tell you that, Joe.' Bargel paused. 'The army's on the streets, restoring order. Most people don't know what the hell's happened. There's been a newspaper blackout until things are completely under control. This country came close to stepping back over fifty years. The measures we've taken are extreme but we want to make certain there's no likelihood of the past ever happening again.'

Volkmann looked away towards the window, then back at Bargel. 'There's something I don't understand. Erica's father was Leibstandarte SS. Why wasn't she contacted like the others?'

Bargel nodded. 'She was on their list all right. But it was quite a list and she was only one of many. From what we can gather Winter himself was responsible for making an approach to her not long before he was murdered. But he didn't make her a priority. Maybe he thought the girl wasn't important enough. Or because he had known her personally at Heidelberg he knew she wouldn't be the kind to help. Besides, Winter himself had become disaffected long before his own people decided to get rid of him. He'd have known the girl would have been killed if she had refused to co-operate.' Bargel shrugged. 'Whatever reason Winter had, it probably saved her life.'

Bargel saw the strain on Volkmann's face and stood. 'We'll talk again, Joe. For now, get some rest. I owe you a great debt of gratitude. Not only me, but the country. I just want you to know that.'

Bargel crossed to the door and smiled over at Volkmann. 'I'll tell the girl you're awake. She's anxious to talk with you.'

The snow had started to fall as they travelled in the taxi from Heathrow, but by the time they had reached the neat square of Victorian houses it had stopped.

Everywhere white, deserted. New Year's Eve.

The flight from Frankfurt had been delayed and he had telephoned from the airport, told the old woman he was coming, heard the surprise in her voice, saying how good it was to hear from him.

When he told her about the girl staying a few days, he recognised the excitement in her voice, like the young woman on the beach in Cornwall he always remembered, with her hair tied back and the smile on her lips and the aura of happiness that made him know why his father had married her. A strong, happy woman who had fought the darkness and won.

It was four o'clock in the afternoon when the taxi pulled up at the top of the square. Darkness falling, the gates of the tiny park open, branches heavy with snow, here and there erratic footprints where a child had strayed and an adult followed. But no one now. Empty.

He led Erica in through the park gates, placed the two overnight cases beside the bench, brushed away snow. As she sat beside him, across the white wasteland and through the trees he could see the house, lights on already, a plume of grey smoke rising faintly from the chimney.

There were lights on in other houses too. Candles burning, Christmas trees winking in the twilight through fogged windows, the vestige of Christmas. Another eight hours and a New Year.

A pigeon cooed in the branches above. A fir tree rustled. The sound of beating wings.

Erica said, 'The house. You never told me which one?'

Volkmann pointed to the red-bricked house and Erica looked at it for a long time.

'It suits you.'

'How?'

She smiled. 'Solid. A little old-fashioned. But dependable.'

He smiled back and Erica looked about the park.

'This is where you played when you were a boy?'

'Yes.'

Erica closed her eyes and said, 'I can picture you, you know. From the photograph I saw in your apartment.'

'Tell me what you picture.'

'A boy who is quiet and very serious. A loner, but curious. And a boy who loved his father and mother very much.'

'You see all that?'

She smiled again. 'It's what I picture.' She opened her eyes, brushed a strand of blonde hair from her face, looked across at him. At the handsome face she wanted to touch as he looked silently about the snowy landscape.

She said, as if reading his thoughts, 'This place, it's special for you, isn't it, Joe?'

'I used to come here with my father.'

He felt the touch of her hand; the silky warmth of her fingers entwining through his. Comforting. He wondered how he had ever doubted her.

She said, 'His pain, it's been repaid now. And the pain of all the others who suffered.'

'You believe that?'

'Yes, I believe it. Because you stopped it happening all over again. And now you can bury your father's pain.'

Volkmann looked at her face. He took her hand in his, brought it to his lips, kissed the cold fingertips, then he stood up slowly, looked about the park.

'I'd like to believe that.'

Through the trees, he could see the house. She would be waiting.

He looked down at the blue eyes watching him.

'Come. She's expecting us. And I'd very much like you to meet her.'

She stood and Volkmann picked up the overnight cases and they started to walk back across the park towards the row of red-bricked houses.

The suite on the top floor of the Hilton Hotel had a clear view to the mountains beyond the city. It was a cold, clear New Year's Day in Madrid and both men sat by the window. There were no buildings overlooking this side of the hotel and the men had taken all the necessary precautions before their arrival.

The younger of the two was in his early thirties, lean and fit-looking. His briefcase was open and a sheaf of papers lay on the coffee table in front of him.

The second man was in his early fifties. His tanned face looked haggard and tired after almost two days without sleep. The hotel computer recorded his name as Federico Ramirez but the man had changed passports and tickets twice in the last twenty-four hours during his connections from Asunción.

He wasted no time on small-talk nor offered his young visitor a drink.

'The number of arrests and detentions, you have the latest figures?'

The younger man glanced briefly at his notes before speaking. 'We estimate twenty-three thousand, as of midnight last night.'

The face of the older man betrayed no emotion at the figures and his visitor carried on talking.

'But the situation is still fluid and the figures may increase. By how much we don't know. Apart from those on the list, the authorities are simply pulling in those with a strong past record of support, so it's likely they'll be released if charges can't be pressed.'

The grey-haired man said impatiently, 'And the cells, how are they holding up?'

'In the eastern region, they remain pretty much intact. The other three points of the compass are the ones really affected. But the damage isn't that great. We've been relatively lucky.'

The grey-haired man stood up and said sharply. 'Lucky? What happened, Raul? How the hell did it go wrong? We were that close.' The older man held up two fingers, the tips close together.

The younger man sighed and looked at his superior. 'You got the preliminary report in Asunción. I'm afraid it's the best we can do for now. Over the next few days we ought to have a clearer picture. Certainly the man and the woman, Volkmann and Kranz, were largely responsible.'

The young man paused, then leaned forward. 'But something positive has actually come out of this. Something that wasn't in the report you got. I wanted to tell you personally.'

'What, for God's sake?'

'Many of the rank supporters didn't really believe we would attempt what we did. Now that they've seen it can happen, they're more determined than ever to carry on.' The young man leaned forward more eagerly. 'We were unsuccessful this time, but when it happens next time we'll be even more prepared. We'll have learned from our mistakes. You know the western democracies can't sustain their problems. Immigration. Unemployment. Recession. They're already crumbling. It's only a question of time before we try again.'

'What's the estimate?'

The young man shook his head. 'I can't give you a definite answer on that. Not just now. But in the meantime we continue to try and strengthen our position.'

'I can confirm that to Asunción?'

'Absolutely. You know we have the resources. It's really only a question of time.'

The grey-haired man sat down and lit a cigarette. 'Do we know what's happened to Schmeltz's body . . .?'

'Five days ago it was cremated. And buried in a forest near the Polish border.'

The grey-haired man sighed and shook his head. 'The man and the girl, Volkmann and Kranz, how did they find out?'

'A photograph they found at the Chaco house of Geli Raubal. That was the clue they worked from. That and the journalist's death.' The young man looked across at his superior. 'You want us to take care of them?'

The grey-haired man thought a moment, then shook his head. 'Not right now, Raul. But later, I promise you, they'll pay the price.'

The grey-haired man looked at his watch and then his visitor. 'You're flying back to Germany this afternoon?'

The young man shook his head. 'I have a meeting with our friends in Paris first. Their immigrant problem's getting worse. They're interested to hear our damage reports and our future intentions for co-operation. The same with our contacts in Rome. Hass is already on his way there. And you?'

'London tonight. Then Asunción, via Rio.'

The young man looked at him. 'They've got the preliminary report, but impress on them we still go ahead with our plans. Assure them of our determination, sir.'

The older man placed a hand on his visitor's shoulder. 'I'll let them know, don't worry, Raul. And thanks for coming.'

The young man picked up his briefcase and replaced his papers and clicked shut the security lock and thumbed the numbers. He picked up his overcoat and the grey-haired man led him to the door.

They shook hands firmly and the young man checked the corridor before stepping out.

He had pressed the button for the lift and the doors had already opened when he heard the grey-haired man call after him.

'And Raul . . .'

'Yes?'

'I almost forgot. Happy New Year.'

'The same to you, sir.'

Afterword

In the winter of 1941, ten years after Geli Raubal was found dead in her uncle's Munich apartment, the Nazi authorities in Vienna issued a secret instruction that the girl's grave and those around it in the Vienna Central Cemetery were to be completely destroyed. No reasons were given and the order was carried out.

To this day plot 23e remains, an unused expanse of green in the midst of a cluttered maze of family vaults and graves in the old Central Cemetery. Whether the remains of Geli Raubal are still buried there is a mystery. There have been numerous and recent attempts to have the remains found and exhumed but the Viennese authorities have consistently delayed granting permission, thus prolonging the mystery.

In the months and years after the girl's 'suicide', several people claimed they knew the truth behind her death, a 'secret' that had ultimately led to her murder.

All died violent deaths, including the journalist, Fritz Gerlich, mentioned briefly in this book.

But what was the 'secret'?

There are clues.

In late 1931, one month after Geli Raubal's death, Erhard Johann Sebastian Schmeltz, a fervent Nazi and a close friend of Adolf Hitler, disappeared mysteriously from his home in Munich, along with his sister. The couple were never seen again in Germany.

Seventeen years later, and over two years after the war had ended, a former Waffen SS officer, wanted by the then American CIC for his involvement in the disappearance of a quantity of Nazi gold bullion and for secretly transporting it to South America, wrote to a friend in Munich from his new home in Asunción, Paraguay. In his letter he said that he had been shocked to come across the sister of an old friend from before the war, in a remote town in a region north of the Paraguayan capital.

The friend's name was given as Erhard Schmeltz.

Accompanying Schmeltz's elderly unmarried sister, the writer noted with some surprise, was a pensive, dark-haired youth no more than seventeen.